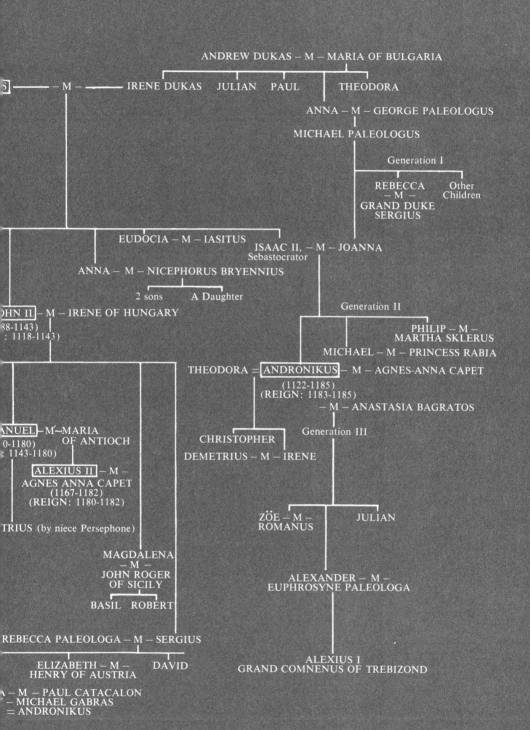

ANDREW DUKAS — M — MARIA OF BULGARIA

S — M — IRENE DUKAS   JULIAN   PAUL   THEODORA

ANNA — M — GEORGE PALEOLOGUS

MICHAEL PALEOLOGUS

Generation I

REBECCA   Other
— M —   Children
GRAND DUKE
SERGIUS

EUDOCIA — M — IASITUS   ISAAC II, — M — JOANNA
                        Sebastocrator

ANNA — M — NICEPHORUS BRYENNIUS

2 sons   A Daughter

Generation II

OHN II — M — IRENE OF HUNGARY
88-1143)
: 1118-1143)   PHILIP — M —
                               MARTHA SKLERUS

MICHAEL — M — PRINCESS RABIA

THEODORA = ANDRONIKUS — M — AGNES-ANNA CAPET
            (1122-1185)
            (REIGN: 1183-1185)
                  — M — ANASTASIA BAGRATOS

ANUEL — M — MARIA   Generation III
0-1180)   OF ANTIOCH
: 1143-1180)   CHRISTOPHER

ALEXIUS II — M —   DEMETRIUS — M — IRENE
AGNES ANNA CAPET
(1167-1182)
(REIGN: 1180-1182)

TRIUS (by niece Persephone)

MAGDALENA
— M —   ZÖE — M —   JULIAN
JOHN ROGER   ROMANUS
OF SICILY

BASIL   ROBERT

REBECCA PALEOLOGA — M — SERGIUS   ALEXANDER — M —
                                   EUPHROSYNE PALEOLOGA

ELIZABETH — M —   DAVID
HENRY OF AUSTRIA

A — M — PAUL CATACALON   ALEXIUS I
  — MICHAEL GABRAS   GRAND COMNENUS OF TREBIZOND
  = ANDRONIKUS

AGAINST THE FALL OF NIGHT

AGAINST THE FALL OF NIGHT

 MICHAEL ARNOLD

DOUBLEDAY & COMPANY, INC.
GARDEN CITY, NEW YORK
1975

Library of Congress Cataloging in Publication Data

Arnold, Michael P.
    Against the fall of night.

    1. Byzantine Empire—History—Fiction. 2. Comnenus
family—Fiction. I. Title.
PZ4.A756Ag   [PS3551.R54]   813'.5'4
ISBN 0-385-05691-5
Library of Congress Catalog Card Number 72-89292

For Richard and Anne Arnold

Contents

Nothing moves toward that which it cannot reach.

—THOMAS AQUINAS

AGAINST THE FALL OF NIGHT

OMNIA CONSTANTINOPOLIS SEPULCHRUM EST

Incipit: Annales Secreti de Nicetas Acominatus: According to Divine Wisdom, the sack of Constantinople, as those few other events where history visibly turns, was an accident.

The Latin armies under the suzerainty of the Marquis Boniface de Montferrat, Count Baldwin of Flanders, Theobald of Champagne, and Louis of Blois arrived at the gates of our city, 23 June 1203. They came from Venice, where they had intended to embark directly for Palestine, until the German Emperor Philip, opportuned by his wife, Irene, sister of our recently deposed Emperor, Alexius IV of the House of Angelus, sent his ambassadors to the blind and bitterly anti-Constantinopolitan Doge, Enrico Dandolo. The Germans proposed the armies divert to the "Kingdom of the Greeks" (as we are inaccurately and somewhat nervously distinguished in the West) and reinstall Alexius—himself a usurper.

Now, this Dandolo, as I have said, personally despised us, for reasons which will become obvious in their time, and politically abominated us, as do all citizens of the Republic of St. Mark, for they are brokers of our wealth, and brokers by definition are servants, and servants by nature are resentful and thieves. Dandolo, however, is not alone to blame, any more or less than Philip, a careful man happier in title than power, extending little but his prestige, and that little enough, for he knows one's reputation is a limited arsenal, a poor one, easily rendered empty by a single assault.

Land and treasure became the objectives of the Western armies perhaps in the belief merely to Latinize is to sanctify. Men cannot live with their own evil. At any rate they are haunted by virtue. It is not the path to heaven, but hell, which is circuitous with rationalization—the false canonization—of one's intentions.

Thus when Geoffrey de Villehardouin, representing perhaps half the conniving armies, arrived at Venice to arrange transportation to Jerusalem, a game of sanctimonious dissimulation—perfectly mutual—was played. The Doge and his henchmen senate demanded 85,000 marks, an impossible sum, as no kings—hence their royal treasures—were involved in this venture. Dandolo thereupon suggested an alternative: embarkation in return for the capture of Zara, a great port on the Dalmatian coast, which threatened Venetian hegemony of the Adriatic. As for the mission to Constantinople, Dandolo, with his blind eyes the color of the sea at noon, pretended the interest of one legal sovereign for another. But he knew—he could not have helped knowing—he was sending the Latin knights to Byzantium as one sends malicious children into an unguarded warren of vulnerable fawns.

It is the fate of the ruled to wait and suffer, of the ordinary men of armies to suffer and die. Only the royal players win and lose; the human lives they manipulate are helpless. It is no great wonder the despotate of Persia was the origin of chess.

In Constantinople, in those days of late spring, 1203, we waited quiescently, as some men you see who are soon to undergo surgery. They fear the pain; they expect death; they can scarcely speak of hope, or, if hope they have, it is no more than the wish to be done with this terrible, inevitable experience, dead, at worst, but beyond dread.

The Angelus Dynasty, successors to the last of the Comneni, the awful and wonderful Andronikus, had ruled by then for eighteen years. They had not sought the throne, but having achieved it by accident, this family, whose harm lay in their innocuousness, of indifferent origin, save one ancestress, a sister of the beloved St. John Augustus, succumbed to the royal morbid choreography of jealousy, injury, ambition, and incestuous murder. To have observed these mediocrities, awkward, small, and supercilious, performing the Imperial dance of death, which has its own grandeur, was to comprehend the final degeneracy to which rulers of our once great Empire had descended, the degeneracy of the inverted principle of monarchy as held by the Senior Angeli: that it had better and sooner destroy the Imperial patrimony than share or relinquish it. (Apparently there is a point among some unreasonable men when revenge and self-destruction become indistinguishable.)

The first months of the third year of the new century, as we anticipated the coming Latins, were all of a piece, the final measure of what
we had lost and endured since Andronikus. The city, which in the century and more of the Comneni had numbered nearly two million souls,
lost by emigration a half million and half that again before the next
spring. Civil facilities were everywhere understaffed, when not inutile. As
a result of constant changes of autocrats the Secret Police were ubiquitous. The city constabulary were indifferent when not extortionate. Every
purchasable item was subject to inflation. The great families were leaving New Rome in its decay, emptying their palaces of treasure and returning to their vast domains in Lesser Asia and Thrace, North Greece,
and Macedonia or the deep-water security of the Archipelago. The Angeli themselves, unwilling to lay their personal fortune at the service of
the state, had pawned all that was movable in that exquisite miracle
raised by the Comneni, Blachernae Palace, and returned five miles across
the city to the droop and dust and chaos of the old Sacred Palace complex.

We of the Senate—those of our rank remaining in the city—met each
day in the grand colonnaded building opposite the entrance to the mighty
Augusteum, the great mosaic square it shared with Holy Wisdom Cathedral and the main, the military, entrance to the Sacred Palace, Chalke
Gate. We met, as men do, with nothing to do, waiting in the silence for
the detonation we knew to be inevitable. We met to await our terrible
visitors, who came, indeed, by the many thousands we had imagined,
but scarcely, of course, the thousands our fears had conjured. And yet,
you must understand, any army of constituted purpose before this stupendous city, surrounded by seventeen miles of triple Cyclopean walls,
threatened in egregious disproportion to its number.

Constantinople was, in fact, defenseless. The regiments of Asia and
Europe—the Optimati, the Bucellari, the Charsinian, Seleucid, Cappa-
docian and Peloponnesian—comprising the three great Imperial legions, of St. George, St. Michael, and the Virgin Mother of God, had
been disbanded. The cost of mercenaries was out of the question: the
landed families had taken their household guards with them and would
not recruit provincial armies and send them back for metropolitan defense. The city police were not soldiers; the six thousand men of the
Tagmata, the Scholarian, the Candidate, the Excubitor, Archontopuli,
and Varangian divisions were for the defense of the Imperium. There

was no way to enforce conscription and no desire to be conscripted. There was only the desire to crouch in a corner—and wait—alone, with one's fears.

The first week in July, the deposed Emperor Alexius IV and his father, the Co-Adjutant and Senior Augustus, Isaac II, blinded, as every school-boy relishes, by the reigning usurper, his brother, Alexius III, arrived from their estates in Thrace and lay the secrets of the city's military defense before the accursed French.

On 17 July 1203 the armies of the Latins made their first assault upon Constantinople. Representatives of the Venetians stood their horse at a great distance watching the first battle of the walls. With so few soldiers for our defense, primary use was made of incendiary naphtha, shot from catapults upon the war machines, the unprotected heads of infantry, and at the frantic massive hooves of Percherons carrying their knights. Our losses were negligible, but the population, who would not themselves resist these mercenaries commissioned by the family which ruled them, rioted. They filled the Augusteum, a hundred thousand strong, demanding the abdication of Alexius III. The Senate was invaded (including the toilets—nothing is sacred) and some of us carried out as champions, delegated to go to the Emperor and command his deposition.

Deputized, we passed beneath Chalke Gate, through the Bronze Hall, where immemorially the military household took their pledge of allegiance on the accession of a new Emperor, amidst the endless, ugly military architecture of the Scholarian Barracks, the Tricilinium of the Candidate, the Onopodion, and the huge three-story ceremonial halls of Daphne Palace, nine hundred years old, reeking of grime and wet stone, dancing with dust and shot by Herculean bolts of light descended from the high-arched windows near the ceilings. The roar of the rioting Constantinopolitans which itself drowned out the ululation of exquisite war —the real thing—at the walls barely three miles from the palace, was now distant and only apprehensible as thunder is, barely, behind great mountains. At the entrance to the last hall of Daphne, the colossal gallery of Justinian, we were met by the Sacred Consistory, the Emperor's Council. Its president, the aged Duke, Nicephorus Paleologus, Alexius III's Finance Minister and the man who perhaps more than any other dealt Andronikus the least political but the cruelest of personal betrayals, said to us, "He's gone. It's over. That's all. Branas is guarding his escape at the Imperial yacht basin. Open the gates of the city. But warn those military pimps, Rupen and Cantacuzenus, if they dare to enter with Their Majesties. Branas has no intention of allowing their collaboration with the Latins to go unpunished. He intends to kill them both."

Kill them he did. While Isaac and Alexius Angelus got their fickle triumph a few days later and poured monies, holy relics, state jewels, gold and silver objects of all conceivable shape and use—bedsteads, tables, knives, swords, reliquaries, icons, crowns, statues—into Latin hands, five hundred wagonfuls of treasure as compensation for the knights, as well as trade monopolies for Venice, Alexius Branas, the morganatic husband of the last Comnena Empress, Agnes-Anna, gathered a score of soldiers devoted to him and with a daring which charmed the population when Alexius IV would have preferred to manipulate their outrage, kidnapped the Co-Augusti's generals, decapitated them somewhere in the city, and sent their heads and boiled, bifurcated penises to Louis of Blois, who tossed out the latter and had the former cleansed, skinned, polished, coated with gold, and kept by his bed as a memento mori.

The Co-Emperors were outraged, but the Branae were beloved and much admired for their fidelity (though they seemed always faithful to the least popular rulers, a perverse virtue), and Duke Alexius was, beyond all else, matrilineally a Comnenus, his wife a Comnena Basilissa and herself a Capet, aunt of the most prestigious, if not the most powerful, knight now encamped before the city, Louis of Blois. Besides, however brutal and stupid the act in principle, there were none who believed the buried, headless trunks had deserved much better fate than they were served. The Branas incident served as a warning to the reinstated Emperors that a third Alexius or a fourth, an Isaac with eyes or sightless, was hopelessness to hopelessness, their rule scarcely absolute, their reign indubitable only in its uncertainty.

The Latins did not go. They did not make preparation for Jerusalem or Paris. They did not dismantle their war machines, not even to save them from the severity of winter, the cruelest and coldest in memory, and there were men alive who had been children in the reign of John II. The city suffered as though under siege, which perhaps it nearly was. The Metropolitan Prefect labored bravely under conditions which required remedy on the order of miracles rather than merely effective administration. But what supplies reached the city, despite harassment and thievery by the Latins—or bald appropriation—went directly to the Sacred Palace. What was not consumed there was sold at extortionate prices to the populace, proving, as one of my colleagues put it not too inaccurately, "speculator's blood still flows in the Imperial veins." (In truth, the Angeli had commanded the food to reach the people at wholesale prices; rather their agents metamorphosed philanthropy into thievery.)

And so, into that last winter we passed, snows deep, cold bone-chilling, supplies limited when not extinct. No fuel, no food, no police. Vandalism and murder were rampant, a man's life for a loaf of bread or a cross word. The demented Angeli set their Secret Police about: arrests were swift, numerous, and often resultantly lethal. Criticism of one's lot was considered seditious; a joke at Imperial expense—and Constantinople, like all capitals, had lived too long with rulers not to be amused and rarely awed—was *lèse majesté* and due for capital punishment, here, where in the quarter-century reign of St. John not a man, not one, was put to death by the state.

Finally there was madness. On the kalends of January a great mob broke through the line of the Scholarian Guard thrown up before the Hippodrome. They entered the vast stadium, quickly pocking its undefiled field of snow, and toppled the titanic statue of Athena Promachus, which sixteen hundred years before had been set atop the Parthenon at Athens. The adamantine bronze colossus, whose imperturbable eyes had watched great history for more than a millennium, swayed, cracked from its foundation with a stupendous moan, and, eliminating the very air in its fall, leaned down, and down, down, down, and smashed upon the arena floor in a hundred thousand pieces. (Old metal and frail; many were killed by its propulsive shrapnel.) She was brought down because she faced the west, because, of course, it was her genius which had been beckoning the Latins, the accursed and homicidal Latins, and now, to be sure, Constantinople would be free again.

The ringleaders of the riot—and those punishable by association, which is to say, the guiltless utterly—were filched out by the Secret Police through the co-operation of frightened or spiteful neighbors. One hundred were burned in an auto-da-fé, that most dread of Latin importations into our land (adopted, it is said, from a Celtic religious rite). The cremations were conspicuously attended by the Co-Emperors and their diminished court and as pointedly unattended by the Dowager Basilissa Anna and her Consort, Branas.

Public executions are a popular pastime, and the Constantinopolitan population, like any, dotes on the spectacle of righteous gore, their inclination for spilling viscera and inflicting pain delivered to them by the state which justifies it and consequently frees them of the necessity of compassion. Only in those rare instances when state and audience disagree (i.e., the condemned are the people in their entirety) do these fatal punishments become a test of government. This was a time of such acrimony and there can be no explanation for the publicity the Angeli arranged for these chastisements, except perhaps the arrogance of the ignorant who, when threatened by all odds, stupidly threaten in return.

It was the end of the Angeli. Within two weeks there was revolution and the Co-Emperors were deposed and murdered.

This is how it came about. The Empress Anna, Dowager though but thirty-two years old, had publicly divorced herself from the regime and loudly announced she was considering self-imposed exile, when the Co-Emperor, Alexius IV, signing for his father and himself, remanded her to the Buceleon Lighthouse, her husband to the Imperial dungeons. For myself, I never much entertained very great affection for the young Dowager or her husband—she, though indisputably courageous, too humorless and politically self-centered, regal to the point of stultification in personal contact; he, too lumpish, choleric, a little frightening—but distance lends enchantment, and the population held these personages in much esteem as sacrosanct remnants of the old days, the days of the Comneni.

Now the deposed usurper, Alexius III, had a daughter who made much the best of it a marriage to another Alexius, Alexius Dukas, a member of the oldest noble house in the Empire (though its senior branch had been collateralized by the Comneni, the junior branch survived through a feminine member of their line). This Dukas lost no love for his Angeli in-laws, whom he looked upon as parvenus as well as usurpers. He had frankly married into the family because it was regnant and influential; the family had married him because he possessed the Dukas name and the wealth and legend as well of the Comneni, all of which he kept at a distance, withdrawing himself and his cosmopolitan, unhappy wife to his estates in Thrace or the vast ducal palace, jointly inherited by all direct descendants of Alexius Comnenus, at Trebizond.

Having learned of the imprisonment of his kinswoman and former Empress, Dukas collected his household troops and began the march to Constantinople, his declared intention, the throne of the Angeli. On the road so many Emperors and would-be Emperors had taken before, he gathered adherents, men desperate as they always are to participate with giants, to taste celebrity and climb from anonymity. Word of the coming army—which was less than an army but more than a mob— reached Constantinople. Adherents, in pay or merely excited, fomented riots. Small Latin contingents used this as excuse for raiding, firing, and looting some of the suburbs. This enraged the populace beyond partisan violence to wanton mayhem. With the incandescent insanity of those in outrage who know no fear, a mass of incalculable number brought down Chalke Gate and murdered any soldier who stood in their way. They charged through the otherworldly confines of the Sacred Palace— perhaps more ethereal for being tattered if no less rich—looting little, looking for their Emperors. Indeed they found them. At the farthest end, the fortified walls of Buceleon Palace supported the roped-together bodies, still alive, of the two Basilei, lowered, delivered as it were, by a group of treacherous, terrified ministers. Archers punctured father and son with arrows so grossly that when, late in the day, they were taken down, one could not be distinguished from the other.

And so the people went out to meet their new Emperor, the only logical—which is to say, available—successor, Alexius V. And no doubt the Latins looked on, and wondered and conferred among themselves. I was reminded, not inappropriately perhaps, of the death of my son, illegitimate, but my only heir, in 1184. Only eight years old, no more, but I have never seen a body put up such a fight, in delirium and out of it, against extinction. I watched his being burn itself out—in pain, which is the fire of the fight, a child gone hairless, covered with tumors, wracked by the collapse of his innards, all this needless agony before its terminal surrender.

How strong the body is that it will summon such torture merely to die. So it was with Constantinople.

No sooner had the Patriarch placed the crown upon Dukas' head than a commission from Baldwin of Flanders arrived at the Sacred Palace demanding further reward for efforts of the previous summer. The Emperor refused. It was, on the Latin part, simple, calculated, diplomatic theatrics, and it signaled the dread inevitable. Daily skirmishes took place without and within the walls, day by day increasing in their brutality.

Enthroned, Alexius was frantic and confused. Perhaps even an uncommon emperor would have failed, but then the populace remembered the first Alexius, of the House of Comnenus, who found the Empire no less beleaguered and before he died left it the largest, soundest, most cohesive political force in Europe. One reads, one recalls, one considers, and possibly the comparison was not unfair.

For three terminal months we endured the fifth Alexius, his good intentions and his lack of ingenuity. Despondency became abysm. The last noble families emigrated, some to Trebizond, the third city of the Empire, to which the Comneni had retired following the martyrdom of Andronikus, some to the Morea, some to Nicea, the one dominated by the Paleologi, the other by the Lascarids. Many more thousands of poor left the city to wander the countryside bewildered and beaten or as predators. To all intents and purposes, the Senate disbanded.

Myself, I was honored by emissaries from the Grand Duke Alexander, son of Andronikus, who offered me refuge at Trebizond. I refused. My brother Michael, Archbishop of Athens, sent his own black-cowled agents with a similar petition, which I similarly refused. I could not leave. To forsake Constantinople would be to forsake myself, for the entire city was my stoicheion, that object with which each Greek believes his life to be bound. Such does love, like God to Adam, inspirit the inanimate. At length, I acceded to the pleas of the Dowager Basilissa Anna and took up residence in her apartments at Magnaura Palace.

The Latins have a saying: *Fortuna, imperatrix mundi,* Fortune is the Empress of the world. When she departs, there is only the chaos and spasms of an heirless, ruleless humanity waiting for the tumble and damnation and death at last and no movement—no hope, no despair, only stillness.

Now, during the revolution of January, the Latins took advantage of the turmoil within the walled city to cross the Golden Horn and take possession of the two separate districts of Galata and Pera, an easy effort, brisk as carving parboiled fowl, for the twin quarters possessed the double disadvantage of isolation and a great host of Western merchants, who found it more economical to supervise their businesses at Constantinople in person rather than by commission through agents. From the Galata towers they watched us on the opposite side of the waters, day by day, twitching, waiting.

On 23 March, Baldwin sent one last supererogatory demand in his own name, that of his fellow counts and their allies, the emissaries of Enrico Dandolo. Alexius V refused outright. Retaliation, of course, was the implicit consequence.

No one really knows how secret negotiations become public (though here, I suspect, paid agents of the Latins sought to further demoralize both the crown and the population), but on 27 March new riots broke against Alexius. On 29 March the Grand Chamberlain arrived at Magnaura with a guard and spoke privately with the Basilissa Anna and her Branas. By evening what treasures were transportable were moved to Buceleon Palace and the imminent escape of the Imperial harborside. Magnaura's residents—including myself—arrived behind the wagons to be greeted by the appalling news that the Emperor had fled on the previous day. For twenty-four hours the Empire, the body, had been living without a head. There had been no formal abdication, and to a man, not a man would take the crown for himself. For the first time in 874 years, 10 months, and 15 days, Constantinople had no ruler.

On 12 April 1204 the massive iron chain which stretched from wall to wall across the Golden Horn was cut. The Venetian navy sailed the inlet and took the harbors. At the far end, the armies of Baldwin and Theobald crossed Blachernae Bridge and entered the city through the nearby gates, which were powerfully and hopelessly defended by a citizens' army. Meanwhile Louis and Boniface were carried across the Golden Horn, at midpoint, by ships of the Latin merchant fleet. Bridges were thrown from the poops to the Phanarain Towers, soldiers crossed them, threw open the gates, and allowed the infantry and transported cavalry into Northwest Constantinople, there to meet a phenomenon of light and mist such as no man had ever seen before (nor have I ever again observed). Though the morning was not unusually warm, and there had been no rain in many days, the air beneath a cloudless peacock sky was filled with angelic little puffs of steam dancing, rising, under the sun.

In this unnaturally serene, almost heavenly state of things, the holocaust of blood and fire began.

The entire western portion of the city was put to the torch at once. Here were mostly tenements, seven stories high, close together, precarious, and housing perhaps 200,000 souls of which, that morning, as many as 70,000 were returned to God, for souls were all that was left when flaming walls stopped collapsing and fires, late in the evening of the second day, extinguished at last for lack of human fuel and timber. Of all the Latins' wanton acts—and there is not ink nor parchment enough to record them one by one—this was the most perverse. There were no treasures here, save Blachernae, which on Baldwin's orders went untouched pending the taking of the entire city. The firing of the tenements was the fitting, symbolic prologue to carnage—apocalypse as irrelevance.

The churches of Holy Savior at Pantokrator, Holy Savior at Pantepopte, St. Theodosia, the Virgin Pammakaristos, St. John in Petra, St. George, Holy Savior in Chora, and most revered, St. Mary of Blachernae, were looted, defiled, fired, and their priests and nuns crucified beneath burning walls. Hundreds of thousands of dogs, cats, and donkeys were slaughtered. Mothers in term—I have examined hundreds of reports of this curious depravity—were split open and forced to eat their aborted fetuses before being decapitated. The Convent of the Almighty was invaded, looted, its nuns subjected to mass rape and murder and the whole establishment brought down by fire. The monks of the Monastery of the Almighty were crowded into the courtyard and massacred by a blizzard of arrows and axes from the roof. By early evening of the first day 150,000 Constantinopolitans were dead and a quarter of the city gutted or aflame.

The Latin armies now converged and began the march south and east along the Mesa, the widest and most beautiful street in the world, where the most splendid statues of antiquity had stood upon pedestals beneath arcades, untouched for nearly a thousand years. Adamantine, graceful, unself-consciously sensual, gathered from throughout the Roman Empire to enhance Constantine's brawny, shining, brand-new capital, their nudity was diabolical to Latin sensibilities and therefore hacked to marble dust. The Cathedral of the Almighty, raised by the Comneni, was entered, its golden iconostasis torn down and divided, its altar of mother-of-pearl, pearls, rubies, and diamonds dragged with great effort into the courtyard, pried of its jewels, and tossed into the street. Soldiers relieved themselves upon the floors and walls of the Holy Place, broke open the tabernacle, and urinated upon the Sacred Host. The fabulously jeweled Gospel was torn apart in an effort to get at the treasure with which it was bound. (Among the devout, but illiterate—and there is no reason to doubt the piety of these men—one can only presume that which

is holy in the native tongue ceases to be so in any other.) The sarcophagi
of the Emperors St. John and Manuel and John's Basilissa, St. Irene,
were shattered, their gorgeously dressed mummies plundered and
tossed in an incestuous heap. But this was minimal damage done to
Imperial remains compared to the morbid havoc—beyond description—
committed in the gigantic Emperor's crypt, much resembling Hadrian's
tomb at old Rome, behind Holy Apostles Cathedral. There, seven hundred years of Basilei and their families were dragged stinking and
akimbo, limp, brittle as glass puppets, into the air, the accursed air so
alien to the horrible dead—and there robbed and desecrated. Had
corpses voices the cries should have been as comparable to hell.

Around midnight, the first two thousand of twelve thousand wagons
of transportable riches left the city. Toward dawn of the second day, the
depredators arrived at the Augusteum, having burned or ransacked
along the way every library—a hundred, two hundred—every museum,
every market, every house, every archive. What the human mind lost in
those hours from Democritus to al-Biruni is unaccountable and irreplaceable, and I should weep the rest of my life for that alone, but what is
mourning for books when teacher, pupil, and the very school itself have
suffered the same depredation. Hector? John the Baptist? Naomi? But
there is all Troy, Christ himself, Naomi's children.

As the Augusteum was invaded and the Senate engulfed by flames,
the sun rose blood-red above the city where the rotting of the corpses
and the infestation of disease had already begun.

A dozen whores were brought over from Chalcedon, wine was poured
down their throats until they were sodden, whereupon they were dressed
in patriarchal robes got from the vestry in Holy Wisdom Cathedral and
forced to burlesque the Greek Catholic Divine Liturgy. After this, the
cathedral was given over to Boniface's and Baldwin's best soldiers.
Again the iconostasis was demolished and plundered of its jewels. The
altar of forty thousand pearls and solid-silver base was assiduously
stripped and melted, as were the gigantic gold cherubim. The Gospel
stand, a life-size silver swan with wings of sapphire, was never seen
again. The tabernacle, hangings, statuary, and carvings were pried,
pulled, torn, and divided. Soldiers cast dice in the Holy of Holies.

In the Hippodrome the bronze was stripped from the colossal ancient
Egyptian obelisk on the spina. The golden dolphins were hacked apart.
The enormous statues of the dioscuri, Castor and Pollux, were demol-

ished and melted on the spot. The four bronze horses were presented to Venetian representatives (and now bestride the lintel of St. Mark's Cathedral—fittingly, since the design of the Basilica is that of Holy Apostles Cathedral to the last mosaic). The hundreds of statues of Christian saints which lined the third tier of the arena like a tiara of holy soiled spikes were one by one, with the laughter we have known as children, turned end over end and shattered upon the pavement, far, far below. The column of Platea, consecrated by Pausius the Lacedae-monian following the great ancient battle, inscribed with the names of the thirty-six participating states and coiled with the famous sinuous snakes, could not be toppled, but the serpentine heads were, anyway, hacked off. The apartments and zoos and training rooms beneath the arena—the stables, cisterns, sudatoria, cloakrooms, saloons, workshops, breweries, and booths—were raided, looted, attendants subjected to bloodbath and finally burned.

While the depredations moved ever closer to the Sacred Palace, at the Golden Gate, the Gate of the Emperors, many miles away to the south, dismantling took place. The stupendous medallions were pried loose, fell, fissured, and became a rainbow of pebbles. The great bronze ele-phants were worked loose by hammers and winches, lowered by pulleys, sectioned by axes, and melted. The Statue of Victory which fell during the reign of Michael III, the Phrygian, and was replaced with one even more artful, fell again and for all time. The enormous golden cross of Theodosius, which fell during a storm in the reign of Justinian and was replaced by that same Emperor, was lowered with great care and melted by watchful eyes into gold bricks of staggering weight and satisfying size and so divided. Finally the bronze superscription of Theodosius, in let-ters the full length of a grown man—HAEC LOCA THEODOSIVS DECORAT POST FATA TYRANNI/ AVRA SAECLA GERAT QVI PORTAM CONSTRVIT AVRO —were separated from their stone dowels, taken down, and melted also.

Now, the Golden Gate opens out onto the Mesa, which, in time, passes the Monastery of St. Theodore of Studium. There was the enshrined head of John the Baptist, one of the most precious relics in this city which had carried European civilization and its mementos on its back for a thousand years. This, too, in its reliquary of gold and all manner of jewels, was carried off, along with our beloved and miraculous Icon of the Blessed Virgin from the Church of St. Mary of Blachernae, the Veronicon—the towel with which Christ had wiped his face and left its imprint, on the way to Golgotha—the True Cross, the Spear, the Crown of Thorns, the Sponge (object, as the Latins did not know, of the only moment of mercy at the Crucifixion, since as every Byzantine schoolboy understands, the sponge was the Roman soldier's canteen, carried in the helmet and soaked in vinegar to purify the water), the manuscript of the Gospel of St. Matthew which had been buried by St. Mark with the body of Barnabas (in return for deliverance to Constantinople, the Bishop of Cyprus was given the dispensation to wear purple and carry an Imperial staff rather than an episcopal crozier), Mary's robe, the robe of Christ, the bodies of Mary Magdalene, Andrew, James. All these relics, relics by the thousands, and all their sanctity, like God's love and protection, left the city, the soul dying with the body.

All our lives we are taught good the greater power than evil, forgiveness superior to revenge. Yet when the means between both these ends is life or death, what is the power and what the superiority, when evil, by mortal elimination of the good, laughing at forgiveness which is only self-disarming, triumphs to infest the earth. For myself, to pardon these men would be an act of evil greater than their sin was evil. A nun, drawing on a list, told me of children whose families had been murdered before their eyes. Many would then wander the streets, dazed beyond saving, until encountered by Latins, whereupon they would be violated—naturally or unnaturally—and dispatched thereafter with a knife. Fathers saw their sons beheaded; mothers their babies swung by the feet and exploded in bloody pulp against the walls of a church where they had gone for sanctuary. Warehouses were spared and their owners confiscated. Whole families were sliced at the knees and forced to run the length of a field or a street until they died from loss of blood. Eyes were gouged, limbs lopped, lives eliminated like garbage. No one was spared, not the beautiful, nor the saintly, the hideous, the evil, the uncommon, the plain, not the aged, nor youth. Lives were ended indifferently; good lives and worthless lives. Corpses were piled in slaughterhouse heaps and each, though indistinguishable in the smelly sameness of death, with a story to tell, but above all with the aspiration to continue to exist now voided in the putrefaction of clay.

With the Basilissa Anna, her Branas, her honorary court, and those remaining members of the court of the four Angeli—mostly the elderly (left over still from the Comneni) who did not know where to go—forlorn, pampered children deserted by their master and mistress—with freedmen, retainers, eunuchs, clerks, and slaves, I attended the last Divine Liturgy in the Imperial Chapel at Buceleon. We had come together to insist we loved God though He cast us down. The tragedy of earthly life is the vanity of anticipation, that things can be possessed, and death is something which happens to others.

There was weeping, only a little, occasionally a betraying cough. But there was never a sign of weakness from the Basilissa toward whom all eyes turned for deliverance—if not from harm, then weakness. As the once-crowned Vicaress of God on Earth, less than divine, more than human, the anointed Autocratrix, our only living touch with heaven, the only sign our abandoning was not entire, her tall frail form was the heart of our courage. And it was then I understood with momentary revelation and renewal of the familiar God sometimes grants us, what it is to wear a crown. Comparatively she was a young woman, an alien child brought to our land and crowned before her tenth year. In the havoc of this night each damage done the city was damage done her appointment, her charge, with no one alive to share her responsibility or sense of ruin. Both were hers to suffer—it does not matter we did not accuse her; she believed her mandate blasphemed—but of a suffering she dared not display, while we, frightened, awed by her consecration, gathered round her for the solace which her feminine sense of compassion, her pride, and the debt she owed God would not let her deny us, however failing and frightened her own heart. Amongst royalty pride is not an affectation but a life's meaning. *Explicit: Nicetas Acominatus.*

Agnes-Anna, her head a little to one side, stands before the court and servants, staring up at the vaulting iconostasis, before which float cloud racks of incense. Her face exhibits a delicate uncertainty, the distress, not fear, of supernal haughtiness. She has been an empress from childhood. She is the daughter of Louis VII of France and his third wife, the marvelous Alix de Champagne, one of the most beautiful queens of the previous century, a century of beautiful queens. Her skin is startling white, her hair as startling black, her eyes, the Capet eyes, blue-gray, enormous, limpid—the eyes of Louis of Blois, which are somewhere in the city winking at the horror at which these eyes wince. She wears the stoa of an empress, blue-purple, fretted at its borders in gold and tiny pearls. Behind her and to her left, Branas watches the back of his wife's body—the most delicate aspect of a woman. In the distance a tremen-dous explosion takes place. Anna starts, but rigid Imperial discipline prevents her turning, and by her example, those rising from their knees keep their place. Branas' dark eyes, beneath blond hair, cut straight across his forehead in the Latin style, squint approvingly at his wife, while his mouth frowns with ineffable pity.

The Patriarch and his co-celebrants come out from behind the iconostasis, the Holy of Holies. Anna receives the Eucharist. To her scarcely concealed consternation, the Patriarch is assisted to his knees. He kisses Anna's hem, then, with arthritic, knotty, immaculate hands on her shoulder, brings her forward and bestows the Kiss of Peace. Be-hind them a servant comes up to Branas who listens for a moment, then moves up to his wife—the Patriarch has continued Communion among the rest of the congregation—and escorts her between the assem-blage to the chapel doors. Along the way she smiles, she touches shoul-ders, now and then hesitating a polite instant, uncannily not a moment more nor less than necessary, while someone kisses her skirt.

At the doors stands Count Boniface de Montferrat, unspeakably filthy with blood and dust, an ancient statue with Verdigris patina and eyes of ivory and obsidian. Anna stops short and begins to turn back.

BONIFACE. Lady, I come as your protector.

Branas holds her still. She turns, her face stolid and deadly.

AGNES-ANNA. Sir, you not only lack compassion, but all sense of fit-ness.

BRANAS. Anna, in God's name, prudence.

Her words, spoken with striking quiet, are the slow choking of emo-tion which is too much emotion. She speaks in perfect French.

AGNES-ANNA. Monseigneur, I tell you this. If I could open my veins and rid myself of my Frankish blood, if I could forget the day I was called French, if I could expunge from my memory this language I speak now only to make clear to you the nature of my curse upon you, your colleagues and your soldiers, thieves and murderers, as you are, I would die, sir, as saints die—ecstatic.

BONIFACE. Lady, you speak as you must.

AGNES-ANNA. Sir, I speak for my people who haven't the dispensation to spite you unpunished.

Branas leans close to her and whispers.

AGNES-ANNA. Then you speak with him. I don't know how you have the heart to use me so.

As Boniface is about to make obeisance, she turns away, re-entering the chapel, quivering, offering her hands to two noblewomen. Anger— the unexpected which royalty dreads—has finally broken her.

BRANAS. Sir, you must forgive Her Majesty. She is both a queen and like you, French-born. It is her nature and her call to be an unforgiving Greek. If I may—there is a favor we would ask of you.

BONIFACE. Whatever service we can offer.

BRANAS. Could you provide escort from the city for one of our citizens? A Senator, a man of letters. You must guarantee us the safety of his person and his papers. He is the historian of my mother's house.

Branas beckons a servant.

BRANAS. Ask Count Acominatus to come to us.

The servant tiptoes, almost minces, along the nave of the very large, quadruple-domed chapel. He signals from the congregation a short, slender man of indeterminate middle age, who limps toward the doors. His eyes are the eyes of an icon's or a child's, empty or preternaturally alert, in any event an observer's, not an actor's. While they await him, Branas and Boniface consider one another. They are men of similar, essentially sanguine disposition, and rarer in Boniface, a fighting man of the Latins, who, like all Greeks, is well read. They are not leaders, only generals—therefore their society is international—the engineers and technicians of power. They ought to have been friends.

BRANAS. We have no Emperor. My wife will not remount the throne. Do you intend to take it?

BONIFACE. Baldwin will be elected from among us.

Branas' eyes pinch—in malice or bitter amusement. He smiles.

BRANAS. Yes. Elected.

Nicetas Acominatus approaches. When he speaks, his Greek is pure, Attic and lovely. His voice is of pleasant middle register, his pronunciation inflected with a sense of theater, or rather the writer's thorough knowledge of the weight and place of each word.

NICETAS. I have not made Communion and it cannot be urgent, my dear Duke. In six hundred years, with few exceptions, the only haste a senator has displayed is the rush to a toilet after peroration. Claudius Galen was right in almost everything, though he should have noted a politician's wind is in his kidneys, not his lungs.

Branas does not smile. The Duke is not humorless nor especially haughty, but it is obvious he only tolerates Acominatus. Himself but half Imperial—the wrong half—he has not the confidence to accept this man's admiration of his mother's family without suspecting a fellow collector of their celebrity—perhaps a more disinterested competitor. Besides, he entertains the activist's mistrust of the intellectually incisive and the large robust man's condescension toward the small or frail.

BRANAS. Sir, you will collect your manuscripts and whatever else you may wish to take with you and leave the city with the escort the generous Marquis has provided for you. You will go now.

NICETAS. It is a sin to save books while men burn.

BRANAS. In the end, sir, it is all that may be left us if we all burn, and we may. For God's sake, Acominatus, we've lost everything and our books as well. At least as long as you live you can replace your own manuscripts. Now go. And God be with you.

Branas winces. He frowns. Suddenly—if it will only last a moment it is no less real—there is the brotherhood between these two men before their common conqueror, both forced from the life of power and control they have known into the anarchic unknown of a future without petition.

BRANAS. God be with you, Nicetas.

Emotionally, they embrace. Branas makes the Sign of the Cross.

Incipit: Nicetas Acominatus: Under the surprising protection of Boniface de Montferrat's soldiers—their surprise and mine, no less—I left the city of Constantinople after midnight, 14 April 1204. I have not been within its walls since (though about two years ago I passed it aboard ship—and felt as one observing a lover across an abyss). I do not expect to see it again in my lifetime. I know I will not.

We crossed the waters to Chalcedon with little incident and no communication whatsoever, for my valet's second language is Chersonese Russian, mine, for the sake of scholarship, must be Latin and Arabic, and our guards spoke French, but with none of the roundness or precision of their masters. I had left by the Imperial yacht basin so I was spared, by God's mercy, the city in its final devastation. The Sacred Palace and the terraced hills upon which it is built concealed all but the topmost points of flames. It was only as we withdrew more and more eastward that we saw what the arrival of Latium had done to Megalopolis. Fire—from rim to rim: columns, domes, the great heads of colossi vanished from the skyline above which floated, ascending to the west, a vast columnular nimbus of smoke, lit beneath with infernal ruby light. I tried to accept this aspect from which we drew away, with that toward which I had sailed on a bright morning nearly forty years before. The two could not be reconciled. What had become of that invincible, glittering city? Was it to this we had been arriving, all the while arriving? It is little wonder oracles are mad. I turned away, feeling my heart torn out of me, and went to be by myself, somehow solaced by the direct line the dipping prow made with the full pearl moon.

Boniface's escort took us through Chalcedon, which was subject to less slaughter, but as much sack and venal atrocity, for this was—had been—the pleasure city of the people and the Emperors. We rode through the streets, my manuscripts in a commandeered wagon serving as a cushion for my seat (coming as close, I suspect, as I ever shall to following the suggestion of my critics). Half-naked, wholly drunk molested women walked alleys in a daze of satiation and despair. Corpses were few, unburied, rigorous, their accusatory, unclosed eyes staring up at the glittering salt of the night sky.

Toward the outskirts of the city, we saw a bawling, blond child, in bloody rags, meandering from wall to wall. Our soldiers cursed him and threatened him with their weapons. In primitive French I called out to them to stop or I would return to Constantinople by hook or crook and report them. I asked the child his name and where he lived. What I finally comprehended was that he had no family—they had been murdered—or he had had only his mother, who had been murdered. I took him with me, and despite his indescribable stink, his lice, I hugged him close, consoling him, kissing his rank hair many times, for in the heartbreak of that night he seemed to me the genius of my beloved city and I longed to comfort her, to put my arms about her, assuage her ache, and console her agony.

We left Chalcedon before dawn and rode out into the countryside and the blessed peace of an earth unburdened by catastrophe. Christos Gennate Castle, the first great domain of the Comneni beyond Constantinople, was a day in the distance. About midmorning Boniface's soldiers stopped our progress. They had come this far and they wished to return to the city. I thanked them with nods and indeterminate, peaceable gestures. They withdrew their swords from their sheathes. One edged his horse closer and toyed with the reticule hanging from my belt. I am no swordsman and I did not argue. I untied the bag of gold and gave it to him. His colleague came up beside him and with the tip of *his* sword described my belt of gold and pearls. I gave him that. I gave him both my rings. Then they cut the harnesses of our horses and pulling them along raced back toward Chalcedon while my valet, myself, and the boy watched from atop the wagon, now useless. I climbed down, my charges followed. We pulled the wagon till dusk.

In the twilight, the enchanted part of day, we rested beside the wheels. My valet had brought few provisions, for we had expected to be at Christos Gennate before supper. As we ate meagerly, in the quiet, we were roused by horsemen. Even in the distance their pointed helmets, pale leather uniforms, and curious pure white belts and headbands—so ghostly in the silver half-light—marked them as Turks, scouts, far beyond the border of the Iconium Sultanate. There was nothing to fear. We crawled out from beneath our shelter and hailed them. Surely our wagon must have seemed to them a pileful of treasure, for the Turks are not gratuitously bestial and there is no other explanation for what followed.

They came up to us at speed, and without a word one of the horsemen beheaded my faithful valet, Thomas: thus the death on a field in Asia, hidden from the boy lying thirty years before in the fields beneath the walls of Novgorod, wondering where, when, and what form his end might assume. Then the child. His arm came away with a clean swipe and he fell crying in his own blood. I was chased by a third Seljuk until at last I felt something like a sting, something like a tickle, in the middle of my back. I heard ringing, the countryside faded before my eyes into accelerated night, and I lost consciousness.

When I awoke—it was not long after—I heard their foreign, unmistakably furious shouts. Slowly—I was far enough away for my movement to be scarcely noticeable—I opened my eyes. The wagon was being ransacked, my manuscripts and records thrown up to the dark blue heaven of night, cut and trampled by dainty hooves upon the still hot dirt. (Vanity of vanities . . .) I rose on my feet, and for all my light-headedness and nausea, I ran toward my attackers shouting at the top of my voice, waving my arms against their destruction of my life's work. Now the Turks, like all Moslems, are deeply superstitious with a particularly morbid streak. When they saw me, I suspect the scouts took me to be my own enraged ghost coming at them in necroid vengeance. They turned, spurred, and dashed away.

The child was still alive. The cut had been clean. There was blood though, much too much blood. I struck flint, ignited one of my manuscripts, and cauterized the whole stump. Then I lifted the child and began to walk. I walked through moonrise and beneath the stars. At first the child moaned, and then he was quiet. And all the while I could not divorce him from Constantinople. If I saved the boy, I saved my beloved city, my lovely city, my stoicheion, my life. In the dark I reached that point of the horizon when the towers of the Comnenus' great fortress, Christos Gennate—Christ Is Born—with beacons fired, rise like twin blazing eyes. I collapsed with Constantinople in my arms, at the foot of the tremendous bronze gates. *Explicit: Nicetas Acominatus.*

Nicetas awakens, momentarily blind, focusing his eyes to behold a man of great height, perhaps fifty, given to the stoutness, not fat, of once active musculature. With his salt-and-pepper hair and nearly classic Greek regularity of feature, he would be very handsome indeed, save two glass eyes stare from ruined lashless rims. The sense of speaking to an animated icon or a transfixed mask is unavoidable and, one suspects, ultimately unnerving.

NICETAS. My dear, dear Prince.

The son of Andronikus feels for a seat, a campstool of leopard and ebony, placed by the bed by a servant to whom he nods dismissal. He reaches into the air toward Nicetas, who takes his hand and kisses it. Into Nicetas' hand he places a lethal crescent-moon brass knife with an Arabic haut-relief superscription along the handle.

ALEXANDER. A souvenir of your adventure.

NICETAS. What is this?

ALEXANDER. That, sir, was found in your back when we found you by the gate. Or rather the Household Cavalry nearly trampled you to death finding you. What with the Latins and reports of Turkish incursions, we've been sending out scouting units three times a night.

Excitedly, Nicetas remembers.

NICETAS. The boy!

ALEXANDER. The child's dead. He'd been dead for hours. You were carrying a corpse. Who was he? Yours? I thought you'd taken orders.

NICETAS. A waif. No one. Lost in the streets of Chalcedon. He probably would have survived there.

ALEXANDER. What happened?

NICETAS. What one expects in time of war. Montferrat promised me safe conduct to you and meant to keep his word and did as far as it goes which does not extend to the honor of his henchmen. They robbed us, took our horses, and left us with a wagonful of manuscript.

ALEXANDER. Did they do this?

He gestures toward Nicetas' prone body.

NICETAS. We pulled the wagon many miles. When we stopped—toward evening—to rest, we were attacked by Turk scouts. They thought the wagon was full of treasure.

ALEXANDER. It was. But that's a secret between us Greeks. I'll send out a party to retrieve them. Were you following the roads?

NICETAS. Oh yes. Due northwest from here. What news is there?

ALEXANDER. Curious. We have an Emperor at Constantinople. Baldwin of Flanders.

NICETAS. Yes, I know. Montferrat told me before I left. I asked him. He didn't offer the information, I assure you. He seemed none too happy for it himself. I don't suspect his heart is entirely in all this.

ALEXANDER. Then he is more irrelevant and more cruel than the great beasts of this world like Dandolo and Baldwin who are wholly understandable because they are demented. Boniface's carnage has a conscience and, for me, that is twice as tormenting to the victim. It is foolish to ask the devil why he is wicked because, of course, it is his nature. But to die, knowing your murderer regrets your murder, knowing he had a choice—and he knows it, too—that's adding insult to injury. If men must be wicked I prefer the Baldwins to the Montferrats of this world. Don't you?

NICETAS. What of Anna and Branas?

ALEXANDER. No word. I presume they're under house arrest. By the way, you are now in a secessionist province. My kinsman Lascaris has declared an Empire of Nicea and himself Basileus.

NICETAS. Have the Paleologi assented?

ALEXANDER. Unexpectedly, yes. The old man has sworn for Theodore. Times change and thrones, too, but the Paleologi remain fixed—the first to *follow*, always.

NICETAS. And you? Will you declare for Lascaris?

ALEXANDER. I cannot. It's a matter for diplomats, now. In my absence my son has seceded Trebizond and its territories from the Empire. Good enough, too. He wants me to take the throne.

NICETAS. Will you?

ALEXANDER. Unequivocally I will not.

NICETAS. You are the oldest of Andronikus' house.

ALEXANDER. I've had enough of thrones in my life.

NICETAS. What will you do?

Alexander shakes his head, smiling.

ALEXANDER. Return to Trebizond and offer obedience to my son—most emphatically support him. Probably once we leave this wonderful castle, it will go the way of the others. Pity. In four hundred years—or nearly—it was never entirely empty of Comneni. Ah, what does it matter. My father saw this coming, Nicetas.

NICETAS. Not all of it, Your Highness.

ALEXANDER. Well, nothing quite happens as a man predicts. That's prophecy, which is to say quackery. I'm speaking of deduction. And now—now those same Greeks, Nicetas, who have abjured to the Latins claim my father at the root of this devastation. But they're wrong. It is their hesitation not his experiments which have ruined us. He would have been the first to accept responsibility, had his ideas been proved pernicious. Rather the ruin was accelerated because his designs were aborted with his death. Responsibility, yes, but blame belongs squarely with his murderers.

NICETAS. Prince, men are desperate when their fates are disagreeable. Though seldom after good luck, they will inquire after the bad. For every punishment has its reason and its chastiser, does it not?

ALEXANDER. My father never believed in such nonsense.

NICETAS. That is true, Your Highness. Your father possessed what few men do: persistence—despite belief in a world of coincidence only. That is courage of a sort.

ALEXANDER. Is it? Or a form of moral ratiocination—to accept any means toward one's ends.

NICETAS. I assure you, Your Highness, as for your father, it was quite the reverse. Especially when he reached supreme power, the web spun downward from each of his acts, made him triply sensitive to his methods.

ALEXANDER. You think so? I had quite the opposite impression. So did the Empire. Hence this—all of this. What a rogue, what a very great rogue. Yet how I loved him, Nicetas. Even despising what he sometimes did, how I loved him.

NICETAS. All men loved him, Your Highness.

ALEXANDER. Did they? Explain to me, then, his death. Justify it.

NICETAS. *Capax imperii nisi imperasset.*

ALEXANDER. What is that?

NICETAS. Something from Tacitus. "He would have been an ideal ruler had he not ruled." In the end, Your Highness, frantic men prefer legends to solutions, for wondrous men are often the sum of wonders expected than realized.

ALEXANDER. In the barracks there's a young trainee, a shepherd's son, I believe. He plays the flute like an angel. I've heard him in the night. He merely wants to slice men's skins when he already pierces their hearts. Shall I send him to you?

NICETAS. Said, Your Highness, like a soldier who ought to be a poet.

ALEXANDER. You flatter me, sir. No, no. I'm rather a former soldier who has the withal to admire poets, for which little I thank God. Nicetas, have you ever killed a man?

NICETAS. No, Prince.

ALEXANDER. Sometimes when I think on it, neither did my father. After any consenting fashion, I hasten to add.

NICETAS. Then we should have full bellies and empty coffins. It seems to me quite the reverse.

ALEXANDER. You did not know him as I did.

NICETAS. Nor you, Your Highness, if I may say so, as did I.

ALEXANDER. Yes, I suppose it is one thing to be the devotee of a great man and another to be his son. One is beguiled, the other is obliged.

NICETAS. I knew what was deplorable in him, too. Believe me. But deplorable by whose standards? One man's sin is often merely another man's limits. I served him to the end, for all my timidity, because it was something large to do, something very great in which to participate, to lift oneself to the immensity of his vision, because the deed was the size of the man in whose behalf it was done. I think you do confuse your father with your sovereign.

ALEXANDER. As my father confused all men with himself. When I say he never killed a man, I speak of premeditation against another—a separate being. I'm certain in some divinely blind way he believed in no other but himself. For the rest, we were recognized only as extensions of that self, its ambition, excitements, passions, vengeance, frustration. If you died as some consequence of his actions—if you were betrayed or humiliated by him—it was, for him, a matter of indifferently inflicted pain, as one removes lice from one's hair and crushes the life out of it between one's fingers. Truly he was the embodiment of the ancient warning of our people to the world: "We Greeks were born to know no rest and give no rest to others."

NICETAS. In all this, you speak nothing of his love, his compassion.

ALEXANDER. Of his compassion—what you would call his compassion, I would call his offended sense of order.

NICETAS. And his love? It, too, was without validity?

ALEXANDER. It was like a whale, Nicetas, which cannot help consuming the space round itself. It was enormous—and curiously sterile. Do you know, I think it made little difference to him whether or not he was loved in turn, and yet it is capacity to love, in whatever form, which most haunts me. I had rather him a brute; his loving makes him seem vulnerable.

Alexander shakes his masklike head and lowers it.

ALEXANDER. I damn him and adore him because he was no more than a man, extended on either side of the balance most men attain and believe they have done well to attain—and they have.

NICETAS. He was the light of our lives, Your Highness, and, like all flame, scorched as one chanced too close to the source.

BOOK ONE

 Fortuna, Imperatrix Mundi

I

Incipit: Nicetas Acominatus: "Who is more content at his death?" said Andronikus. "The happy man who asks, 'So soon?' or the suffering man who says, 'At last'?" He smiled a smile, serene as a woman's, lips parted to reveal teeth sturdy and white as a child's though he was approaching his sixty-second year, eyes distant not with an old man's reverie but in ironic meditation. He tapped the pillar perfunctorily against which his hand had rested, then looked about—Holy Wisdom Basilica in the winter morning light of January 1184.

He said to me: "By way of example, consider the builder of this church, which the Moslems say will be consecrated to the one Allah only on the Day of Judgment. Consider Justinian. To everything he aspired; in nearly everything he failed. He alienated rather than convinced all manner of heretic. He won the West as a gesture rather than sensibly fortifying the prosperous East. As for his famous Codex: he embalmed Roman law; he did not renew it. When a man lives long enough on a throne, he soon reaches the triune delusion which is incipient royal senility: He is indestructible, infallible, and irreplaceable. Justinian became hated not because he was inept, but because he had contracted a sovereign's most dread disease—a killing sense of his own legend. His precedent as sanctified despot—he was the first Emperor, and Theodora the first Empress, to be portrayed with halos—was to make of his successors, whatever their inclination, despots also, unless they seemed lesser men to begin with. He is the last, illustrious pan-*Latin* Emperor. He has the legend he wished for himself but only because by doing so—by squandering resources and alienating the West—he made it impossible for any man following him to approach his circumstances. But his dream haunted and ruined his successors from his day to my cousin's. Both Manuel *and* Justinian *were* imitators, make no mistake, looking over their shoulders, and like all imitators, rather than the truly inspired, they touched surfaces rather than depths, as imitation has not the motive of necessity. Manuel too turned from the urgent East to the seductive and fatal West, in which consequences, we live now and I now rule."

In the way of all conversation with royalty, I tentatively interrupted him, at which he, as was customary, said, with a nod, "Please."

"But, Divinity," I said, "if we can say a man's glory *is* his aspiration rather than his achievement, Justinian was undeniably great. You may never reach the stars, but if you do not aim for them, you will not even miss."

"True enough, my boy, though one hesitates to claim glory of any sort as a prerogative of the monarch—whether heritage or legacy. Still, in one measure, both literally and figuratively, Justinian did indeed achieve his Coelum Empireum Habitaculum Dei et Omnium Electorum. I am speaking, of course, of this church, which is not the largest in the world, only the most beautiful—and careless and bold in its vanity. Consider: Justinian broke Egypt and Syria, paving a Moslem inroad, to assure the luxury of materials. Yet have you looked closely? Look here: These crude initials of stonecutters and monograms of artisans, shamelessly memorialized where the humility of man ought to reign. And here again. Stone plaques of fabulous weight and value: serrated by the tools which sliced them and left unfinished, and look, here, the corner chipped away and the next panel carved to fit the damage. Look, there, scatological mottoes, those tiny letters at the bottom—and the accompanying caricatures of fellow workmen. The architectural conception is traditional and superb: an enormous square buttressed on either side by immense aisles, at either end by the great apses each of which blossoms and becomes terminus in three more apses, the problem of hiding the dome's support solved in an exquisite syncopation of curves and its own beauty. But scarcely an arch is perfect, scarcely a line uncorrupted. Details are wondrous, outlines perfunctory when not slovenly. Capitals are flamboyant, columns sheer as ice, bases the shame of a child's hand. What is in shadows is miserably sloppy or altogether unfinished."

In a sense, Andronikus was accurate enough. What has stood seven centuries was constructed seven times sooner than the care it deserved. What should have been God's glory alone, like Constantinople itself, served to monumentalize its inceptor. (If you dispute this, look again when next you are lucky enough to visit: The intertwined monogram of

Justinian and Theodora is everywhere—including the urinals in the Imperial and patriarchal vestries.) For all the jewel-gorged sacred icons—in the hundreds—for all the shimmering silk hangings—immense masterpieces of the weaver's art—what do you first see in the courtyard of the Basilica but the monster equestrian statue of Justinian? ("Yes, yes," said Andronikus, "though it has never been clear to me whether he takes horse to beat the worshipers to God's blessing—or precisely, as possible, the reverse.")

And yet—of course—and yet . . . Few architects have so limpidly concealed their genius as Anthemius and Isidorus, sheathing solutions of size and support in heavenly disguise, calling attention away from house to purpose. From without, Holy Wisdom is ponderous, weighty, confused, asymmetrical, and—were it not for the extravagant majesty of its size and height—almost ugly, scarcely inviting. But then so is death—the door to heaven. For heaven it is, within, lustrous with four acres of gold, glowing roseate in the light of six thousand candles. Gleaming pillars and panels of green serpentine marble, Theban porphyry, granular blood-violet stone, Phrygian and white-spotted marble, silver-veined Laurentian and Lybian gold-streaked stone, rise arch on arch, half-dome on half-dome, circle on circle to the utmost crown, the gigantic cross-encrusted cupola of gold and jewels, the largest closed dome in the history of mankind, swelling from the curved square of thrusted pendentives like a titan's bubble, iridescent, from cusp to cusp, the shrunken sphere of heaven drawn to earth, uncannily incredibly free of support, there, as it were, by a miracle.

No edifice in the world has been raised with such care for its illumination from sunrise to dusk. Each hour of the day possesses its signature of olympic citron bolts, titanic sun spikes, focused, refocused, cross-hatched, dancing, flickering, from the latticed windows of the dome, the apses and subapses, the galleries, the unexpectedly pierced walls, patterns like elegant, sensitive fingers of the blind, searching out the church, betimes creating such nimbuses of light between springing and summit, the whole no longer seems attached to earth, but only about to settle—or to ascend.

Indeed, it is this sense of being surrounded by air—open, gold-soaked, vast—contained at once and infinite, which more than any other—a building, not a building, a vision about to become fabric or vanish—makes transcendent the experience of this church. Like the walls those seventeen serpentine miles of walls which protected the city and its heart, this cathedral—Holy Wisdom—was something greater than its makers, creation at the fundamental, and as nearly close to the eternal as the imponderable may aspire. Neither the walls nor the church ever failed us; rather, in failing ourselves, they were surpassed.

"Shall we go up to the dome?" Andronikus said. Without waiting for my assent—he need not command when he had been gracious enough to request—he signaled a Varangian, those ever present protectors of the Imperial family, whose scarlet-and-gold-cuirassed figures he had known since his birth as Grand Duke and Prince of the Blood Royal (the latter title a West European distinction, adopted by the Emperor's cousin and predecessor, Manuel Augustus).

By a series of sinuous staircases, smelling of dank stone and then again, acridly, of dry wood, lit from unexpected apertures—and that light pale and cold as moonbeams on a snowscape—we made our way round and upward to the great cupola. At a double door, Andronikus stepped aside, and the Varangian—taller even than the Emperor's six feet and six inches—shot the heavy wooden bolt. The last barriers were drawn back. A topaz bolt of light filled the hollow and ignited our three persons. Before us, revealed in nightmare perspective—so close as to nearly break apart into abstraction—was the colossal mosaic cross: almighty, overwhelming. Beyond the arched windows on the opposite side of the dome lay the visible junction of Europe and Asia. The guard allowed the Emperor and myself to enter.

Andronikus leaned against the balustrade, and almost at once began to weave dizzily—consent before the siren of height. I grabbed his arm and concealed that impertinence with one spoken. "Easy, Lord. You haven't your grandfather's wings yet." At once, I said, "Forgive me, Sire, I did not mean that." He smiled. "Oh, I'm sure you meant it. Rather you did not mean to say it." He paused. "And you're right. I haven't Alexius' wings. I doubt I ever shall. He knew what it was to live a life beneath a throne before he took it. He grew wings to rise to it. We, his children and grandchildren, had no need of them—or thought so."

As a governess nervously ruffles through a chest for anything to amuse her charge, I said, "You know, Augustus, your grandfather was asked once to name the predecessor he most admired. His answer was immediate and to everyone's surprise, Vespasian. Irene Augusta is said to have commented, 'Ah yes, Vespasian. You *would* choose him. A pagan peasant.' At which your grandfather protested, 'But, madame, he was a genius.' She said, 'He had no sense of majesty.' And again your grandfather protested, 'That did not seem to affect his authority.' 'Beggars,' she said, 'could approach him without a salute.' 'Well,' he said at last, 'in that, I flatter myself, we are similar. It only goes to prove Vespasian was not a solemn ass, nor am I for choosing him.' "

The Emperor burst out laughing, like an egg exploding from a smashed shell. "Oh, that sounds like him, all right. Her, too."

"And whom do you admire, Lord?"

His eyes passed from Olympia to mischief. "Whom do you think, my boy?"

"I doubt, anyone, Your Majesty. I think—like Jehovah—you have it in your nature to be jealous. Too jealous to have other gods."

Indifferent as he was to his membership in the Imperial house, he could not escape its traits—that is, his upbringing—any more readily than a tree will cease to be a tree because it is leafless. His smile was gracious, frozen—perfect for a diplomatic reception—a mask. It sat easily—it *was* gracious, *and* a mask, indicative of nothing. In an instant he had passed from mischief to incisive majesty. I presume I had gone deeper by insight into his nature than was acceptable to him. Quite simply he did not wish to be knowable. Whether it delighted him or distressed him—both, I think—there was no one alive whose riddle more men wished to solve. A line comes to mind now, in a letter he once wrote to me: "Any man—or woman—who thinks he knows me and may draw my soul through a flaming hoop is sadly mistaken. I would kill him or estrange him on principle."

The light in his eyes became infernal. Until I turned away, he did not speak, and when he did, he was hoarse. "You're quite wrong, Nicetas."

"Who, then, Augustus?" I tried to pretend I believed him. He believed my pretense, or desperately pretended to. He would not leave himself understood. With an autocrat's disdain, he could escape at any moment; the door at the back of the cage was held open for him. But he would not move. The challenge lay not in escaping capture, solely, but escaping before his captor's eyes through the *locked* end of the cage.

"Not so much a man," he said. "An idea. Phaëthon."

"I would have thought Prometheus."

"Good heavens, why?"

"His suffering in man's behalf."

"Then you're doubly wrong. Why should I want to suffer for my fellow men? Besides, Prometheus was not bound to the Caucasus for the revelation of fire. Remember? Rather because he knew and would not disclose the name of the usurper of Zeus' throne. Pure politics. In any event, there is something greater than dying for our fellows, and that is the infinitely more ennobling act of dying in the effort to enlarge oneself. When Apollo offered Phaëthon any favor, he chose for one day to drive the chariot of the sun across the sky, for one day to bring light to the world."

"He chose rashly, Augustus. He was warned not even Zeus could control the great steeds of the sun. He did not listen. He was overwhelmed, he fell, his body ablaze, from heaven, struck by a thunderbolt hurled by his own father."

"Which is more admirable, Nicetas? The offer and the common sense to refuse, or the daring of the attempt. Think of it, if only in your fancy. Those first moments racing out of Olympus, overtaking the east wind, climbing above the banks of the clouds which limit the ocean, then up and up, ascending the blue vault of heaven. . . . Even to die on the way, but for a moment, or a lifetime, to assume something greater than oneself, greater than any man besides yourself will attempt, and only because he fears death or defeat sooner than later, to open the door of the cosmos or at least leave the scars of your effort upon its hinges."

" 'Here lies Phaëthon who drove the chariot of the sun-god, who failed as greatly as he had greatly dared.' I understand, Your Majesty." And I did and I was obviously moved and, for that, he was offended. He had not yet escaped. I would let him. "How ironic, Your Majesty. Do you know which of your ancestors saw something of himself in Phaëthon —the less flattering interpretation, I might add."

He frowned. "Who? I don't know of any. Who?"

"St. Isaac Augustus. After his abdication."

"Not really."

"Somewhere in the *Confessions* he says—let me see—'When, like Phaëthon, the reins of the state proved more than my hands could control, God in his mercy did not destroy me, but lifted me bodily from the chariot and set me back upon the earth to dwell in humility upon one's second chances.' "

Andronikus smirked. "I don't call that mercy. I call it humiliation."

Like many strong-willed people, he was incapable of seeing compromise as a form of strength. "Isaac didn't. I think he saw those years after the renunciation as one of triumph."

"A form of heroism, I suppose, though scarcely to my taste. However it emerges you cannot conceal a man's fire; sooner or later it enflames the very sanctuary which conceals it—even if it is greatness as a matter of survival rather than enhancement—a waste."

"Nobility is scarcely a waste, Your Majesty."

Almost at once his lips parted to refute me. And then he shrugged, as though it were of no matter.

We were facing east toward the Augusteum, the sun full upon the Emperor's figure, his expression once again pensive as he stared down at the numerous figures crossing the marble chessboard of the square. He said, "You can always tell the bureaucrats from the tourists."

"How is that, Your Majesty?"

"In cold weather like this the official wears the least possible protection against the elements so the tourists know he's about some errand from one warm room to another. How grown men play." He shook his head and sighed, then he looked to the left and pointed toward the Senate Building—and beyond to Magnaura Palace and its gardens. "My grandfather died there. At Magnaura. And there"—the whole hand with its single jewel, the coronation ring, pointed to an auxiliary gate near the Senate—"my uncle and my father rode out to repossess the palace as Alexius' heirs." Once again, he sighed. "I envy my elder brothers little —Philip, scarcely, and Michael, poor Michael, not at all—except perhaps, they knew Alexius. Philip actually *remembers* the man." The Emperor seemed awed. "Can you imagine? He remembers Alexius. He remembers that day." Then he turned and looked down and away to his right, as if, as it were, in response to the alarmed murmurs which followed the ascent to the ambo of the Patriarch of Constantinople sixty-six years before.

II

It was 5:30 in the afternoon when, one hour after administering to Alexius Augustus the viaticum—the traveling provisions of the soul about to leave the body—His Holiness John IV Agapetus declared to the congregation of Holy Wisdom, miserable in anticipation, "My dear children, he who was terrific in war, wise in justice, always in God's light, is with us no more." We are told men and women wept—and children wept to see their parents weep—and wandered about the city's streets, dazed, saying, "Our Father is dead. Who will protect us now?"

This is not so naïve as it sounds. After thirty-seven years on the throne, grandchildren nearly the age of their folk at the time of Alexius' accession, could hardly imagine a world without that short, brawny figure with his painful impediment of speech, which was soon forgot in the majesty and generosity of his presence. According to Alexius' private physician, who is not given to exaggeration or sentimentality, at Orphanotropolis, among those lamed and leprous and lunatic, abandoned old veterans, widows and orphans for whom he built a city within a city specifically for their care, the only solace they had ever known, mass hysteria ensued. Here, where Alexius was second only to Christ, and more immediate—for he had rescued the people when, it seemed, they had been abandoned by Heaven—there was no consolation. Into the night, every church in this city of churches was thronged, and the tears were as one.

This was civil grief borne for a man few mourners had ever known—in effect, a myth, as their grief was a form of mythopoesis—large, ambiguous, pervasive, submission before the inevitable. Bereavement was intense, but without personal reference—save the memory, perhaps, of a distant figure, glowing like a lily, on a white steed, the blind smile of a small man surrounded by giants as he entered a cathedral. Beyond this, nothing. God abided; the Emperor lived; the seasons passed. Alexius' two score years on the throne had diminished the memory of the ephemeral reigns which had followed the end of the Macedonian Dynasty—five emperors in one generation. He had been nearly omnipotent. He had seemed, in time, immortal. Now he was gone, as storms go and the snows melt, and rivers flow home to the sea. There was shock at first, and wonder and, eventually, in repose, a morose weight upon the soul from day to day and sleep to sleep as one contemplated the vulnerability of life at every level of creation. A chastening experience—emotionally and spiritually.

No such continence existed among those most personally affected—that is, the Imperial family. Here, where grief was startling, constant, pointed, were the pathetic distractions of state: individual ambitions, the intricacies of accession, and the ceremonial duties of those by blood and marriage believed to be vinculum between earth and heaven.

The most alarming factor at the end of Alexius' life was the visible fracture of the Imperial family into two groups, one mastered by the Basilissa Irene and her son-in-law, the Caesar Bryennius, the other by her two surviving sons, the Porphyriogeneti, John and Isaac. The Sebastocrator Isaac I, now sixty-six years old and gradually retiring from public life, ironically made such division possible by sharing his Vice-Regency with the Heir and the Caesar. The Grand Duke Nicephorus, at fifty-nine an elegant, lonely old bachelor, remained above faction, whilst the Grand Duke Adrian and his brothers-in-law, the Caesar Melissenus and Prince Taronites, never having truly recovered their stations after the Diogenian Conspiracy of 1094, like all ciphers had become passive political objects, bestirred only to attach themselves— and then, carefully, for protection, not power—to the most obviously legitimate authority, any authority in any event.

Alliances did not precisely assume the configuration one would have expected. Prince Rodomer, though Bulgar born and the Basilissa's cousin, took the side of traditional primogeniture, which was neither so "safe" nor without required courage as it seemed. As he had gradually transferred his attendance from Alexius' side to John's—no doubt, with Alexius' approval—he was marked for disenfranchisement by the Irenian faction should their plots succeed—a possibility to his last breath, which the late Emperor took quite seriously. The great commanders—Humbertopolis, Marianus Catacalon, the Aaroni brothers, Kamytzes and Taticius—with the expectable exception of the Empress Dowager's first cousin, George Paleologus, both open and in secret favored the Heir and left no doubt they would initiate a bloodbath if his legitimacy were usurped. (Had you asked these generals why they so chose, they would have answered "Law and tradition"—law, which is the clay, and tradition, the kiln in which the army is baked.)

Surprisingly, Felix Branas, the Minister of Justice, was an Irenian possibly for no more weighty reason than he was uxorious—so was the great Justinian—and his wife was one of the Dowager Empress' ladies-in-waiting. As for the Porphyriogenetae: both Theodora and Maria allied themselves with John. Haughty and intelligent themselves, they may have sympathized with the injustice of masculine succession and supersession their sister Anna suffered. But the pride which encouraged them was their father's—he who had himself prevented usurpation by Bryennius' father—and they had no intention of being bullied into, or conniving in, the elevation of their brother-in-law to the devolution of their own name, the splendor of *their* birthright. For that they would gladly suffer their mother's disapproval.

Her younger daughters believed they knew, as the world did not, Irene Dukas Comnena, Augusta, not so much favored Anna or loathed John —as parents, arbitrarily, sometimes will—but detested their father in life and death, detested him the forty years of his fidelity to his mistress, Mary of Alania, who in her still beauteous, gracious presence repre- sented all else from which the Dowager took affront.

Maria and Theodora—and not any less sympathetically, if ruefully, their brothers—understood their mother's position to be final—an irrev- ocability because it was founded not in logic (if that were so, the Dowager could have taken the same satisfaction in the well-beloved Crown Prince, as had her husband), but in hatred born of thwarted tenderness. (No one ever doubted Irene had loved and been awed by Alexius from the day of their betrothal.) Affection can survive indif- ference; it cannot live in humiliation.

All families are essentially their own law. Whether they consider themselves fortunate or not, those most unified are usually under the jurisdiction of one who administers favor and punishment, who is ca- pable of ostracizing the wrongdoer whose authority is crossed at a risk not worth the reward. It is true, while Alexius' mother lived and shared his rule along with the first Sebastocrator Isaac, Adrian and the princes Taronites and Melissenus succumbed to Imperial conspiracy. It is also true they were wrecked and hollow men before her death. It may be supposed, in fact, the dissolution of the family came about for the very success toward which the Empress Mother urged it.

For the more than three score descendants of Alexius and Irene, thriving by midcentury, it was very difficult—be he or she Porphyriogene- tus, Grand Duke, or Grand Duchess—to distinguish between the venera- tion allowed their anointed relation and themselves. Indeed, the difference was negligible, entirely, in terms of public demonstration, and nearly so according to monarchical metaphysics, since all derived the respect due them from what Andronikus called—irreverently, perhaps, but accurately—the "same sanctified groin." If corruption is the elimination of tension between evil and its object, the achievement of one's ambitions as often eliminates discipline, compassion, and a sense of proportion. Those same dynasts who may have approved of—or in his place, little differed from—the policies of their enthroned Kin saw nothing obtrusive in their contempt for him based on little more than the manner in which he cracked and noisily consumed an egg.

III

At seven o'clock precisely, messengers were dispatched to the four corners of the city, and the Empire, announcing Alexius Augustus' death. This was no mere formality: the proclamations to governors and mayors were signed by John II Augustus, a first significant step in sealing off the Regency from any further machinations of his sister and his mother. Then, some time before midnight, the entire Johannine faction, under heavy guard, crossed the Augusteum and entered Holy Wisdom Cathedral. There the new Emperor pledged before the Patriarch the immemorial words:

> I, John Alexius Porphyriogenetus, of the House of Comnenus, believe in one God Almighty, Creator of Heaven and Earth. I confirm, acknowledge, and approve the apostolic and God-guided decisions of the ecumenical and local councils together with the constitutions and definitions of these, also the privileges and customs of the most Holy Church of God. Furthermore I confirm and approve what the Holy Fathers of the Church have instituted and defined as sound, canonical, and free from error. At the same time I vow to remain always the faithful and veritable servant and son of the Holy Church and to be both her defender and avenger, to be considerate and philanthropic, and, so far as law and custom allow, to inflict the death penalty as sparingly as possible. So I vow, so I swear, so help me God, before these, God's holy servants—upon the Lance, the Cross, the Nails, the Crown, and Shroud of Jesus Christ, my Lord and Redeemer.

Before leaving Holy Wisdom, he named his brother the Sebastocrator Isaac II, with the concurrence of their uncle, who renounced his title and declared his retirement.*

The Grand Duke Nicephorus records for us, without comment, what was perhaps the most crucial moment of that crucial day, 18 August:

> About a month after my nephew's accession, quite as smilingly as possible under the circumstances, I asked my niece's husband, the Caesar Bryennius, why he did not leave the deathbed as had the Basileus John, and proclaim himself and Anna Porphyriogeneta. He seemed almost delighted, relieved to tell me, as a man purging a great revulsion. "Easily answered. Had the Dowager Empress not conducted herself like a gross fishwife, I might have acted. But the sight of my chiefest adherent remonstrating your brother while he took his last breath was simply too much for me, too much.
>
> "One who will not let a great man die kindly will never allow lesser men to live in peace. I thought and thought to myself: 'You will blacken your name, your great name, your father's and your forefathers', if you so much as wink at Augusta's conduct. You shall never be respected, and a ruler who cannot summon respect can only be a tyrant.'"

Years later, Bryennius—probably having forgotten his immediate reasoning—frankly confessed, when he did not take the throne at noon, several hours before Alexius' death, he lost it forever.

But yet another estrangement, deeper and perhaps more personal, took place in that moment. The Sebastocrator Isaac II, Isaac Porphyriogenetus, describes a long conversation between himself and Bryennius, following his momentous reconciliation with the Emperor—effected by none other than the Caesar—in 1137. The self-perception is uncharacteristic:

---

* In a memorandum written shortly after his accession, Alexius, seeking to honor his eldest surviving brother, described the office he had created for Isaac in terms, more accurate than flattering, hence the warning at the end. "In all manner of authority and ceremony the Sebastocrator is to be considered a semi-autocrat, if that is not too much a contradiction in terms, responsible—only on certain, specific occasions—to the Emperor, otherwise plenipotentiary in his powers. The Emperor can abrogate his acts but not countermand them before execution, and the office is subject to dismissal, though such penalty, of its nature is not operable by the Emperor until the errors, which certify his vice-regent's ineptitude, are manifest, if not irrevocable. Thus I do not advise my son or his heirs to consider the office of Sebastocrator either inheritable or an obligation. Rather it ought to be the pleasure of one who entertains implicit trust in the man he appoints. Isaac and I are indivisible. It must be that close."

Bryennius said to me, "Somehow, whilst the old Emperor was alive it seemed to me something of a game—crucial, but a game. Or perhaps a gamble would be the better term—the same high stakes, the same exhilaration in suspense, and the motivations, at heart, capricious. Always there was the Old Man to decide amongst us or decide not at all. I'm certain we were children in his eyes, our machinations frivolous while he bore the weight of rule, from which there was no escape. Besides, there was a great difference in the attitudes of Anna and your mother toward Johnny, as averse my own." He tapped my knee. "Mind you, I am not saying this in the light of all that has gone since but rather with a perfect memory for what was.

"I could never join them in their terrible boil because I too much admired John. I suppose I was rather in the position of the Old Man against my father. Unlike Alexius, however, I hadn't sufficient belief in myself to destroy my contender. And honestly, it seemed to me, in some fashion, your father was omniscient. Nothing concealed in my heart could be kept from him." I suggested it may have been the hot eye of his own guilt. He nodded. "Perhaps. Perhaps. In any event, after his death, my feelings became even more ambivalent. You know, many have said it is Orthodoxy which holds the Empire together. I have often posited quite the reverse. It is the Empire which unifies the Church. Should, God forbid, we ever fail, the Patriarchates will fracture into their component, autonomous bishoprics, with all native customs overwhelming the sense of Universal Church. It was the same in the family when the Old Man died. Everyone went so far and no further while he lived, and he held us together in his single person. But no sooner was he abed and passing on than your mother became a barbarous harridan and Johnny was pulling the Imperial sigil from his father's hand." I reminded him of the truth of *that* event. "Well, that is what you saw and Johnny told you. I suspect something else—usurpation. You saw the Old Man raise his hand in blessing. I saw dismissal, a curse. But that is by the way. With John's accession, as we all turned, something turned in me. I no longer had the heart for it. With the Old Man's death, and John's mounting of the throne, it was no longer the game I called it. We might only undo his son with pain—blinding him, regicide, usurpation, civil war, the ruin of all your father achieved. My *own* father's ghost would have risen to curse me."

That long day of which they all often spoke ended when the Imperial morticians arrived to prepare the body. As for the factions, they remained almost literally in a state of siege, with but the Patriarch and

Duke Michael Paleologus—the Dowager Empress; nephew, but more to the point, the new Sebastocrator's father-in-law—as go-between. The Bryennii remained, with the body, at Magnaura. The Johannines occupied Buceleon, Daphne, and the Military Barracks.

His Imperial uncles insisted the new Emperor, in these first days, could not possibly decree the usual elaborate burial rites for his father. They would, by tradition and ceremonial rubric, require constant attendance. The new Sebastocrator, however, said the obsequies must go on. Alexius was too well loved by the people. It was their right to say farewell and honor him as he deserved, to which the Grand Duke Nicephorus responded angrily, "Of his body, no matter. The only honor it deserves is sepulture. As for reward to the soul we all loved: it can only be given in heaven, and anything less is presumption, if not detention, on our part."

In the dialogue of 1137, Bryennius told Isaac:

> Let me reveal something to you. You shall probably be surprised. The night of 18 August and the days following, which saw Rodomer and Melissenus and Taronites, as well the *real* power brokers, your two uncles, running about, so certain and so frantic of our schemes, were quite pointless. Everyone would have done better to sit by the bed of poor Uncle Adrian and soothe his last hours. (Amazing, isn't it? How little we know? There's no doubt his brother's death—the brother who punished him—took what spirit was left from your uncle, and killed him sooner.) In fact, we had no plans. I refused to conjure any, and God knows, Anna really was terribly upset—and your mother was like a rock. She'd shorn her hair and veiled herself, like a good widow, but I think it was rather the realization of what she had revealed of herself in those last hours for which she appeared so positively mortified. No one would ever forget, and the cold dignity which had drawn men to her was forever shrived.

John had known power in these past two years, but now he was sole heir to the sins and riches of his own decisions. It was one of those crucial moments of an inherited Regency when the previous generation—whether consciously or not—confuses their chronology with prerogative, and the young Heir, uncertain in those first hours, surrenders. Knowing the love his uncles felt for his father, he believed their views, most likely, the most judicious, for they were contrary to the glory Isaac and Nicepho-

rus would sooner shower on their brother's memory. Therefore the new
Emperor decreed the minimum any Christian may expect after his death:
a Requiem Liturgy at the Monastery of Christ and immediate interment
in the crypt prepared for him. No obsequies, no lying in state, no reception of mourners, no funeral feast. It was, in fact, the first and last
decision in which the Emperor deferred to his uncles. The people were
outraged, and in the following weeks the Bryennii put this to good
effect. The Grand Duke Nicephorus writes of those days—in our last
view of him in a purely historical capacity:

I was warned over and above again by my nephews the situation in the
city was too uncertain for me to go about. They meant well, but I chided
them, calling them great flatterers if they believed my person was quite
worth anyone's trouble. In truth, I found the palace suffocating—physically and mentally. Usually when summer lingered—as that summer of
1118, one particularly lovely—we moved to Hieriea Palace with its sublime breezes and faience-bricked lakes. This year, of course, such
peregrination was impossible. But more than that, my brother's memory
was irrelevant at the Sacred Palace, saluted, but no more, as things must
be during the inauguration of a new reign. I wanted time to dwell on my
grief, to accept it in quiet. In the Imperium, there was not and could not
be that leisure. So I went where men may live more slowly: among the
ruled, who mourned my brother most truly. Quite unescorted I rode
about the streets of Constantinople, as always humming with life, in as
constant state as ever of being torn down and built up once again. (I
remembered the architect Adrian Lecapenus' words, "We tend to think of
a metropolis as permanent, when that is true only of the great buildings,
which are many in a city as large as Constantinople, yet, in the collect,
comprise no more than two percent of the total. And this ratio, mind you,
is higher than any in the history of cities—including Old Rome. In fact,
a city is an idea with certain physical manifestations, comprised of districts which take a generation to begin, flourish for another, and devolve
in the third.") In the warmth, in the sun, in the scent of the sea, out of
the ongoing life, I tried to comprehend my brother was gone. But it is
impossible to imagine annihilation. Occasionally I was recognized by
someone who would come up to me and kiss my hands without a word,
as none were necessary. I fancied—whoever ruled—there was a unity now
between the Comneni and the people, for one never becomes so united
with another as in the mutual endurance of a great pain. Just as from love,
the ultimate perfection, there can only be descent; from pain, the ulti-

mate imperfection, there is but the leap—into oblivion, or something finer. As love ends in pain, so the successful test of pain must always end in some form of love. Indeed, high and low, afraid and fearless, the compassion born of pain—that this man suffers, has suffered, as much as I— is the primary force of love. In time I took to visiting with she who mourned my brother as much as I: his beloved Mary. There was not a moment of weeping between us, only the serene grief of those who have lived long enough to know love is no bulwark against death, and yet it is all we have and no more to be discarded because it is futile than any other consolation in this life to which, after all, we are born only to die. Love in fact is more momentous than death when it teaches us a sense of urgency, the value of things before they are taken away.

On 8 March 1119, in the last controversial act of a woman whose life had been a crucible of controversy, Mary Augusta Dukas Botaniates, born of the House of Bagratid, became the Grand Duchess Comnena. In a ceremony at the Oratory of St. Stephen, attended by the Emperor —who signed the dispensation for consanguine impediment in the first degree collateral—and the new Empress, Irene II, the first and second Sebastocrators and their wives and the Caesar and Caesarissa Bryennius—the first record we have with any hint of accord following Alexius' death—the sixty-two-year-old bachelor, the Grand Duke Nicephorus, married the sixty-four-year-old former Empress. (Andronikus once told me that his father, shortly thereafter, asked Mary, slyly, if there seemed to be much difference between Alexius and his younger brother, and the new bride, holding her third husband's hand, her eyes agleam mischievously, replied, "Yes," and then paused, "he's taller.")

It is sadder to report the gossip of the court, which, in the previous midcentury, dominated by vigorous sexagenarians and septuagenarians, would have otherwise been quite delighted with the match, gave it about that the only reasons Mary had forgone her higher, erstwhile title and married the "old debauchee" was to retain the financial support of a member of the Imperial house or give the bastards she had borne by Alexius and kept hidden at Pentegoste Castle all these years the same name and rank they would have received from the Emperor had he legally been their father. The first proposition is absurd, since Mary's inheritance from two Imperial husbands, an Imperial son, her state endowment as former Empress, and, no less, the sums Alexius settled upon her, left her perhaps the single richest individual agent in the whole Empire. The second accusation, while more spiteful and less absurd, is most unlikely. Children born illegitimate to Alexius and Mary are nowhere documented, or, in person, survived or even suggested by contemporaries. *Explicit: Nicetas Acominatus.*

Candles. Heights which vary. Tall as children, thick as an infant's torso. Hundreds. Glittering ellipsoid tips, flickering, flailing this way and that. Chant and antiphon, priest and chorus, song on wing, dancing from stone to stone, gold to gold, on high to the jeweled circumference of the Christ-encrusted domes of Cathedral of the Almighty. In the middle of the school of fire, on a silver bier, is the embalmed and gutted corpse of His Imperial Highness, the Grand Duke Adrian. Kneeling at golden prie-dieus are his nephews, John Augustus and Isaac Porphyriogenetus, and their eldest sons—the Sovereign Heir, Alexius, a child pretty only for his youth's softness and the wonderful manicure of his appearance, and the Grand Duke Philip, six years junior to his cousin's twelve years, but already lithe and tall, resembling his maternal Paleologi forebears. Behind the children, also kneeling, is Count Leo Auxuchos, "Auxuch," the Emperor's former Governor and second only to the Sebastocrator in his confidence. At length the group rises as one; as one, grooms step forward and hand the Imperial party into fur-lined capes. In file they move between the candles, lean forward, and kiss the icon in the hands of the corpse, then its forehead, then its lips. Only the Heir hesitates at the last, his eyes wide at first, then narrowing curiously. Gathered again at the foot of the catafalque, the party moves through the line of censers and monks, between the assemblage of random mourners to the vast doors of the new cathedral, built by the Comneni with the intent of supplanting Justinian's Holy Apostles as Imperial sepulcher and Holy Wisdom as setting for Imperial ceremony. Beyond the stupendous portals, unwinded snow falls gently, languidly. The brothers, their sons, and Count Auxuchos step out into the cold, white, lenient night. Pages and attendants dismount their own horses and wait upon their masters. The two young Grand Dukes, all awe gone from them like wind whistling out of a canyon, draw snowballs and pitch them at the torches affixed high on the purple columns of the gigantic cathedral. An entire detachment of Varangians, the Imperial bodyguard, lining the huge chessboard square, alternating torches with the double-headed axe, the rhomphaea, move forward to encircle the dynasts.

ISAAC PORPHYRIOGENETUS. Come, boys, mount up.

The Grand Dukes obey at once, as sons of soldiers and royal children, used to the instruction of ceremonial, usually do. The Emperor's eye is caught by what he believes, apparently, to be a flaw in Philip's bridle. He leans to catch it, inspects it—nothing—and leaves go. At a small nod from the Emperor, the square before Pantokrator erupts with the thunderous hippomanic tattoo of hundreds of men on the hoof.

ISAAC PORPHYRIOGENETUS. You know, I never really liked him. Awful man. Deserved his fate.

JOHN AUGUSTUS. Isaac, you've no sense of decorum.

ISAAC PORPHYRIOGENETUS. Sense enough where it counts. Dead or alive, but more important, dead, a man's reputation's the sum of his actions and not his intent, which may be no more than self-excuse. His actions alone affect us, and it is for them we hold him responsible and so mark him. Uncle Adrian's reputation is red off the bellows and turning cold as his corpse, and for me, he was an ingrate and a traitor to his own brother. In fact, Papa gave him better than he deserved.

JOHN AUGUSTUS. Isaac, if we all lived as heaven intended, we would offer no disappointments and never need rely on another man's mercy or, for that matter, God's.

The Emperor smiles to indulge his younger brother as he remonstrates him.

JOHN AUGUSTUS. At any rate, the man is dead and you're extraordinarily unfair. He cannot defend himself.

ISAAC PORPHYRIOGENETUS. He had time enough while he lived to explain his provocations.

JOHN AUGUSTUS. But he's dead, Isaac, and our judgment no longer has meaning. Let us be more timely. You know, Papa always appreciated—however dully—Uncle Paul's efforts in behalf of the Empire's finances. Trouble is, he rarely followed the advice given him. But he was not entirely insensitive to waste. He made some attempt to forgo a millennium's accretion of ceremony. I suspect he failed, or anyway little succeeded, because his approach was hesitant and conservative. He confused persistence of the oldest traditions with intrinsic worth, as tradition is the sincerest form of complacency. Well, death persists, too, and greed and sorcery and the Paulician heresy. He meant well in his attempt to preserve what he believed valid. Unfortunately, it was an act which succeeded in curing all of the symptoms and nothing of the illness. God above in all His glory is impalpable. I am no more than His servant. My commission comes from God and I can ask no more distinction, visible or invisible, than that.

ISAAC PORPHYRIOGENETUS. What is it you wish to do?

JOHN. Banish *all* court ceremony, even that upon my personal attendance, and all public ceremony, again without the exception of my attendance. No pageantry save that for the Great Holy Days.

ISAAC. You could not be more provocative or parsimonious were you Paul Dukas' Finance Minister and he your King.

JOHN. Were my uncle my King, I would sooner be a cobbler.

AUXUCH. If I may say, Sire, Alexius Augustus' policy was neither so irresolute nor spendthrift as Your Majesty seems to think. Ceremony is glitter and baubles are for children. This is true. But it was your father's intent not so much to appease his courtiers as reduce their desires to those which children fancy to distract them and finally render the aristocracy nugatory. Often he told my father, "It's expensive, but God knows, sooner this extravagance than any more sin of civil war, as in the Time of Troubles, when we cut up our own carcass for our enemies' delectation." Between the throne and the nobles, Divinity, there must be, shall we say, an abyss of awe which cannot be crossed, so that attendance of His Majesty becomes a privilege with its own form of reward and station. By this nobles jockey for servitude, not autocracy.

John listens intently, one of his most admirable, flattering, and, on occasion, misinterpreted habits. He gives Auxuch's advice a proper little silence, then shakes his head.

JOHN AUGUSTUS. That is out of the question. All things my father did, he did in virtuous innocence for the state and the state alone. No malicious act was possible to him. He was blithe because he could be none other. I have another choice—and really I have no choice at all. I cannot make children of my subjects in order to gain their obedience. Their acquiescence to my policies must be free, internal, logical, because they *perceive* what I mean to do. Otherwise nothing I accomplish can survive if men are made fools to achieve it. A man's vision dies with him unless he leaves behind a race of disciples.

IV

Incipit: Nicetas Acominatus: We look back on the third Comnenus
Emperor through the inescapable glow of his canonization, but it is his
extrinsic good which is ecclesiastically memorialized, not his internal
struggle. This fact presents a problem to the historian who is obliged to
describe the journey toward beatitude in which light he writes. But John
Augustus' is not really a journey. Rather, closer to the hagiographer's
heart, he issues forth, fully formed. His soul has direction without movement. He is radiant and sapient without struggle, compassionate without the experience of having himself struggled. Curiously he does not
resonate throughout his time to ours in any religious sense.

Bluntly put, one cannot be inspired by one who, from the telling of
it, passed from holiness to holiness and on death took wing for heaven.
That is not man, but superman, and so far beyond a student's spiritually
willing, fleshly weak self, he may be effectually dismissed. If one is
behooved to imitation, it is by the example of another no more and no
less a man than you and I, extended by will, by sacrifice, by denial, by
pain. Andronikus once described to me the Perchersakia Lavra, the
Monastery of the Caves, at Kiev. I believe I am correct in stating it was
the only example of Christian piety which left him awed. He explained
that beneath the Dnieper River, which fronts the monastery proper, is
a tunnel lined with rooms in which are sealed those monks who have
triumphed utterly over the flesh. Their meals are gradually diminished
until, sustained for a little in spirit alone, they die, their cells become
their tombs. I think it is this sense of contest—men, whose antagonists are
their own selves—which we miss in a hagiography.

Andronikus once said to me: "Serenity was more than a mere characteristic of my uncle, it was his genius. He was not tragic, complex, and
pretentious as was his successor, my cousin, Manuel. His, rather, was
a purity, as my grandfather was reputed to have had; both born, shall
we say, functionally sinless, incapable by design of the vulgar or cruel.
His insight into motives of men was marvelous, but without passion.
There was something truly angelic—sympathetic, but detached—in the
manner in which he attended us all. He possessed what I have always
yearned for in myself: ultimate outward intensity, which is action upon

the world, and ultimate inward rest, that ability to withdraw in a crowd and consider all action, including one's own, as from a great height. I have never known one more ripe than he. My father was vivacious and lived at many levels. The Emperor was as deep but not so volatile. I should compare one to all the manifestations of the changing seasons—that is, my father—and the other—my uncle—to the constant earth itself upon which those changes are manifested."

It is significant Andronikus binds Isaac to John complimentarily. Throughout the twenty-five years of John's reign, even in the years of their estrangement, the brothers remain the dioscuri of the Comnenus Dynasty if not all Byzantine history. Not even their immediate predecessors, their father, Alexius, and their uncle, the first Sebastocrator Isaac, who throughout the early years and nearly all their middle age lived somewhat in their mother's shadow, were so thoroughly partnered in the public mind.

As befitting the father of Andronikus, and save his son, he is the most controversial—or in the least, misunderstood—member of the senior branch. Had he succeeded to the throne, it is implied by his character, we should have had a more rounded, exciting, cynical Emperor than we possessed in St. John. Insofar as I am able to judge as a historian, which is to say, an observer of men at extremes, those qualities of wit, of culture, the man's very variousness, might have been the first victims of his assumption. We cannot know how the Augustate might have altered Isaac. Some say he would have been a tyrant—benign, but a tyrant. Yet I suspect it is only the ingenuous—and the bards—who believe despotism is the logical political extension of the arrogant, the amoral, the brutal, or the maniac. It is just as often the consequence of the lethargic, the unimaginative, the prig, and the spiritually arrogant who confuses his policies with his person and misconstruing their rejection or failure, perceives only political threat. (Indeed as a tyrant's only motive is power as a means not an end, any diminution of his authority is the only failure he recognizes.)

His uncle, the Grand Duke Nicephorus, once spoke of him thus, in a letter:

> As an adult, Isaac is all I could scarcely have expected of him during his youth: refined, devout, personally impeccable and politically amoral (which is to say, all his actions pointed toward the effect of his brother's

Regency), a good poet, a prudent warrior, and an excellent leader of men. As a child he was a hellion of all sorts with the promise of atheism, avarice, illiteracy, and recklessness to come, and no one to punish him as a grown man. He asked insolent questions of his religious tutor and usually landed a bite on the arm or leg of secular professors. He took to horse at the age of four—already uncommonly tall for his age—and as of seven years made it his pleasure to ride, *mounted,* into an Imperial Silentium, the full court assembled, thereby, as all scrambled to catch him, raising a havoc the likes of which had not been seen since Basil the Magnificent's Eudocia assembled two hundred reformed whores to present them with gold and diplomas, and one anonymous doxy doubted, in the most physical and profane terms, the regeneration of a colleague (the seconds of the audience make superb reading).

Even young the boy often amazed me with occasional inferences of sublimity. Once, I remember, the son of the Archadmiral Landulf, whose playmates included Isaac and John, shattered some fabulous antique in the gallery of Justinian at the inopportune moment his father and I and several aides were coming down the enormous vaulted corridor. I saw the accident plainly, but Landulf was uncertain. He nevertheless deprived his son of the benefit of the doubt and began to lecture him sternly. The Heir Apparent stood mute before this example of adult rage. As for the Heir Presumptive, he marched up to his father's highest captain and spoke boldly. "Sir, you misjudge your son. It was I who caused the accident." Then for good measure: "You may report it to His Majesty." What for me is simply astonishing is not the act of defending a playmate—though touching it is not remarkable—but that I sensed with incontrovertible certainty Isaac was giving Landulf as good as he had given his son, that on the *edge* of the age of reason, he knew the Archadmiral—in the awful way of grown men before exalted little Princes—blamed his boy only because he dared not blame the Porphyriogeneti, and would have done no differently had he actually *seen* Isaac or John cause the accident.

Fifteen years after this incident, Princess Martha Vatatzes, who had been intended for Isaac, in what would have been a real love match, died in a riding accident. We were all worried for the boy's grief. There is a streak of excess in the Porphyriogenetus which now and then obliges him to foolish acts. A hunt had been scheduled many weeks previous for the day following the funeral. Isaac had been assigned to "attend" his father. He had not appeared in public or amongst the family since Johnny told him of the Princess' death. The morning we arrived at Villa

Rufiniana, however, the Porphyriogenetus was at the gate to greet Alexius, all in readiness. He was red-eyed, but no more than that. Throughout the day he was solicitous of everyone, convivial, successful in his game, humorously critical (though the humor was noticeably less biting than usual) and even drank with us (though moderately as was his habit) at the day's end. Before retiring I took him aside and rather gracelessly said, "For God's sake, boy, you're so intent on making everyone comfortable, you couldn't possibly make them more ill at ease." He stared at me with the most confounding mixture of coldness and helplessness I have ever beheld and said, "What would you have me do, uncle? It is pointless and vulgar to reach for sympathy and nothing will console me Martha's absence. We need consider nothing inevitable, but we must accept the occasion. Nothing can turn us back and it is as a child to weep save in one's closet."

According to Andronikus, his father was least famous with either parent, which would seem to conform to Nicephorus' portrait. Isaac was indeed a solitary man, neither begging affection—which is a contradiction in terms, really—nor giving it, save assured it would be returned in kind. Rash actions by which he stood in adolescence became considered decisions by which he abided, no matter the consequence, in his maturity. He was called cold, unapproachable, prejudiced, and rigid by some; gentle, subtle, profoundly tolerant, and of the utmost integrity by others—usually by those who knew him personally and at length. Andronikus once called his father the typical Great Courtier, meaning, I suppose, the highest servant of a ruler, of whom much is spoken and little accurately known, for he is too busy in the state's behalf to defend himself against those from whom he shields the Regent (thus arousing their enmity and gossip).

Their aunt, the first Sebastocratrix, Irene of Alania, writes of them:

Not so surprisingly, it was Isaac Porphyriogenetus who led John the way to a normally more yielding, mischievous childhood. I should have been alarmed otherwise. Every mother I know wants an angel for a son, but give her one and she begins to suspect in that passivity, a kinky unquiet which, not subject to the run of normal emotions and outbursts, cannot be taught control, so that, at last, if the boy is aroused—worse, as a man —he may strike in disproportionate anger—merciless, murderous, vicious, and unscrupulous. (Hence, many a wretch is indeed a "good boy" to his mother.)

In truth, there has always been a subtlety between the two brothers
which is quite beyond my powers to describe. As children, there was
never any dispute about John's seniority and the deference due to him,
yet Isaac was plainly the "leader," the deviser of their adventures, which
Johnny followed with a fixed glee and frequent giggles no matter the
situation. (My niece Anna warranted in those moments, her brother resembled an idiot.) They are wonderfully devoted to one another, though
I cannot imagine a greater difference between two men. I have never
been much attached to my brother-in-law's second son, but then, in that,
I stand at the end of a very long line. Not that I haven't made my assaults on his affections, but that he has repulsed them (and there again I
am one of many). He is without compassion for other men's weaknesses.

Yes, who does not know of his excellent poetry and his philanthropy
and the many kindnesses to his staff and his suite? Yet is it not significant
these praises are offered defensively, in behalf of that self-righteous
giant? Of all the comprehensible good which can be said of him, it is
this: he reveres Johnny. As for my august nephew; the most cynical
courtier is beside himself with reverence, a *serious* deference. Alexius
knew some of this awe—especially at the end of his life—and suffered it
with a blend of toleration and grace. I know Isaac Porphyriogenetus
would have accepted it without a smile as his due. But John, who did
away with kissing of the boot or the hem, seems still amazed when a
peasant kneels in something like religious ecstasy to kiss his hem. Then
my nephew places his own hand on the poor fellow's head and turns his
face away with a look which seems to be pain, seems to be embarrassment, seems to say, "Why me?"

I do not say Isaac would not have been a good emperor, and possibly
as great as his brother, only that Isaac would have stopped at nothing
to come by greatness. Once, I remember, John said, "If we have not the
laws to be certain a fool will be obeyed, we have not the means to maintain a wise man upon the throne." To which Isaac responded with an
awful vehemence, arm extended to a pointing jeweled forefinger,
squinting balefully, "That's preposterous! If we have not the means to
remove a fool from power, the genius which could replace it is irrelevant." Compare this with words Johnny wrote to me in 1110: "It seems
to men so natural to remove morality from the affairs of state in order
to gain their ends. Yet what assurance have they in their unscrupulousness that their antagonists shall not do likewise? Amorality is anarchic
because it denies a common reference with which men may come to
terms, equably with other men. If there is not that public founding, that

mutual consent, all that we do is in vain. Papa's ministers think me either a lunatic or a prig. In the one, they attempt to intimidate me, in the other, they dread my accession (whether for the state or themselves, it is not clear to me). But I must have the courage to be different, to be humble without allowing myself to be bullied. I am not attempting to be virtuous merely to be different and remarkable. I had thought virtue would offend no one. Apparently, in a world such as we live, it is most suspect. Yet I feel, however onerous my conduct seems to these people, it is the only possible manner in which I may act and the only meaning in so much chaos. We have lost more good deeds for sniggering than lethargy. The struggle to be good makes men uneasy, I suppose, because, in the tension of the spiritual flight, to remain airborne, the man who will act morally is unpredictable. It is, rather, the evil soul which is predictable, for it arrives at its meaning, loses all tension, its alternatives obvious, the moment wickedness is chosen. The *good* man cannot be called good until his death. Simply put, there is only one way for men to be virtuous and too many ways to be wicked." A few days after receiving this letter, I sent him this passage, which, I was moved to note, he had copied in tiny script and secured in a locket he always wore from that time forward, with his icon. It is from St. Symeon, the New Theologian: "And by what means then have saints shone on earth and become lights in the world? If it were impossible, they too could not have achieved it. For they were men as we are. And they had no more than we have, except their resolution for good, fervor, humility, and love. . . . Therefore, acquire this yourselves and your soul, which is now stony, will become for you a spring of tears. And even if you do not wish to take the difficult and narrow way, at least do not say that such things are impossible."

The Emperor rose, we are told, like his father before him, before dawn, spending several minutes in prayer in his private chapel. Then he would collect his sons, Alexius, Isaac, and Sergius, and meet Isaac and Isaac's eldest, Philip, at the riding track of the old Sacred Palace. Afterward, the brothers would attend Divine Liturgy, breakfast, and either separately or together meet with the Imperial undersecretaries to consider appointments for the day. If it were a Holy Day, one brother or the other, seldom both, represented the throne, at morning festivities. The first set of correspondence was attended to, and thereafter interviews with ministers or the reception, perhaps, of an ambassador. Lunch was taken uncommonly early in the day, after which the Emperor diverted himself with reading, a siesta, or more riding, "while," says Andronikus, "my father visited his latest mistress, with each visit mini-mizing the likelihood I should ever be born to the Sebastocratrix Joanna Paleologa Comnena."

The afternoon began with a second portfolio of correspondence *ab* and *ex cathedra,* and the examination of unending, sometimes superflu-ous reports of the Imperial bureaucracy. A second set of interviews usu-ally followed and with that, adjournment for dinner, if to a formal banquet, together, if not, apart. After dinner John heard Divine Liturgy for the second time, usually, as it deeply pleased him to, in the ordinarily nearly empty Holy Wisdom Cathedral, the splendid Patriarch John IX making it a special point to celebrate.* Afterward, John and Isaac usu-ally met with the Caesar Bryennius, more often than not for the second or third time that day.

The Imperial brothers had begun by attempting, somewhat warily, to co-opt their sister's husband and ended by depending upon him for his untold abilities in managing the bureaucracy. They realized the great risk in granting the Caesar control of government machinery—Isaac against his better judgment, John from a typically deeper perception of the boundaries of trust beyond which a man would not pass—for who controls the bureaucracy is half the way by sabotage or competence to the throne. Still they gave Bryennius the power, much as Alexius forgave his antagonists—perhaps with that in mind—and he seemed to have grati-fied their best expectations.

For working members of the regime, for palace servants, for mem-bers of the merchant class—whom, like Andronikus, the Emperor and Sebastocrator prodded to join the Imperial service—for the Orphano-tropolites—in a sense beside society—and the poor with whom they came in contact—in a sense, beneath society—there was no act too gracious for the brothers to lovably perform. For the court, however—indeed, the en-tire aristocracy—John's accession was a bitter sequel to his father's reign, "which," as the young Sebastocrator has one critic putting it to

---

* This custom became widely known throughout the city. The poor, who rarely glimpsed this Emperor—less public than his father—began to attend vespers themselves in ever greater numbers. The Emperor did not in the least mind—and was rather moved—but at length the crush became too great, and the Varangian commander, responsible for his final safety, asked John to use one of the numerous churches in the palace complex.

him, "may have been a struggle, but it was a happy one." "Indeed," as Isaac notes, "it was free-wheeling as well as happy, if not prodigal."

> My father, like most children of great wealth—and even when the parent is parsimonious as my grandmother—was rather more indulged than he may have realized or wished to admit, especially in his political ambitions, for which, then, no sum was too dear. As such, money was for Alexius something which could always be got, in whatever amount. He was not indifferent to it, by any means, only to its source. As Emperor, he extended this attitude to the court. And worse: A prideful man, and a kindly one, he could never refuse to be generous. The very idea of illiberality was offensive to him because he himself had all his life received whatever he asked, whenever he asked for it.

With the thoroughness of a great critic, if not a revolutionary, who does not hesitate, as might have his father—a restorer—to use power so sweepingly, John Augustus, in a stroke, canceled eight incremental centuries of court ceremony.

Besides the offense this gave to traditionalists for whom Imperial choreography was as sacred as Divine Liturgy (as Patriarch John reminded those who flocked to him in petition, it was not; and further reminded them, its actual sources were Hellenist Roman, Zoroastrian Persian, and Pharaonic Egyptian), the crush of such an austere fist also knocked the means from beneath many hundreds of courtiers whose only *function* was ceremony and only livelihood, quite frankly, parasitism. (Most of the latter were old men and women, who, though senile in all else, could still perform the most intricate ritual, which was, by now, as much their instinct as hunger or the need for sleep.) Also caught, though not so nearly undone, were the master goldsmiths of the city, as well as its jewelers and weavers.

To this decree, the Caesarissa Anna and the Dowager Empress, now living at Porphyriogenetus Palace, responded that, for themselves, they would welcome all refugees from the Imperial court at their own, and intended to continue the hallowed dignities. Of course, there was a great flight, at which the Emperor informed his sister and mother—significantly not through Bryennius, but by letter—if they intended to maintain themselves and others so profligately, they could not expect an increase in their privy purse or the establishment of a public one, which was for the Autocrat's attendance, solely. Whether reluctantly (there is, in all sincerity, that possibility) or pretending to be reluctant (sincerity extended by rhetoric), the Dowager Empress and her daughter shortly released all but a few of the aristocratic immigrants from the Sacred Palace.

The expected lowering of tax levies, however, did not arrive in this same year. On the advice of Auxuch—on whom the Emperor relied nearly as much as on his brother and whose erasure from Isaac's memoranda resembles John's from his sister's *Alexiad,* and for the same reasons—the Emperor instead took the less drastic step of proclaiming a moratorium on all outstanding debts within the Empire. Unfortunately, this act caused greater confusion than joy, and the benefits were minimal.

As anyone could have foreseen, those who at once benefited were the antipodes of the rich and the poor, which is to say, the most irresponsible, those perpetually in debt, purchasing too much and possessing too little means to pay for it. Merchants of really immense wealth—that is, with agents or friends in the administration, who warned them of impending legislation—suffered least by calling in all loans, quickly instituting suit before deadline, and refusing new debtors. The lesser businessmen were substantially hurt—especially contractors, hence workmen—and almost as a group, Jewish bankers—save again, the great ones—giving rise to gruesome rumors of an anti-Semitic Autocrat and impending pogroms.† "Leave John to that slave and your iniquitous, swaggering younger brother," the Dowager Empress wrote to her eldest daughter at Thessalonika, "and I assure you within a year any further effort on our part will be unnecessary. The people themselves will set you on the throne."

By February 1120 it became clear the only real antidote to this half-hearted—and unsuccessful—cure was indeed some form of tax abatement. In preparation thereof, John took two momentous steps. Against Isaac's advice, the first of the more notorious disagreements between the brothers, the Emperor placed a moratorium on the construction of Blachernae Palace, "the Jewel Box," as he called it, and an unconscion-

---

† Isaac, who relished the consequences of the "Persian's Wisdom" (as he contemptuously referred to Auxuch), advised his brother to make haste in reassuring the Rabbi of Constantinople, or the city would lose its greatest finance houses. This John did at once, and probably rescued the capital from complete fiscal collapse. N.A.

able drain on Imperial revenues.‡ Then, against the advice of Marianus Catacalon, his Archadmiral and brother-in-law, and to the profit, he hoped, of native merchants and the government's tolls, John abrogated the Venetian Trade Treaty of 1082.

The abrogation was unusually popular, politics and finances aside. Despite forty years' residence many Latin merchants of the second generation, taking their cue from the first, persisted in acting impertinently to every Greek—high or low—they encountered. Neither alien conquerors nor native princes, they persisted in the manner of both. Then, too, the Emperor's move had not seemed a militarily foolish strategy, since to all appearances, Norman Sicily no longer presented the threat it had on his father's accession. What *was* unwise was the lack of inclusion of Genoa and Pisa in this Imperial reneging. Their advantages, it is true, were scarcely comparable, but to a ruined man, a street vendor has more privilege than he.

Almost at once, Venetian armadas began raiding the Aegean and the Adriatic, in acts which were nothing less than piracy. Yet there was no disputing this, the greatest sea power in the world, and, in August, the treaty was restored, the only advantage to Byzantium a negative one: the Emperor had refused a malicious, retaliatory demand to extend the privileges.

This episode may be described as the single greatest diplomatic humiliation of John's reign, and it could not have been at a less propitious moment. The discontent which had been mounting since Alexius' death, the unity which his person, as has been said, symbolized, during the first long period of the Empire's rehabilitation, the absence, too, of a common enemy to inspire a common amity and now this errant submission to Venice, combined to convince the Bryennii faction the time was ripe for supplanting. It is for Bryennius himself to tell the story, as recorded in a private memorandum in 1137, the year he died of cancer.

> I shall make a clean breast of it once and for all, and I shall not mince a word or the vice of any participant. The plot was conceived in autumn, 1120. September, I believe.

‡ The economic situation of the city was not improved by the dismissal, implicit, of so many artisans, craftsmen, and contractors and their laborers. They—or rather another generation—would not return to complete Alexius' great work until the accession of Manuel, the Emperor's youngest child, born, if irony needs be, in the same month. N.A.

At the time, a marriage had been arranged by Lord John between my eldest son and Militsa, daughter of David II of Georgia—a most splendid match. The date of the ceremony was set for February 1121, and, to be sure, the nuptials—who much favored their august uncle despite my wife's prolix hatred—were not informed of the plot, since they were to be the innocent diversion. (That is to say, the guiltless always play a better part.) Whilst the means were devised, I should add, I was assisting the Emperor in the preparation of a chrysobull which would forever forbid capital punishment by the state.

I must say I count those days of 1120–21 as the unhappiest of my life: a great palpable gloom through which I moved as one bewitched. Even today, the mere sight of Porphyriogenetus Palace—to which, since, I have never returned—is enough to evoke in me the same sort of dread and relief as a man imprisoned and later freed must experience when he passes the place of his former incarceration. . . .

Surely what amazed us all and finally gave me the motive to become estranged in all but declaration from my wife—*that* proved a fortuitous wisdom—was the Dowager Empress' refusal to recognize or to join the conspiracy when she learned from Anna it was to end, as it must, in the murder of both her sons. That revelation took place at Petrion Convent in which Irene was making retreat. She listened patiently to my wife and, at first, with the usual admiration and fervor in her responses. When the final nature of the plot became clear, however, her eyes swelled with the same terror I once noted in my daughter, when, smug and dissimulating after mischief to which I was secretly witness, I confronted her with the intent, at once, to punish; or, perhaps, the same terror I saw by the Emperor's deathbed, when not all the frenzy in the world would stop the inevitable from occurring.

My wife, the Caesarissa, is a profoundly perceptive woman—we all know that—yet I think she is one who does not know what to do with all the ore of her insight once she has mined it. A prospector, then, not a goldsmith. She saw her mother's horror, yet she could not stop herself. She only spoke more quickly, with more force, became more vitriolic, as if to overwhelm her mother's coming condemnation. At long length she was silent, not with the blazing apostrophe of a leader among devotees, but by stops and starts, as one relinquishing herself unwillingly to criticism.

Irene said, "So I have nourished a murderess."

Anna blushed, as only her mother, the great consenting coddler of her life, could make her blush. She began to speak, but Irene silenced her with an almost imperceptible movement of her beautiful hand.

"And I have cozened a snake. How well I remember the day I thanked God my brother-in-law, George Paleologus, was my champion. Now *he* would kill my sons." Anna attempted again to speak, but her mother croaked at her, attempting to control a shout: "Be quiet! I would contend for you, and I have, at great cost to myself, let me tell you, against anyone—even your brothers. I might have wished my own sons deformed, or elsewhere, anywhere, playboys, fools, anything to allow you the Regency. But I have never wished them dead, or done to death." She lifted her hands to her face. "My fault, my fault."

My wife seemed to be of two minds: she was obviously stricken by her mother's tears, her own about to fall. At the same time she was struggling for a last measure of dignity which was gone if her mother's tears recognizing her personal responsibility for corruption of her own child were valid. They must not be recognized, or consoled. Weakly, my wife said, "Mama, there's nothing left to me, but this."

The Dowager Empress brought down her hands and looked at me with the eyes of a dead fish: glittering and hard. "Do you consent to this, Nicky?" Agonized, myself, I allowed her an indeterminate expression of helplessness, and, lifting my hands, turned them up. "Go away then, the both of you, and if you do what you seem about"—she raised her hands to heaven, but spoke without emphasis—"then take with you a mother's curse."

I need not describe my wife's turmoil at that moment, how she knelt weeping before the Dowager Empress who was as stone—until I lifted her, saying, "Come, let's go."

Now, I have often wondered at Irene's sincerity. As far as I have been able to learn, she did not go to the Emperor with news of the plot, the very shadow under which we all lived from that visit to the contemplated day of assassination. Perhaps she did not wish to implicate her daughter in a crime she believed, at the end, would never take place. Anyone of goodwill, which, however painfully, I believe myself to be, seeks some virtue in the life of the most errant man. I should like to think better of Irene than I do—especially now as I sort my memories before the end. Yet—in the peril of my soul—I cannot.

What then was the Dowager's motive in cursing Anna, and after a fashion, accusing herself? Perhaps in that wicked way of little religious minds, she attempted to keep God's punishing hands from her own head —as though God listens rather than *perceives*. I think the woman honestly believed she ceased to be complicit by disclaiming herself on the one hand, and accusation on the other.

For myself, I played the perilous, perhaps futile game—quite in the hope (or horror) of the Empress' revelation—of marking the attitude of the Emperor and the Sebastocrator toward me. My reasoning was, of course, ambiguous, errant. If the Imperial brothers turned on me, I could only presume myself compromised and be obliged to join against them. If their kindness remained unshaken, it behooved me to tell them of their peril before they became its victim. Why did *I* not go to them at once? Perhaps, in part, for the same reasons Irene could not bring herself to compromise her own daughter: on the supposition of a crime so ghastly we believed it beyond Anna's sensibility to commit. But then, I well knew her supporters less scrupulous. Did I, at any point, desire her success and my own enthronement? Yes, qualifiedly. As a child too strictly raised wishes the death of his parent, and, as quickly, thinks better.

As the day of consummation of the conspiracy grew nearer, I prayed. Heaven knows for what: Irene's revelation, Anna's death, Auxuch's spies? I slept little, grew weak, yet I would not leave the side of the Emperor and the Sebastocrator as much as work and protocol allowed. Finally, three days before the wedding, 6 February, while the eminent victims and myself were sitting at our usual evening conference, I made my decision. I remember, as I rose to close the doors into the antechamber, a feeling of extraordinary light-headedness, as if my brain were somehow severed from my body, within it, but detached, afloat.

Then I did something completely to my own surprise. I fell to my knees in the center of the room and with nothing of the intricate casuistry I had rehearsed, said, quite baldly, "Your Majesty, Your Highness, I wish to confess a plot, myself complicit, in which it is the object to murder yourselves, place my wife, Anna, upon the Imperial throne, and raise me to Supreme Power as Autocratic Consort." I recall the brothers looked at one another, almost impassively, though the Emperor's left foot began to shake uncontrollably as it did in any grave moment.

His first question was quietly given. "When?"

"Monday, John. After the wedding. The plan is to waylay and assassinate both of you as you leave Pantokrator."

Isaac almost smiled. "Propitious marriage."

The Emperor said, "Yes. Why *then?* How unthinkable for the children." He signaled me up from my knees and into a chair.

I did not move back from its edge. "I don't believe either of you realize how unapproachable you've been for the last three years, mostly secluded, otherwise constantly guarded. An occasion such as this should have been an excellent opportunity." In the following hour, I gave names, and details to the best of my knowledge, and at its end, it seemed to me, I had awakened from death on the other side of infinity.

When it was over, I left my chair again and prostrated myself upon the purple marble cross set into the red malachite floor, and kissing it, said, "I swear by the God who made me and the death by which I shall be overtaken, no sin in my life do I more abjectly regret than this. I swear further, by my own hope of heaven, my children are in all ways innocent and ignorant of this terrible venture. Whatever becomes of myself and my wife, I pray you, Divinity, have pity upon them."

I heard footsteps moving up to me, Isaac's. He said, "You scum."

And then the Emperor's remonstrance, *"Isaac!"*

To my own horror, I felt my body revolt. Rising quickly from the floor, I moved to a corner and vomited. Afterward, whether it was the mortification of this act or the real agony in my stomach, I was on my knees again, sobbing. I remember only the smell of my own refuse, my hands upon my face, the rings upon my fingers become like pincers.

Then Isaac lifted me and said, somewhat more sympathetically, "Come, you're ill. We'll leave this room."

Though not indifferent to my very real misery, the Emperor told me to return to Porphyriogenetus under the pretense of continued complicity.

On my arrival home, my valet called Anna to me and she, whom, after a fact, I had as well betrayed, was as loving and as solicitous to me as ever, remaining by my bed well into the night, tending me.

On the day of the wedding, not even my wife's fellow conspirators remarked upon the increased guard round the Emperor, Empress, the Sebastocrator, and Sebastocratrix *within* the cathedral.*

Now, the plan was brutal and morose: to cut down the Varangians which preceded the brothers from the cathedral, and follow with regicide. The key, according to old George Paleologus, was cutting off any further egress from Pantokrator. Twelve Varangians, even twenty, could be undone. If the rest of the guard were allowed to enter the fray, there might be a possibility of rescue. There was indeed.

---

* For the first time in many years, it may be added, the Sebastocratrix Joanna was noted to "cling" to her husband, though whether adoring or merely in fear for him we are not told. Marriage to any member of the Imperial house is splendid enough to make any spouse grateful. Surely the Sebastocratrix had long ago reckoned herself too fortunate as the Second Lady of the Empire and dismissed the possibility of divorce. "But," says Andronikus, "it required a great many people who wished my father dead before my mother ceased to wish it herself. From these few weeks of toleration or tenderness, needless to say, I was given the opportunity to be born the following year, 1122. Of course, by then my parents were thoroughly annoyed. They were back to their old rancor again and, I should imagine, no more desired this reminder of the previous year's vulnerability —political and emotional—than a priest his drunkenness the previous night." N.A.

During the night, Excubitors were sent to the cathedral. I am told it was an ominous sight, these hundreds of armored soldiers forming a cordon sanitaire round the entire building, torches and braziers flaring, throwing the lines and loops of Pantokrator into fantastical perspectives. At dawn, the soldiers vanished, it was thought, to the palace. Instead, they had retired to the Cantacuzenus mansion across the street. An additional contingent of Varangians arrived and Pantokrator was once more encircled. That facilely, that cleanly, the plot was foiled. None of the henchmen, none of the soldiers from Porphyriogenetus, would dare approach.

To protect the Emperor and the Sebastocrator still further, it was thought prudent to have them leave by a side entrance, returning to the palace, quite literally in the middle of a Roman square. By this, my son was married happily, nothing seeming amiss, whilst the conspirators, desperate all, were not certain whether they were the dupes of coincidentally stricter protection for the Emperor, or revealed and ruined, by implication. The answer came upon us that evening.

Throughout the city there were arrests. When the Scholarians arrived at Porphyriogenetus, my wife and I were in our suite on the second floor, rooms designed originally for the Autocrat Constantine VII, who built that beautiful palace, so loathsome to me now.

I vividly recall my wife before the fire, still lovely in her jewels and gown, which, stunned by the lack of event of the afternoon, she had not yet bothered to remove. She was without any aspect of usual tantrum; rather, still with the immovability of ultimate failure which knows not what to do next, save welcome death, which, stubbornly, will not come. At that terrible sound of cavalry in the courtyard, the initial panic of the servants, and the battering of the door, Anna looked up. The expression upon her face remains with me yet in the life I have left to live. All in a trice, there was amazement, fear, and the sudden comprehension of my betrayal. Perhaps she knew my culpability the moment the conspiracy failed; it took the jolt of consequences for her to connect the two, much, I imagine, as a mathematician will suddenly surmise, after long cogitation and relinquishment, the theorem which binds antagonistic concepts.

Explicit: Nicetas Acominatus.

Anna looks up, appalled, at her husband, who is staring at the silver and cedar doors, with the complete calm of one who knows the origin of an alarming noise, and its destination. Hypnotically, he pushes back his sleeves, of deep purple velvet, the huge scallops lined in pale blue silk, a gesture by which anyone who knows him would tell you of his anxiety. It is a moment before he realizes his wife is watching him. She is shaking in little spasms, the pearls at her ears clicking like chattering teeth.

ANNA PORPHYRIOGENETA. You. You have done this to me.

She rises, her hands throwing her weight against the arms of her chair. Bryennius frowns upon his wife, then looks away.

BRYENNIUS. One's troth in his family is an obligation, Anna. It ought not to be mocked as you have mocked it.

ANNA PORPHYRIOGENETA. And my faith in you as my husband? My father's faith in you as a son? You, lifted from disgrace, by my blood.

BRYENNIUS. Madame, one should seek to make an emperor only when the throne is vacant. Once there is a worthy sovereign he should not be overthrown. It is as simple as that. I have found your brother worthy, and can be worthy myself, of your father's generosity only as I honor that opinion.

ANNA PORPHYRIOGENETA. Then be *damned,* you hypocrite!

BRYENNIUS. You were not meant for the throne. Your brother is anointed. He takes precedence over us all, over me as my sovereign, over you at court and throughout the Empire, as I did in wisdom to forfeit your atrocious scheme. You are, I fear, rash and arrogant, and I forgive you as wholeheartedly as, I am certain, at this moment, you detest me.

ANNA PROPHYRIOGENETA. And you are a repellent and immoral opportunist, who have betrayed me and my family at every crow of the cock which was our kindness to you.

BRYENNIUS. Have I indeed? Then this was an opportunity for betrayal which would repay all generosity to me, in degree.

She expectorates full on the floor between them.

Incipit: Nicetas Acominatus:

My wife, the Caesarissa, is one of those, I have so come to the conclusion, not really intelligent, only opinionated, with a fatal streak of sentimentality which is excess. She idealizes what she favors and caricatures what she loathes. She has never had a friend in the world because she is incapable of moderation and diplomitesse. She is not subtle even when she attempts to be subtle, for she italicizes. She is condemned to the hell of the conceited and the obdurate, who do not and cannot learn from their failure, for, unable to keep a distance from their actions, they personalize, to the point of insult, the ruin of their stratagems.

Secondary conspirators were subject to confiscation of all property, save that to which they were banished, that is, their own estates farthest from Constantinople. These included all those names, especially George Paleologus', which ring so heroically from Alexius' reign. (Though, once again, in the case of Paleologus, punishment was ameliorated, by passing on his patrimony to his son, the Sebastocrator's father-in-law, Michael.) But when all was done, Anna Porphyriogeneta, under house arrest in the same apartments in which her father died, remained the Emperor's most undoubted problem, as for that matter did Bryennius. The former the Emperor knew not how to punish, the latter whether or not he ought to punish. Finally, there was the Dowager Empress who had made herself complicit by her silence.

Isaac wanted death for Anna, exile for Bryennius, and incarceration under the veil for their mother. John, however, meted out punishment less brusquely, almost tentatively. He did, indeed, command his mother take the veil, and then, within a month, his sister, also. In April he confiscated Anna's vast inheritance and signed it over to Auxuch.

Now, Andronikus insisted this was the beginning, however resolved, of the estrangement between his father and his uncle. Isaac Porphyriogenetus was genuinely shocked that monies and properties left privately by the father to the daughter should be turned over to one who was not a Comnenus and, moreover, sufficiently rich in his own personal fortune. I have it on the son's authority that Isaac, face to face, threatened to sew Auxuch in a sack and drop him in the Bosporus if he did not return Anna's properties to the crown. Too discreet, and wily yet, to inform the Emperor of his brother's threat, Auxuch, indeed, forfeited the estate back to the Imperium, with the advice, either clement or calculating, they ought to be held in trust or immediately divided between the Caesarissa's children. To be sure, Isaac's threat reached the ears of the Emperor, with the end result, John's confidence and admiration of Auxuch knew no bounds, while his disappointment in the Sebastocrator —the practitioner of extremes beyond which there is no return save capitulation or oblivion—was total. (If I seem, myself, less than willing to praise the Emperor's adviser, it may be for the unhappy reason I still bake somewhat under the fire of Andronikus' prejudices, or the honest conclusion Count Auxuchos ought to have returned the gift on reception —at once, not at length.)

As for Bryennius, suiting the punishment to the crime, his chastisement was as ambiguous as his sin. Much has been made of John's forgiveness, but this seems to me more supposed than fact. The Emperor was a good man. He was not a fool, though fools confuse the two. If Bryennius were truly repentant, that was to the profit of his own soul. But for too long the Caesar had been the rallying point—active or passive, in name, if not truth—of every reasonably and unreasonably disaffected grandee or bureaucrat. His presence at Constantinople was, quite simply, intolerable. And so he was sent into useful—but unmistakable—banishment as Governor of Trebizond, the first to establish that great city as the traditional place of exile for members of the Imperial family. In the years until he returned to court, he performed admirably, in every way, his functions. Yet there was no mistaking the taint of dishonor which remained with him the rest of his life, nor the saddening fact that two generations of those among the Empire's most high-minded families, the Comneni and the Bryennii, had contested one another, leaving precisely the same name ruined, one heroically, one in knavery.

In August 1121 an embassy arrived from the Roman Pope, Calixtus II, seeking John Augustus' intercession with Heinrich V in yet another Petrine and Imperial battle for right of investiture of bishops. Consenting to the absurdity of assuming the Pope's behalf—which can only be compared to a man requesting an arsonist to assist him in putting out a fire since it is the first fine point of our law that the Emperor shall nominate the Orthodox patriarchs—John made clear his own condition, quid pro quo: the establishment of a committee, composed ecumenically of Greeks and Latins, meeting at Old Rome and New Rome semiannually, for purposes of seeking a reunion of the Western and Eastern rite. Such are the contradictions which make of diplomacy more amusing reading than Petronius. If it were possible the divisions of Christendom should cease, what would become of the Basileus' prerogative over bishops, averse the Pope's? I am reminded of Andronikus' musing, "If every state acted in externals according to its internal legal currency, diplomacy would trip upon the cynicism of its own bones. Men would be unintelligible to one another, and even wars, which begin and end with diplomats, might vanish." *Explicit: Nicetas Acominatus.*

A month-old child, swaddled in fine linen, lies asleep in his cradle. A man's bejeweled hand reaches down and very gently lays by the side of the mummiform infant a small golden icon attached to a chain.

VOICE OF JOANNA. Oh, come now, Isaac. That sort of thing only goes down well with your brother. I know too much and the child too little to be impressed.

Joanna's fine hand reaches down to take up the talisman.

VOICE OF ISAAC. Don't touch it. It was my father's. It will be his stoicheion. A truly fair child. You're an excellent vessel.

VOICE OF JOANNA. I assure you he's the last. If there's another, he'll be a bastard. How shall we call him?

VOICE OF ISAAC. It is said Hermes rubs the moly, the magic herb which conquers the hearts of men, across the lips at birth of the children he favors. I think it well here.

There is some pleasure in the Sebastocrator's voice as his hand reaches down to touch the child's cheek. Eerily, the infant's eyes open slowly.

VOICE. He shall be baptized "Andronikus."

v

Incipit: Nicetas Acominatus: John Augustus called war "the devil's entertainment." "Somewhere," he once said, "the devil sits aside and laughs. Even in the thick of battle, I think, betimes, if I turn very quickly, I will find him behind me, with his death's head smile. Or if I glance from the corner of my eye, I will catch him somewhere near the sun, obscene and dark and gleaming. He knows the intoxication of murder, the obnoxious sense of power one feels in killing a man. He knows we are so seduced, we have found it necessary to excuse its sin by inextricable incorporation into the nature of our dealings with our fellow men. Pillage is pillage; rape is rape; blasphemy is blasphemy; but killing is sometimes murder and sometimes war."

The glory of his reign is the gradual reassertion of Greek hegemony throughout the Balkans, Lesser Asia, and Palestine. At his death, in 1143, nearly three quarters of the immense Empire of Basil II, the Great, had been regained. Yet again and again we are told by his contemporaries to conclude for ourselves, he dreamed neither as his father nor his son. Alexius was an archon, son of archons, and despite his regret, which was real, he loved the adventure and surprise of war, the contest of ingenuity, the black and white of antagonist and protagonist in an otherwise indeterminate world. Drums and trumpets stirred his memories and his ambitions.

Manuel, on the other hand, less ingenuous, was more culpable, his view of the agency of war quite ambiguous. If his grandfather dreamed of Alexander as a votary dreams of his saints, and in some manner harkened back to the equity of the Macedonian camp, wherein the King asked nothing of others that he did not expect, ultimately, of himself, Manuel—this great, extravagant, and finally deluded man—looked back to the days of Justinian—not as inspiration, but challenge—to its awesome pageantry and twilight bravado, to its reach and its glamour. He loved all men and could not understand why they did not wish to be ruled by him. Reluctantly he answered dissent with war.

John is somewhere between the two. He never thought of war as anything but a gruesome business and the most awful responsibility of his crown. When he returned to Constantinople from a campaign, he acted more like a man come from dispatching his favorite horse than the greatest general in Europe or Asia. Only once did he allow any of his victories to be celebrated in a public triumph, and then under the duress of politics. He did not refight old battles in his armchair. The cheers with which he was always greeted by his regiments, to whom he was nothing less than the incarnation of Michael of the Hosts, visibly distressed him. "The only pleasure war gives me is its conclusion," he once said.

Yet he never rushed a battle to its end, or a war. Because he considered himself, as Imperator, a sinner (he fasted a month after every campaign, living on bread and water), he took war too seriously to waste it. That perhaps is the key to his mastery. The resemblances to his father are evident. He entered the forefront of battle. He thirsted with his men as they thirsted, hungered when they lacked food, and would have walked when they walked, save he knew the sight of himself mounted on his pure white Arabian stallion, lifted their next foot when a trudging Emperor mightn't. If he lacked his father's camaraderie and panache, by which the soldiers fought as if for a great friend, he nevertheless instilled the sort of awe absent since Heraclius I or Leo III. If Alexius'

men fought so as not to disappoint him, John's armies could not conceive of defeat when led to battle by a clement, if slightly aloof, god, or
very nearly a god. Alexius welded his armies by amiability, John by
piety.

These first years of war—between 1123 and 1129 up to the moment
of dissolution between the Porphyriogeneti—are of a piece. Each man
comes into his own, and by that individuality estranges himself from
the other. Nowhere was this more apparent than John's refusal—when
absent at war—to grant his brother plenipotentiary powers in direct distinction to their father's practice and the Sebastocrator's prerogatives.

The answer lies, I suspect, in the further distinction we have made
between the Comneni as subjects and the Comneni as dynasts. John was
born to the crown. In a subtle sense he was separate from all men, and
dedicated, as a bull calf bound for sacrifice in Old Rome, from birth.
Isaac describes it:

> Whether he was born with it or the promise of that to which he was
> born made him so, there seemed round my brother an indeterminate
> "space," at once cautionary and tranquil, aloof and fascinating. Nothing
> passed through that boundary, save by his consent, and nothing reached
> him by that passage which was not, in the meantime, purged and trans-
> figured, as a frenzied soul passes through the flames to reach heaven,
> removed of all earthly dross. He never seemed to condescend; he was
> capable of real, intimate, and simple joys and filial love of the richest
> and most abiding texture and yet he remained apart, inviolable, un-
> troubled, in the profoundest sense. He *reached* to us. He did not blend.
> He reached as God reaches from heaven and inspires one with his love
> yet remains unknowable, indivisible, not wholly giving of Himself.

A man such as this could not comfortably share his throne, as did his
father, any more than he could possibly share his eyes, his appetite, or
its satiation. Alexius had known that special unity of an ambitious family, whose spirits rose and fell with each member's success. John had
known the jealousy, cynosure, and disparateness of a family ultimately
arrived. Alexius could be generous and rely on others because he had
known, along the path to supreme power, practically, the convenience,
and morally, the virtues, which trust in another via delegation of authority may produce. As his father's heir, John knew neither necessity.
Not that the son was obtuse and the father more lenient, but that John's
father was an emperor and Alexius', a mere duke. And so we observe,

while John adjures Isaac from the field, Isaac, with a very real sense of exasperation, is charged with all of the responsibility of ruling the Empire as his namesake and predecessor, but with scarcely a quarter of the freedom to act that his uncle knew. He was forced to satisfy his obligations and his brother, which was not the same thing. One testily written —and uncommon—postscript runs:

> Johnny. It is your duty before God at this juncture to execute a war and mine to be caretaker of the state in your place. As I would not presume to strategize from the Sacred Palace, for I cannot possibly know the terrain and flow of the enemy's position and their intent from day to day, I beg of you do not contend or direct me in matters with which I deal —for your good cause—from moment to moment. Believe me, I remain, ever your loving brother and subject, Isaac.

Now in December 1122 the Pechs, who had felt the crush of Alexius' spurs and spanned a generation in their recovery, once again crossed the Danube ravaging Bulgaria as they passed south. When John charged his wife's dissimulating second cousin, Stephen II of Hungary, with their advance, he was not merely looking for someone to blame. Stephen had indeed sent his agents among the Pechs, if not in the hope of setting back the Empire by thirty years, then at least diverting and perhaps ending its Balkan hegemony. So long as Byzantium remained strong from the Carpathians to the Iron Defile, Hungary was little better than a victim between the two cudgels of the Holy Roman Empire and the East Roman Empire.

The Emperor did not leave Constantinople before March 1123, but then he moved at forced speed, in consecutive engagements at Adrianopolis, Philippopolis, Sredetz, Nissa, then east, in June, to Tŭrnovo and final carnage at Sillstria by the Danube. He did not return to the capital until late July, first calling Stephen from Stuhlweissenburg, to meet with him at the Tsar's palace, Ochrida. It was a long journey, and in its length, instructive. Stephen did not refuse.

The Emperor did not openly castigate the young King—young enough and surly to precisely turn on a lecture—but suggested reassertion of the "Perpetual Alliance," as he wrote ironically to Isaac, between Hungary and Byzantium. The twenty-two-year-old Apostolic King consented, and the treaty was signed with great pomp in the Palace Square, at Ochrida. Its most signal point was the right of Byzantium to "rectify"

Hungarian foreign policy, at any time the safety of the Empire or the Kingdom seemed subject to external danger. A magnificent hunt afterward which John had planned with the thought of ameliorating the humiliation of his wife's kin was, however, canceled when the Emperor received urgent dispatch from the Sebastocrator that their mother, the Dowager Empress Irene, was dying.

It is the sort of irony which, probably, would have brought light to the eyes of Alexius, that his wife followed him, presumably to heaven, on the fifth anniversary of his own death, 18 August 1123, at the age of fifty-seven. Her end was unnecessarily cruel. For a year a tumor had been swelling on her throat. At the beginning there was little pain; at the end the Dowager was conscious of nothing else. Those who visited her deathbed invariably speak of an "acrid" smell, which they could associate with nothing in their experience. During her last days, attended by Anna—whom Isaac now nicknamed the family's Messenger of Death— she was lucid and practical and prayed constantly. There is no record anywhere of her last meeting or meetings with her two sons, by which we may draw the conclusion they were tentative and painful, at best. What indeed does a monther say to children she never favored and to whose death she might have consented? What in turn do the forsaken children say to her? No tears, one would think, for tears would be unkind. Great silences, perhaps, between irrelevant words, silences in place of implicit apologies which cannot really be loving, and at best only generous and humane for a fellow being facing the death of us all. The last words of her final delirium are her epitaph. "Pity, pity," she repeated, "ashes, ashes."

Throughout the following year, in Serbia, numerous separate uprisings took place, the heritage of the short-lived, would-be Bodin dynasts, those ambitious, arrogant, brutal warlords whose memory had become since Alexius' reign the rallying cry of other, similarly ambitious aristocrats. In a group these native grandees turned now to an unregenerate Stephen of Hungary for assistance. And the King gave it, supporting their desire for separation from the Imperium (one presumes, with the ultimate point of forcing them to recognize Hungarian overlordship), at least until the Emperor marched east with a force of fifty thousand. Then Stephen's advisers took hold and refused to execute his promise, convinced such mischief would draw Imperial anger of the like unseen since Basil II punished Bulgaria one hundred years before.

This campaign, by the way, was the first in which Crown Prince Alexius was given a command. He acquitted himself, by all accounts, wretchedly. The Emperor wrote to his brother:

> Your nephew at eighteen is a born infantryman. The very idea of making a decision which will affect others weakens my son's knees—as there is no further resolve to be dispersed. He is, otherwise, such a little bully that this curious fear in the face of responsibility quite mystifies me.

Far happier was the increased reputation of the Archontopuli Regiment. This cavalry unit, you will remember, was initiated by Alexius for the sons of those military aristocrats killed in war. In the course of his reign it was extended to include sons of metropolitan aristocrats, as the late Emperor preferred a median between Constantinopolitan nobles more militarized and the archons of the provinces more dependent on the court. In describing the campaign of Belgrade-on-the-Sava, the Emperor wrote:

> I have great news for you. Those poor clowns, the Archontopuli, have, at last, I think, come into their own. Now you must write at once to Bryennius and tell him his Alexius commands a splendid body of men. Tell Militsa, too. When one thinks how, previously, they were Papa's despair. But then he should have foreseen the inevitable devolution of a corps of well-born young fellows into something like a club with all the worst vices of young captains and charming roués: drinking, swaggering, boisterousness, elaborate practical jokes, lack of discipline, and more strategy given to the consummation of trysts than upon the battlefield. In forty years it has become the tradition of these nitwits to perform more wretchedly than their predecessors. It seems to have been expected of them, as butts of the army, and they were only too willing to oblige. Papa, as you know, was terrified of putting them into action. He once said to me, only half-jokingly, I think, "I wouldn't know how to explain it to their mothers should anything happen to them." As for myself, I simply refused to take them with us last year, by which they were very wroth. They petitioned Alexei, who petitioned me. I told our dear nephew I would never use those fools again until they were proved less irresponsible, and better apt to fight. The army has no need of jesters. It was then, as you know, for reasons which may now become clearer to you, Alexei took them off to the estate he inherited from the Old Duchess Bryennius below Adrianople and put the whole lot to some awesome maneuvers. Still, when we reached Belgrade, I decided to use them as

reinforcements rather than in the main attack. I am given to understand they took great umbrage in this. In any event, as the slant-line has been in use for eight years and thus subject to contesting strategies by opposing generals, another formation, one nearly as successful, was attempted by the Serbs, wherein the heaviest possible attack was exercised upon the archers from both left and right, encompassing the entire turn of their aim, so that, thus diverted, a whole company could circle and attack from behind. It was at this point the Archontopuli achieved apostrophe. I released them against the flank and they annihilated the Serbs. Our nephew later told me, "What a test, uncle. I think we went into battle everyone for himself, everyone more intent on performing well than adequately within the unit. Then, I think, when we knew our own proficiency (it was like a miracle, I swear it), we came together. We stopped fighting like champions and started fighting like soldiers." I told him he had learned a great secret, vis-à-vis the training and deployment of men, and thereafter never to forget it. I think he will be a very great general. Would I could say as much for my sons.

This same year, two marriages were made, one compensating the other. In order to seal the years of peace with Sicily, the Emperor welcomed into Orthodoxy and the Imperial family, Prince Roger of Otranto, nephew of the Duke of Sicily, whom he married to the Crown Prince's twin, Magdalena Porphyriogeneta. As was become the custom, he created his eldest daughter Caesarissa and her husband, who took the name John, her Consort. It was, in fact, a most unpopular marriage despite the young man's charm, the willingness with which he adapted to Greek custom, and the astonishing rapidity with which he learned both demotic and court—or Attic—Greek. The history of this animosity was quite simple: even dead, Bohemond of Sicily and Antioch, Alexius' chief antagonist, stank fearfully behind anything and anyone Sicilian.

The Emperor's choice of a wife for the Heir, however, was gratifying in the extreme to all Greeks, the Princess of a native Orthodox house, Natalie Melissenus. In some ways it was an unusual move, a look backward, for Alexius had seemed to set a precedent for foreign marriages. Unfortunately the only Orthodox Princess beyond the Empire was the two-year-old Anastasia, daughter of Crown Prince George of Georgia (who in the following year, 1125, ascended the throne on the death of King David II). While it is true such a betrothal between the infant and the seventeen-year-old Heir would not have been unheard-of, it might

have proved politically and personally dangerous for Alexius Porphyriogenetus.

The Sovereign Grand Duke, it seems, was showing all the earmarks
of a second-rate libertine, i.e., one without at least the leavening of cynicism, and—perhaps pursuant to the former—a fourth-rate intellect. A
certain incipient sensitivity gleamed feebly in the Prince, but no sooner
did he comprehend how it disarmed people than he began to use it as
a weapon by which to attract, then brutalize, friend and critic alike. It
was rightly believed, if there were any hope for the Heir, it was not in
the way of postponement of marriage and consummation for, at minimum, thirteen years. The hiatus, without at least the steadying influence
of a wife, and the reassurance to the state of another Heir, would only
lead to the further dissolution of the Porphyriogenetus character and
reputation. Andronikus, in a memorandum to me, wrote of this man
and his marriage none too flatteringly:

> Manuel once reminded me (I recall nothing) how his eldest brother
> would make it a point to catch him, George Bryennius, my brother
> Michael—so frail—and myself at play. He would then accuse us of some
> incomprehensible misdemeanor and before we could explain ourselves
> —naturally impossible—beat the living daylight out of us. It's not diffi-
> cult to compare his practices with those of certain guards I recall at the
> court of Mas'ud Shah. As for Natalie: she was discreet, gracious, and, it
> seemed to me, always unhappy. Very pretty. I especially remember her
> red hair and dark blue—sublime blue—eyes. During the first years at
> court, after our exile, I made a special effort to attend her, which natu-
> rally gave rise to rumors I was my father's son and well into establishing
> my place in the next regime. Once or twice I provoked a smile from that
> dear girl, but nothing more. Poor thing. At length, I became quite bored
> with her and no longer paid her court. No, that is too cruel. But one can
> only attend a mannequin so long before activity on one side and unre-
> sponsiveness on the other makes a fool of a troubadour. As an empress
> she promised to be distant and uninspiring. As a matriarch she pro-
> duced two magnificently healthy daughters and four dead sons, thus
> promising the throne would fall on my cousin, Sergius.

That same new Heir Presumptive was married in 1125 to Rebecca
Paleologus, the half-sister of Andronikus' mother, the Sebastocratrix.
Seventeen years at the time of his nuptials, Sergius Porphyriogenetus re-
flected himself scarcely any better than his elder brother as the scion

of a saintly couple. Andronikus called him "the coldest, slyest, most sullen, stiffest moral and intellectual bigot" he ever knew. This is fascinating, since Sergius, like Andronikus' brother Michael, was a bleeder, and quite coddled throughout his childhood. One would have expected this man, whose children were to figure so importantly in the following reign, to be a deal more limpid, with the semi-invalid's instinct for pain in others and—since he could not himself be cured—an equal instinct toward correctable wrong. Then again, given the unending variations of human response, it may be, he sought to counter his born weakness with a miscalculated sense of "character." Rebecca was his complement and the self-appointed reproof to her half-sister/aunt: a narrow, languid girl who equated sin with sweat and submitted herself to her husband with a dutifulness which surprised no one. She gave him five children: Eudocia, who would marry two of Manuel's greatest generals, Paul Catacalon and Michael Gabras; Elizabeth, who would marry Henry of Austria; Constantia, also twice married, to Count Theodore Dasiota (who said of her, "Imperial Princess or no, she is so dissolute she ought to be walking on all fours") and James Cantacuzenus, who reformed her (or satisfied her); John, Manuel's Master of Robes, whose own daughters would marry the King of Jerusalem and the Prince of Antioch; and David, the most famous and pathetic, the last man to stand between Andronikus and the throne.

VI

In 1125 John Augustus left for his campaign in the Little Caucasus with the physicians' confirmation that his Empress, Irene II Augusta, was suffering from cancer. The Sebastocrator, too, was preoccupied by his Consort, whose "problem" was the antipode of the Empress'. The Sebastocratrix had become notorious, and for her husband this was much to the point, as the people of the Empire became aware of their beloved Basilissa's mortality. The contrast of her arrogant, extravagant sister-in-law flouting her adultery, persisting in her usual banquets, a prerogative of men, her seminars wherein she invited doctors of the university as well the great wits and poets of Constantinople to Porphyriogenetus Palace for an evening's pleasure, was politically imprudent and publicly an insult to the Empress' suffering. "But what do they expect? Fifty million souls ought suddenly to walk on tiptoe and whisper?" she was heard to ask. "No one loves the Empress more than I, and no one knows better that Her Majesty could care less how her death is awaited. It is only between heaven and herself to prepare that noble soul to meet its Redeemer."*

In the autumn of 1125, Isaac resorted to measures against his wife least likely to be productive, publicly spurning Joanna at a reception for ambassadors from King George III of Georgia, arrived to seal the betrothal between Princess Anastasia and the three-year-old Grand Duke Andronikus.

With the extraordinary charm she could summon on a wink in the state's behalf—"almost, it seemed, a conscious satire of charm," said an eyewitness—Joanna entered the throne room and approached Isaac as his serene wife. As she started to speak, he turned on her and said, "Madame, I shall not see you again until you mend your ways. You are shameless." Then he gave her his back. "She continued to smile," wrote the Sebastocrator's sister, Maria, Princess Catacalon,

> that marmoreal smile of state receptions, that smile we're taught to smile in place of boredom, disgust—or even in place of real but retarding interest. But her eyes, those eyes, so wide, did not see, and were so stiffly fixed as nearly to be crossed. She moved away in rigid, graceless little steps, quite unlike her usual regal glide. Once or twice in my own life I have been so insulted by those I respect. I knew what she felt. One appears to be bewildered but one is not. Rather one is overwhelmed by a sense of solitude of the self. One dreads drawing any further attention one's way by the least movement of the body. Who is staring? Everyone. Who has heard? Everyone. Are they talking of you? Of course. It is a staggering effort to move through such scrutiny, merely to leave a room. One's desire is to be alone, to hide from the merciless light of such exposure, the vulnerability of your soul so precisely noted. I could compare such an experience to the bursting of a blister caused by fire. If you peal away the degenerate tissue, you find the new pink skin below sensitive to so much as the cool of your own breath. Once, when I spoke of this to one of my ladies-in-waiting, she said, "But, Your Highness, you appear in public nearly every day of your life." I did not respond, but I have since thought about that remark. It seems to me now the difference

---

* It is presumed the reader will catch the same archness with which Joanna satirized the Empress in a series of privately circulated poems. The most notorious compared Irene to Penelope, weaving her charitable gifts by day and stealing them back from the beggar's bedside that night so as to have more to give on the following morning. N.A.

between public life and public insult is the distinction between cynosure and curiosity; in the one, there is a living bond—if it be no more than the envy for an emperor's daughter—in which the subject remains recognizably human; in the other, there is conscious exclusion, the objectification of the victim to the exclusion of all feeling, as the aspect of destruction is always fascinating to us.

Interestingly enough, and perhaps personally mortifying, Joanna had her greatest adept in the Empress Irene, as introverted women will often admire—betimes blindly to a fault—their more extroverted compeers, whom they usually term "brave." Though weakening day by day (it is reported in the seventh month of her illness, she began to lose both weight and her hair, in alarming measure, while cruel sores appeared upon her body), she was still Autocratrix without whose signature to the right of her husband's or the left of the Sebastocrator's, not the most innocuous legislation was valid before God or man. The Basilissa, normally so shy—or perhaps too preoccupied—wrote an indignant letter to John detailing the incident, as reported to her. Then she asked for Isaac's attendance.

Of his sister-in-law and the interview, the second Sebastocrator wrote:

The Empress is utterly without affectation. She is, rather, the holiest woman I have ever known, a contemplative miscalculated as an empress. She is not one to amuse, and it is difficult to love her, for she is too inward, and yet my affection and respect for her, even awe, is without end. Within a year of her arrival her charities were already legend among our people, high and low alike. Great sophisticates mind themselves in her presence, and the guileless and poor believe her to be a saint. Perhaps I do myself. When she appears in public, she evokes something I have never seen before, something like hysteria. Whereas most Imperial personages, in their best luck, evoke applause after obeisance, Irene in her transcendent serenity raises the yearning to *touch*. Numerous times, John or Count Auxuchos or I have been obliged to send extra contingents of guards to protect her progress through the streets.

When I received command to attend her I was so appalled at the thought of a dying woman of such famous goodness (servants could no longer leave her presence without bursting into tears) being brought near this lurid situation, I at once suspected my wife's tales. This was ungenerous to both women: Joanna because she would sooner defend herself than petition a champion she had belittled; Irene because her natural charity at once sympathized with the shorn lamb (or rather in Joanna's instance, the spurned sow).

She received me on a chaise, covered with a silken blanket, on the terrace of Buceleon's Imperial apartments. It was a warm day, the colors lovely. She did not embroider, but, as was her custom, sewed clothes for the children of Orphanotropolis. She was attempting to concentrate on her needle as I approached, attempting to be stern, for which she was too weak or too poor an actress. She offered her hand without looking at me, then brought it back to her sewing. "Isaac," she said, "I am wroth with you."

"This grieves me, my dear. What about?"

"You know perfectly well. Must men tell you who you are? Alexius' son, my husband's great Regent. You are the state. As you act, we are defined. Now you have mightily offended your wife, and so all wives, including myself."

I took her hand from the sewing, and held it between both my own. "My dearest, you are above other women, as the moon above the night."

"Don't condescend to me, Isaac." She withdrew her hand and the needle flew. "Everyone condescends to me. Especially now. They think me miserable and cater to me with every earthly toy. They think to entice me from thoughts of death with precisely the *wrong* things. Where was I? Yes. Or rather no. That is precisely the point, Isaac. I am only a woman, and I am only a wife. How could you insult me so? You are John's deputy. Joanna has been mine, uncomplainingly and competently for many years when I know—oh, with her lively mind—she would sooner be elsewhere."

"Madame, as you put it that way, I am at odds ends with myself."

"I am not thinking of revenge, but the loneliness of your poor wife."

"Irene, come now, even you . . ."

Finally she stopped her sewing and looked at me, her eyes, like all the very ill, wonderfully luminous. "I know of no *other* woman who loves you more, Isaac." She said this with a *drôle* sense of double entendre worthy of the city's most *soigné* matron.

I countered her unkindly. "I know of no other woman who loves you less. Why ought you to defend her?"

She smiled. *"Varium et mutabile semper femina.* We are past understanding. You have said so yourself in your poetry. When a man is humiliated, he may seek revenge, and society will applaud him. When a woman is humiliated, it is usually thought to be deserved and she is petty and vindictive if she means to retaliate. I have written to the Emperor of your conduct."

I started to speak. She lifted a needle-poised hand. "There is only one way you may prevent his interference. If I may write to John tonight of reconciliation, private and public. Go now to St. Stephen's Oratory. I believe they are saying liturgy. Joanna is there. Come back with her to me."

I need not add that like most women of a mystic nature, Irene was at once marvelously practical in matters practical—perhaps the distance from worldly things—and hopelessly sentimental in matters of sentiment —perhaps too neatly cocooned in her own goodness. In any event, I took the autumn walk to the oratory, prepared to bring Joanna back at the point of a knife to satisfy this otherwise superb, foolish, dying woman. Whatever it was—the balminess of the day, my sympathies sharpened upon the Empress—I was deeply moved by the liturgy, as I am usually in my softer moments, by those choristers who could wring tears from a stone. Joanna's sense of poetry is, I fancy, as strong as my own, and she seemed as moved, as she stood in the little gallery, her reddish-purple mantle, trimmed with gold, resting about her face like a sublime madonna—of which there could be no aspect further from the truth. Afterward I met her at the foot of the stairs—nothing to her surprise— kissed both her hands, begged her forgiveness—quite businesslike—and said, "Come, madame, we shall return to our sponsor."

The Empress died the following January 1126 both too ill and too gruesome in appearance to have any but her last request fulfilled that she be attended by none but the family and the Patriarch. Andronikus dimly remembered being quartered with his brother Michael, Isaac III, the thirteen-year-old heir to the Sebastocracy, and Manuel, occasionally visited by a somewhat more chastened Joanna and an utterly wretched Natalie. "I recall," he said, "at one point Manuel turned to me and said with that self-importance of children greedy for inclusion in any event of great and mysterious maturity, 'My mother is going to heaven,' and with that, my cousin Isaac burst into tears and ran from the room." Andronikus' father tells us the only sadness the Basilissa admittedly reckoned was the leaving behind of these children—including Julianna, but seven, and Eudocia, ten—which is somewhat ironic since even her late father-in-law, as all contemporaries, agreed on her distracted motherhood.

Despite the coldest, whitest winter since the dread Cuman onslaught of 1091, the people gathered in numbers beyond anyone's memory for the Augusta's funeral. Isaac Porphyriogenetus describes it:

The silence was uncanny. Even the wheels and horses' hooves were quietened by the snow. All along the route to Pantokrator, there was a ground swell of gasps as if the sight of the Empress' coffin were finally confirming her death. You could hear too the frequent hacking of men too much moved and embarrassed in their display of emotion. Those who attempted to touch the coffin did so in graceful, almost fleeting movements, running up, reaching with just a brush of the fingers, and it was enough. The Varangians did not attempt to stop the people, and they were few in any event. The rest, I think, were too stunned by the emptiness which may incur in the deprival of one human life.

It was the Patriarch, not the Emperor, who requested a convocation of the Patriarchal Synod, not two months after Irene's death, for the purpose of instituting canonization procedure in behalf of "this best and purest Basilissa who ever reigned." Profoundly moved, the Emperor consented. And so this daughter of a Latin Catholic saint became a saint in the Church to which her marriage had brought her, the first officially canonized Comnena, and a far more likely beatific figure than the last Empress of the same name, so commemorated, Irene of Macedon, usurper and child-blinder, but restorer of icons.

The Empress' death divided rather than brought closer the two surviving sons of Alexius or, shall we say, marked the beginning of the final long stage of the dissolution of their relationship. With Irene's passing, the Emperor became more inward, if not inscrutable, than ever, and preferred to rely on the calm and competence of Count Auxuchos, though in no way did he lessen his brother's powers or seem to disavow him in word or deed. Politically, there is no reason to believe in a breach of policy. Isaac, at worst, argued, but always followed the Emperor's intentions. It may even be said, his own latitude of activity and prerogative increased.

Perhaps it was that the death of the Empress, denying the Emperor a perfectly attuned companion, rather emphasized the differences—emotionally and temperamentally—between the Imperial brothers, who, while manifestly loving one another, could not be more of a mirrored pair than their wives.

Undoubtedly the most surprising consequence, which Andronikus directly attributed to the Empress' death, was the metamorphosis—keen, though not complete—in the personality of the Sebastocratrix Joanna. Now she becomes, or begins to become, the more familiar, worldly—but discreet—matron of Manuel's reign. Her son once wrote of this event:

> How to explain it? Consider that my mother was never an insensitive woman. All her life pampered, all her tantrums indulged, she may have come to some sort of reckoning of herself by my aunt's deathbed. You can caricature good which seems so ludicrously inadequate to the bitter, sophisticated, but not unsympathetic eye, in this ocean of wickedness. You can ridicule it, but you cannot deny it. Nor would my mother, essentially an idealist—as her satire indicates—want to. It may be the sight of Irene, ravaged beyond recognition, brought my mother up short. We tend to think of the virtuous that the good they do is their own reward. We scarcely expect them to be punished by the Great Invisible. Injustice, pain without meaning, if pain is punishment, and punishment is justice, will either pierce the most sardonic soul—which dreads, as any other, moot suffering—or condemn it forever to insensitivity and anarchy. Years afterward, my mother referred to those days of January 1126 as "the spanking I'd all my life deserved. Plotinus was wrong: as long as the good suffer, there can be no great melody in the spheres, for that fact offers discord against the tune the stars sing."

Though still irritatingly superior in manner—hence a virtual target, whether or not she realized it, for the upcoming generation—Joanna thereafter displayed a repose of attitude and activity which made her suspect among some friends and an object of derision among others (this says as much for the friends as the earlier personality which attracted them).

Between the Sebastocratrix Joanna, her half-sister, the Grand Duchess Rebecca, and the Crown Princess Natalie who generally shared the upbringing of the remaining five Imperial Princes and Princesses, Manuel Augustus once told me, his brothers and sisters preferred the mother of Andronikus: "Like all children, we scarcely comprehended the loss in our mother's death, myself especially as the youngest. It wasn't too long before she became something quite impalpable, something between a few personal notions and the great legend of saintly charity, a saintliness not very well conveyed, I fear, by that dour, ice-cold portrait in Holy Wisdom. Of our mothers, as we called them, Rebecca seemed to

us too meek and at the same time too harsh, too humorless. I don't
think we displeased her. We simply never seemed to touch her. Natalie
was sweet, but she imposed her mourning for my mother upon us, long
after we had survived our grief. My aunt Joanna was the best, very
firm, frank, incapable of condescending, a beautiful and a glamorous
creature—the two are not the same. We did not fear her. We were in
awe of her, which is a wonderful thing."

The Emperor in his turn was equally as solicitous of Isaac's children,
conferring upon the Sebastocrator's three sons the Orders of St. Demetrius and St. Sebastian and procuring for them from Venice the Order
of St. Mark (normally only Porphyriogeneti might wear all three). He
quite encouraged the betrothal between his youngest nephew, Andronikus, and Princess Anastasia and even paid for the magnificent train
which brought her from Tiflis to Constantinople, to live, from the age of
six, in the home of her betrothed, to be raised by his mother. Still again,
when Andronikus, at but the age of five, in what he later called his
Epiphany, showed, untutored, within a few months' span, an aptitude
for languages, for mathematics and music, John Augustus, happily
amazed, called in the best tutors from throughout Europe and the
Levant, as well as Constantinople, to "encourage and discipline this
gift from heaven."

Indeed, whatever it irked the Sebastocrator, the Emperor personally
supervised the education of Isaac's youngest and favorite. In one letter
written from Lesser Armenia, where John, as usual, received weekly
tutorial reports on his nephew, he wrote to his brother:

> The doctors say Andronikus is either the work of the devil or preter-
> naturally blessed, which is as I prefer it. I confess I am at a loss to ex-
> plain it. There is something too unsettling about such genius in a child
> who has not lost, yet, all his first teeth, though whether intelligence shall
> become wisdom is another matter entirely. But one thing, dear brother,
> we must never set him too much apart from the others the moment he
> raises his head from his lessons. If we can avoid it, we must try, though I
> have noticed imaginative children are never lonely (imaginative adults
> are seldom anything else). He is one apart already. He senses, I think,
> his own brilliance. Should he remain segregated, he will become inured
> to the limitations of lesser men and, by that, become alienated, or, I fear,
> use them cynically. This must not be. He must become one who leads by
> the light he exudes, not the contempt born of that light. One teaches,

the other is a betrayal of his humanity by betraying the humanity of others. I think it time, by the way, despite my absence, you begin riding lessons for Manuel and Andronikus: they are, as were you, unusually tall for their age, and should have little trouble. Soon we shall have them with us each morning for our usual constitutional. . . .

During this Armenian expedition of 1128, the Emperor called down Bryennius from Trebizond to a personal interview, their first confrontation in seven years despite the Caesar's semiannual visits to his wife and children at Constantinople, begun in 1124. Reckoning punishment enough and proof of repentance in Bryennius' unimpeachable personal conduct throughout his governancy, John promised his brother-in-law permanent return to the Imperial capital and a place at court, perhaps as early as the following year.

On reception of the minutes of this interview, the Sebastocrator sensed a slip of the ground beneath his feet (or the imagined slip; in many ways, his fall was self-inflicted). At once, he suspected Auxuch's hand. We do not know. We have not the evidence. Even were the Emperor to follow the Count's advise, vis-à-vis clemency for the Caesar, we cannot precisely say it was meant as counterweight to the Sebastocrator. The problems of interpretation are this: both men are culpable. Auxuch was in too controversial and illustrious a position to be impeccable. Isaac's mistake—born of his precipitous nature, which could burn his subtlety to crisp—was an inability to distinguish between the Count's influence and his own very real practical power. The Emperor's attitude may have indeed altered toward his brother with his wife's death, but, as had been said, not in the matter of prerogative.

And here is where the flaw of dynastic rule comes to play. Isaac, as Sebastocrator, might have continued happily indifferent, assured by oath and diadem of his office. The brother could not. The most subtle change of emotional attitude toward him might—or might not—be indicative of gross political change. (His poetry of that period, about a dozen utterly beautiful, elegiac songs—"*too* elegiac for a man of thirty-five," said Andronikus musingly one day—reveal, rather curiously, the ingenuous and poignant bewilderment of a man who has passively accepted betrayal.) †

---

† The intimacies of the last quoted letter may be discounted, at least insofar as a profile of the Emperor's attitude toward his brother. Even Irene II was wont to point out the remarkable difference between her husband's personal self-containment and what amounted to volubility in his correspondence. Seemingly for this innately inward man,

With a sense of personal doom friends and critics found more alarming than melodramatic—for quiescence was so unlike him—the Sebastocrator continued in his office, scarcely cheered by the further hopeless task, with which everyone sympathized, of attempting to introduce the Crown Prince into the machinery of government (with Sergius, he was far more successful: "He is decisive and he loves power; unfortunately he is also stupid," the Sebastocrator noted in his journal). Indeed, Isaac increased his work load nearly to the point of mania (in some instances in the fear his legislation would be compromised if not initially shepherded by its creator), and Joanna, who knew the difference between a man spent by his mistresses and enervated by overwork and anxiety, herself became distraught for him.

When the Emperor returned from Armenia, in October 1128, he was horrified by the "ghost" (his own description) which greeted him at the Golden Gate. Six foot four and ordinarily capable of bending an iron bar without a change of expression, the Sebastocrator was slender as a scythe and, at the age of thirty-six, had gone almost entirely gray.

Now, John Augustus possessed an agile mind, a compassionate nature, and a way with men which melted them to his design. Here, however, he was like a great runner expending all his energy and technique in the wrong direction and exasperated each time he encounters, head-on, his challenger. No argument will convince him *he* is contrary, since the track is elliptical and the finish of the course might just as well be the beginning. Ideally, which is to say, with an intelligence and symmetry the subjects of history seldom share with its telling, he should have noted Isaac's behavior, confronted him with it, sought explanation and allowed him the same reassurance the brothers lavished upon their ministers. It might have been that simple. Instead, the Emperor misinterpreted what he saw, looked no further, and with utmost sympathy and love, exacerbated the situation, by alleviating Isaac of some of his "overwhelming" responsibility—thinking him too proud, no doubt, to confess his own exhaustion—and so fought fire with flood. At this, one may imagine Isaac's state of mind.

---

distance left nothing but the memory and John's opinions of the recipient, both bathed in the glow of affection provoked by absence, i.e., an objectification, an assurance against the sometimes painful accidents of personal encounter with which a man, treated as nearly semidivine from birth, found it difficult to cope. "For my uncle," Andronikus once told me, *"distance* was the bliss of love. And then he could be rapturous." N.A.

The unforeseen compelled the actors. In December a cholera epidemic was introduced into the city. At first, John refused to leave Constantinople, which had been placed under quarantine on rescript of the Sebastocrator and Prince Alexius Bryennius, now Prefect of the City. In an Extraordinary Petition, however—with, most likely, the ominous accession of the Sovereign Heir in mind—the Sacred Consistory, to a man, asked that the Emperor remove himself to Hieriea Palace at Chalcedon, or preferably, further still, to St. George's at Nicea. The Emperor, according to all witness, more distressed than ever in anyone's memory, agreed to retire to Chalcedon. Isaac, meanwhile, remained in the city, whose gates closed on 2,500,000 citizens.

There is, of course, only so much as may be humanly done against endemic disease, even with spectacular planning and the best effort of the vigorous and victim alike. When far worse you are forced to run the duration of a plague on a metropolitan scale, you must deal with the panic of entrapment, of such pitch and size as can be remedied only by an act of God.

On 12 January 1129 riots occurred in the poorest quarters of the city, Petrion, and within two days spread to the Venetian and Amalfitan Quarters. On the fourth day anarchy touched the boundaries of the Blachernae District, threatening its harbors and warehouses, the two Imperial palaces, and a newly established business district. Before nightfall, the entire waterfront was in similar danger. Aristocrats and merchants, for once with a common cause, stormed Porphyriogenetus Palace, already under guard against the usual hooligans of every civil disturbance, imploring the Sebastocrator to put a stop to the depredation of the mercantile and administrative hearts of the city. Cold as such a petition seemed, it must also be remembered, the riots hampered any possible aid in those areas where its very lack had been, initially, the accelerator of hysteria.

Isaac crossed the Bosporus and spent the night with the Emperor at Hieriea. The Sebastocrator insisted, later, that his brother entrusted him to end the rioting by whatever means he could with as "subtle" (Isaac quoting John) a use of force as possible. (Writing much later, he asked, "How may force be subtle: a blow is a blow and one dead man is dead as all the men dead and gone before him.") On arrival at Porphyriogenetus in the morning, the Sebastocrator signed the release of the Constantinopolitan Garrison into the city (which, incidentally, insured their presence for the duration). He could have warned the people; he could have pleaded with them, but it is unlikely that those who are ripping officers from their saddles and tearing open their bodies from throat to crotch are inclined toward reason. Judiciousness becomes not even moot, but ludicrous.

Thus, to the 100,000 who died of the Epidemic of 1128–29 may be added the estimated 2,000 more souls dispatched to heaven by the city soldiery. The Emperor, on hearing the news, was appalled. As always, the sight of massacred bodies must have suggested a greater number than the Imperial commissioners realistically tallied. Unfortunately it was early exaggeration rather than later fact which was reported to John. It was then he performed what remains the single most extravagantly dramatic act of his reign.

Against all advice and the implication of forced detention, he took ship across the Bosporus, disembarked at Buceleon, and, with no more than a dozen men to protect him, rode into the still rioting Amalfitan Quarter. The sight of the Basileus in the square before the sacked Botaniates Palace stopped ruffians in their tracks and brought those whom fear had sequestered in their homes on the run. The Emperor sat, still as the Justinian equestrian, beneath the Labarum of Constantine and the Pallium of the Virgin. When a vast crowd had assembled, he told his two trumpeters to sound their horns, and in the silence, rose in his saddle and bellowed, "So this is what you have become, my children. Physicians risk their lives to save you, soldiers to keep any further contaminant away, fellow citizens to feed and serve you, priests to give unction to those otherwise beyond hope, and you dance like beasts of prey around them. Down on your knees! Now! Before God! Pray His forgiveness!"

After six days of lawlessness, the law worked hypnotically upon many; others were conquered by the Emperor's voice, which they had never before heard. His words may as well have been commands from heaven. He went from quarter to quarter of the city and spoke thus, divinely imperious, at once obeyed, and quelled the disturbances before late afternoon. Whether Isaac might have done likewise is moot. The Emperor with his nimbus of anointment arrived, let us not forget, when both the heart and vivacity had gone out of the demonstrations, nearly a week and some two thousand deaths after its beginning.

Now, Isaac knew his brother was in the city before the end of the morning, and according to his eldest son, Philip, his outrage was monumental. His description is interesting for its denouement:

My father's real temper—not the professional exasperation most people mistook for his temper—was alarming in the extreme. He simply was not the same man. Or perhaps he was, for even when calm I had often noticed his eyes, as my brother Andronikus'—it is difficult to say—they *lurked*. They were the eyes of a great febrile animal of the North: gray, enormous, with very thick lashes, and precisely like an animal's—almost no visible white. When anger overtook him and his mouth opened wide in a roar or grimaced in disgust with a display of fine white teeth, those eyes, that mouth, the furrows of irritation connecting the two was the aspect precisely of a lion or a wolf at the end of his tether. His fury, moreover, was, while physical—intensely so—curiously, horribly static. He did not throw objects, but rather punched or kicked them in tight, savage movements: legs from under tables or chairs (including one of silver, I remember, which ordinarily took three servants to move), clean holes straight through chests. He would slam the panels of bolted doors so fiercely they would splinter, crack, or come loose, smash mirrors and crush vases with a downward swing of his fist (one, I recall was a positively priceless diatreton, or cage cup, of red-and-gold-colored millefiori glass, set in crystal, set in turn in a trellis of sapphire-colored glass, given by the Emperor Trajan to his Governor of Egypt and returned to New Rome as a gift to my father from the Fatimite Caliph).

Whatever damage he did, however, he might survey later with wonder, never with embarrassment. If you attempted to hold him down, he did not fight you, but pulled away and continued his rampage. Reasoning with him was, to say the least, impossible. If you spoke, he would rush up to you, utter some withering epithet and you shrank from him, as at any moment bolts might fly from him and kill you indifferently.

Only Andronikus, from boyhood, could quite literally stop our father short in the midst of his violent paroxysm. I sometimes think my brother was born without any sense of fear whatsoever, quite as dangerous as being born without a sense of pain—which is a warning, not a flaw—for even at that age of six or seven, Andronikus could counter Isaac Porphyriogenetus with a display of ferocity equal to, if not the superior of, the sire's. (I see them, not so many years later, their two heads strained toward one another, two eyes deadly, each jaw drawn wide as though about to decapitate the antagonist with a bite.) And though my father never struck Andronikus, Andronikus several memorable times struck my father. As for instance that day in 1129 when he freed himself from my mother's hysterical grasp and jumped upon Isaac's back—I have the image of a mountain cat—kicking him, biting him, scratching him, pulling at his hair, his beard, pummeling my father's huge head with his small fists, screaming, "Stop! Stop it at once, you madman, do you hear?" My father at once ceased his rampage and sought only to free himself from my brother, at length flinging him away, as an elephant would toss a cheetah at a tree, before himself collapsing into a chair in tears, moaning, "Cain, he is Cain. He is no longer my brother. He is Cain."

The Emperor John entered the gates of Porphyriogenetus Palace about four o'clock in the afternoon, near sunset. He had not eaten since the previous evening and scarcely slept. So he bathed, napped, and dined, before calling the Sebastocrator to him after vespers. It may have been the perfectly natural conduct of a tense, exhausted man. It may also have been the intentional delay to reason with his own temper, or that pause of a sophisticated politician who knows perfectly well the stay of a confrontation is both chastisement and a superiority.

We may sympathize with both men: with John, who in the successful, bloodless termination of a great civil disturbance was of no mind to indulge the fatal decisions of an impetuous minister on the verge of breakdown; with Isaac, who honored the consequence of primogeniture even as he was its victim, who possessed the sharp pride of the younger brother of a monarch, which pride is quite all he may have with his name, and losing that, loses all. *Explicit: Nicetas Acominatus.*

Beyond the slender arched windows, an accretion of snow is gradually rising on the sill. Superimposed upon the darkness beyond are the ascending triple hoops of a chandelier. Within the room, the high burnish of the verd antique floor also repeats the image of the lamp—in concentric circles—directly above it. Repeated six times, between the windows and at each end wall, against fields of gold, are the great Imperial bicephalic eagles holding sway over serpents. The Emperor is standing at a table, drawing his pen—it is the only sound—across the bottom of a document. He conveys the hurriedness of one about to be interrupted, and shortly there is, indeed, a knock. He speaks in a clipped fashion, either to conceal his mood or because his mind is still distracted by what he is writing.

JOHN. Come in.

The doors of beaten gold, ivory, and cedar open inward. Count Auxuchos—the elder—steps into the room and in the same movement stands aside.

COUNT AUXUCHOS. His Imperial Highness, the Sebastocrator.

JOHN. Leave us, if you please.

Isaac enters. With a bow in the direction of the Presence, the Count leaves the room, securing the doors, softly, after him. Isaac is stolid, not intentionally, but as the aftermath of outburst. He moves up to the bronze and marble table. Raising his eyes in a frown of concentration to a document above the one on which he is writing with his left hand, the Emperor offers his right, bejeweled only with his marriage ring and the blazing ruby of the coronation sigil, to be uncustomarily kissed. Isaac lifts the fist a little higher, touches it with his lips, and drops it rudely. The Emperor returns it to steady the document, pauses, either considering Isaac's insult or determining what further to write, nods imperceptibly, straightens, leaves the stylus aside, and walks to the center of the room. Hands on hips he considers Isaac, not angrily, almost with curiosity, quite as if he were a stranger, as perhaps it is so.

JOHN. Now, are we so far apart I must follow you like a governor paying for the damage of his charge in a tavern or a bath? There was a time when you acted so assuredly in my place the deed was done before I could finish the command, which was never a command between you and me.

ISAAC. Things as you wish them are a command for all men to follow. That is the nature of your anointment, Johnny. I cannot join you in the loneliness of autocracy and *I* cannot follow after *you* with guesses, which is all it has ever been, however fortuitous the conclusion. For me, it is no longer obedience, but degradation. Or rather, I am degraded as I obey. I am no longer asked to do what is right, apparently, but what shall please you. That is not my way.

JOHN. Wherever had you got that idea? That is the attitude of a flunky, which I trust you are not.

ISAAC. But I have been in contest with a natural toad—Auxuch—and that is an unfair advantage.

JOHN. You fear his precedence?

ISAAC. I despise the man and therefore his precedence.

JOHN. Well, we very often despise those we fear or wrong. This is unworthy of you. For God's sake, Isaac, be more narrow-minded and less prodigal with your hatreds.

He smiles.

JOHN. Be ingenious and hate only those who may do you real harm.

ISAAC. I know my enemy well enough. Do you?

JOHN. That's a madman's talk.

ISAAC. You will be pleased to know your nephew and yourself agree completely on the verge of my sanity.

Isaac pauses, closing his eyes momentarily, as though preparing for a great effort. When he speaks his usually low voice is high and very tense.

ISAAC. John, I shall race you the purpose of this interview. I offer you as of this evening my resignation.

JOHN. You *are* mad. You cannot renounce the Sebastocracy. Where is the law which says you may do so against my will.

ISAAC. Where is the law which says I may not. There *is* no such law.

John taps his chest gently.

JOHN. Here is your law, and he says you may not. I did not ask you here to retire you but to seek explanations for your actions yesterday.

ISAAC. I have no explanations. I would not offer them if I did. You must trust me to their integrity in your behalf. I acted as the occasion disposed me to act.

JOHN. With massacre? Come now.

ISAAC. What is it you are thinking of, Johnny? Your reputation? Or the expediency of saving this city from the mayhem into which it was nearly fallen beyond hope.

JOHN. Very well, if we have come as far as accusations, then I ask you what it is you want of me more than I have given you. No man has the right to dispute you, but I. I am, therefore, asking you for the rationale of a desperate action, which did not seem to me necessary. This is not to punish you. Only to convince you you were wrong, convince you here—

He taps his skull with uncharacteristic agitation—

JOHN. —where it matters, so that you will never again, of your *own* accord, take such measures, in my name or your own. Or are you so proud you have ceased to learn?

ISAAC. I am too proud to usurp your throne. Be glad of that.

John has arrived by the table again. He is startled, frowning visibly.

JOHN. It is not in my power to give you more.

ISAAC. If not, whose is it? Tell me and I will go to him. There have been fraternal Co-Augustates.

JOHN. Indeed, as legacy, not self-created. I repeat: It is not in my power, Isaac.

ISAAC. It is in your power, certainly, just as it would be in mine from now forever more to refuse such an elevation, even were you so disposed, because you have forced me to ask it. You are no more disinterested than Marcus Aurelius when he appointed Commodus, his son, his heir. You are as vain as the rest, Johnny. After all, it is not the state but yourself.

JOHN. Don't you see you have more power as my Sebastocrator than as junior Augustus. There would be no concert between us for the good of the Empire. Only a rivalry. And what of our sons? Shall we then quarter the state and quarter it again to satisfy their legacy and leave behind only fratricide and chaos?

ISAAC. Ah, reduction to absurdity—the last refuge of inadequate argument.

JOHN. I don't know which disappoints me more, these insults and insinuations, or your very ingratitude.

ISAAC. Yes, yes, how crude the desire for position seems to those whose own ambitions are fulfilled. Johnny, if I were certain martyrdom *were* a token of a man's sincerity, I would kill myself before you to prove my gratitude. You have missed my point. I will not defend my actions yesterday because in that you question my right of choice, my authority, and seem to doubt either would be put in any way but service to yourself.

JOHN. I do not doubt your ends are mine, I only know your means are not.

ISAAC. That rabble this past week confused destruction with petition.

JOHN. And you confuse the silence of death with the consent of obedience.

ISAAC. Well, then, as I've said. You shall have no more arguments. You shall have Auxuch and Bryennius.

JOHN. Do you dispute me him as well?

ISAAC. Must you select for confidants our proved enemies?

JOHN. Yes. So did Papa, so shall I. Yes. And sooner than curse him I would light a candle to lead the devil himself from darkness.

Isaac shakes his head, lowers his head, and sighs.

ISAAC. I am of no further use to you.

JOHN. How can you, who know my loneliness, leave me to this? How can you of all men, my own brother, use me so?

ISAAC. Perhaps I am no more than weary. I have the alternative of renunciation of my duties. If I am not being too cruel, though accurate, I *am* aware you cannot do likewise in your own behalf.

JOHN. You *are* weary, then rest.

ISAAC. It's too late.

JOHN. You speak like a brute or an infant, expecting sympathy and giving none. You *know* how difficult it is for me to say these things. Isaac, I implore you.

He extends his left hand for his brother to take. The Sebastocrator steps back, his head tossed aside as if glancing from a blow, pain upon his face, his own hand upheld momentarily in its own beseeching.

ISAAC. I'll have no more of this, no more.

For an instant he looks down and away, dazedly, as though bethinking himself, blinking quickly. He turns on his heels, throws open both doors, and leaves the study.

VII

Incipit: Nicetas Acominatus: "Have you ever known nightmare?" Andronikus once asked me. "I mean true nightmare, a reality so painful, sleep or death seems infinitely preferable to waking hours not to be borne. I've known it many times, but the first time will always remain for me the most vivid, when my father and my uncle became estranged and we were forced to leave the Imperial court.

"A snowy evening, I recall, and Michael and I had already been put to bed. Suddenly we were awakened and dressed by our nurses. We were taken to our parents' apartments where Philip and my mother were speaking to some servants while my father and several of his undersecretaries, and, to my surprise, my aunt Maria and her husband, Catacalon, conversed in passionate undertones. Fur cloaks were thrown over my shoulders and Michael's, and my mother said we were going away. Only those words—we were going away—and nothing more. She seemed angry and I remember she was especially acrimonious with my father, whenever he spoke to her, throughout that night, and the next day, until exhaustion, perhaps, made her reconsider or else accept what was done as done and to make the best of it.

"We left Porphyriogenetus by ways I had never before known, ignominiously, as I now see, or rather fittingly, by the back. Though I had begun riding lessons the previous autumn, and protested, my father muttered, 'Not for what we're about,' as he took me into his seat. In all there were about a dozen riders, saddle packs stuffed, and two horses with any manner of objects—mostly gold, I suspect—secured to their backs. And so in the night, in the snow, in the cold, we were off, all power, position, amenity, luxury, honor, abandoned as simply as that.

"We left Constantinople by Xylokerkos Gate and followed the walls to the Justinian Bridge, crossed the Golden Horn, and at Galata took ship, horses and all, across the Bosporus to Chalcedon. I see it all: the sputtering torches, the snow which I had never known to be less enchanting, and those pitch waters, hardly visible, only glinting now and then by some alien light. I still feel the cold and the wind. The snows in Russia were twice as distressing in my maturity, because they reminded me of the night of this earlier exile.

"I wanted to sleep. I wanted to be warm. Oh, but I was an Emperor's pampered grandson then, never denied a moment's indulgence, unable to bathe without three attendants or dress without two, the water tepid, not hot, the clothes to my own specifics of texture and design or I refused to wear them. (Had I been one of my servants as a child, I would have murdered me in my sleep.) In any event, I thought perhaps we were going to Hieriea, my favorite palace. But I had known the route from infancy and this was not the way. The night and the storm even prevented a good-by to its spires, domes, and crosses, its huge pennants with our family's escutcheon, raised when one of us was in residence.

"It is here the nightmare takes shape, or, we might accurately put it, the ordinary, which we prefer to call the real, ceases to be. I remained unnaturally awake. I knew the rest of the world was dreaming. There is a great loneliness in such an hour. And for the first time in my life I sensed a panic beyond the doings of my own mischief, the panic of adult issue over which I had no control and for which I did not want to suffer the consequences, as a conscriptee loathes to fight a war begun by the Emperor and his generals over issues he scarcely touches and shall never understand. I count that night as the first stirring within me of a loathing that any man should interfere with the processes and destinies of my life. If I am led to ruin, so to speak, let me have no one to blame but myself and I can accept the consequences.

"I heard my father say—I can feel his chest and belly resonating against my back as he spoke—to either my mother or one of her ladies, 'Madame, the only consolation we have in this is the hope one day we shall be able to laugh while describing it.' That is the last thing I remember. It seemed I closed my eyes for a moment (I can still recall the *sense* of it being only a moment), then my father's hand gripped my shoulder and I heard him say softly, 'Andronikus,' very softly, 'look, Andronikus,' and to my astonishment I opened my eyes directly into the sun, rising above the head of the steed on which I was riding. I was enchanted. I have carried that vision with me to this day.

"You must remember these factors which mitigated our flight and distinguish it from my own, much later in my cousin's reign. My father was the Emperor's only brother and had been, for many years, Heir Presumptive. I was but one of seven Grand Dukes and as many lives from succession to the throne. I was, in some degree, a wastrel, though not of my own choice. My father was Sebastocrator of the Empire. I was accepted at Galitch, as an exalted, politically innocuous, refugee. My father was accepted at Mas'ud's court precisely because he could be of use as an instrument of foreign policy. I need not tell you, *that,* by itself, made every hour of every day of every year of his exile a humiliation. He was a Roman emperor's Roman son, and the very thought of his being utilized as a threat to the fatherland was abhorrent. Of course, my father quite forgot his presence in your native city was as much a distress to the great Shah. Half of Iconium's population was Greek and here among them suddenly was the Vice-Regent of the Empire which, even in the third generation, they had left only in the way of enfranchisement but not here, not in their hearts. (Heaven knows, you're proof enough of that.)

"Wherever we went in those first weeks, we were accorded prostrations. Hosts vied for our attention, recidivistic aristocrats and hysterical priests who believed Isaac Porphyriogenetus had come to rescue Iconiate Asia from the Turk yoke (the Greek yoke ought to rest as lightly). Even many of the disaffected at Constantinople whom in better days my father would not have spit upon (and they knew it) sent their agents or came themselves to plot agitation. While my mother was almost pleased, almost reassured, by this commotion, my father was disgusted by it. I think he was relieved when Mas'ud Shah placed us under police surveillance, which is to say, house arrest of sorts, which did not really end until we left Iconium. He gave us the old Exarch's palace and furnished it quite lavishly. By this, at least, we were comfortably secluded from the worst fools and sycophants, native and Constantinopolitan.

"What almost everyone refused to take seriously—though it was all too true—was that my father wanted nothing further whatever to do with politics. It is hard, admittedly, to believe it of a Porphyriogenetus, but then it was precisely the sort of gesture only an emperor's son would make. Others must earn their power, an Imperial prince is born to it. For that reason, I should think, what is his by birth becomes his to keep or relinquish without a second thought, without, that is to say, the sense of failed effort merely to gain it.

"What a man he was. When elated, his joy was like cold sunlight, brilliant but never cloying. When dejected—as here he believed his life gone for naught, himself disgraced in a foreign land—it was like living with the brother of death.

"For his own peace of mind—though others dismissed it as eccentricity —Isaac insisted all servants, even Turks, speak Greek, or he would not accept them. He all but locked my brothers, my mother, and myself in our apartments to prevent us from going among the people (which we were permitted to do so long as we were accompanied by 'governors' from the royal court). He was equally rigid about whom he would entertain. (He adored your parents, Nicetas, because they were virtuous and apolitical—which perhaps is redundant.) In sum, he did all he could to prevent Moslem ways from entering our household, as it had entered the households of the Latin Palestinian principates. Not because he was a bigot, as the Latins, ironically enough, are bigoted, but because he was the son of Alexius Augustus, born in the purple, baptized in Holy Wisdom Cathedral, and crowned Sebastocrator.

"Yet the contagion was almost unavoidable. Both my mother and he, as poets, fell in love with Arabic rhythms and delighted in the elegant, sinuous appearance of the language upon the page. They insisted that to Greek, Latin, Hungarian, and Russian, I add also a thorough grounding, written and spoken, in the Arabic tongue. (Lucky for me, of course, when my own turn for exile was appointed.) In time my father could even say that the sensuous beauty of Arabic music would have left Plato tearing out his hair. After a thorough study of Moslem architecture, which, at first, he had thought too pretty and insubstantial, Isaac determined it marvelously in advance of our own, with ingenious solutions to lightening the arch and opening walls as an antidote to giganticism. So, too, he was enchanted with the uses to which exquisitely intricate, nonrepresentational patterns could be put, relieving large rooms of their emptiness and small rooms of their oppression. (Indeed, when Manuel again began Blachernae, he saw to it that my father's suggestions were incorporated into the new design.)

"Well . . . these things might distract him for a time, but really, it took so little to incite his misery. Once, I recall—it must have been as late as 1134—one of the old gardeners from our summer estate near Selymbria walked all the way to Iconium—isn't that incredible?—to give my mother and father a large chest of seeds which he had carefully prepared during the previous two years, from the flowers which grew in the gardens round the palace. Afterward, my father, so much moved, was glum for weeks, speaking morning, noon, and night of the splendid days when he would leave the heat of Constantinople for the breezes of Selymbria, followed by a wagonful, he said, of state papers to be considered during his sojourn.

"Worse times were to follow. Insofar as Michael's submission to Allah, well, I never mock a man's belief. Whatever enables him to face the most important event of his life—his annihilation—with dignity, even if it be dignity via a fiction, ought to be respected. The most wretched aspect, otherwise, in the world, is that of a man afraid of his own death, from which there is neither rescue nor mercy. Desperation is such a merciless tyrant, sparing least of all the dignity of its victim. It is more than I can bear to watch. What, after all, is God but the light by which a man thinks he sees his own short way in the infinite? The flame is quenched and infinity goes on.

"In truth, I think it may have been my father's contracture of a tutor in astronomy which set Michael on the path to submission. The fellow was a Moslem, of course, despite my father's policy, for he was the best of his kind, and between prejudice and perfection my father usually chose the latter. Both Michael and I, therefore, had access to many splendid treatises which were not otherwise available in Greek, or even in Arabic, at Constantinople. For Michael, the possible multiplicity of creation, of other worlds and other peoples and suns so distant they no longer seemed suns to us, but stars, was simply staggering intellectually and religiously. I shrugged and now and then felt bewildered and more often than not assured myself if God could create one man and one world—in itself a considerable achievement—he could create many. My theology, probably because I was no longer tutored by the great doctors at Constantinople in rigid and pervasive doctrine, was supple and subtle enough to reconcile these collisions with biblical dicta. But my brother had already been confirmed in the Church, with all the panoply attending such an occasion for a grand duke, and, as invalids will, he found meaning for his suffering in an imitation of Christ. When this under-pinning, this sense to his pain, was removed, he was desolated. Because his theology was taller and more intricate, it was easier to bring down.

"Now, Michael noted the serenity with which the Moslem astronomer accepted these facts and asked him how this could be. The doctor an-swered him, at first, I think, in all innocence, with quotations from the Koran, no better, no worse, no more sly, no more cognitatively specious, than our extrapolations from the Testaments in similar events. He was satisfied by so little. He was like a lover on the rebound, so tortured by the voiding of the meaning of all which had gone before, he must re-affirm himself elsewhere, quickly, without further thought, or he will be overwhelmed by meaninglessness—after which the next step is suicide—and a man's desire for self-preservation is his sincerest.

"My father was appalled. That hardly needs imagining. He had a great fondness for Michael. He could afford not to be bitter because he had stronger sons to carry on his line, which Philip and I, indeed, have done, legitimately and illegitimately, with liberality for all. When Mas'ud learned of Michael's intention—deeply moved in that artless way of the most sophisticated Moslem encountering one who seeks submission—it was decided none but he, the Shah, was fit to stand sponsor for the grandson of Alexius Augustus. This impressed Isaac not a whit. In truth, it only made things worse, for my father knew enough about Islam and the convoluted mores of its world to reckon that among the Moslem princes, from Nisbis to Tangier, Mas'ud Seljucis was politically en-hanced by this magnificent Byzantine religious capture. And this, pre-

cisely as possible, was what my father dreaded, believing his name at
Constantinople would surely be ruined, as well eradicate any last chance
of reconciliation.

"He poured scorn on Michael, who suffered it with the intrepidity, if
it is not too much to say, of an early Christian. Oh, you could see the
glow of self-righteous suffering in his eyes.

"The conversion was, moreover, a source of real estrangement between my father and mother. Joanna was, I think, secretly charmed by
its novelty and, in any event, a *Madonna misericordia* in her attitude
toward Michael. She had already read several lives of Mohammed,
enough to ask intelligent questions of Moslems, and now she had a fish
of her own to fry and serve her guests and enhance her reputation. (Not
born Imperial, there was always something of the social entrepreneur
about my mother.) Beyond this she was too self-centered intellectually
to take seriously another man's opinions unless they pointedly threatened her own."

I believe, from this, I learned as much as historians shall ever know
of Isaac Porphyriogenetus' exile. There is a curious—and thorough—
silence, everywhere, concerning this time. About four years ago through
an old family friend, I wrote the Procurator of His Majesty the Sultan's
Archives at Iconium, requesting he examine the rolls for the years 1129
through 1137 for any mention of the Comneni, relevant to the Porphyriogenetus' residence in the city. With typical Moslem generosity—unlike
Christians they seem honored by the trust of a favor—he executed my
request more thoroughly than I had the power to thank. Yet having
himself and his secretaries perused every document between the years
1128 and 1142—the year of Michael's marriage to Mas'ud's beloved
daughter, Princess Rabia (named after the Sufi ascetic of Basra, who,
when asked if she hated Satan, replied, "My love of God leaves me no
room to hate Satan")—he discovered no entries save those relevant to
the Sebastocrator's housekeeping (duly copied) and, in 1136, the establishment of a second household for "His Imperial and Royal Highness,
the Grand Duke, Emir, Michael," which, of course, implies Isaac's scorn
surpassed his sympathy. Letters abound, thereafter, between Michael
and Mas'ud, but fairly those of a father to an adopted son, much in need
of consolation. They are affectionate, impeccable, and quite devoid of
politics.

VIII

Now, in 1130, with the consolidation of Norman power in southern Italy, Roger Guiscard had himself crowned King, Christmas Day, in the Cathedral of Palermo. He had warned no one and asked no one's consent, not even Pope Innocent II's.* But no sovereign—save the Pope—would recognize his title, which is to say, everyone recognized his threat.

This nephew of the adventurer Robert, tall, strapping, handsome in that thin-faced, sloe-eyed way of Manuel Augustus (both men suffered some hilarious putations of mutual genealogy), was called the Pagan by subject and enemy alike: by his enemies because he was indomitable (those whose power we loathe we often ascribe to the devil's strength); by his Christian subjects because unlike all other West European rulers he tolerated Moslems and Jews.

He suggests his notorious uncle in his wonderful affecting energy, his ingenuity, his single-mindedness and the all-round international loathing he could provoke. In truth, it is that external animosity which certified his crown, for there is nothing like a common enemy to make a king. If Lothar of Germany detested him because he effortlessly annexed Abruzzi, revealing the dangerously extended line of the German Empire; if Byzantium according to its traditional claim of Sicily (half Roger's population was Greek) declared his crown fraudulent and usurped; if the North African Moslems instituted jihad against him, then Roger could turn a besieged people's fear to a subject's loyalty and make a monarchy-of-a-dukedom and seem to allay their anxiety by satisfying their pride (the quickest way to a narcissistic Sicilian's heart).

The man was a wonder, and, like Andronikus, a reconciliation of contradictions because he existed and thrived. At his coronation, which followed the Greek rite, he wore a *divitavisson*, woven with an Arabic inscription, received his crown from a Latin Catholic bishop, and greeted first the Rabbi of Palermo, as he left the cathedral. He announced, in his first days, he was without preference for creed in the

---

* The Pope, however, belatedly blessed his accession lest Roger request the benediction—and thereby acknowledge the Papacy—of the anti-Pope Anacletus. In the next month His Holiness turned worriedly to the German King Lothar II, bidding him come to Rome to be crowned Emperor, as a makeweight to Sicily Resurgent. N.A.

service of the state: Latin, Greek, Jew, Arab, were invited to join his administration (hence within a few years he had the finest running bureaucracy in West Europe). Himself, he was an atheist. He was personally abstemious—save in sexual alliances—but his new palace was so magnificent (he patronized only Moslem architects) Manuel nearly bankrupted the state for two years to outdo him in the completion of Blachernae (and did, just barely). Ambitious against the Greek Empire, he nevertheless adopted its ways and the aptitude for work and personal supervision of its sovereign. Between sailing upon a man-made lake with his many concubines ("a demented immoralist," commented Lothar in a letter to John, who in turn was heard to say—surprisingly, since he had taken vows of celibacy—"as though a man needs be insane instead of merely venal to enjoy more than one woman"), he emasculated his gentry, gave more power to the bureaucracy, welcomed merchants to dine at the palace with promises of import quotas (presenting lower taxes for dessert), and allowed cultural autonomy according to the majority population of each city or village, though never to the point of encroaching on the rights of minorities (and there were constant visits of justiciars to insure his tolerance as fact).

It hardly need be added, John Augustus considered the resurgence of Sicily the bitterest eventuality of his reign. For the next four years he was forced to war, Janus-faced. He would leave Constantinople to direct campaigns in West Greece against Roger's repeated attempts to invade the mainland. Always victorious (which is more than can be said of the newly entrenched Almohades of Northwest Africa who lost to Roger, Tunis, Mahdia, and Sfax), he nevertheless considered every moment and every soldier at Dyrrhachium "a waste of human life in all its aspects and directly attributable to the unjustifiable aggression of this pretentious thief who calls himself king" (John to Lothar). In any event, after supervising the initial stages of the Adriatic Watch, he would return to Constantinople for a short respite and to consider any decisions awaiting him otherwise too important to be left to Auxuch or Bryennius (or one of the ministers), and which, previously, had been prerogative of Isaac in the years before 1129.† Invariably, he remained

---

† For instance, in 1131, a delegation of Hungarian nobles, unable to wait at Constantinople, took horse to Dyrrhachium to inform the Emperor a palace revolution was imminent against Stephen II, and the late Empress' cousin—Stephen's uncle—wished to take the throne. From the field, the Emperor gave his full approval to the candidate—an old

at the capital something less than a month, before he was off again, east
now, against the Danishmend Emirs over an issue as lucid as his wars
with Roger, to wit: aggression against the Empire. These are the engagements which led to the decisive wars of 1135 through 1137, at which
end a very ambitious confederacy of petty rulers found, to their horror,
they had advanced no one's cause save the Constantinopolitan Emperor's. And this is irony bordering on the sublime, for John, rather
than initiating events, in all ways was at their cat's paw, attributable,
perhaps, to the fact the man was functioning at less than his best,
quite simply spent after nearly twenty years on the throne, throughout
most of the second decade without Isaac. Bryennius tells us in 1137:

> Two years ago, I should say, the transformation was complete. The
> Emperor's life was one without personal diversion—or even personal
> meaning—totally at the service of the state. There was no one, or so he
> believed, on whom he could rely—including myself—with anything like
> the immense trust he had been able to posit in my brother-in-law, the
> Sebastocrator. On those broad shoulders had previously rested half the
> burden of the Empire—perhaps more than the Emperor, in one of his
> rare vanities, might be willing to admit—and it had been carried, if I
> may say, more sensibly, with a feel for objectivity which was the distance
> of one who did not believe the state would collapse if, for a moment,
> he amused himself or left to a lesser functionary a lesser decision he
> could have made himself. (The omnipotent, I find, are, by far, more
> jealous of the minor prerogative, to which they ought to be indifferent,
> than their autocratic powers, which are taken for granted.) In any event,
> he could not, in his weariness, but resent the Sebastocrator as irrespon-
> sible. With each day's exhaustion indignation grew. At the age of
> forty-seven, the Emperor looked sixty, as his father at sixty had seemed
> much older. His hair was almost entirely gray, and those once luminous
> eyes were dull, as if he never caught enough sleep, as I believe, it was so.
>   The Praetorium, the bureaucracy, the hierarchy of the Church—all
> those who came into some contact with His Majesty—were deeply wor-
> ried for his health and peace of mind, yet no one dared break protocol
> to broach the subject of the Sebastocrator's return, which, really, was
> the only solution. (As for Auxuch, I do not think it was in his interest
> or his own peace of mind to invite the return of the Porphyriogenetus.)

---

friend. With this support, the conspirators forced Stephen to abdicate the following month.
Yet it had nearly been too late, the complotters discovered by their extended absence on a
matter to which Isaac could have given consent in the Emperor's place. N.A.

After a fashion, let it be said, the entire court was coincidentally pleased by my nephew's sensational conversion to Islam, which, it may have surprised him to know, in the quiet of his establishment at Iconium, was the talk of every capital from Russia to France, from Denmark to Egypt. We were pleased because Unspoken Names suddenly became a matter of public irrepressible discussion. Indeed, its importance to any but Michael himself was magnified for obvious purposes of keeping Isaac's name before the Emperor. With Michael's submission, indeed, the six-year-old crust of silence was smashed and events began to move again toward reconciliation.

I sent the Porphyriogenetus and the Sebastocratrix and their sons gifts and letters on their name day, which were unacknowledged and returned through my intermediary, it is true; but in time, a correspondence was struck by my sister-in-law and her sons—infrequent, yet a beginning. The subject of reconciliation was unmentioned. That, however, was implicit, and could come later.

When, during our first Cilician campaign, it was rumored—and I think it only a rumor, though one never knows—the sons of the Porphyriogenetus, Philip and Andronikus, and their Seljuk guards—the latter fact just errant enough to make plausible the rest—had fought, disguised in the Imperial army, it is significant, hysteria ensued throughout the camp in a search for their persons. I then discounted the stories, as my youngest nephew could not have been more than thirteen years old at the time. I had not seen him since he was a child. I did not know. Now, at fifteen, he has the physique of a man, which, more's to the point, he *controls* like a man, not a large and awkward adolescent. (Indeed, there is something too disturbingly self-aware about that boy.) He promises to be as broad as his father and his technique with sword, shortsword, spear, mace, and arrow—though full of patently Turk eccentricities—is even now so finished, as bespeaks several years' training. Though Augustus dismissed the notions of his nephews' presence, he was obviously tense with expectancy throughout the day the rumor reached full cry, seemed to start with every entry into the Imperial pavilion, and was visibly disappointed when rumor had to go, in a manner of speaking, unsubstantiated.

One of the first things I asked those young nephews of mine on our meeting was whether or not they had indeed been present in Cilicia, against the Armenian rebels. Philip started to speak, but his features were still too indeterminately blank in that last instant before our expression follows on our words, when Andronikus, with a short, sinuous, unnaturally commanding wave of his hand, silenced his oldest brother. "Tell me, uncle," he said, "what's the pleasure of mystery?" I said, "It's revelation, nephew." He spoke slowly, his eyes still as a snake's transfixing its prey, his mouth curled in a tight smile which made me want to strike him. "Oh no, uncle. Confess: for the perpetrator, the torture he inflicts upon his victim with his god-like refusal of solution. I think we'll not answer you."

IX

Now, on 21 August 1131 Baldwin II, last of the original Crusaders of 1097, former Regent of Edessa, King of Jerusalem, died without male issue. His patrimony took the form of four daughters, two who were but children, Jovieta and Hodierna, and two, whom the Emperor called the Scylla and Charybdis of the Levant, Alice and Melisande.

Alice had married Bohemond II of Antioch, on his majority and accession to the Principate, in 1124. From any aspect, it was a wretched match: Alice was everything one would expect of a soldier's eldest daughter: stern, taut, ambitious, humorless. Bohemond was everything one expects of a boy raised by his mother and crowned before he could crawl: irascible, domineering, overindulged, petty, pompous, and easily bored. Shortly after the birth of their daughter, Crown Princess Constance—their one radiant justification in the eyes of history—the marriage ended in all but political fact. In 1129, mixing detestation with ambition, Bohemond sought to take advantage of the death of Alice's maternal uncle, Prince Thoros I of Cilicia, by establishing his wife as Princess Regnant of that secessionary Byzantine province. Unfortunately, he was forced to confront similar ambitions in the Danishmend Emir, Gahji. In the ensuing war, Bohemond and his entire army were massacred (to no one's surprise or regret). Mistrusting his daughter, Baldwin II, with two years to live, sought the Regency of Antioch—in Constance's behalf —for himself. Alice, true to her nature, contrived to call in the Governor of Persian Mosul, Zengi, to counter her own father. Her request was intercepted, and before his death, Baldwin had locked away his startling progeny in her dower city of Lattakieh. The time is 1132.

On her father's death, Melisande, now Queen of Jerusalem, was ad-

vised, which is to say, instructed, by that gross and canny quinquege-
narian dissipate, Louis VI of France, to marry Fulk of Anjou, a
practical, not very subtle knight, haughty with the honor of his name,
as only the near royal can be. This should have been of little matter to
his Consort, save an eventuality ensued which brings tears to the eyes
of the French: Fulk fell in love with his wife, who was already quite
passionately beguiled, thank you, by one of her late father's aides, Hugh
of Puiset.

The rest is lurid, to say the least. Fulk contrived to have his wife's
lover charged with treason and challenged to defend himself in the
tournament lists, the Latin's likely, brute replacement for jurisprudence.
Hugh survived and so, guiltless, was pardoned, on the further condition
he exile himself to Europe. Two days before his embarkation he was
stabbed by a knight, claiming revenge on the sullied honor of the Sovereign Queen. He seemed to recover, but at Sicily he died. Through the
agencies of grief and unrequited passion, Melisande was instantly metamorphosed, accusing Fulk with the murder. To exonerate himself, Fulk
took the logical, if crude, step of putting the assassin to public torture.
With his last breath, the accused denied the King's complicity. Yet what
would a monster be, if not closed to logic, intrepid, relentless. In the first
two years of his reign, the King, rather like a man turning down his marriage bed each night to successively discover a knife, an asp, a snake,
and poison, uncovered four plots against his life, all richly hatched by
his Queen. Four times he forgave her. When death did not overtake her
husband and grief did not overcome Melisande, she was left, then, in
the enviable position of one to whom irrevocable wrong has been done.
The Queen squeezed from her still ardent husband the last drop of recompense, which, by definition, would never be sufficient for forgiveness,
in the form of his consent to her every wish. Her most impractical desire
was, of course, political: the reinstatement of her beloved sister, Alice,
as Regent of Antioch. The time is 1135.

It is at this moment, Byzantium and the Turks begin to close in on
the Latin states. Zengi of Mosul moves from the east, Byzantium from
the west.

John's intentions toward Antioch began with Cilicia. Quite simply
the Emperor was not reconciled to the secession of the huge southwest
province under the Rupen family, and intended to have it back, not so

unlikely an eventuality in the turmoil still brewing over accession to the princely throne at Tarsus. As a means of distracting the Emperor, Alice, restored to the Regency of Antioch, offered the Heiress, Constance, then eight years old, in marriage to Manuel Porphyriogenetus, then fifteen. Her barons, however, correctly apprehensive of an Imperium which claimed not only neighboring Cilicia, but vassal rights over Antioch, refused to consent to the alliance, and asked the intercession of Fulk, who, nothing loath to repeat the pedophilism of his own ventures, at once sent ambassadors to fetch the thirty-six-year-old Raymond, youngest son of the fabulous William IX of Aquitaine, born in the year his father disastrously ventured east to Jerusalem, as the only fit bridegroom for Antioch's next ruler. Alice was forced to withdraw the Constantinopolitan betrothal, and John Augustus, having just married the heir to the Sebastocracy, Isaac III, to Francesca of Hungary, once again annealing hostility in the north and leaving him free to face the south again, did not conceal his diplomatic fury at this slight from what he called the "Latin's capriole mentality."*

In two campaigns, of 1134 and 1135, the Emperor ended Cilicia's brief independence. The first year, he chose to leave the Rupens, leaders of the insurrectionists, in power, in the hope as plenipotentiary governors, they would combine ambition with loyalty and provide the antidote to their fellow rebels. Instead, before spring 1135, they expelled the Imperial commissioners and went into pitch battle with the army of occupation. In this second campaign, which lasted to October, John took Heraclea, Tarsus, Caesarea, Militene, and then marched south on the local capital, Sis, where he disenfranchised the aristocracy, and sent their marshals, the Rupen family, to Constantinople and a life of state-financed luxury which, with public pretension and private uneasiness (since they did not refuse the remuneration), they called their "intolerable exile."

The reaction, everywhere in Palestine and reaching to Baghdad, was one of intense alarm. The Emperor's ambitions were now variously interpreted by each of his enemies through the dark glass of their own fears, which is to say, the Emperor now possessed all the advantages of unpredictability. *Explicit: Nicetas Acominatus.*

---

* The capriole is the battle technique of the Latin horse, in which a leap is executed on all fours followed by a swift hind kick. N.A.

Through the white streets of Iconium, crowded with the progress of its citizens, in white, still whiter than the walls, and the accent, every- where, of gold—palanquins, burnooses, staffs, knives, doors, spears, chariots, carrying chairs, bridles, saddles—Mas'ud Shah and Isaac Por- phyriogenetus proceed to the Exarch's palace surrounded by the Seljuk King's Household Cavalry. The Shah is pale-skinned as Isaac, paler even, with that characteristic calcimine tint of aristocratic Moslems—not the sallow to pink of Europeans, but the true white which is the absence of color so nearly as to be the phantom blue of ice. His eyes are the Arab's eyes, deep set, doelike, dark, feral, dancing between what ap- pears to be irrevocable cynicism and tragic disappointment—the look of an ingenuous maid as she starts from her chair and falls back again, waiting for the lover who never comes. His nose is an aquiline beak, his beard neat—Greek—his mouth pinched, though the effect is not unpleas- ant—rather that of a man lost in thought and about to give an answer. He is not small, but he is slender, and gives the appearance of being dwarfed beside the gigantesque Imperial Prince, who leans to him, deferentially in his saddle, as they converse, in Greek.

Without warning, Isaac reins his horse. He is staring ahead, stock- still. Before the entrance to the Exarch's palace is a small contingent of Varangians in dusty, but formal dress. They are attracting a crowd— Greek and Turk alike—for their size, the beauty of their persons and uniforms, and no less, the meaning of their presence. Resolute, Isaac begins to turn his horse. Malik extends his breathtakingly bejeweled right hand to the bridle and—with surprising strength—stays him.

MAS'UD. Prince, in the name of God, and all that is good, go and meet with your brother.

Isaac's cheeks flush visibly. His breath is spastic.

ISAAC. My brother is here?

MAS'UD. Not the Emperor. I would be sick with insufficiency if he were. It is the Caesar Bryennius and your father-in-law, Duke Michael. I received them—and gladly—this morning. If I am ultimately frank with you, will you do as I ask? Not as I command, as I ask?

Isaac turns from the Varangians to the King.

MAS'UD. Sir, I have maintained two decades of peace in Lesser Asia, giving and losing much to do so. This was my coronation promise and it is one I have kept. I do not prescribe to the theory a people are proud when they are imperialistic. The Prophet has said, "He is the best of men who loathes power." My forefathers drove our people for a century in unremitting war. If my successors wish to match them, *Keleisate,* so be it, as you Greeks say, but so long as I live and reign, my life shall be dedicated to the respite of my people. Now Constantinople under the aegis of your awesome brother has become again the most powerful single factor in the Mediterranean lake. He has bested my detestable Danishmend brother and his own ungrateful Cilician children. I have not the heart to challenge him, and as you are here, the offense to him is implicit. I could dismiss you from my kingdom, but where then would you go? To the West? To Frankish Syria? I think not. For the greater the esteem in which the Latins hold you, the truer your contempt—and the more dissimulating—and the greater your profit, the truer your betrayal of the fatherland and the unhappier you shall be. Remember the words of your worthy Bishop of Hippo, "It is a great liberty to be able not to sin; it is the greatest liberty to be unable to sin." That is the superb freedom you shall have if you return to your brother, the Autocrat.

Mas'ud releases the bridle. With a hesitation which is perceptible Isaac moves forward between the lines of brown-leathered Seljuk cavalry. At the gate, he is unrecognized by the Varangians, who are probably recent recruits. But the commander, Paul of Chernigov, recognizes the Porphyriogenetus at once and hastily calls his men to present arms. Bethinking himself, he approaches Isaac with a look of calculated expressionlessness. But something snaps when he reaches the Sebastocrator. So close to the huge figure, he is truly moved. He bends forward and kisses the buffed boot of the Emperor's brother.

PAUL. Christ be praised, Your Imperial Highness, to see you again, alive and well.

Isaac, too, is moved, squinting in the sunlight—though rather from rapidly deteriorating eyesight than too much light. He glances toward a frankly curious and expectant Mas'ud, catches himself, and straightens in the saddle, speaking to Paul.

ISAAC. I never liked you, Paul and my father never trusted you. I pray this is not an indication of the sincerity which awaits me within.

Incipit: Nicetas Acominatus: With the repeated success of the Governor of Mosul, Zengi, against Antiochenes, Tripolitans, and Jerusalemites alike, it became more imperative than ever to the Emperor that the matter of suzerainty over the city on the Orontes be settled or (he feared, incorrectly) the expense suffered would be the Moslem overwhelming of Christian Palestine.

In March 1136 John Augustus left Constantinople with an army of fifty thousand, which, by the time he had crossed half Lesser Asia, had swelled half that again. His express intent was the capture of Antioch and the assertion of his sovereignty as liege lord.

Presumably this was the opportunity Bryennius had awaited to begin proceedings for reconciliation between the brothers. Taking with him Duke Michael Paleologus and a small band of Imperial guardsmen under the command of one of the Caesar's oldest and most trusted followers, Paul of Chernigov, this remarkable sexagenarian—suffering the first throes of the disease which would kill him—rode all night from the vast Imperial encampment at Laodicea, arriving at Iconium the next day to be immediately received by Mas'ud Shah, plainly eager to be rid of an eminent prince, whom he found after seven years' residence he could neither use nor deplore. Bryennius writes:

> The King assured us he would arrange the meeting by noon, as he realized our absence at the Praetorium should have already created an uproar. Indeed, he kept his word. While we awaited my brother-in-law, we were reunited with the Sebastocratrix. Duke Michael was bitterly disappointed his grandsons were absent, both visiting with his namesake.
>
> While we talked of—what else?—old times, Isaac, with a splendid throwing apart of both doors, which led me to believe he had suffered a long wait and taken a deep breath before doing so, entered the room. He looked magnificent, though I was touched to notice how his vision —never good—had become impaired further these last years. From the lack of response in the eyes, I knew at thirty feet he could not tell Michael from myself, though there is a world of difference and fifteen years between us.
>
> Michael came forward; the Porphyriogenetus' eyes cleared and deepened, and, with minutest pause—to measure mutually the calculation or lack of it—the two men embraced. And then I was profoundly moved when, he, who had, for so many years, been wary of me, embraced me too. For all I know, he may have had knowledge of my illness, whose end is not very distant from this writing. Indeed, there is nothing like the certainty, one's forgiveness need not be long-lived, to induce one to extend it in the manner of a friend forever.
>
> It goes without saying, he was somewhat taken aback—in fact, I almost thought our mission lost—when he learned the Emperor was not ex-

tending a pardon. Rather we were asking the Sebastocrator to petition the Emperor in his own behalf. I said, "He will be amenable, Isaac, and more than that, deeply joyed, but it is you who must go to him—as a loving brother and a subject, which is to say, his offender. Even were you ultimately in the right, in the face of your actions"—I held up my hand—"and I assure you I would not presume to sit in judgment—"

But he interrupted me in spite of himself. "Let us be open with one another, Nicky."

I nodded.

"He went so far, as I recall it, to command you come to him from far Trebizond."

I said, "True. But had you ever thought my sin against the throne was specifically legal and definable? I could not presume to ask for pardon."

He shook his head, his expression perplexed. "I am disturbed by this and I cannot quite understand why."

Paleologus spoke. "If you cannot articulate what disturbs you, I suggest you look to your prejudices." He paused. "Isaac, you will see for yourself: His Majesty has changed immeasurably in these last years."

"Can eight years make such a difference?"

Paleologus nodded. "If not, what can? He relies on no one, suffers almost no man's advice and appreciates no man's admonishment afterward. And not all of us agree with his policies, especially in the matter of war"—he paused—"even such a general as myself."

"But that Persian does, I'm certain."

I interrupted: "Leave Auxuch be. He is probably the only one among us to exercise the least restraint on Johnny. Do you know he's already dreaming of the Mesopotamia."

He started, "That is plain madness."

"Indeed it is. And your loathsome Persian, moreover, who has about as much Persian blood remaining in his veins as I've had from birth, has been the only one to gainsay him or protest an economy which relies—or shall, if we continue in the present direction—on the artificial vitriol of war to sustain it."

"That's no news to me." He was angry and he was warming to it. "Johnny's always been rather dim financially. He never listened to Uncle Paul's tutelage the way I did. And perhaps I ought to point out to you I fought for the same principle during my years in power. I similarly dissented. It says nothing for Auxuch but that he listens well and grasps the logic of the best advice secondhand. I pray you do not credit him with my good sense."

We talked, thus, until late afternoon, at which time we were obliged to return to the Praetorium. The Porphyriogenetus would not give us a specific answer, but he seemed to be on the side of consent. We decided the most propitious moment for a public act of submission should occur at Antioch, if the Emperor were triumphant.

At this, scratching his forehead with his second finger, his eyes filled with the first amusement we had seen since our arrival, Isaac said, "Oh, I should be more certain, if I were you, Johnny will be victorious at Antioch, then I will submit to him."

Afterward we proceeded directly to the Sultan's palace where a Writ of Neutrality had been in preparation the entire day. This was Mas'ud's suggested excuse for our disappearance. Rather redundant to the action, it guaranteed the King would not interfere with the Emperor's attack on Antioch. We returned to Laodicea, where John seemed pleased but somewhat bewildered by our efforts at Iconium. He did not ask if we had visited with his brother. I think he feared the answer.

What Isaac never told his kin, nor even Mas'ud—and that which was the cause of his hesitation—was existence of an offer from Zengi of Mosul, which would place at the Sebastocrator's disposal the armies of Baghdad to achieve nothing less than his accession to the Imperial throne. It was, in truth, to this purpose that Philip and Andronikus (a singular point of trust, in spite of his age) were absent, meeting at Michael's villa with an intermediary, an Aleppan merchant who did no more than convey a letter detailing the scheme by which, as Isaac later told his youngest son, "I would betray the fatherland, then rule it in accord with Baghdad's instructions."

Why the Porphyriogenetus allowed the suggestion to proceed as far as it did is perplexing. Perhaps in his heart of hearts, there was something like a whisper of consent. In any event, by the time his sons had returned, he knew his own mind. As the letter was handed to him, Andronikus told me, he did not even read it, but scrawled across its face, *Obtempero*—I submit—underlined it twice, and, in a deed whose only extravagance turns out to be its unexpected clumsiness, sent the document to his brother: their first communication in eight years.

Its effect can only be compared to that of an earthquake. The Sebastocrator may have meant to be large in his action, magnificently dramatic, perhaps inspired by his renewed study of the Poet which produced in these same months those two famous jewel-like essays on the transformation of the Homeric epic in modern times—but the effect of the gesture depends upon the audience for whom it is intended. John Augustus was by no means unsubtle or blind to aesthetics or unmoved by great deeds. Yet in the solitude of his position since birth, living all his life a step below and then at the pinnacle of earthly power, the glamour and vivacity of autocracy, which other men would imitate in small, scarcely seemed credible to him. Supreme power was a burden, a very "ordinary" thing, and all politics, besides, a serious business, a quiet one, in which nothing impetuous or considered save in repose is to be tolerated. He was not blind, but so to speak, color-blind. Nothing grand, sentimental, or fantastical could resound off his "political soul." He could not see below the superscription to the act of extravagant homage and apology. Simply, traitorously, his brother had consorted with Zengi, and he thereupon refused any talk of reconciliation, whilst Isaac waited, bewildered and then bitter, but still anxiously, on letters from Bryennius, which were more abashed than enlightening.

X

Now, Raymond of Poitiers, on his marriage to the eight-year-old Constance, foiled the designs of Princess Alice and her Patriarch, who had foreseen the Consort as their tool. Instead, he became Regent for his wife, forswore all oaths taken in France, and owed himself to none but Fulk of Jerusalem, to whom, indeed, he owed everything.

Knowing very little of the history of Antioch or its enemies, save that which he learned from manuals and portfolios sent by representative ministries and read to him during evenings on his journey east, the new Prince sought a stand against John Augustus, who became the first reigning Emperor in more than five centuries to officially set foot in the Holy Land. Moreover, he commanded an army whose like had not been seen in engines and numbers since the days of Basil II. When it was unleashed in all its pulverizing weight against Antioch, the city suffered four months' excruciating siege, at the end of which capitulation became inevitable.

Before surrender, however, Raymond sent messengers to Fulk to gain the King his liege's consent. As Jerusalem that same summer had suffered defeat to Zengi at Montferrand, Fulk was more than eager to recognize the superior suzerainty of Byzantium over the great city, and thereby reach an alliance which, he foresaw, would carry with it the promise of Constantinopolitan military aid. Alexius would have smiled at the sudden indisputability of Imperial claims. Jerusalem even sent his Constable to stand proxy in a separate oath of vassalage.

On word from Fulk, Raymond ordered his intermediaries to the Praetorium with a writ of total surrender, which may have saved him his throne from a people disgusted with a ruler who inaugurated his reign by putting Antioch to such trial. (Raymond would have done well to practice his swordsmanship less and learn more of his subjects. Antiochenes, with their largess, their incendiary tempers, their appetite for novelty which is a low tolerance on boredom, are notoriously the worst possible candidates to endure siege.)

It is said, when news reached Constantinople of the recovery of its "Elder Sister," the city went mad. Thanksgiving liturgies were held in every church, after which citizens rushed into the street to dance. Bonfires were lit everywhere, and not a few tenements went up in smoke along with their occupants (so one man dies because of an event hundreds of miles away and by worlds separate from his own self-interest). Palaces were thrown open to rich and poor alike in banqueting and entertainment. It was like a second Easter. The Senate, at once, voted a triumphal entry on the Emperor's return. (Wiser than effusive in a reign which had known not one and dangerously separated the people from the sense of such wars as their own. Bryennius tells us Auxuch was behind this move, and it speaks well of him.) Finally, in the tenderest moment at least one kind wag remembered him for whom Antioch had been a paramount concern. Scrawled across the sarcophagus of Alexius Augustus in red paint was found the legend "Rest; it is done."

John, however, did not enter Antioch, and would not, for another year. Contemporary historians tell us it was Bryennius' advice to assume the city by stages. Though native Antiochenes were in the majority, power now lay in the hands of Italians, Sicilians and the French, whose resentment against an overbearing victor might be put to advantage by Raymond of Poitiers.

The Emperor settled for private oaths, taken in the Praetorium, and then instructed Raymond, Edmond—Fulk's Constable—and Raymond's erstwhile ally, Joscelin, Count of Edessa, they were to raise armies with the intent of marching in a line with Imperial forces first on the province of Shaizar, then Aleppo, and finally Damascus. The campaign would commence spring, next.

With these startling words, John turned his army north and west again and marched across Lesser Asia, nearly three-quarters Byzantine again, arriving in Constantinople in October. He was appalled by the extent to which preparations had gone forward for a triumphal entry and, it is said, upbraided Auxuch—the only record we have of anger against this supernally trusted servant. Auxuch patiently, and rather cannily, pointed out how much more willingly the people would support the Emperor's proposal of a Holy War on Damascus if he were to show himself, in all panoply, as the great warlord. There was, moreover, the goodwill of the army to consider—denied, at worst, pillage, at best, entry into the city they had captured. We see a touch of Alexian pragmatism in the Emperor's consent. *Explicit: Nicetas Acominatas.*

In the unexpectedly warm November sun, a white Arabian stallion is led forward, its neck encircled with pearls, its frontlet and breastplate studded with sapphires, rubies, and emeralds, its dainty hooves prancing out a tattoo of hysteria in the midst of these scores of thousands of troops to the fore and aft of the Abramite Monastery. Within, in the Imperial apartments, where, time immemorial, Byzantine emperors have spent the night in prayer and fasting, previous to a triumphal entry, John, dressed in golden mail, sags noticeably and uncomfortably as two portions of a golden breastplate are placed against his back and chest, then secured along the sides and atop the shoulders with silver greaves. He is handed gloves of scarlet leather sewn with pearls. He turns to Byrennius. The old man is sipping from a goblet of crystal set in a filigree net.

JOHN. Nicephorus, how the devil do you propose to receive the Host in three hours if you drink wine? Gluttony.

BRYENNIUS. Not gluttony, only thirst. And not wine—

He taps the exquisite cup—

BRYENNIUS. —only water. Even our Lord's thirst was slaked at the First Sacrifice.

JOHN. Well, then, imitate him in full. Try vinegar. Come, let's get this over with.

The Varangians, in gold and scarlet; the Lancers of the Excubitors in gold and blue; Scholarians in gold and green carrying shields dis-

playing a golden eye in a golden circle; Cubiculars, Protospatars, in blue and white; and Senators in white and gold all await the Emperor. Presently the doors of Abramite open as its bell begins to toll. The dozen trumpeters on horse before the entrance repeat a dissonant four-note blast. John Augustus' golden armor is struck by the sun as soon as he appears. Over his shoulders he wears a white velvet mantle, its lining woven with abstract scarlet rosettes, secured below his throat by a colossal ruby, repeated on his golden helmet. Unceremoniously, he carries his gloves in his hands. Swords arc and skirts rustle, as soldiers salute and civilians kneel. The Emperor mounts up. He is handed the Sword of Constantine by Michael Paleologus. With more discipline and duty than the requisite strength he hefts its five feet of gold, emeralds, and pearls upright, setting the pommel in an ingenious contraption fitted into the horn of his saddle. Followed by his suite, then the Imperial guard— the civilians shall walk—the procession begins the march from the suburb of Hebdomen to the Golden Gate.

The first quarter mile of the half-mile procession has marched ahead of the doors of the Monastery of St. John the Baptist of Studion before —in the precise center—the Emperor arrives and dismounts. He is cheered from the roof by hundreds of well-born students of his alma mater and, as well, several dozens more, who, neither rich nor aristocratic, have been admitted at his urging under Imperial scholarships. Once again, with little forethought—protesting his disgust with it by breaking protocol—the Emperor looks up, smiles, and waves the hand which holds the gloves. The boys roar. One student nearly falls—the Emperor starts— but he is caught. Bryennius follows the Emperor with a wave of his own. A canopy of purple silk and gold is held by four Varangians above Augustus as the seven-hundred-year-old encaustic Icon of John the Baptist is carried out to the Via Triumphalis. The Emperor kneels, as it is told, giving thanks to God for his victories and praying for the Roman Empire. It is one of the few simple moments in so much panoply. The million persons lining the avenue are suddenly silenced, by waves, into the distance. All about stand with heads bent, while the Autocrat alone is on his knees. When he rises, a eunuch, bowing deeply, approaches the Emperor and—in a compromise agreed upon during rehearsals—receives from his hands rather than lifts from his head the sovereign helmet with its Cyclopean ruby. Two more eunuchs remove the white mantle, and the General of the Scholarians receives the Sword of Constantine, with which Basil I crossed and raised to the nobility Alexander Comnenus, nearly three hundred years before. Thus disrobed, the Emperor is no longer warlord and commences to assume the image of Christ. His sons, Alexius and Isaac, the Porphyriogeneti, step forward, receiving from Constantinopolitan Grandees a combination mantle and dalmatic of deep purple, with which they clothe their father. Manuel, the youngest and tallest—and attempting, diplomatically, to slouch before the short, slender Emperor—presents his father with the massive cross-topped Imperial tiara, and John crowns himself. The Caesar Bryennius hands the Emperor a golden taper, with a candle, and takes up another, already lit, which John touches to his own, thereby symbolizing himself as the Light of the World in Christ's place. This is the signal. The entire Via Triumphalis bursts into flame beneath the sunlight, as tapers which have been dispensed among the people for the last week by order of the Prefect, John Dukas Bryennius, are lit—one neighbor touching his own to the next and on and on and on, along the Way to the Augusteum. Alexius Bryennius presents his uncle with the cruciate scepter, and thus, his hands rather clumsily filled, the Emperor ascends four purple velvet steps to remount his steed. Six enormous, beribboned, flammulae icons now precede him.

The Augusteum. At least a quarter million people are drawn up behind spear-carrying Varangians. Two extremely wide paths—that from Holy Wisdom to Chalke, and the Million Arch to the Senate—intersect, forming a cross. The magnificent chessboard slabs of marble are hidden beneath tons of flower petals; every wall and gate has been festooned with serpentine boughs and wreaths of autumn bloom. On the Emperor's appearance a great cry goes up and follows him during the slow progress to the ancient chapel of Theotokos, dwarfed by the soaring white pillars of the Senate Building.

In the vestry of Theotokos, John stands half-naked in his white silk bloomers. The hair on his chest and limbs is completely gray. With his left hand he grasps the right bicep and flexes his obviously strained forearm. Bryennius has presumed on an old man's advantage—he is certain, at least, of unction on his deathbed—and broken his fast. He now munches happily and fastidiously one by one, on a cupful of almonds.

The Emperor surveys his shoulders, pulling them forward a little with the grasp of his opposite hand, and shakes his head at sight of the deep red grooves worn by the breastplate. Loosening the silk cord which secures his undergarment, he exposes his hips just below the line of the first gray pubic hairs. Auxuch, in the uncustomary role of valet, enters, carrying the Emperor's white chalmys.

JOHN. Look at this. Just look. These bruises will be weeks healing. If you were so damn set on this absurdity, the least you might have done, is have that wretched armor recast on my mannequin.

AUXUCH. Yes, Divinity, I shall remember it.

JOHN. Don't bother. This won't happen again.

BRYENNIUS. Not true. This is as nothing compared to a successful venture against Zengi. Am I not right, Auxuch?

JOHN. Then I promise you I won't enter Constantinople until I am given a guarantee of dignity, which is to say simplicity.

Auxuch hands the chalmys to one of the attendants and reties the bloomer cord at the Emperor's waist.

Under the sunburst bolts of Holy Wisdom, the court and as much of the population as can be admitted without a crush are assembled. Along with the hidden Cathedral Choir of two hundred voices and two hundred more of the Palace Choir—composed of those best voices among sailors of the Imperial yachts, and members of the Scholarians, Excubitors, Varangians, and Cubiculars—the assemblage sings the anthem "Hail, Autocrat of the Romans" ("delight of the universe, whom the Trinity has led to victory./Incomparable Commander, Guardian of the World, mayst thou henceforward/Coerce the nations by the holy weapon of piety alone") while the Emperor passes from the Imperial vestry half the length of Holy Wisdom to the porphyry dais, surmounted by his throne, whose cedar body is invisible beneath an over-all crust of rubies, sapphires, emeralds, carnelians, opals, aquamarines, diamonds, and pearls. Towering above it is a huge gold double-barred Patriarchal Cross. He is followed by his sons and his suite, but absent are the fan-bearers, the military icons and standards of the regiments which, on hearing of it, he had absolutely forbidden within the cathedral. He is clad in the traditional chalmys. Rather than the traditional purple mantle, he wears a luminously beautiful dalmatic of iridescent opus plumarium. *He is, of course, without a crown where Christ is King. Divine Liturgy begins. He motions Bryennius to him.*

JOHN. I received a letter this morning. From Isaac's son, of all people.

BRYENNIUS. Philip? Michael?

JOHN. The youngest. Andronikus. What do you think of that?

Bryennius, leaning by the Emperor, waits. John seems to bethink himself and has nothing more to say. The Caesar retires to his place.

XI

Incipit: Nicetas Acominatus: From the moment John Augustus left Antioch, Prince Raymond proposed to disrupt the Emperor's plans. In this, he was to be assisted by Joscelin II, Count of Edessa, one of those marvelously clever fellows in whom irony is mistaken, too often, for indifference. Such men as Joscelin appear to follow—or, anyway, accompany—the more vigorous and avid like Raymond. In truth, all the while, they have led by subtle guidance. The stillness of calculation seems to surround them, and since they never *move,* they may always observe—and observe that which is best to their advantage—as one who enters a room wherein maids are frantically searching for a brooch, which is in plain view, catches sight of it, takes it, and departs. Such men never warn, they strike. Of course immobility may lead to improvidence, no less than success, since it is essentially the ethic of the opportunist. Vision and preparation, or preventative action, save foreknowledge of the nearest door or the quickest path from battle, are unknown to them. Unhappily, Joscelin was to have this insight into his own character much too late to stave off disaster.

But that was the unknowable future. In 1136 the Count perceived in the intentions of Raymond of Antioch—a colleague he thoroughly detested as "half lost to barbarism and the other half not worth rescue"—his own profit. If Aleppo were taken, it would surely become part of the Antiochene fief, an increase in power intolerable to the County of Edessa. To be sure, the only possible solution was the ruin of the oncoming war initiated by the "Holy Yokel," as he termed the Emperor. Equally to be sure, Raymond was easy material for one so sinuous as Joscelin. Thus these two unlikely men joined hands: Joscelin in the belief he was destroying Raymond, Raymond in the belief he was gaining a helpmate to yet prevent the Emperor's suzerainty of Antioch, each in the vanity of his own efficacious manipulation of the other.

On 7 April 1137 the combined armies of Constantinople, Antioch, Edessa, and Jerusalem marched on the Shaizarine Emirate. During the week-long march, the future was foretold in the conduct of the Edessan Count and the Antiochene Prince. They refused to attend staff meetings and rather, as soon as the camp was founded, proceeded each night to drink themselves insensate, also profoundly offending the Emperor with the legion of prostitutes—not courtesans, streetwalkers—in their suites. They refused to partake of, or supervise, dusk or morning maneuvers and set their men to singing bawdy songs during liturgy. Fulk, who, albeit his uxoriousness, was seeming to grow splendidly into his Kingship, was profoundly ashamed of his vassals. My dear late friend, Bishop William of Tyre, the greatest historian of the previous century, compares the actions of these former fellow Latins to those of vicious and disobedient schoolboys annoying their master not to gain his attention by punishment, but to distract him from his task.

Once the siege of Shaizar commenced, on 14 April, ignominy surpassed mischief. While the Greek line was harassed, neither Count nor Prince would order their troops into battle. While the Emperor fought among his men, horsed and unhorsed, these worthies, it is reliably reported (if we may trust William, and we may), diced in silken robes, drowned their hangovers in renewed drunks and fornicated like bulls in a barnyard. William recounts a pause in battle during which the Emperor, filthy with the warrior's detritus, of dust, blood, and sweat, entered Raymond's incense-heavy tent, come himself to implore the nobles to battle:

> With miraculously mild manner, he prayed them show more spirit in the effort which they had consented to undertake with him. As he who was wealthier than they by far and had kings and great princes under his dominion did not ease from battle but exposed himself to its wounds and perils in the service of Our Lord, they ought not to do less. . . .

The great bishop and historian may have read equanimity in that episode, but those who knew the Emperor have told me the bite of his irony, not very exquisite, increased in proportion to the seriousness of an issue.

Yet, as we have suggested, not all the Latins conducted themselves so wretchedly. Fulk fought with indisputable bravery and deployed his forces brilliantly. In battle he was, as they say, in his element, and a master. And something more. He was a man of North France—dour, pious, honorable, not subtle, but always sensible, trustworthy, and stubborn to a task. For that he still believed in the Crusading idea and the heavenly behooving of alliance against Moslems. As King of Jerusalem, he also knew he was less a man of politics than participant in something like legend. It was not the power he wielded but the ideal he experienced which moved him. From his unsavory beginnings as cuckolded Consort, he was transfigured into something shining. For that he won a real friendship with the Emperor which lasted to the end of their days, both dying similarly and suddenly in the same year.

Fulk's pleas to his vassals fared no better than the Emperor's, and one suspects that the very act of both sovereigns in seeking out Raymond and Joscelin only confirmed the latter two—if their mockery and renewed insouciance is any indication—on the course they set for themselves. The manliness and the humility of both King and Emperor had meaning precisely because of their anointment. Exalted, they were yet patient and gracious, pointing up all the more reprehensible immaturity of their vassals. It is not very difficult, in turn, to perceive shame and jealousy in Raymond and Joscelin. Even if that envy were not fully articulated, as an animal's panic is not self-conscious, they could act upon it, as animals will respond to their fears, without knowing why.

On 2 August the Emperor, in concert with Fulk, decided to treat with the Shaizarenes to the exclusion of Joscelin and Raymond. In fact, he commanded the two to leave the Praetorium and return to Antioch, where, significantly, they were to prepare the city for his entry and their own public oaths of vassalage. After a peace treaty was signed with the Emir, which included annual payment to Byzantium of five thousand pounds of solid gold, 8 August 1137, the Emperor himself followed the route to the Orontes débouche. At Antioch he once again consented to pageantry, though now with a vengeance. Surrounded by his four sons, courtiers and officials he had called from Constantinople, the Emperor was welcomed at the great gates by Raymond and Joscelin and the Patriarch. The Marshal of the Court read the official welcome, whose arabesque floridity suggests Joscelin's literary hand:

Antioch welcomes Thee as Lover of Christ, as Athlete of the Lord, as Zealous Fighter against the barbarians, as carrying the Sword of Elijah; it wipes off Thy sweat and softly embraces Thee. The whole numerous population pours out, of every age and both sexes, to accord You Your triumph, as You shine amidst us, Our Brightest Star. . . . Be of good cheer, O men who love Christ, and those who are pilgrims and strangers because of Christ. Do not fear any more murderous hands. The Basileus Who loves Christ has put them in chains and broken to pieces the unjust sword. Thou has cleared for them the way to the earthly and visible Jerusalem and has opened Thyself to another more divine and broad way: that to the heavenly and holy Jerusalem.

Explicit: Nicetas Acominatus.

Nicephorus Bryennius leans to the Crown Prince Alexius.

BRYENNIUS. Prose or poetry, nephew, that's the worst piece of shit I've ever heard.

Alexius giggles—then starts suddenly as Sergius kicks him with his spurred foot.

Incipit: Nicetas Acominatus: The Imperial banners were then raised over all official buildings and John Augustus entered the city, Joscelin and Raymond afoot, leading his horse. The Emperor heard Mass at St. Peter's, then moved to the Palace of the Caesars, the vice-regal seat once occupied, according to Diocletian's Reform, by the Caesarean Heir to the East Roman Imperial Throne, then later by one of the half-dozen most important officials in the Empire, the Governor of Greek Syria. Now, an Isapostolos, for the first time since the wondrous years of Heraclius, took the steps of the establishment at a clip and entered the bronze doors depicting the life of the Chief Apostle, Peter. *Explicit: Nicetas Acominatus.*

Unaccompanied, as is their habit, the Emperor and the Porphyriogeneti, Alexius, Isaac, and Manuel, pass round the huge, three-tiered colonnaded curve of the ancient Antioch Circus. The fantastic heat of the Levantine summer's day is not yet upon the city, and with it the stench of Symeon Harbor. The dawn sky, above the riders and above —high above—the coronet of statues overlooking the circus, is glimmering and nacreous: the blue still to be breathed into it. The air is pre-

ternaturally clear. Everything suggests renewal. The Emperor and his sons pass within the colonnade and begin a semi-circumnavigation between the tiers to the entrance of the floor of the stadium. Their horses' hooves clatter on the ancient marble pavement. The gloom is oppressive and decidedly emphasized by the resounding echo. They pass vagrants, sometimes entire families, huddled in sleep.

To their surprise, the doors of the passage leading to the stadium are thrown open. It is narrow and high, cut through the first vault of seats, a tunnel, nearly, which would be dark as night but for the vista beyond the archway: the spina, the opposite curve of the stadium, and the incandescent tip of the sun's disk which throws the entire row of statues into umbra. John egresses first into the stadium and notices in the distance a young man taking a magnificent palomino round the far end of the spina. Elsewhere along the tiers there are yet more vagrants, some asleep, some risen and, for lack of anything better, watching the racer.

ALEXIUS. So much for that. We should have had the guards here, at least to clear the place.

Manuel follows the rider with the interest of a connoisseur.

MANUEL. He leaned too much on the turn.

In echo of the Porphyriogenetus' words a young voice from above and behind bellows across the stadium.

VOICE. You leaned him too much on the turn! Too much! You leaned!

The rider, still too distant to be distinguished clearly, stops his horse, raising dust, glowing like gold in the low sunlight. One can just discern the movement of his head as he makes out the figures of the Emperor and Porphyriogeneti beneath the source of the voice.

VOICE. Good way to lose speed or cause a fall.

MANUEL. So much, Papa, for diplomacy.

JOHN. Greeks.

The rider starts toward the Imperial family at an easy trot.

VOICE. Now what's the matter? Andronikus? What's the matter?

The rider does not answer. The sun has risen by a half. From behind, and above John and his sons, there is the sharp drumming of hooves on stone as a horse descends the stadium stairs and at length appears round the protruding entry. Its rider so uncannily resembles the late Alexius Augustus in all but diminutiveness, the Emperor audibly gasps. The young man turns on the sound, and blushes, and gapes.

PHILIP. God help us. Uncle.

The three Porphyriogeneti, the Emperor, and Isaac's son turn to
watch the oncoming rider. Years from now, Manuel, in words which
will not be recorded, shall say: "He came toward us as the whole disk
of the sun rose above the coronet of the Antioch Circus and flooded
the stadium in light, the most perilously beautiful boy I had ever seen
in my life. Not beautiful in the sense of effeminate, but feminine in the
valuable sense of being self-aware, self-contained, indifferent, perfect,
one who would grow bored with compliments, not doubting their sin-
cerity but exasperated by the similarity, which increases him not a whit.
Marcus Aurelius speaks of it: 'Whatever is in any way beautiful has its
source of beauty in itself and is complete in itself: praise forms no part
of it.' He was one of those for whom his own good looks are simultane-
ously a pleasure—he was too intelligent to be entirely vain—and a toy
with which to tempt and beguile others who take beauty too seriously.
His dark hair was blown back by the force of the ride toward us, a trans-
lucent nimbus lit by the light of the sun behind him. I recall his head a
little to one side, in frank curiosity, and those eyes, those enormous gray
eyes, almost blue, with lashes nearly as long as the steed's upon which
he was mounted. His legs and arms glistened like the horse and his
mouth was sealed, though smiling a knowing, clement, indulgent smile
such as I have seen on very old men and the lips of certain statues un-
earthed in ancient temples between Delphi and Aegina. Animated in
the face of a fifteen-year-old boy, it was uncanny, awful, exhilarating—
like a vision of God. Such is the ideal which has followed me from that
day to this. I know—he used you and me as one would wait upon a
candle and toss away the nub; but his ardency was real, and it was shin-
ing and the light by which he came to know himself. It was ephemeral
only as the flight of all earthbound things tossed at the sky is ephemeral."

Incipit: Nicetas Acominatus: By now Bryennius had but one wish: to
reconcile the brothers before his death. Thus, while the Emperor fought
at Shaizar, the Caesar wrote to the Sebastocrator and told him to come
with his wife and sons to Antioch. He describes it in his final memorandum:

They arrived 8 August, and I settled them for their stay in a villa at
Daphne, lent us by an ambitious Genoese millionaire, who desperately

wants a license to open an agency at Constantinople, which shall be given him though I have directed the Interior Minister to wait a year before issuing the patent (how strange to think I command an act now which shall not be executed till I am clay). Too summary a compensation might lead the fellow to believe in his own influence at court, and he would become a pest. A good wait will humble him or at least discourage familiarity—save as a petitioner, frantic and irritating, for whom things are done to be rid of him, with orders at the gates against readmittance.

If there were any doubts the merchant was precisely a merchant and no more, they were dispelled by the decor within. He had attempted to imitate the classical luxury of the Early Empire and rather succeeded in burlesquing it. Where walls were originally muraled, the Signor washed them in bright red paint. Where marble once reigned, it was supplanted by gold, and where gold was once used with the precision of a jeweler's knife, it was now laid on with a trowel. Joanna called it "a rich man's bordello and a poor man's heaven."

I must admit, however, the equanimity I suggest—including my own— is deceptive. From the beginning, this venture has seemed threatened with failure. When Isaac learned he was not in Antioch on the Emperor's consent to his submission that—rather it was my intention to force brother upon brother—he was, at once, for returning to Iconium. It took the Sebastocratrix and myself the whole of the afternoon to convince him to remain. The very gist of my argument was that this estrangement would continue indefinitely unless something bold were done to end it.

"You know Johnny," I said. "You yourself once told me, you perceived, for all his activity, a passive nature, even a fateful one."

"I told you no such thing."

"You didn't? Well, I thought you had. Very well, it must have been someone else. I mean to say I sometimes think Johnny takes refuge in the distance the autocracy allows him. I think if he could he would sooner live in a world without personal encumbrances and obligations. I'm certain of it. He is not callous as Anna thinks. He loves a very few and the rest to him are unknowable. He does not like people, which is not the same thing as disliking them. He has neither your force nor the old man's charm, and he knows it." I told him I was not implying the Emperor was pleased to be rid of him, but perhaps in his heart of hearts relieved that the only man, his brother, who came as close to being his legal equal as one can be, or, in the least, by the prerogatives of blood might intrude upon him both personally and intellectually, as no other man might and never a woman at all, had seen fit to estrange himself.

"If that is what he wants, then I have less need of him than he of me."

Joanna was irritated at this. "Now you speak like a child. Only children demand affection before co-operation."

In the evening we received word the Emperor was on his way from Shaizar. Isaac blushed with anticipation and refused to say whether he would stay or go, but staying whilst he refused.

The Emperor arrived last Monday and last Tuesday took nominal possession of the city. Then, Wednesday in the morning, before I could broach to him Isaac's presence in the city, ease him, as it were, into the longing to be reconciled, he encountered Philip and Andronikus at the Antiochene Circus. Apparently things went well and Manuel especially hit it off splendidly with Andronikus. Yet, hard as it is to imagine, John asked after neither Isaac nor Joanna.

When he returned to the palace, he called Paleologus and myself to him and affected that cold-blooded aloofness which he assumes in place of anger, usually when he is being presumed upon personally, which he confuses with *laesa majestas*. He told us of the events of the morning, and threatened—that is too harsh—*implied* banishment, which is to say, commanded us to arrange Isaac's return to wherever it is his brother wished to go, to remain in his exile.

Paleologus, to my astonishment, drew himself up and uttered words I should never have thought to hear a subject lambaste upon an emperor before I died—well, there is a first and a last to everything—"Why, you stubborn, conceited, sinful prig."

John grimaced, pointed to the floor, and said slowly, "Ask my pardon while I still have it in me to give it you."

Instead, Michael bowed from the waist and began to leave.

I stood up as soon as the little strength I have would permit me and said, "This is too absurd. Stay, Michael. John, what is it you intend to do? You will pass your brother by, as he has come this far to ask your for-giveness? If he is stubborn and prideful, so are you. He has become more limpid in both. Will you not yourself? Or God will surely have His say over it and it will be none too favorable to either one of you." I smiled and continued: "And you forget. I am soon to be an agent in—I pray—the celestial realms. Do not send me there with such fresh resentments in mind or I shall have a say, too, before God, and my reference will not be kind."

He was touched for a moment, but he collected himself. "He has con-sorted with my enemies. Loyalty is the lifeblood of the dynasty. There is no state without loyalty and no loyalty unless it is to me. I bind our di-verse peoples in each man's duty to the throne."

"Yes, Your Majesty. Remember that. And remember, too, it is your integrity as both man and Emperor which gives currency to that duty. I have spoken myself hoarse explaining to you the meaning of the Zengian letter, if that is what you mean. You are being stubborn, John, and more than that, laggard as a Christian, as a forgiving Christian—you the very animation of earthly Christianity. Your father forgave me my wrongs against him and so have you. Is this what it has come to mean? I, who am not of the blood, am less peccable than one who is? Then, just so, my wife has been veiled for sixteen years not for the gravity of her crime against you, but for the irrevocable and helpless accident of her genesis."

He turned his face away. He was silent much, much longer than a man's considered deliberation, rather as though he had lost track of time entirely, which for me meant logic had ceased to play a part in his decision. I would wager all the minutes left me (which are fewer than my sins) the struggle within him was one of pride, quite as pernicious as Isaac's—in fact, I sometimes think, the birthmark (and possibly one day, the ruin) of this remarkable family, with whose fate my father's, mine, and my children's has been inextricably bound.

To reconcile himself with his brother, he must have thought, would be a public admission—or a private one, if only among his councilors—that in his own adamancy (especially these last two years) he had inflicted pain. Now, it is no great deal for a man to confess unintentional harm, even when it is an admission of stupidity or arrogance which led to such cruelty. But if an emperor admits to such a loss of logic and feeling, he must measure recantation in the degree which it shall affect his moral authority—pertinent consideration for one such as John Augustus. (And it is true indeed, we find admirable otherwise ordinary men who ripen with recognition of their flaws, while we suspect the flexibility and renewal of those who presently hold power and humbly act likewise.)

At length he spoke. "All right. I shall see him. I promise you nothing."

In the evening, then, escorted by Varangians, Isaac, Joanna, Philip, and Andronikus arrived at the Caesarean Palace. Save for the guards there were otherwise no official notices of welcome or station. It was prudent. Those of the court at Antioch did not know how to greet him, going down on one knee, as befits a Prince of the Blood, but not reaching to kiss his hands, as is proper in greeting a Sebastocrator.

I greeted him at the doors to the private audience chamber. Joanna was on his arm, in fact leading him in this diplomatic posture, since his sight is failing at terrific speed. I did not nod to him, slightly less in rank, as Caesar to Sebastocrator, but embraced him lightly as a relative. I kissed Joanna and each of the boys' shoulders. One of the guards rapped twice upon the floor and I heard Michael's voice consent to entry. As the doors opened I could see John take the three short steps to the little dais and throne set in the corner of the chamber. His face was flushed, which is a habit with both brothers when highly excited. When he saw Isaac blindly peering about the room, his face quite fell. No one had told him of the oncoming blindness and the secret was intentional. Sympathy is scarcely a basis for a reconciliation, and as it is, quickly deteriorates. Joanna led Isaac closer to the Emperor and finally the Sebastocrator's expression resolved itself as John resolved in his field of vision. The giant got down on his knees without a word and prostrated himself. "God forgive me," he said, "the offense I have given you, my brother and my lord." "God long ago forgave you, Isaac. It is I who am laggard in the eyes of heaven. I ask God's forgiveness for this, and yours." Isaac rose to his knees and John offered his hands to kiss, which Isaac grabbed with both his own, fervently. Naturally as can be, the brothers passed from this posture into an embrace. I am glad I lived to see it.

Explicit: Nicetas Acominatus.

In the silver night Manuel and Andronikus are atop the roof of the Caesarean Palace. Above them is the whole blue bowl of the firmament, the fainter stars overwhelmed by the light of the moon, full and perfect and turning about the zenith. The youths are improvidently without mantles and sit with their knees gathered. Only Manuel's eyes and brows —large, sensitive, and exquisitely molded—are Comnenian. He is, otherwise, discernibly the descendant of Bela Orseolo, whose Venetian blood it is which gives life to the spurious descendants of Hungary's St. Stephen Arpad (the original dynastic line having died during the childless marriage between Stephen's daughter and Peter Orseolo). The fine long nose, the small, almost feminine mouth, the ovular face, and the chestnut hair and high cheekbones are his mother's. It is a wonderful face—open, handsome, with touches of wit and melancholy. It promises to take a beard well. Andronikus has the Comnenus head—large, squarish, with its wide and vigorous chin—and like his father and his great-grandfather, the Nobilissimus John, he also possesses the height to carry it in proportion—as his uncle, grandfather, and great-granduncle, St. Isaac, did not. Otherwise, like Manuel, he resembles his mother's line and especially his great-grandfather, George Paleologus: enormous gray eyes with a luminous depth, the result of a more pronouncedly concave iris, sharply arched brows which give the face an expression of misleading aloofness. The bridge of the nose is high, anchoring the forehead, yet the nose itself is long, straight, and almost delicately refined at the base. The lips are large, but startlingly articulated. Manuel shall be correct in determining, as he remembers it, the beauty of this youth "perilous." He is unusually handsome, by all means and any standard— and yet, depending upon his mood or yours, your position or his posture, the coquetry of light and shadow, these splendid looks may seem soft or brutal, that of an angel's or a hedon's. Even without expression, perfectly still, his aspect has no repose, which seems the contradiction of beauty, if beauty is symmetry, that which is fixed. His face shifts like a prism held up to the light. It possesses liveness; *it seems not quite graspable at a glance, at war between the voluptuous and the precise.*

MANUEL. Do you believe in dreams? the foretelling of great things? And small things, too? Once, a few years ago, I misplaced a splendid knife which no one could find. I was quite heartbroken. And then one night, in a dream, I saw precisely where I had left it. And in the morning I found it where my dream had promised. As if by magic.

ANDRONIKUS. Do you believe in magic?

MANUEL. Do you? We're more than reason, aren't we?

Andronikus raises his eyes to the stars, his smile may mean wistfulness or resignation. It suggests a great secret, or perhaps detachment, tenderness, perhaps.

ANDRONIKUS. Are we? What more? . . . You know, the annals tell us when St. Isaac was governor, here, in 1054, a great star appeared in the heavens, burning night and day. Imagine that. Think of what these stones have seen of all who have marched upon them. Out there to the east is Persia, and there to the south, Persia, and to the west, Rome, and to the north, New Rome. Two immemorial enemies facing one another, for a thousand years beneath. . . .

MANUEL. Beneath what?

Andronikus shrugs and lies back, starting only a little as his back touches the cold stone.

ANDRONIKUS. The greatest enemy: anonymity. Think of how many men have lived and died and seen those stars who alone remember them.

MANUEL. Shall you be a poet like your father? Perhaps write a great epic and glorify my father's reign, and my brother's?

ANDRONIKUS. I hear you study medicine. Is this true? Why?

MANUEL. Because the workings of the body fascinate me. You asked a moment ago what more we are than reason?

He extends his arm and pushes back the loose sleeve to the shoulder.

MANUEL. We're this. We're flesh. All that stands between your reason and oblivion, the animal part which is the resolution of all powers in the resistance of death.

ANDRONIKUS. And yet, if I were to plunge a knife into you—or you into me—your self-consciousness or mine, however immense, would expire in a moment.

MANUEL. But that is what is most difficult to accept. I suppose I study the physician's art in the hope of learning the great secret which lets self-consciousness live or die on such fragile terms.

ANDRONIKUS. What great secret? A man dies as a fine chariot is smashed, in collision, regardless of intellect or beauty. What is there to know, but that the body, which is the vessel of the mind, can take incredible punishment save when it is struck at the carotid, the heart, or the liver, dismembered or crushed. Your animal part is but a tool, and like the chisel of Phidias is the agency which reveals immortality without itself being immortal. A tool. An animal does what it must; a man does what he intends.

MANUEL. Christ sanctified the body. For all time.

ANDRONIKUS. Last year I had a tutor I particularly disliked. Whenever he asked me a question and I suggested an alternative—not incorrect, only substitutable—to his prepared answer, he would argue me blue in the face to prove me wrong, and when I would not relent, he would say to me, "You'll learn, Your Highness, you'll learn." He was not so much intellectually conceited as too unimaginative to consent to other possible answers. He never seemed to realize an argument would circle on itself, infinitely, if you attempted to prove one possibility was more likely than the other. Let us be fair; I will not make you acolyte to my ideas if you will not make me acolyte to yours.

XII

Incipit: Nicetas Acominatus: "I think I led him a merry chase," Andronikus once said of his first encounters with Manuel. "I was im-

possibly arrogant, even unctuous, and had he been less good-willed—
not docile, but innately kind—he would have resented me. Instead he
was challenged.

"I suppose what most offended him was my lack of inquisitiveness,
of rapture, as regards Constantinople. He could not help but feel for it
a great love, even a passion, I shall never remotely experience. To me,
it is an agent of rejection filled with the many, who, excepting the good
Byrennius, and my grandfather, Michael, did nothing to help us. In
any event, Manuel's position in the Imperial brood was something like
a Grand Master of Courtiers. Responsibility had already been given to,
if not wasted upon, his older brothers, and not much was left for him
but pride of place and whatever diversions he preferred. He was quick
to temper, I think, because he was, more often than not, inactive, or
active only to some point he set for himself, which is to say, exaggerated
effort to little purpose. His taste in all things, and his manners, when
not ruined by his temper, were so polished as to be almost feminine in
refinement. He was dazzled by anything out of the ordinary, including
myself, because his sense of boredom was extremely acute."

And Manuel once said, "He was, in truth, always a little apart. A
child, alien in an alien land, he, not Michael, was the most irrevocable
effect of his father's exile—not allowed to be Greek as he was born and
certainly not Turk in whose lands he was raised. He could set my father's
hair on end with some of his opinions. Once John Augustus commented
in his presence something to the extent, 'So long as there are many nations, there shall be war,' at which my cousin, then sixteen, said, 'Uncle,
I think it not the confusion of diversity which causes war but the insistence on similarity.' Can it be any wonder all of us felt as though we
were being observed, every standard of our culture noted and smiled
upon. What others call his insolence, I call—more accurately, if you will
permit me—his separateness. The intensity of his existence is incapable
of annihilation. It is not rooted, as ours, in pride, but the quest for a
unity, a consummation, the repose in oneness he has otherwise never
known. He who abhors the final laws of dogma searches for them more
than he realizes. Once he said to me, 'I don't fear death. I love life. Death
means nothing to me save it removes from me those I love, who give
meaning to my love for life.'"

Between these two men, whose activities, arguably, decided the fate
of the East Roman Empire, there is such a confusion of ideals and be-

trayal, surreptitious affection and overt hatred, their entire lives blur, so that perhaps only a history even more distant than mine from the events shall distinguishably separate the threads of motive. There is a tendency—I am not alone—to dwell on those early years, as if the key is there to be discovered which will open the door on all that followed. But this is not history. It is myth. We no longer seek men, but archetypes, much as these antagonists thought of one another if not themselves, even if, as Andronikus once said, "The most fatal mistake a man makes is to think of his enemy, if he must think a man his enemy, in terms of cliché." Perhaps, indeed, it was not the confusion of diversity but the insistence on similarity which configured the duel between these two men. For archetypes are singular and do not admit the subtlety of synthesis.

On 20 August, Manuel and Andronikus traveled with a small band of guards, King Fulk, and several of his courtiers, 235 miles from Antioch to Little Galilee, where, in a small house near the sky-blue sea, a Jewish family had for a millennium passed down a robe said to be that of Mary, Mother of Christ. For eleven hundred years, in every generation, a virgin daughter had been born to receive it. Now there was none but an old spinster—virgin unto death and the end of her line—who wished the garment to be translated to some Christian church.

The Emperor could not travel, in safety or dignity, without his army, and the army could not enter the Jerusalemite Kingdom without dire political implication, much less to forage the first good harvest after five years of drought. When the King had explained these factors to John, the Basileus at once ended for himself the hope—so long cherished—of a pilgrimage to Jerusalem. It was Fulk's immeasurable generosity and friendship for the Emperor that he was allowing the relic to be conveyed to Constantinople, as a gift of recompense.

And so, at Nazareth, on the twenty-third, the two young Megadux attended Divine Liturgy at Annunciation Church, then, with their suites and the King's, walked on foot to the house of the Jewess where they received the robe. As Andronikus himself once told me, both Princes were so entranced by the lively spinster, not at all the sanctimonious dame they had expected, it was in their mind to sojourn most of the day, while she, the envy of that holy village, acted—through a translator—as guide to her King and two Imperial Grand Dukes of Byzantium.

"I became less and less stiff," Andronikus recalled, "less aloof, if you like—certainly Manuel thought so—as the day wore on. Of course, his critical eye on my every move helped not a whit. He scarcely seemed to understand I had never before acted as the Emperor's representative in public. At Iconium we had been little better than unusually privileged citizens. Of course my father never had any sense of the social contortions of the court. After a fashion, my brothers and I received as common an upbringing as a merchant's son, whose blood is not sanctified, whose touch is not talismanic, and who does not live his life from ceremony to ceremony. I was stiff as a stick, and in such situations which threaten awkwardness, I tend to be short-tempered. I remember at some point, King Fulk took my shoulder as we were leaning closer to inspect an apostolic relic, and I snapped, 'Don't do that,' and it was reported to the Emperor by one of Manuel's suite, and on my return I received a short but significant lecture on self-control, for which, publicly, at least, my cousin never lacked—never a meaningless or a less than graceful gesture. The unexpected inspired him, or seemed to. I remember vividly there were tears in the eyes of the Jewess as she presented the Virgin's robe to Manuel and he said, 'No tears, madam. You mustn't. It passes from family to family beneath the same roof, for our God and your God are the same.' His reputation for gallantry is well deserved, but it is born on the rumor of these superb little gestures, not, I think, his 'great' political acts."

They returned to Antioch, where John, Greek kindness to Latin kindness, commanded the robe be displayed for adoration for a week in St. Peter's Cathedral before it was embarked, the center of magnificent ceremony, for Constantinople. Just as its rescue had been significant in the inclusion of Andronikus, the pageantry in the midst of St. Symeon's stench marked the first appearance of the Emperor and his brother in eight years. Most observers took it as an indication of full reinstatement.

This is not entirely true. One even wonders, if the Sebastocrator had not fast been approaching blindness, how much less—or more—the reconciliation would have been mitigated. It is, in fact, doubtful the Emperor —who considered Isaac's exile a dereliction—was of a mind to trust him again so confidently as previous to 1129. Yet several factors combined to throw much of the weight of previous authority upon the Sebastocrator.

The first circumstance was Bryennius' death, at Constantinople, in October. Those men were few in whom the Emperor even provisionally confided, and toward the end, the habit of the Caesar had become stronger than suspicion. Quite besides, his mastery of the bureaucracy, if less incisive than Isaac's, was, in its own way, as adept. (He tended, by far, to be less sensitive to corruption and delay, which he considered the occupational hazards of government.) The second factor, more ambiguous, it is true, but no less crucial, was the Comnenus "birthmark," as Bryennius called it, pride. In the short of it, the bond of two men mutually blessed by the Patriarch in the belly of their Mother Autocratrix, their heads held under the State Imperial Crown before they had lived as many minutes as they had taken deep breaths, asserted itself.

"My uncle," Andronikus once told me, "was pleased by the change in my father: his calm, his circumspection—those qualities Augustus most appreciated in his advisers and which my father, for all his genius, had conspicuously lacked. He moved closer to his younger brother than ever before. He did not realize Isaac Porphyriogenetus' prudence was that of a man who having crossed a frozen pond and suffering the ice to break beneath him, never again trusts the same path. One night, the Emperor said warmly to my father, 'Perhaps it is necessary for those who love one another to fly in opposite directions to learn the strength of the chains which bind them.' My father was appreciative, but I suspect nothing the Emperor ever again said or did could seal the wound of mistrust he had opened in Isaac's soul."

The final factor in assuring Isaac's reinstatement was the elimination of Auxuch, secured, it seems, apparently by the latter's own improvidence.

Little Christmas, January 1138, the Heir to the throne, without his father's consent announced the betrothal of his eldest daughter, the thirteen-year-old Grand Duchess Zoë, to Count George Auxuchos, Auxuch's ward and nephew. All the Constantinopolitan aristocracy was outraged for the usual reasons: privately because one son or the other had not been chosen; publicly because Auxuch seemed to have taken advantage of his proximity to the throne, though it was well known the Crown Prince had effected the match after brazen opportuning and conniving by the Senior Countess George, Auxuch's sister-in-law, and an abomination to him. Yet the Emperor, perhaps rightly, felt his trusted adviser could not have been ignorant of the plans—nor of the

Emperor's more splendid alternatives in mind such as Crown Prince William of Sicily—and should have put a stop to them at once.

The eunuch's power was enormous, and if John should die suddenly —always a possibility with a warlord as monarch—there was the danger he might place Zoë and George on the throne, installing Natalie as Regent and himself President of the Sacred Consistory. (The Emperor was aware it would be of little matter to replace his eldest son, who was no one's favorite and all too busy assuming the prerogatives of an heir to found a real power base.) Andronikus once said in language more crude than I shall repeat, a eunuch is cut twice, once to advance himself and the second time when he can no longer be trusted. If it were guilt by association, and nothing more, or anything less just, from the moment of publications of the bans, Auxuch's power began to wane. Even could the marriage have been stopped, it was the principle, not the fact, which ruined him.

The Sebastocrator could not have been more content, but, in truth, more than his resurgent career and Auxuch's discomfiture turned on that marriage. Kindly as John was to his sons and daughters, he realistically considered his eldest male a rank failure. Until the Auxuchos incident, however, he had never confronted his son or countermanded him. Now the Emperor requested his Heir break the promise of marriage. Alexius, aware he had been duped, both humiliated and stubborn, refused. After a month, the Emperor ceased to protest and the betrothal was allowed to stand. But from that moment of consent, John began to consider the possibility of leaving the throne to his second son, Isaac, or his youngest and favorite, Manuel Porphyriogenetus. It would be an unprecedented step and a dangerous one, as the semi-invalid Sergius— who was out of the question for the succession—he knew to be profoundly canny enough, and cold, to manipulate Alexius against either one of their younger brothers. However these questions occurred to the Emperor, there is little doubt he must have put them aside in the knowledge, at fifty, born of a line of long-lived males, he had many more years to reign and to decide. *Explicit: Nicetas Acominatus.*

In the winter rain, Manuel and Andronikus are admitted to the courtyard of Palace Comnenus, while their horses are taken off to the stables, where, more than sixty years ago, the young Duke Alexius bid his groom run, before himself being taken off to Buceleon dungeon as an enemy of the throne. An old footman stands at the open doors. As the Grand Dukes ascend the stairs, he bows.

FOOTMAN. Good morning, Nobilissimi.

At this use of the antique rank for Grand Duke, Andronikus stares at Manuel, who smiles.

MANUEL. I told you. It's like stepping into the past. But wait until you meet *her*.

They are greeted by a majordomo, who bows to Manuel with a confident familiarity, and to Andronikus with the mildest exaggeration due one who is august but unfamiliar.

MANUEL. Good morning, Count. You see, as I promised; I've brought a new swain for the Augusta.

MAJORDOMO. Your Imperial Highnesses are too kind to attend Her Majesty. And may I say she has missed you, Manuel Porphyriogenetus, most intensely.

As the youths begin the trip to the second-floor apartments, preceded by the majordomo, Manuel whispers to Andronikus.

MANUEL. He's ten years younger than her, and she's more lucid.

ANDRONIKUS. How old is she now?

MANUEL. Eighty-three. Are you nervous?

Andronikus shakes his head as they enter an apartment, and an old woman seated with her back to the visitors hands her embroidery to a serving girl, who sits by her, holding the many-colored threads, notoriously bored. The crone is up from her chair almost as the doors part. Plainly she has been anticipating her guests. She turns. The jowled, wrinkled, high-boned face is still somewhat recognizably that of the Mary of Alania of legendary beauty. She holds out her arms to Manuel, rather a little affectedly.

MARY OF ALANIA. At last.

She embraces him—and it is a real grip of affection—then kisses him lightly on both cheeks. Manuel, noting his cousin's disapproval of such effusiveness, edges away without taking a step and grasps Andronikus' hand, then their aged grandaunt's.

MANUEL. See here who I've brought you, Aunty. You remember Uncle Isaac's boy, Andronikus.

Plainly she does not, but she is too elated by this intrusion into the solitude between herself and her servants to be anything less than gracious. Andronikus, whether consciously or instinctively, senses this, and, at once, an intentionally dazzling smile appears on his face. There is a communication of gestures more rapid than speech and more valid.

Mary, with a tiny, surprised, grateful look of the eyes, lifts her hands, with artificial gaiety, to be kissed. Indulged and accompanied, flattered and protected all her life, she is rather bewildered to find that now she must face old age and death alone, grasping at minutes the way a poor man downs a feast, momentarily satisfied and ultimately melancholy.

Forty years later, Andronikus, in words which Nicetas will record, but not enter into his history, will say: "She really had very little intellect. She only acquired the patina of intelligence from her own authority and the great men she attracted. I could not help but be certain, she who was never before teased must have suffered terribly death's teasing, as the old expect death on every turn. What's worse, the very indulgence of the many more years given her only extended the agony."

MARY OF ALANIA. Oh yes. Yes. Now I *do* remember. Oh yes. Isaac's boy, the one he was so certain was rubbed with a moly by Hermes.

ANDRONIKUS. Did my father actually say that?

MARY OF ALANIA. Oh yes, he did. Do you still wear the icon he gave you?

ANDRONIKUS. Indeed, Lady. It is my stoicheion.

MARY OF ALANIA. It was your grandfather's, you know. It was removed a few days before he died. It seemed to irritate him. I gave it to him. Did you know that?

ANDRONIKUS. No, Lady. But it pleases me.

This is said with a blush, a hesitant drop of the head as the eyes are lifted, a shyness so melting, it would seem, to any but an old woman, less real than what it was in fact: exaggerated imitation by a boy who has observed this affectation work marvelously between some other man and his mistress; one who is becoming so inflamed by the adoration which is being lavished upon his own face and body—the first initiation of conscious sexuality—he has become indiscriminate in his quest for seduction, by charm, by wit, by touch, by glance.

And Mary is caught indeed: it is obvious—perhaps only because Andronikus is momentarily the more scintillant of the two—she sees her son, Constantine Dukas, who in no way resembled either youth, save in youth itself. Forty-four years have passed since his death. By now, he should, himself, have been an old man. But other old men do not remind the mothers of their dead sons, for in dying, the child's age is buried with him and it is rather the concept of the child which haunts the parent.

MARY OF ALANIA. Come, let me serve you both.

MANUEL. No, aunt, we cannot stay long.

She is visibly disappointed, her hand still in midair, gesturing toward some unseen refectory. Andronikus glances furiously at Manuel, who, he seems certain, has dissimulated out of jealousy. What's more he has done so at the expense of a lonely old woman. Only one raised in the seclusion of exile could be so quickly sympathetic to another's isolation.

ANDRONIKUS. Nonsense, Lady, he lies. We have all the time in the world, and I, for one, should be pleased to stay.

Unfortunately, the visit is, willy-nilly, ruined. Mary, who has known the ways of men all her life, recognizes she will spend the balance of their stay as referee between the two youths who will compete before her now, argue between themselves afterward, and make for her what had been anticipated a diversion, a chore. Had it been a battle for her attentions she might have dreamed a little and played the flirtatious arbitress. Instead Manuel resents Andronikus' revelation of his lie and the favor he has found with the old woman. Andronikus resents Manuel's cruelty. There is no war without an audience. That, Mary shall be. And acrimony between the young is the unkindest presentiment before the elderly, too aware of the end of everything, too weary to suffer in any degree the real, if only momentary, conceits of hatred.

XIII

Incipit: Nicetas Acominatus: The Sebastocrator was initially established with the Emperor at Buceleon, though he now considered his real residence—both winter and summer—Hieriea Palace, at Chalcedon. He could still see colors and shapes when he returned to Constantinople, and the massive cream façade of Porphyriogenetus Palace had so much distressed him, it was unthinkable he should return there. Hieriea also presented the advantage of the sound of the sea, its scent, too, each morning before assuming his burdens.

In the late winter of 1138, Conrad Hohenstaufen, nephew of the Emperor Heinrich V, German anti-King and contestor of Emperor

Lothar II, was elected—which is to say, he bought and bullied his way—
to the throne of the Holy Roman Empire, fast on his enemy's natural
death. At once, he dispossessed and placed under ban Lothar's son-in-
law and putative successor, Heinrich the Proud, who died in any event
the following year, leaving his son, the Lion, a heritage of exile, war,
and bitter gall, indeed. Saxony was given to Conrad's kin Albert the
Bear, and Bavaria to his cousin, Leopold, Duke of Austria and father
of Elizabeth Comnena's betrothed (the marriage was arranged that
year by her father, Isaac III).

John was wary of giving support to the Hohenstaufens, having gained
accord with Lothar II against Roger of Sicily through many years' exchange of ambassadors. It was the Sebastocrator who pointed out to his
brother that the German Imperial Italian possessions were in no less
danger as Conrad's than as Lothar's and the mutual assistance pact
ought to stand. He therefore advised immediate recognition. In truth,
it took all Isaac's force of argument to keep the Emperor on a steady
diplomatic path. Circumstances had fearfully changed—or fearfully as
things seem at first—since the year's previous superiority of Byzantium.

When Imperial commissioners arrived at Antioch to assume administra-
trative control, for instance, Raymond—with Joscelin's agents, or in their
thrall—instigated riots of such devastating ferocity, it was deemed unwise for either the administrators or their escorts to enter the city. When
the demonstrations persisted for week after week, the Emperor ordered
his representative back to Constantinople for "consultation."

Then, too, Innocent II, who had earned Conrad's enmity by recognizing Lothar as an ally against Roger of Sicily—and now turned to
Roger against Conrad—sought to drive a wedge not only between Palestine and Byzantium but between the two Emperors. At Rome, 28 March,
a bull was issued ordering all "Celtic" regiments to leave the service of
the "Orthodox Autocrat" under pain of excommunication and interdict.

Technically and specifically, by inclusion of the word *interdictum*,
this warning embraced the vassal states of the Holy Land. On one level,
it was Innocent's answer to John's assumption of Antioch. On another
level, we detect the hand of Raymond in concert with his wife's cousin,
Roger; on a third level, the purely fiscal interests of Genoa and Pisa,
seeking to counter Venetian hegemony; and, finally, on a fourth, France
and her King—or rather, her King's King, Suger of St. Denis—who considered the loss of the Antiochene Principate too intolerable to Frankish

prestige. As though matters were not complex enough, the ubiquitous Zengi of Mosul, recognizing a common fool in Raymond, and, in Joscelin, a man who had acquired a dangerously false sense of his own intelligence by too long manipulating inferiors instead of challenging equals, made tentative promises of alliance against Constantinople. Both Joscelin and Raymond readily accepted his quarter and, of course, the Moslem Prince began, at once, eating his way along the limbs of Latin Syria to rescue the still beating hearts of Edessa and Antioch.

Finally, six days after issuance of Innocent's notorious bull, Bela II, the Emperor's friend, kin, and frequent correspondee, and quite as much Constantinople's protégé, crossed the Danube, marched on and sacked Branchiero, a lovely fortress town of about ten thousand population. It is a general fact of history that empires suffer a curious immobility, more often than not the defender than the aggressor; like elephants, they have reach, but no spring. With Conrad attempting to secure his hold on the Holy Roman throne and John beset by the Pope and Antioch, it is apparent Bela esteemed himself secure enough to nibble without notice at the knee of the Elephant from the East.

The Emperor left Constantinople at once, reconnoitering with the armies of Thrace and marching north. He engaged Bela at Vidin-on-the-Danube, in a battle which has become a classic for military strategists. To wit: While Bela pounded the Imperial center, John gradually deployed the left and right in wider and wider movements until the Hungarian's line of retreat had been cut. Thereupon he moved up reserves in the center and closed the right and left wings. The enemy was surrounded and a massacre might have commenced, save John sent an agent under a flag of truce to the Hungarian Praetorium, offering one last chance of surrender. The most famous letter the Emperor ever wrote contained what must be the most striking passage one warrior has ever addressed another:

> You and I know, if it comes to a massacre we need have no fear for the safety of our bodies, though we may well dread the peril of our immortal souls. Bela, my dear friend—for I shall continue to call you that till you tell me not to—true greatness in a man is the assurance that in any act, if he has not achieved perfection, he cannot be imagined to have strived any more completely. It is not enough to satisfy St. George of the Battles. You must remember, as I, Christ watches us in all things and we have no

right before heaven to satisfy a grudge through the ill use and massacre of innocent soldiery, yours and mine, who follow us, and obey us, as they believe God has ordained it.

The Apostolic King of Hungary capitulated and John was both munificent and subtle in the matter of indemnities to be paid not to Constantinople, but directly to the ruined city for reconstruction. Also Bela's grandchild, the ten-year-old Prince Boris, youngest son of Crown Prince Geza, was to live at Constantinople, betrothed and eventually married to Sergius' daughter, another Grand Duchess Elizabeth, honored or a hostage, depending upon Hungary's conduct.

On the Emperor's return to the capital he received the additional good news that Fulk refused to bow to the Pope's interdict for the most guileless of reasons, and perhaps the most profound, his sense of honor. It was a daring measure for a Latin Catholic king, not so much between himself and Rome, nearly two thousand miles by sea, but between his authority and the gainsay of his own priests, who could undermine him, now, with a clear conscience, surely another truncheon with which his Queen might beat him. *Explicit: Nicetas Acominatus.*

The Sebastocrator Isaac II sits in a chair beside his secretary's desk, forehead in hand, eyes closed, dictating so softly—not to disturb the work of the eunuch's two colleagues—as to be almost inaudible. The doors to the terrace behind him are thrown open against the heat. The room is illumined only from that light without. Beyond the terrace balustrade, deeper into the distance, are the cross-topped masts of Buceleon Harbor, shimmering in the noon heat. A gentle knock sounds on the inner doors.

ISAAC. Enter.

A court attendant opens one of the doors, backing against it, as Andronikus passes over the threshold. The young Grand Duke crosses the room.

ANDRONIKUS. It is I, Papa.

The blind man sits alert in the direction of the voice, like all sightless his head strained a little forward, his lids half lowered over useless eyes. Andronikus comes up to his father and kisses him on the forehead and the hand. The Sebastocrator clears his throat.

ISAAC. I've a few things to say to you. I shall not take much of your time. You've given Manuel the Arabian intended for Philip. Is that true?

ANDRONIKUS. Why, yes, of course.

ISAAC. Well, then, it's done. But now your comptroller tells me you've asked for an additional note to purchase another. I thought it a courtesy to inform you personally that you shall not have it.

ANDRONIKUS. Very well, Papa.

ISAAC. Let me explain. Your uncle intends to keep this court as free of cliques and power blocks and hysterical agents running between one or the other and profiting in the fall of both. In that, I concur. Factions round any one of the Porphyriogeneti are intolerable and will be crushed commensurate with the seriousness of their intent.

ANDRONIKUS. Alexius' train is longer than Uncle John's.

ISAAC. The men who surround your cousin are either so absurd as to be irrelevant or so errant as to be anyway, constantly under surveillance or else superficially appointed by His Majesty or myself.

ANDRONIKUS. There's no need to explain. I understand. I presented Manuel with the steed because he wanted it and I knew he would treasure it.

ISAAC. That is, most likely, true.

ANDRONIKUS. Then why on earth do you admonish me?

ISAAC. Because sentiment, however exquisite, plays no part in an impeccable reputation. Andronikus, you know the Emperor is heartsick about the succession. Your elder cousin's attitude is deplorable, and until some way is found to counteract the chaos he promises, we must seek to prevent the rise of factions on just such future stirrings, whether for or against him, whether formed round a candidate without our family, in which case they are entirely inimical to us, or around the Porphyriogeneti, myself, Philip, or, for that matter, you. You are to keep in mind, realistically speaking, you stand in succession to the throne after Alexius, Isaac, Manuel, and Philip. For the foreseeable future you will remain in that position, since it is unlikely Alexius will have an heir and Sergius' boys cannot inherit that from which their father is excluded. I bid you remember this. Henceforward, however sincere, give no favors. Accept none.

Incipit: Nicetas Acominatus: Alexander, Andronikus' eldest son, once said to me: "It is odd how my father has acquired a reputation for inflexibility, even a lack of imagination, because his convictions have not changed in forty years. Even though those opinions are entirely out of the ordinary, perhaps heretical, the similarity, indeed, between what he said as a youth and says now as an elder are taken as a sign of his superficiality, rather than his depth. Why is it men suppose the wisdom of old age, if wisdom it is, must be a complete rejection of the ideas and ideals of one's youth? If he is the genius men thought him as a young man, why, then, must he conform to some definitive abstraction of old men in his old age? That is not distinction, but sycophancy. Throughout his life, even at the abysm, the worst waste of his potential, there was always the feeling, 'This man is beyond the implications of his actions.' In a letter my father once wrote to me from Persia he said, 'Between the essence and the consummation is carnality: the eternal estrangement between the idea, which is impermeable from matter, and man, who must die, if he does not yield.'"

His father also said, "The difference between youth and old age is that in youth we have neither the courage nor the patience to accept tragic coincidence without a cry, and in old age, we have no other choice."

At the age of seventeen, in 1139, Andronikus was neither the dealer nor the victim of unfortunate circumstance, but the chief personal beneficiary of his father's reinstatement. His brother, the Grand Duke Philip, who like most first sons of trenchant men was antipodally mild, almost melting, has written:

> What was more natural as my father's authority assumed its former vigor but that we should be surrounded by the same opportunists and petitioners who pestered my cousins?
>
> Once, I remember, as Andronikus and I were riding about the countryside near our villa at Selymbria, an old woman with the harshest face I have ever seen stepped in the way of our horses and offered up a small rolled document, one of those which all illiterate villagers procure from their barely literate priests. She jerked the scroll in Andronikus' face with a curious, very grim sort of resentment, as though daring this son of the mighty *not* to give her what she asked. My brother was so startled, and the woman's demeanor so foul, he did precisely what I would have done. He knocked the petition to the ground and rode on apace. Now, Andronikus has my father's same brooding sense and I knew better than to trouble it. I caught up with him and glanced at his profile. His cheeks were rippling with fury. We rode on a few feet more, and I said, finally, "Imagine."

With that, he looked up, squinted ahead bethinking himself, turned and spurred his horse, and rode back to the old crone. She was already on her own way in the opposite direction and would not speak to him. He followed on his horse. I still vividly recall the hand of that black-robed figure making a gesture of dismissal and disgust toward the Sebastocrator's son. At length, Andronikus dismounted and took hold of the woman. She tried to break free and even bit his hand. Still he would not let her go, and then she seemed to relent. They spoke shortly and she handed my brother the retrieved petition, then fell on her knees and kissed his hand. When she looked up he made the Sign of the Cross over her. Then he rejoined me. (She watched us, I noted, as we continued down the road.)

I asked, "Why did you do that? You know what Papa will say."

"I have an idea. I don't care. What are we here for then? Her request was just what you might have imagined. Two sons died in the last Hungarian campaign, her farm is worked by her daughters, and none too well, and she wants a tax abeyance, which the mayor has refused. I shall see him this afternoon."

"He'll tell Papa."

"We may just as well face this now as later." He lifted the petition. "These are the same taxes which pay for your fine clothes and mine. We're in *her* thrall."

"That's absurd." He stared at me with the same fearfully contemptuous expression of which only our father is equally capable. "Oh, don't be such a stupid bastard." He softened. "I ask you to think logically. Papa's incorruptibility is his own. But what in the name of heaven will he make of us by rendering us so powerless as to secure the justice in so small an iniquity even as this? It's concubinage, and I shall be no man's catamite. What would that woman have thought of me had I gone on? I won't be thought any the less by any man high or low than what I think to make myself. I won't have sins *imposed* upon me."

Indeed, my brother did not go to the mayor of Selymbria that afternoon, but, as I was informed, rode direct to Constantinople where he asked an interview with our uncle, with whom he left the petition. Afterward, as one would expect, there took place a tremendous row with my father, and as always, in the ambivalence of their arguments, Andronikus was given his way. He never to my knowledge abused this privilege. Certainly a merchant or a courtier, seeking this concession or that sinecure, would have received for his pains my brother's marvelous smile, which, without any commensurate merriness in the eyes, was as chilling and impassive as a death's head.

From these early acts of minor justice arose the first legends of the People's Prince. As bees have their way of informing one another of a motherlode of nectar, so do peasants from city to city, across the countryside, the length and breadth of an empire. Eventually the young Grand Duke was besieged wherever he ventured. In time, something akin to the hysteria which followed his canonized aunt followed him. His looks, his dash, and the access to power he allowed through his own agency were everywhere discussed. The aristocracy thought him an ambitious little cynic prompted by his father; the people thought him a saint. He often said the people could not have been as overwhelmed by him as he was by the advantages taken against them, when they did not otherwise suffer indifference. His first fame was ingenuous in its origins. Politically, however, its implications were intolerable. If any Comnenus should have been among his citizens, it was the Heir, not his youngest cousin. This subtle damning was noted by Alexius' clique.

"You may call it, I suppose, my baptism in the sanctimony which exists at the summit of power. At the time I was only resentful, miserable, appalled. These measly little acts of grace and favor were disapproved of by precisely the people who should have attended to them. Of Alexius and his creatures, I should say it was jealousy and no more. But the more exalted bureaucrats and courtiers resented my coming to them with these little matters either because it was beneath their dignity or reminded them of their own remiss or, for all I know, reminded some of them of origins they wished to forget. How I hated them then. Now, while I cannot excuse them, at least I see I suffered my own presumptuousness in that contempt. How smug of me from the essential security which is that as a Prince of the Blood to fret another man's lack of charity.

"But what bewildered me most then, at the end of this ridiculous incident, was the conduct of my father and my uncle. Isaac alternately ranted and smiled and told me I was not to any longer pester the Imperial ministers or members of the Sacred Consistory or Praetorium. If I did they were instructed to disregard whatever I demanded or petitioned. My uncle, to his credit, was at once more frank and uneasy. He said it was repellent for him to stop my good works, but there was simply no denying the poor shadow this cast on certain parties—Alexius, of course —who were, anyway, incorrigible. Then, of course, he disappointed me by saying there *were* lower echelons specifically appointed to deal with the very problems I otherwise presented to those with matters of far greater import to attend. I would have asked him, 'And what would those matters be?' yet, to be sure, I could not. It seemed to me then I was confronted by a horde of autocrats—great and little, real or *soi-disant*—seeking to protect themselves from the lowest and most helpless they should have been quickest to serve. Only Manuel came to my defense, but rather from love than conviction, which irritated me the more. Together we went off to Oeneum to hunt."

He never quite lived down that sojourn on the Black Sea. Both his game and his manner must have been uncommon. The reputation he engendered during this one stay persisted nearly forty years so that, when returned from exile and at once banished from Constantinople as Governor of Oeneum, his coming was dreaded and his clemency a surprise.

His cousin, Nicephorus Paleologus, has written:

> Here was this fellow, who only a few weeks before had been the champion of the downtrodden—or so it seemed—now going after the most helpless of all creatures. It was not that he tortured his prey, or was inept so as to cause needless suffering—indeed, he dispatched his game with deft mercy—but that he was excessive, killing what he could not possibly eat and hunting down beasts who ran from him. The greater the display of carcasses at the end of the day, the more appalled we, his companions, seemed, the more satisfied he seemed to be. I decided then and there his convictions were so deep as to approach insanity, or else he was the very sort of aristocrat he affected to despise, one of those enervated by indulgence and lack of struggle, who assumed roles, quite convinced of each—the saint, the butcher—as no more than a diversion. Or else he was merely Greek, a man, inexplicable, only more so. For it must be said, while we, clement young hunters, drank ourselves insensible, were rude to servants, merciless to whores, full of practical jokes against guards or any traveler unlucky enough to find himself on the road past the Imperial villa, Andronikus either slept, indifferent to us, or banished himself to walk the grounds beneath the stars, or, if sitting among us, then as one entranced. And I do mean entranced: that inward radiance which seems to muse on some chance insight of great irony. He has not, to my knowledge, changed in any way and I don't know which I find the more implausible: that he is now fifty-five and so juvenile or at eighteen he seemed so old.

Since it is Andronikus whereof we speak, it is not surprising Manuel's description of the sojourn differs, but only to compliment:

> For the first time I saw my cousin disappointed or, as he would put it, "imposed upon." He was miserable quite the whole length of our stay and I was hurt for him and could do nothing. Andronikus then, as now, withdraws—that is the only way I can describe it—when he is thwarted. He intensifies the isolation which is grief, by closing off others, and with that, their consolation. In truth, he is the only man in my ken who is offended by any attempt to assuage him. It is as though you are presumptuous in even pretending to surmise the depth of his unhappiness, which you cannot possibly know, and any sympathy is insufficient unless it is a direct remedy to the problem at hand. But it goes deeper still: whether or not it is intentional, he seems to impress you as resenting your lightheartedness—or your contentment—though it be on tiptoe, if he is miserable. Perhaps it is only *his* glowering, and your imagination, but self-consciousness, a sense of awkwardness before him, is inescapable. Indeed, these moods are so memorable that ever after, and whenever his frame of mind—the better one—returns to normal, you seek to entertain it, preserve it, indulge it. This I think is the secret of how he gathers people to himself. No effort is involved because men will always pursue the exclusive sooner than the accessible.
>
> A more serious consequence of our stay at Oeneum was, however, the infamous unpopularity he served himself among the local nobles. His arrogance toward them was really astonishing. I suspect its origins to be prejudicial: the local gentry were the same as those at Selymbria who had complained to my father of his nephew's "rabble-rousing." I suppose as he sensed many men fancied his charm, his only retaliation was to deny it. This attitude has not changed. I find it singular a man with such insight and sympathy for the mitigated lives of the poor and helpless should deny the same thoughtfulness (in both senses) to his peers. It seems to me to make nonsense of his compassion.

XIV

The year 1140, which saw Zengi, true to the implications of his alliance with Antioch and Edessa, swallow the provinces between Mosul and Palestine, was also witness to a series of Imperial nuptials and betrothals of no little consequence to the future.

At Iconium, the Grand Duke Michael married Princess Rabia. By continuous post, the Emperor John bid Duke Peter Exazenus, returning from another unsuccessful attempt to install himself as Imperial commissioner at Antioch, detour to Iconium and invite the Grand Duke and his royal Seljuk bride to reside at Constantinople. Almost eagerly, Isaac Porphyriogenetus concurred. It is probable he had forgiven his son renunciation of Orthodoxy on his own reappointment, and, anyway, his gainsay of the marriage had more likely been political rather than religious. Unhappily, in one of those eventualities which may visit any family, Michael had taken more seriously his estrangement. He no longer had any desire but for the most superficial of reconciliations. He was too generous to refuse generosity, and he promised to come to Constantinople in the summer—and so he did—but resettlement was out of the question.

During the visit of the Grand Duke Emir, the eldest brother, Philip, was married to Martha Sklerus at Holy Apostles Cathedral (Holy Wisdom, at the time, was undergoing one of its infrequent refurbishings). Of this occasion, Andronikus said, "I spent the greater part of the ceremony watching Michael. He was the most sentimental of us three. That is, he possessed my parents' sense of poetry deprived of curiosity and discipline. He thought in cliché. I should find it hard to believe he was not a little harrowed by this first experience within a church in something approaching a half-dozen years, and then, as an alien. Later I asked him what he was thinking, but he only smiled—a little sadly—and shrugged."

By far the most important marriage—or rather projected marriage in the form of formal betrothal—was that designated by the Emperor for his youngest son. This is how it came about.

John Augustus sent ambassadors to Augsburg as signatories for the Alliance of the Two Empires, which had been reconfigured to each Emperor's satisfaction. The ambassadors had received specific instructions to ask for the hand of Conrad's young sister-in-law, Bertha, Countess of Sulzbach, in behalf of Manuel Porphyriogenetus. (Conrad himself was childless.) The Holy Roman Emperor assented, in principle, to the marriage, so that negotiations for the betrothal could begin and the alliance would not be impeded at the last moment. Otherwise he was far more reluctant than one might have been led to expect.

As it was the Constantinopolitan Emperor who asked for a marriageable relation, the German Emperor could not but give the best, the richest heiress in the Holy Roman Empire. Yet Conrad felt he was not much better than wasting Bertha on the Autocrat's politically insignificant fourth son. Hence, for two years after signatures were put to the betrothal, the German Emperor tergiversated, setting up ridiculous demands, and, on reconsideration during the time consumed by exchanges of offers and counter offers between the Imperial courts, relenting and returning to the original points of the great contract. John Augustus was incensed, but the time would come when, precisely as possible, the roles of Constantinople and Augsburg would be reversed.

As for Manuel, he was at first indifferent, and then, on first reports of his bride-to-be, even a little apprehensive. "How is it," he asked his brother, Isaac III, "I who am the least member of the family must suffer the most political and loveless of marriages?" Of all the disappointments which seemed to befall him as the youngest son, this was the most abject.

From the beginning, Manuel was a prince of blazing ardor and limpid charm, the very sort most inspired by—and most needful of—a glamorous woman who assumes the place (and gives point to his actions) which should have been taken by articulated ideals. For it must be said, withal his study of medicine and astrology, Manuel was of average, if not lethargic intellect. According to Andronikus, "He was one of those who have no patience with learning for its own sake. He believed in great secrets rather than the progress of thought. In other words he believed he might come upon a totality which would open to him all existence—a great ecstasy—as a poor man comes upon an object of great wealth lying beside the road. Well, ecstasy is for the naïve, who cannot perceive the tenuousness of all things, including the ephemerality of their enchantment, and Manuel was too much of a child to recognize the sum of all men's thoughts is a portion of the warp and woof of those questions, which, each day to the most distant generation, all men will recognize and ask again."

The Porphyriogenetus' betrothed was scarcely the woman for such a prince. You can see her portrait today at Nea Church, where canonization rites elevated her—as her husband's mother, father, and maternal grandfather—to sainthood. She seemed more like an icon in life than the icon itself, which has softened her features, humanized them with a touch of sadness—or is it bewilderment?

This woman, who awaited her matrimony two years at Sulzbach and three at Constantinople, remains perhaps the most misunderstood of the Comnenae Imperatrix.

Coldly beautiful, aloof only because she was too proud to suffer the deadly laughter of overly civilized Constantinopolitan aristocrats, suspicious, believing that any situation which revealed her as awkward was not the result of her own deficiencies but the successful strategy of spiteful enemies, suffering the delay of a marriage by an unexpectedly elevated husband whom she loved passionately from first sight, yet who, himself, only respected her and treated her with the indifference of splendid manners he allowed the least of his subjects, unable to give that husband the heir for which he was bound to her (and thus to bind him by gratitude, if nothing else), it is little wonder this woman so soon folded into hypochondria, mysticism, and charitable enterprises which surely killed her sooner than her time (and occasionally that phrase does hold a certain relevance). How improbably, and yet how inevitably, she was complicated by Constantinople.

Her pride was born of the county in which she was raised and her sister's marriage to the Holy Roman Emperor, yet how little Sulzbach meant at New Rome, some of whose families could trace their descent in the Patrician order to the days of Septimius Severus. She possessed that curious Teutonic frigidity toward all "outsiders" who were any but her family, in a society which thrived on social intercourse. She was prurient, and suffered excruciating scandal amongst a people who were at once the most devout and depraved in the world, adulterous in the morning and attending Divine Liturgy, with the fervor of ascetics, at noon. She was demure, like most German women, only before those who wielded a power greater than her own or her husband's. To the rest she was imperious long before such manner was authorized by the crown set upon her head. Finally she was without a sense of humor, hence a mark for flatterers and a poor foil in a land of wits.

Yet all this is to deny her most eminent qualities, those which made her at once admirable and a victim. She possessed not Irene of Hungary's tragic sense of philanthropy. She was Martha with her good deeds. She simply believed no man should suffer what it is in another man's power—be he a stranger—to cure: poverty, hunger, homelessness. Acutely conscious of her own dignity, she was sensitive to the dignity of those, the poor and ill, who had not money or blood with which to allay the world's contempt. She was also remarkably clear-eyed in the belief a man, whatever his condition, has the right to the practice of the faith in which he was born and, to that effect—the first act to bring her worldwide fame—she established at Constantinople the first orphanage for Moslem children, who had otherwise been baptized before entry into a religious home. Then, too, if she bored her husband, she was a rallying point for the rest of the numerous Imperial brothers and sisters, aunts and uncles, nieces, nephews, cousins, to whom she opened herself with a warmth which would have amazed those residing in Constantinople's palaces. The nobility would never understand her essentially German dislike of frivolity, and she as a German would consider any woman's activity beyond the hearth frivolous in nature. Andronikus once said of her: "You begin to understand the ancient Teutonic practice of blood feud. Family was the only reality for her. Only those bound by blood or God could truly be themselves amongst themselves. The world was an intrusion, demanding artifice or arbitration. Bertha was sensible, always clement, and she interceded for us all, endlessly. I never knew a harsh word—to or concerning anyone—from her lips." Finally, she bore with sublime resignation the worst humiliation it is possible for a regent's consort to suffer—the lack of a male heir—and suffered it in a manner so public, "her right to suicide," as Andronikus' wife once said, "was unquestionable."

The reader may be wondering, while we speak of marriages, of the betrothal of Andronikus to Princess Anastasia of Georgia. Perhaps it is best here to bring events up to date.

The evening Isaac exiled himself, the Princess, the same age as Andronikus, was, but for her little retinue of Georgians and Greeks, left mistress of the vast Porphyriogenetus Palace. At once, the delicacy of her position was subject to considered parley at the Foreign Ministry and within the walls of Buceleon. To return her to Georgia was unthinkable. (Indeed, it is remarkable she was not then betrothed to Manuel, for she already gave promise of becoming that perfect, inspiring creature he was forced to find beyond his marriage.) Instead the Emperor personally wrote to King George assuring him he wished for the Princess "some magnificent new betrothal in lieu of that which she has lost."

> I cannot adequately express how well we love her. Though but a child, she shines for Tsargrad like an evening star. We cannot part with this treasure and we shall not. I urge you to give consent she remain at Con-

stantinople. It is my promise her upbringing will be no less than a queen's. Indeed, I have this day commissioned my late and sainted wife's former Mistress of Robes, the Protovestaria Emerita Helen, Duchess Cantostephana, to continue her upbringing and education and withal at her disposal is all the resource and beauty of Porphyriogenetus Palace, with which the young Princess is much familiar and much loves.

In truth, of course, John scarcely knew the little Princess and rather than glowing like an evening star over the city, she had never been seen in the streets of Constantinople, and only distantly when her intended Imperial relations of the same age were present in one of the great cathedrals during a Holy Day. More exactly, the Emperor was cognizant George would never allow his daughter the insult of return to Tiflis without seeking compensation in the form of expensive emolument or even outright revenge, by ceasing to be the bastion of the Empire's northeast borders.

Then, too, time counts quickly in a child's upbringing. After so short a stay, Anastasia's Greek was now more accomplished than her native tongue, and, pursuant to that, her matriculation, her manners, and her tastes were on their way to becoming pronouncedly Greek. It would have been an insufferable cruelty to uproot a child for the third time before her tenth year. Surprisingly, it was the Crown Princess Natalie who thus admonished her father-in-law, and John, perceiving the truth, was probably only too pleased to add some honest personal feeling to what was otherwise a deal of cold politics served over the heart of a child—royal or not.

When Isaac returned from exile there was hardly a question the betrothal was to be revalidated. Yet the Princess did not return to the care of her mother-in-law-to-be, but continued to live at Porphyriogenetus with her "guardian," the Duchess Cantostephana. Indeed, she led a life of almost incomparable freedom for one of her age and station. Like the most headstrong of heiresses who are also orphans, she had taken the high road to do as she pleased, whenever she pleased, and whatever she pleased, short of scandal. The Duchess had no control over her charge and was alternately bewitched and intimidated by her.

Between 1137 when Andronikus arrived at Constantinople and 1144 when he was married to Anastasia in exaggerated splendor at Holy Wisdom (Manuel's first annunciation of return to the ancient ways—insofar as an extravagant, well-populated court—which he could afford since his father's economies had left the state staggering under the burden of its own replenished wealth), the Grand Duke and the Princess saw one another on but nine occasions, five times in the year before their nuptials. "She was agreeable to me," Andronikus reported tersely. Manuel, however, writes with the lovingly envious detail of one distracted as he can be by his own unhappy prospect. (He begins with an extraordinary portrait of Andronikus' mother.)

When my aunt Joanna returned with her family to Constantinople, she stepped rather lightly at first, uncertain as to her personal authority. I believe she had sooner died or retired to her wonderful gardens at Selymbria than exist where she was not the cynosure of attention. It was not enough for my aunt to be the most powerful woman at court. Far more important that she reign over the city's matrons and intellectual life, that she set the tone and standard of society. It must have then been unsettling to Joanna to realize she was too old to be acceptable to trend-setting youth and too young to preside over the great social dragons, maliciously of a mind to revenge themselves against her own scandalous early years. I suppose for a poetess of her real stature, the very idea of decay was repugnant in the extreme—the antithesis of the nascent, creative idea.

And so my aunt was only too happy to herself dismiss the "social crows" and recherché young and resolve to initiate her own set of "fashionables." The keys to this independence were her sons and myself. She bid us bring our friends to Palace Paleologus, where she stayed when in the city. There she indeed presided over banquets and games and symposiums and flirted with prompt regularity. Andronikus was in gross collusion with her and I cannot imagine a son extending so uncritically a hand to his mother. It seemed to amuse him to indulge her and he more often than not escaped this or that function at hand, having "led the lambs to the slaughter," as Judas goat or procurer, I shall never know.

I must say, I have never suffered my aunt very well. The handsome Paleologus features translate poorly in a woman—at least to my taste. I thought Joanna mannish and domineering. Of course, she had such transcendent faith in her own charm, it was precisely the single-mindedness of the faith and not the charm itself which overwhelmed you.

Invariably, as Andronikus withdrew, so did I. His mother is perhaps the least likely model of the sort of woman who would please him, or so I would have thought. But once he said to me, "She is the perfect woman for my father, and because she is so, she is most nearly the most unlikely. They are both passionate, intelligent individuals. Their singular misfortune is that they have so much in common they take one another for granted and fail in the subtlety which recognizes the differences comprising their individual natures, the differences which take easy offense."

Of Anastasia, she was as independent as her betrothed. This was to the good, for Andronikus was one, like his father, who preferred the self-contained in a woman, only more consciously so. And what could be more natural for my cousin whose chiefest cry is not to be imposed upon? He is too honest and too compassionate to allow a woman to believe he is either possessed by her or cares to possess her forever. A woman who seems to slip from him every so often allows him the test of choice: now and then he might let her slip and slip a little more and slip away entirely. Love for him must remain the voluntary offering it is purported to be or it is but another set of chains which binds him to the earth rather than releases him to the stars. Anastasia was luckier than she knew in the nature which prevented her capitulation, at once, to my cousin. For that, she held him longer. Her unhappiness began when in loving him so passionately, she offered him the tyranny of her own slavery.

Explicit: Nicetas Acominatus.

Bertha-Irene arrives at the Augusteum with her train, escorted by John Augustus' brother-in-law—the ambassador sent to fetch her—the dashing, elderly Count Constantine Angelus. Though she had progressed through decorated streets in which trumpets were sounded, organs struck, aromatics and flower petals tossed beneath the feet of her horse, the Countess seems less reassured than terrified by the enormity of her welcome. The size and sheer numbers of Constantinople, moreover, to a young woman who has never seen a city greater in extent or more densely populated than Regensburg or Prague, can only have the effect of numbing confusion or agoraphobia. At the equestrian statue of Justinian, she is assisted in her dismounting by Count Angelus. Of course, none of the travelers show any sign of fatigue or journey, since—the Count playing their host—they have spent the previous two days in seclusion at Villa Rufiniana. With a smile and sweep of his hand which is reciprocated by the least twitch of the Countess' lips, Angelus indicates the cathedral doors, opened out to her, towering.

ANGELUS. Madame, if you will.

BERTHA-IRENE. Oh, Count, I am so afraid.

ANGELUS. But, ma'am, we are all your friends—and soon your family.

With Angelus on her arm, the Countess of Sulzbach ascends the short row of stairs. In honor of her new country, she has donned its dress—or at least its current fashion: a wide-sleeved, belted gown of magnificent green and gold brocade, whipped with ermine. Over her flowing hair, secured by a headband of pearls, she wears a diaphanous shawl, which trails upon the ground behind her in numerous little folds. At the door she is greeted with inauspicious coldness by the Patriarch Cosmas. He is scarcely moved even by a little compassion when as she kneels to kiss his hand, he perceives her own trembles violently. With his puffed-out chest and his head thrown back, the Patriarch looks the bigot he is. . . .

Angelus assists the Countess to her feet. Four Varangians move forward with a gold-tassled white canopy. The Countess begins the endless trek to the dais at the opposite end of the cathedral, between the craning lines of the military and metropolitan aristocracies, arrived for this rare gathering of the court and a glimpse of the Western Emperor's relation. Between the congregation and the gathered Imperial family stands quite alone a breathtakingly beautiful little girl, garbed in white silk, which is accented with little ruby rosettes. Her abundant raven hair is parted at the center and topped by a skullcap in the form of a net of pearls. Her eyes are brilliant blue and they are wide, but she holds them wider still in an expression of innocence, which one is almost tempted to say is itself the denial of innocence. She is, perhaps, six years old, and her sense of self is not that of a child momentarily the center of attention, but inward, serene. With a perfect curtsy, she offers the Countess a golden taper, round whose base are white flowers. Insolently still in the child's hand, the flame all but flickers out in Bertha-Irene's. The Emperor notes this with a sympathetic wince of his eyes. The little girl notes it with the fascination of one who has just made a wager with herself as to when the candle will topple and smash—what a jolly mess— upon the floor. Andronikus, watching the girl rather than the young Countess, suppresses a smile. Before the dais, Angelus speaks, holding up Bertha-Irene's free hand in presentation.

ANGELUS. Your Imperial Majesty, I have the express honor to present to you, Her Grace, Bertha, Countess of Sulzbach, who has, this day, consented to embrace Orthodoxy and enter into betrothal with His Imperial Highness, Manuel Porphyriogenetus.

Quickly, Bertha-Irene scans the faces of the many men and women who surround the Emperor. Rather cruelly, Manuel remains impassive, hence, anonymous. Alexius considers her with affectedly appraising, squinted eyes. He is a man who confuses the lure of his position with personal charm in his success with women. The Countess' eyes, reflecting the light of the candle, pause on the Heir's. She is impassive, and is suddenly surprised when Manuel, slim, tall, handsome, wearing a white robe with a flamboyantly thick, diagonal purple band bordered with pearls, steps from the assemblage and descends the dais.

In the Western fashion—to a few murmurs—he raises the hand which Angelus has let go and kisses it.

MANUEL. Madame, I greet you with great joy.

Bertha-Irene curtsies, graceful, grateful, suddenly calm and quite lovely.

BERTHA-IRENE. Your Imperial Highness.

With exceeding thoughtfulness, Manuel removes the wavering taper from Bertha's hand and gives it to an attendant, before they ascend the stairs to kneel before the Emperor and receive his blessing.

Manuel and Andronikus stand to either side of Irene in the crowded Imperial vestry of Holy Wisdom. The clusters of many-colored silks have the aspect of bouquets—or a bazaar. The people stand in small groups, speaking softly, above which Bertha's voice—sweetly pitched, but guttural—is unfortunately audible. It is not her natural way of speaking. She is simply new to the Greek language and as yet too uncertain of vocabulary and syntax to modulate what she says. The Countess' eye catches on an extraordinarily attractive young woman with pale hair and dark eyes.

BERTHA-IRENE. And who is that woman?

MANUEL. Anastasia, Princess of Georgia.

BERTHA-IRENE. And where is Georgia?

MANUEL. If you sail the Black Sea, east, from this end to its antipode some six hundred miles, you are in Georgia. Anastasia is the daughter of its King and Andronikus will one day marry her, won't you, Andronikus?

ANDRONIKUS. One day. Surely.

BERTHA-IRENE. And you do not court such a beauty? Ah, where I am from, men would sing songs to her.

MANUEL. Oh, we sing songs to the great beauties of Byzantium as well, and my cousin is all too certain too many have been sung to his betrothed. She knows it and he knows she knows. Pity.

Manuel notices Bertha's alarmed expression—either scandal or perplexity—and says no more. They are approached by the little girl who handed the Countess the taper during the reception. The child's pace has slackened. She is wary. She knows her most notable enemies are those on the brink of maturity.

MANUEL. Countess, I don't think you've been formally presented. This is my niece, Her Imperial Majesty, the Grand Duchess Theodora. My brother Isaac's little girl.

BERTHA-IRENE. And you are the only one of your grandfather's grandchildren here today. No doubt because you are the prettiest.

MANUEL. Or the best politician.

ANDRONIKUS. Or the worst bully.

THEODORA. You're unspeakable!

She lands Andronikus a kick beneath his knee which produces an "oomph" from its victim. The Grand Duchess Francesca arrives on the run.

FRANCESCA. Are you hurt, Andronikus?

THEODORA. He's not hurt, the brute. He's rude.

FRANCESCA. Find your governess and return to Daphne at once. Countess, please forgive us.

BERTHA-IRENE. It is no matter, Princess, believe me.

ANDRONIKUS. Don't send her away, Francesca. I baited her.

FRANCESCA. It was scarcely the response of a well-born young lady.

ANDRONIKUS. It was *precisely* the response of a well-born lady, under the circumstances.

With a perfectly serious face, Andronikus bends to the little Grand Duchess, lifts her limp hand, and to her open-mouthed astonishment, a perfect little mouth, sets his lips to her fingers.

ANDRONIKUS. Will you forgive me, Theodora?

The child blushes red as a rose and runs from the room. Her mother quite obviously approves Andronikus' gallantry, unable to see the wit in its exaggeration. She draws herself with a single breath into the role of the next Sebastocratrix.

FRANCESCA. And tell me, Countess, what do you think of Constantinople? I suppose you are as amazed as I when I arrived. But no matter.
All is lovable here, as I have come to know, and soon you will, too.

With a nod, she is off.

MANUEL. A word of warning. Never attempt to converse with Francesca. She asks all questions and answers them. Nothing lost, nothing
learned.

*The Crown Princess Natalie approaches. In the years since her mar-
riage to Alexius, she has gained the composure—if incapable of wisdom
—of one resigned to an unhappy situation. There is a distracted look in
her eyes—weariness, perhaps, perhaps despair. Her smile seems effortful,
if not unnatural, as though manifested, now and then, because it is the
only proper response, one tool of a splendid set of good manners, so
profoundly instilled, they would function were she unconscious. She is
inoffensive, which is not to be confused with the conscientiously good.
None of her thoughtfulness, therefore, is innate, but rather recognized
by her as a duty. Left to her own devices she would probably expire in
quiet apathy. Instead it is her obligation now, in place of her deceased
mother-in-law, to be gracious and thoughtful as an empress ought, and
so she has imposed these virtues upon herself. She is more polished and
more aware as she moves from group to group—such ubiquity unthinkable at the time of her marriage. As she stands before the Countess,
Bertha-Irene drops a profoundest curtsy. The Crown Princess stands
immobile, garbed in deepest Imperial purple, touched discreetly with
scarlet and gold silk at the edges.*

NATALIE. Countess, I hope you have found nothing of the day or ourselves too trying. Perhaps you would like to rest now.

BERTHA-IRENE. Madame, I have been meaning to ask you: For whom
is it that you are in mourning, and may I offer my condolences?

*Several people turn on these words. There is a ghastly hush. Manuel
steps away an infinitesimal fraction as if to disassociate himself—and
only Andronikus seems amused.*

Incipit: Nicetas Acominatus: Of course, it has become legend: the
extraordinary misapprehension given Bertha-Irene to ask Natalie after
whom she grieved. Her ignorance of the Imperial purple (and, perhaps, Natalie's visage described by Andronikus as the aspect of "one
who has swallowed something very hot") brought about a question

which seemed to nearly everyone present dreadfully ominous. Even the least superstitious catch the shiver of possibility from the words of brides and the dying. Why it is, no one can say—save, perhaps, few greater steps are measured than those into the unknowns of marriage and death.

If the usual ways of men are any indication, it is likely the remark—repeated rather for its gaucherie than its morbid significance—was soon forgotten, and only remembered later as events founded its supposed prescience.

But there were other words that day, far more momentous, as told to me by Andronikus: "Toward late afternoon, when the second reception —that for the court—was coming to an end, my cousin Alexius marked me out and asked me where I was headed. In truth, I had intended to stay that night at Buceleon. I sensed, however, he wanted to talk, and this so surprised me and aroused my interest—he seemed quite without connivance, even urgent—that as I knew his destination was the Villa of the Paleaticum at Chalcedon, I said, without a second thought, 'Hier-iea.' He seemed to smile at this. 'Really? And I believed you such a mother's boy. Well, you never know.' (Like everyone else he quite mis-interpreted my reasons for residing with my mother. I loved my father deeply, but we argued constantly. When we had nothing at issue, our silence was that of a truce, not calm, and made Isaac, sensitive to its nature, uneasy.)

"In any event, there was something in Alexius' manner—a wit, if you will—so unlikely, so disarming, I meant to follow.

"Natalie was not at all surprised to see me as we boarded the yacht. I remember she was attended, simply, by her two daughters, Zoë and Elizabeth (how on earth a sylph like Zoë ever gave birth to that pillow-bellied prince of hers, I'll never know). She dismissed them as soon as Alexius and I arrived. Then, as we sailed out of Buceleon Harbor, across the Bosporus, the setting sun at our back, we talked of many things.

"I could scarcely believe my ears. Granted Alexius was Alexius and now and then offensive as an unbathed saint is offensive—helplessly—but in the long and the short of it, he seemed more artless and at the same time more serious than I had ever known him to be. Even Natalie seemed altered, more authoritative, more original in her remarks. (What a pity history almost never changes its mind about you.) Well. What it seemed to come down to was that Alexius knew his reputation and his father's opinion of him and regretted both—a piteous confession for a man of thirty-six years. Somewhat insolently I said so. Incredibly, he smiled and said, 'Is it? Andronikus, a king's son is treated like an infant until the day the king, his father, dies.' He went on: he had had numerous discussions these past two years with Patriarch Cosmas. My opinion of that mule must have registered in my face, for he said, 'Yes, yes, he makes the flesh of all too many men, including my own, creep. But, he's pious enough. And do you know, cousin, he is the only official in Church or at court who has ever *reproached* me my desertion of responsibility? The eye of his criticism is but that one day I should fulfill them.'

"He paused a moment, looking off starboard, his mother's pale beautiful profile, drawn by a thin silver-vermilion line of low sunlight, going to ruin. (He looked ten years older than his twin, Magdalena.) He said, 'I must do something, do you know? Your father is blind and working himself to death, and my father is too blind not to see it and too proud to confess his own exhaustion.' Natalie interrupted him. 'Andronikus, if the Emperor dies before Alexius can prove himself again. If that happens—' Like many husbands, he finished his wife's thought (I was, by the way, amazed at the equanimity of their union, which, like everything else that day, seemed to me to have been resurrected from catastrophe). 'If that happens, you know the accession will be disputed, and only your father will stand between myself and disenthronement. If he, in fact, is then alive. If not, then I am all too vulnerable, as is the state, to civil war.'

"I asked whom he feared. I thought he would say the obvious—Sergius, who for all his incorrigible arrogance and small purview was insinuating himself with my father and my uncle. Instead, he said a name I had never remotely considered, his brother-in-law, John-Roger. Granted, a few years more upon me, and I would have seen, at once, the logic of his remark. Either someone was thinking brilliantly for Alexius or Alexius was forced by the circumstances of his early waste to come to terms with himself before it was too late. Consider: Magdalena was his twin. Her husband was the nephew of the King of Sicily. What further qualifications were necessary? In one throw the Houses of Comnenus and Hauteville-Guiscard were united, and with them, their mutually vast resources. Against whom? Take your pick. The Seljuks, the Holy Roman Empire, the Palestinian states. There was no end. The very idea was positively megalomanic. And then my cousin told me the generals of the army and almost all the nobles of Asia and the Greek mainland were ready to supplant him. Consider this, too: For the West, no further threat of invasions from Brindisi; in the East nothing less than the eradication of the Turks.

"I said to him, 'What can I possibly do?' and perhaps I meant it both rhetorically and actually. 'For one thing,' he said, 'my agents believe there is a possible plot to assassinate Papa and either make me complicit or blind me in any event. It may be mere talk. I don't know. But my father treats his personal security much too lightly, indifferently, and I think that must come to an end.' 'Alexius, my father disparages my advice the more worthwhile it is. I can do nothing for you.'

"He pulled an ivory, gold, and jeweled knife from its sheath and began cleaning and paring his nails, which I thought disgusting. 'True,' he said. 'But anyone can see you have great influence over Manuel and Manuel has Papa's ear in a fashion I do not.' Natalie spoke, 'The point is, we know so little. Oh, Andronikus, you must help us.' But I hadn't the foggiest notion of what I might be able to do. For the first time in my life I experienced the inner frenzy of a man who must stand still in the face of an oncoming, dreadful event, either too large or too amorphous to be prevented.

"Natalie leaned forward a little and patted my hand. My feelings must have seemed plain enough. 'You're so young. Perhaps we are wrong to ask this of you. But others must know and what little can be done *must* be done.' I said, 'Lady, I fear you've sought out the helpless themselves to protect you.' Alexius seemed distressed in what was, for him, a mild, unlikely way. None of the usual tantrum. 'Truer for us all than you know. Now we shall pay the penalty of fools.' Those were among his last words to me—at least the last I remember. I never saw him again.

"During the night I sent a message to Manuel asking him to come to Hieriea in the morning, to bring none of his suite. It was urgent and secret. I remember waiting for him in the garden, gazing at the statues collected from ancient Greece by Rome and from Old Rome by Constantinople, set on their high pedestals, immaculate, adamantine, so gracious in their sensuality, the billowing marble robes of some, worn so thin by a half-million days, the sun passed through the stone as through a leaf. I was struck, I recall, by the fact all the statues faced the morning sun. I wondered if this were an accident or the dreamy wit of Hieriea's architect, who had planted his tender joke eight centuries before and waited for me to catch it. Manuel then arrived to interrupt these thoughts and we went in to breakfast.

"He listened to what I had to say, and at first he scoffed, which I had dreaded because it was a reflection on my judgment as well as his eldest brother's integrity. But I persisted and convinced him, I think. He asked me, 'What must we do?' I said, 'What Alexius says to do, warn your father.' 'I don't know what to make of it. You say he's changed and I trust you, but you've heard the stories of what's gone on these last days at Paleaticum.' I knew: There were rumors, probably true, of incredible orgies, persisting day after day, with the participation of the Crown Prince. I argued Manuel. 'How much would you trust a man whose metamorphosis is so complete and sudden? That's whim, not change— the supersession of one set of beliefs for another, as one changes the sheets on a bed.' I smiled. 'Besides, who are we to say debauchery impairs a man's competence.'

"In the following weeks, Manuel and I became rather bored on the subject of Alexius' regeneration and the desire for concessions to the Emperor's safety. Men simply pointed to the goings-on at Paleaticum and with that also discredited our fears of assassination. And then Alexius died.

"I shall never forget how we learned the news. Manuel and Philip, Isaac III, my cousin Nicephorus Paleologus, Basil Angelus, and perhaps a half-dozen others, myself included, were about to leave Satyrus Castle and sail to Sinope where the Governor had invited us on an elaborate hunt, transparently to score points with the Emperor's sons and kin, despite the inherent danger of entertaining nearly a dozen young gentlemen already notorious throughout Constantinople.

"I remember vividly I hadn't felt too well that morning—I suffer warm weather poorly—and I had napped for an hour with the result I was perspiring and more light-headed than ever in the torrid heat. I was quite foul in mood and foul to everyone. I recall the sound, so unmistakable, of the courtyard filling with numerous cavalry. Someone sent an attendant who returned with Prince Cantostephanus, the General of the Scholarians. He kissed Manuel's and Isaac's hands, which I thought strange, then kissed Philip's and mine—which I thought stranger still, since he and I had shared a whore not a few days before while he soddenly regretted his inability to accompany us to Sinope. He straightened and told us we were to return to Constantinople at once, and under escort. Something terrible had happened which it was not in his power to reveal. 'How serious?' I asked, since everyone else seemed struck dumb. 'I can only tell you, Your Highness'—I cocked a brow at that, but his face remained impassive—'an embargo has been placed on all ships both leaving and approaching Constantinople and Chalcedon, and all gates of both cities have been closed.' Manuel spoke up. 'That's enough. Let's go.' He turned to our companions. 'Sorry, gentlemen. Another day.' As he crossed the room, he glanced at me and there was a moment between us of real mutual guilt. If the ports and gates had been closed, then there were men on the run. From what? Assassination? Successful or failed? Or, in the worst resort, were we ourselves suspect?"

Alexius John, of the House of Comnenus, Sovereign Heir Grand Duke of the Byzantine Empire, was found dead at the foot of the Green Staircase, so called because it was carved from gigantic blocks of verd antique, in the Villa of the Paleaticum, 10 June 1142. The body bore no marks of violence, and according to his valet, Igor, he had consumed no food that morning, complaining of dyspepsia and lack of breath. An autopsy was nevertheless performed, attended, as the law prescribes, by the Emperor, his sons, and Philip and Andronikus as proxy for their father. The top of the skull was removed, the brains examined; the jaw smashed and the mouth considered, the chest opened, the rib cage broken, the heart, liver, stomach, kidneys, and lungs extracted and placed on golden trays, the entrails in an enormous golden bowl, for the physician's opinion. Findings were at once pronounced, as here, the cause of death was natural.

Andronikus: "It was impossible to believe he had not been murdered. And yet, that is often the way of coincidence. He had merely suffered unpropitious heart attack. When afterward I spoke to Natalie who, to my surprise, was somewhat bitter at the prospect of never becoming Empress, she, who knew, said it was God's will, and I ceased to have any suspicions."

Unfortunately the rest of the Imperial family did not. Fortified by rumors, and rumors of rumors and the early warnings of Manuel and Andronikus, and despite the postmortem, the entire Imperial administration lowered a crushing silence on all inquiry. Whatever the infallible

evidence of the corpse, the government acted precisely as though something shameful or perilous or treasonous had occurred, so that, long afterward, when many were free to speak it, there was no official story to
counteract the numerous legends.

On a personal level, the death of his Heir struck the Emperor more
vehemently than anyone had expected—perhaps himself included. If a
crown prince suffers thoughts of the patricite, the father, it may often
be forgotten, suffers, too, a great and multiple guilt. On the one hand,
he resents his son's resentment and yet realizes its validity; on the other,
he must contend with his own jealousy for the power he wields and his
responsibility to the state, to share that power—to train his successor
eminently—the moment he attains majority. To this, add John's personal
displeasure with his son. And what is displeasure with another man but
wishing him away, however indifferently, dead?

Throughout the summer, the Emperor seemed to fail, and there were
genuine fears for his survival. He became a recluse; he left all power to
the Sebastocrator; he spent day after day weaving in prayer. The family
was overwhelmed by this extravagant grief because they were too certain of the Emperor's nature to doubt its sincerity. He had decreed the
court go into mourning, and so it did: donning a pure grieving white
from which no one could have foreseen it would not emerge for two
years.

As always, what draws a man from the self-indulgence of excessive
grief is inescapable responsibility. Here, the heritage of reconquest which
John had nominally meant to pass on to Alexius was still threatened
by Raymond of Antioch and Joscelin of Edessa. Whoever his successor
would be—and throughout the year the Emperor refrained (perhaps
superstitiously) from naming him—he did not intend to leave him wars
east and west.

In the previous year two events had ominously served up the infidelity
of the Empire's allies. The first followed the death of Bela II of Hungary. On ascending the Apostolic throne, his son, Geza II, now a
widower, married himself to a Serbian princess, which, as the Sebastocrator Isaac said, "really means he has married himself to the designs of
the Serbian nobles. Once again Hungary can no longer be trusted to
our cause."

To the east: Fulk of Jerusalem, in 1141, disowning both his vassals,
Joscelin and Raymond, who were now the very victims of their non-

aggression pact with Zengi, sought his own mutual assistance pact with the Damascene Emirate. The move was unavoidable, however unfortunate it looked to Constantinople, which, eight hundred miles distant, could not practicably be depended upon for immediate aid should Mosul's warlord march on the Holy Sepulcher. Offense to his friend, the Emperor, was not really in the King's design, but he was prepared to take the consequences for acting to protect himself against those enemies drawn too near by his irresponsible Latin colleagues.

More and more roused by the possible disintegration of his achievement, the Emperor was resolved, according to Andronikus, to crush all the Latin principates, save Jerusalem, and to that end, marched from Constantinople 15 September 1143. For the first time on campaign he took with him his own youngest son and his brother's, who remembered: "As we were leaving the city, my uncle turned a little in his saddle and looked back at those walls which, as everyone points out, stubbornly refuse to diminish, no matter how far you ride, until finally they sink, hallucinatorally, as if of their own weight, beneath the horizon. I thought he looked wistful as a child leaving home forever. I recall thinking precisely that." As he spoke the next words to me, Andronikus looked down and away with uncharacteristic, open emotion. "It was the last time he ever saw the city of his birth, and over which he ruled so brilliantly."

XV

She appeared in the heavens in November, as we approached Tarsus ascending higher, gleaming brighter, growing larger, each evening, a star such as no man remembered, though Mary of Alania told me of its like in her childhood. It seemed to be arriving, undaunted from infinity, the celestial about to descend upon the earth. In its wake it drew a trail of its own stuff, uplifted, immense, complex, dazzling, yet behind which the blue-white stars still visibly winked—even the delicate little Pleiades, the most beautiful constellation in the heavens. It seemed never to move. Each night, transfixed by its beauty, impossible to sleep while such an event occurred, I thought nothing in creation so wonderful, so vast, could suffer diminishing as mere harbinger. The greatest beauty, if we follow Plato—and we would do worse to follow others—is but the poor reflection of its Idea, the symbol of greater perfection still, which is

beyond man's reach but not his yearning. And I thought: if we must reduce this colossal, glittering visitor to a mere presage, let it be of hope—
why else this feeling of elation as one beheld it?—in the knowledge that
coincidence, which may lead to misfortune, may also, as indifferent as
this star, so bright and magnificent in its progress, achieve fulfillment.

—Andronikus on the comet of 1142

The Emperor's march across Lesser Asia took three months due to
the fact he made it an Imperial Progress, sitting in state and justice in
as many cities as possible, investigating the machinery of government,
here and there making small changes or inaugurating wholesale purges,
altering local laws on the spur of the moment, or taking this particular
flaw as the key to a more widespread problem and instituting a chrysobull applicable to the entire Empire.

For Andronikus and Manuel it was an unforgettable lesson in the art
of rule. It must be remembered that at Constantinople the Emperor was
usually secluded from both son and nephew, save by interview, on a
state occasion or during a hunting holiday, which was more and more
rare in these late years. Unless he sat enthroned in the Chrysotriclinium,
when the objectives of justice or legislation were previously arranged,
they scarcely ever saw him as Monarch Regnant. "Laws are first conceived—like bastards—in closets," Andronikus said to me, and he was
quite right. But these three months, son and nephew beheld the very
image and activity of Autocracy, ideals and expediency weighed by intellect put at once to purpose as everywhere the Emperor was attendant,
"considering, concluding, pronouncing his decisions, affecting in a moment whole generations of men. It was the activity of one, at once, in-
herently great, humane, assured, and unself-conscious. It was beyond
earthly rule. It was godly. Only a man who had wielded absolute power
responsibly for so long, one superbly grounded in the often tiresome details of state could have so well extemporized. When I recall my uncle,
I prefer to remember him as he was in those last months: so vigorous,
so wise, the very icon of earthly majesty."

His assertion to the power of Antioch came to less profit. Once again,
for the third and last time, Raymond's agents instituted riots with the
cry: "Sooner the Pope's tiara than the Emperor's!" Nearly the entire
population took to the streets to prevent the surrender of the city to Imperial commissioners.

For more than a thousand years Antioch had seduced and mastered its conquerors. She was like a great courtesan who could refuse no one and disappoint no one. Witty, now languorous, now temperamental, wise, willful, absurd, exalted, no vanquisher till the Latin could alter her or resist her nature. Now, in the first century of the new millennium, under the heels of a new sort of hero, incapable of subtlety, indifferent to the exquisite, not sensual, only bestial, avaricious but not self-indulgent, survivors of the pagan male Gallic countryside and contemptuous of the essential feminine of the idea of city, this magnificent metropolis was metamorphosed physically and in her peoples, beyond recognition, as the curvaceous mistress of kings enters a convent to emerge shrewish, bigoted, sharp-featured, sharp-tongued, monotonous, and gray. Acrimony toward Constantinople was now the habit of a generation. Children were born hating Byzantium the way you and I are born with brown eyes. ("She will die now," Andronikus once said to me, "mighty Antioch will die. A city which loses the capacity to impose itself upon its inhabitants ceases to be creative, becomes stagnant, and dies.")

On 15 December, at a meeting of the Imperial General Staff, it was decided to postpone siege operations in the face of the coming winter and—a virtue of delay—thus allow Raymond time to reconsider the issue of authority before it was too late. There was no reassurance the second offense against Antioch, by Byzantium, would end clemently as the first. It is also likely this hiatus allowed the Emperor himself time for reconsideration. He was extremely hesitant about destroying even a portion of Antioch to gain it. In part, the city's venerable reputation gave him pause; in part, the damage to his reputation if he should initiate bombardment. Then, surely, Antioch would have to be occupied, exacerbating hatreds and wasting thousands of soldiers in that dullest, most gruesome duty of all.

Let it be said for all Manuel's pursuant Latinophilism, he never forgot those days outside the great city, nor the greatness of heart John displayed in his unwillingness to accomplish the dream of Constantinople at the cost of needless suffering and bitterness. He was longer on vengeance and shorter to forgive the House of Guiscard and Poitiers for the insult they so cynically dealt his father—insults which took on a special poignancy, as they always do, when, unbeknownst, they arrive so close on a man's personal tragedy.

On 19 December 1142 death struck against the Imperial family for the second time in seven months when Sergius Porphyriogenetus died of injuries sustained five days before at Constantinople.

While riding in procession, as his father's representative on 13 December, the Grand Duke had been approached by a man who had burst through the lines of soldiery, keeping back the crowd from the Mesa. Apparently the poor fellow, zealous, not malign, may have wanted nothing more than to touch the Imperial Prince. Sergius' steed was startled, reared and threw its rider, then fell upon him, bolting upright, but too late. The Grand Duke, who had all his life to be guarded against bruises, suffered numerous broken bones in the lower half of his body. After nearly a week of indescribable suffering, he was gone.

Both the Sebastocrator and his nephew, Isaac III, were informed the "assailant" had been found with a knife on his person, which, though sheathed, did not preclude assassination (nor did it imply murder). Was he a lunatic? an agent for others? (which did not preclude lunacy). The Emperor had abolished capital punishment, and with it, any form of torture, since that, too, might lead to death. Even Imperial assassination was not exempt, and Sergius was, according to the Emperor's as yet unchanged will, still the Heir by tradition of primogeniture. Torture was the only tool by which the truth might be made known. Both the Sebastocrator and the new Heir Apparent, Isaac III, requested specific instructions from Antioch.

Andronikus: "My uncle was unforgettable. Somehow he had to see beyond the mist of his own grief and put himself to the test of his own principles, to cast aside the natural desire for revenge against a man who was, intentionally or accidentally, the instrument of his son's death. He asked Manuel and me to come pray with him. He was not surprised Raymond—one of those hunch-shouldered, overmuscled hulks who turn the whole body as though the neck were immovable—had not at all offered his sympathies, indefatigable boor. But the real Heiress, Constance—she must have been, then, sixteen—secretly visited the Praetorium with two of her ladies. She bid the Emperor come enter Antioch, in disguise of course, and receive the Host in his son's memory at St. Peter's Cathedral. Much moved, my uncle, holding her small hand in both his own, said, 'Dearest child, I see now it was a sadder day than we had ever imagined—for Constantinople and Antioch—when you were disabled from marrying my son.'

"Constance was such a darling little creature—blond-haired and blue-eyed, cornflower blue (I dreamed of them for days)—a sentimental child. She wept when the Emperor thanked her, thus. John had superb charm when he chose to use it, and I think it may have been real regret she had lost so many days of perfect beguilement by this handsome, elderly knight—'the supremest knight in Christendom,' as he was called even by the Latins. (It was curious, by the way, to watch Manuel watch Constance with a confusion of rapture and regret. Between this dazzling peach and the hard marble beauty of Bertha there was scarcely a contest in his affection. He loved Constance at first sight, and I have often wondered if he did not really marry her in marrying her daughter.)

"In any event, we accompanied the Emperor, along with three Varangians—all of us garbed as Pilgrims—on foot, to St. Peter's Cathedral. Although the Church now celebrated the Latin rite, it was, of course, an Orthodox cathedral and neither the icons nor the iconostasis had been removed, so we were quite at home. There we prayed for the repose of Sergius' soul, without the benefit of prie-dieus, hard on cassocked knees on the stone floor.

"But, let me tell you, it was glorious to watch my uncle at his devotions. There was, then, something unearthly about his rapt concentration, the sense of certitude, the sense of mission. He was, I would say, a mystic. Once he said to me, 'Nephew, if I could impart to you what I feel when I am at prayer, something at once spiritual and yet so palpable, the so-called material riches of this world are crude and lusterless by comparison. I feel a joy, so great, and at once so quiet, my soul is all but bursting in its fullness.' Obviously, he did not pray, he dreamed, which is the reward of the mystic, and like all dreams, the experience was inward, sensual, fulsome, ripe, and more often than not, ecstatic. I myself never saw him rise from his knees, but that he was assuaged or renewed. Those moments in St. Peter's are a perfect example. The Emperor returned to the Praetorium, all vengeance drawn from his heart. He wrote at once to my father instructing him to imprison the culprit and 'treat him.' I shall never forget him dictating these words in a clear, almost exultant voice—'no worse than any other prisoner and no better. Question him, yes, until he drops off his feet, for all that. We will pray God does not give him too much patience and the uncertain length of his incarceration teaches him to speak, if, indeed, he has anything to say.'"

Andronikus neglected to mention what Manuel several years later imparted to one of his ADCs, who imparted it to me, to wit: The two young Grand Dukes argued with the Emperor over this very issue. Manuel wished the death penalty, this once, restored. Andronikus suggested the whip or water torture in the end might be more clement and more productive than a limitless consignment to a dungeon. Manuel had said, "It is a matter of state. Nothing malicious is intended." At this the Emperor reminded his son he would only *sign* the death warrant. Other men would carry out the execution and that is the corruption of agents, who must inure themselves to the pain they inflict, or death. "That is the only way such men may live with their own cruelty." Manuel said, "But isn't there a line which must be drawn between private intent and duty to the state?" At which Andronikus spoke before the Emperor, "In a great state, cousin, if not a perfect one, no line need be drawn." The Emperor smiled upon his nephew and said, "Behold the deep Greek."

When the Emperor once again requested permission to enter the Kingdom of the Holy Sepulcher, and make pilgrimage at Jerusalem, Fulk Anjou once again refused him, with the same excuse offered five years before: He could not support the Imperial army necessary to accompany the great Sovereign. The Emperor was on the point of conceding he would travel, as into Antioch, in disguise with no more than two bodyguards, but neither his generals nor the Varangian commander, who assumed final responsibility for his safety, would hear of it.

Andronikus once spoke of this episode: "When Fulk's letter arrived, my uncle took this supreme denial with a composure which was incomprehensible, and all the more poignant to me. I remember he was so eager, he left the pavilion to meet the messenger, wearing only a thin purple chalmys, which outlined his body in the strong wind. When I think of it, I feel myself the chill of the silk. The Emperor broke the seal as the letter was handed to him. At once, his face fell, and with a look of resignation and hurt, he handed the parchment to Manuel. No hope dearer to him had existed than the thought of seeing Jerusalem. No man loved Christ more sweetly. He said, 'We'll leave for Tarsus, then, at the end of the week, for winter maneuvers,' and re-entered the huge red and gold Praetorium. Manuel offered me the letter to read. I could scarcely make out his figure I was so blinded by tears. Before I completely lost control, I ran to my own tent.

"My cousin followed not a moment later, the letter still in his hand. I sat in a chair, my face buried in my hands, sobbing like an old woman. He repeatedly patted my shoulder and said, almost shyly, 'You mustn't. You mustn't. Papa has had many worse trials than this. He mourns Sergius more than the absence of Jerusalem. Someday we'll revenge him, I promise you, you and I together.' I paid him no attention. At such moments his facility for taking consolation from the future of which he had no right to be so certain, fairly irritated me. But then he said to me the most lying words, or else, the most stupidly ill-considered, any man ever spoke into my ear. He said, 'Listen to me, Andronikus. There have never been any secrets between us—and now I will tell you the greatest of all. Papa is going to declare me his Heir when we return to Constantinople. He told me this last night, swore it before the Icon of Blessed Paul the Proto-Anchorite. And I promise you this: When I am Autocrat, I will make you my Caesar—not titular, but plenipotentiary—for you've a wonderful heart and a bold mind and I shall have need of you all of my life.'"

Forty-two years later, recounting the event to me, as we walked in the unparalleled gardens of Blachernae, the then Emperor, Andronikus Augustus, turned to me to emphasize the point, and said, "This I swear to you, Nicetas, is what he said to me." He paused. "That day, when we were young," and he paused again, "so long ago." He absently kneaded the head of one of those hideous mastiffs he bred and kept simply because it pleased him to be treated with singular devotion by one so ferocious (the day after his murder these dogs were butchered with axes, saws, and arrows). He said, "I pray you, Nicetas, if you mean indeed to write a history, don't reduce all that was between Manuel and myself, thereafterward, as born of this incident. All meaning in my life has been the intent to wield power in such a manner as it will benefit the land into which I was born. The rest is irrelevant. I would sooner no nations and bow before one philosopher king, but until that day, we must accord what is given us. I have sought the answers which would best benefit my fellow men in the here and now. If they are sufficient and good they may last and, lasting, contribute to the days of a future wisdom. This is the nature of my contention with Manuel. Even should I have been made Caesar, we were irreconcilable because events proved our differences were not material or emotional, but ideological, even aesthetic: differences of perception.

"In time, though his heart and soul—as he believed it, and I doubt not his sincerity—were to the greater glory of Byzantium, he was divorced from the people, who had no meaning and were not the state. We would be saved, he believed, not by our own personal resurrection, but through the vigor of the Latins he loved and despised, like myself. He saw the people failing and allowed them to fail, imposing saviors from without because by denying the state exists only to serve its citizens, by believing their only duty to himself, he denied the humanity and precluded the regeneration of all Byzantines. He could not conceive, if aliens rescued the state and remained, then it would no longer be New Rome. If they departed in some future time, there would be none but an enervated population, incapable of taking their place and frantic with their own incompetence. Such a people as has been left me to rule. Regeneration must be willed from within, and I fear—though I will not surrender to it —there is none of that left in our Empire, only a hoarding against some awful day of immigration.

"While my cousin lived, his incredible staying power, which some confuse with venerability or prestige, kept his people in check, that, and his dreams, which were hypnotic, and the love his person and his longevity had engendered as a matter of course. But, really, what could he know of his people, buried in the heart of the most splendiferous ceremony since Diocletian, who was, at least, cynical about it and had the motive of majestic distance after the accessibility and assassinations of the Era of the Barrack Emperors. What could he know of the world beyond the Imperial palaces, or the coteries which surrounded him in the field, who sought to please him because he was, after all, the Emperor, deeply in the center of concentric circles of bureaucratic and ministerial pillagers who depended upon his continued authority to continue their malfeasance which crippled the state and blackened his name. What did he see of the people but their backs as their bellies were prostrated in the winter slush as he passed them in the streets.

"Oh, I know what you historians will say of me: that I inflamed and degenerated those people and released the mob to rule. But is that true, Nicetas? I may have used their antagonism toward Manuel's wife and Heir, but I did not manufacture it. The contumely existed already, like a cloud: against the emptiness suddenly revealed at the top, against the venality of the aristocracy, further corrupted by Manuel, against the gainsay of his policy, his Justinianian Revival, which had no place in a contemporary world, in which Byzantium may be a light—and better than that—but cannot be an overlord, and has no right to be. Worse still, my cousin initiated such vitiating conquest not because he was obliged to, but because the old Roman claims behooved him. In a world of new kings, themselves uncertain of their titles, he flaunted his superiority, and those men were offended. Now with the spell broken by his death, those thrones are poised against mine, while I must contend with an ever more demanding—because desperate—nobility, a beaten peasant, a bankrupt treasury, a merchant class in shambles, and my own family, too long Imperial to prevent dynastic interests, which are their own, from superseding the state's.

"If Manuel's accomplishment was as soundly foreseen and as great as that of our grandfather and his father, why did the state begin to desiccate with his corpse? If it were sound, why did it not survive him? You will say the unity of a man's vision dies with him; *I* say the measure of the integrity—the selflessness, if you will, of a man's vision—is in its ability to live beyond him. He imitated Justinian in more ways than he knew. While I would scarcely consider myself as great a soul as the good Maurice—last of the House of Justinian—I believe I am prepared to meet his same wretched end. In place of ideals, my cousin chose glory. Maurice had no choice, and neither do I, but to live with the consequence of another man's dream.

"In fact, let me make a prediction, which is not any indication of my prescience, but the degeneracy to which our people have succumbed in that they are so ruined, at the moment, so still, their future may be predicated. If I fail or fall—as Maurice after Justinian—we will enter a dark age. If I fail, then the problems are terminal rather than curable. If I fall, it can only be by consent of the mob in another man's hands, and I assure you, that man will assume the state not as executant to serve it, but as executor to disperse it.

"I have risen to power on the mob's shoulders. I was the first, and so, by degrees, I am the least corrupted by that factor. But to consent, in whatever degree, to the anarchy which seeks a father, which is the mob, is to consent to its authority. Whom they make, they may break. I have re-established a precedent, to gain what I must, to do what I must. I am not a fatalist. Nothing, I believe, is meant. I accept what *is* as the only indication of what must be done, and what's done as irrevocable."

And yet he sighed then, and said, "If only I had come to the throne sooner. If only my father had remained Sebastocrator or my cousin Isaac taken the crown for himself and Manuel not galloped across Asia leaving me to fester, for all he knew, in a dungeon or a cave. If only my uncle had not died so irrelevantly." But he did not say the words I had most expected—"If only Manuel had not become Emperor." Instead, looking into the discernible disk of the setting sun, he said, "I did love my cousin deeply, Nicetas. He was perhaps the last great seeker after glory in the ancient mold. Glory. There is only one glory which is a man's, and that is the full exercise of his intellect which shall expand the possibilities of existence, for himself and other men. The elephant is stronger, the horse more regal, the tiger runs faster, the dog quicker catches the scent, birds can fly and the eagle has a greater breadth of vision, the tortoise lives longer, the lion is a more prodigious sire, fish take felicitously to their waters and the whale is momentous, the peacock more exquisite. The only valid contest and conquests between men is in their heads. Glory. My cousin was such a child"—he sighed again—"such a child."

The Emperor arrived at Tarsus on 4 January 1143. For all the solicitous care of his attendants, he became ill the second night in the Governor's palace. Andronikus thought he caught a chill, for the weather was unusually hard along the Mediterranean that winter. In the next several weeks he seemed unable to unwork the grip of a high fever and a hacking cough. Manuel reports he seemed mortally exhausted, disappointed by the events of the previous year, still freshly grief-struck for his sons, and, as Andronikus once told me, "conscious of the future in a way he had, probably, never been before. *Then* it was only to plan and eagerly anticipate the results. Now the unknown years of Regency stretched forward to oppress him, a whole ocean of responsibility in which he must swim, with no promise of rest till an end in death." It is said he spoke much of his father and often wept on the uncharacteristic, heavy side of sentimentality.

By late February, his health, at least, was totally restored though he continued to suffer moods of profound depression. He attended to the correspondence which always flowed, unstoppable, between Constantinople and the field, and on the twenty-seventh day of the month, signed a revised version of his will naming Manuel Porphyriogenetus, "my most beloved son, Sovereign Heir Apparent to all the realms of New Rome, as Lord Basileus, Augustus Imperator, and Autocrat." The testament, which—presumably—may still be seen in the Imperial Archives at Constantinople, bears the signatures of the Grand Duke Andronikus, Duke Nicephorus Paleologus, Prince Alexius Bryennius, Prince John Dukas Bryennius, two ADCs, the Metropolitans of Sis and Tarsus, the Governor of Tarsus, and members of the Imperial General Staff. Copies were dispatched to the Patriarch of Constantinople, the President of the Senate, and Isaac II Sebastocrator. The fourth copy was to be kept by the Emperor's person.

In all this, there was not even a note of explanation to Isaac III, who, unlike his namesakes and predecessors, was less forceful though no less conscientious. He accepted his father's decision, at least outwardly, with complete equanimity. Why the eldest surviving son should have been surpassed for the youngest has no answer in political or emotional reason. Isaac was most like his father in demeanor and thoughtfulness, Manuel most like that which his father might have wished to be in his idle hours. These were the two sons the Emperor had always loved best, and his decision to leave the Imperium to one and the Sebastocracy to another is founded in a motive so guileless and simple, it must be accepted at once.

Two days previous to the signing of the will he dreamed a dream which is probably the most effectual in our history save the Great Constantine's. Two angels appeared to him and unrolled a scroll on which, in gold, were printed the letters alpha, iota, mu, alpha, which, of course, spells the word *blood*. If one pulls the first letter from the names Alexius and Ioannes, includes Manuel (and his son, Alexius II) the anagram becomes clear. The Emperor believed the dream to have come from God, a prediction of the continued rule of the Comneni and an imperative from heaven as to the naming of each successor.

In the spring John Augustus penned a last note to his brother:

Dearest Isaac. It is now eight months since I saw you last—leaves have flown and snow has flown—and now there is a great stillness—you sense it everywhere, sense it in the depth of your being—before the quake of spring, the warming, the first deep breath of the earth as it begins again to awaken.

Do you remember when we were boys and our nurses—in those first springs—would take away the sable and velvet and drop linen or silk over our shoulders and shod us in sandals instead of boots and stockings—and you and I and our dear Simon would run in the wild, secret gardens and paths near the deserted Palace of Justinian? Remember the great vines along the North Wall you and I would climb—Simon, somewhere, pouting below—and from which we would peer into the windows of that haunted mansion? And what is it we saw? Bolts of light of the sun of our youth, defined by the billions of dancing particles of dust, shining upon the huge and empty audience hall, bereft of all its former treasure save the golden walls and the gigantic portraits with their enormous, enchanted, distracted eyes which, nevertheless, seemed to stare at us, whether to accuse or frighten or in a plea for freedom or to be remembered, I was never certain. Once Papa came with us and found an ancient attendant who unlocked the doors and together we walked those halls. How alien it seemed to look *upward* at the portraits? And then there was no doubt: they were meant, in their giganticism, to terrify.

It seems when we are young, we run, and when we are old, we dream of the time when once we ran.

It is hard enough I must war against Antioch and harder still she will prevent me from celebrating Easter at Constantinople. I shall miss the intricate swirls of bread baked round red-rinsed eggs which recall to us the Passion of Our Lord, the roasted goat and good wines after Communion, the soaring enchantment after midnight Saturday when Christ is proclaimed risen, the Procession of the Icons on Tuesday following, or the children's choir of Orphanotropolis on Maundy Thursday. We will have some of this at Tarsus, but it shall not be the same. Constantinople is the city of Christ's glory and all other cities are but her reflection, as the glee of spring is but the crudest implication of the beatitude which shall be ours in confrontation with the Beatific Vision. Oh, Isaac, for that rest, for a little rest. This chase after a portion of equity and peace, is so elusive, so exhausting.

So then, I send you my blessings against the time we shall be together again, firm in the belief, in the joy of Easter at hand, unhappy days are passed. Pray to God He gives us strength, teaches us ever-renewed compassion, grants us wisdom, and allows us the Light that, in the years of His Mystery, we do not pass on completely governed by darkness. If He will, again and again, however briefly, allow us a little exaltation, we shall risk any great grief until the day of everlasting sleep comes upon us, the little sleep, the little slumber, the little folding of the hands—to sleep. Farewell. John.

A hunting expedition had been planned, since the beginning of March, by the two young Grand Dukes, a surprise to divert and relax the Emperor before the return to Antioch. They had had the full co-operation of the Grand Chamberlain and the Imperial Master of the Hunt. Magnificent steeds, some standing as high as sixteen hands, had been brought from Constantinople along with many of the Emperor's favorite hounds. Provisions were made for every eventuality and carefully stored. Colorful pavilions were shipped from the capital and also a stock of poisoned arrows, with which the Emperor preferred to hunt, since a wounded animal too much distressed him and he had not the heart for a coup de grace. (From the point of view of the Imperial bodyguard this was just as well: game in pain might charge dangerously.)

What followed is described by Andronikus: "We presented him with a fait accompli on the morning of 27 March and he joined us within the hour, delighted and, I think, touched. (My uncle was one of those people who are always surprised others think of him when he is not thinking of them.) We rode off at once into the Taurian Range. It seems to me now—and I know it is but an emotional superimposition—we swept away too quickly, without a second thought. In truth, it was unlikely for the Emperor to act so devil-may-care. In the previous two years, especially, he seemed to have become obsessive in the care of his responsibilities. As an Autocrat is, by definition, omnipotent, he could in fact begrudge himself his very sleep in his search for work. You sensed, previously, had my uncle relaxed for a moment, he would have been miserable, believing himself without the right to diversion, neglectful.

"But that spring day, he bound off with us like the most irresponsible youth—namely, Manuel or myself. Perhaps our surprise for him even seemed like a concurring omen to his new mood. We hunted for two days before the black one, 30 March.

"Is there no way to give weight to his death? Must it be without meaning? So effortless, so absurd? We were after a cat about midmorning. My uncle caught sight of her and removed one of the poisoned arrows from his quiver, his horse still on the move. He told Manuel, our cousin, Bryennius, and myself—the four of us farther ahead of the others—to wait. He fitted the arrow into his bow. About twenty feet ahead the cat caught sight of him and disappeared through a hole formed of three boulders. I remember seeing the Emperor's shoulders shrug, his horse still moving. Then I see it: He removes the arrow from the bow to replace it in the quiver. He lifts it behind, and drives the point, by chance, between his vest and his back. We hear a small sound of bestartlement as the razored tip, the poisoned tip, slices the skin. That's it. The end of everything.

"Manuel once told me, I groaned at that moment, or croaked, but so loudly its echo rebounded off the stones. All I could see, all I knew in the entire world, was the sight of that back suddenly straightening. My cousins and I reached him and he was already turning. It seemed an infinite wait, and I asked myself: What will the face of death look like?

"Impassive. No—more subtle: a little twitch at the lip, almost the suggestion of a shy smile such as one not well used to personal attention. But otherwise—save his hands, suddenly tight on the reins—impassivity. What does a man say who knows he will be dead before an hour turns? Manuel came up to his father's side, towering over him. In a simple gesture he bent his head down to his father's shoulder. John momentarily embraced him with one arm and kissed my cousin's forehead, and in the softest voice imaginable, said, 'We'll go back now.'

"That ride to the pavilion I count among the most nightmarish incidents of my life. We cantered down the pass, head-on toward the rest of the hunting party, some forty others. We did not stop and they parted for us, bewildered. I heard Bryennius say to the first riders, 'The Emperor's been wounded, we're going back to the pavilion.' And then the futile gallop began, Manuel to one side, myself to the other, waiting for him to fall, which he did not. Rather, he folded against the saddle pommel, little by little. I made the decision. I raised my arm for the halt and grabbed the reins of my uncle's hunter. He raised his head to me, weakly. 'A wagon, uncle?' He shook his head. 'Not necessary.' His face was like chalk, his teeth gritted in pain. Manuel dispatched someone in any event.

"Three or four mantles were tossed onto the ground, two of them fur-lined, I remember. I pulled the saddle off my horse and we covered it with more mantles, folded. Then Manuel and I, gently as possible, took his father from the steed's back. Strange how until that moment I had never realized how slim and small he was. He attempted to walk, supported by our arms, but his knees folded. I swept him off his feet and carried him the rest of the way to the place we had laid for him. Almost at once he began to shiver, probably the first convulsions. Two more mantles were offered to cover him. Manuel and I knelt on either side.

Manuel said, 'Are you in great pain, Papa?' And my uncle said, 'Bearable. Confess me.'

"I removed the gold icon from my neck, the one I wear now, and handed it to Manuel. My uncle weakly brushed my hand with his own. His breath was becoming spastic, but he managed to say 'How wonderful. Papa's.' I lifted his hand, so calloused from horses' reins after nearly a half century in the saddle, and I kissed it with fervor. At that moment, it seemed all good was going from the world, and I must touch it before it departs. Behind the Emperor's head Manuel took my other hand and pressed it tightly. He held the gleaming little icon before his father's eyes while they exchanged responses. The rest of the hunting party stood about, stunned beyond action.

"It was my cousin Alexius Bryennius who had the presence of mind to say, 'Gentlemen, let us pray for the Emperor.' So there, on the cold, arid ground, the Military Grandees knelt, while Bryennius led them in devotions, either by oversight or too kind, refraining from prayers for the dying.

"When my uncle and my cousin were finished, the Emperor seemed to muse. 'So much to do, so much.' Manuel still grasped my hand, but he did not look at me. His eyes would not move from his father—and they frowned curiously, as if the outward sign of an impossible inner conundrum he was considering. Impossible, indeed, for within moments, at the age of twenty-three, he would ascend the Imperial throne. On a day begun like any other.

"My uncle gasped the words 'Don't forget Antioch. . . . Make amends with Fulk.' He tried to catch his breath. 'Venice. . . . Follow your uncle's wisdom.' His head fell to one side, not in unconsciousness, but very obvious despair. 'Terrible . . . terrible for your poor sisters,' and he shuddered and died and the archons prayed on, unawares. I cleared my throat and I was even startled by the sound of my own voice which cut through the orisons with an edge of conscious disgust, as I said, 'Gentlemen, His Imperial Majesty is dead.'

"Suddenly I felt as though all the life had gone out of me, or rather, as if I had spent what life I had in speaking those words. I relaxed my hand in Manuel's, but he only gripped it more tightly. And I knew why. The moment he so much as turned his head, he would slip helplessly into the Imperium, for the canons say the Empire is never without an Emperor. With the stoppage of one man's breath the office passes reincarnate to his successor, whoever his successor may be. If he occupies a cradle, he is nevertheless an autocrat. Whether he rules matters not half so much but that he reign. Coronations are a formality, crowns are baubles, anointment is a baptism in rancid water. When my cousin moved—movement, which is life, the signal of his existence—moved to look at the generals who were now standing, gathering closer, in that instant he would become Basileus.

"But my cousin was refusing to lift his head. I could see it. He was extending the moment of himself as son before the father to be obeyed, as if, so long as he stayed bowed before the corpse, my uncle's death would remain a progress and not a finality, releasing the father from and impelling the son into the burdens of Autocracy. Perfect stasis, which I, for one, could not abide. Whether motion bodes good or ill for me, I prefer it to stagnation. And yet, my logic, as I remember it, was the logic of a dream, inane but real in its effect upon my emotions. I sensed in myself a great resentment. I somehow believed—and perhaps in some strange way it was so—it fell to me to make him Emperor. And in a brief epiphany, I loathed my cousin for it. I saw that of the grandsons of Alexius Augustus I was the only one fit for the throne: clear-eyed, harder, wanting to act not by tradition but by logic, as acting and logic were the only reasons for being. Only three months had passed since I first lived with the possibility of Manuel's accession. But for this catastrophe I might have expected twenty years more of accustoming myself. I might have rejected my cousin entirely or taken complete hold of him. Instead I had to let him go—to the Autocracy, to ultimate power, when he could not even wield his own servants properly. I had to release him to a world of influence, not merely my own, to a world of flattery such as I would never give him, to the world as its cynosure. I possessed him and now I was obliged to relinquish him.

"With my free hand I closed my uncle's eyes, repelled by the resistance of the lids and the hardness of the spheres beneath. I kissed his lips, still remarkably warm, as if in sleep. I lifted his hand once again and kissed that, too, and pulled off the ruby sigil, which came away easily. And then I rose, pulling Manuel up with me, and I passed behind the Emperor's head and knelt before my cousin and kissed the hand which still grasped mine, then opened his fist, as if, indeed, it were the dead man's, and slipped the surprisingly small ring on the second, the third, the fourth finger and kissed the hand once again. I raised my eyes to him, but he was looking distractedly at the ground. I said, 'As for me and my house, Augustus, we shall be yours, faithfully, unto death.' I had done what was expected of me, but scarcely, after that revelation of envy, what I had expected of myself.

"I stood away then and allowed the others to pay homage. I looked about me for a moment, then down, of course, my eyes drawn, as in a whirlpool, to my uncle's corpse. I heard murmurings and reassurances to his son in my ear. Despite the heartbreak and loneliness which follows the death of a good man such as John II—the sense of less heart and less charity in the world—here was begun, so soon, the clear-eyed, cold-sober calculations of the realignment of power, only intensified.

"It was worse still in the evening, when the Praetorium gathered. Nothing of the man, nothing of loss. Only very sensible questions. Should the eastern borders be fortified against possible attack by Zengi, who, in my uncle's death, had lost his most formidable antagonist? Should the West fleet be placed on alert against possible attack by Sicily? Should the armies of Thrace guard the North Defile against Hungary? Should the Constantinopolitan Garrison enter the city to assist the constabulary in the event of unrest? Poor Manuel. He sat it all through long after sunset, while undertakers arrived from Sis along with the remaining members of the Varangian Guard which had left Constantinople with the Emperor eight months before.

"As far as I know, notification of my uncle's death had not even been dispatched to the capital, yet he lay hours dead, outside the pavilion, in the unusual cold—it had been a false spring—to prevent further desiccation until the embalmers went to work. I left the meeting halfway through—and caught Manuel's disapproving glance. (It mattered little to me; if he had the least power of disapprobation over me, he had all power over me.) Outside, under torches, honor guards, and a praying priest, my uncle's corpse remained, covered by a purple pall which was actually his blanket. I prayed at the makeshift bier, stood up, and pulled back the cover from his face. His cheeks and eyes were sunken. His lustrous silver hair moved in the wind.

"So we cannot reckon the future. If we could, we should not, even then, escape despair, as death, anyway, is at the end of everything. Probably the foresight of Universal Oblivion would drive us mad, though madness I think might be preferable to annihilation. Whatever Manuel became now, it was his choice to be. Indeed, as Autocrat, he was the only man alive who might make a choice. In absolute power you may come as close to freedom, absolute freedom on earth, as it is possible. You may still live with the terror of the unforeseen, but you are the animation of response to it; you may act from perfect repose, as for that, a god would do. I cannot express to you the bitterness I felt. I looked up at the stars, those few visible in the silver glare of a half-moon. There is a rhythm, an ineffability in creation, which is its perfection. No human can feel its part unless it be from repose. Otherwise this beauty, this ineffability, is but a taunting to the busy and the weary. To all but the truly free, aesthetics are an irrelevance, and beauty an excess. So I was doomed as Plato was doomed beneath this same sky.

"I stared at my uncle's face, no longer animated by that spirit which had behooved my love for him. I quite suddenly realized that love is but the reminder of one's mortality, and one is only loved against just such a day as this. We love because love ends. After that, it is love no longer, but grief, which we confuse with love. Love is creative and you cannot share with clay; you can only mold it, which is as often what we do with our memories of the dead. If love is a reminder of one's mortality, then it is a consent to death. How the stars, then, must laugh at love. Without love, one is free at least to confront the stars on their own cold terms. To accept love is to admit the universe has overwhelmed you. Unloved, you are dispersed, loved, you are diminished by those who believe that in loving you they have defined you, as, after a fashion, they have, according to their own prejudices. You are smaller and more mortal still in the night.

"In all this, there was only one source of redemption: the consciousness of those stars and the moon above my uncle's body could not be measured. That which is incorporeal is infinite. A truth lives, remains unalterable, even when stars die. They may have laughed at Plato, but Plato may laugh last at the stars. Perhaps it is, then, mortal deeds can be immortal, if only as memory. Or so it seems. After all, what's life worth if we're not captivated by questions, themselves a source of creativity?

"It is not hard to understand my train of thought. Death must not come to the great in our lives. It is too much the reminder of our own vulnerability. Too much death. Death under the mat and death in corners and death behind the door and death along the street, beneath a rock and within the waters. We must convince ourselves death has a plan. Otherwise, reminded even towering lives are mortal, it is simply too much to bear. A lesson in vanity: a little poison, a scratch, the exposure of a little viscera and it is over: the holy internum dies before the light of day. In the night we are born, in the night we live, and we die into the night.

"After Manuel ended the meeting, he called me to him. We walked and conversed about the day's unbelievable events. He wanted to leave a guard with me, for I preferred to continue my stroll and he was understandably weary. I bantered. I said it was only his life that was all-precious now, and mine, only in its proximity to his. And really I wanted to be alone. So he returned to the Praetorium and I was kidnapped and my life changed utterly from what it might have been.

"It was about a half mile from the encampment. They appeared over the tip of an incline. They were brigands, plain brigands. I would have thought them remnants of another age, my grandfather's time or even earlier, but not alive and flourishing in a garrisoned Greek Asia. They were Turks, though between themselves and Mas'ud there was as great a gap as between men and the moon. They were small, savage, smelly, brutal, and stupid. They had approached the encampment, as wild animals will, warily, to forage. Strange, my first thought was not fear, but a sort of wonder: how had I passed in a matter of moments from the ultimate safety of my cousin's company to this peril? I even thought: 'Why, I'm going to die,' a little incredulous, but nothing more.

"Well, I turned on my heel and started running. Not to outdistance them, I assure you, which was anyway impossible from the look of those hard, mangy little ponies. I was hoping to tempt one of the Turks at least close enough to pull him from his horse—a hostage, a weapon, or even the animal itself on which to flee was what I wanted. Unfortunately, I tripped and sprawled and that gave them—eight or nine men—the opportunity to make a wide, impenetrable circle about me. You know, I had always sympathy for an animal trapped by too many hunters, but that was the compassion of observation. Experience ceases to objectify and gives new insight into the feelings of the victim. (I suppose only a poet otherwise has the intensity of imagination to perceive the emotional possibilities of a situation, suffering them without enduring the circumstances.) I got to my feet, my heart about to explode, racing too fast, in a panic, while I ran from here to there and back again, seeking an escape, ducking their swords or truncheons, braced for a blow at every moment. It was still unexpected—and for that, perhaps, merciful—when it came."

When Andronikus did not arrive at Manuel Augustus' tent by mid-evening, the new Emperor sent a servant to fetch him. The servant returned to say the Grand Duke was absent from his pavilion. "Only a little alarmed," Manuel dispatched three or four guards into the surrounding hills to search for his cousin by the bright moonlight. For two hours deferential and gradually more urgent cries of "Your Highness" and "Prince Andronikus" echoed through the mountains. Nigh by midnight, the full contingent of Varangians and even a few of the generals followed on one another among the gorges and valleys. Manuel, in a document now lost to us, hauntingly recalled looking into his father's dead face, now blue by the moon, now amber by the torches, while a strong wind shot through the camp carrying voices calling his cousin's name "as though summoned by ghosts or the weavers of Fortune's loom." Manuel was urged to bed. It was expected the Grand Duke would be found, and the new Emperor must, above all else, leave for Constantinople by sunrise. So the Heir slept, following what he thereafter—and often—described as "the longest day of my life."

About an hour before dawn he awoke to the sound of the search party trudging back to camp. The moon had set and there was no purpose in looking further for the Prince. It was probably valid criticism and not merely the years' resentment when Andronikus said, "I would have sent them out again with torches, told them to keep up the search until mid-morning. In the smug safety of an Imperial encampment, it would scarcely have occurred to someone I might have been waylaid and with every moment carried farther and farther away."

Of course, to the victim nothing was so urgent as his rescue. The Grand Duke was in the right to criticize the carelessness of the Praetorium—probably the result of exhaustion—but not its intentions. In later years I think he confused the motives of those, including the Emperor, who then, seemly as possible, would have been glad to be rid of his overwhelming presence with the genuinely heartbroken companions of that first adventure. In 1143 he was too much loved and admired as a grand and brilliant young Imperial prince—"Comnenus Attar," he was called. We must remember, as even Andronikus infrequently admitted, his own misfortune could not have arrived at a less propitious time. Indeed, his was one of those ancillary disasters following almost inevitably from the distractions, the carelessness and miscalculations subsequent to one greater.

The Empire had still to be plunged into mourning. These guards, and the generals, and even the Bryennii brothers had faced, as Andronikus, one of the most grievous days in their experience and forgone sleep in the face of the oncoming, long, forced trek to Constantinople. If judgments were impaired—and just so Andronikus' may have been, walking alone in the night—if the men, however unhappily, chose for themselves the less arduous alternative of a little rest and leaving behind a guard of some forty Varangians to search the area in the following days, if Manuel was urged not to remain ("They said to me, anything I could do was not of such matter I could not be replaced by someone else; but I was indispensable at Constantinople"), if it be all this, then forgiveness is the word for all.

Manuel did everything he possibly could. Andronikus once said it was his cousin's first failure of will to succumb to the advice of his General Staff and leave. But it seems more likely to remain would have been obstinacy. Had he remained, even in the likelihood Andronikus would soon be found, it would have seemed an extraordinary personal gesture, and nothing more. (In fact, two months were to pass before the recovery of the Grand Duke. Would Andronikus have charged his cousin less if he had departed after a month?)

And so, scarcely knowing what to think—even considering his cousin had committed suicide—Manuel dispatched a second note to Constantinople on the heels of the first and most momentous Message of Succession, informing his uncle of the disappearance of his son. Then, shortly before noon, much of the encampment left upstanding for the remaining Varangian search party, the new Autocrat of New Rome set out for his capital behind his father's body, sealed in lead and resting on a wagon covered in purple velvet, beneath a canopy of white and gold, donated by the late Emperor's good friend, the Metropolitan of Tarsus.

To anyone who participated in that journey, every step of the four hundred miles was harrowing. The time to Easter Sunday was on everyone's mind—and, too, memories—poignant and heroic—of the late Emperor, now that the initial shock had worn away and one would have to come to terms with the times-to-be without him, the realignment of lives, which is, in truth, the essence of mourning. But most touching of all were the hundreds of thousands, the millions of people along the way—slave, peasant, and nobleman alike—who lined the road to the Imperial capital, in grief and last respect for the late Emperor and in some degree curious about his successor whose life as the youngest son had previously been of little publicity. *Explicit: Nicetas Acominatus.*

An irradiant full moon, the paschal moon, a very few, the very brightest stars against the deep and beautiful blue of the sky. A dolphin-shaped cloud, transparently silver at the limb, swims across the night. Beneath this panorama, soldiers in formal dress bestride the top of the Golden Gate, the Emperor's gate, at Constantinople, torchbearers and sword-bearers alternating with banner-bearers. To either side of the massive bronze doors, shut tight, are the members of the Senate, the city aristocracy, and representative members of the archonate. Complete silence, but for the sharp snap of flames, the susurration of the trees, the whipping of the standards, and an occasional cough.

A tattoo breaks the quiet as hundreds of hooves crack against cobblestones. Scarlet and gold Varangians ride up to the gate and with stunning precision break from marching formation into presentation, lining the last hundred yards of road to the gates. There is a short pause and then the sound of chanting preceded by the Church hierarchy and a multitude of canons carrying tapers, bejeweled icons, and a gigantic crucifix as the dead Emperor, released from the lead casket, his body incorrupt, is drawn forward on a golden and purple catafalque by eight white donkeys. In the center of a sea of mighty candles, shrouded in purple, bordered with ermine, crowned on a bed of white silk, his corpse shakes in its progress with the oneness of massive wax. Twenty feet from the gates the catafalque is stopped.

Now the new Emperor comes forward. Manuel rides a white stallion, his father's. He wears the crown of Justinian the Great—perhaps a purposeful choice—an incredibly heavy solid-gold band, bejeweled and pearl-encrusted. He is clothed in a white, weighty, silken chalmys, tight along the arms, high on the throat, and a purple cape, open on the right, brooched with an enormous pigeon-eye ruby. . . . Stairs, covered with purple velvet, are set beside his horse. Auxuch, who has been shifted into the still powerful post of Imperial Grand Chamberlain, succeeding his father, steps up to the young Emperor, his eyes roughened and shrunk by tears, his lips trembling. He offers his hand, wrapped in a silken napkin, to his dead master's son. Before taking it, Manuel grants him a short, small, reassuring smile.

The Emperor grips the hand of his Chamberlain, dismounts, and takes the stairs at an unceremonious clip. A Canon of Holy Wisdom presents the Gospel, which Manuel kisses reverently and without further ceremony, walks away, to the threshold of the Golden Gate. There, the Caesar John-Roger, whom Manuel but curtly acknowledges, presents a purple pillow on which reposes a golden hammer. This, Manuel takes up handily, and three times—so resoundingly as to dent the precious tool—strikes the gate. From within comes the voice of the Prefect of the City, his brother-in-law, Duke Stephen Cantacuzenus, Julianna Porphyriogeneta's husband.

CANTACUZENUS. Who seeks entrance?

MANUEL. Manuel Augustus, a citizen of Constantinople.

CANTACUZENUS. Then enter, Manuel Augustus.

Ponderously the gates swing back. Beyond the walls, along the Via Triumphalis, as far as the eye can see, to the Forum of Bovi, half or more of Constantinople's population stands in the night, many on the opening of the gates, lighting up tapers in a magical effect. Waiting on the road, each beside a white stallion, are the Sebastocrators, Isaac II and Isaac III. The younger man takes the hand of his uncle and leads him forward. They stop before the new Autocrat and mutually sink to their knees. Isaac lifts the hem of his brother's chalmys, bejeweled with a line of rubies, pearls, and gold thread, kisses it, and places it in his uncle's hand. Isaac II kisses the hem. Manuel's hands reach down to help his uncle rise. Though he takes an aesthetic's delight in it, one of the more curious aspects of this young man's affection for ceremony, already noticeable—it will never be absent—is that he has not the actor's imagination and is frankly too guileless to endure it with a mime's stately and intimidating grace, pomposity in the least pejorative sense. He is not trained to it from the cradle like his father, and so it does not become him. Rather like his grandfather, he is not "slow." Everything is as it should be—he makes not an awkward move, but like his grandfather, he seems rather brusque, eager to be on to other things. There is no lack of dignity, but there is indeed a lack of grandeur, as though in going through with this he were indulging the entreaties of children. As he raises his uncle level, he speaks hoarsely, whispering.

MANUEL. It will be well, uncle. I promise you.

There is nothing but a squeak and tears from the older man. Manuel grasps Isaac's hand ever more tightly for one reassuring moment, then steps back, frees himself, as touched as he may have dreaded, and somewhat dizzy. He is also at a loss as to what to do next. John-Roger comes forward with his horse and, saved, the Emperor mounts up at once without waiting for the others. And suddenly the stifled sobs of Isaac II and anyone in the vicinity so moved are overwhelmed by the sound of clinking metal and creaking leather, whinnies and hooves dancing on cobblestones as horses become accustomed to their riders' weight and balance, and pass on.

The dead Emperor's body having been transported to Cathedral of the Almighty where it will be prepared for further obsequies, Manuel, his mantle billowing like a great dark bird of prey in his progress, approaches the iconostasis of Holy Wisdom. It is an hour before midnight and Easter services are about to begin. The Heir quickly mounts the ambo where he is met by the Patriarch Cosmas and a canon, holding up from bended knee an open Gospel over whose left page a card, with the coronation oath, has been placed. His right hand on the right page, Manuel intones in a clear, firm voice the words which formalize his accession.

MANUEL. I, Manuel John, of the House of Comnenus, believe in one God Almighty, Creator of Heaven and Earth. I confirm, acknowledge, and approve the apostolic and God-guided decisions of the ecumenical and local councils together with the constitutions and definitions of these, also the privileges and customs of the most Holy Church of God. Furthermore I confirm and approve what the Holy Fathers of the Church have instituted and defined as sound, canonical, and free from error. At the same time I vow to remain always the faithful and veritable servant and son of the Holy Church and to be both her defender and avenger, to be considerate and philanthropic, and, so far as law and custom allow, to inflict the death penalty as sparingly as possible. So I vow, so I swear, so help me God, before these, God's holy servants—upon the Lance, the Cross, the Nails, the Crown, and Shroud of Jesus Christ, my Lord and Redeemer.

BOOK TWO

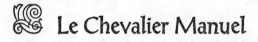 Le Chevalier Manuel

I

Incipit: Nicetas Acominatus: And so, in the year which would have marked his first Jubilee, John Augustus returned to Constantinople to be entombed, and his son, crowning himself in the most sudden and sparest of circumstances in the first hours of Easter morning, began his fabulous, disastrous reign, one of the most fateful in our long history.

Manuel's first resolve was what might have been expected of one, headstrong and the youngest in a family, unused to the prerogatives, the exceptions and expectations, which are the authority of an heir or even an elder sibling. He intended to be a "true Autocrat," which, with his idealizing and sentimental imagination, he saw not as the assumption of all power and responsibility for every decision—not a writ passing without his examination and signature—but rather, at no time in his reign should he seem any man's tool, as, indeed, he never did.

To this end, he meant to make himself less accessible than his "sainted father and grandfather of Blessed Memory." To this end, he initiated under Auxuch a commission which would re-establish the ceremony and style of the Imperial court, choosing as his standard the almost suffocating protocol and asphyxiating magnificence of the time of Constantine VII. To this end, though always gracious, he became somewhat more condescending, which is to say, he practiced an impassivity *interrupted* by kindness, which otherwise intimidated his father's advisers. To this end, he evolved a policy of surrounding himself with advisers who might never outshine him, who could be eliminated without loss, who in their dullness made his decisions, by comparison, seem inspired. "My cousin was never malicious. He was incapable, anyway, of acting from malice," said Andronikus. "He did not go about this quite so coldly as it seems in retrospect. Rather, it became the motive, virtually an instinct, by which he chose his council. Thereby he could dismiss the prophets of doom—those men whose advice he would not allow—as merely resentful and uninformed. It was no satisfaction to any of us, our predictions proved correct. We had better been poor prophets and good servants."

Manuel's first official acts were instituted on Easter morning, before attending Divine Liturgy for the third time since midnight. First, he wrote to Mas'ud Shah at Iconium, requesting aid in the search "for Our Dearest Cousin—and through his kin, yours—the Grand Duke Andronikus." Mas'ud consented with an alacrity and conscientiousness which was the shame of the Varangians left in the Taurian Mountains. In an extraordinary breakdown of discipline, members of this elite corps had turned to spending their days hunting, drinking whole stores of wine at al fresco banquets, and intimidating nearby villages, if not actually involved in extortion. (When news of their activity reached Constantinople, they were replaced, recalled, scourged, and deported to their homelands. Precious days had been lost which not even the competence of the Moslem search party could compensate.)

The Emperor's second act was to institute a Second Court of Inquiry concerning the guilt of his brother Sergius' alleged assassin. Not a man at court doubted this was the precedent to re-establishing the death penalty in the Empire.

About two weeks following the Imperial accession, the Sebastocrator Isaac II, in what he believed was a mere formality (unlike the action of his predecessor, who had been sincere, even eager, to be rid of his office), submitted to the Emperor, his nephew, his renunciation of the Sebastocracy. It was accepted. If Andronikus' father was appalled, the entire court was thunderstruck, no less the second Sebastocrator's admiring disciple, Isaac III, on whom the responsibilities of Interior, Police, and Transport Ministries, as well as the office of Imperial Comptroller, now fell like a rock. But the Emperor could not be moved, in fact was only more resolved at the suggestion of criticism. His uncle's resignation bluntly eliminated two problems at once. In the first, the implicit seniority held by Isaac II after what amounted to a Co-Regency with John II; in the second, the term of office of the Sebastocrator. Ought it to be lifelong? Or the length of the brother's reign, which is to say, not otherwise be conferred on any but a Porphyriogenetus? Isaac I's resignation, and now that of Isaac II, finally settled the matter by insinuating a tradition. What no man could have foreseen, of course, as

Manuel settled the beautiful silver, pearl, and sapphire rayed crown upon his older brother's head, was that the third Isaacian Sebastocrator was also the final one. The Emperor's absolute monarchism and his brother's mere competence, as well the lack of Porphyriogeneti in the following generation, devalued the office, then left it without a candidate.

Andronikus' father, it need hardly be added, from that April day forward, until his death, fourteen years later, counted Holy Week, 1143, as the blackest of his life, incomparably worse than any hour of his exile at Iconium. Within a day he had lost his brother and—it seemed so— his favorite son and youngest child, and not thirteen days later, his authority, "insolently retired," as he put, "at the age of fifty-one by a twenty-three-year-old emperor who had never served a day's apprenticed rule in his life." (If such words reached Manuel—in all likelihood they did —one may imagine the reaction.) To be certain, Andronikus' return at the beginning of the summer was an unexpected and joyous recovery, but the very length of the young Grand Duke's absence had metamorphosed anxiety into the certitude of grief so that by late May the scars had taken their toll. There were men I knew, personally, honest courtiers, hugely sympathetic to the second Sebastocrator, who swore he aged, within two month's time, as drastically as his father, in Alexius' last years, going from gray hair to white and a hearty constitution to that of a fragile giant.

And there was, of course, the testimony of Andronikus himself, who was, he said, "appalled by the change which had taken place. At twenty-one, one does not expect to encounter an old man for a father. And, by heavens, my father was *not* old. There are many things for which I cannot forgive Manuel, in the sense of true forgiveness: the recognition beyond the outward act to the inner intent—and the callous indifference to my father—is one of the many. It is one thing to dismiss a man who is useless: the victim may thereafter be bewildered, but that is the punishment of the obtuse. It is quite another thing to enforce inutility upon a vigorous, just, and experienced regent, which, beyond all question, my father was. It seems to me singularly odd, my cousin, so cognizant of the Imperial dignity, could treat so callously one, like himself, a Porphyriogenetus.

"The aftermath is, of course, a matter of history. Manuel proceeded to turn round virtually every edict, every strategy, every economy, intended by our grandfather and his father (and often suggested by my own). Do you know we spent the last fourteen years of my father's life keeping from him these awful truths? We allowed him to believe though he were gone, his policies, at least, survived so that he would not also suffer the worst pangs of the man who is told all his life and his hard work—and no less his brother's—was for nothing. What did I tell him in place of the truth? I told it to him straight as I would have ruled: as a continuation of my uncle's and my grandfather's intentions, subject to my own revisions and exclusive of certain ideas I long entertained and in which I knew my father to be in complete disagreement. Of course, it was necessary to keep Manuel and my father apart even on a personal basis to prevent discrepancies, and to restrict those visitors to Isaac to a faithful few whom we could thoroughly indoctrinate into the deception. Unfortunately, this restriction produced, on my father's side, outrage at the infidelity of so many, deserting him once his power was gone (from outrage, he passed to misery, and then, misanthropy, so that at length, even our most trusted friends lost the desire or the ability to tolerate him). On Manuel's side, my mother, my brother, and I, in all sympathy, told him of Isaac's lack of eagerness in maintaining any relationship whatsoever, even privately. My cousin's bewilderment, to his credit, never became antagonism. It remained an open wound, which he constantly attempted to ameliorate and we were forced to sabotage. After all, my father was the only man of the previous generation who might admonish him by his Christian name, and mean it. But that is all scarcely the tragedy it is to make of a great and busy man's life, as my father's, one of emptiness. I ached for him whenever I looked on him, listening to his reader, walking the fields assisted by his valet or his faithful Barnabas. Nothing could compensate him or myself this enforced decadence."

In May the Second Court of Inquiry into the guilt of Sergius Porphyriogenetus' accused assailant reached the only conclusion its members understood was expected of them—indeed it seemed to be implicit in the convocation: the prisoner ought to be subject to torture, even at the risk of death. There were, otherwise, no possible means of learning the extent, if any, of a widespread, subversive plot against members of the Imperial family.

Manuel, it is said, was tormented by this decision. We may believe it. For several years I was mystified by the sincerity which so many of my colleagues ascribed at the time to the young Emperor's distress. But

Manuel, though he had less compunction in the utilization of the instruments of torture and death, had genuinely admired his father's rescript against capital punishment as "whatever its implicit flaws, the very acme of civilization." Now to cancel that writ was to undo one of the very virtues for which he meant to have his father canonized—and any path which leads to sainthood is at once instructive and an admonition.

Peering deeper still into Manuel's motives, we may ask ourselves if he did not conceive the Second Court as a man acting in behalf of his better judgment against some repellent course in which his suspicions behoove him. That is literally the meaning of a man being of two minds about an issue. Unfortunately the Emperor's very authority acted as a bellwether. His own crown defeated his best intentions. The Second Court, intelligent men all, but also ambitious, and attempting to please the new Autocrat in hopes of their own advancement, believed, quite rightly, such a board of inquiry was unnecessary unless it was the Basileus' wish to reinstitute capital punishment—and so they served him.

I have said we may believe these mitigations against the Emperor's callousness. There is very good reason beyond mere supposition. Among his personal papers found after his death was this note to himself, dated 1143, which Andronikus much appreciated as "worthy" of his cousin:

Question: Is an absolute king above morality in what exclusively benefits or deprives the Imperium, whose person I am? Or is that king answerable to imperatives, the exemplar of morality and due to repent— even suffer punishment—in the event of transgression? Either I am less a man, a beast, for whom good and evil are irrelevant, or I must be more —by consecration and because of it, their animation. This Empire is entrusted to me by God, and if I fail at any point, I am thus answerable to Him. If I refrain from allowing torture and possible execution, it should be an act of great mercy, and Christ does say, "Blessed are the Merciful." Yet, if there are men against the state, a great danger, and I do not root them out, if the state fails, then in the selfish endeavor to personal virtue I have betrayed a heaven-sent trust. So angels fall from heaven in their self-congratulation. Is there no alternative? What must I do? What can I do? Before God, I am as dust. How dare I then, dust, condemn a man to pain and to oblivion? Which shall be the greater strength? Mercy or inflexibility? *This* is what I must ask myself: not whether it is a greater or lesser sin to execute a man in the state's behalf, not whether the state, by his death, shall profit, but whether I have sinned threefold because I could not find other means to protect our Holy Fatherland. I am thinking now of that perfect state in which a man need never act against his virtue, such as my cousin spoke of outside the walls of Antioch. My grandfather reached this decision, but once, for death. How did he come to it? But then, what would another man's advice gain for me? The decision is still mine, right or wrong, and it shall repay my soul with very little consolation.

Finally, there was one excellent economic advantage for not re-establishing the death penalty. In place of torture, blinding, or execution for all gross crimes, John Augustus, who was not above mixing piety and his purse—or, specifically, the state's—had instituted a process of formal confiscation to the Imperial Treasury of all personal lands and treasures owned by the malefactor, if he possessed wealth, or, if he possessed but the shirt on his back, remanding him to the State Public Works. Ironically, this had proved intensely unpopular, as many a spouse would sooner be a rich and grieving widow than an impoverished wife, while an impoverished and condemned man would sooner an absent hand than work without pay. Such a threat nevertheless served the state well.

It is significant those urging Manuel to restore the death penalty were the civilian aristocrats, whose fortunes lay primarily in mercantile areas and personal property rather than the land. The archonate and the majority of the General Staff, those most accustomed to slaughter, who knew, in full, the measure of death, were against the re-establishment of capital punishment. The reasoning of the latter group bears investigation.

Immemorially, the military has been autocratic and concomitantly, the most tradition-bound of institutions. Even the smallest changes, wherein unchallenged obedience is paramount, carry the scent of anarchy. To the military, the man who occupies the throne is not so much Autocrat or Basileus as his age-old title, Augustus Imperator, i.e., Revered Generalissimo. Only this legal descendant of Julius Caesar possessed the prestige to alter laws, to end a tradition or void an apparently imperishable canon. The General Staff which Manuel inherited from his father admired John as a strategist, loved him as a fighting comrade in the thick of it, and, in the most literal sense, adored him as the living incarnation of Demetrius of the Battles. Indeed, it is probable their supernal self-control the day of the Emperor's death was a final service to the deceased Augustus, an honor due his memory rather than self-aggrandizement. Against the massive weight of precedent going back to that most bitter biblical dictum of official revenge John II had abolished capital punishment throughout his Empire. At first, these men had obliged him only because he was the Vice-Regent of God on Earth and, like God, occasionally inscrutable. In time, as they beheld no increase in crimes of the first degree, no more and no less than before, man's usual wickedness, they accepted the absence of mutilation and execution as the ultimate Christian beneficence, and final proof, if proof there need be, of their Chieftain's greatness.

With this acceptance, it can easily be imagined the effect of Manuel's turnabout in that same generation. For these men—whose principle was death, yet for once on the side of magnificent clemency—*this* was anarchy, whim, a lack of self-assurance in the successor, and, more's to the point, a desecration of his father's goodness. Unfortunately the displeasure of his generals whom he commanded-to-be-obeyed, in the army upon which his autocracy rested, reached Manuel. Such a challenge was intolerable. It should, then, come as no surprise, the membership of the Praetorium as it was now constituted was destined for purging.

The alleged assassin of the Grand Duke Sergius died on the rack without confession or accusation. (It is presumed the somewhat vague plot of the pro-Sicilian faction, mentioned by Crown Prince Alexius to Andronikus, which sought to install the Caesar John-Roger as Emperor, died with John Augustus.) At once, Manuel went into retreat at Pantokrator Monastery. When he emerged—knowing his reputation, in some degree, had suffered diminution—he did not return to the Sacred Palace. To many, it seemed as though the apparently innocent blood spilled, against John's hopes, was the final stain upon that vast agglomeration of churches and palaces and arsenals, grown only more cursed in their indomitability. The new Emperor moved into the Sebastocrator's Palace, as Porphyriogenetus Palace came to be called, and a few days later signed the commission to complete Blachernae.

As if to further compel hope after so inauspicious an inauguration to his reign, on 7 June Manuel received word his cousin Andronikus had

been rescued, "only a little worse for wear," as Duke Stephen Cantacuzenus wrote, "underweight, half-naked, and smelling to high heaven
of savage life."

II

"What saved me from the first, I believe, was my, if you will, flawless
Arabic," said Andronikus during one of our first conversations, for indeed I was curious about this episode which constitutes the beginning
of his legendary indestructibility. "You might say, if those brigands had
any thoughts as to my origins—whether or not they knew the meaning
of the standards flying above our encampment—they took me for a Cau-
casian Turk, probably an Armenian or Danishmend. That, at once,
tempered their treatment. More subtly, because I spoke their language
I was never objectified as I might have been. There is a special brutality
we allow ourselves against the utterly alien. I might have been murdered
casually or insofar as I am concerned gone to a fate worse than death,
for one of the first things I heard on awakening, bound stark-naked
over the back of a horse, was discussion of the possibility of *castrating*
me and selling the remains to a slave merchant in Seleucia—obviously a
black marketeer. No more appalling prospect could have prompted me
to action. Mind you, with my face pressed against the odoriferous flanks
of that pony, I said, in Arabic, 'Gentlemen, I shouldn't do that if I were
you. My uncle is a powerful prince in these parts and he will be very
angry.'

"For one reason or another, I had no desire to announce my name or
my station. I can no longer say whether I feared they would be twice as
cruel to me—in that way of the powerless when the powerful come into
their hands (I've never doubted that inclination, whatever fiction other
princes are pleased to live with)—or I feared they would deliver me for
a price to some Danishmend official who, in turn, would imprison me
until I was ransomed by Constantinople. I am even willing to admit I
may have been a little eager for the adventure. I was certain I would be
rescued within a few hours or a day, at most, and equally certain I could
live by my wits until then.

"I suppose with that sort of aristocratic malingering I deserved the
two months which followed. Look how, in a moment, *I* had objectified

my captors. In a fair governancy men are not driven to become thieves, and to a truly sensitive man, a highway robber ought not to be thought picturesque. Shall I be honest with you? The privileged abhor the robber because he will take away what they possess, and the helpless pretend to decry the robber because they have been intimidated or momentarily appeased by the privileged. In truth, the helpless envy the thief who has exercised the final choice left to him by an inequitable society: anarchy, the refusal to live by laws which are the instigation of a few individuals to maintain their good fortune at the cost of most other men's stagnation. I can scarcely say I tolerate the thief—he is a negation, not a solution—but I *do* respect him.

"In any event, my first mistake was underestimating the resources of my captors. They were not henchmen of any aristocrat, but nomads forced to live off their wits, which kept them sharp. They had no real leader and an argument preceded every decision. I calculated that was a real danger. For example, two or three opted at once for death on the logical grounds I was a great oaf (why is it men think only the diminutive are incisive?) who had fallen, without a valuable to justify me, into their hands. In this sort of captainless group I could easily imagine those three showing up their colleagues by killing me in my sleep.

"When I complained of cold, someone threw a mantle—or a blanket—over me. No man was ever privileged to such a stink as that cloth possessed: sweat, grease, semen, old food and the garbage which pours from either end of the human form, bad wine, bad beer, and God knows what other conjuries. On second thought I would have preferred pneumonia to suffocation. But that is what I remember most vividly of the first days: the smells, the filth. Anything you touched seemed to have a layer of viscous dust. At first I was surprised, for I had thought even the poorest Moslem was immaculate as the most hygienic Greek aristocrat, not because they were so inclined, but because Allah so obliged them. When I saw them pantomiming their ablutions before prayer, I understood.

"They took me deeper into the mountains, to their caves which served as a semi-permanent encampment for their women, if wives, and their children. We arrived by dawn and I was thrown, still trussed, into a corner by four men.

"I had never known my body to be so contradictory. I was exhausted and yet alert. I wanted to urinate and I thirsted. I wanted to move my bowels and I was hungry.

"For the first time I began to consider the possibility I might not be rescued. I lay there caught between the vise of two alternative visions. Either I was the subject of intensive search or I had been abandoned. If the first, then I was prepared at any moment for the sounds of commotion at the entrance to the cave—and perhaps my own death. Why not? As these people might be slaughtered in any event, they might take me for company. If the second, then, between surges of hatred for Manuel and envy for those in the world I knew, going on to splendid, ordered futures, I saw myself maimed, sold into slavery, and spending the rest of my life—even ending it—attempting to return to Constantinople to prove who I am and never succeeding—waste, all waste. (In ways I never dreamed, the latter proved all too true, didn't it, Nicetas?) It was my first encounter with personal desolation and, for that, remains the most memorable, if only because its circumstances remain highly colored. As I grew older, colors became grayer and finally monochromatic, the desolation less hysterical, but more oppressive, and the sense of waste, all too real, pervading, overwhelming.

"Heaven knows how many hours passed, but I was awakened from some sort of stupor by giggles and Arabic terms of endearment and a pair of hands stroking my shoulders and waist and buttocks and legs. I opened my eyes to the coarsest, fattest woman I had ever beheld. When she attempted to kiss me on the mouth, I moved away, still trussed, as best I could. No more giggles. She slapped me brutally and nearly lifted me off the ground in an effort to rearrange me more suitably to her intentions. Her object was not intercourse but fellatio, which Moslem women seem to favor. To this day, I've no idea whether the woman believed I possessed dionysiac potency or knew from the beginning what was happening and was delighted to oblige (I've bedded aristocratic girls with stranger practices). In any event she swallowed a whole day's piss, a relief for me almost indistinguishable from orgasm, which I was also willing to give her in sheer gratefulness, save at that moment one of my captors—a deeply tanned little runt with a broken nose and black teeth and one of those small, hard bodies which instantly reminded me of an old mongrel—not pretty, but hardy—entered the cave and began kicking her as she tended me. *He* tossed *her* from the shelter, quite a feat. Then he knelt by me and said, 'Are you all right?'

with more apprehension than concern. No man's beggar, I answered him in kind, 'As well as you allow me to be.' (I must tell you that although we were speaking the same language there was all the difference between his vulgar accent and my pure Sultan's tongue as between vernacular Greek of the Constantinopolitan streets and the Attic speech we affect at court.)"

At this point I reminded Andronikus that legend had it he became friends with his captors and in the ensuing weeks improved their strategies, weaponry, fighting technique, and so forth. (To be quite honest, I repeated these stories to annoy him since the hour was extremely late and though exhausted, I was in the worst possible position: his house guest, who could not retire until dismissed. I have noted that to effectively conclude a ruminative session which really has no beginning or end, but drifts in weight and interest like waves of the sea, one must ride the host from topic untiringly to topic and generally comment monosyllabically until he utters those magic words, "But I've tired you; I must let you go.")

The Grand Duke—the year is 1178—snapped at my rumor-mongering. "That's absurd." Then he smiled. "Attractive, but absurd." I said, "Something like Caesar making friends with the Aegean pirates and all the while promising to return one day and kill them?" Andronikus said, "Which he did—which says little for him." Thirty-six years later the circumstances of his rescue still moved him to grief and anger. "I had nothing to do with that obscenity. And I never quite forgave Stephen Cantacuzenus for what he did. I hadn't become friends with that riffraff, but I pitied them their desolate existence, hand to mouth, and their helpless ignorance which could not break the circle of their misery.

"When the whole South Coast of Lesser Asia was alerted in my behalf and Mas'ud sent in his cavalry, my captors became hunted. I pleaded with them to set me free, for if they were found with me, they would surely suffer terrible consequences. Well, they suffered the true curse of the lower orders: they were their own most abject victims, very stupid and very clever. They suspected I was merely trying to free myself at their expense. I had become their burden and an oriflamme to anyone who discovered us—and yet they would not let me go.

"And then, at last, we were one day caught out. It occurred very uneventfully. A scout simply appeared at the entry to a ravine in which we were encamped. I saw him and warned the others to flee. At that point, of course, it was all too hopeless. They would simply be run down. They bound me with ropes for the first time in weeks, and I thought at first they would present me as a hostage. But something—not honor— heaven knows what—something, perhaps generosity, the lingering of habit which came as close to affection as they might feel, perhaps the fact they were, like all savages, only brutal, not unscrupulous, perhaps kismet moved them, prevented their using me. Like the grim mules they were, they gathered together all their possessions, including myself, and attempted to run.

"Within an hour Stephen was upon us at the head of a mixed cavalry of Greeks and Turks. Their first victim, by an arrow in the back at a hundred yards, was a fine, fat little nine-year-old boy, Ibrim, who'd brought me extra food in the night and generously offered to pick off the lice which had infested my hair in return for tales I told him. Come full circle, I was bent like a sack over the pony I had ridden shortly after capture. Still I shouted like a madman for Stephen's men to stop. Revenge wasn't necessary. I was saved. But the soldiery shoved spears into bellies and ripped them up to the throat; they pierced and hacked and trampled to death forty-two men, women, and children, and when Stephen got to me and found me sobbing, he didn't understand. He just didn't understand.

"I was pleased when the Turks from Iconium insisted on burying the dead. We left the scene of the massacre by late afternoon. I proposed to ride the pony over whose back I'd been slung on those first and last days. Stephen—meaning well, I suppose—offered me his horse. I was adamant; actually I'd grown quite attached to the stinking little beast, whose descendants survive in Philip's stables at Selymbria. Stephen, however, commented, 'It's a horse fit for a beggar.' I asked in all innocence, 'He won't notice the difference, will he?'"

The young Grand Duke was taken at once to Iconium where he recuperated at the palace of his brother and sister-in-law. Two weeks later he set out for Constantinople, stopping for several days at Christos Gennate, which, though maintained and staffed now by the Imperial Steward, had been left to Isaac II in his brother's will. There, Andronikus was reunited with his father and learned why Isaac had taken up residence, "as far as possible from that accursed city." The Grand Duke's surmises may be imagined. There were perfectly logical factors, distinct from one another, for the length of time it took to find him and, on the other hand, his father's cashierment. Yet in his mind the two events became inextricable. Once, when I attempted to reason with him on these points, he nodded and said, "True, possibly true. Probably true, but irrelevant, now. I am what I am today because I believed *then* Manuel had hoped to be rid of me—and *did* rid himself of my father because of—or in—my absence. I never trusted him thereafter. I ascribed to him a duplicity of which, of course, he was incapable."

He returned to Constantinople as a hero. The Emperor, it is said, was beside himself with joy and commanded Te Deums be sung in all the city's churches the morning of his cousin's arrival and himself—unprecedentedly—met the Grand Duke at the Golden Gate. ("I have no doubt," said Andronikus, "of the sincerity of his delight. Only my cousin was too aware of the metaphysical heights from which it came. His presence at the gates was not an impulsive gesture borne on love but one, considered, meant to honor me. It was condescension in the subtlest degree. Sooner a private libation at Rufiniana.")

At once Andronikus was drawn into the splendid, petty life of the reviving court. Implicitly, he was the Imperial favorite and his power should have been enormous. There is not a minister who does not gainfully employ some relation or companion with access to the Emperor in his leisure, when he is most amenable to suggestion and the consent to plans the administrator may have presented for decision weeks or months before. But the Grand Duke's effectiveness as a favorite was mitigated by his own Imperial birth, which allowed him a detachment conducive, at best, to disinterest, at worst, to irony and mischief rather than bribery and errands. Furthermore, his experience with the Taurian brigands, his father's cashierment, but above all that quality of his person which one of his first mistresses described as "a singularity—in the Latin sense of apartness—and a characteristic of certain aspects of nature of awful brightness and beauty which are fatal to touch but must be touched after all," served to make him a most unlikely favorite. Indeed, there were factions, even then, which sought to undo and replace him with a more amenable power broker necessary to a resurgent Imperial court.

"I sometimes wonder," said Andronikus, "if Manuel was not slier than I gave him credit, if it was not his aim, after all, by reconstituting the court to castrate, once and for all, the aristocracy, as any eunuch is cut, and for the same reason: to promise efficient exercise of power without the threat of usurpation. So long as this or that noble fought for position of Protospatar or Protovestarius or fretted because the Grand Chamberlain had not tapped his shoulder the previous week and pronounced those deathless words, which, if there be a hell and I go to it, will ring in my ears, eternally, 'It is His Imperial Majesty's wish that you accompany him on the hunt next Monday,' then my cousin could go about his covetous assumption of all power (which is not my argument, only what he did with it). In any event, I believed I sensed some such reasoning from the beginning and that, along with my instinctive revulsion of the too effusive welcome he had given me, determined me not to debase myself. I knew if I attempted to advise him, he would assume his most disarming air, which seemed to suggest I was disappointing him like all the others, ambitious rather than his consolation. If you please."

He spat into the brazier beside which he sat, one leg settled over the arm of a chair, document in hand. "The poet-essayist Tetzes once told me he found it impossible to create in the midst of physical disorder. Everything—notebooks, references, ink, and paper—must be neatly at hand, every vase, every icon, every chair before his eyes where it ought to be, all errands of his day completed. When I chided him with acting like a punctilious clerk and asked him why, he said in that portentous but sincere way of his—you remember (he was one of your tutors, wasn't he?)—'Because the strain of creating out of spiritual chaos is great enough without the distraction of physical chaos before me. There is a balance so small it is scarcely to be believed between the winning and the loss of an original thought. In that moment when it arrives out of a sea of impressions, out of the void, as it were, more a feeling than an articulation, the difference between its escape and leashing to words may be as small as the silent interruption of remarking a chair out of place.' Well, Nicetas, God knows, the true artist is the closest thing men have to gods, and I consent to whatever processes or eccentricities they practice in order to create. But for a ruler, Manuel or myself, order—real or imagined—merely lack of contention of sycophancy—is not only luxury; too much of it may make a man downright morally flabby or falsely secure. It behooves a regent's sense of discipline to teach himself to function in antagonism—indeed, he will be the more incisive for it—to function in a madhouse, if necessary.

"Well, my cousin created the madhouse, all right, an extravaganza to shame any event which takes place in the Hippodrome, to wit: Blachernae. But no sooner was it blessed and occupied in 1150 than he locked all the doors and the gates against the world and proceeded to rule an empire from the aspects of Philopation Park. I find it significant Blachernae was impregnable to riot. That is to say, it was impregnable to any man's opinion but its overlord's."

What neither young man seemed to understand—with all of Aesop's blindness and none of his insight—was that those qualities which had attracted Manuel to Andronikus, initially, now estranged him. Independence, revolutionary ideals are exciting and lovable in an equal. In a subject, however, Manuel believed a difference of opinion implied supplanting, as many a man, unsure of himself, believes a beautiful, intelligent woman designs only to humiliate him.

In the matter of Manuel's forgiveness, Andronikus was, it is not too much to say, self-centered, the consequence of his intellect and his pride. His sense of personal justice was belligerent. Thwarted once, he was beyond compensation. His nearly four-decade confrontation with Manuel was the first example of this characteristic, to wit: he would have made a better Emperor than his cousin; Manuel knew it; he knew Manuel knew it, and it was Manuel's obligation to forgive him, since it was Manuel—unwilling to use him, unwilling to seek his advice, much less crown him Co-Augustus—who was ruining him, a great wrong for which the Emperor must pay and pay, in all things, great and little.

So between these two there existed till death and beyond it, an overwhelming, indissoluble fascination, as feline beasts in confrontation across an abyss beneath a starry night, uncertain of what they see, are yet helplessly fixed in their attraction toward one another.

III

Bertha-Irene presented—for Manuel alone—a clear problem which he solved very clumsily. With his accession to the throne, his betrothal now possessed enormous implications, as the Emperor Conrad's first letter was quick to point out. "Let it be a sign of the unity between the two Empires and the two Houses of Hohenstaufen and Comnenus, that you soon marry my wife's dearest heart and sister and recognize thereby the permanence of our alliance, of constant friendship, and I will love who loves you and call my enemy who calls you his, arriving at your side, sword in hand, with all the forces of the West Empire to assist you."

We may only suppose why Manuel on receipt of the letter—of which the above is an excerpt—did not proceed to marriage and consummate it at once. Instead suddenly propelled into responsibility—personal and political—for a policy and a marriage initiated by his father—the latter accepted none too happily by himself—he delayed as Conrad had once delayed.

"I suspect," said Andronikus, "his reasons were emotional which he, as monarch, could disguise as diplomatic. Absurdly, he dared to question our alliance against Sicily. He scarcely seemed to recognize—or willfully would *not* recognize—that in his very assumption, the whole world had shifted, save where it was *most* advantageous: in Conrad's willingness to maintain the Alliance of the Two Empires. When my uncle died, he died the greatest general in all Europe and the Levant, dreaded by King Roger and Prince Zengi alike. Our entente cordiale with Germany—the very cornerstone of my uncle's and my father's last years—was not merely a weapon against Sicily, but against ever-feckless Hungary, while we confronted Palestine and Mosul. When Fulk died a few months after John—and with him the only responsible Latin prince averse Zengi—it was all the more imperative to protect our northern and northwest flank should the need arise to march east."

Fulk's death, like John's—perhaps more so—could not have arrived at a less propitious time. His generalship and his person gave meaning, in turn, to the alliance between Jerusalem and Damascus which comprised the Jordan River Watch, before which even Zengi hesitated. The King's heir, his eldest son, Baldwin III, was but thirteen years old at his father's death—an exquisite youth, now winsome, now grave, with a mind the delight of his tutors, and, even so young, of a grace and chivalry which brought tears of joy to his father's vassals. Yet no force on earth could anticipate his majority or prevent the damage which might be done in between by the Dowager Queen Mother and her charmless cousin, counselor and Constable, Manasses of Hierges.

In sum, Manuel was now alone in the East by virtue of his exalted position and its attendant responsibilities. Acting on these advantages, in the late summer of 1144, Zengi marched and laid siege on Edessa.

Now, in the years since the first Latin occupation of Palestine and

North Mesopotamia the native Orthodox and Moslem populations had come to accept their Norman overlords and were prepared to resist the enemy in behalf of West Christian princes. For a month previous to the Edessan siege, our redoubtable Joscelin had had information to the effect of Zengi's intent against his domains, and yet, incredibly, he neither provisioned nor garrisoned his capital nor even informed his Constable until a week before the Governor's army appeared. Meanwhile he took his pleasures at Turbessel Palace, his favorite retreat. William of Tyre once suggested to me his own theory that, on the contrary, Joscelin was not irresponsible, but too scrupulous. According to William, Joscelin hesitated to risk the native population in defense of the Latins. But that, for me, is the specious thinking of a military chaplain. Citizen defense—as it is willing—knows its own limitations, is more apt to follow orders than the veteran who too self-confidently knows his own business and by its very nature, engenders an enthusiasm, a staying power, which is enormous. Indeed, when the Mosul Prince established his siege before Edessa's mighty walls, the population so proved this, manning the battlements in a sublime display of unity and courage. And it was only when the siege was begun that Joscelin, still at Turbessel, had the presence of mind to send ambassadors to Antioch and Jerusalem.

At Antioch, we may note, Raymond, Joscelin's erstwhile colleague during the Johannine episodes, turned up empty hands, cold-bloodedly refusing aid and expressing the good hope "his cousin might rot in the hell he's made for himself," as though the wisdom of the ages had coursed through Raymond and gone unheeded in Joscelin. (When Edessa fell, and Raymond, in consequence, was next to be threatened, he informed his fellow princes he had not gone to Joscelin's rescue because the Count, in favoring the native population—a small portion of which, he did not add, were Moslems—had himself become an infidel and unworthy of "pious, Frankish swords.")

At Jerusalem the reception was, at once, more earnest and more sympathetic. The Dowager Queen, herself born in Edessa, was eager to be of help. Unfortunately, her Constable had so profoundly offended her barons, which is to say, the army, she was weeks, instead of moments, convincing them the fall of her native county was a common alarum for Latin Catholicism in the Levant. Even then, only a few hundred knights volunteered for the venture. More astonishing still, the

Jerusalemites did not start north till mid-November, rested three weeks at Tripolis, where they were feted as heroes, and did not arrive at Edessa until 18 December 1144, the day the city fell and was given over to a week's sack and carnage. At this tragic news the Knights of the Kingdom of the Holy Sepulcher, who were never closer than three miles to the walls, simply turned round and marched home covering the same five hundred miles in eight days, whereas previously it had taken them forty.

On 26 December 1144 the Governor-Prince of Mosul entered the gates of Edessa, formerly the bellwether between Constantinople and the Moslems, fulfilling now a similar function between the Moslems and the Latins. The first significant Frankish city had fallen to the East.

What followed was exemplary. Zengi commanded the pillage to cease and returned all fixed property to its rightful owners—if, indeed, they were still alive. He freed all prisoners, made compensation to those who had thought themselves ruined, and, in a speech read in his presence by his herald to the assembled citizens, guaranteed all civil rights, including the freedom to worship as any man pleased. The Jacobite Metropolitan, Basil bar Shumana, the only man of rank present, accepted these guarantees for the Count. By these means Zengi intended to prove to a generation of Syrians who had known only Latin rule and Latin tales of Moslem atrocity that Allah was indeed as merciful as Jesus. And even did he fail to convince new followers of the submission, he certainly proved himself in all ways superior to that morbid incompetent, Joscelin, who fled fifty miles northeast to the west bank of the Euphrates where one of his few strongholds remained.

"The news of Edessa arrived at Constantinople the same night Anastasia miscarried our first child. It was an extraordinarily harrowing time for me," Andronikus remembered. "Manuel had given us Hieriea Palace on our marriage—that really *was* from the heart because he knew it so close to mine. In the evening he came across the Bosporus to dine with us privately. Or very nearly. He brought along with him Cosmas to bless my wife's womb. That was tantamount to risk emptying it before term. Anastasia despised Cosmas and so did I. There was not a trace of charity in the man, nothing but the cold eye of the careerist cast upon the Christian poor, who somehow had no right to hunger in such stark contrast to his sumptuous dinners at St. Michael's Palace or wear such rags as did not complement his patriarchal vestments. A true Christian snob: one for whom sin was a matter of bad taste. Ah, but among princes and dukes, and especially that night in the bosom of the Imperial family, he glowed—in that same repellent way mushrooms glow on a rotting trunk after a rain. His smile was the same smile I've seen on Egyptian pederasts.

"Well, we were halfway through a strained dinner—thanks to Cosmas —when Anastasia, her belly blessed and probably revolted, turned white as chalk. Two of her ladies-in-waiting helped her from the refectory, and an hour later, a boy was born dead, placenta previa. Sometimes I fill the air with what that child might have been.

"While we waited outside Stana's lying-in, most of the General Staff arrived with news of Edessa. It was a hideous shock for us all. Though I personally cared little whether the province was claimed by pagan Russians or the fish of the Caspian Sea—it had always been traditionally Christian even if of a heretical bent. During the worst invasions of the last century, it had never surrendered or been captured. Now this; quite disheartening. Cosmas, of course, at once pronounced it the judgment of a righteous God, at which Manuel cleared his throat and suggested the Patriarch return to St. Michael's and pray before the most revered icon of battles, the Hodigitrea, or as I like to call her, Our Holy Mother of War. I should have gone, myself, to sit with my wife. Instead, I believed that in the importance of the moment and the fact decisions would be made under my roof, my cousin would see fit to include me in what amounted to a meeting of the Praetorium.

"So, while my poor wife lay ravished in her apartment, I sat for three hours with His Majesty and my friends, who in private life otherwise hung on my every word. Each time I attempted to offer advice I was granted the polite indifference due an exalted nonentity."

I commented how unlike him this was. "Yes, my dear boy, but you must remember, I was still young then. I was even foolish and sentimentally devious enough to believe my cousin and my friends would have pity on a man who'd just lost his firstborn and attempt to distract me with attention. Once or twice, when Manuel suggested an expeditionary force to Edessa, Stephen Cantacuzenus and Alexius Bryennius even looked my way, for they knew I had argued—futilely—precisely to this policy the previous autumn, and only changed my mind when it appeared none of the Latin states would complement us with their own numbers.

"I've no idea why that particular night struck me as any greater a humiliation than the previous nineteen months. Perhaps it was the entire luckless day: the loss of the child, this unconscionable waste of time when I should have been with my wife, and the usual official insensibility extended to me, when I dared to speak with the prerogative of a grandson of Alexius Augustus. In any event, I waited until Manuel was speaking and then, with purposeful rudeness, stood up and said, 'If Your Majesty will excuse me, I must attend my wife.'

"As I was leaving, I was certain I heard John-Roger mumble, 'Not true; he's simply had to piss for hours like the rest of us—lucky man.' There was a little laughter, very soft, and on that I stood stock-still. I anger not at all now. But when I was young—ah, there, you never saw such eruption. Nothing mattered, least of all Imperial etiquette. The silence which waited on my turning was the first pleasant vengeance. From what I know of my grandfather, he would have let such an incident stand and proceeded from the room, leaving his antagonist to consider what vengeance he would pursue. Instead, I rushed over to an ancient shield with its brightly polished cross swords, pulled the weapons from their hooks, and tossed one of them to John-Roger. This is of course the greatest possible offense one can make in the presence of the Sovereign, and several of the generals rose, admonishing me, either annoyedly or plainly traumatized by my *lèse majesté*. John-Roger looked down at the sword as though some particularly repellent animal had died by his chair.

"'Pick it up,' I said. 'Pick it up, you perfidious bastard. I know all about you.' Manuel rose and said, 'Andronikus, that's enough. You've lost your senses.' When John-Roger did not move—now that I think of it, he seemed not so much pusillanimous as superbly in control of his own temper, which only made me the angrier—I dashed at him and slashed the arm of his robe. Several people attempted to grab me, but I wielded the sword in huge arcs. That was it. With the most hideous shout of animal anger I've ever heard out of man, the Caesar grabbed the sword and started for me. There were cries of 'Oh no' and 'Madness.' Well, we got as far as crossing the swords when Manuel leaped from his chair and while the others warned him, came up to us, and with those incredible arms and hands spanned the space between us, grabbed both our wrists, then twisted and squeezed them mightily until we dropped the weapons.

"Do you know what my first emotion was? Rank envy. It was a superb and courageous response to the crude and dangerous act of a child, namely myself. It would appear I deserved other men's indifference, and in a world of appearances, this is all that matters. I lifted my cousin's hand, kissed it, and left without his dismissal." *Explicit: Nicetas Acominatus.*

Andronikus moves down the length of Hieriea's reception hall—the largest till Blachernae—across a floor of mosaic medallions—eagles, dragons, peacocks, aurochs, stags, and ancient barbarian faces—between huge, soaring columns of red malachite—defining the nave and side aisles—at the foot of which are enormous vases of turquoise faience, now empty, but filled with flowers in season. Twenty-five yards behind him a servant chases a cat-sized rat which he smashes with a shovel. None of the attendants about their tasks or the master of the palace turn on the sound as the man scoops up the rodent's carcass and leaves the hall. As Andronikus ascends the staircase of silver-striated white marble and blue, he is stopped by one of his wife's ladies, one of those elderly, plump yet still petite and highly excitable relics of an earlier age, whom someone almost married. At a distance, despite perfect acoustics, her words are incomprehensible, no more than a series of rapid squeaks followed by Andronikus' exceptionally smooth and pleasant tenor. After a few moments he pats the woman's shoulder and pulling back, not lifting, the skirts of his deep blue, silver whipped robe, continues up the stairwell, his boots making a short shuffling sound against the stone. He descends a long corridor, its walls of angels and prophets against a field of gold, his feet crossing marble, then intricately patterned carpets which in West Europe are still too exorbitant for any display but upon a wall. At a set of gold and red lacquered doors, he knocks. They are opened inward by one of his wife's Georgian girls, who, after nearly twenty years' residence at Constantinople, is Greek as any member of the court —and more so.

ANDRONIKUS. Is Her Highness awake?

LADY-IN-WAITING. Yes, Your Highness. She has asked for you several times, but I told her you were with the Emperor. Your Highness, is it true about Edessa? But how terrible.

ANDRONIKUS. Not so terrible. The worst has passed.

LADY-IN-WAITING. I was there, once, as a child. Strange to think it in the hands of Saracens.

She crosses herself and waits for Andronikus to do the same. He does not.

ANDRONIKUS. It's still a free city. What have they done to the child?

LADY-IN-WAITING. Madame's confessor, Father Andrew, is holding a service. He will be buried in the chapel vault.

ANDRONIKUS. Very good. Go and tell them to wait until I arrive.

LADY-IN-WAITING. Will you receive the Host?

Andronikus grants her a look both familiar and wry, then passes through a set of silver doors into Anastasia's suite. She is attended by a midwife and two nuns.

ANDRONIKUS. Please go. The Princess and I would like to be alone.

Anastasia stares at her husband, her eyes glittering in the half-light, but passively, more of a sickly shine than the expression of inner life. When the doors close she lifts her head once to settle it more comfortably and speaks to the wall opposite the foot of her silver and quartz bedstead.

ANASTASIA. The Princess has *been* alone since before midnight. And you were with the Little Dragon, I was told. For what? How did he humiliate you this time?

ANDRONIKUS. Stupid to talk about it. I drew a sword on John-Roger.

She turns her head away, disheartened. Andronikus seats himself on the bed and takes his wife's hand.

ANASTASIA. I could have hoped the boy had lived if only to spite Manuel.

ANDRONIKUS. I quote Augustine, "To confess that God exists and at the same time to deny that he has foreknowledge of future things is the most manifest folly." Perhaps He heard you and struck down the infant.

ANASTASIA. Don't be blasphemous. He has mightier enemies and means than a baby's death as the instrument of revenge against a fool like me.

He leans forward and kisses Anastasia's cheek, his expression suffused with sympathy and charm, to which his wife responds with a grateful look of her eyes and a hesitant smile.

ANDRONIKUS. Are you in pain?

ANASTASIA. None at all. I feel like a peasant. Will you do something for me, Andronikus?

ANDRONIKUS. Anything in the world. What shall it be?

ANASTASIA. Take this icon from my neck. Put it with the child.

ANDRONIKUS. Why do such a thing? It was your mother's. You treasure it.

She raises her head and lifts the back of her hair for him to loosen the clasp.

ANASTASIA. Because he nearly lived. He breathed a few moments. Because we'll scarcely remember him and he's died without a name, and abandoned. This morning he was warm in my belly and now they're using crowbars to pry apart stones so that we can put him in the cold dark. I hadn't the time to love him, only the idea of bearing him. Let him take something into the grave which I treasure. Let me feel the pull back to him; let me feel there is something here I have left behind which meant so much to me.

He loosens the clasp and pulls away the gold icon.

Incipit: Nicetas Acominatus: ". . . Later, as I entered the chapel for the burial service I found a coldly polite Manuel, Stephen and the Bryennii and Helena's husband, Anemas, being somewhat more sympathetic. Father Andrew, my wife's confessor, sang the service. I think besides Kamaterus, he is the only priest I ever cared for personally. By that I mean, of course, as a man beyond his habit, not as priest among priests. But what a world away from my indomitable and recherché Patriarch. He was a Georgian and old, when he accompanied Anastasia, as a child, to Constantinople. He was little and wizened and white with the most serene face I have ever beheld, more than childlike, for no child's face is ever serene—except the ill. He had a way of looking up at me, his head a little to one side, those brilliant blue eyes absolutely uncorrupted, his lips in a half smile to which I could not but respond in kind. When I would say to him, 'You know what a sinner I am. You mustn't waste your old bones upon me,' he would say, 'God loves you and I love you too, Prince,' and I would reply, lifting my eyes for a moment, 'As for that, I can't be certain I love what is for me undefined, but I love you very much, Father, as does my wife.'

"And I did. One wonders how a man arrives at such beatitude. Mere passivity is a ride to corruption or indifference. What was he like as a child? What did he suffer to retain such purity in a failing world as ours? I don't think it was willful blindness, which is the defense of hypocrites such as Cosmas. Perhaps it is living long enough to become patient. In any event, it pleased me Cosmas had been dismissed earlier in the evening, for he would have superseded Andrew and defiled the infant in the short, dead space between his mother's womb and the grave."

I asked Andronikus, I remember, if Manuel spoke to him after the service. "Only the most perfunctory consolation. Then he left at once aboard his yacht and crossed the Bosporus to the European side. The next weekend, however, Bertha arrived—ostensibly to visit with Anastasia, of whom she had grown very fond. But she insisted I stay by her side and talked with me at length, with both of us, and so I knew she had been sent by Manuel, which quite amazed me since he had scarcely anything to do with her. To use her even in a semi-official capacity was to renew speculation of imminent marriage, even though he had already begun that great alliance with his niece, Alexius' eldest, Elizabeth Persephone, whom you knew in the considerably less notorious, more austere guise of the Duchess Branas." *Explicit: Nicetas Acominatus.*

IV

Incipit: Nicetas Acominatus: It was Manuel's decision to reinforce the east border. The Praetorium consented to this wisdom, and to its effect several regiments and another army of engineers were dispatched from Constantinople in March 1145.

Andronikus: "I would have concurred in the garrisoning of East Asia, save Stephen let me see the reports of our agents at Edessa. Said el-Din, the Emir's eldest son, and according to rumor an immensely decent sort, had been appointed Governor-General by his father. This was most wise if Zengi was serious about implementing a truly clement policy in all reconquered cities. The appointment is to be taken as evidence he was.

"Manuel did not want war, but he wanted a show of strength, which is rather like confronting one gang of toughs with another in the hope the aspect of challenge will give them pause. In the challenge is an implicit insult of inferiority, and thereby, war is bound to occur. If my cousin meant strategy on the side of peace, he should have been more discreet, less public. Perhaps I ought not to give him the credit for such breathtaking deviousness, but the thought occurred when he appointed me second-in-command to Cantacuzenus, he might mean to sacrifice me, meanwhile silencing my complaints of inactivity. Ah, but that's too convoluted and self-centered even for my way of thinking.

"As I finally had access to him *officially*—with this campaign I was made a member of the Imperial General Staff—I told him to send an ambassador to Iconium and inform Mas'ud of his intentions. He declined. It would have been well had he not. Certainly it would have prevented the insanity which took place at the end of the year. The Shah was under great pressure from his generals at the time. I know this from my brother's letters which I showed to Manuel. One can understand their fears. They were surrounded by a Byzantine sea, and they bordered, as did we, the County of Edessa. They were confronting, moreover, a new Emperor, whom they did not yet know how to trust, and suffering that curious anxiety—almost irascibility, almost paranoia—of a new generation of military, born, trained, and matured throughout a long period of tranquillity. For these Seljuk generals, a Byzantine army flanking them north and south, might just as likely turn on them, which, in truth, is what happened. Highly significant, is it not, that nearly twenty-nine years of peace between Iconium and Constantinople ended within the first twenty-nine months of my cousin's reign?"

Andronikus had neglected to mention why a defensive measure degenerated into an offensive war. No sooner had the support troops left Constantinople than Manuel invited to his capital the Danishmend Emir to initiate a formal peace, which had never been accomplished between the two states. He was seeking, on his own initiative, and without consulting the Foreign Ministry, something like a diplomatic coup. It has never been made clear whether or not he intended to include Iconium in what should have been, by all logic, a tripartite pact, since the Sultanate was by far the larger of the two Turk states in Lesser Asia. It does explain why he refused to allow Andronikus to inform Mas'ud of his intentions on the east border. What followed was a quite classic—and fatal—misunderstanding. The Shah, as Andronikus pointed out, was being urged by his generals to mobilize his own troops. When the Danishmend Emir, traditionally Iconium's enemy, arrived at Constantinople, the final argument snapped into place for the Seljuk militarists. It was then this most pacific Shah gave the order his own frontiers should be manned, and it was only a matter of time before skirmish began between Byzantines and the army of Iconium.

Andronikus: "I did everything I possibly could to maintain discipline, but it was my first command. I was still learning. Cantacuzenus was all along the east borders with engineers, repairing old fortresses and establishing new ones, so day-to-day activities were left at my discretion. I even considered decimating the ranks if so much as one Greek should be proved to have attacked a Turk—any Turk, in uniform or out of it. The situation was pure tinder.

"Finally, on my own, I wrote to my brother Michael, enclosing a letter to Mas'ud, swearing to him by all he considered holy, we had no designs against him, that I was at a loss to explain Manuel's entertainment of the Danishmends, but I could assure him it involved no betrayal of the 'constant, sacred understanding between the people of New Rome and the Seleucid Kingdom.' For all I knew of Mas'ud, he may have believed me. But his generals were onto the scent, much too eager to take advantage of appearances. They gainsaid him. They desired to win back the lands we had in turn re-claimed from them, while many of our own Imperial General Staff were of a mind to make a final drive against the Turks and sweep them altogether from the face of Lesser Asia.

"I must tell you I was frantic because war seemed so inevitable. I knew if it began it would take a generation to end the round-robin gestures of attack and revenge. Every attempt I made to prevent it was contested at every turn. Have you ever noticed how militarists acquire a glazed eye—if not a glazed brain—in the time just previous to holocaust? They will accept no logic but that which confirms their own arguments, which is the end of their own ambitions and fears. All men move toward the doom of war in a trance. All those errors which lead to hostilities possess the inevitability of insanity.

"What was necessary to prevent this breakdown was decisive action at the top, *rule* from the men who were consecrated to rule—and never mind the nonsense about the honor of the state, on one hand, or a regent's reputation on the other. But Mas'ud was old and distracted. And Manuel was young and eager to put my uncle's overwhelming reputation behind him. The sources from which I sought championship were as dry and introverted as their lackeys. I was made at instead from all sides. Unbeknownst to me, Stephen had written to Manuel complaining I was destroying the morale of the troops, which was true rather more of the officers itching for battle and advancement. As for the common soldiers: I believed they really liked me. I went among them. I was honest. I did not condescend to them and I did not allow them to become too familiar—not because I looked down upon them but because there is a line of discipline I myself found difficult to maintain with those I knew too well. It is twice as hard to send a friend to the forefront of battle as it is hard enough to send a stranger—to affect a life so momentously.

("By the way, one morning, outside my pavilion, my guards found the carcass of a dog decapitated so swiftly and violently its feet were still in running posture. I knew to the last man the captains who committed this charmless barbarity. I also knew they would have me believe it significant of the discontent of the NCOs or the infantry.)

"At any rate, a copy of my letter to Mas'ud was forwarded to Manuel. How it was come by I have no idea—probably spies he had set on me from the beginning. For those pains I received no answer from the Shah but a very lengthy rebuke from my cousin reminding me diplomacy was his initiative, not mine. I was merely his servant, free to act only within the constraints he had set for me. It was the most frank and harshly worded document he ever sent to me." Andronikus smiled. "At least he never put anything of the sort in writing again.

"I saw no point in changing my tactics. To be perfectly honest, in the end, it was not logic, but plain stubbornness. There were several border skirmishes—and, of course, the men were allowed to defend themselves, though I was at pains to discover who initiated the attack and to punish any Imperial soldier so at fault.

"About two weeks after Manuel's first letter there was a major battle —it simply swelled—on the westernmost Cilician border. I relied, believe me, on my aides, far more experienced in strategy than myself, until Cantacuzenus arrived. At length, we were victorious and I wanted to release the prisoners as a gesture of goodwill toward Iconium. 'If we do return them,' Stephen said to me, 'they'll go back to Iconium as did the Bulgarians to Samuel under Basil II—with one eye to every nineteen blind.' At the beginning of April, when Stephen departed for another inspection tour, I freed the Turks, twenty eyes to every ten men, and told them, in their own tongue, to inform Mas'ud, it was Manuel Augustus' desire for peace between the Seljuk and Roman states, as peace had previously existed between us these past three decades.

"Of course, I was challenged by my aides, by anyone in the least official capacity, and for one of the few times in my life, I insisted upon my blooded prerogatives as the grandson of an emperor and son of a sebastocrator, to maintain both discipline and silence. Of course, no sooner had my critics obeyed me than messengers were off to Stephen and to Manuel, and within a week I received a letter—no, a note—from my cousin, curtly demanding my resignation and ordering me to return to Christos Gennate—not Hieriea, Christos Gennate—until further notice.

"I remember as I was leaving the camp an old foot soldier—he must have been in his fifties—stopped me and said, 'Prince, I know what you're trying to do, I know, and let me tell you, your grandpa would approve. I fought under him at Damalis. I know. He'd approved.' I can't tell you, Nicetas, how this warmed me. I thanked him and grasped his shoulder, refusing to let him kneel, and took his name like a proper general. Usually, of course, these names are thrown away no sooner than a man is out of sight. But I've never done that. As soon as it is in my power I return a kindness. I sent this old veteran an icon—very small, you could hold it in your hand—of cloisonné and pearls, which was in the room at Christos Gennate my grandfather had occupied as a boy. I also saw to it he got a cash bonus which I knew the poor fellow would squander. At least I hoped he would. Every man deserves one turn at profligacy."

Throughout the spring, Andronikus "festered" at Christos Gennate. He was allowed to come to Constantinople only once, and then, not to the court, but directly to Holy Wisdom for the funeral of his aunt, Anna, who had to all intents died, really, twenty years before when forced to take the veil. Yet she was a Porphyriogeneta, had been betrothed to a Co-Augustus, and had remained a Caesarissa until her death, which must be followed by Imperial obsequies.

"How ironic it shall be," said Andronikus when he allowed me to examine the original manuscript of the *Alexiad,* left to him by Manuel Augustus, "if she, the most forgotten of Alexius' children at the end, shall, through this, be the best remembered." "Even above the Comnenus Emperors?" I asked. "Why not? What is a ruler but a caretaker, and an empire but the day-to-day administration of municipal services, one solution forgotten as quickly as the next problem arises. When we are gone and this Empire is dust and ruins, there will still be the word, this word." I complained of his aunt's inaccuracies, her self-serving, her misrepresentation of John II—or rather, her lack of presentation, whatsoever. "An abominable diatribe," I said. "She caught something of my grandfather, nevertheless." I said I doubted that beside Alexius' own memoirs, which Andronikus had even then begun to edit. "But if we hadn't the *Muses,* something of the same man shines through this. The autobiography, moreover, will be suspect because no one shall believe its objectivity. Here, however, is someone else's word, my aunt's against my grandfather's. For now, hers is the last word because it is, in effect, the *only* word."

On 12 April 1145 a lightly armed Turk company—escorting tax revenues to Iconium—was set upon by Byzantine soldiery, plundered, and slaughtered. In retaliation the Seljuks attacked an Imperial regiment—"stationed like a child's taunt" (Andronikus)—at Lake of the Forty Martyrs. Of two hundred men, twenty-five survived for ransom. On 23 May, Manuel declared a state of hostility against Mas'ud and marched on Iconium at the head of an army of fifty thousand.

In one of our last conversations before his murder, Andronikus said to me, "Beyond the unacceptability of Manuel's Turkish venture in the mid-forties in terms of failed common sense or visible result, save the conditioning of our people to a perpetual state of war which would culminate in the ultimate disaster of Myriokephalum, there is another point to be made, by far more significant. As he passed through Asia, adored by the peasantry, confirming him in the belief he could do most anything and emerge unblamed and unshaken, I happen to know he was planning legislation favorable to the aristocracy vis-à-vis land tenure, which is to say, precisely *against* those same poor souls in the dust by the side of the road which led to Iconium. It has always seemed pathetic to me his wars were so popular amongst the poor. I suppose the Turks were someone for them to hate—a diversion from their own misery and the real villains: the aristocrats from whom there was no recourse.

"Well, while I hunted the preserves at Christos Gennate, accused, so it was reported to me, of cowardice for not joining my cousin in Holy War, Manuel reached and captured the suburbs of your native city. He was actually that close to total conquest when he made, I should say, the mistake of his lifetime. The famous false agent was captured and informed a General Staff—so amazed by its success it had become anxious rather than daring—of oncoming reinforcements, whereupon my cousin too readily pulled back several miles, a strategic error neither my grandfather nor my uncle would have committed. Of course, by leaving Iconium uncaptured, the possibilities of peace, and a quick one, were facilitated. This was more than ever necessary when the real thing broke upon us: rumor of a new Crusade, soon to leave West Europe for the East."

At Iconium—this, previous to the taking of the suburbs without the walls; in fact, the direct inspiration for that onslaught—there occurred what John-Roger, no partisan of Andronikus, once called the most thrilling moment of his life.

On the third morning of battle, as the Turk line was drawn up facing south, and the Greek line, facing them, north, in the perfect, terrible silence before the order to advance, Andronikus appeared—"from nowhere, out of thin air," as Manuel later described it—took the sword and shield of the first Imperial cavalryman he encountered, and before anyone could stop him—if anyone tried to—rode up to the space between the two armies and challenged the Turk generals to personal combat. When none accepted he called his father's former protector a lily served by eunuchs and Allah, the god of women. Finally one general accepted his challenge.

Both men dismounted, the Seljuk suddenly dwarfed by the tremendous size of the Grand Duke. Perhaps realizing the absurdity of the sight— and later judgment of its fairness—Andronikus called for a second Turk. Emboldened by his colleague's acceptance, another general appeared. John-Roger says Manuel was beside himself "with jealousy, fury, apprehension, and awe." The duel, two to one, lasted only a few minutes. When it was over, both Turks lay dead where they fought, and the Imperial army was hysterical with admiration, bouncing their standards, their icons, clattering shield and spear together, tossing their helmets sky-high, and chanting the name in rhythm of Alexius Augustus' youngest grandson. Andronikus rode up to the soldier from whom he had borrowed the shield and sword and returned both without a word. In the tumult, the cavalryman, now the envy of his brothers with such "sanctified" weapons, kissed the sword's pommel before the Grand Duke's eyes. Andronikus, who, by the way, had all along been insolently garbed in leather hunting dress, not battle mail, then passed along the front ranks of the line and approached his cousin. As the Grand Duke dismounted, so too, to the delight of the army, did the Emperor, an unparalleled honor, even for a kinsman. Andronikus embraced Manuel and, according to John-Roger, seemed to be in tears. "In all the shouting

I couldn't possibly hear what they were saying, but all at once, Manuel was talking very quickly, attempting, obviously, to convince him of something. More than once Andronikus looked back at the two corpses lying in the great space between the armies and his expression was most woebegone."

Andronikus: "Plato speaks of the big lie, and the bigger the better. His implication seems to be, people will accept—even against all logic—mendacity from their leaders because government is their only recourse from anarchy, and it is more consoling to believe in what seems unlikely than to accept the enormous malice and consequent irresponsibility of a state suffering under the heel of corruption and untruth. A similar suspension of judgment—though less maliciously initiated—takes place in the acceptance of the dramatic gesture, which may otherwise seem whimsical, or else intolerable, especially in a prince, who uses the spectators' reaction toward a calculated effect. As for the great to-do I caused at Iconium: it was as puerile and crass as the audience which saw it as noble and the war which brought them together. It was a frankly political gesture, as any of the careerists could have told you—probably infuriated—but one so accurately aimed at the body of the army, I became their hero and inviolable. All to the good, since, with my conduct vis-à-vis Mas'ud, as well my freeing of the Seljuk prisoners, I had shown myself to be, if not antimilitaristic, then exceedingly selective in which ventures I believed we should become involved.

"There was another reason the archons were beginning to range against me, however. War was their means of barter with Manuel—the more of it, the better. To that end, Manuel would require huge levies of men which the military nobility would gladly supply so long as my cousin increased their power over the peasants and concomitantly decreased their taxes.

"Insofar as the civilian aristocracy, I was not much more kindly tolerated, because in the public mind I was beginning to emerge as a real alternative to Manuel. This was a comparison not easy to suffer: either among the Grandees who knew my views on a lavish court, or the Imperial confidants who depended upon my cousin's rigid definition of aloof autocracy to maintain their own influence.

"At Iconium, in any event, all went perfectly—more so than I had dared hope—save the second Seljuk general to enter the field against me was Prince Ishmail, whom I had known and trained with when he was a divinely laughing, witty youth and I, an exile at Iconium. Did he recognize me? If so, why did he step forward? His face before I killed him—a kind of unearthly irony—will haunt me to the end of my days. But Fortune left me no choice. As she has always favored Manuel she has abominated me—the only woman I have never been able to seduce. I have since told myself the contribution Ishmail should have given his state, and that, I to mine, made a necessity of his death. But that sort of hindsight really won't do at all. I think of us as boys and wonder what we should have thought one bright afternoon at play had a seer told us: 'One day you will meet each other to the death.' "

The Emperor returned to Constantinople with the plunder of several cities and the name of his cousin on every man's lips. In every way, both baggage were controversial. Alexius and John Augustus were exceedingly wary of the policy of sack. Most often they expected to reincorporate into the Empire whatever city they took; hence to leave behind a smoking, pillaged hulk—Roman soldiers sated, native citizens burning with resentment—was, in the long run, politically too expensive. Manuel has often been criticized for bankrupting the Byzantine Empire in the gratification of his own personal pleasures. This is egregiously unfair. But it is well—and no less unfortunate—to point out this Autocrat of the most civilized society on earth, breaking his grandfather's and father's precedent in allowing his men to pillage wherever they conquered, added considerably to the state's financial burden as he was obliged to rebuild whatever he re-claimed.

The second problem with which the Emperor returned to his capital was, like the first, to remain with him, throughout his reign: his cousin, publicly and impulsively forgiven and for that stronger than before. Yet to Manuel's amazement, Andronikus seemed not to challenge him, but rather relinquish himself—unenviably, save among those who care for these things—to the role of the city's leading bon vivant, fashion plate, trend-setter, party-goer and party-giver. At length Manuel may have believed Andronikus chastised by the previous year and tamed. The Emperor was suspicious, but he was, at length, appeased.

Once when I asked the Grand Duke Philip of this absurdly wasted period of his youngest brother's life, he smiled and said, "Wasted? Waste, my dear fellow, is a matter of choice. You may decide between these two explanations. Either Andronikus had no choice, or he never for a moment acted without calculation. 'Behold the deep Greek,' as my uncle once said to him, or of him, I don't know. Perhaps for that time of desuetude, there is no answer, or one so subtle we shall never know it. The best *I* can offer you as an explanation—beside the fact my brother has never been above pleasure no matter how errant, or basking in popularity, adoration, from any source—is that he may have hoped to ingratiate himself with my cousin as a magnificent nonentity, and in Manuel's disarming, influence him less obviously." The Grand Duke shook his head: "He's too profound for a meaningless life, a life which is not useful, which does not test him. There's always been a power in him too immense to tolerate void. Like water, he seeks to fill whatever space he occupies. A great man forced to act the great nullity, forced to become a great nullity.

"Have you ever noticed how he listens to people? There is a stillness and a silence about him, a readiness to absorb, so absolute you feel yourself quite stupid or presumptuous if you haven't something to say commensurate with his attention. And if you haven't, when you're finished, he looks up, in something like a daze, quite honestly at a loss for words, though the less insightful used to call it an inability to suffer fools. This, once, was taken as a sign of haughtiness, and this, together with his good looks, his wit, and his real taste, made him attractive to just the absurd sort who collect otherwise aloof souls as friends because they see in such company their own exclusivity. Another sort attracted to my brother was the matron helplessly beguiled by glamour, who nearly faints before speaking and melts when spoken to. Such people followed Andronikus as fleas follow a dog. Really, it was most amusing to watch them circle round him when he became morose. Lapdogs yapping at a mastiff is a fair analogy. Then these people were certain his introversion was their fault and attempted to make amends, following him ever more closely, when he only wished to be alone. He once suggested to me, only half humorously, I think, he was delighted when Manuel imprisoned him, as it forever discredited him in the eyes of these poor, frivolous, ephemeral souls. The simple fact is that my brother always has more to give you than you to offer him, if you know how to tap the lode, if he senses in you a seriousness even beneath your laughter."

In this year, at long last, the Emperor took as his wife and August Basilissa, Bertha-Irene of Sulzbach, a marriage accomplished nearly too late to its original purpose. If it had been meant as vinculum to the Alliance of the Two Empires against Roger of Sicily, then the Crusade of 1147 rendered it nugatory almost at once. Conrad had grown pardonably disgusted with his colleague's tergiversation. Giving fuel to flame, Manuel had sent as ambassador to the German court to explain the delay the insufferably arrogant Prince Basil Melissenus, Eudocia Comnena Melissena's grandson (his chief recommendation). A mission of such diplomacy called for the superior finesse of our greatest diplomat of the previous century, Constantine Angelus, who had died of old age between securing the betrothal and observing its consummation.

"Sending Basil," said Andronikus, who had actually petitioned Manuel for the mission, "was a guarantee of insolence and ineptitude since our dearest cousin in the second decree, completely misunderstanding the nature of the German Imperium, was quite certain any Melissenus was the superior of an elected German sovereign. Just so, Angelus would have been careful to cater to the implicit insecurity of such a position."

So it happened Hohenstaufen and Melissenus loathed one another, and in his last interview Conrad continually referred to Manuel as "our dear brother, the illustrious and glorious *King* of the Greeks," and added, "Tell your master, he and I may both make the same mistakes, but I only make them once." At this point, the Bishop of Wurzburg interrupted the Emperor and offered to go to Constantinople to intercede: to end the betrothal, altogether or in marriage. The Bishop's charm and tact, once arrived, accomplished the latter, and Manuel promised to invest Bertha-Irene at Easter and marry her in the coming summer. As Andronikus once said, "It is a strange fact, a winning personality could sway my cousin when logic had already surrendered to his stubbornness."

V

On 15 September 1146 'Imad-al-Din, called Zengi, Prince of Mosul and Aleppo, Conqueror of Edessa, was smothered in his bed not by an Edessan agent, his generals, or Nureddin, his ambitious younger son, but by three drunk pages and an equally inebriated valet. So history is, infrequently, altered not by the men who intend to make it, but by those who stumble into its waters and find themselves floating with the best.

The story goes that Zengi, himself quite in his cups, had retired to sleep, when he was awakened by noises in the antechamber. There he found his valet, who had a weakness for wine and boys, succumbing to both. Too drunk himself to shout any but a few epithets and a promise of dire punishment, he retired once more. It is not difficult to imagine what followed.

It was a fortuitous murder, scarcely mourned by anyone. Not by Zengi's generals who believed he had overextended himself. Not by his nobles who loathed his austerity and the taxes which financed his wars. Not by the people who paid for the campaigns with blood and still more meager earnings. Not by his sons—either the generous elder, Said, who believed his father another Attila, or Nureddin, an unappeasable fanatic who believed his father was not relentless enough in the way of jihad. Not by Manuel or Mas'ud, who had everything to gain, nor last, not least, and most important, by Joscelin of Edessa.

Almost at once, on receipt of the news, the Latin Count sought to regain his capital. With new vigor, he attacked the city which was governed by an appointee of the clement Said, who had gone on to inherit Mosul (Nureddin receiving the crown of Aleppo). Needless to say, the natives of Edessa, for whom Zengi's clemency after the sack had been not so much too little as too late—even cynical—opened the gates to their former Count. The occupationists were massacred to a man. Joscelin then called on Antioch and Jerusalem to assist him in keeping what he had regained. There was not time enough for his brother princes to respond. Nureddin, disgusted with his brother's governor, marched with holy vengeance at the head of an army of one hundred thousand against the ancient bastion. At once he laid siege as tight and suffocating as the pillow fatally pressed upon his father's face. To complicate and dishearten the defenders of the city, there were virtually no arms to be had, Edessa having been shorn of all weapons of war during the capture of 1144.

It is nothing, let us say, for a man to acknowledge his errors. Even villains may do that—usually quite cheerfully. But there is no sight more moving than a man who rises above his errors to rectify them, especially if they have led to the hopeless predicament in which he finds himself. The scorn which is poured upon Joscelin's memory, even now, over a half century later, is at once smug and un-Christian. It is indeed tragic that, at the end, when he might have succeeded—and Europe, perhaps, avoided the havoc of the next years—he was on every side deserted, as the next-to-final episode of his life became a magnification of all the flaws which had preceded it.

In November, recognizing he was without the means to continue resisting the siege, unwilling to leave his people to the barbarity of Nureddin's call for unconditional surrender—which could only mean submission, slavery, or execution—Joscelin proposed to fight a diversionary sortie, while fifty thousand Edessans attempted to leave the city—literally by the back—and vanish into the countryside. It was a brave, mad move, but there were not sufficient troops for the venture and too many tongues amongst the population to keep a secret which might save them. Most of Joscelin's company was overwhelmed. He himself escaped to Samosata Castle, there to meet an end at once unexpected and exalted, which we shall, in time, come to, and then the real butchery ensued, unseen since the Latins took Jerusalem. That terrible day thirty thousand men, women, and children—the old, the sick, and the lame—lost their lives, while nineteen thousand captured survivors were remanded to the slave markets of Aleppo. Only one thousand men—and only the men—survived to tell the story at Jerusalem, at Tripolis, at Antioch, Constantinople, Palermo, Paris, and Speyer. In retrospect, we may now see it was a milestone event, after which the principates could but defend rather than conquer, pulling back and back, until they turned, at length and as one, on Constantinople.

It was the first fall of Edessa, however, not the second and more abject defeat, which reminded Latin Europe of its responsibilities in Palestine. There were now commercial as well as family ties, beside the overriding factor of the prestige of a Roman Catholic Holy Land which bound the West, literally body and soul, to its defense. And, to be sure, there was still the wondrous, mystic lure of that most sacred portion of the earth whereon Jesus' feet had trod.

The ingenuous would say it was in the latter spirit and no other that the good friend of Louis VII's ubiquitous Suger, Bernard, Abbot of Clairvaux, preached another adventure in the Holy Land in 1145. Rather this remarkable scholar, ascetic, and church reformer, who had refused the Papal seat, sensed with rare insight that the fall of Christian Palestine might seriously tamper with the integrity of the western Church he had so recently and almost singularly purified.

Thus with an eloquence which, if the minutes of his speeches be correct, would cause stones to sprout ears to listen, the abbot delivered an impassioned declaration before his King and a vast audience at Vézelay, 31 March 1146. He called upon all Christians, everywhere, to journey once again to the Holy Land and renew their souls as well exert their swords to the submission of the infidel to the one, true, revealed Faith. It is unfortunately to be remarked the stink of enforced conversion which had never entered the minds of the first Crusaders had taken its root among their descendants (though Bernard cannot be accused of outright bigotry; his influence alone protected the Jews of the Rhineland from the virulent anti-Semitism of the German nobles).

Louis, then and there, took the cross (though we may be certain he had long contemplated the decision and approved the context of Bernard's speech beforehand). This man, whose daughter was to marry two Byzantine Emperors, was something of a mystic and something like a schemer, full of the introversions, suspicions, secret sins, moroseness, and inscrutability of one trained by priests. He possessed a small soul of intricate turnings. He had no jealousy in him, save for his rightful prerogatives, but he stored resentments like a squirrel and possessed the patience to delay revenge till the optimum moment. He was married to a most unlikely Consort, the niece of Raymond of Antioch, Eleanor, Heiress of Aquitaine, a duchy larger and richer than her husband's kingdom.

(Andronikus once described the Queen of France as "one of the most unsettling women I have ever known. You simply couldn't get to the bottom of her, not because there was very far to go, but because she constantly wrenched it to one side like a small rug pulled from beneath one's feet whenever she sensed you were on to her. Her few outstanding qualities—and I have a sinking feeling they were her only qualities— were exceptionally contradictory. She was a bully, yet she seemed to throw herself under any strong hand in her vicinity. She was without question a nymphomaniac, and yet intolerant of the least sign of moral turpitude in others. She was excitable, but without passion. She could be crushed with the least criticism—and quite self-piteous about it—yet I have never known anyone to spare less the feelings of others. Her tongue was fire out of control and apt to be fueled by attempts to put it out. She had not the least patience—or sympathy—for another man's hurt. Manuel thought she smiled at him a little too often and poor Bertha shrank in her presence. She scarcely paid any attention or respect to Louis. 'He is something you'll have to forgive me for,' her manner seemed to imply. Soon enough we knew the reason. As for the King: he reminded me of a rat: he seemed to hunch; he was repellent and yet fascinating. He reminded me of a clerk. Yet no clerk ever possessed such a leisurely, calculating, cynical mind. Eleanor was too self-centered to realize his silence had nothing whatever to do with weakness. He was not sinister, though he seemed to be. Certainly he was without generosity. An undemonstrative misanthrope.")

When Bernard preached another oration before the Diet of Speyer and the Holy Roman Emperor, on Christmas Day of the same year, there was, of course, renewed urgency, for the first survivors of the few, from Edessa, had reached the courts of Europe to tell of horrors, which, for once, could not have been less exaggerated.

On a personal level, Conrad was not about to allow Louis the historical precedent of being the first King Regnant—or the only one—to visit the Holy Land. If Louis, moreover, could force or convince his greatest vassals to accompany him—Henri of Champaigne (whose daughter, Alix, he would one day marry), Alfonso-Jordan of Toulouse, Thierry of Flanders and his brother, Robert—Conrad intended to have in *his* train more shining nobles still: his half-brother, Otto, Bishop of Freisingen, Henry, Duke of Austria, Welf of Bavaria, Hermann of Baden, Henry, Bishop of Toul, Stephen, Bishop of Metz, William of Montferrat, and, by his side, his nephew and Heir Apparent, Frederick of Swabia. To be sure, these supernumeraries provided not only luster but enormous numbers, required for a great offensive against the Moslems.

In the spring of 1147, in two massive jealous paths, the armies marched across Europe to Constantinople, their eminent leaders departing under the most inauspicious circumstances. Conrad's Empire was direly threatened by the heathen Slavs, still moving west, a problem scarcely rectified by the absence of the great barons. Louis, in an equally poor presage, had burned a church to the ground, killing many women and children, in his zeal to capture a criminal who had taken refuge therein. If Louis had, at all, any second thoughts about the Crusade, they were forfeited when Bernard declared the Pilgrimage to be his penance.

Manuel's first order of business was the elimination of all distractions, most infamously—and unnecessarily—the fruitless war with Iconium. One of those temporary pacts, sworn by both parties to last for eternity—which a danger may sometimes seem—was quickly signed, the issue of indemnities scarcely haggled. (Later, when the Latins had suffered at the hands of the simultaneously undistracted Seljuks, Manuel's treaty was taken by the West as the act of an anti-Christ.) The armies of the Greek mainland were placed on alert, though in no manner whatsoever were they to take the offensive against the Latins. They were to consider themselves "ushers," meant to keep good order.

Now, while the cavalry of the French and German armies were undoubtedly well trained and disciplined by second nature, the infantry, unfortunately, included a great number of lay pilgrims, hastily armed, who were poorly fed and left to sleep in any passing field. It was these poor souls who caused the worst damage and reopened the wound of hostility between the West and citizens of our own Empire. There took place the same plunder, burning, infrequent rapes and murder as in the Crusade which had preceded this by nearly a half century. (One town was brazenly occupied by the French, who quartered their horses in the village church.) Generally, if an Imperial garrison was nearby, our soldiers, though outnumbered, attempted some rescue, which thereupon brought on interference by the Latin horse. In that event nothing less than a full-scale battle ensued between Greek and Latin Catholics.

Andronikus: "Memorable days for us all. The year began ominously enough when Manuel deposed Patriarch Cosmas, something he should have done the moment of his accession. Of course, my cousin's reasons for cashiering that wretch were neither a matter of ethics or politics but, not surprisingly, personal in nature. Cosmas hated Bertha, as unreasoningly as one lacks an appetite for certain foods. He mistrusted her as a Latin and a Latin Catholic, and he was vocal about it in an entirely vulgar, presumptuous way. As Bertha was now Empress, Manuel was careful to maintain her position as rigorously as his own. It's true he indulged Persephone's rather mistaken pretensions as the eldest child of a dead crown prince, quite grossly, giving her a court and a discreet diadem—as though the family, save myself, wasn't scandalized enough by uncle and niece bedding down together, though they were nearly the same age and more like cousins—but it was still Bertha's signature on all state documents, Bertha's presence at all state occasions, which manifested the legality of things. Besides which, Manuel was careful never to be less than courtly and kind to her. (It is useless to say he ought to have peered deeper. He knew his wife's great goodness, that she was worth a dozen Persephones. Unfortunately, sexual appetite has taste but no conscience.)

"In any event, Manuel convened a synod and Cosmas was cashiered, but not before he publicly cursed the Empress' womb against the birth of a male heir. It was the act of an unredeemable clod. I can't think of any gesture more humiliating to a woman so private and demure, who had already suffered, sublimely, her new husband's adultery.

"When we had news of the oncoming Germans and French, Manuel, besides placing the mainland armies on alert—wisely, I think—commanded a much needed repair of the walls of the capital which had not been tended since our grandfather's reign. His interest in the Latins—real curiosity—quite surprised me and was due to Bertha's influence which, in some respects, was greater than most historians realize. Besides formalizing his natural compassion toward at least a modicum of social legislation, she introduced my cousin to many Western social concepts. Since they were no more than cordial in public or the semiprivacy of the family, I imagine she worked on him in the afterglow of Imperial Duty, which he performed upon her five times monthly. Manuel was quite taken by it all—from the idea of courtly love, which I find amusing, to that of battle chivalry, which I find revolting. All quite diversions for children, but new, and my cousin found them delightful.

"It was, for instance, the custom of every Latin knight, as soon as possible after his marriage, to do some great deed in honor of his bride. In that order Manuel decided he would proclaim himself leader of the Crusade as soon as Conrad arrived at Constantinople, and go with the Latin armies to Jerusalem. Bertha was much moved, and the family took to calling him Le Chevalier Manuel. He was too ingenuous to catch the sarcasm."

Whatever Manuel's plans, they were dashed hopelessly by the political realities which overwhelmed him. The Germans' progress from the crossing of the Danube, as they moved south to Constantinople, became again and again more intolerable, until the Emperor was forced to send Nicephorus Paleologus north with an unusually harsh letter which stated that "unless depredations cease at once, We, Manuel, Autocrat, Divine in the eyes of Almighty God, shall consider Ourself in a state of war with the Testator of the Carolingian inheritance."

The warning was heeded and the rest of the way to the Imperial city was, for all practical purposes, without incident. It is said Conrad, rather more used to anarchy in his own Empire, in proportion to the distance one placed between oneself and a ruler, was, at first, puzzled the Basileus should concern himself with what amounted to the conduct of men in open countryside. It was not long before he realized that the pervasiveness of Byzantine civilization extended beyond city boundaries.

And so, for the first time in nearly a thousand years, two Christian Emperors met face to face. Andronikus, as a member of the Imperial court, was, of course, present.

"I must admit, even I was somewhat moved by that day which stands out as a tiny isle of comity in a sea of spite. But let it be so. Better men memorialize such events as these, which are really trivial, than wars and assassination and ruin."

As the problem had never before arisen, the etiquette of the occasion had to be established, as they say, from scratch. The most important question was implicitly settled in the decision to treat the event as something more than a courtesy: Should Conrad be greeted as King of Saxony or Holy Roman Emperor? The answer, as Andronikus once suggested to me, may have rested as much in Manuel's attraction to the glamour of the occasion, even if it destroyed his own uniqueness, as his desire to indulge Bertha-Irene Augusta, whose pleasure in seeing her brother-in-law was a means of allaying his own adulterous guilt.

Andronikus: "It was unerring graciousness on Manuel's part, and, in a way, fitting, he chose to meet Conrad, not in state, at the palace, but before the open doors of the Golden Gate so that the two of them could enter Constantinople side by side. Word to this effect was relayed to Conrad and he was properly pleased by the honor—as well he might be—though he refused with great regret Manuel's offer of Magnaura Palace, preferring to lodge in his own pavilion, with his soldiers, outside the walls. Of course, any Byzantine knows you do not, no matter your preferences, refuse the hospitality of a roof, without giving abject offense, but we let it pass as ignorance of our culture.

"Well, on a sunny day, Manuel, my cousin Isaac, Sergius' brats—David, the spectacular monster, and John, the covert one—John-Roger, the Bryennii, Philip, and myself, among heaven knows how many others,

surrounded by Varangians, followed and massed behind Manuel at
the Golden Gate, while arriving in the distance with perfect German
punctuality was Conrad and his army, which had been instructed by
our master of ceremonies not to pitch camp until both Emperors entered Megalopolis.

"About fifty feet from us the great din of the thousands marching
stopped. There was a pause, and save for the murmuring of the crowd
along the Via Triumphalis, you could hear the wind in the grass. They
were an impressive sight, indeed, these Germans, in their dress helmets and formal armor, beneath their red-crossed, white Crusaders'
cloaks. Plumes, horns, spikes, huge Percherons, and dancing-eyed stares
—that is what I remember.

"But more vividly still, I recall my own feeling of vulnerability. Here
we were, surrounded by our ruby-earringed, gold and scarlet Varangian giants, ourselves in immaculate white and purpled silks with pearl-
dropped cameos of Manuel at our shoulders, seated not atop mighty
chargers, but our long-lashed Arabian darlings. A chill entered my
bones that day which has never quite left me. It is not their jealousy
we must fear, Nicetas, but the utter alienness between us, which, I
think, nothing shall ever bridge. It was the confrontation that day of
intellect, taste, material refinement, and scrupulousness with the austerity, brutality, illiteracy, and the indifferent havoc of primeval force.
I believe all Byzantines felt the same feelings as I, though to a man,
we never discussed it. Perhaps it is one of those revelations so horrify-
ing that to articulate it is all too readily to confirm it. It was one of the
few times in my life I've known real dread and I can tell you I didn't
like it one bit, as it was to no purpose—this undefinable, sinking fear,
which required all one's strength to keep one's balance while crossing
an abyss above panic.

"How odd—and fitting then—my eye flew to the man who would
dominate Manuel's future and, it appears, my own, Frederick, called
Barbarossa, who was not then red-haired, but a tow-thatched blond
suffering a hideous case of sunburn. The calculation of his demeanor
was as obvious as, I used to be told, was mine, before men stopped
attempting to predict what I would do. You know, of course, his height
and breadth have expanded with his reputation, and so has his beauty.
In truth, he was shorter than Manuel, much less myself (it must gall

him I am the tallest Emperor in history*). He was also gaunt and almost willowy. His eyes were of a startling beauty and intensity—I'll admit that much of the legend—but unfortunately, they were crossed and, worse still, rested above high—almost Slavic—cheekbones and an extraordinarily pinched and prissy mouth. He reminded me of some few, very hard, indomitable women, rather than a man, now that I think of it. He sensed I was watching him because suddenly he turned to look at me—or perhaps he was merely searching out the companionship—or the challenge—of other tall men, which I often do myself as I enter a room. I smiled. He was startled. I turned away and spit.

"Just at that moment we were distracted as the Emperors' horses advanced an equal distance toward one another. Manuel extended his hand before he arrived beside Conrad, who seemed obviously pleased by this assent to the Latin gesture of friendship. The German Emperor said in careful, awful Greek, 'Greetings, Your Imperial Majesty,' to which Manuel responded in Bertha's well-drilled, flawless German, 'Your Imperial Majesty, I am pleased to welcome you to New Rome,' to which Conrad replied in German, 'Yes, I am very glad to be here, Augustus.' So much for deathlessly appropriate words to the occasion.

"I suppose what most surprised me about the German Emperor was his age. I don't know why, but I had expected a much younger man, and here was this immaculately barbered older fellow at least as old as my father. I think Manuel was no less surprised and even a bit put out—otherwise, as we called it, petulant—since Conrad's seniority placed my twenty-seven-year-old cousin at a manifest disadvantage. There is a respect—if it is only shyness, if only defensive insolence—we pay age, if only because we presume the old possess the condescension of years, and surely less the excesses of youth. So it may have seemed when my cousin was confronted with this austere regent in dress of silver mail, wearing not a trace of jewels save a wedding band and his coronation ring, while Conrad beheld a giant in chased golden armor, wearing a fantastically elaborate winged terristra cap and a short purple chiton bordered in pearls and precious thread."

In the afternoon Conrad was reunited with his sister-in-law, whom he seemed to hold in some real affection. He was plainly gratified

---

* Almost. Andronikus was 6′6″ to the 6′9″ of Magnus Clemens Maximus Augustus (A.D. 383–385). N.A.

by her acceptance amongst the Greek Imperial family. As it happened, Bertha-Irene played a larger role during her brother-in-law's sojourn than might have been foreseen.

Manuel appeared to vie between an eagerness to be gracious and an almost frantic desire to pull the Germans out from beneath the city's walls and float them across the Bosporus to Asia Minor. Conrad was plainly insulted by the implications of the Basileus' fears and at the end of the first week refused to re-enter Constantinople.† It was then Bertha-Irene took it upon herself to act the intermediary between the German Emperor and her husband.

Seldom had a woman a more thankless task, and it is here the Augusta begins to shine in her quiet way as the noblest Empress of the Comnenus Dynasty. She possessed patience, real heart, and a practical if not remarkable intelligence; besides which, a sense of responsibility and those qualities most necessary to an intercessor: the ability to present opposing views to opposing parties without seeming to take sides, and such unimpeachable decency as her very taking on of the errand becomes itself a recommendation of compromise. (It may even be said, until the first great break between the cousins, in the following decade, she served to placate and anneal and often reconcile Andronikus' and Manuel's immense and mutually abrasive personalities. The former himself once said, "I often thought something was lost between Manuel and myself when she died, and for years I could never quite name it. Now I know. The spirit of generosity, of which Bertha reminded us—and into which, perhaps, she shamed us.") The Empress succeeded in assuring Manuel that Conrad had no de-

---

† A notorious example of the crudity of which Manuel was sometimes surprisingly capable was once recalled by Andronikus. It portrays a guile so obvious—and born of such guilelessness—the machinery of the plot was less offensive than the implicit accusation of stupidity in its victims. "My cousin, at one point, sent to Conrad's camp a survivor—I like to call him a professional survivor—of the Edessa massacre. This fellow had repeated his witness over and over again from palace to Hippodrome, to the streets, so much so, he had ceased to have any feeling for what he described. Finally he spoke from rote, with rote gestures and rote emotion. 'I saw a man lying on the ground, twisting in agony, his face unrecognizable as human.' Head bowed. He can barely go on. 'I saw a child with empty eye sockets wailing his way blindly down a street,' and so forth. By the time he was sent to arouse the Germans, who had no intention of venturing anywhere near Edessa, this fellow was accepted in the best of homes, where he told his story still again to matrons, weeping over their luncheon. When Conrad learned the man's background—after shedding tears himself (sooner insult an enemy than move him under false pretenses)—he was outraged by his brother-in-law for sending him such a fraud. Well he might be." N.A.

signs on Constantinople, nor was any insult intended in refusing to accept the Autocrat's leadership of the Crusade. Equally, she convinced her brother-in-law that Manuel was not chasing him into Asia in a vengeful spirit. Rather, the German army was an intolerable presence in a city of two million, garrisoned, by its own law, with no more than twenty thousand troops. Would such a threat be any less allayed by the presence of Louis' army? And, indeed, had Conrad's proved itself quite so trustworthy on crossing the Danube?

The Germans traversed the Bosporus at the beginning of October and began the final trek to the Holy Land. Unhappily, the fate which awaited the Crusaders of 1101 undid, as well, those of 1147. Unused to the semiarid country and the heat of a lingering Asiatic summer, the soldiers roasted beneath their armor and the pilgrims withered from starvation; both died of thirst. Even before the enervated army entered the borders of Iconium, it suffered from the gadfly guerrilla tactics of the Turks. Then, unexpectedly, on the morning of 26 October, in the hills near the South Meander—precisely the terrain which could prevent use of the Latins' best weapon: the massed charge of the cavalry—Conrad's army was surrounded and, to all intents, destroyed. All lay pilgrims, unarmed, were killed, as well as 90 per cent of the infantry and nearly half the knights. The leaders of the expedition escaped unharmed and in the shock which follows paroxysm, marched to Ephesus, where Conrad, heartsick and ill from the ravages of the previous weeks, fell to bed and claimed himself ready to die.

When news of the disaster reached Constantinople, Manuel, Bertha-Irene, Andronikus, and Anastasia boarded the Imperial state drummond—with its five banks of oars, the fastest ship in the world—and sailed throughout the night to the ancient city of Mary's ascension, arriving on the morning of 4 November. (During their two days' sojourn they took up residence at the Archepiscopal palace.)

Andronikus recalled, "Manuel was always at his best, which could be quite melting, when neither pride nor politics complicated his relationships. When we arrived at Ephesus, we found the Holy Roman Emperor laid up in an inn, unbelievably, his General Staff in complete chaos, and what was left of his army broken in discipline and spirit. One's heart quite went out to them all. While Manuel sat with Conrad, the Empress, Anastasia, and I toured the camps. Rather thoughtfully,

Bertha asked the Latin Catholic chaplains to celebrate two hugely attended outdoor masses, one in the morning—a Requiem for the victims—and one in the evening—a Te Deum for the survivors. Anastasia and I attended both, and Bertha seemed to be amused at our tentative responses and the self-correction of our three-fingered, right-to-left Signs of the Cross. I must say I'd never known her to be so completely at ease, as during those two days. But then, to be sure, she was among her own, and the sight of her, in a silver and purple dress with the delicate, unostentatious little rings and earrings she favored, was indeed something like a vision from heaven to the grieving Germans. This gratified her immensely. Unhappy herself—in a situation she could neither alter nor enforce—she seemed pleased whenever she could cheer others. If her mere presence could accomplish this, then she was tirelessly public though it much distressed her sense of privacy."

The double Imperial party set sail for Constantinople on the morning of 7 November. Manuel promised to send provisions to the remaining knights and infantry, who were to march to Nicea and encamp on the grounds of St. George's Palace. The Basileus, meanwhile, doctored and diverted his brother Emperor at Buceleon, while at Hieriea, Andronikus was enlisted to entertain the Heir Apparent, Frederick of Swabia.

"They were the longest two weeks of my life. Bertha chirruped about how wonderful it was we two young Princes were becoming friends and, for once, I could have choked her. Even through my limited knowledge of the German language, I perceived Frederick as a complete ass, everything a civilized man is not. He was just stolid enough and limited enough and prudish enough and arrogant enough to offend everyone. Much of the time with him was spent attempting to explain that the only insult he had just suffered was in his imagination—if he had one. You know the sort. He was one of those foreigners who, because he can't understand the language and makes no attempt to understand the culture or grant it integrity even though it is alien, believes the entire country a plot to humiliate him—self-centeredness on a grand scale. One morning, toward the end of my Calvary, when I accompanied Frederick on his daily visit to Uncle Conrad, Manuel took me aside and with a look in his eye, said, 'I hear you and Swabia discussed the *Eumedian Ethics* till late in the night.' I looked twice again at him, and when he burst out laughing, I said, 'Very funny. He's not a man.

He's a coma.' 'Patience,' Manuel said, 'patience. I appreciate the trial you're enduring in the name of the fatherland.' I'm certain Manuel's elation was nothing less than the belief he had the measure of Conrad's Heir and the rule of Europe fast in his hand for the future. I can, therefore, almost take pleasure in the surprise Frederick proved to us all."

By mid-November, Conrad was recuperated enough to rejoin his troops at Nicea. No sooner had he left than Louis of France arrived with an army vaster than the Germans and, as Andronikus put it, "with the stink of Sicily still clinging to his boots." Of course, he was referring to the nonaggression pact Louis had signed with Roger on his southerly, leisurely way to Constantinople.

On 23 November, while the King of France approached our walls, Roger of Sicily and his admirals made a multi-pronged attack on several western islands off the coast of Greece, chief among them gigantic Corfu, succeeded in their capture, and proceeded to invade the mainland. The news reached the city, fittingly enough, during a banquet attended by Perfidious Louis (as Constantinopolitans soon named him), who had just sworn vassalage to Manuel, subject to any lands he gained in the Levant. (When at Antioch, Queen Eleanor, at the behest of her uncle—and, briefly, her lover—Prince Raymond, decided to divorce the King to marry the Heir Apparent to the English throne, Henry Plantagenet, she claimed Louis Capet's fealty to Manuel and her consanguinity to Raymond threatened Antioch's independence, and in a splendid gesture of self-sacrifice proposed by this to dissolve her French marriage. Of such women, lawyers are born.)

It is said that same evening, as the French returned to their tents, his barons urged Louis to forsake his venture to the Holy Land and take Constantinople. It is not unlikely his narrow, glittering mind for a night dreamed itself enthroned in the Sacred Palace, or, better even, between the rising staggeringly bejeweled walls of Blachernae, in which a proud Manuel had acted as guide that same afternoon. But then Bernard's interdict hung heavily upon this man, whose first obedience—as a pupil —had been not to God or ambition, but to priests. To make certain Louis' aspirations did not exceed his conscience, Manuel resorted to a rare example of Imperial dishonesty. He circulated agents through the French camp with tales of Conrad's wondrous success in Lesser Asia, a lure the French, the prideful race, were certain to heed. (They had been in Sicily or at sea during November and were unaware of the German catastrophe at Meander.)

Within a week, on the Asiatic side and arrived at Nicea, Louis learned the ghastly truth from Conrad. As a perfect example of Latins as guests, the King proposed, thereon, to sack St. George's Palace from top to bottom, burn it, and pillage the city, which, for a brief time, had been capital of old Roman Empire. Conrad, not so much admiring Manuel's ruse, or himself honorable, but loathing Louis, convinced the King he had been "outsmarted by a bigger sneak than yourself," and revenge was to no purpose. The two men parted wary friends with the promise to meet in the Holy Land the following year. Conrad returned to Constantinople where Manuel decorated his brother-in-law with the Order of St. Sebastian and provided ships which took the dwarfed German army directly to Acre in the Kingdom of Jerusalem.

Louis, meanwhile, unlike his pragmatic self, spurned all further Greek aid. He paid with a quarter of his army lost to Turks, who invaded Imperial territory, depredated the French, withdrew to the Taurian cliffs, and left the third and most ubiquitous of the Four Horsemen, Famine, to do the rest. At Adalia, on the southern coast of Lesser Asia, the army took ship for Antioch. The Greek maritime fleet charged such exorbitant rates, Louis refused to pay for a whole horde of lay pilgrims, thus stranded four hundred miles from their destination and two thousand miles from their home. (They became a drain on the city's philanthropy, then a danger to its safety and, at length, the Governor of the Cibyrrhaeot Province, of which Adalia was the capital, received permission from the Emperor to deport them back to France, along with their aggravated anti-Byzantinism.)

There is no point in following this stumbling and finally abortive venture in any detail. As to its original intent—assistance to the beleaguered principates—of that, nothing. There was much talk of an attack on Nureddin's Aleppo, which never took place, and a siege of Damascus which lasted all of four days and proved diplomatically disastrous, since that Emirate was the only Moslem power to have made peace with the principates and, on several occasions, acted as their bastion. In truth, the Campaign of 1147–49, which cost the lives of more than 150,000 people, accomplished nothing but the exacerbation of Palestine, which was troubled enough before this irrelevant upheaval.

Conrad was obliged to rebuild his shattered forces at precisely the time he could least afford it, during the Slav incursions on his east flank. Of his shattered health, there was no hope.

Raymond of Antioch had disagreed with Louis' "Faith or Death" propaganda—a rare glint of wisdom—and then totally antagonized the King by advising his mistress-niece to divorce her husband and marry the English Heir. (She did, and throughout the years she was Henry II's Consort she was hated by her island subjects, whose language she could not speak and whose culture she regarded as beneath her refined contempt.)

Raymond II of Tripolis, Raymond of St. Gilles' great-grandson—via the illegitimized line of his eldest son—successfully engineered the assassination of his granduncle, Alfonso-Jordan, Count of Toulouse, whose sentimental visit to the land of his birth was looked upon as nothing more than a plot to claim Tripolis. When Alfonso-Jordan's son and daughter attempted to avenge their father, they were haphazardly captured and imprisoned by Nureddin for twelve years.

As for the Prince of Aleppo, who at the outset had seemed to have antagonized enough kings and armies to give even his own religious frenzy pause: he did nothing, as much the signal of his disgust as his intelligence. One well-mounted campaign against the Latins might have served to unify these "baboons" (as he referred indiscriminately to all Christians and Jews). He would not give them the advantage of a common enemy.

On the face of it, the Byzantine Empire seemed to have escaped this bloody, irrelevant event with the fewest wounds. There were Roger and the Slavs to deal with, which we shall come to presently, dangers of no mean proportion, but by no means hopeless. It was the contemporary view, held especially by Manuel's all too readily admiring courtiers, given the circumstances, he had guided the state through these frantic events with a maximum of discretion and a minimum of force. Surprisingly, the leader among those praising the Emperor was Andronikus himself.

For once I think the Grand Duke's willingness to be just with his cousin was uninsightful. But then, he was a prisoner of his time. Only now, in retrospect, can we see that beneath the chaos of activity, round about, but never at Constantinople, there took place the great failing of Byzantium's prestige.

For nearly a thousand years, our Empire had stood second only to Jerusalem as, shall we say, a Christian Mecca—the largest, holiest, wealthiest city on earth, often besieged, never captured, whose Emperor may have been the object of gainsay by the West, but remained the legal descendant of Octavian Augustus. To all men Constantinople was the inviolable fountainhead—and, as often, the fortress—of Christianity. But beginning in 1054, Western Europe resurgent and that indifferent schism having occurred, growing wider and more irrevocable every year, New Rome lost its luster. Or perhaps it might more accurately be said, the Latins lost their awe, which must always precede assault. As my dear friend Bishop Eustathius of Thessalonika once said, "The single greatest problem we have to contend with is this: The Latins think the world is not big enough for themselves and us." I would not demur. It is because the West Christian antipathy was so unconscionable, so forced, we may accept the insight of the Metropolitan, though we must call it something other than a problem. When a man tells you it is his existence or your own, there is no solution but the most negative, the annihilation of one or the other antagonist.

The Crusaders of 1097 and 1101 blamed their failure on Alexius, which was specious in the extreme. The Crusaders of 1147, mainly the French, as much convinced by their failures as by Raymond of Antioch, accused Manuel of contrivance with the Moslems. One was an accusation of neglect, the other, of conspiracy. Louis was certain of it, and, as it proved, Frederick of Swabia harbored the thought in his heart. The Sicilian Guiscards would, of course, accept any half-truth or untruth as provocation against its inherited enemy. It is significant our very right to exist was in such question by 1149, that Bernard of Clairvaux—the only man whose esteem had increased since Vézelay—without turning a hair, could preach still another Crusade—offer, indeed, to lead it himself—which, but for the disinterest of an exhausted French chivalry, might have been mounted not against the Moslems, but Constantinople itself. (When news of this extraordinary proposal reached Constantinople, fifty thousand citizens gathered on the Latin Church in the Venetian Quarter, defiled it, and burned it to the ground, while the police stood by and did not interfere—on orders, it is said, of the Sebastocrator himself. Later the Emperor apologized to Venice and built a new church, though from private funds—he let it be known—not the state's.)

VI

We must return now to midwinter of 1148.

When the Latins had departed Constantinople, Manuel had hoped, at once, to mount a force against Roger of Sicily. To this end he required the Venetian armada and to that end was willing to make any concessions to the Republic of St. Mark.

"My grandfather set an awful precedent," said Andronikus. "And my cousin was one of those who in fear resort to precedent rather than ingenuity. In such situations he ceased to think clearly—and that is when originality counts most. I tried to make it clear to Manuel no concessions to Venice were necessary. The Doge would never allow Roger to keep Corfu, which meant, in effect, the control of the Adriatic Gates. But Manuel was quite certain, if Venice freed Corfu, they would keep it, and he was, besides, in a panic to commence operations. My advice, both blunt and urgent, was taken as a return to my old ways of interference and a complete lack of consideration for the burdens with which he was shouldered. He seemed to indicate I had betrayed him. No basis in reality, of course, but he suffered nevertheless. In that, I couldn't even pity him.

"He called in the plenipotentiary ambassador and after two days' parley at the Villa of the Paleaticum offered Venice a second district in Constantinople and still a fourth dock—not a bad trade for Corfu. I nearly went mad. It was so obvious this unnecessary remuneration would antagonize Genoan and Pisan merchants, infuriate our own citizens, and cut deeply into our own revenues.

"I would have preferred to go on to the estate in Thessaly left to me by my grandfather, Michael Paleologus, ostensibly to refurbish the palace, more accurately to sulk, but then came the Slavs who were intruding upon Hungary and the German Empire. Obviously with an eye to our preoccupation with Roger on the left and the Crusaders on the right, they crossed the Danube and set to pillage the province of Bulgaria. Manuel, with a whimsy which drove me to tears of frustration because I could catch no rhyme behind his antipathy one moment and attention the next, appointed my cousin Nicephorus Paleologus and myself com-

manders for the Northern Campaign, which, I suspect, he considered
not much more than a piratical raid.

"I remember just before we began the last meeting of the Praetorium
previous to leaving for Bulgaria, he said to me, 'I know you think I
should not have compensated Venice for her fleet, but suppose she had
suddenly turned and allied with Roger? The advantages I have given
her here are by leaps more valuable than anything Sicily can give her.
She will serve us now, not gain on us. We can fight now with a clear
mind, which is half the battle.' I was about to admit to the possible wisdom in this when he said something which took my breath away. 'Perhaps eventually we may even carry the campaign against Roger more
deeply into his own country with Venice as ally instead of vigilante.'
I was appalled. That was the first mention he ever made to me of the
Great Scheme which was to alienate Venice from us from year to year
until nothing was left of the alliance but memories and the resentment
of its betrayal. How could he seriously believe the Republic of St. Mark
would allow Constantinople any sooner than Palermo to control the east
and west banks of the Adriatic?"

But for Andronikus' short, immensely effective generalship against
the Slavs, whatever the Emperor preferred to believe, there would not
have been the possibility of even a holding action against Sicily. Andronikus was never more than a competent strategist. Yet, by virtue of
his person—his size, his daring, which all witnesses called manic, and
that history of independence, which the lowest men in the army envied
and loved so well—he was, even so young, a figure almost mystically
revered: George of Battles come to life. If his fellow generals—who
were also fellow courtiers—were wary of him, every other man, officers
on down to the ranks, was ready to die for him, "though to be sure, I
preferred a less lethal form of tribute."

The Campaign in Bulgaria lasted from early January to the end of
March. Manuel remained with the forces until mid-February, then,
leaving Andronikus and Nicephorus to supervise the final sweep across
the Danube, himself passed south to take up residence at Demetrius
Palace, Thessalonika, where the armies of the West were massing to
march against Robert. In May the Emperor sailed at the head of the
Imperial fleet round the tip of Greece and reconnoitered with the Archadmiral of Venice and his armada. (Andronikus was later told that
when the tips of the majestic fleet ascended the horizon in the west, Man-

uel turned to his aides and said, in an extraordinary breach of dynastic etiquette, "Gentlemen, my cousin would have us go into battle without giving assurance—or gaining, at least, the neutrality—of that colossus.")

Roger proved more formidably seaworthy than anyone had imagined, and the combined fleets of Byzantium and Venice were at work—with not complete success—the better part of May and June throwing a blockade around Sicily and the West Coast of Greece and its islands. Unfortunately, there was more animosity than co-operation between the allies, due to an incident which had occurred during the first sea battle off Corfu.

According to the records, when Manuel had left ship for the island, about a dozen Venetian sailors and an African of enormous girth boarded the Imperial yacht, slaughtered the servants and Household Guard, dressed the black man in Manuel's robes, and hilariously paraded him on deck in a burlesque of court ceremony. When the Emperor returned unexpectedly, he was both shocked and insulted—as well he might be—and demanded of the Venetian Archadmiral the execution of these worthies. This was refused. All Greeks were grossly offended, and the alliance, henceforward, came close to its own internecine war.

In June, Roger battered his way through the Aegean fleet and reached the east shores of Greece. He sacked the suburbs of Athens and passed on to Thebes, which was totally destroyed, its silk factories burned and its unparalleled weavers carried back to Sicily as slaves, there to supervise the initiation of master silkworks which would, in time, rival Byzantium's. (Our own were rebuilt—this time, at Constantinople. It may be said, along with the failing economy of Trebizond—due to the diversion of trade routes south to the newly accessible ports of Palestine—the loss of Thebes, and with it the European monopoly of silk, proved one of the most serious fiscal problems of Manuel's reign and was never satisfactorily solved.)

The Emperor left the fleet and ordered Paleologus and Andronikus south from Bulgaria. At once, he drove against Roger. There is, of course, an urgency fighting on one's native soil which no conqueror's army can ever know. In three months, attacked from the north and west, the King of Sicily was swept, landward, three-quarters across the breadth of Greece.

When Manuel received word Conrad was on his way home from Jerusalem, "having forsook the absurdity of Latin Syria," he dispatched his fastest yacht to divert the German Emperor to Thessalonika, left the scene of battle under the command of both his cousins, and proceeded himself, at once, to Thrace. The Alliance of the Two Empires was more than ever necessary and the Basileus meant to reassure its viability. But he had not counted on the unforeseen.

As he told me many years later, "I was shocked by the German Emperor's appearance. It is my absolute conviction that unholy Pilgrimage killed him before his time, and so ruined our mutual hopes for Europe. We concluded a definite pact to join in an assault against Roger's Italian possessions some time within the next two years, but Duke Frederick, the Heir, was against such a venture and quite open in contesting his uncle. Even then. He suspected, as I, that Conrad was dying, and had not the decency to bury him before contradicting him." Manuel smiled in recollection. "It was then, you know, I wished I'd brought along His Highness, the Grand Duke Andronikus. He seemed to be the only Greek who, in some way, could silence that oaf."

Despite the German Heir's opposition, the mutual assistance pact was signed and deposited—or given for deposit—in both Imperial Archives. To seal the union, Sergius' daughter, Elizabeth (not to be confused with Manuel's mistress, Elizabeth Persephone), was given in marriage to Henry of Austria.

It is said, when the Grand Duchess received word she was to leave Constantinople for "the barbarous north woods," she threatened to commit suicide or become a nun. In contemplation of either event, her mother, Andronikus' Aunt Rebecca, was ready to perish in tears. She allowed her daughter to write one letter of protest to the Emperor. If he refused to change his mind, she must consent. A month passed. The petition became a correspondence. Manuel remained adamant, but so did his niece. In letters which crossed, Manuel sent and Rebecca asked as intercessor, Andronikus, the only relation to whom Elizabeth would listen.

"I was rather surprised, and a little annoyed, by the errand, taken from the battlefield to the boudoir. I could scarcely imagine why either my cousin or my aunt thought I should have any influence with Veta. In truth I treated the matter far too lightly. I thought it incidental, but then it is just such incidents with which one must live, either as subject or dynast in an autocracy.

"When I arrived at Constantinople, Rebecca told me point-blank (and did not doubt it) her daughter wouldn't marry Heinrich and leave Constantinople even if Manuel prevented her from marrying anyone else. I told her Manuel was too kind to take such retaliation—and he was— or so I believed he was too resolved in his desire to be adored to risk being loathed. I warned instead that our August Cousin would *resent* Veta and that might be more intolerable than the Viennese *Föhn*. I asked her why my cousins, John or David or for that matter her sister, Eudocia, did not speak to her. My aunt's words were apt of our condition under Manuel: 'Good heavens,' she said, 'you know Veta won't listen to her brothers. She'll think they're trying to protect themselves and their positions. As for Eudocia, it will be too easy to say she's been lucky enough to marry Paul Catacalon and remain here. Oh, and it's true, Andronikus. My poor darling gone off somewhere hundreds and hundreds of miles from all her friends, and her family, from *civilization*.' I said, 'Not to say the least, civilization. But why should she listen to me, aunt? For a fact, I'd sooner tell her to stand her ground.' Then she said something which quite surprised me, 'But you know we all look to you.' And perhaps realizing what she had said, she decided to reinforce her words. She leaned to me and touched my forearm. 'Someone *must* face him with the truth.' 'I mostly fail in any event.'

"She snatched back her hand and with a deep breath seemed to possess strength, more *opinion* than I had ever known. I had noted something like its promise seven years before when—to everyone's surprise— she and Natalie had pleaded for the life of Sergius' assailant. Quite suddenly I felt a real warmth toward my mother's half-sister. Free of Sergius, she had become a woman of considerable integrity. 'Must we all be like that detestable child Persephone who has broken Natalie's heart? Must we worship him falsely as a false god to gain his favors? He's shut us all out, Andronikus, not just yourself. But he *is* the consecrated Autocrat and we cannot contend him.' 'Rebecca, he is inviolable only if you believe in a God who has made him inviolable. Without such a God, he is not sacrosanct.'

"Now she disappointed me. She said, 'Oh, you mustn't speak like that. There's nothing to hold back the chaos.' 'That's not true,' I said. 'Athens was a democracy before it was a tyranny and Rome a republic before it was an Empire. And Athens believed herself the height of civilization, as did Rome, as do we.' Almost in a panic, she said, 'But we are the light of the world.' I smiled and I said, 'And by the light the darkness is defined. But what is its source? What have these centuries of absolutism achieved? Whatever glows burns at the source. And what is that fuel but the enervation, the corruption, if you will, of our race. If one man holds all the power, then it is to him we must address ourselves, and what is the end but servility and cynicism. And what is the future of cynicism but the extreme of self-interest as each man pushes aside the other to make his way to that one man, the Emperor, and win his favor. You, all of us, we mustn't be afraid of alternatives. We only fear anarchy because too many men confuse it with cruelty, since most of us have no desire for freedom, which we confuse with license. In the absolute power which falls to each Basileus is absolute discretion. What one Emperor promises, the next may deny. Because he embodies all power, he has the choice, it is true, to make great changes. *Our* only true choice is that to obey or disobey him.'

"Once again she touched my arm. 'Listen to me. You must keep these thoughts to yourself. I know you have given serious consideration to what you say and I have neither the intellect nor the courage nor, for that matter, your way with words to dispute you. And neither have many others. You would put fearful thoughts in a man's mind and there are those who would respond with their fists, destroy you, if they cannot turn you to their own way of thinking. There are also those who do not care what you think but who would use your convictions to condemn you. Whether or not I assent to your ideas, I grant them your virtue, and for that, I fear you would never deny them if challenged.' 'We shall see,' I said. 'You mustn't worry about me.' She smiled, almost coquettishly. She was not made for the gesture. 'Oh, but I do. You and Manuel are both, I think, good men, and that is what terrifies me so. Manuel is very jealous of you, but he loves you. Nothing could be more dangerous for you. It is too easy for jealousy to be offended and love to feel betrayed —and that obverse is hatred and the cruelest retaliation. Your grandfather Michael worried for you on his deathbed. Papa warned your mother you must be more discreet. "Jealousy," he said, "is a passion, and all passions are illogical, impetuous, and destructive. Manuel will destroy that boy one day. He will regret it sincerely, but he will destroy him."'

"I could dismiss Rebecca's argument, with indifference, if not, as she put it, the fist. But I had loved and respected my maternal grandfather. He was not an intellect, but he had wisdom and he was incorruptible.

His warning, which I had not known, quite chilled me. I might have been in the intolerable position of having to bare my fear, but something in Rebecca—a watchfulness, a waiting for it—stayed me. At once, I resented her and became insouciant. I said, not coldly, 'Well, I have traveled all this way to see Veta, not discuss my own perils. Where is she?'

"Whether or not I was given pause by my conversation with her mother, I surprised myself by the council I gave my cousin. Whether or not it was rationalization, I no longer treated Elizabeth's feelings with the seriousness they deserved. Intent is the foundation of meaning, and meaning that of action. I did little more than mouth duty to Veta, who was quite brokenhearted, when I should have gone to Manuel and, at least, conveyed to him the reality of her suffering. In the insight of my twenty-seven years I was certain hers were the tears of a child, as though there were a certain level of experience one must reach before he earns the observer's consent to the depths of his grief. Well, the observer does not matter and all grief is as deep as the man who feels it."

Elizabeth was commanded to leave for Vienna before her uncle returned to Constantinople, a slight, absently made or intentional, which Rebecca never forgave. The Grand Duchess was not present to welcome her brother-in-law's triumphant return, 11 February. Claiming herself seriously chilled (one wonders if the double meaning was intended; as Andronikus often said a slier version of his mother's wit increased with his aunt's age), Rebecca sailed south to the Island of Rhodes and the most fabled of the Paleologus estates, the Castle of Roses, while her daughter passed north to the indelicacies of the Austrian court, and a marriage which began with the introduction of the hand of the Archbishop of Vienna between the newly wedded couple in their nuptial bed to be certain intromission of the Imperial virgin was complete.

VII

Once I asked the greatest of Andronikus' generals, Michael Branas, how likely might have been Manuel's victory had he been able to join forces with Conrad in the summer of 1149. He responded thus: "I think victory would have been incontestable. I was Nicky Paleologus' aide-de-camp and I was in a position to know. Our own forces were exhausted, but they were also exhilarated with triumph. A late winter's rest and spring maneuvers and there's no question but that we should have had the advantage in every way, spiritual and numerical. You must remember Roger had lost half his forces or more in the retreat across Greece. Had His Majesty, the Emperor Conrad, come down from the north, our strategic positions would have been unbeatable. It cannot be enough emphasized Manuel's plans in Italy depended upon the maintenance of an alliance with Conrad. When the German Emperor died and Frederick succeeded him and began to deny all bonds between the Empires, Manuel made the mistake, I must say, of proceeding with an invasion whose practicability had been nullified. At the same time, it is to be admitted, some show of strength was necessary against old King Roger whose ability to place one army after another in the field was nothing short of miraculous."

What Duke Michael neglected to mention was that the source of Roger's strength was Paris rather than heaven.

Louis left Palestine in complete disarray: Alfonso-Jordan dead, his murderer, Raymond II, in disgrace, the heirs of Toulouse in bondage at Aleppo, the Anjou-Lorraine dynasty of Jerusalem alienated, and Raymond of Antioch exposed to the fury of Nureddin. (Indeed, on the day following Louis' departure from Symeon Harbor, the Prince of Aleppo marched on Antioch. Raymond met him—and death—at a suicidal, heroic stand near Fons Muraz. The Prince's head was sent to Nureddin's capital—Manuel once suggested it should have been sent to Louis, the rightful conqueror—and all prisoners slaughtered, as the Moslem warlord believed Raymond's forces were but the vanguard of a much larger army, supplemented by Germans and the French.)

While the East blamed Louis, Louis, to be sure, blamed Constantinople, and in a fleet sent by France at the cost of two years' taxes to bring its King home, he sailed direct to the Imperial city and laid siege by sea and land. This three-week war, like the Crusade itself, was muddled in intent, confused in execution, and costly to French mortality (and incidentally served to turn its leaders against that second attempt preached by Bernard).* When the siege was lifted, Louis asked to meet with Manuel. Andronikus, in this, one of his periodic intimacies with his cousin, promptly estranged himself again by urging the Emperor to

---

* It is reliably reported whenever Louis beheld Marine fire blasting out of the Greek siphonophores, the King would fall flat on his face on the deck of his ship and scream, "Lord, Lord, Lord! Have mercy on us!" N.A.

receive the King. Instead Manuel, in incredible dudgeon, refused, calling this most abstemious of the Capets a "whoremongering son of a whore, an anti-Christ, and a liar." What Louis might have said to Manuel, perhaps the truce he might even have offered, is a matter of speculation.

Many years were to pass before the King of France and the Autocrat of the Romans were to have words again for one another, and, by then, events had so altered, it would be irresponsible to argue from hindsight. So Louis sailed to Sicily and reaffirmed his military and fiscal devotion to the descendants of a petty, penniless count to whom his great-grandfather, Henri, would not have given the board and bed of his kennels. With this support, Roger could continue to plague Byzantium till the devil took him.

Andronikus thought Manuel's treatment of the King would have been much different, diplomatically wiser and more generous, had the Imperial family, at the time of siege, not suffered a ghastly personal grief in the suicide, with her lover, Prince Basil Taronites, of Caesarissa Magdalena, twin of the late Crown Prince Alexius. "After all, *I* was clearheaded enough. It was my cousin's duty—the 'burden' he so much talked about—to raise himself from the distraction of mourning and serve the state with an eye to its best interests. But then I mustn't be too harsh with him, for his grief was real and it was inconsolable, in the strictest sense, the grief which cannot be assuaged because it is founded in deepest guilt beyond forgiveness. No man could accuse him—or had the heart to, if he dared—more than he accused himself as directly responsible for his sister's and Basil's death. And he sought me out and I lent him my consolation because, unwitting, mine had been in some degree the final argument against which his fatal stubbornness turned.

"Basil, you see, had all along favored me. He was nearly twice my age and devoted to the throne through our family (his grandmother was my grandaunt). He had worshiped my uncle and my father, and he was, above all things, guided by the well-being of the state. When Manuel cashiered Isaac II and estranged me, Basil was of the few to contest him. For that I could not help but love him. He was one of those small men—like my grandfather and my uncle—who, without the questionable advantage of size, must continually assert themselves, all too alert to condescension. He served Manuel faithfully, but he was my friend, and he approved of my beliefs and he was quick to make both factors known. In truth, he was sometimes embarrassing to me, taking up certain causes which might have been better served by silence, or inaction.

"Through Basil I came to know my cousin, Magdalena, who, otherwise, because of our extreme age difference should have remained something of a stranger to me. She was, in disposition, most like her father, and a perfectly elegant foil to Basil's abrupt masculinity. They were supremely devoted to one another, and having been lovers for ten years, their relationship was mellow as well as passionate, an alliance of utmost simplicity and enviable serenity, save the single flaw: they were not married. Heaven knows, their adultery was grounds, then and there, for dissolution of the respective marriages. Basil's wife, who was Magdalena's First Lady-in-Waiting, had long ago released her husband to the Caesarissa, and their children were of no especial prejudice. But on the other side there was the pride of that wretch, John-Roger. Though he was bound moreover by Orthodox vows, I suspect he retained the Latin Catholic distaste for divorce. True, there was the ban of consanguinity as Basil and Magdalena were cousins in the second degree, but that is scarcely an impediment in light of an Emperor making love to his niece.

"Four of the years Basil and Magdalena were together they pressed her brother to consent to the divorce and he would not give it. It was more than dynastic dignity or John-Roger's whispers. The Caesarissa's sons, though not disapproving on a personal basis, were also behooved to gainsay their mother in *their* desire for a position in their uncle's court.

"Once I was truly of age, I took up their cause. I sensed this was bound to set Manuel against them for whatever I espoused he belittled. His favors to me, his consent to use my talents, had to be voluntary. He must never allow himself to believe he was convinced by me or obliged by an act I might perform. As I say, my espousal may have been the death knell, altogether, for the Emperor let it be known he intended to make Basil Military Governor of the Russian Chersonese, which was tantamount to exile. (This was in the same month when Persephone presented her mother Natalie with a mortifying grandson-nephew—incestuous decadence.)

"Well, one fine day, when no one expected it, Basil and Magdalena swallowed poison. They were discovered by servants, *my* servants, in the evening. They had begun their entry into death hand in hand, but the pain of the poison—it must have been particularly vitriolic—had contorted them and the rigor mortis was hideous. How unlikely, one thought, this darling, harmless couple should be driven to the grandeur and excess of such an act.

"I broke the news to Manuel and I forgave him, in part, because his guilt was penance enough and his grief was immense and if I dared to loathe him only a little, it would release *all* the bitterness I was amassing toward him. Even then I could feel it, like a subterranean river within me."

I asked him why there was no memorial tomb to the Caesarissa. Where was she buried? He looked at me, quite surprised. "Are there really so few suicides you do not know the practice of our merciful Church? Stakes were driven into the hearts of both Magdalena and Basil, their bodies burned, their ashes triturated and blended and scattered to the winds." He was thoughtful a moment, his expression as stone. Quietly, very tersely, he said, "I like that better, perhaps," and I was not certain whether he was thinking in the general or the particular.

He was silent a long while, then he roused himself and said, "Since death seems to be our subject this evening, let me relate to you something which occurred a few weeks later, during Louis' siege.

"One day I was riding to the watergate of St. Amelianus. I passed an old woman following a covered stretcher carried by municipal bearers which the poor hire to take their dead from the city. Or *did* hire until I ordered the service extended gratis, without tips, though it has since been reported to me the bearers threaten to drop the corpse unless given an extra fee—the usual victimization of the poor by the poor. In any event the streets were being cleared ahead of me as is usual for the progress of a member of the Imperial family, and among the people, as I say, was the corpse, its carriers, and the one old woman, all removed to one side. My eye fell on the old lady and she gave me a smile I have too often seen among the downtrodden: a real smile, the head to one side, like so, but such sadness, and the lips trembling, and the eyes so hopeless. It just pierces one to the heart.

"I stopped. I asked her name. (I have a poor head for these things, which is why since my accession I keep a secretary at my side when I venture into the city.) Well, she explained to me the body beneath the blanket was her grandson who had been killed the previous night, not

by the French, but in an accident, while helping to repair the great catapults at the walls. He had been her only living relative or means of support and she kept referring to him as 'my honey,' 'my darling boy,' 'my
angel.' One of my ADCs, moved, I'll grant him, probably attempting to
exorcise *his* helplessness before such need, said, I shall never forget,
'Better it is she grieve for this one boy than the Emperor mourns the
whole city.' Under my breath, I said, 'Shut up,' and dismounted and . . .
I had no idea what I could, what I might, do. I simply could not assent
that a city, even an Empire, was worth this old woman's grief and that
boy's life cut short. And yet what's a failed state but all mothers grieving for their sons, for all their children. Really, there's no answer.

"Rather for anything else to do, I approached the litter and removed,
to the belly, the blanket covering the boy. A handsome, strong young
fellow who looked to be in perfect sleep. It took an effort of the imagination to think him as dead. The body was smooth, too compact, well
muscled, ready to spring. But there was blood at the base of the skull.
He was dead indeed. The old woman asked me to pray, which considering the moment and the publicity—a crowd had gathered—was repellent
to me. Manuel would have gone grandly on, having smiled down on the
mud, twice as adored because he had acted precisely inhuman and indifferent as a vision. There *I* stood, at odds ends, embarrassed, inadequate as my ADC before such pathos. I had spent a morning exercising
and steaming and being pummeled by a masseur and I had no intention
of kneeling in the street. I had been on my way to the walls to oversee
the progress of battle before returning to the palace for dinner with the
Emperor (and his morbid reminiscences of Magdalena), who had not
seen them do to his sister's body what I had seen. And what was in store
for the grandmother, here, before me, but burial without a priest or a
coffin because she hadn't the money, and a return to heaven knows what
hovel, a little meal, and the constant shock of little habits in preparation
for her grandson's presence or return, which were no longer necessary?

"Between my horse's eyes—a part of the bridle, a good place for it
—was a small gold and pearl icon of St. Demetrius. I unhooked it and
gave it to the old woman. 'Put this in your grandson's hands, as custom
tells us.' Then I asked one of my ADCs for his purse and gave this too
to the old woman and said, 'Now listen to me, Granny. Your boy died
brave as any patrician in defense of the city and deserves a proper
burial. These two soldiers'—I signaled forward two of my Excubitor

Guard—'they'll go with you. You find a coffin-maker and buy the best, and put your boy in it. Then go to the cemetery of St. Theodora and pay the gravediggers and the priest in the chapel. He'll repeat the Requiem service. These gentlemen will make certain of that. Then they'll take you to Orphanotropolis. Would you like to go there? You would, wouldn't you? I'll have Father Paul notified. He's going to expect you before sunset, now, so you be prompt.' From the look of her face, I couldn't tell whether she was amazed or even if she comprehended what I was saying. Later, I thought of the precise coincidences which had landed me beside her. Had she been notified earlier of her grandson, had I tarried—as I was tempted to, I remember—only a little longer in the sudatorium, all would have been seemless for her and she would have been otherwise consigned, I am sure, to beggary. You see such women in the streets all the time. Yet why had she to lose everything before even this mild windfall of which I was the agent? And what of the millions whom I shall never know, who continue to suffer? I tell you, Nicetas, there are times when I would blithely offer my own obliteration if the world would be rid of its misery. And there are times when I would see the world obliterated because it seems to exist only to be miserable."

VIII

In the evening of 30 May 1150, three thousand tapers were lit, a chorus began to chant the Divine Liturgy of St. John Chrysostom, and the consecration ceremonies of Nea Church were begun, and with it, a week of celebration unlike Constantinople had ever seen or shall ever see again.

While the whole vast city shone like an island of stars with torches, the members of the Senate, the court, and the military aristocracy, privileged to be invited, had arrived at the huge white marble façade of Nea. Upon entering the cathedral they were given silver copes to don for the duration of the liturgy and after which they might keep as mementos of the occasion. Within the cathedral they discovered the intent behind this unusual gift. Garbed in silver themselves, standing on a floor of silver-striated white marble, they looked up past ice-blue marble pillars, at walls of silver and mother-of-pearl paneling, chandeliers of silver, a towering iconostasis of etched silver decorated with more than a half-million pearls and white opals and above the entrance to the Holy of Holies—the one relief in this lustrous, shimmering sea—a seven-foot cross of diamonds, sapphires, and lapis lazuli.

Andronikus remained forever aghast at this "flawless example of effeminate excess, this celebration not of Christian humility, but Imperial extravagance, with worse to come," but we may be certain the majority of the congregation that night were nothing if not astonished by the splendor their young Emperor and his priest-architect had wrought. Surely, before the sack, Nea rivaled in magnificence, if not size, Alexius' Cathedral of the Almighty (though it certainly had not the relevance, since no monastery or hospital was attached to it).

But, as Andronikus said, this was a mere prelude. The following morning, 31 May 1150, 819 years after the founding of the City of Constantine, and the inaugural of the nuclear Sacred Palace, Daphne, the New Sacred Palace, known the world wide as Blachernae, was consecrated by the Patriarch in ceremonies lasting until late afternoon, upon which commenced seven days of celebration, which, even Manuel was heard to remark, somewhat reminded him of the final orgy of Sardanapalus.

Blachernae, in fact, had stood completed and almost entirely furnished since February. The Emperor, however, with his fine eye for the event, had chosen to commence his occupancy on the most meaningful day of the civic calendar. If he could attempt to rival Justinian rivaling Solomon with Nea, he could likewise challenge Constantine. With Blachernae, he surpassed everyone—not the least, as we once promised (and he no doubt promised himself) Roger's fabled domain at Palermo. Fifty-five years after its inception by his grandfather, as the gleaming bronze doors—each panel twenty-five feet high and fifteen feet across —were trudged back to admit its occupants, Blachernae, on the face of it, announced to the world the revitalization of the oldest European throne under this, its 118th occupant since Octavian Augustus.

In truth—as we see it now—it was the end of one world and the beginning of another. Nea, Blachernae, Pantokrator, the Colossal Cross of the Constantinian Forum, the rebuilding of the city's arches, all seems rather a reassuring reminder or a harking back, of the dreams of youth in the sleep of the old. (This is not to say we were doomed to fail. The Silver Age of the Comneni was not an omen, but a consequence. We are—or were—a very aged people. Our last hope seems to have been

Andronikus. Had he lived, we might have survived even more bravely than before, but it would not have been the Byzantium of previous history.)

Just as one man may bring senility and the other wisdom to old age, there are certain signs in a people which are a warning, if not the last word. While one man grows old at sixty, others infuriate their children and delight their great-grandchildren at eighty. Who's to say it did not seem like the end with the rise of Phocas or the fall of the Isaurians? But there rose Heraclius, and still again, Michael Rhangabe. When his line quickly expired, there came to the throne Basil I, the Magnificent. Yes, it is true, one man may single-handedly heave history to a new course, but whether it is luck or genius which means his success, there must, at some point, coalesce other circumstances to his advantage: the will of the people, the unselfishness of the nobles, the weather on a day of battle, perhaps the accidental death of a potential enemy, a good harvest, the fiscal viability of the state, any or all of these factors, and more. Coincidence is all, and, in a sense, no act has been committed in a void since the creation of the universe.

In every way we see now, much as we consider the last days of one we knew who carried a fatal disease secretly to his death, our Empire was approaching its terminus. The buildings, the conquests, were not significant of vitality, but tumescence; the alliance between the military and civilian aristocrats was not a selfless compromise to the end of civil peace, but a mutual degeneration, wherein one took on the worst attributes of the other, in a collusive raid for state favor; the quiet of the peasant was not the effect of his contentment, but the consequences of his oppression.

Constantinople was the jewel of the Empire, but its brilliance was become singular. While Manuel decorated his immediate environment, which was his capital, he paid scarce attention to the other major cities —Thessalonika, Trebizond, Sinope, Nicea, Ancyra, Ephesus, Nicomedia, Sis, Miletus, Dorylaeum, Smyrna, Adalia, Candia, Rhodes, Athens, Nicosia, Famagusta, Thebes. Constantinople was a jewel, to be sure, but more enticing for the desolation of its company. Manuel endowed the City as few Emperors before him. But what did those riches depend upon save war and taxes, compromise with the archonate at the expense of the peasants' sons, the shifting of the tax burden from the aristocracy to the merchant class and farmers, who were attempting to survive without sons, or sons forced to march across their fathers' fields to enforce the law, no party precisely pleased to see its monies translated into marble or annuities for a favorite, illustrious name rather than government services. Buildings rose, indeed, beautiful buildings, but they served to conceal growing slums, not to eradicate them. It is a significant fact poverty and unemployment were rife in Constantinople during the latter half of the twelfth century, which coincides with the resurgence of the mob.

The poor of the cities and the poor of the provinces, the beset farmer and harried merchant, might say of the failing government and its regent: "If only the Basileus knew of this." But from that, it is only one more step to the statement, "He's made a venal choice for a servant and he does nothing about it." This is to completely misunderstand the responsibilities of a minister, or a clerk, or a tax-gatherer, for that matter, in an autocracy. But the sense of the statement holds. Two comments of Andronikus, spoken at random come to mind again: "A King is someone to blame," and, "If a ruler would be omnipotent, he just practicably be omniscient." Of the latter statement, we know such powers of ubiquity cannot be, though we as subjects would have it so in our rulers. The best one can hope is that a regent has the insight to raise the very best men, and those men their undersecretaries of like persuasion, and those men their clerks similarly, that the virtue carried down through each appointment will not be too much diluted. It is in the former statement, the King as scapegoat, we find the greatest gap between the man and acts, or consequences of those acts, done in his name. Of no one was this more true than in the person of Manuel Augustus.

Aside from court ceremony, when majesty was of the utmost, he was a man of limpid graciousness, wry humor, and vivacious curiosity. Away from his throne, this Emperor, who did adore panoply, could not have been more informal. He who in public rode or was carried or walked in august isolation, in private preferred the visiting functionary to sit opposite him or partake of his favorite manner of interview—Andronikus' too—a walk beside him in the magnificent gardens of Philopation, Varangians fore and aft at a discreet distance.

My memory of my own first interview with Manuel is vivid example enough of the Emperor's unfailing, always courteous charm. A twenty-year-old stripling who had risen too fast to the post of Confidential Secretary to the third Sebastocrator, I had spent most of the previous evening in the ghostly beauty of Nea, praying I would not make a complete ass of myself, on meeting this man who had existed more as legend than reality for me, having ruled for three decades and now acknowledged the premier sovereign in Europe and the Levant, not by mere precedent, but politically, as him by whom others set their strategies. Like most citizens I had never seen the Emperor *move* save according to the rigid proscriptives of ceremony. I could scarcely imagine that this tall, rather slender, insuperably dignified figure even led a private life. And yet, I knew on Bishop Eustathius' recommendation he had taken a more than superficial interest in the schooling and careers of my brother Michael and myself.

In the morning, that dreaded morning, I gathered the documents I was to explain in detail to the Emperor and took the long walk from Blachernae's administration wing to the Imperial wing, through those astonishingly jeweled, flower-bedecked halls. I was met promptly by the Imperial Chamberlain, Nicephorus, who conducted me along more galleries still and through rooms, each more indescribably magnificent than the last, until I was certain I would confront a god in a tabernacle, not a man. At the last doors, of gold—each decorated with an enormous bicephalic eagle in cloisonné of carnelian, jasper, and obsidian—my knees were shaking, an affliction I had heretofore believed a literary convention.

The Chamberlain did not signal the Varangians. No man would dare approach, much less be allowed to approach this study, were he not inscribed in the Emperor's appointment calendar. Nicephorus knocked twice, lightly, and the voice which I had previously heard so infrequently, I could only afterward approximately recall, said, "Come in." The Chamberlain pushed open the priceless doors and I found the Autocrat of the Romans, His Imperial Majesty, Manuel Augustus John Comnenus, standing like a petitioner before the desk of his seated secretary, his fingers drumming its gold-banded edge, as he frowned, attempting, apparently, to remember something. Offhandedly, without looking at us, he said, "A moment" (he *was* then human, capable of the uneventful act), frowned more deeply, looked up at me—blushing and shaking— which must have completely distracted him, said, "We'll finish later," then strode forward to meet me.

He was garbed in a profoundly purple chalmys. Close to, one noted an appliqué of Imperial eagles in the similar same colored velvet thread.

He wore no jewels save a wedding band on the same finger as the Imperial sigil. His step was light at fifty-four years and his hair thick and attractively gray. I had never before beheld a man whose face radiated more serious, pure, and childlike goodness. Having often beheld the icons of his canonized parents in Holy Wisdom, I could see his mother's physical refinement, but his father's coloring and ingenuousness. All of his movements had a spring to them—leaving little doubt he had been positively rejuvenated by his second marriage and the birth of his son six years before.

He offered his hand for me to kiss, which I did so, reverently, as he said, "At last, the young patrician from Iconium whose praises Eustathius continually sings in my ear, am I right, Nicephorus?" "To the letter, Divinity." As he raised me, the Emperor covered my hand with both his own. (They were enormous and calloused.) He said, "How good of you to come and elaborate on those documents I returned. I'm afraid His Imperial Highness, the Sebastocrator, believes me gifted with second sight. I can't make heads or tails of what he wishes me to do." He considered me, still silent, still shaking, made a signal with his forefinger to the Chamberlain, pulled the portfolio from beneath my arm, laid it aside, and said, "Come, my boy, you must meet my son. He's in the garden. Come." In the following half hour I spent with Manuel and the future Emperor Alexius II, the Augustus proceeded to allay my timidity and incite in me a love for him, and an awe, which has not failed to this day.

It is little wonder, then, Andronikus was so ambivalent about his cousin. So am I. "His intentions were indisputably removed from realms of ever *meaning* to harm, which makes his failings, perhaps, all the more painful." This is Manuel's tragedy most succinctly, and yet Andronikus extended to it, only infrequently, his sympathy. Neither man, it may be said, assumed the power with a conscious eye to egotistical self-gratification. Both were men of action, and they ruled according to their natures, Manuel in the extravagance which he believed by enhancing him, enhanced the state, Andronikus in the austerity—born of philosophical conviction, certified by years of imprisonment, exile, renegadism, and personal suffering—which seared away layer after layer of the lavish accouterment and an aptness for luxury which is a dynast's birthright. Manuel could not have maintained a greater distance from the people were he God Himself. Andronikus was accessible to all and, for that, perhaps, sacrificed the mystique of majesty which was his safety, becoming the first Emperor since the founding of Constantinople to be murdered not by a military or palace cabal, but by those subjects, the very powerless, he sought to defend.

While I, by no means, release Manuel from the historian's condemnation of the man who, by decision after decision, incorrectly reasoned and disastrously concluded, spun the breeze which became the whirlwind over the land he loved passionately, still I permit the first sovereign I served the reality of his personal integrity and selflessness. He was stubborn, yes, and shortsighted, yes. Incapable of waiting on his strategies, too quick to act on them if they initially proved unsatisfactory, he was sometimes accused of hypocrisy, which was alien to his nature. He was not insightful, but he could see pain and was eager to anneal it, if it were possible. He was informed rather than a real intellect. He had dreams, which are irrelevant, rather than vision, which is to the point. But above all, he lacked what Andronikus possessed in the abundance which was his cousin's burden as well as genius until he reached the throne and briefly ruled, the power of logical extension, an overview.

What, then, was the nature of this court at Blachernae, whose Emperor sat in state upon a throne of solid gold, encrusted with every conceivable precious stone, beneath a gigantic representation of his own crown, banded in diamonds and pearls, suspended the long drop from the golden ceiling of the throne room by golden chains?

It was, as might be expected of a successor who ascended that throne still young, and whose father had died in middle age, predominantly youthful, profligate, hedonistic, cynical, lavish, and "delightful," as Andronikus said, "as long as you were unaware of what was going on outside."

Alexius Branas, the morganatic third husband of Agnes Anna Augusta, once told me his father used to refer to the midcentury Imperial court as "a stud farm." The Duke was probably closer to the truth than he realized. The religious climate was notably a matter of fervent devotion at prayer and abject absentmindedness afterward. The moral consequences can be imagined. Adultery was notorious and usual; its risks were minimal—mostly of the jealous cuckold (if he were interested enough to be jealous and not, himself, otherwise allied). Even the urgency born of sense of sin—not denied—was spice to passion. The only disapproval engendered was against those instances of bad form: of being caught at one's peccadilloes, or publicly flagrant, or too serious (the suggestion of divorce and remarriage), or vengeful (the lover who would destroy his mistress when he discovers she has another lover besides himself). One might not be noisy, or graceless.

A very pertinent example of one who was thus condemned and nearly ruined is to be found in none other than the career of the Emperor's mistress, the Grand Duchess Elizabeth Persephone.

In the beginning all that had been possible to lavish upon his niece, short of making her Empress (a position to which she believed herself entitled as the eldest grandchild of John II), had been, one is tempted to say, squandered upon her by the Emperor. A colleague of mine, both witty and assiduous, once spent the spare time of several months computing from the novels of Manuel's reign precisely the wealth, all told, spent on his mite-too-haughty, demanding, beautiful niece—"the golden apple," as Andronikus once called her for her outer loveliness and inner density. Upward from small personal gifts to the presentation of Magnaura Palace and the courtiers to fill it (who had to be clothed and fed and amused), the sum was so staggering, none of us, at first, could quite believe it: an unbelievable year's standard budget for the Imperial government. (But perhaps the harshest cost could never be tallied: that of the Empress' humiliation and desertion by the court and no less her niece's affrontery, brazen even beyond the prerogatives of a born Grand Duchess.) It is little wonder, then, Persephone and the "counselors" who owed their fortunes to her position jealously guarded the access of any comely, compliant woman to the Emperor's presence. As always, even the personal relationship of an Autocrat—as it must be in his sphere—was metamorphosed into a proposition of hard power.

Unfortunately—and for some fittingly—the Emperor's eye the first summer at Blachernae fell on his wife's Zoste Patricia, or First-Lady-in-Waiting, Eugenia, Duchess Exazena, according to all descriptions a woman of really extraordinary loveliness and serene temperament, whom Bertha-Irene found particularly cordial. Persephone opportuned her Imperial lover against such an alliance and, inevitably, only alienated him the more. At length, she was urged by her coterie to do away with the young woman, murder by act or consent. Persephone refused to hear of it and even exiled—she had the power—several of its most eager advocates. But by late autumn Manuel's attentions toward her had altogether ceased, though not his financial support. For all one can surmise, the Emperor might have continued to indulge the mother of his illegitimate son all honors and pleasures. Like most women in her position, however, Persephone was not of a mind to trust a former lover's generosity. In November, while Manuel was absent at Turbessel—of which, more—Persephone's agents murdered Eugenia in the presence of the Empress herself and Andronikus, whose words follow:

"Eugenia was warned Persephone had commissioned agents to kill her in Manuel's absence, and appealed to the Empress for protection, which Bertha gave without any further discussion. This means, finally, the assassination should, if successful, entail *lèse majesté* of the most profound offense, since such a crime before the Basileus or Basilissa is by itself implicit threat of regicide.

"The night of 17 November, one of Bertha's pages arrived at Porphyriogenetus and somewhat boldly sought me out in the apartments of my cousin Eudocia, Sergius' daughter and Paul Catacalon's wife, pleading with me to come with him to Blachernae. He kept saying, 'There's great danger, awful danger, Megadux,' but when I asked him to explain himself, he only said the Empress was terribly frightened and wished me to come to her. At once, I knew, and rather than waiting for a horse to be fetched from the stables, left the boy behind and took his.

"When I arrived at Bertha's apartments at Blachernae, there were no guards to stop me. Obviously they had been bribed—heavily: these were Varangians—to disburse at the critical moment. Within, there was only the Empress, two maids, a page, and Eugenia, immobilized, terrified.

"I remember as I entered, Bertha, normally the least demonstrative of women, who always moved tautly, ran up to me and threw her arms about my neck, saying, 'Thank God, thank God.' I said, 'Where are the guards,' and I was furious. 'I don't know,' she said, 'I don't know. I can't trust anyone to come and I daren't send my children to find more.' (She always referred to her suite as her children.) I said I'd go after some myself, but she clutched me back with a fierce 'No!' I cursed myself that I had not indeed ordered a horse from Porphyriogenetus' stables. Automatically, two members of the Household Cavalry would have been dispatched with it.

"Can you imagine any group more vulnerable than ourselves? Not even a decorative sword in sight, and myself, quick from my cousin's bed, quite weaponless. So we began piling furniture in front of the doors.

We stripped superb tapestries from the wall of another room which I then attached to the lintels, so that, in effect, if the assassins got through the door, they should be momentarily confused by these blinds which would cover them. We repeated this at the five remaining entrances (the suite contained fifteen rooms) and threw open all the doors between. Then I scoured for anything that looked remotely lethal. Chairs and tables, some quite priceless pieces, were smashed for the truncheons the legs might provide. The most exquisite jeweled vases were piled up as missiles. And then we waited.

"And, of course, we had forgot something. After about an hour of intolerable anticipation, we heard a noise and Bertha clapped her hand to her mouth, saying softly—as though she were amazed in a small way—'Oh, my *God*. I'd forgotten. The servants' entrance.' *'Where?'* I hissed, and before she could reply, a half-dozen men—all Excubitors, my own regiment—had entered the room in which we stood. I lunged for them as the women screamed. I took a knife, right here, near the collarbone. I don't know how it happened. I never saw it, but I was in such a rage it scarcely stopped me. I growled like a dog and went straight for the fellow I thought had attacked me, pushed him against his colleague, and was ready to crack their heads, when something landed on my own and I fell in a daze, pushing the knife more deeply into my shoulder.

"I was conscious, but the rest is a confusion of shouting and running and at some point Eugenia was murdered. Though I have no recollection of it, Bertha said my eyes were open. Her two maids had run and hid wherever they could. The page was wounded. Bertha herself put Eugenia behind her. The leader of the assassins told her to step away. She would not. In one movement he wrenched her aside and drove a knife into Eugenia's throat, and it was over. I will grant you men who murder are not about to observe amenities unless they are demented, but this terrible episode serves as well to show the vulnerability, if not irrelevance, of Bertha's position, undermined not so much by the excesses of Manuel's philandering, as the implication it left like a riptide in its wake.

"The next thing I clearly remember, I was lying in the Empress' bed, there was a commotion of many voices beyond the doors, and round me were ranged two nursing sisters and the court physician. Bertha notified Manuel of Eugenia's death in full detail. She refused to ever again enter her Blachernae apartments and I don't one bit blame her."

There is every evidence to suggest the Emperor's affair with the Duchess Exazena was nothing more than an infatuation which would have ended and returned him to the grateful familiarity of the Grand Duchess Persephone who had borne such a short, tantalizing distance from legitimacy, a son. Rather the Exazenus scandal was more permanent in its consequences. Wherever it touched, the murder was a disaster.

On Manuel's return he took custody of his Imperial bastard and exiled the mother to Pentegoste, which the Dowager Empress Mary Augusta had ceded to the Emperor on her ninety-fifth birthday that same year. He was obliged to double the guard round the Grand Duchess against the sworn vengeance of Eugenia's brothers, who themselves, having hoped to rise with her, promised to kill the murderess, if they be killed in the attempt (they were not, nor did they succeed, and in time, instead, became sworn enemies of the dynasty). The six Excubitors who had committed the deed were burned alive and the Empress' Guard cashiered and deported. Persephone's Magnaura clique was disbanded, most in exile to their country estates, some few suffering the confiscation of all possessions.

Manuel's reputation suffered too, for the first time in his reign and seriously, so much so as to affect the dynasty itself, whose moral integrity had never been questioned since the accession of Alexius. The consanguinity of the alliance, only one degree from incest, was in itself deeply disapproved of. This was only aggravated by the unusual unpopularity of the Grand Duchess Persephone and the real affection of the poorer classes for the Empress. Now Her Imperial Highness was proved to be a murderess, and the Empress had nearly become one of her victims. Persephone's enemies and a surprising number of Constantinopolitans sought a stricter justice than the Emperor gave or was prepared to give. Briefly, Manuel's popularity plummeted.

News of Andronikus' heroism, on the other hand, spread like wildfire, and the Grand Duke made it a point to go out among the people and receive their admiration, accruing it to his family. (Somewhat sourly the Emperor asked if the public was aware of his cousin's alliance with Sergius' daughter, and "how well *that* would go down, if they knew.") In a more substantial gesture still, the Dowager Crown Princess Natalie, against the Emperor's prohibition but overwhelmed rather more by shame for her daughter, cut her hair, removed her shoes, donned sackcloth, and as public penitent walked from the Gates of Blachernae to the Convent of the Word where she took the veil, ostensibly in penance for Persephone's wickedness, though she had long been of a mind to thus retire from the world.

As for Persephone: she was to resume her alliance a few years hence, and it was to last until discretion by the bedside of the dying Bertha-Irene demanded Manuel put her aside (by then, of course, she had already begun her affair with Michael Branas, which was consummated in marriage). Not so unexpectedly, this episode altered her personality almost beyond recognition.

Given the length of her exile, the respite from the superficialities and human swirl of the court, separation from those dark eminences round her—the sort of sly, ambitious men and women, kings and queens of the closet, who play cats' paws with the mighty with the malicious revenge of the little against the large (and Persephone was a perfect foil: too sure of her place to examine herself or those about her)—her separation from Manuel who seems to have been the love of her life and her only diversion (she was that rare Comnena: without intellect), the Grand Duchess had ample leisure to dwell on her crime. In four years, of course, every aspect of a deed may be thought through until it becomes obsession. Ironically this was classic punishment, if punishment is meant to teach and rehabilitate.

In effect the Grand Duchess began her years at Pentegoste with her father's worst faults in her baggage. She emerged with her mother's patient wings. The woman who returned to Manuel was deeper, calmer, *good*, but not less vital. "Hers was not the mere virtue," said Andronikus, "of rectitude which is never tested, but that which rises from a confrontation and triumphs over personal iniquity—not the chastened quiet after penitence, but the worldliness which promises active compassion." Yet for the rest of her life the Grand Duchess remained haunted by her crime against Eugenia Exazena. She suffered constant nightmares, and became hopelessly and fervently devout in the way of those who believe they are anyway forever damned.

When in 1176 he heard she was dying of cancer—then scarcely fifty—Andronikus wrote to Persephone from his own exile—then in its second decade—this remarkable letter:

My Dearest Persephone. It is with great alarm I have learned of your recent quite serious decline. This, Philip writes to tell me, and too, your very unnecessary desire for my forgiveness for an episode which I would have had you strike from your memory many more years ago than I have years before me. I am, frankly, quite troubled by your dwelling on this event, and this seemingly interminable purgatory to which it has led you. Perhaps you will think it presumptuous of me to counsel you in the ways of heaven, and yet, as I am outside the flock, it may be I can see its workings and its essences somewhat more clearly than one who lives day to day with their jurisdiction. From this vantage point, I would tell you, it seems to me most unlikely the Jesus Christ in whom you believe has not absolved you again and again by your example and your repentance, which is indisputably sincere and, I think, morally grand. I think, my dear, Christ is apt to be far more merciful than we dare imagine in his judgment of the motives which compel men to their deeds. It is true nothing can undo what is done. The error, as we may call it, remains in historical effect. It also remains an active agent of evil, *only* if one refuses to learn from it. Perhaps that is the nature of all religion: the emergence from ignorance of the consequences of our evil. It cannot be said of you that you have remained in darkness. Your example is incomparable. Yes, I know: we may share our joy, but our fears are our own—which is the nature of solitude—and I doubt anything I say to you will serve to lessen your anxiety. It has been twenty-six years since that terrible evening. I cannot say I myself was saved for any great venture or profit, yet what man would willingly sacrifice a moment of his life? As long as one lives, there is infinite possibility. So long as there is possibility, there is also hope. This, I ask you to remember. There were many alternatives for you to take in 1150. You took that which, without realizing it, perhaps, was most significant of renewal. It is not my intent to belittle an event which has so long and enormously grieved you, but, I should ask you: if you cannot be guided by the thoughts of the victim, how can you presume to guess the thoughts of the Judge. Therefore, dearest cousin, I implore you with all my heart, rest easy and give yourself up to the clemency of the Christ in whom you believe—he shall scarcely cease to exist for others by my denial. And remember, if such a reprobate as I have not the heart to bear you any ill will, it is far less likely to be believed of a just and merciful God. Andronikus.

(Two notes: first, the letter was never delivered to the dying woman. When her sister Zoë became aware of its source she delivered it, unopened, above the objections of Michael Branas, to Manuel, who read it and had it deposited in the Imperial Archives, whereupon many years later it came into my possession—after being used by Andronikus' enemies as proof by his own hand of his atheism, which they believed rendered him invalid as the Champion of Orthodoxy, hence as Emperor. Secondly, Andronikus related to me only a few years later the circumstances round the death itself of the Grand Duchess: "I was told though she asked for him, Manuel refused to attend Persephone's deathbed. It was more than likely so, though not born of any lack of feeling. He was married then to Maria-Xenia and totally infatuated with her. Well, he had also been in love with Persephone, when they were both young, and I think he could not tolerate the sight of this wasted woman as a mirror of his own mortality. No fellow, at my age, as his then, wishes to remind himself or his bride of half again as many years, he is no longer young. In truth, he did not fear Maria's jealousy, but loss of the pathetic illusion of youth regained which Maria's affection gave to him.")

IX

The event which removed Manuel from Constantinople during the Exazenus scandal—indeed, allowed the assassination to take place—was an unforeseen campaign against the Seljuks which rather served to prove the delicate balance between the Imperial and Moslem states.

The origin of this brief war lay in the death of Joscelin II, Count of Edessa. Earlier we said it was indeed tragic that at the end, when he succeeded in proving his own integrity, he was scorned and alone. Yet in his solitude is his transcendency, as, in the end, deserted and tortured beyond any memory of inhuman brutality, Andronikus' death was to redeem him in the eyes of his murderers. Finally, at the end, Joscelin fulfilled the promise he had, all his life, otherwise wasted.

His Calvary did not begin promisingly. From Samosata Castle he is said to have loudly rejoiced the passing of Raymond of Antioch, who himself overtook the heroism which had always escaped him till Fons Muraz. But one can imagine the laughter dying into anxious silence as Joscelin realized the consequences of the loss of nearly half of Antiochene Syria and the one remaining warrior-knight still enthroned in Palestine. Raymond of Tripolis, growing immensely wealthy under his

Genoan and Pisan advisers, was indifferent to him and Baldwin of Jerusalem still under his mother's tutelage. Thus abandoned, also by circumstances, Joscelin resolved to swear fealty to Mas'ud Shah and protect the northwest portion of the Edessan County, which was all that remained of what was formerly the largest Latin principate.

All at once, he was beset on his entire east flank, which bordered the Euphrates: to the north by the ascendant Ortoquid Emirate and to the south by Nureddin (precisely against whom the Ortoquids were rising to protect themselves). Joscelin spent the last months of his freedom in battle. Rather contrary to human experience, as he fought, beleaguered, against all hope—such intensity could not be constantly maintained and despair must have touched him in moments before sleep—his wife, Lady Beatrice, who had previously abhorred her husband's irresponsibility and estranged herself, returned to him with their three children as a mark of devotion and encouragement.

For this "remarriage," Joscelin, her knight, presented the Countess with a feat which none of his colleagues had previously accomplished: a victory over Nureddin and even the capture (for ransoming) of the Prince of Aleppo's ADC. In the next three months, until May 1150, but for sorties with the Ortoquids, he was left in peace and actually made a state visit to Mas'ud who pronounced himself perfectly charmed by Beatrice. On his return to Turbessel, he was given word of Nureddin's approach at the head of a monstrous force of 200,000 men.

His last war, his last week, was in the execution of guerrilla tactics. And then, by chance, he was taken in ambush in the company of a dozen of his bodyguard, each of whom was garroted before his eyes. Joscelin himself was carefully spared, bound in irons, and sent to Nureddin, who tied him behind his horse and forced him to walk—and sometimes run, or be dragged—in the kicked-up, suffocating dust, 250 miles to Aleppo. At night Joscelin was whipped—expertly: to cause pain, but not to wound—before his meal of gruel. He was left to sleep without blanket on the open ground, which may serve a man like ice in the plummeting cold of the desert night.

After being paraded through Aleppo he was given the choice: blinding and imprisonment for the rest of his life, or else abjuration of the Christian faith. He was not tortured save the torture of free choice, and in the end, he refused to renounce Christ, lost his eyes, and was tossed into a dungeon where, nine years later, he died in chains having never known again any but the fetid air of his cell. That is his end: a long uneventful wait for the death which did not come soon enough. When told the full story by Beatrice herself, who had made inquiry following the translation of her husband's corpse to Jerusalem, Andronikus said, "The nature of a man's belief, foolish or sublime, does not matter. If he is willing to die sooner than deny it because it is that which gives his life meaning, then his authority and his courage stand higher than other men who live and die without challenge. But what a long way he passed from the silken, dissolute figure at dice with whom my uncle pleaded to enter the battle of Damascus."

From the moment of her husband's capture, Countess Beatrice spent futile months attempting to arrange ransom. Hearing of it, Nureddin sent her an anomalously sympathetic letter explaining to her the nature of her husband's incarceration. No ransom was acceptable. The justice against Joscelin II was final. Swearing herself against all Moslems, unable to defend the immediate lands, which the Prince of Aleppo had left to her after her husband's capture, Beatrice offered her still endangered ground not to her husband's liege, Mas'ud, but to Manuel, in exchange for a huge pension and a Greek guard. The Emperor, delighted by hegemony without a lance struck accepted the offer against the advice of all his courtiers including those most sycophantic. Andronikus' comment stood for all: "He's overtaking a war, not a province."

Mas'ud's son, Crown Prince Kilij, was infuriated by the contract. Ruler in fact, if not precedence, for a father too old, too sick, and too muddled to care, he had no intentions of being bound to mistakes suffered for filial piety, and he demanded, in Mas'ud's name, Manuel swear fealty as Pensioner of Edessa to the King. The Foreign Ministry dismissed the idea out of hand. Kilij put the arthritically illegible signature of his senile father to a document of war, and in the autumn the Emperor was forced to campaign against the Seljuks. In the long run, despite Manuel's success against Iconium, it would have been far better to have signed over Turbessel. The following year, in a surprise attack, the Ortoquid Emir, at the head of an army of eighty thousand, overwhelmed and captured the town, the castle, and the surrounding countryside. The Dowager Countess and her children, including the nominal Heir, Joscelin III, were forced to flee, penniless, to Jerusalem, but the damage done Byzantium in the agency of its Emperor was subtler and even worse. Previous to the Ortoquid victory, Manuel's policy had seemed triumphantly correct, so much so he had ceased to listen to the advice of his generals or his court, no matter how disinterested. By the time of the Edessan incident he could not make the connection between error and effect. "My husband," Bertha-Irene is once reported to have said, "cannot see that justice is not always prompt, but it *is* certain."

When he returned to Constantinople in December, he, of course, found his new mistress murdered and Persephone, with good reason, dreading the consequences. (We need not ask ourselves if, before the assassination, the Grand Duchess had expected the Emperor to trip indifferently over the corpse of Eugenia Exazena on his way back to her bed. Passion, indeed, has a logic like insanity, which has a logic all its own.) No wonder at the end of his life Manuel often compared himself to Agamemnon as a man whose tragedy after so many victorious years was not himself, but his family (and perhaps such a conclusion of self-excuse is the final tragedy).

After he had exiled Persephone, the Emperor devoted himself—at once as apology and recompense—to the Basilissa Irene. Together with Latin members of the Imperial army, he even initiated a courtly tournament in the Hippodrome, the first ever held in the history of that stadium and a far cry from the lavish successors which would be celebrated during the Emperor's marriage to Maria-Xenia of Antioch.

Nothing, that first time, went quite right—or quite wrong. The long stadium had been designed and built for chariot racing, not tournaments. The spina interfered with the spectators to one side or the other, and the great hairpins at either end could not accommodate the running length of the horses, though it was wide enough to accommodate several hundreds in hand-to-hand battle. Of course, these would have been serious flaws if the audience of Constantinopolitans had the least idea of what they were watching. In the end, it was scarcely important. The gesture was conceived with the Empress in mind and she enjoyed herself immensely, at once flattered and touched. Manuel, too, was gratified by her reaction and resolved to increase still more his attentions to his wife.

The Empress in turn resolved to serve herself up as a more glittering Consort. She took a greater care—to which she had previously given none—in clothes and jewels and the social life of the city, startling untold numbers of aristocratic and previously resentful matrons by inviting them to Blachernae, where they cooed and bowed respectfully and afterward sniggered and tore the Empress apart. So, too, Irene attempted to imitate her sisters-in-law by becoming somewhat more literary, which led, unfortunately, to two embarrassing incidents.

For guidance she had turned to the Emperor's aunt, the Sebastocratrix Joanna, who recommended to Augusta the two acknowledged lions of their day—though from opposite ends of the jungle—the poet-essayist John Tetzes and the poet-novelist Theodore Prodromus (or as the latter liked to style himself, Ptochoprodromus, Poor Prodromus, though he was immensely rich). Now, whom other hostesses must entice, the Empress could command, and naturally both men arrived promptly at her fairy-tale villa in Philopation Park.

John Tetzes was, of course, the master poet and greatest literary commentator of the previous century. It was my very great privilege to be his student, and like all budding litterateurs, I measured myself against him until, exasperated with my own insufficiency, I was certain he was, if not a fraud, vastly overrated. It is only since I have come into my own reputation, I quite frankly admit myself self-assured enough to acknowledge that I stand upon his shoulders—as do we all—and only wonder at my own previous tantrums. His words still ring in my ears: "The point is, my dear, I may be a wretched stylist, but I shall never be a hack. I don't write to specification and never shall. Yes, of course, I write to be read, but I write to be read on *my* terms—or else what's the point of writing at all? If you've nothing new or interesting to say, be silent. We go to a writer to see things his way—there's a choice: we don't have to— or we go to the ever similar Ptochoprodromus to remain unlit and untaught, and see things our own way, our perceptions unenlivened and unenlightened—in fact, embalmed. That *is*, you know, the beauty of human communication—that each of us, by sharing ourselves, may make one another more than we were before." Of course, John was very poor. I supported him in last years and, on learning of his plight, so did Andronikus till his own death. To be sure, his audience of intellects somehow believed poverty enhanced his integrity, while those who knew him only by name respectfully believed he was above complaining about his growling stomach and roach-filled tenement room.

Poor Prodromus, as they say, needs no introduction. He is the author of that undeservedly famous piece of sentimental bombasticity, *Rhodanphe and Dosicles,* which Andronikus, after reading the first four stanzas, accurately described, I think, as "something vomited up by a lapdog." *Rhodanphe and Dosicles* (there are still men and women alive who curse their names, which followed on its publication) is an amateurish attempt to equal *The Epic of Digenis Akritas,* the greatest poem of love and war in our history. I knew Theodore, also, and though I never liked him, I was alternately fascinated and repelled because I was never quite certain just how serious he was about himself. Contrary to his writings, his wit was sharp and incisive. How it became the man to succeed in that which he eminently did not deserve: literary success. His uncle was John II, Metropolitan-Archbishop of Kiev; hence his connections were impeccable, and though he disowned them, he was sure to use them. His loudest adherents were not intellects, but wealthy matrons who otherwise never read and to whom he was a flaming banner of *their* literacy against those snickering mental worthies who praised Tetzes, themselves jealous of Prodromus' wealth while contemptuous of his spiritual prostitution. (They might have relented somewhat if they had read some of Theodore's scurrilous pieces satirizing his "ladies" which he showed to me one drunken night.)

The reader need scarcely be told Bertha-Irene was not of the necessary sophistication to deal with these two temperamental gentlemen who saw each other as the refutation of all meaning in their careers. In his most hopeless, hungry moments John believed Theodore the triumph of mediocrity, proof of the absurdity of sincerity and the striving for art at the expense of material happiness in the only life one has to live. In those rare moments of solitude, away from his claque, Theodore held John—in misery and envy—as a noble accusation of the superficiality of his life, as one who had the strength to forgo the moment in return for the promise of artistic immorality. Let it be said Tetzes considered the invitation to Blachernae as interruption of his work, something vaguely like an honor, with the promise, somewhere, of a little money. Prodromus considered the invitation the summit, the crown, the final consent to his career, which, in a way, it was, since he had spent more time social-climbing than at his desk, and court life is, of course, *sine qua non.*

The somewhat unlikely symposium at Philopation lasted—miraculously—about two weeks, at the end of which John, suffering from dyspepsia, disgusted with the dancing obsequiousness of Theodore, and in despair over his neglected work, proposed he pay more lasting tribute to the Empress by dedicating to her the work—research completed—he was about to begin when called to the palace: that which became his monumental *Allegories on the Iliad*. Offended by the suspicion John was thinking of something else while talking to her, by his terse, true, unsmiling observations (proof, of course, of an impatience which was the consequence of his distraction) and the brutal carelessness of his clothing and toilette, Irene was frankly glad to be so diplomatically rid of this irritating creature and offered him 12 golden bezants for every notebook he filled.

Prodromus on the other hand was so witty, so charming, so impeccable, so *comme il faut,* so sympathetic, she did not hesitate to show him the poetry she had written in the years since her arrival at Constantinople, verses which Theodore praised as the very incarnation of Sappho. (Her niece, the Grand Duchess Eudocia, Andronikus' mistress, called them "something more than speech and very much less than song.") Indeed, Prodromus began to call the Empress "My Dearest Sappho," even in public, until several very pointed looks from the Grand Chamberlain and a certain noticeable distance in the Empress herself reminded him precisely who he was and what he was. As tribute to her, Prodromus lifted several unpublished poems from his files—Eudocia said it was from his morning trash—and presented them to Irene Augusta, bound and inscribed, for which he was handsomely rewarded.

Tetzes, on the other hand, was incapable of releasing from beneath his pen anything which he considered less than his best. As with genius this was a matter of both pride and obsession. He chose large paper and wrote in his small fine hand to show his seriousness. The work, which remains one of the literary milestones of the previous century, took a year to complete. By then, Irene was simultaneously pregnant and happily back at her charities. When Tetzes presented the work to the Empress, who greeted him as a stranger, he accurately if awkwardly suggested these ten notebooks were worth another man's one hundred. No money was forthcoming. Tetzes limped to the palace to ask Bertha-Irene why. He was received not by the Empress, but her comptroller, who informed our greatest living writer he would receive, as prearranged, 12 golden pieces per notebook—120 bezants in all—or nothing. Twice more Tetzes protested, and on his third venture to the court, he was altogether dismissed, without payment, his manuscripts returned to him.

It was the beginning, not the end, of a cause célèbre, which still festered when I arrived at Constantinople in the mid-sixties. Theodore's usual good fortune and John's ill favor was used by many poor writers—or writers forced to earn their pay by praising their patrons—as the truncheon with which to finally smash what was left of Prodromus' intellectual standing. In truth, I think, these supposedly sober mental worthies capable of seeing so many shades of gray they could not wash their linen without a second thought, acted somewhat too harshly and precipitously, which leads me to believe their motive was as much righteous indignation as the intolerable tension of envying a man's success, whose works they despised with considered reason.

When the literary praetorians were finished with Ptochoprodromus, they went after their own aristocratic patrons—these, the most literate and generous in the world, the likes of the Sebastocratrix, her sons Philip and Andronikus, whom one can imagine perfectly bemused wondering what on earth had got into their friends, as they truly considered such writers. Yet the final words were still Tetzes' and Prodromus' (the spark which set the conflagration, the Empress Irene, was, by then, dead). In a monograph written in 1167, Theodore made an unexpected reference to his antagonist, thus:

> Tetzes is condescending toward the ignorant as though intellect were an endowment rather than a discipline. There is something, after all, to be said for the crude, clear eye of the unschooled against the too subtle vision of the learned. I fear, moreover, though John George never speaks less than the truth, he possesses no sense of discretion. He does not measure his admonishments according to the time, the place, and the person. He is equally brusque to all with the consequence he sometimes obscures his wisdom by a false impression of resentment. A little honey will never dilute learning, but lubricate it.

So, too, John responded in an essay, by way of passing:

> When unfavorable opinion reaches him, Theodore Vladimir confronts his critic with a smile: he seems neither angered nor insulted, but wistful, rather as though resigned to be proved again and again correct in his mistrust of fellow men. Beware, my friends: it is not the understanding of resignation you perceive in the exhibition of those teeth, but a vindictiveness which will one day burst, if it has not at this writing. Prodromus is one of those who creates his tormentors and retaliates without conscience, or, conversely, creates his victims and calls himself mighty—confusing authority with malice. He admires intellect, it is true,

but admiration too often takes the final metamorphosis of jealousy, which is rather proof of a lack of faith in his own fair mind. As for the late and most assuredly mourned Empress: while I cannot be said to have known her intimately, as Ptochoprodromus has, I would wager they were two of a kind in their own respective fashions. She impressed me in the brief time I knew her as one of those who, if not allowed to help you—in *some* way—seemed to accuse you. These are personally very troubling people, for there is no way to be rid of such Samaritans, finally, but to rebuff them and leave them ultimately to repeat the same mistake and so on until death or final embitterment. It pains me to say, such is the nature of men my heartless art will outlive her heartfelt charities. Just so Theodore Vladimir—or, as he has now taken to calling himself, *à la russe,* Feodor Vladimirovitch (he wears his pretensions like colored scarves: depending on his moods)—he fails to see the distinction between celebrity and the man who is celebrated. His self-delusion is either greater than I thought or his powers of insight, always at a minimum, finally failed. He cannot see his acceptance amongst the social lions of this city has nothing whatever to do with the talent he once believed himself to have possessed. Only *he* seems to remember it. Rather he is rich and famous and the very powerful get on best, understandably, with their kind, taking in one another's glory to assure themselves of their own. Yet, I would refrain from congratulating myself for my lack of riches, as young men congratulate themselves in the morning for rising early. It is true, nevertheless, the older I become, the less materially inclined I have become, with only a little regret, only occasionally, only once in a while, desiring to be a little more comfortable, but not too often. I possess still the great gift God has given me, for which I am thankful. I have my eyes and my ears and I have never been obliged to pawn my books. I can still write, though I can scarcely walk, but it is enough. In the end, finery and too much food and social amenities and gatherings in the country and the city serve only to pass the time, however pleasurably—that is no excuse—of men who have nothing else to do. I part with each hour of the day most niggardly. The ambition to set down one's perceptions and beliefs has, for me, become more important even than great friends, medicines for my aches, warm rooms, or the allaying of petulant loneliness. I do not mock these things: a life lived well is an art in itself, but the discipline which reaches depths cannot be divided. It is, by nature, monomanic. Prodromus, in this light, *is* an artist and I congratulate him his achievement. I assure him, he will be remembered—via my essays.

X

About a year before her death at the turn of the century, I spoke to the Grand Duchess Eudocia Comnena Catacalon Gabras of that period when she had been the mistress of the then Grand Duke Andronikus. I expected she might be reticent. I had not seen her for almost twenty years and I was scarcely prepared for the regal, beautiful, bejeweled old woman who leaned her lovely white-haired head against the golden back of her chair and smiled in delighted reverie. "Heavens, he was the most handsome man who ever lived, and the most wondrous, the most attentive. Of course, you know he was such a *large* man." She said this with a circular upraised movement of her beringed fingers, with the sensuous savor of one describing a particularly gratifying meal. "People would instinctively step back as he approached them. And you know, their first impulse was to treat him like a bull, a gross, insensitive bull. For *them*, he sharpened himself all the more. He seemed amused. Perhaps he *was* a bull, but his ways were as labyrinthine as the paths to the minotaur. And, of course, the irony of it is that beside him all other men were beasts."

I asked her how the alliance began. "It was in the autumn of '49— or was it '50? I don't know. In any event it was the most magic of my life—not exciting, mind you, but *enchanted*. I was like an animal, if I may say. I put aside all logic, all propriety, all sense to remove myself from danger or prevent myself from giving offense to others. It was not a conscious impetuousity. I simply didn't care. I lived for my cousin and through him and I existed only to be with him again and when I was with him I dreaded the moment when we would have to part. Even when we were apart, I sensed he *hovered* over me. (Once when we were staying with his mother at Selymbria I told her of these things and she only smiled in a curious way, almost a sad smile, but after a fashion full of pride her son could provoke a woman so, and said, 'Well, my dear, now you know the meaning of obsession.' 'Yes,' I said, 'and I'm not certain I like it.')

"Curious how I confused our alliance with an intense religious devotion, and even death. As for the piety, I suppose I wanted to be grateful to *someone* for having him. The thought we were in love by chance was *too* intolerable. It made one giddy. Then too, I worried for him, *I* hovered over *him* when he was not with me. I had to think he was under some divine protection. He was such a reckless man otherwise. I remember one crepuscular winter sunset so very vividly—once again at Selymbria. For some reason he was called away for the night and we lingered and could not part and he wept and I wept. I was certain he could not love me as I loved him. And no doubt he was certain I could not love him as he loved me—I would like to hope so, though I doubt it. We were dreadfully miserable that afternoon as we rode away in opposite directions. Then he called my name and I turned and he only looked at me —I see him against the snow and violet-pink glow of the sky—and I *knew* in that moment he loved me, if only in that moment, and though it was the happiest of my life, why, do you know, I wanted to die." Fifty years later her amazement at her feelings was still fresh. She bethought herself and then shrugged—such a light, graceful little gesture with those shoulders. "I suppose the thought of death is never very far from any experience good or bad, and as we may slip out of life from the top *or* the bottom, if we are very lucky, we will fly from the heights. Why not consent to death in ecstasy rather than despair or resignation?

"He could hurt me more than he knew. I suppose I was sentimental somewhat, being young, and preferred to think of our love in the most exalted terms. Simply nothing else would do. Well, he had a way of deflating those pretensions. I said to him once, 'I think love is the most spiritual of our essences,' and he said right back, almost coldly, 'It's the most animal, my dear, preserved in its purest state—and thank heavens.' "

I laughed then because the Grand Duchess' imitation was so exact, because the corners of her lips curled down and then up—like a ram's horn arrow (a Paleologus feature)—which, together with her childlike, elongated two front teeth, was so precisely and attractively like her former lover's smile.

"Oh, but Count, you don't know how a remark like that wounded me. I loved him with my whole heart and soul. I would accept from him any humiliation, any remonstrance, though no act of his was ever intended as such, for all that they were; I would do whatever he wished, anything to prove my love for him. What is it Sappho speaks? 'Like a windstorm/ Punishing the oak trees/ Love shakes my heart.' When it was over, I don't know whether it can be said I left much of myself behind or took so much of the alliance forward with me—yes, that; it is more positive—in the sense, later, I was constantly distracted, reminded, withdrawn from the present into the past or, perhaps, making the past present. Since then, of course, the dross of those days has been washed away. The consequences I dreaded I have lived beyond, and I am no longer tormented. I remember that time with such sweetness, for it could never occur again. The circumstances were once and irrevocable: our youth, our beauty. Nothing was expected of us and we were easily forgiven because there were years ahead to make recompense."

She was silent, looking away, a little smile of reverie and pleasure playing upon the countenance of her lips and eyes, her still slender, white-garbed body in perfect repose, arms upon the arms of the chair, the still elegant, lengthy fingers hanging limp. She seemed, then, old, but old in the sense of ripeness, of fulfillment. When she spoke, her voice was from the distance of her memories. "We were lucky too. We were cut clean—that death I wished for in the pink sunset in the winter at Selymbria. I can even say now, when my uncle and my brothers conspired to send him away from me, I was almost relieved." I asked her if she held the Grand Duke responsible for the death of her brother David. The wonderful expression vanished. She was inscrutable, her eyes lowered. "Yes. But it doesn't matter."

Andronikus: "Someone once said—I no longer remember who—I was the most unlikely lover who ever existed. The fellow then went on to explain I was one of those too ambitious and too introverted to maintain the frivolity of a paramour. But wit which must be footnoted is like opening a jeweler's box to find a description of the contents which are not there. I rather dismissed the observation as the inaccuracy of one of those polysyllabic illiterates one sometimes encounters, who because he turns the conventional on its head believes he has discovered a new truth. Anything looks different upside down. The distinction, as I understand it, is not between my ability to love and my ambition, or love and my personal metaphysics, but between spiritual obsession and lust. I've had carnal thoughts on the field of battle, at funerals, while a surgeon extracted a tooth, as a starved outlaw crawling in concealment on my belly across the countryside. I've used lust as a weapon against nightmare, despair, and then again, carnality has now and then used me to poor effect. We often speak of the spiritual unity between men and women, but I would be willing to wager the real commonality is in their passion, which is indistinguishable, rather than their so-called intellectual compatibility, which is the source of their individuality. We are similarly animals and especially angels.

"Once my father gave me some words of sound advice: 'My boy,' he said, 'women are like the rarest game: to catch and make a meal of one fowl is a pleasure; to consume a whole flock is to invite indigestion and ennui.' I have often thought of lust as something like anarchy and of love as the imposition of order upon that chaos, as the tree which throws its roots in all directions becomes the hut which was implied in its being.

"The first time I allowed passion without calculation to disorder my life was, of course, my affair with my cousin Eudocia, which, believe me, I found far more notorious myself than its naysayers. I sometimes think —but not often; it is difficult to recall my own motives in the tumult—I was committed to our alliance perhaps more eagerly and completely than, knowing myself now, seems very likely. It was the appalling interference of Manuel and her brothers which determined me more than ever to do what I liked. What possible right had these people—*not* disinterestedly, to threaten us, counsel us, command, or even attempt to destroy us? A little affection and a little bedding down. It was the sheer irrelevance of the situation, its innate privacy, bringing about the wrath of the Emperor and the malice of her brothers which affronted me. Did I love Eudocia? After a fashion, yes. I loved her, but I loved my wife, too, who, I may remind you, was then with child—our eldest, Alexander.

"Anastasia accepted the situation, or seemed to, but then Anastasia's pride was the deciding factor of all her actions—perhaps the very reason I so much appreciated her. She would not ask me to refrain from Eudocia because that implied my fidelity was thereafter a matter of probation rather than volition, a ravaging really of the very meaning of love.

"Something changed in me the night of Eugenia's assassination. I had, myself, come so close to dying. Had I not turned one way or another or my assailant's wrist been deflected by his own clothing or his own excitement—or his colleague's fall, I seem to remember—I would not be here—for some, a blessing.

"I know there are others who, following so narrow an escape, would have found renewed the meaning of life, would have found God, or the pleasure of simple things—I am not mocking them—and forsworn ever, another wasted moment. But do you know, to me, the awkward aim of that knife represented nothing so much as the epiphany of the absurdity of existence, its fragility against which there is no defense. Not many nights thereafter I had one of the most vivid dreams of my life in which I was forced to cross a gorge, on a slender plank, blindfolded. As in the way of dreams, I could see the long fall below me, but it did not matter because all my senses were responding in a manner as though I could not. I could warn myself of the dangers, but I could not prevent them.

"It has seemed to me, since, everything matters and nothing matters and confidence is for the naïve, for children. If I am forced to point to a time when I realized what I had long sensed—the tenuousness of existence, its lack of seriousness—I would choose that moment in my twenty-eighth year. Is there anything more wonderful than the mind which is conscious of itself—and anything more ridiculous than the slender threads which bind it to life, which are, so simply, cut.

"In any event, the more Eudocia and I made concessions to propriety or politics, the more, not less, we antagonized her brother John, not because he was a prude (quite the opposite: he practiced on his whores in secret while trumpeting a public morality which made him the laughing stock of the family), but because Rebecca, their mother, was profoundly offended. Mere adultery, I suspect, would not have raised my aunt's hackles so. Once again it was our consanguinity—in the first *and* second degree since Eudocia was a first cousin through her mother and a second through her father. Rebecca would have preferred Prince Paul Catacalon, Eudocia's husband, to contest me—at length, my aunt could be that much of a cynic—but Paul was too intimidated by her title to contest his wife who I happen to know couldn't have been kinder to him. John, despite his father's disinheritance had been reaffirmed Heir Presumptive to the throne. It was in his gain to destroy me under the apron of his mother's outrage. He was clever enough or suspicious enough—I would never say insightful—to scent something of danger in my political beliefs. On a personal level, he fiercely resented my popularity with the army and the constant indulgences Manuel extended to me. John was like one of those tyrannical little maidens who give little, yet must be told constantly they are loved and pout stridently if their lovers so much as look at another woman. Somehow he felt all that was given me was stolen on its way to him."

Having divested himself of his niece, the Emperor was now in a clear position to demand Andronikus relinquish Eudocia. He created Prince

Paul Governor of Thrace and ordered the Grand Duchess to follow her husband to Demetrius Palace at Thessalonika. She did. And Andronikus followed her. He commanded Eudocia back to Constantinople and Andronikus to make a state visit, with Anastasia, to Iconium, where in December 1151, at Leila Palace, the home of her brother-in-law, Michael, the Grand Duchess gave birth to a son, whom as Andronikus described it, "in a small fit of vengeance, I named after the founder of our House. Magnanimously then, I asked Manuel and Bertha to be his godparents. They accepted. When the Patriarch submerged my boy in the font of the Imperial Chapel I could imagine Manuel with visions of keeping the child's head under. But the boy was dipped vigorously and came up screaming and Anastasia and I heard his bawling—a little to our relief, small as that sounds—just outside the doors."

To honor the birth of the nephew of the King of Georgia, the Emperor used his baptism as an excuse to promulgate an edict granting those Russian monks who had previously lived within the community of Mt. Athos an establishment of their own, St. Panteleimon.*

"As soon as I returned to Constantinople," Andronikus recalled, "I resumed my alliance with Eudocia, if only to spite her brother and my wife, both of whom for obviously differing reasons seemed to be congratulating themselves their mastery of me. In truth, these last times together were somewhat uncomfortable. I knew what was coming and I could no longer care, which was really an awful thing. But I was thirty years old, the very best years of my life were passing without any fruit, save a son, whose existence now impressed upon me a ponderable sense of the future I had never before known, a sense of rushing away and waste and nothing served between save the accomplishment of Manuel's most successful and willing castration. No amount of political ornamentation can disguise the fact that Manuel exiled me when he made me

---

* Before the year 1152 was out, Manuel was to serve his priests a less palatable course. Faced with combating a clergy once again grown lax, wealthy, illiterate, and undisciplined, he decided to reinforce the novels of Nicephorus II, breaking up monasterial domains, making mandatory the ability to read and write, forbidding otherwise the consecration of former outlaws (who sought sanctuary for a time in this manner and would think twice, henceforth, if put to the books), also the establishment of new foundations or grants to old ones. In the next breath, unfortunately, he went against his own decree setting up a monastery at Constantinople, under strict budget of the Imperial Treasury, to serve as a model and allowed Andronikus' father, now sixty, to build another at Vera, in Thrace, where the former Sebastocrator would take the tonsure as abbot and hoped to be buried. N.A.

Governor of Cilicia, yet for that I was almost happy to go. Eudocia had nothing to do with it. Rather, after fifteen years, he and I had grown quite weary of one another, dangerously weary. The weariness which is indifference to pain, given or received. I had begun to be capricious, to taunt, almost against myself, to be a little cruel and a little insolent; but, then, it is only so long as ideals and dreams, one's ambitions, can hold before the desiccation takes place. Like all things sweet they spoil most acridly.

"And Manuel was beginning to respond in kind, by stops and starts and hesitations of affection, progressively more resolute and harsh and suspicious. Yet without plots or political interference to certify his fears he could do no better than to place a great distance between myself and all source of power, namely himself. So he made me Governor of Cilicia and expressly commissioned me to put down the insurrection of Prince Thoros of Armenia as clemently as possible, which is to say win the secessionist back to the Empire after humiliating him in war, a bankrupt policy both my grandfather and my uncle had previously attempted with the Rupen family to the same abject end."

On his way to Cilicia, Andronikus stopped at Christos Gennate to present his son to his father. Against Manuel's orders to proceed at once with his commission, he remained with his wife and child, by Isaac's side, for a fortnight. "Three days after our arrival, my mother joined us. It was the first time for Sandro—and the last—three generations of heirs were together. I don't think I've idealized those three weeks. They *were* lovely. Strange how my father's mortality affected me. He seemed not to move before my eyes but that he was a step closer to death. All at once he had become for me so desperately vulnerable in his years. I remember one day I accompanied my father to the little church down the road from the castle, which immemorial had been our ancestral place of worship. . . ." *Explicit: Nicetas Acominatus.*

With his left palm cupped under Isaac's left elbow, his right arm round his father's shoulder, Andronikus leads Isaac along the russet-colored pine-needle path. They pass from bolt to bolt of sunlight, followed by the Sebastocrator's "faithful Barnabas" and the Grand Duke's bodyguards, everyone on foot, the old secretary in quiet conversation with the two Excubitors. Andronikus' expression is remarkable, an aspect almost never seen by the world: mild, guileless, gentle, almost radiant; Isaac's is nearly all pain, but resigned, even tolerable, while his son is close-by.

ISAAC. I have only one wish, you know, before I die.

ANDRONIKUS. I know.

ISAAC. It may be God draws you into the darkness so that you may perceive the light more clearly. You rely too much on yourself. Your beliefs are a candle flame held against the disk of the sun which is the immortal truth.

ANDRONIKUS. But a candle is light in my hand, which is all that concerns me, rather than the sun, which is aloof. I would go willingly—sooner than believe myself delivered—into the darkness.

ISAAC. I only fear, without God, you are bound so capriciously to life. I think it is because you do not believe God loves you, that you do not believe yourself singular in His eyes, you chase so insatiably after celebrity.

ANDRONIKUS. Immortality. To be inconspicuous is very like death.

ISAAC. Is that why you have come to resent my brother's son? Because both have come to him like a gift and you must earn them?

ANDRONIKUS. Do I resent him? Is it so obvious?

ISAAC. It is *very* obvious. Your mother says you come close to baiting him like a cruel hunter when you are in his company.

ANDRONIKUS. Perhaps I only mean to draw him out. Sooner an open enemy than one with the charm which in its perfume conceals the fact it is also vitriolic when swallowed. I shall never know what became of us.

ISAAC. You became men, Andronikus. You know you will die. You know your own solitude, and now you know as you never could before, in that solitude, there are others. They are the world, which is at stake between the two of you, the world as you would see it. And the world watches. From that, there is only one conclusion. Two men who fight before a third will become shy as the irrelevance of their argument becomes obvious, or, certain of their premises, become vindictive, more resolute, seeking the cheers of that audience, both controlled and seeking to control it.

Incipit: Nicetas Acominatus: ". . . As Isaac and I talked on the way home, I noticed a repose in my attitude of which I had never previously been aware. Previously in our conversations you could have drawn blood along the rasp in my voice. But it was more than that. In no sense whatsoever condescending, I knew I was being kinder to him, more tolerant by far of his opinions—even seeing some of their logic if I could not act upon it—than I had ever been before. I no longer challenged him or felt superior to his prejudices. My father, for instance, was overwhelmed by a sense of sin. Well, you know, I have always considered the first mark of a civilized man his realization of the distinction between sin and crime, and the second, that sin does not exist. In fact I was repelled by his breast-beating though I did not show it, as I would have, once. On balance, however, my father was a wise man, after a fashion, a genius. That genius never deserted him, though its constant fire in an ailing frame wore him out. (One last thing. You may think it by the way, but somehow the incident has remained with me more than thirty years from that day to this, I don't know why. During that walk from the little church to the castle, we sat for a while on a fallen trunk and I remember watching an ant carrying a dead moth across the entire width of the road. This enormous burden, so many times its own weight—or so it must have been—across the equal, let us say, of something like a mile. As Isaac and I talked, I watched his brute feat in awe. And just as we were rising, my father took a step and crushed both the ant and its burden. Odd, isn't it, I felt an unbearable pang? I felt something fail before that absurd, enormous effort and indifferent death.)

"At the end of nearly three weeks, I received a terse letter from my cousin to leave at once for Cilicia. He was, he said, quite mystified and unhappy with my—I quote—illegal tarrying—close quote. So I said good-by to my mother and my son and my wife—and to my father, whom I never saw again."

XI

In July 1152, shortly before the Empress was about to reach term, Manuel Augustus ordered one of the most sacred relics in Christendom —the stone slab on which Christ lay in his tomb—translated from the Cathedral of the Holy Sepulcher at Ephesus, amidst incense and torches, day and night, to Constantinople. When it arrived at the harbor of Drungariou Viglae in an extraordinary act of public imploration to God that his wife conceive an Heir, the Emperor, dressed in a rough black wool penitent's cowl, carried the huge stone on his back the half mile to Pantokrator Cathedral, where it was set before the tomb of his canonized parents. Then, alone, throughout the afternoon and into the evening, knees to the stone floor, the Emperor prayed not only for a son but, as he had promised his Basilissa, for the soul of the Emperor Conrad III, who had died in February. The following month the Empress gave birth to a daughter, Her Imperial Highness the Grand Duchess Maria Catherine Porphyriogeneta, whom the Imperial family, in this sea of Marias (and Eudocias and Theodoras and Elizabeths and Irenes), immediately, distinctively, and gratefully called Catherine, as shall we.

On the assumption heaven is above all boundaries, Manuel had good reason to propitiate his former earthly ally. On 5 March 1152, following obsequies, Conrad's nephew, Frederick, to no one's surprise, was elected German King at Frankfurt, and four days later was crowned in the Carolingian vault at Aix-la-Chapelle. His apologists, at the ready with their bought pens, at once commenced burnishing his reputation to a high glow, though it is certain this stolid, brutal, conceited prude was chosen less as the reincarnation of Carolus Magnus he believed himself to be than for the mix of his blood (Hohenstaufen-Waiblingen on his father Frederick's side, Welf through his mother, Judith of Bavaria), which promised an end to the atrociously violent rivalry of the two most powerful families in the Empire. Conrad had seen this and forced to choose between the devil and the deep sea—i.e., Frederick or continuation of the Empire-wrecking feud—recommended his nephew as Heir.

Now, Frederick had seen and heard, at Constantinople, just enough to confirm his belief in absolutism as the only fit tool for his will, and he went about substantiating his authority. As there could be only one Lord of the World, for a beginning, he addressed Manuel in a letter responding to the Basileus' greeting of his "Imperial brother," as Rex Grecorum rather than Imperator Romanorum or even Imperator Romanorum Orientalis. At the same time, with a marvelous blindness, which denied his insolence but obviated his lack of self-assurance, having divorced his wife Adela, whom he did not crown Queen, he requested Manuel send him a bride from among the Comnenian Grand Duchesses. Unfortunately our own Emperor's hauteur offended, Manuel informed the German ambassador he would sooner marry one of his nieces to Nureddin than to Frederick, and thereby cost the state lives and monies as the Alliance of the Two Empires was shattered and fell in the middle ground between Frankfurt and Constantinople, which is to say Hungary, once again to be flattered, threatened, battered, and raised again in the role of buffer.

Not content to offend a man whom, had Frederick been a little more insightful, he would have seen was impressionable as talcum, the German Emperor, displaying the aptness for feud learned at his parents' knees, interfered in a dynastic quarrel taking place in Denmark, naturally deciding in favor of the anti-Constantinopolitan Svend. Our ambassador, present at the time of the usurpation to conclude a treaty and recruit Varangians, was ordered to leave the capital, Roskilde, and when he was not quick enough about it, the kingdom itself. Then again while Frederick made enormous concessions to his local nobles to free himself to fight the East Slavs—repeating Manuel's error—he treated those who formed the basis of his claim to the Roman Imperium, the North Italians, as conquered aliens fit only for the knout if they were impertinent and the tax collector if they were loyal. The consequences of this injudicious disparity of rule was to have untold consequences, in time, for Byzantium.* Finally after alienating the Pope on matters of prerogative (i.e., failing to ask for confirmation of his election), he actively antagonized his territorial neighbor and spiritual superior, Eugenius III, by having the anti-Pope, Anastasius IV, canonize that most unlikely saint, Carolus Magnus. Eugenius in turn threatened to deny Frederick a coronation, and Frederick, truly into his element now, responded he would make alliance with Eugenius' foremost enemy, Roger of Sicily.

Incredibly, this monstrous, impetuous upsetting of the European diplomatic scheme occurred within six months of the German Emperor's accession. At the end, if offense were profit, Frederick stood rich and alone, unable to move, having thwarted, insulted, or manipulated so variously, even his potential allies mistrusted this dervish. Any alliance is a matter of self-interest, but there is always something to gain as well as give. Frederick's right hand promised almost no advantage worth the

---

* The Italians had, of course, learned the folly of Empire long ago, by creating the greatest and losing it—perhaps in sheer exhaustion. They have since refused to take politics seriously, least of all politics in its most pompous and malicious form: despotism. Since there is no better way to offend superciliousness than by familiarity, graffiti began to appear in response to the Emperor's propagandists, of which the most famous was *"Barbarossa: tanto buon che val niente,"* or "Redbeard: so good he's good for nothing." Thus wit, not fear, gave the German Emperor the sobriquet by which the world knows him. It is only coincidence his name is so incestuously similar to our Greek word for foreign or rude, i.e., *barbaros*. But then nothing Greek served him well. N.A.

outrage his left hand raised. This served Byzantium better than his active challenge against Manuel's Italian campaign. Plans of the Imperial General Staff proceeded, therefore, with the following spring as a target date, when it was hoped the first Constantinopolitan Emperor in half a thousand years would set foot in Italy, the boot of Europe, or even Sicily, the rock Italy is about to kick.

All that might prevent Manuel from moving west was the extensive damage he believed his cousin to be drawing in his wake in the East.

"I really can't be sure," Andronikus once recalled for me, "but I believe my second-in-command, Magdalena's son, her eldest, Basil, was set upon me as a spy. I suspected it so and was more amused than angered because the boy was so limpid, one of those who blush at the least cross word. He really wasn't quite that sensitive, I think, but rather in a constant turmoil between the polarities of a heroic ambition and the awful suspicion the world thought him a bungler if not a fool. You know the sort: every act is performed as though under the duress of examination. The moment I guessed his role, I was very careful to be *very* cordial. Such people are not always spiteful—Basil wasn't—but there was no point in giving his potential antagonism a handle with which to beat me. Then again, I served myself ill enough. There was no need."

There are no excuses for Andronikus' conduct in Cilicia, only explanations. Almost from the first, he made reconciliation with the insurgent Thoros impossible. The Grand Duke Basil describes the event which was to cause Constantinople two armies and six years more of intermittent war:

> About a month after our arrival, during the battle at the Lampron Defile, despite Andronikus' lackadaisical strategy (his fighting serving to inspire the army whereas his command nearly destroyed it), we were fortunate enough to inflict heavy casualties on the enemy's left and, more important still, to capture no less than Prince Stephen, Prince Thoros' brother. My aides and myself were on our way back to the Praetorium to present him to Andronikus, when he attempted an escape instead of acting honorably in defeat as should have become his station. And so we bound and gagged him like a common criminal. By the time we reached camp I thought his eyes would burst from his head; his face was actually scarlet (the temper of these people is legend). Well, we stood him before my cousin who, I remember, seemed more amused than excited—perfect counterpoint to the infuriated Cilician. Himself

covered with dust and blood and sweat, he calmly slit the seal on a communication, as apparently he had been about to do before our arrival. He said, "Ungag him. He looks as though he's about to swallow his own head." The moment we took the silk away, the Prince expectorated full in my cousin's face. I recall Andronikus' head was a little to one side, his eyes at the corners as though listening, in passing, to someone behind him. His expression was unchanged. All of a moment—an endless one—he plunged the knife with which he had opened the letter into Stephen's heart. The Prince screamed horribly and crumpled in death, grotesque in his ropes, at my cousin's feet. My cousin looked round at all of us, still expressionless, but somehow daring us to accuse him, turned, and re-entered the pavilion. This was murder, and something beyond murder. He sheathed that knife in Stephen's breast with no more thought than cutting into a loaf of bread.

"I felt no guilt then," said Andronikus of this infamous episode, "I feel none now. It was a sudden expostulation, deliberate, but passionate —not vindictive. It had only a little to do with Stephen's aristocratic spittle. Rather, I think, he seemed to me the very living image of my fortune, my nemesis. His feet were my exile, his wild eyes my absent wife again with child, his hands, which would have killed *me* given the opportunity, the consolation of my son, his trembling, separation from my father as he daily slipped closer to death. He was myself in this dusty, forever rebellious corner of the Empire; he was day after day of battle with the promise, if I were triumphant, I should remain in Cilicia forever to administer petty bureaucrats."

Looking off in the direction of the long shadows of the late summer afternoon, Andronikus' expression darkened. His head weaved momentarily and he winced a little in some remembered pain. His voice lowered and he mused, "Odd, I haven't thought of that incident in so many years. I would like to feel something, but there seems to be, for me, no resonance in the act. Only a vague revulsion—I can still feel it—in the nauseating little instant when the flesh you violate resists—and the resistance communicates itself the length of your weapon to your hand and arm—before all gives and the blade sinks as if having gathered your strength, descends with its own life into the hot internum."

Quietly, I asked the then Emperor if perhaps he was not accusing himself unnecessarily. I asked him to consider the circumstances: having just arrived from fierce battle with the usual exhilaration and exhaustion of the battle-weary, his judgment may have been as lax as his temper keen. Prince or peasant feels an extraordinary insult in what is perhaps the foulest gesture of contempt a man can make. Quite besides, Prince Stephen was complicit with aristocrats against the lower orders served more kindly by Imperial rule. Mightn't it all have been impetuosity rather than malice?

At my rationalization he seemed to be very amused, smiling perhaps the same smile which was the last thing Stephen ever saw. "You don't seem to understand, my boy. There was never any question of malice. It was slaughter, unfeeling, as the butchers who bind a cow in the Forum of Theodosius and slit its throat. I tell you there have been acts which I have committed which I could more easily excuse and have indeed regretted. But this: its evil is in its emptiness. Perhaps from this tyrants are born who would kill and kill again to find somewhere in a field of corpses their own remorse."

While Andronikus inferred meanings in this incident which—if not the act itself—would haunt him so anomalously all his life, Manuel drew only one conclusion, the irrevocable, intentional alienation of Thoros. This is not so unfair as it sounds, for while the Cilician Prince fought in the vigor of his grief, Andronikus seemed altogether to relinquish his responsibilities. He left the Grand Duke Basil to preside over the General Staff—a commission for which the young man was neither intended nor prepared—and ceased to take part in the strategy or performance of battles. Without his presence, the army fought poorly. This, and strategy of little insight and no daring, resulted in serious Byzantine losses.

In civic spheres the Grand Duke was more himself, but without the grace of which he was quite capable, alienating rather than persuading. When the Metropolitan of Sis wanted to bring to trial a small congregation of Paulician heretics, long protected by Thoros' fellow nobles and —with the usual exaggeration of fear—believed to be the vanguard of an army of apostatical missionaries set to overrun Cilicia the moment it passed from Imperial hands, Andronikus threatened to hang the Archbishop from the walls of the city. Testified Basil:

> He told His Eminence to release the heretics at once or answer to him most direly. After the interview—from which the Bishop departed enraged (as much by my cousin's calm as his proposal to rescue heretics) —I asked Andronikus, "Why do you defend these people? They corrupt the truth of Orthodoxy." Surprised, he said, "If Orthodoxy is the truth

it will survive the corruption. If not, so much the better." I asked him in a friendly way, "Why should it matter to you—of all people—what men believe?" He said, "Basil, I loathe bullies, and the Bishop is a bully." "He's defending Mother Church." He looked at me with awful contempt, and then he softened, and smiled, and patted my shoulder, "Just you worry about your own virtue. Mother Church is quite equipped to take care of her own." But I persisted, even though he seemed to be growing impatient. "Heretics sow division, Andronikus." "*No, Basil.* Men who call other men heretics are divisive."

On receipt of a letter of complaint by the Metropolitan, in which the Bishop went so far as to state the Grand Duke had been receiving agents from the Iconiate court (actually his brother Michael's equerry) and Baldwin II of Jerusalem (a grain merchant who had contracted with Andronikus' quartermaster), Manuel Augustus was more than ever certified in suspicions of his cousin. He sent an angry letter to Andronikus and a countermand which allowed the Metropolitan to try the heretics (Manuel's tolerance extended to Moslems, Jews, Latin Catholics, and even atheists, not to those perverted within the body Orthodox). Furthermore, he placed the Grand Duke under the surveillance of the Secret Police and in a gesture of rank public mistrust, removed Anastasia from Hieriea Palace across the Bosporus to within the city walls and Vlanga Palace—an exquisite tenth-century structure built for the mistress of John I. In effect, Andronikus' wife was hostage—under house arrest— against his conduct.

In a letter attached to the memorandum of Basil Guiscard which we have been quoting, mention is made of this last incident:

I am forced to respectfully suggest to you, uncle, that either you allow Stana to return to Hieriea or, in the least, remove her guard and find some pretext for informing Andronikus this has been done. Really, you are misinformed of the realities of the situation or there exist those who are purposefully poisoning you against our cousin. The Metropolitan is an arch liar, a careerist, and a more notorious bigot than any I have ever known, and while I would be fain to allow Christ's enemies to roam free, I must concur with Andronikus this is not the time to make an example of these wretches who have lived peaceably under the auspices of Thoros and his colleagues. If the Prince is ever to be reconciled, we need not arm his supporters with arguments and proofs that a return to Constantinople would mean the introduction of religious despotism—

and, by extension, civil despotism as well. Moreover, I must tell you, Andronikus is scarcely in the mood to be further antagonized. He has become, by turns, sullen and capricious, and I feel it is building toward something disastrous. If I may say, uncle, you have, on scant proof, insulted his loyalty, and an insult great or small arouses antagonism all the same, for a pebble may trip up a man and kill him, as soon as the boulder in a landslide. If you insult a man, he is still disciplined enough to be cunning. If he is outraged, he is bound to be gross and make mistakes. . . .

("Either he has forced Basil—with a knife at his throat—to write this letter, or my nephew has suffered not the wounds of battle, but the amputation of his judgment." This was Manuel's comment on receipt of the above note. Many years later courtiers still vividly recalled the Emperor's anger. One fellow, who drew me into a corner, said, with a wide-eyed expression and an urgent conspiratorial whisper—a curious habit of aged sycophants—"Oh, His Majesty was certain the Grand Duke Basil took His Imperial Highness' defense in revenge against his mother, the late Caesarissa. Nothing could change his mind, either, insofar as his cousin. He was certain Andronikus was deliberately setting out to ruin him in ways great and small.")

All suspicions were confirmed when Andronikus, on Twelfth Night, 1153, deserted his command and fled to Antioch. Later, he was to say, with grim humor, "As the Magi passed west, so I passed east," but that is the captain's giddy braggadocio after he has brought the ship through a storm, or else the actor's trivialization of his deed so that men will marvel all the more. In fact, as the Grand Duke's beloved Theodora (then sixteen) once told me, "It was an upheaval, really. It gave the Imperial livestock months of cud to chew on." She smiled wickedly. "I thought it was perfectly marvelous. Everyone followed my uncle like sheep, but for this one jackal. I hardly knew him then (I hadn't seen him since I was thirteen). I only knew *of* him, as did everyone else. And somehow—as witness to the kind but belittling indifference with which my uncle treated my father, who was, after all, the Sebastocrator and his elder brother—I was pleased, even then, someone was alive to antagonize and irritate Manuel, whom I always found just a bit *de trop*."

It was an altered Latin Confederacy to which Andronikus fled.

The Christian Levantine states had rebounded astonishingly well after the disasters of the late forties. At the time of Andronikus' arrival, they were dominated by a single young man, and a most melting one, at that: His Royal Majesty King Baldwin III, Advocatus Sancti Sepulchri, then twenty-two years old and, with no exaggeration, the purest flower of Latin chivalry, as beautiful as a woman, as pious as a saint, gallant, literate, compassionate, witty, ardent, strong as Samson, flirtatious as Pan.

Once again, the Grand Duchess Theodora, who was to become Baldwin's Queen: "I sometimes think it is well my husband died young. Once I thought Andronikus should not have grown old either—that he was what Baldwin might have become. But no. The other day you said something quite pertinent. What was it? There were times when you must remind yourself you are speaking to a fifty-eight-year-old man because the Grand Duke seems to you so young? If by youth you mean passion, flexibility, curiosity, wonder, then you are quite correct. But Baldwin was that other youth—the sentimental ideal of which poets speak and whom one scarcely, if ever, encounters. Andronikus is the reality of youth—impetuous, novel, inexhaustible, whimsical, too serious and not serious enough, at once dissimulator and almost offensively honest, questioning, adapting, contradictory, infuriating, and hopelessly self-centered. Baldwin was the ideal of youth, youth perceived in retrospect: he was a boy, a perfect boy, and as an ideal, how shall I say it, stagnant. An ideal cannot be altered. It cannot fail and it does not grow. All of his qualities, which nearly drove one insane with infatuation, would have been irritating had he carried them on into middle age, had he lived, like a rose, to decay. It is not that he *lacked* certain perfectly admirable traits—as we say a man lacks wisdom or charity, the implication being that he may be taught both—but that he possessed none of the potential for maturity. He was fit, seamless as good armor. There was, quite simply, no room to grow, to change."

This knight of legend could scarcely have blossomed in circumstances other than those peculiar to his birth, his station, and his inheritance. For all he rather disliked his mother's Constable, Manasses of Hierges, whom we have already mentioned as the ogre of the Jerusalemite barons, the latter's stewardship of the kingdom had been impeccable. It is doubtful Baldwin, had he been of age, could have as successfully guided his legacy through the disasters of the Franco-German Crusade. In the following four years, Jerusalem was allowed a welcome respite in which to regain its strength while the Prince of Aleppo concentrated on Edessa, then the Ortoquids, then Damascus.

The young King would have been perfectly happy to march his troops into mock battle or real battle and leave the management of the king-dom to his mother and cousin, save his barons, longer on resentment than wisdom, urged him to wrest complete authority for himself. It was an easy task to convince such a trusting fellow against his own good nature, for the "trusting fellow" is really a more flattering description of the inconstant man, led by the latest argument from one firm conviction to the next. First the barons purported that Melisande's generosity to the Church was ambition as much as piety, since the good bishops might, for her continued support, find an excuse to render her eldest son's ac-cession invalid and name Almaric, his seventeen-year-old brother—three years short of majority—as King. More to the mark, they also argued the Dowager Queen, by her parsimony and disinterest in the army, was endangering Jerusalem (which though in the long run might have been an accurate accusation, in the halcyon years after the Second Crusade was decidedly specious). This touched Baldwin's very raison d'être and he promised to take the power. His initiative, however, proved some-thing less than vigorous.

At length it was decided by the barons to destroy Manasses and pre-sent the King with a fait accompli. Since it was the Constable who, for all practical purposes, ruled, Baldwin would either lose his inheritance altogether and confess to the world, at twenty-two, he was either in-competent or uninterested, or become King in effort as well as princi-ple. Antipathy between Baldwin and Manasses was thereupon increased in a series of manufactured incidents which would have tested even the best will in the world to endure. The Constable was banished. Feeling his oats, Baldwin demanded his mother surrender Jerusalem. When Melisande demurred and Almaric argued his elder brother, the King marched on Jerusalem. The gates were thrown open by the people.

Thus this personally courageous and immensely popular young man —rather lacking in will, though not application—was in the enviable position of being surrounded by hard, brilliant, ambitious soldiers, who would follow him anywhere so long as he would rule (and probably too blinded by his light to note the lack of heat at its source). Fortune added to his authority in quick course. The same year he assumed the power—1152—Raymond II of Tripoli was murdered by members of the

Assassin sect (who had assisted the Count in the overanxious murder of his European kin, the Count of Toulouse). In a rare note, it might be pointed out the murder was, for once, not by commission. Rather, it seems, the Assassins were declared enemies of Nureddin, and Raymond had begun negotiations, in secret—or so he thought—with the Governor of Aleppo. This would not do. The county, the guardianship, the regency, passed during the minority of Raymond's son, Pons, to his vassal lord of Jerusalem.

Now with two great fiefs to protect, either Baldwin or his advisers realized the dubiety of the position of Antioch, which, since the death of Raymond of Poitiers, had been ruled by its lineal Heiress and Princess Regent, the exquisite Constance, in behalf of her son, Bohemond III. Right and left this most eligible and desirable young woman had refused suitors, declaring she would only marry a man she loved. To this end Walter de Sant-Omer of Tiberius and Galilee and Yvs, Count of Soissons, were dispatched from Jerusalem, and, surprisingly, the Caesar John-Roger, was proposed with a wink by Constantinople.

Andronikus: "One, she told me, was too ugly, and the other did not bathe often enough. 'Your cousin, John-Roger, is handsome and immaculate, but he is too old.' I protested, 'He's not yet fifty.' And she said, with a knowing look, 'I'm not yet thirty.' A lie of course. She was precisely my age, thirty-one." While the Grand Duke was still at Antioch, Baldwin sent his mother and his aunt, the Dowager Countess Hodierna of Tripolis, to commend his cousin to her duty rather than pleasure in taking a husband. "She asked me to sit with her when she received her aunts, and while the ladies protested, she reminded them an Imperial Grand Duke was higher in station than any save the Dowager Queen. Poor Constance. Her years with Raymond prejudiced her against herself. If she hadn't been such a darling, I would have said she got precisely what she deserved."

Not the remark of one himself spurned. That which was between Andronikus and Constance was never more than a delicate and abiding flirtation. One wonders, then, if the Grand Duke, at once disinterestedly and affectionately, did submerge his vanity before woman long enough to warn the Princess what was obvious to all save herself. An arranged marriage, her husband as petitioner, would have left Constance in a superior, not to say entirely dominant position. He whom she chose bound by her emotions would place the lady herself in thrall. If the

Grand Duke did not advise her thus, I suspect it might have been because he hoped himself to be chosen—if only to refuse—against such competition.

No sooner, in truth, had Andronikus, on Manuel's command, departed than an impoverished French knight, one Reynald of Châtillon, appeared, all white teeth, fair hair, blue eyes, bad temper, and empty head. Constance—true to her word and to the horror of the aristocracy of Latin Palestine—promptly fell in love, married, and, unfortunately, lived to regret it. Like most weak men, he masqueraded his own uncertainty beneath public bluster and private cruelty. Constance and her four young children—Bohemond, Baldwin, Philippa, and Maria—especially bore the marks of his tyranny precisely because he was beholden to them. He replied to the admonitions of the Latin Patriarch by having him beaten, coated with honey, and exposed to wasps, and warned the King of Jerusalem, whose vassal he was, not to interfere with his rule or command him contrary to his own designs, for Baldwin would then be considered an enemy within the borders of the principate.

Constance's barons did not protest and she could not go to them to gainsay her husband, though she was well within her rights as Regent for the rightful Heir, Bohemond III. The reason for their alienation was aboard an Imperial yacht bound for Constantinople during the same week which saw the arrival of the infamous Reynald on a cargo vessel. While Constance and Andronikus had carried forward their flirtation, they were unaware an ocean of dissent swirled round them. The barons of Antioch had been appalled at the thought of the Greek Emperor's Greek cousin as their potentate. The Latin Patriarch, Aimery, who would, with lacerated back and wasp-bitten body, soon flee Constance's real suitor, Reynald, feared loss of his power as the Princess' adviser and supplanting, perhaps, by a Greek bishop (he would have done well to inquire on Andronikus' policies in Cilicia). If, as Andronikus once said, "a man's life is the ripeness between calculation and luck," then Reynald could not have arrived more opportunely.

Yet it is one of the most fascinating "ifs" of the previous century how the future might have turned had Andronikus, as he was quite capable, pursued his flirtation with Constance into seduction. Ironic that while these two royalties bantered poetry and glances at one another, they never realized the weight history might give—and does now, negatively—to their diversion. There might have been some question whether the

Emperor would have consented to the divorce which would have allowed his cousin a rule of his own. Yet a Greek prince of Antioch, one is forced to surmise, would override any hesitation. The likelihood Andronikus' restlessness born of a frustrated ambition might have been in some measure satisfied was too attractive a prospect for the Emperor. The Grand Duke might have ended his days as a great defender of his domains, an apt administrator, and—even Fortune smiles—the step-father-in-law and step-grandfather of two Augusti of the Byzantine Empire. All things being equal, a symmetrical, serene, and ubiquitous second half of a life begun in such scintillating agitation. But no. The times he might have overseen as Patriarch, he quenched instead. The man of a becalmed old age was consumed instead, as Cronos consumed the flesh of his flesh, in the rebel. The Empire he sought to alter and preserve has since fallen. The lesser domain of Antioch still stands. The yacht which Manuel sent to fetch his cousin may be said to have carried away an entire alternative future of the East.

"I remember," he said, "the day I left, Constance asked me to meet her little girl, Maria, and herself in the gardens of the Caesarean Palace. There had been rain in the morning, really a torrent, and the petals of the flowers had flown everywhere and adhered to everything, especially the marble, quite lovely. There was no place dry enough to sit, so we walked. I carried Maria in my arms, yes. She was then, what, seven, I believe, a beautiful pale-haired child, one of those very early indulged in their beauty and beginning to be aware of some unusual power in their person, if they can scarcely understand it. I told her of the Hercules Clock at Constantinople, the great over-life-size figure of gold which strikes the hours, not very accurately. I understand, on her arrival here, it was one of the first things she asked to see."

The time was 1183. That little girl he recalled had lived to become one of the most controversial Empresses in our history, and was now dead. He shook his head, whether in regret of wonderment he should have been the instrument of her death, I cannot say and would not have asked. "Her mother," he said, rousing himself, "carried with her a wreath of flowers, which she gave to me as a keepsake, and a ring. The one I had preserved in wax, though understandably it was lost in my travels. The other I wore until I met Theodora. Really, she was a remarkable woman, what her people—the French, not the Antiochenes—call *du chien,* that somewhat conscious allure—light, never offensive, and entirely flattering. The innocuous, pretty little maid so charmed by my uncle became a bright, secretly lustful, secretly willful creature, with an element of languor I find most attractive in a woman. When she was silent, whether bethinking herself or listening to someone else, her expression assumed such a *rapt* concentration, the merest trace of a smile —an enigmatic smile, not one of amusement. Remarkable woman. We talked of the *Iliad* and the *Odyssey,* fittingly, which I had persuaded her to read. She thought the epic of the Trojan War a lot of interminable gore and the travels of Ulysses frivolous. I attempted to convince her they were metaphors of life itself. She asked if the metaphor were implicit. I asked if it mattered. Their universalism was not in their analogies, but the genius out of which they were crafted. Metaphors are the pertinent reflections successive ages behold in the mirror of finished art, which is the only way a work becomes immortal. The metaphor is the accident, not the essence of literature. If it seems too obviously imposed, then it is no longer art but pedantry, and local. I remember I said, 'The two poems are among those few achievements so great that once given, the world is thereafter unimaginable without them.' She said, 'You seem almost jealous.' I responded she was quite accurate. At length she agreed. 'I have read these words, as you asked me, and'now I am glad. I feel quite civilized.' She was, as I say, the most remarkable woman I met until my cousin Theodora."

He sighed. "Well. From the warmth of Antioch I passed to the cold slush of Constantinople at the end of winter. As I sailed into Julian Harbor, the city, for the first time, seemed to me personalized, and I loathed her every stone."

Andronikus traveled under guard from Syria to the Imperial capital. Once arrived, he was passed in a deeply hooded cape across the city to Blachernae. "I was not allowed to see my wife, my son, or my newborn daughter, Zoë, at Vlanga. I remember as I rode by the palace, I noted the extra detachments over and above the usual Household Guard.

"Curious. That morning, in my boot, I found a pebble, a good-sized one, which had nagged me all the way from Antioch and somehow escaped falling out each time I knocked the sole. I carried it in my hand halfway across the city and then tossed it into a puddle. Absurd, isn't it? That gesture bothered me. I kept thinking of that little stone of the Antiochene earth dashed into a cold alien street and I felt immense regret. Curious what one is bound to recall." *Explicit: Nicetas Acominatus.*

XII

On the polo grounds of Blachernae Palace, in the cold, beneath the clouds, Manuel, drenched with sweat and still breathing hard, canters his pony in aimless little circles. The Grand Duke John Sergius receives a jeweled goblet from a servant and carries it to the Emperor. Manuel receives it with a nod, unsmilingly. He catches sight of Andronikus and his guard entering the grounds. He looks directly at his unhooded cousin, then sips the wine. Several players dismount and move up behind John. The Emperor's nephew has the real aloofness of humorless power. The men behind him, obviously his coterie, like all creatures, attempt to imitate their master's manner and only come up stolid. As Andronikus separates from his guard and rides up to the Emperor, John Sergius bristles.

JOHN SERGIUS. How dare you approach the Emperor on horseback. Dismount at once.

Manuel smiles tolerantly at his nephew.

MANUEL. John, one day he's going to cut your throat. Stay, Andronikus.

Manuel gives his horse a gentle spur and takes a few steps toward his cousin, extending his hand, which Andronikus, with real affection rather than reverence, kisses. The Emperor is at his most charming.

MANUEL. It is good to see you again.

ANDRONIKUS. And you.

MANUEL. Not a twitch in your voice. Even an arrow quivers a little when it hits its target.

ANDRONIKUS. Shall I say God steadies a man in a righteous cause?

MANUEL. You might—if you believed in God or were so much the hypocrite as to consider your cause righteous.

ANDRONIKUS. Then there is nothing I shall say in my defense, Sire.

Manuel snorts out a laugh.

MANUEL. There's nothing you *could* say, you rogue. Come, let's ride.

The Emperor empties the goblet in his hand and extends it to John Sergius.

MANUEL. The wine is bad. Every drop of it.

The Emperor and the Grand Duke move off slowly through the wooded park which surrounds the field.

MANUEL. Are you abreast of what has happened? Thoros has taken Sis.

ANDRONIKUS. And Basil? Is he all right?

MANUEL. He's on his way home now with what remains of the army.

ANDRONIKUS. Very well, I accept the blame for what it's worth.

MANUEL. Andronikus, *why?*

ANDRONIKUS. Is this rhetoric or curiosity?

MANUEL. *Have* you an answer? I should be glad to hear it.

Andronikus smiles all too ironically. He is unwontedly radiant.

ANDRONIKUS. There is no explanation which you would accept as valid. Perhaps right now you ought to have me taken to the cellar and beheaded.

MANUEL. You're insolent. Or else irresponsible; but if you are serious, then you are mad.

ANDRONIKUS. Only in respect to other men's sanity.

MANUEL. Then until there is a world of Andronikuses, you are eccentric.

ANDRONIKUS. I am what I am, Manuel. And I told you what to do. Right now, have me taken to the cellar of the palace—

MANUEL. *Silence!*

Andronikus, for once abashed, winces. Manuel is silent, staring ahead, meditatively. At length he speaks.

MANUEL. You speak of your own death with such affectation and bravado. What of the men who have died because of your activity in Cilicia? Only that which *you* hold seriously seems to be worthy of your compassion or whatever dignity you allow things.

ANDRONIKUS. Those are not my thoughts. You presume.

MANUEL. Do I?

ANDRONIKUS. How can you know my mind, Manuel? I don't know the mind of my valet and, God knows, he's a simple enough specimen.

MANUEL. What is it you want of me? Favor? What have I denied you? I love you. You know that, and for that love I've outraged many. Indulgence? I've forgiven you acts for which other men were sent to the Buceleon Ravelin. You know that, too. Responsibility? I sent you to Cilicia and lost it. What is there left for me to do?

ANDRONIKUS. I love you, too, Manuel. But I don't want your indulgence, and I don't want your favor and it is not responsibility a sovereign can give his subject—only errands.

MANUEL. Is it so intolerable to you that one must lead and others follow? Would you expect any differently if you were Emperor?

ANDRONIKUS. Probably not.

MANUEL. By rights, for your actions in Cilicia, I should confiscate your property and your personal fortune and send you into exile. But it would be to no purpose. If I exiled you, one day I would have to call you back, as nothing you have done merits a lifelong estrangement. And if I confiscated your estates, it would bring needless suffering to your wife and children, though I could place them in my tutelage. I really have no choice but to take the gamble that one day you will have pity on the burden I carry and be of real assistance to me. I leave for Dyrrhachium next week and I cannot let you remain here. Gabras is at Belgrade and still recovering from the pneumonia he suffered this winter. He must be replaced and the Hungarian frontier guarded against an attack from the north. I think Geza and Frederick are in collusion. I am creating you Military Governor of Belgrade and Brantizova and I expect you to guard the entire Balkan Defile while I am in the south and in Italy.

ANDRONIKUS. Whatever you wish.

MANUEL. You're not surprised?

ANDRONIKUS. It's still exile.

MANUEL. From what, Andronikus? What is there here for you?

Incipit: Nicetas Acominatus: "It was a curious interview," Andronikus recalled, at another time, of his reunion with the Emperor after Cilicia. "Half lecture, half warning, and entirely inexpressible on my part. Out of it, of course, I became Military Governor of Belgrade. I thought at first his forbearance was simply an act of propitiation to God. After all, Bertha was about to give birth to a second child and he would scarcely want to offend heaven by his lack of charity. And yet there was something deeper, something unsaid I could not quite touch.

"He came to dine with us that night at Vlanga as a mark of complete exoneration. He was trying to be good, to be clement even, to understand me. And yet I sensed in him a wariness which had not been there before, very real, a tension, a readiness to spring. I pitied him, and out of love for him I tried to be kind and gracious, bland, I suppose, as he would have it. And yet as he sat there before me the subtleties of the interview became clearer.

"Quite obviously, he had planned, long before my arrival, to send me to the Hungarian border. What had occurred between us that morning was false. His impetuous manifestation of clemency and affection a matter of strategy, to win me after apparent chastisement, by his mercy, which he could give or withdraw as it pleased him. Perhaps it was also an attempt to silence me in the issue of his Italian campaign, against which he knew I was unalterably opposed. Manuel saw it as the natural expansion of aggressive Byzantine power. *I* saw—ask any man alive at the time who would listen to me—only needless death and expense and alienation everywhere. We would give Sicily a justification for *its* aggression, whereas, heretofore, it had none. Venice, whose fleets we had bought so dearly, would range against us, and might even join Sicily, if our successes were opportune. Louis was allied with Roger. Who was to say Frederick would not ally himself with both to share their spoils against us? I would have contested my cousin for all the good it might do, but he had disarmed me with his forgiveness—for a fact even made me weary with it. I had not yet lost all and so gained the free voice of the dispossessed."

Uneasily reconciled with his wife (who wrote to Elizabeth Comnena Jasomirgott, the Duchess-Margravine of Austria, she had fallen again under the spell of "the disconcerting directness of those eyes which men are supposed to leave behind in childhood"), Andronikus did not meet with Eudocia during his short stay at Constantinople. On 6 April 1153 he left the city in the company of the Emperor and the Army of the West, somewhat uneasy in the midst of the military pomp and publicity, since he was aware the population did not quite know what to make of him after his conduct in Cilicia.

There had been a delay in the departure of both the principals due to the birth of the Emperor's second daughter, Magdalena Porphyriogeneta, for whom Andronikus and Anastasia stood as godparents. "One courtier," Andronikus remembered, "who, only much later, I realized, must have been one of John's creatures, told me there was bad feeling against me in the army, as well among the Constantinopolitan populace, a marvelous absurdity, since short of invasion of the city—and I'm not so certain of that—our citizens could not have cared less about the loss of a province somewhere in the far corner of Lesser Asia. Of course, I

was also told the Master of Robes and Heir was infuriated he had not
been chosen godparent to Magdalena Porphyriogeneta—oh, the little
honors of that court!—and held me responsible. To tell you the truth,
I expected my own assassination somewhere between Constantinople
and Belgrade. I was stupid enough then, and affected enough, to welcome my own murder and the remorse my cousin would feel. It took
only a little extension of that logic to realize no sooner out of sight than
out of mind, and well rid of me."

As Andronikus had foreseen, Venice refused to assist Byzantium in
the expedition to Italy. Roger, however, did not extend his friendship to
the Republic—an unlikely lack of opportunism, which may be credited
to the old King's firm autocracy and failing brilliance (which source
was senility, not syphilis, as some insisted; every woman this prodigious
satyriac violated was subject to a physician's vetting)—and so the Doge
was left in the unhappy position of watching two great powers at war,
knowing the victor would turn on Venice—Sicily for maritime ultimacy,
Constantinople in revenge.

Frederick, however, was quite another story, quick into the Sicilian
breach, while, with marvelous awful offhandedness, also sending his
agents to sow discord within the papal principate. In the audacity of this
man's schemes was a megalomania, a fixity, which suggests, if not as-
sures, success. Unfortunately Frederick still had not the armies to confront both the Pope and Constantinople and Eugenius III, at wit's end,
anyway, removed from the Vatican spiritual arsenal, its most powerful
weapon. If Frederick did not cease all collusion with Sicilians and
against the Patrimony, the Pope would never crown him—"anywhere
or ever"—and would, furthermore, demand the election of a new Emperor, which, if not carried out, would result in the excommunication of
Frederick from the Roman Catholic Church and the interdiction of the
whole Holy Roman Empire.

Chastened, Frederick agreed to meet with His Holiness at Lake Constance, where, in a period of about a week, a treaty of mutual conciliation was devised and signed. Frederick would withdraw his agents from
the papal domains, and himself from alliance with Roger of Sicily. In
return, the Pope would crown him, at some future date, at Rome.

Thus, Manuel had his wife's nephew to thank that as he set sail for
Brindisi, Western Europe was in a state of self-inflicted diplomatic

paralysis. Venice would not join either Roger or Manuel and so she would not call on Frederick, whom she feared would attack the Republic. Frederick had just made peace with the Pope, who feared Roger would march on Rome. Roger had been disabused of Frederick, and Louis of France would offer neither himself nor his vassals in a war which in no way was to his interests.

In this superb situation, Manuel confidently met the navy Sicily sent against him and in a week of battles destroyed half its fleet. On 31 May, that most propitious date, the Emperor set foot on the antique Italian land which is the source of the Roman Imperium. On shore, surrounded by the dragons of the House of Comnenus, the bicephalic eagles, the icons of Orthodoxy, he knelt and kissed the "venerable" earth, praying for the success of his army. Those very few who were old enough to remember their great-grandfather's or their grandfather's tales of the Byzantine retreat from Sicily in the previous midcentury were in tears. Those young enough for their history lessons to be fresh still in their minds, were understandably exalted. The Emperor called forth the Commander of the Maniaces Regiment—named for that last Military Governor of Sicily whom his own ancestor, St. Isaac, had vanquished in a usurpation attempt—asked for the man's sword, and plunged it into the sand with the words "I claim this province and the whole of Sicily as land rightfully Constantinopolitan, to be reconquered by the sword, under the protection of Demetrius, George, and Michael of the Battles, and our patroness, Mary, Virgin Mother of God."

The Emperor then marched north and throughout the summer, between the swamp and the heat of the incandescent Italian solstice, took the enormous province of Apulia, which forms the boot of the peninsula, and its magnificent capital of Bari, which he entered, 5 September 1153. At Constantinople, where men would not demonstrate against a general who had lost a province, more than a million citizens poured into the streets to celebrate the Italian victories. Manuel was declared the New Digenis Akritas, Alexander Reincarnate. Astrologers, all of whom were, of course, under ban by Orthodoxy, foretold a Christian Empire which would stretch from shores of the Black Sea to the Gateway of the Atlantic (and, in a way, they were correct, if untimely: the present Emperor at Byzantium, Henri of Flanders, is indeed part of a Latin Catholic union from Greece to Spain).

Andronikus: "The news reached me at my summer palace at Brantizova, and do you know, my first reaction was a shake of the head and a whispered congratulation on the wind to my cousin. No matter how he seemed to trip over his own schemes, he came up off his knees to win and win again." His remark is one which hauntingly compliments another made to me by Michael Branas several years after Andronikus' death. "What if I told you, more often than not, I felt sorry for Andronikus? Sorry because I sensed he was right in nearly everything he said, his eye as pellucid as those of other men were blinded or partially blinded by greed, by ambition, by bitterness, by complacency. Can there be anything worse than possessing—shall we call it—intellectual second sight, and being repudiated by the present only to be proved, in the long run, precisely correct? Nothing can make amends for the contemporary ostracism. He failed in small things, I suspect, because his longer vision was impatient of details which are usual to a man such as Manuel, who took each event in isolation. Andronikus might have succeeded in his great objectives given time and circumstance, but he was submerged by the avalanche of consequences of his cousin's reign. He saw all and attempted to stay all. His task was superhuman, and he was not. A man may alter history, but he cannot control it. Manuel's ultimate failure was that he saw too little. Andronikus' tragedy was not his martyrdom, but that he saw too, too much. And we, happy souls, are the mean between these two extremes."

Andronikus: "Not too long after the herald, as I ordered him, proclaimed victory in the streets, I heard the same celebration which, much magnified no doubt, was taking place at Constantinople. I ordered a Te Deum sung in the Cathedral of St. Anna and attended it myself along with Heinrich of Austria and my cousin, Elizabeth, who were visiting me in a private capacity. When he heard the news, Jasomirgott, whose laconic, droll, insightful self I liked immensely, said, 'Well, it's only begun. Now your cousin must waste an army in defense of that squalid land, and now my cousin, I'm certain, will leave His Holiness' side and help yours to dismember the rest of Italy, even at the risk of excommunication. It is not for nothing Frederick has placed a statue of Janus, the two-faced god of gates and doors, above the entrance to his palace.'

"I must tell you, by the way, the change in my cousin Elizabeth was quite instructive to me. She had adopted Western dress, which reached Constantinople a few years later, less daring—and less flattering—in the translation, until Maria-Xenia, like Theodora, eluded all pretense of modesty and opened the neckline to the breasts, dispensed with a veil, and allowed her hair to be combed loose and hang bountifully. But the accouterments were little compared to the change which had taken place in my cousin's heart. She was wonderfully happy, but more, she possessed the surprised and grateful warmth of a woman who had not *expected* to be happy. But something told me of an element of restlessness. She had always a sly tongue, but heretofore, it had been reserved for the pompous or contradictory or the ironic. Now there was an edge, a harsh frivolity, often but not always successfully repressed, and the tendency, infrequent but perceptible, to mockery—against herself or someone out of earshot, for all the graciousness she had just displayed him. Something told me she did not want to be content, that she was rankled by the furor she had caused before her marriage because now all men would smugly say they had been correct in treating her as an abominable, spoiled child. In fact, she had been within her rights to act just so and would any day relinquish the ducal throne of Austria and sooner return to Constantinople. Her pride, in effect, was the cost of her happiness.

"It did not take very long for me to make the connection between her position and my own. Brooding upon it, I was suddenly horrified by the apparent acceptance and complacency I myself had manifested. More and more that interview at Blachernae seemed to me ruin than redemption. To be acceptable is to be nugatory, which is to say I might no longer be considered a threat, an alternative. Here it appeared I had assumed rightful subordinacy to an Emperor I believed would antagonize the world against us at the cost of the Empire's internal well-being—efficient administration, the freedom of the peasants, the curbing of the aristocracy, state services for the poor, and support of the industrious middle class. Here it appeared I had taken my place amongst the parasitical court, who gained everything and did nothing, lying in the sun like gross, steaming beasts breathing fire only when cowed servants demurred.

"You must understand until that moment, the idea of conspicuously and notoriously undermining my cousin to the point of wresting the throne from him had been no more than a daring and seductive thought at the back of my mind. I had, theretofore, looked upon it as a last resort, and an unlikely one, and a real evil since it was not an easy thing to cast aside my upbringing in Orthodoxy which held the Emperor the animation of supreme power on earth, and his undoing the foulest crime. You may escape belief in God, but not the idea of God, insofar as vestigial admonitions of sin from childhood. Yet was it not the greatest Patriarch of Constantinople, Nicholas Mysticus, who said that from autocracy the only recourse is revolution, that if the Emperor falls, then it is proof he no longer possessed heaven's mandate? A torturous way of turning back a Basil or Alexius, but then what's to be done if heaven does not speak except after the fact?

"No sooner, however, than I had decided the depths of my contention, I was assailed by doubts. Was I so inspired I could perceive so purely the reality of things, whereas other men were blind? There was always the possibility, no matter how I argued with myself, I was tautological and dissimulating. Perhaps Manuel was correct and the world was there to be conquered if we were not conquered in turn. Perhaps I was merely jealous and my reason specious, for the failure of human vanity is that it will bend any refutation of its prejudices, just so, to fit them. Was my concern for the powerless and suffering a canonization of my greed for power itself? All men want to rule. How was I any different? Once, I remember, I asked the incorruptible Tetzes, 'Do you write because you must or to be celebrated or to open a man's eyes to what he has not seen before?' And he said, 'All three—and for money besides.'

"Raise the poor and the rich are more secure; succor the powerless and the mighty need not waste their strength in oppression: any man of minimal logic would consider it so."

Andronikus shook his head in obvious wonderment at his own, earlier ingenuousness. "Heavens, how simple it all seemed, when one did not take into account the animadversions of other men. Several months later, Little Christmas, the sixth of January, I attended liturgy in my capacity as Governor-General. Afterward I dismissed my party and remained seated on my throne lost in thought, while the deacons and the Archimandrite Stephen went about their final chores. I particularly favored Stephen because he reminded me of Father Andrew, short, with a bulbous nose, small thick hands, and deep-set almost effeminately sensitive eyes. A true Balkan peasant's face: squat and ugly in youth, I should think, but cherubic in old age, and he was very old, and, unlike most hierarchs, most holy—or perhaps only old enough to have outlived those competitors for the flesh, ambition and sexuality. He approached me, smiling a little uncertainly—he was somewhat afraid of me, I don't know why—and either unaware or uninterested in Imperial etiquette, said, with marvelous gentle irony, 'May I dare to hope since we celebrate the birth of Christ there has been a rebirth of Orthodoxy in the heart of Your Imperial Highness?' 'I fear not, Monsignor.' He said, 'A great pity. What a catch you should be. I should thank God on my knees for a week.'

"I rose and took his arm and together we walked the length of the cathedral. I said to him, 'There is great peace and beauty here. I prefer the solitude it offers me.' 'Had Your Imperial Highness ever thought there might be a compulsion deeper still?' I had to smile. 'No, Monsignor. My pleasure is aesthetic, I assure you, not divine.' 'One is not exclusive of the other.' 'No, indeed. You are quite correct.' 'The Emperor is in Macedon. Will you see him?' I doubted it. 'A great warrior,' the Archimandrite said. I said, 'Little enough to report of a man. He makes war. I would as soon use my sword in the dragon's behalf as of St. George. Last September, after that absurd battle on the Tisza, I passed a mound of soldiers' corpses, Hungarians and Romans, indistinguishable and alike. In a flash, I thought: Only a little while ago those men were ten thousand various affections and hatreds, hopes, ambitions, virtues, eccentricities, prejudices, appetites—and enemies—and now they are all the same, all dead. To what end? To what end is any war but that a sufficient number of men who wished to live must die, while those few who survive stupidly wish themselves dead when they capitulate. No man dies in any war for a cause—even as he defends it, or so he thinks—he dies as a statistic for the consideration of generals, like myself, on opposing sides. Not that war is, on occasion, unjustifiable, but that we are truly wicked or inhuman if we believe it is holy or patriotic or gallant. It is to no purpose save a table of cold slaughter. We Byzantines do well to fast after a war—to show some repentance, if not to God, then to man, if not to man, then to give ourselves pause.' He placed one hand over mine, which I had not yet gloved. Awful, isn't it? I noticed his dirty fingernails. I resented the touch, still quite royal enough to resent such familiarity of inferiors. 'Prince,' he said to me urgently, 'I must tell you. There are rumors in the city. There is a question of your safety.' Do you know, Nicetas, I was smug enough to tell him any rumor which concerned me would reach my desk first? The point is, I was too certain of myself to realize if it concerned my safety, my desk should be the last place to find its report." *Explicit: Nicetas Acominatus.*

The gates of the Governor's Palace are trudged inward as Andronikus, three of his ADCs, and a half-dozen guards enter the enormous court-yard, which except for a wide horsepath and a large square at the stairs —lately shoveled and in need of a second go—is snow-covered. The Grand Duke frowns as he espies by the huge bronze doors at least a dozen horses with the escutcheon of the Imperial eagle on their saddle-cloths. His First ADC, the perfect attendant, second-guesses him and turns in the saddle calling to the sentries by the gates.

AIDE-DE-CAMP. Whose horses?

SENTRY. From the Emperor.

Andronikus' expression alters from curiosity to affected impassivity. At the door he dismounts and hands his reins to one of his guards as the second, realizing something out of the ordinary—attendants ought to have had the doors open before the Governor dismounted—slams the huge brass knocker, once, twice, a third time resoundingly.

XIII

Incipit: Nicetas Acominatus: On 27 January 1154 the Grand Duke Andronikus was arrested at his palace in Belgrade and presented a war-rant, signed by the Protovestarius and Heir, the Grand Duke John Sergius, which cited him not on Praemunire Charges, but, in full, for high treason. He was also handed Commissions of Pursuivancy, which allowed his jailers to ransack his personal papers, and he was, further-more, commanded to relinquish all powers to his immediate subordinate who would function as acting governor until replaced, and ordered to present himself, at once to the Emperor, in the field near Pelagonia, in Macedon.

The origin of this extraordinary step is international in its scope, for which we must digress, momentarily, on an errand of clarification.

In Russia, the descendants of Rurik had settled upon a depressingly complicated Rota system of rule throughout the cities comprising the Kievan Principate—i.e., Rostov, Tver, Chernigov, Murom, Smolensk,

Galicia, Vladimir, Ryazan, and Suzdal—by which all sons of the Grand Prince sat, at one time or another, in order of seniority, on the Kievan throne, and otherwise in one of the lesser domains, and so on sons in the following generation, beginning with the eldest male cousin in each family. Unfortunately, if only one reigning Kievan Prince refused to step down and was powerful enough to keep his seat, the Rota, the wheel, ground to a halt. Now, when Vladimir Monomakh died in 1125, this was the genealogical branch he left behind: the eldest son, Msitslav, reigned his seven years, followed by the next brother, Yaropolk. In the following seven years Andrew and Vyacheslav contested the throne, Vyacheslav claiming his elder brother a moron unfit to rule, Andrew eloquently and mightily protesting such defamation.

By midcentury, Prince George Dolgoruky, already an old man, announced that Vyacheslav and Andrew had nullified the Rota term due each. At the same time, Izyaslav Msitslavovitch, eldest son of the eldest son, appalled by the degeneration of Kiev "while senile old men fight for the final prestige of being buried from the Cathedral of St. Vladimir," contested his uncle George and claimed it the turn of the younger generation to begin their round from Kiev to Suzdal. Manuel Augustus favored the rightful successor, Dolgoruky. Geza II, as much to contend Constantinople as content his second wife, favored her brother, Izyaslav, as the true Heir of Kiev.

Year after year, this internecine war progressed with only token outside interference. But then, in a last gasp of malice, seeking to delay Manuel from entering Sicily, Roger persuaded Geza—in return for trade advantages and a lump sum—to urge his brother-in-law, Prince Izyaslav, to attack the Empire on its north (Bulgarian) flank and to this effect, open Hungary to the passage of the Russian army.

All strategies, of course, depend upon the stupidity or predictability of their antagonists. Geza and Izyaslav met at the Apostolic King's hunting lodge at Turda in the Transylvanian Principate and the scheme was put to work, both parties delighted in their gains: Geza enriched and Izyaslav happy to avenge himself against the Basileus who supported his uncle George. In the beginning all went well. Izyaslav attacked Bulgaria via Hungary, and the Army of the East had to be partitioned and several regiments sent north under Gabras. The Emperor's orders were explicit: harassment of the South Hungarian Frontier —which is to say fire, pillage, and slaughter at random. This was nothing less than a punitive war, which Andronikus was expected to continue when he relieved Gabras in 1153. Instead, after a few halfhearted expeditions, entirely on his own responsibility, the Grand Duke brought to an end this "wanton, brutal policy which admonished a king by killing his helpless subjects—rather like punishing a rich man by killing his servants." To assure Geza his reluctance was no mere whim, he rather artlessly wrote the King this would be his avowed policy so long as he was Governor.

Unhappily—and unlikely—on all sides, Andronikus became the dupe of other men's ambitions. Geza, an aggrandizer and bitterly anti-Byzantine, took advantage of the Grand Duke's declaration to attack Vidin in December, a betrayal that Andronikus never forgave or forgot —of Geza, or his successors. (In fact, his hatred of the Árpád-Orseolos became notorious and detrimentally affected his own reign since the Hungarian Royal House was not of a mind to wait on his statesmanship but, perhaps guiltily, attacked the Empire at once on his accession.)

In January a Constantinopolitan agent at Geza's court forwarded a copy of Andronikus' letter to Manuel. It was intercepted by the Grand Duke John, who now controlled virtually all access to his uncle.* With such a document, this neurotic, amoral power-monger now possessed the means of destroying his sister's "ravager" and his own certain rival to the throne should the Emperor die.

Before closing the circle and continuing our narrative, let us stop a moment and consider this man, who, if he did not succeed more than any third party in poisoning the relationship between Manuel and Andronikus, then nagged and ambushed his uncle into taking steps which alienated the two cousins for nearly a quarter century. (To be sure, the Protovestarius would have been quite amazed by such a judgment. John Sergius was, at once, limited as he proved to be ambitious, born with just that sufficient lack of imagination to live his life in honest hypocrisy, convincing himself all acts he committed were in his uncle's interest, when more obviously they were in his own. Nureddin played

---

* Easily accomplished since, as Master of Robes, he was the executor of all Imperial possessions, the Privy Purse, the thirty thousand servants employed throughout all palaces, stud farms, villas, hunting lodges, and country estates. The Protovestarius is sometimes called ironically—though not without respect—"Commander in Chief of the Kitchen Praetorim," which is to say, the final arbiter of the palace staff, including the Grand Chamberlain, the Master of Stables, the Imperial Steward, and Imperial Majordomo. In conniving hands, such power, as is obvious, can be crushing. N.A.

similar havoc with his fellow Moslem princes under the guise of religious purity.)

I knew the Grand Duke personally, and, as one who has always believed the worst that men can be is sometimes mitigated, and even forgivable, on examination of circumstance and motive—even deluded motive—I am forced to say I found John Sergius in every way unredeemable and morally repellent. I realize this is a large statement and it makes me quite uneasy to write it. Yet I experienced the Grand Duke from all sides—public and private—and especially as I was young, waited, anticipating, in vain, on some humane gesture, a spark by which his soul, if only for an instant, might be illuminated, comprehended.

But in John Sergius I was forced to recognize the possibility a man may live fraudulent, perverted, and misanthropic from birth to death. All was self-deceit, lack of conscience, lack of self-investigation, lack of insight. There are, indeed, some men whose innards are like wax—seamless, without complexity—who live by first impressions, who never alter their opinions—and call *that* integrity—who believe their own contorted excuses for the evil they commit. This was John Sergius. Compared to Andronikus and Manuel, whose souls were drenched in light, the one man's nephew and the other's first cousin was all darkness, stagnation, backwardness, insulation, violence, and willful stupidity (and, one is tempted to say, he was proud of it). His was immorality constantly excusing itself by a "higher good." The perfect clerk, he cringed elegantly before the Emperor and was a vindictive despot to everyone else. He was his father—exaggerated and damned. He was vain of his good looks, which, like Andronikus', combined the Paleologi and the Comneni, but they were nullified by eyes which stared but could not express, a mouth which smiled while the remainder of the face was terrifyingly still. He preened. He took delight in other men's fear. For John Sergius a display of cruelty—unimpugned—was the manifestation of power; a lack of compassion, proof of intrepidity. He did not love, he possessed.

The Emperor attempted, year after year, to temper his nephew, to humanize him, but he always ended by succumbing, instead, to keep the peace between himself and his Heir. After the birth of Alexius Porphyriogenetus, and his consequent demotion to Heir Presumptive, John Sergius was staggered only for a time. Then, at his most petty and malevolent, he spent the last of his nearly fifty acrid years to the effect

of one abiding passion. It became this wreck of a soul to avenge himself on the uncle before whom he still maintained a blood-curdling
obsequiousness, by keeping the Emperor from finally forgiving and
calling back Andronikus from exile (which was not accomplished until
after the Protovestarius' death in 1176). The rumors which he carried
to Manuel were not simply infamous; they were more often than not
mendacious. It was he who prodded both the Emperor and the Patriarch
to excommunicate the Grand Duke and Queen Theodora, and then,
using the seal of the most powerful monarch bestriding the Mediterranean, chose to warn each successive Christian King and Moslem
Prince to whom these renegades fled to deport both or face the displeasure of the Basileus. "I respect the right of all men and animals to
life," Andronikus once said, "but just as I would kill a mad dog because it is helplessly capable of nothing but injury, so, had I the
opportunity, I would have murdered John Sergius. Instead, in bed, he
died happy in his acrimony."

So we return to the episode of 1154 via its perpetrator and its victim:
"Curious the peace I felt once the charges had been brought against me.
Inactivity depresses me. The immovability of my situation depressed me
profoundly. The previous six years during which I recognized the power-
lessness and inutility in which I was obliged to live, and to which I was
expected to become reconciled, were, in a way, the unhappiest of my
life."

More so than his imprisonment? I asked. He nodded. "That was hor-
rendous, so alien—and such a constant, *living* mistreatment—or so I
saw it, hatred and the desire to escape consumed me. At least there was
something to act *against*. As unlikely as it sounds, I would prefer those
years to the well-appointed titillation—the raised hopes and repetitive
despair, each deeper than the last—of the early fifties. I can live without
hope if there is no point in hoping. Once I was accused, at least I was
faced with the possibility of the unexpected, of action and response. I
was apprehensive, to be sure"—he smiled, rather *drôle*—"but then what
rejuvenates like anxiety?

"Or like beauty. I remember the first day on the road in the Danube
Valley, it snowed till nightfall. Apparently while we slept there was a
short thaw and then everything froze again. The following morning I
was awakened at the inn in which we were staying. The Varangian

captain, who the previous day had been so grim, said with the anticipation of one about to give a gift he knows will be appreciated, 'Your Highness, come out and see this, if you will, come see.' I dressed quickly and left the establishment and encountered, really, the most opulent sight I have ever seen in my life. For miles round us all the trees of the forest were traced in ice. They had become like crystal. They shone in the sunlight with inconceivable brilliance. It hurt the eyes, and yet one could scarcely look away. All my jailers were thrilled. One youth, his cheeks red and his arms bare, completely oblivious to the cold, kept saying, 'It isn't real; it just isn't real. It can't be.' Aware of their errand, it was very difficult for them the rest of the morning riding with me through that enchanted forest. I felt sorry for them. They were all young, exhilarated by the beauty, and, do you know, for the first time, I felt *old*.

"Well, we arrived at Pelagonia on the fourth day. I wonder now why I hadn't realized the significance of Manuel's move into Macedonia from Thessalonika where he was wintering. He meant to proceed north against Geza to war on the Apostolic Judas not because the wretch had taken advantage of my clemency, but because he continued to be in league with Izyaslav and Roger. Of course unknown to us at the time, a new future began to grow in the tumor in the belly of the Sicilian King which would kill him before the year was out: a slow and painful death, richly earned, including the crude, morbid riddles about precisely the nature of his sexuality as suggested by his pregnant appearance. I hear he asked to be dressed in a monk's robe—like Manuel—at the end. Ah, how all the world loves a repentant sinner who's enjoyed his sinning in the meantime. All well and good in the rich and aristocratic. But ask the poor man and the beggar who haven't succumbed to the narcotic of envy and they'll tell you, all right, what they think about abstinence after a full meal."

His cousin, Basil, describes the scene as Andronikus entered the Imperial encampment at Pelagonia:

The stares of the soldiers, his pets and adorers, told the story. They watched him with a mixture of amazement and resentment—the resentment of the betrayed. Try and tell them it was Hungarian wives and brothers like their own he had attempted to save. But these were simple souls, the misled, convinced it is their own mind from which they act.

In their eyes, he, the greatest soldier in the Imperial army, the Emperor's Sword, as they called him, had disobeyed the Autocrat not once, but twice. The first time, it had seemed like inscrutable mischief, though a few talked of cowardice. Twice and it was treason and anathema. Well, you cannot overcome the prejudices of the common man, and one of them is the suspicion he is, at best, the cat's paw of royalty. Occasionally, against his better judgment, he believes wholeheartedly in a Prince's apparent sincerity. Once *that* is ravaged, intentionally or indifferently, his resentment is unbounded.

What I found truly reprehensible, however, was the conduct of our fellow generals, among them, those who had previously openly praised my cousin. The final motive of their disassociation was nothing more than self-preservation. Worse, in the days previous to my cousin's arrival, they had eagerly discussed his failings. In their critical gusto, they supposed, was the exhibition of their independence. I thought them measly and appalling. With their every word, voluntarily or haphazardly they fell under John Sergius' fist. *Why* must men destroy their heroes? Is it because the exalted remind us of our own failings? Because as long as such men are impeccable we are trapped in our own inadequacies and obliged to worship them? Do we then spring in malice and jealousy rather than justice with the appearance of flaws?

As my cousin rode through the camp on the way to the Imperial pavilion, his head affectedly high in a pretense of impassivity, my heart quite went out to him and I loved him very much. I remembered he was the only member of our family who had truly and disinterestedly attempted to help my mother and Lecapenus, with no thought for the anger against himself he might engender. Only he had attempted to do what was right and generous, humane. Even if he had left me high and dry in Cilicia, all was forgiven in that moment as I stood by the entry to my pavilion and watched him pass. As I left his side, my brother Robert called to me, "What are you doing? Come back!" But I was in something like a trance, the sort which overcomes us when we proceed to dare beyond our own sense of discretion.

I came up beside Andronikus, took the reins from his hands, lifted them over the horse's head, and in the age-old gesture of submission, led him to my uncle's enormous white and gold praetorium.

He said, "Basil, go back, it's to no purpose."

I was giddy. "I'm probably ruining myself, but the company's excellent."

He said, "Thank you." Nothing more.

To be perfectly honest I was a little dashed he had not entreated me still more so I could puff myself up all the more. It is only now I realize what grace there was in that man, God knows where in the world today. When he himself acted, he did so without looking back, without excuse or approval. Just so, he preferred the similar gestures of other men quite as clean. One of his finest qualities, one may say, most lordly, was that he knew how to accept a gift, a sacrifice, in his behalf. He never pretended a false humility which in the end belittled your gesture and forced him to become the grateful nag. Nothing is more irritating than a man who believes *he* obliged you to sacrifice rather than your scrupulousness. It is quite true, in the event, he can never be grateful enough.

Later in the day, I was told my cousin, John Sergius, had expressed disdain for my theatrics—a threat, I surmised, as the Protovestarius always couched his warnings in the mincing dicta of a pompous old bureaucrat.

Andronikus: "Manuel did not receive me on my arrival, so I was remanded to a pavilion of my own, under guard. Of course, the civil thing for John Sergius to do would have been to stay away and in the least keep the dignity of implacable enmity. But no. He was one of those so sincerely obtuse or malicious, he found it necessary to visit my quarters. To taunt me, I suppose. The man lacked the taste of a good villain." *Explicit: Nicetas Acominatus.*

As John enters the handsome red pavilion, Andronikus rises from his dinner. In the subsequent twitch of his lips is the curse upon himself for this display of submission. He beseats himself at once. But John, significant of his advantage, bids him the same with a wave of his hand and an ironic smile. The advantage was recognized before it could be withdrawn and it is all that matters.

ANDRONIKUS. What is it you want?

JOHN SERGIUS. I don't think that's any way to speak to me.

ANDRONIKUS. John, there *is* no way to speak to you. One finds oneself addressing you.

JOHN. Did you have a good trip? Are you well?

ANDRONIKUS. I have a cold.

JOHN. Perhaps Count Theophan can treat you.

ANDRONIKUS. I would appreciate it.

JOHN. I will send him promptly.

ANDRONIKUS. Thanks. But without his medicines. He's your doctor, isn't he? At least he's in your pay.

JOHN. Why on earth are you so jittery, cousin? You must relax.

In fact, quite relaxed—no less by this ploy which John has used too often and too famously—Andronikus points at the door with a cucumber slice he has just skewered and swirled in cream.

ANDRONIKUS. Get out. I have nothing to say to you.

JOHN. That may be true, but you are in no position to dismiss me.

ANDRONIKUS. Is that so?

JOHN. Indeed. You are a prisoner. Not a guest or a courtier. A prisoner.

ANDRONIKUS. World-shaking, your powers of deduction, Johnny.

JOHN. Despite your belligerence, I've come in the matter of intercession. The Emperor wants your confession. I am simply asking you to ask him to forgive you. And he will. I promise.

ANDRONIKUS. My confession he can have any day. But I don't ask the forgiveness of any man. Not of Manuel, least of all you.

JOHN. I can't see your point. Then you will admit to treason as charged.

ANDRONIKUS. I don't call it treason.

JOHN. No traitor does.

ANDRONIKUS. You miss my point. To ask for pardon would be to accept Manuel's definition—which is yours, for all I know—of what is good and just and what is bad for the state. I would then deny the meaning of what I have done as *I* see it. It would no longer be dissent but crime, as you say, treason. And I am not a traitor.

JOHN. The deep Greek again. The Emperor can no longer indulge you your definitions.

ANDRONIKUS. Is that the voice of his exasperation or yours? Manuel won't punish me because he won't make me a martyr.

JOHN. Had you paused long enough in your running to look behind you, you would have observed there is in fact no host at your back, proclaiming your beatification, your message, or your righteousness.

ANDRONIKUS. Never my righteousness. I leave sanctimony to you.

JOHN. Stand up!

Andronikus frowns, disbelieving.

ANDRONIKUS. I beg your pardon.

JOHN. I told you to stand in my presence.

ANDRONIKUS. Go to hell.

His unlikely calm—in fact, his hands are shaking—infuriates John Sergius who makes a rush to drag him to his feet. Swiftly Andronikus lifts a knife from his setting and points it at his oncoming cousin. The Protovestarius stops short. Without rising from his chair, Andronikus warns him in a soft monotonous voice.

ANDRONIKUS. I'll kill you.

XIV

Incipit: Nicetas Acominatus: Once I commented to Andronikus how unlikely it seemed a man such as John Sergius should have been given the power and named Heir by one even more unlikely, Manuel Augustus. The then Emperor shook his head. "Not so. First there was precedent. When Basil I issued the Imperial Constitution, he never dealt with the problem of succession. It's a notorious oversight, and puzzling, until one takes into account the somewhat confused putative parenthood of his own sons. He ought to have decreed the Imperial Inheritance subject to primogeniture or the predecessor's discretion. Instead the *tradition* of primogeniture came into effect—in a way more binding since any Emperor who attempted to codify it would be called self-serving, and oppositely, who promoted Discretionary Inheritance would be called unnatural. Then again, there was pride, as always pride. If a man were the measure of the throne, Philip and I had better claims than any of Manuel's nephews. But my cousin was not about to pass on the accession to the junior branch. Possibly, Manuel wanted a shadow, not a promise. Possibly even, John Sergius was the vent of Manuel's darker side, the prosecuting lieutenant of the always clement king.

"In any event, in a world of dwarfs, as was my cousin's court, a full grown child is king—and this was John Sergius. He used power like a hammer. His aim: to preserve and increase that power, which is all a man needs to give his actions shape and point, however blunt. Nothing else mattered and nothing was immoral to that effect. Thus, if a decent man's contest was based on real principle, and his dissent honorably offered, he was at a distinct disadvantage. Besides, rather like Manuel, John viewed any question of policy as an affront, a threat. He was not really malevolent, but, in a real sense, desperate. Consider it this way:

He believed he was fighting for his life, which was his authority. He had no ideas to die for, only power. Yet that is enough in a limited man.

"My first interview with Manuel began, if awkwardly, well. The Emperor had only himself to blame if he had intended to be stern. He made the mistake of telling me news of my daughter Zoë, that she was the darling of Blachernae and Vlanga, already walking and speaking a few words. 'As precocious as her father,' he said. He was sincere and disarming, and I responded in kind. This excluded John Sergius: in fact, his dour presence became intrusive and even a little embarrassing, and so when I asked to speak to the Emperor alone and John protested, Manuel—probably against his better judgment—was delighted to be rid of his nephew.

"Somewhat more at ease, and much to my suprise, I attempted a new tack. I attempted to be reasonable, rather than argumentative.

"Thus, while the Emperor pretended irritation with John Sergius for declaring me a traitor, without first, as is protocol for an Imperial Grand Duke, submitting proof of guilt to the Senate and obtaining from a quorum in plenary session an indictment on Initial Praemunire Charges (what garbage: if Manuel had said no more to him than 'Do what you think best,' it proved his indifference to my reputation), I pretended both injustice and affront of no matter, at least, I said, in comparison to my manifest at Belgrade. I said, 'Don't you see? Punitive expeditions in which none suffer but the helpless and undefended are for barbarians. They are against all Byzantine rules of war. Declare yourself against Geza and his knights—against Izyaslav, if you must—but not the easy mark of open frontier villages.' At that, he thought a moment, then said, 'Let's walk.' I expressed surprise. You never could tell whether his impulses were real or calculated. I pretended to be artless—but some of my question was sincere. 'Do you want to be seen with me?' He smirked then, the perfect smirk—which, I might add, he had learned from me, which I had copied from my father—which silenced all questions. Then he said something—as infrequently it happened—which still gives me to wonder if he was not open to my deepest motives, as I to his. He said, 'But, Andronikus, pray don't mistake my sincerity for mercy, just as I do not mistake your honesty for ingenuousness.'

"So we left the tent, keeping to the duckboards. He was supremely relaxed, a half-smiling expression on his face—not derisive, but warmly, if inscrutably amused, as though no motive could be concealed from him. He looked at me; he looked at the duckboard before his feet; he acknowledged none of the obeisances made toward him which remained fixed until we passed. His first decade as Emperor had left him not exhausted but seemingly indefatigable. Of course, his person was worlds apart from the semidivinity, whom the peasants believed went to heaven to consult with God every Sunday, but he had the repose of semidivinity just because he was believed, elsewhere, to be divine.

"Compare this with the picture I must have presented by his side. I was tense enough within the pavilion. Outside, I believed myself certain prey for John's agents. I was alert nearly to the point of hysteria and also desperately ill with a fever which I had attempted to conceal since my arrival. The brilliant sunlight hurt my eyes, and so I squinted. I shivered. I was rheumy and continually bringing up phlegm, collecting it with a roll of the tongue and expectorating it to one side of the walk.

"He said to me, 'You know I esteem you more than any other man I have ever known.' And I responded, quite to the point, 'That doesn't mean you understand me.' He said, 'All a man may go by is another man's deeds, or don't you agree?' I told him I didn't agree. If it were true I would have had to call him irresponsible for not condemning me out of hand. And then he spoke again with unexpected aptness. 'Andronikus,' he said, 'had you ever thought to yearn too much for power is to become the victim of those who possess it?' I said, 'You mean the minions who possess it by serving you and have much to lose?' To my surprise he said, 'Precisely. Because, you know, there is a point beyond which I cannot control such people, or I should be their next victim. I can ameliorate their damage. I can occasionally be clement. But I cannot be forever forgiving or they would call me weak.' I stopped him. I took hold of his forearm. 'Manuel: answer me this. Have I ever denied your authority? All I have asked is that you listen to me. What I say and do, I say and do for your good and the good of the state. Your grandfather is mine, and both our pride in resurrecting the fatherland. Have I not that right to serve his memory and his work?'

"Well, that infernal, amused smile vanished from his face. He shook his head. He no longer knew what to say. He said, 'I think you have the potential to be a great man. To be of service to me. That goes without question.' He covered my hand, which still rested on his forearm. 'Be calm,' he said, 'be calm. As you can see, I've charged you with nothing like treason. Of course, I cannot have you initiating your own policy, no matter the good you think it does me or the reputation of the Empire. Geza's ambition refuses to distinguish between the pious and the unholy. Go back to your pavilion. Rest. You really look awful. Come to me tonight and we will have dinner and talk more.'

"I went back to my tent and vomited up blood."

The only time in his life he was ever seriously ill Andronikus counted the most inopportune. In the short run, his pneumonia—apparently, *pace* Gabras, an occupational hazard of winter service along the Danube —nullified any further prosecution for treason, which, for a fact, Manuel did not believe anyway. His cousin, thus stricken, moreover, opened the gates of the usual generosity in the Emperor's great heart. To be sure, there is nothing like a fallen antagonist to inspire pity, but all eyewitnesses at Pelagonia told me the same story: the Emperor's concern surpassed mere sympathy. Manuel was quite overcome at the thought the Grand Duke would die and—a physician himself—when not tireless attending his cousin was in the small chapel within his tent at prayer.

Michael Branas told me many years later, "One afternoon during the worst of the crisis, the Emperor left Andronikus' pavilion, his face like stone. He passed me at the entrance without seeing me. I came up beside him and said, 'Your Majesty?' And he only shook his head. When the crowd of soldiers and officers saw that, I heard a moan spread throughout the crowd and cries of 'Oh no' and 'That's it, he's gone.' Once again I said, 'Your Majesty? Is he dead?' And realizing what was about, he shook his head, to sighs of general relief. There's nothing like death, Nicetas, to win back men's hearts. It's presumed you can do no more harm and nothing you've done really merited this much punishment." He spoke these words in the year 1186, ten months after Andronikus' death. He looked at me with a child's bewildered eyes in an old man's face. "Anyway, it seemed so, didn't it, until last year?"

Michael was not a naïve man—indeed not; he possessed a fine mind and just principles such as few I have ever known—but he was one of those so innately kind, he cannot imagine the lack of kindness, in return, anywhere, of anyone. Andronikus' death had brought him up sharply, had not wizened his generosity, but wounded him, personally and profoundly, as a gentle dog, mistreated, is made wary of the world. After a silence, he looked up. "You know, most amazing of all, when his life was despaired of and Manuel asked him if he wished to receive unction, he consented. All of us gathered round his bed were quite surprised. Or perhaps he was too confused to realize what was happening. I know several times he was in delirium and would complain to his father of the snow. I recalled those words when, later, I learned how the great Sebastocrator died. It made my hair stand on end. I was much moved when the Icon of Maria Sedes Sapientiae was brought to him to kiss, which he did, feebly after receiving the Host. It *is* the truth he passed the crisis that night and began to recover."

"What a stroke of ill luck that was," Andronikus would only recall of his illness. "By the time I recovered, events were seemlessly on their way again. I cannot say I survived much chastened or changed. Rather I was angry and extraordinarily cantankerous as it was possible to be. As soon as I was well, we broke camp. When my cousin postponed for a month his planned attack on Hungary, I dared to hope he had come to his senses. He had not. The postponement lasted precisely a month. In the meantime, we returned to Thessalonika. Eudocia was there and we resumed our alliance.

"What a delightful girl she was, half-seductive, half-mocking, mocking those foolish enough to be seduced by the other half. All the intelligence and assurance, the witty sensuality of a highborn nymphomaniac, to be as blunt as possible. But she was also vulnerable.

"I recall during our time together, she warned me I was under surveillance. Since the Secret Police were under Isaac's jurisdiction, she was furious. She told me to confront the Sebastocrator with this abuse of prerogative. I remember she was quite sure since Isaac was 'the kindest, most malleable man alive' he would do whatever I asked. I tried to explain to her why I could do no such thing. For one, Manuel had placed me in Isaac's tutelage, which meant my cousin was now executor of my estate, passing judgment on all my debts and controlling my annuity as Grand Duke. I had no intention of antagonizing him and becoming completely penniless as well as disgraced. You know, the 'kindest, most malleable' men are just the sort who one fine day, sick to death of such benign contempt, decide to exert their will and manliness over just such a presumably dangerous, actually powerless figure as I then was. I was certain if I confronted Isaac with his nephew's presumption he might see fit to revenge his embarrassment on the audience—the victim, myself—rather than the antagonist. No matter how mild I try to be, no matter the justice of my request, I've noted many people will take it as a demand and resent the intimidation. It's rather a flaw. Perhaps it's nothing more than my unusual height.

"In any event, Eudocia, as I might have predicted, refused to take my reasoning seriously. She confronted not Isaac, however, but her brother, and as a result, came back to me as nearly in tears as I had ever known her. She explained that he had said to her, 'I don't know who I despise more: Andronikus for seducing you or yourself for yielding to him.' I tried to dismiss it. I said, 'I could have told you he'd say something like that. What you don't seem to understand is that suspicion and malignity is your brother's way of life, and rather than confront it, one had best learn to live with it, which I'm perfectly willing to do. He'll learn nothing from the police he did not already presume, which is usually the way of things.' But really, she was quite struck by John's remark. She said, 'No one's ever spoken to me like that. Besides, he's my brother and whatever he's done to us, to me, I've never *hated* him, or meant to hurt him. I don't know why I should feel so surprised or wounded. Johnny and I have nothing in common, but he *is* my brother.'"

In time, an idea, a reputation, gains a life of its own, abided by adherents, detested by antagonists. It is doubtful Andronikus, had he wanted, could have recanted or relented his position. In time, as men began to respond to him, their activities, in kind, engendered their own reality, their own consequences, divorced from, but still attributable to, him.

Andronikus was raised to Imperial visibility when Manuel was raised to the throne. The votaries or champions he gained might implement his ideas because, ironically, they were less closely observed and less powerful, if power be the measure of threat. Men such as the Grand Duke Basil, Duke Michael Branas, and Count George Angelus, among others, neither very notable nor as fair and extravagant as the son of the Great Sebastocrator, were, for those very reasons, privy to all councils and, as members of the Praetorium (and in Basil's case, as a Grand Duke, also a member of the Sacred Consistory), able to offer, however diluted or somewhat removed, something like the same advice espoused by Andronikus, but without the abrasion, which came between his person and the Emperor's, or, for that matter, John Sergius'. It was known, in fact, they favored Andronikus, but, save for Basil's handsome gesture at Pelagonia, they were not frantic in defending his person and by all odds ready to obey the Emperor when he forbade alternatives. They could not, therefore, comfortably be relieved without raising in their own defense the banner of gross injustice.

Whether or not Manuel was distressed by these impeccable termites we cannot say. One may be certain of John Sergius' animosity. And so, on 2 March 1154, Basil was reassigned as Commander of the Constantinopolitan Garrison, which it had been a legal precedent, heretofore, never to assign to a member of the Imperial family. Michael Branas was directed to proceed to Dyrrhachium as Military Governor, ironically, the initial ascent of his great career. George Angelus, similarly disassociated and raised, was assigned to Anchialus on the Black Sea. It should come as no surprise, all three of these men were against the Hungarian reprisals.

More than forty years after the event, Eudocia Comnena Branas recalled the circumstances which gave her to accompany the Imperial War Party north to Zeugamin and her lover's downfall: "They say the motives of the young, if not wise, are at least uncomplicated, rather ardent and ingenuous. For me, that is pure nonsense. After the initial excitement of our reunion, I should be less than truthful if I did not say my cousin and I became bored with one another yet maintained our alliance because my brother, the Protovestarius, was outraged by it. Really there was no choice. It was rather obvious my brother took our alliance as a personal affront and it had quite nothing whatever to do with the offense previously given my mother. So, too, my cousin had now been politically isolated—and really, for that, I didn't want to leave him. There isn't a bone of courage in my body, I think, but if anything happened to Andronikus, I wanted to share his fate. I'm certain the thought should never have passed through his mind, but *I* should have felt irresponsible and frivolous had he suffered any disaster alone. Instead I became the instrument of that disaster.

"Ironic, isn't it? Moved to such a fate and yet we had become oppressive to one another. We argued quite a bit those last days at Demetrius Palace, trifles, nothing, over personal habits, then arguments about the argument. At one point, when my cousin was being particularly cruel in his remarks, I reminded him I could go back to my good husband who would gratefully and faithfully receive me (or so I thought), but *he* could not go back to Anastasia without intervening between his wife and her lover. At that, I bit my tongue. Previously, no one had dared speak of it for fear of what he would do. Well, sir, I'll tell you, I've never seen so many emotions pass through one man in an instant—like the colors of a faceted glass spun against the sun. At first he was stunned, then I thought he was going to strike me. But then, probably to spite my disclosure and my smugness, and the world which might think him so closely allied to its conventions, or to point up his opinion of himself which would never allow him to believe he was replaceable in any woman's heart (he wasn't), or even to make certain I knew a cuckold's horns grew from the inside out—and he realized Anastasia's infidelity was revenge, not appetite—he laughed with real cheer and said, 'Marvelous. Only, when you get back, tell her for me she'd best abort any bastard she conceives, since I'll never, never make a Grand Duke of another man's runt.' Whether it was woman's intuition or womanly sentiment, however, I approached him, then, with stupid tenderness, but he told me to go away.

"Inevitably, though, when the Emperor left for the north and took my cousin Elizabeth Persephone with him, Andronikus told me to make arrangements with my steward to accompany *him*. When my brother tried to countermand me, I had my own steward requisition a pavilion from the quartermaster—not the last word in luxury, nor of the triple thickness with the velvet interface usual to a Grand Duchess' field accommodations—and in the end I nearly froze to death. But it recommended itself later by saving Andronikus' life." The Grand Duchess squinted, as though peering into her own past. Now she pulled tight, with one jerk, the exquisite handkerchief she had been holding between her fingers, glinting with rubies and emeralds. A hangman's gesture, I thought. "How absurd," she said. "The thickness of that army regulation tent was the little space between my cousin's life and death."

At Zeugamin the Imperial forces and the Hungarian army met in an extraordinarily savage clash in which, for the first time in nearly forty years, Alexius' unconquerable military invention, the slant-line formation, was finally overcome. Nevertheless, as Andronikus explained, "Zeugamin was not the end of the use of the slant-line, as, for example, 197 years before Christ, Kynoscephale marked the end of the Macedonian phalanx. In that classic battle, which men shall probably consider and reconsider as long as wars are fought—in sum, forever—the classic occurred, an old strategy was rendered obsolete by a new one: if the phalanx's effectiveness was its immovable, ponderous ferocity, then the answer was, as logic might have told you—if there were any logic in war —agility, constant movement, adaptability, the mountain cat to the rhinoceros. The anonymous Roman commander at Kynoscephale drawing up his right, behind the Greek phalanx, which was nearly triumphant over the Roman left, whether he knew it or not, was standing face to face with Alexander of Macedon, who conquered the world with this formation.

"No such victory, on the other hand, took place at Zeugamin. Geza had mastered no real counter-thrust against the slant-line. He merely proved once again, so long as a warlord had troops sufficiently suicidal in their willingness to gallop over a plain of their own dead, so long as he could command an inexhaustible number of chests to bare their torsos to arrows and heads to axes, he could penetrate the presumably impenetrable."

In the end the King of Hungary was defeated because he wasted three quarters of his army in an egotistical attempt to mount history's horse as the first conqueror of the slant-line, because, lacking insight in proportion to the degree he possessed vanity, he chose incident to conquest. He could scarcely have comprehended the sophistication of the Byzantine Praetorium, its generals much too worldly wise to base a battle on a single group of men numbering no more than a seventh of the entire army, generals taught at the Scholarian Academy in the very tradition of the impromptu strategy which defeated the Macedonians nearly thirteen centuries before. It was not the slant-line, alone, but its effectiveness as part of a vast, living body of soldiery at separate but interconnected tasks, which assured success.

At Zeugamin, of course, there took place the famous exploit in which Andronikus saved the Emperor's life.

I was given probably the only eyewitness by a veteran—a former Varangian—of the Hungarian campaign, who seemed less interested in describing the battle in which he had lost an eye thirty-five years before than convincing me, as Senator and Minister, to petition the Emperor Alexius III of the House of Angelus for abrogation of the new, hysterical law which enforced registration of all portable—which is to say, private —weapons at Constantinople. ("Licenses mean money, Senator, which the rich have got, and we haven't—and they go about at night with their own soldiers. Can't you do something? We know why they're doing this, don't we? They learned a lesson from their own usurpation.") At length, I reminded him I was pressed for time, which I was. Like most veterans he talked a blue streak. (Trained for war, unequipped for peaceful pursuits, they have little to do, indeed, but mull past glories. The problem among the Varangians is especially acute. They are the only elite corps not comprised of aristocrats, and they must face mandatory retirement at thirty-five, unless they are officers, in which case there is an optional grace period of ten more years. If they have not used their approximation to the court—and their code of honor is awesome—the privates and NCOs retire, save for severance pay, with no future and nothing to fall back upon. Most of them, accustomed to the magnificence and noise of court and city, refuse the always open offer of transportation home to their native land and so their sorry fate is usually destitution and chronic drunkenness—a drink for a tale. Andronikus, shortly before his death, convened a commission to consider the problem and recommend solutions. Unfortunately, it was disbanded, without report, by the Angeli.) I must admit, this fellow was sharper than most and, as a Varangian, privy, of course, to gossip of the court as well as the field, but slow to the point, and so I pressed him.

"Well"—he cleared his throat (somewhat abashed, which broke my heart, so that, against my better judgment, I invited him to dinner—which he refused—and offered him a job in my stables—which he accepted)—"you know the Emperor's reputation on the battlefield. He was the despair of the Guard. Something overcame him and he was worse than a man in a passion, which is to say, he never considered the consequences, only the promise. Long ago, I remember, I was courting a particularly young thing. She was a personal maid to one of the Grand Duchesses. Once, Her Imperial Highness was staying at an estate near the farm I had bought for my mother and brother, who died in the epidemic of '73. (Manuel Augustus actually brought them from Russia at his own expense.) In any event, I was in a frenzy to get to the girl and there was only one horse we had—sick as the very devil—but I insisted on taking it and rode the life out of it just to see the lady. While I was entertaining her, the old nag, poor thing, died. When I found it I was in despair not only because I'd have to buy a new horse for the farm—with the money from God knows where—but because in my unthinking, I'd been despicably cruel. Recall the words of Proverbs: 'The just regards the life of his beasts.' The promise, as I said, against the consequences.

"Well, that was the Emperor during campaign. At Zeugamin, when the slant-line was overwhelmed, His Majesty couldn't stand to watch any longer and spurred his horse right into the thick of it. A dozen of us Varangians followed, trying to surround him, but he kept on right ahead of us, and the twelve became six, and the six became three and three became one—myself—and we were unhorsed. The battlefield was more of a horror than usual because one of those sloppy spring snows was falling—you know, flakes big as tulip petals and steam rising out of the ground so you couldn't see the bodies until you stepped on them, and the fog rolling in and rolling out beneath the ramparts of Zeugamin Castle. You know, the enemy here—the fog rolls in, the fog rolls out—and it's not the enemy anymore, but you're suddenly facing your own, just as though a magician's at work and *someone's* laughing and applauding. Well, both His Majesty and me were backed against a pile of huge boulders—I lost the eye then; I don't even remember the moment (later, in the infirmary, His Majesty told me that in all the fighting, he remembered thinking in a flash, I looked like the lead actor in the last act of *Oedipus Rex;* I saw the play about a year later out of curiosity—it was *disgusting*). Like a fool, I called for help—'It's the Emperor, here! Save him!'—when it could only bring on more Hungarians.

"Well, as long as I live I'll never forget what happened next. The Grand Duke Andronikus, nearer than I would have imagined, in the thick of it, himself, heard me, and wheeled around like a shot for a look. He was wearing a blue metal helmet with the silver cross of the Grand Dukes atop, and blue mail, and in that mist, on his big black white-plumed stallion, with his gleaming sword upraised—well, I can't say precisely whether he seemed to me Michael of the Hosts or the very devil incarnate. When he saw us, his whole expression became—I can't quite describe it—something like terror—not fear, but a thrill of astonishment. So he rode down on the men giving it to us. For a fellow who'd been near death's door two months before—and I'd seen His Imperial Highness on maneuvers: he had not half his usual strength—it was just amazing. By the Blachernae Mother of God, I vow he took on four, five, seven men at a throw—lopping off one head, cleaving that unlucky soul in two, this man's arms, giving it to another straight through the heart. If he looked like an angel before rescuing us, he arrived by our side like a butcher, just ghastly with blood. He dismounted and came up to the Emperor and they stared at one another for an eternity, which in a battle is anywhere from five to ten seconds of inactivity, then grasped one another's arm in an odd, shaking way. Very cold-blooded, not even a hug."

If the event is accurate as described—and there is no reason to doubt it since many years previous Manuel had corroborated his cousin's heroism (besides such unknowingly accurate insights as a lack of physical demonstrativeness in both men—quite true)—it is little wonder Andronikus suffered a relapse after the battle and was put to bed with a high fever. The Emperor insisted the army remain at Zeugamin a week longer in his cousin's behalf, a delay gladly endorsed by those men to whom Andronikus was once again Prosopopoeia Invictae. This, by chance, worked to the advantage of a diplomatic settlement between the Byzantine and Hungarian states, since the usual ambassadors could be dispensed with and the two monarchs were able to strike a treaty between themselves and something like a friendship.*

The army took a leisurely two weeks to return to Demetrius Palace at Thessalonika, the slow progress due in part to the immensity of the war train. All the while, of course, documents and ministers were traversing the distance between Constantinople and the field. Ironically, there was once again set up an encampment at Pelagonia, where, in the space of two days, Andronikus' life was irrevocably changed.

Andronikus: "The first afternoon I was able to get some exercise, I took my horse on a canter through the woods. It was a marvelous ride, I remember. Everything was just beginning to bud. The trees dark and damp from a late morning shower with their wispy helmets of pale green leaf pods looking like nothing so much as colossal maidenhair. Several times I thought I saw shadowy figures to either side of the path, and now and then I heard a cascade of rocks, but either I was too slow or 'they' were too quick, for I never caught sight of anyone. In fact, I was somewhat unnerved. I was weaker still than I wished to admit, and in those periods of my life where I've overexerted myself, I'm usually prey to overmuch imagination, of a rather morbid, even fantastical kind.

---

* Geza II was the son of Bela II, Irene of Hungary's first cousin, thus the King and the Emperor shared a common great-grandfather in Bela I and common kin in Manuel's sister-in-law, Geza's cousin, the Sebastocratrix Francesca, Theodora's mother. N.A.

Realistically, I should have marked those 'phantoms' I thought I saw as John Sergius' agents and left it at that. Instead, with a real chill up my back, I became certain they were witches, demons. I was actually frightened enough to stop, to think twice and return to the encampment, quite full of foreboding. I decided to visit with Eudocia. She knew my mood well enough, and she was willing to bed down with me for the afternoon. I was very grateful. If such dread and brooding points up one's solitude, love or lust is the only antidote.

"I stayed past sunset, when one of her women came to us in great alarm and told us the front and back of the pavilion were surrounded by soldiers who nearly hadn't let her pass. This was an impossible situation since Eudocia's tent was not within the official encampment, but some distance apart, worse still, with a river at its back. At once, I turned to my cousin. I am ashamed to say I suspected her of complot with her brother. Her hysteria convinced me she was not, and I think that alarmed me more. She was a woman of enormous self-possession and to see her cracking apart somehow unsettled me. Almost jabbering, she made one suggestion to save myself, which will give you some idea: that I dress in women's clothes and pretend I was the lady-in-waiting who had just entered. Aside from such alarming growth into something like a feminine Goliath, which would convince no one, or the lack of draperies enough to cover me, I rather thought, if die I must, I would much sooner point up the malevolence of my death than the absurdity of my corpse, for all men to remember.

"I took up my only weapon, a jeweled hunting knife which had been my grandfather the Emperor's, felt with my hand along the back of the tent, and then, with a great swipe, cut the cloth from top to bottom. It gave more easily than I had expected—the night air rushing in on me with a chill. I ran out into the darkness with a war cry meant to startle, and dimly perceived the stunned assassins. I crouched, once, then bounded over their heads and jumped into the river about twenty feet below. The cold of the water was simply indescribable, and in the darkness, one of my nightmares realized. For an instant I remembered myself as a child, looking over the side of the ship which took us across the Bosporus into exile one snowy winter night. How vivid it is to me still. Do you know, for a moment, I wanted to let go, to submerge into this icy ink and be done with it, to drown and be done with it. But it was all too physically shocking, too confusing for a death as surrender, as respite, into a final sleep. I found myself, before I had resolved it, swimming downstream and emerging by the torches near the tents of the Imperial pavilion.

"You can imagine the apparition I must have seemed: half-naked, unshod, shivering like a thistle in a breeze. Yet one thing remained recognizable in any metamorphosis: my height. One of the Varangians, an Englishman, whom I knew, Sicco Miller, recognized me. I told him to take me to the Emperor. He said, with a very heavy accent, 'Your Highness—like *that?*' What a mix of efficiency and effeminacy those Varangians can be. I pushed past him—I remember the touch of his gold-on-silver breastplate, so cold—and he followed me in.

"Manuel was at dinner with his companions—among them, John Sergius. Again, as with Eudocia, I knew from the look of his eye the Emperor was innocent. I went up to John Sergius, caught him by his neck and pulled him out of his chair, and without an instant's delay, broke his nose with one punch. A great commotion, naturally. The Varangians came at me and knocked me down, pummeling me with the butts of their spears—gold spears and heavy—me, the grandson of Alexius Augustus in front of the reigning Emperor whose father and my father were brothers. I was still very much the Imperial prince then and the affront, even in my pain, quite staggered me, the betrayal made more painful still by the witness of my cousin who would allow it. But then, to be sure, they had scarcely known what to expect of me.

"From the floor, I saw John Sergius, his face bloodied, his eyes already beginning to close, helped away by his creatures. And there I lay naked, sopping, shivering, and bleeding, too. Manuel stood above me, towering above me, hissing down, 'In God's name, what kind of lunatic are you?'

"And do you know, Nicetas, all the rage went out of me, and the despair of the waters—and their silence—returned. Suddenly I knew the dullness of resignation. Suddenly these people seemed to me strangers and children. Not that I was above them, but that our levels of meaning should never coincide. It was not a matter of compromise or definitions, but irreconcilability. I felt myself as one throwing a tantrum before infants, removed from threat, who merely watched, awed and amused and unconvinced. I can only compare what I experienced then to a feeling one knows when ill and awakening from a poor sleep—nausea, lassitude, an overwhelming weakness in the bone.

"Manuel signaled the guards to raise me. The moment I was on my feet the blood from my nose ran over my mouth and I sneezed and spewed it everywhere. The whole company stepped away from me like hunters who have come upon their kill unexpectedly alive while the dogs have opened its ravened insides. I said, 'Take me away. In the name of God take me away from here.' "

In the vermilion afterglow of the sun, now set beneath the horizon, the then Emperor Andronikus closed his eyes. Behind his head, in the oncoming violet night, the first star appeared.

I said, "Forgive me, Your Majesty." He opened his eyes. "Why?" "Perhaps this is rather too painful." He looked at me with the small amazement, not untouched by irony, of one who acknowledges the gesture, if not the effectuality, of sympathy. He put one hand—with its single jewel, his coronation ring—over mine. "You mustn't feel that way. It seems to me now it can hardly have happened."

At that moment, Andronikus' valet, Leo, a retainer of the Comneni, descended the steps into the garden. He approached us and said, "Your Majesty, there is a chill." With the solicitous tyranny of a servant, he took the cape from his arm and waited for the Emperor to stand, which Andronikus did to indulge him. (I followed, of course, in courtesy.) Leo draped the length of rich purple wool, soft as down, with its gold metallic threads at the border, over the Emperor's shoulders, bowed, smiled coldly to me with a look which said, "Fend for yourself," and departed. The Emperor considered me a moment, removed his cape, and said, "Here, my boy, you're turning blue." It was the gesture of an old athlete too proud of his body to admit its susceptibility to age.

As he fastened its ruby clasp beneath my neck, he said, "There is an old custom, you must know it. When an Emperor threw his cape around a subject, that man became sacrosanct and inviolable to harm." He made a gesture for me to be seated. "Well, now you know what it is like to wear the purple." There was a faint smell in the fabric of the musk-scented creams which the Emperor's masseur preferred.

He was silent as we sat again, and in his eye was the look of—what?—yearning, reverie, and a little fear I have noticed in the old when dusk occurs. For all I know, it may be in my own eye now as I remember that moment in a late August evening when I was still young and stood by a man whose birth was only four years from the death of Alexius I, and those accomplishments which are now the legend of the dispossessed.

The vision of that late day has, for me, the serenity of a dream, though I know beyond the walls of that garden were the gathering circumstances which in three weeks would bring about the Emperor's ghastly death.

"Have you ever noticed how the embers of a gutted fire will sometimes flare briefly, even spectacularly, if only for a moment, before they finally die? I suppose it is only by this analogy I can explain what became of me after I asked, quite in despair, to be taken away. Manuel—how very like him—was quick to catch something in my voice, in the request itself, and made move toward me, his hand already extended, his expression truly compassionate. But I waved him away with a short disgusted gesture. I happened to turn my head at that moment, and looked into the eyes of one of the Varangians, who, from the feel of his strokes—and I marked them his—had taken particular pleasure in punishing with immunity the son of the Great Sebastocrator. There was no warning: white rage suddenly burst like a small sun within me. I punched him below his breastplate, in the groin, which doubled him, and then I brought my folded hands down upon the back of his neck, as he crumpled. Again, there was commotion, and I heard someone say, 'He's dead,' all too obvious in the look of his broken neck. Manuel said, 'Take that man away. Put him in chains.' He had every right to be appalled, though even then I sensed he was less offended by the fact of murder than the murder of a man before his Imperial person."

There is a legend—I have not been able to trace its origins, though I suspect the agents of the Protovestarius—which does not mention the killing of the Varangian or the attempted assassination, for that matter, of the Grand Duke as ascribable to John Sergius. Rather after Andronikus' escape from the Grand Duchess' pavilion, he accused, without cause, her brother, and the Emperor refused to believe his cousin. In turn, John Sergius calumniated Andronikus by professing to have proof the Grand Duke was set to assassinate the Emperor. Forgery is admitted as possible, but the Protovestarius is described as being in mortal fear of his cousin's mistaken accusation and misplaced revenge. The Emperor is described as being of two minds and indecisive, until one day Andronikus, by a chance remark, condemned himself. Supposedly the Emperor came upon his cousin, an Imperial Grand Duke, at the very unlikely task of grooming his own horse. When he asked Andronikus why he so extravagantly coddled the animal (instead of the more obvious question: why was he playing the stable boy?) the Grand Duke is said to have

replied, "I'd lavish any attention on the means of leaping over the severed head of my worst enemy." Manuel is purported to have taken this
as a threat to his own trunkless pate, as John Sergius had intimated,
and then and there, ordered his cousin chained, remanded to Constantinople and the dungeons of Buceleon Palace.

Besides exonerating John Sergius, this legend, which has not a parti-
cle of truth insofar as events took place, or, for that matter, accuracy in
its details of a dynast's pastimes, serves to condemn Manuel for punishing his cousin on circumstantial evidence, with unbelievably capricious
severity.

In point of fact, there was never an episode in which a quip cost Andronikus the better part of the next decade of his life. He was placed
in confinement that April night of an attempted assassination upon
himself because he had murdered a Varangian before the eyes of offended Majesty. Why temporary incarceration became permanent and
abject, we will come to presently. I am certain succeeding generations,
without investigation, are going to pour still more contumely on this
apparent miscarriage of justice than is deserved. True: there is no question, according to the Lex Fundamentalis, the Emperor is empowered
to pardon any man in his realm, priest, lay, prince or slave, of any crime,
including murder, heresy, treason, or usurpation. Also true: however
callous, the murder of any man other than a member of the Imperial
family has seldom been grounds for prosecuting a Grand Duke in whose
veins flows the august blood of Emperors of a reigning dynasty. In effect
this is precisely the charge we would like to presume, but cannot, which
would have been brought against John Sergius had his agents succeeded
in killing Andronikus. (That those soldiers surrounding the Grand
Duchess' tent *were* the Protovestarius' creatures was certified by a board
of inquiry convened a year after the death of the Heir Presumptive.)

By the standards of dynastic justice, which are another world from
that of the ordinary man, Andronikus fell haphazardly into his imprisonment. He was jailed, at first, because a Varangian died by his hand and
this was an offense of Imperial etiquette. What followed in the space
of a few days is rather like the story of the hunter who sets his trap for a
boar, and finds instead a wolf.

It can be said, Manuel was aware his cousin's sensational disputa-
tiousness was based not on mere possession of power, but the uses to
which it was put: that is, resentment most dangerous, the envy born of

the logic of the articulate rebel. He was aware that as an Imperial relative, Andronikus' access to his person was, in principle, a matter of course, and therefore the Grand Duke's activities were, at once, potentially more lethal and a reflection upon the dynasty. It can be said also, if Andronikus lived to challenge him as an alternative, then his own burdens seemed all the heavier under a critic he respected, if he could not always comprehend the criticism. It *cannot* be said the Emperor realized the bias his own vanity brought to any decision regarding his cousin. Conceding Andronikus' sublimity could only degenerate further into recklessness without the discipline of responsibility—and refusing to offer it—the Emperor preferred to punish the symptoms instead of the source.

I am going to present, here, the minutes of the last meeting between Manuel and Andronikus, conducted in strict privacy—save for the secretary, recording in *notae Tironianae*—in the pavilion in which the Grand Duke was kept chained. The reader may decide for himself the Emperor's guilt, or his cousin's, or, most unhappily, the lethal collision of their mutual innocence.

At first His Highness refused to speak to His Majesty.

HIS MAJESTY. I am asking you to listen to me.

HIS HIGHNESS. Say whatever you like. I have no choice. I can't even stop my ears. Is it your orders my hands are not to be free save to eat, with two archers trained on me?

H.M. I'm sorry. You know these are regulation procedures. The guards had no authority but to treat you like the others.

H.H. Like a criminal, you mean. They had the authority, all right. Your indifference.

H.M. I'll see the chains are removed.

H.H. You do and I'll clap them back on myself. You treat me like a criminal, I'll stay one, punished like one. You give me pardon, I'll give you none. This is where I belong. It's where we all belong in an autocracy. There is only whim, not law, and where there is no law, accusation is not necessary to punishment.

H.M. You killed one of my guards.

H.H. Yes. And for that I am sorry. Had he a family?

H.M. A wife. Three sons.

H.H. Then ask Isaac, if you will, to set aside from my estate an annuity for them. Something substantial. Unless, that is, you intend to confiscate my possessions.

H.M. No, I do not.

H.H. Then I ask you to do that much for me. It really was unfortunate. But there's no way to repent, is there? Nothing will bring him back. Of course, were I like you I could ask God to forgive me and, washed clean of the circumspection of guilt, go on to do the same thing once again.

H.M. And are you happier this way?

H.H. Shall we say, what I've done and cannot undo shall not be so easily dismissed from my mind by absolution and the Host.

H.M. Men may just as soon become degenerate with no alternative from their remorse.

H.H. Why am I here, Manuel? It's not the Varangian, is it?

H.M. You are here because I cannot tolerate any longer your disruptive and unpredictable offenses.

H.H. Good. You're frank, as far as it goes. And what have you done as regards John Sergius' attempt on my life?

H.M. That has all been explained. Had you been less than culpable in insisting on resuming your relations with Eudocia against Johnny's wishes, you would not have acted or judged with the impetuosity of the guilty. Those guards were present to prevent you from entering. They were not aware you were already within her pavilion.

H.H. If you believe that, you're beneath contempt.

H.M. Is there no man whose warning you will take?

H.H. I'm beyond warning, Manuel.

H.M. I want you to be free.

H.H. There's no freedom if you must want it for me. These shackles prove it, the material proof of the reality in principle. I was in chains last week, only they were the lighter weight of your condescension. I tell you this as a last gesture of respect because I would never speak behind any man's back. Do you think I could give a man the regard of my criticism if I did not think he knew how to accept it?

H.M. By whose authority do you make yourself arbiter?

H.H. My own, Manuel. Authority belongs to those who have the courage to reject, the intelligence to replace, and the wit to perceive the ephemerality of both.

H.M. My authority is from heaven itself, whether or not you choose to believe it.

H.H. Whether or not I choose to believe your authority is borne on an angel's wings from heaven or on Satan's bright trident up from hell or, for that matter, the incantations of witches in the wood is of no account. The point is other men believe your divine manifest, most men do—and that is why I am here.

H.M. That is not why you are here.

H.H. Isn't it?

H.M. Why must you waste your life as you do?

H.H. I've never wasted a moment of my life. But that is no concern of yours.

H.M. It is my concern. I saved it here at Pelagonia.

H.H. I saved yours at Zeugamin. The debt is canceled. A pretty end to all this, isn't it?

H.M. This is not the end. I forbid you to speak so.

H.H. You have forbidden me everything, Manuel. There is nothing left to forbid. I'm free. For that, much thanks.

H.M. Be serious. I implore you.

H.H. If I were, I'd kill myself. But I am no less accurate.

H.M. This is where your arrogance has led you.

H.H. Not arrogance. Logic.

H.M. Your amorality which is the bastard of your atheism. You have lost all compassion. There is nothing more terrible than a man without compassion. He cannot be reached.

H.H. All that you have said of compassion and its loss is true, but it is you, in your ship of omnipotence on a sea of flattery, who have run aground. You are without the compassion I extend to you because you do not recognize your loss. You live in your world, I, mine. You cannot see my point, I, yours. A fish cannot imagine himself without water, a man without air. If I try to take the fish from the water or you, the man, out of the air, one, as the other, rebels, because his existence is impossible without the environment which nourishes him.

H.M. What is it you want of me, Andronikus?

H.H. Power.

H.M. To do what?

H.H. Since the question is hypothetical, I will entertain you with a hypothetical answer. In the immediate: to use that army which has been so superbly rebuilt not in your absurd hankering after conquest, but to maintain the borders of the late Macedonians which we have nearly regained, save for Sicily—and the sooner you realize that accursed isle is a permanent loss the better—; to rebuild the cities rather than add one more unnecessary monument in our name at Constantinople which already groans under the weight of such extravagant and atrocious vanities; to relieve the poor of taxes altogether, improve state services in their behalf, and tax the aristocrats off the face of the land; to disband the court, favor the merchant class, break up the monasteries and cashier half, if not all, their treasures. Madness, no?

H.M. No. Not madness. But the coldest vision of a state I've ever heard.

H.H. Yes, yes. No color, no trumpets, no affectations by which a bore like Johnny tells himself he's finer, fitter, a repository of grace as the descendant of Emperors, somehow more exalted than the servant who attends him in his bath. He's none of these things—nor you, nor I. We're only luckier. For me, the only consolation is that I could have been anything had I not been a Grand Duke.

H.M. And do you think the oppressed, those unlucky, would bless you for the state you have created for them?

H.H. I don't care for their blessings.

H.M. Let me tell you something: In all you would do, you would open a Pandora's box releasing evils which would bring down the very state you think you mean to save. The oppressed will suffer patiently what seems to them ordained. Reform such as you would have would lead them to disbelieve all order whatsoever. What you lifted a little from their shoulders, they would shake off entirely. And you with it. And why? Because what is no longer inevitable becomes intolerable. Reform is irrevocable, Andronikus. Once begun, it must be all at once, or the oppressed will become impatient, and the oppressors, as you prefer to call us—and you'd best include yourself—will attempt by any means to retrieve the old order, enraging the oppressed still more. Anarchy, civil war, revolution: that would be your heritage to your precious downtrodden.

H.H. If you believe that, you're more depraved than I thought, or more cowardly. You do not seem to understand it would take a greater regent to conquer iniquity than Sicily. But for that, you must first conquer yourself, your fear of the unknown. As you said, reform is irrevocable. And true, the oppressors, initially, might return to the old ways, but never with the previous complacency they knew. We are all apt pupils, even against our will and our comfort. You want—God knows what you want —a return to the days of Justinian. You do not seem to realize that retrospect is pretense, your own, whereas had I the power, and implemented what I believe, and fell by it, too, there would be others, after me, enlightened by my example.

H.M. That is unlike you. Why should you care what comes after you?

H.H. And there is the difference between you and me. Once, I cared, as you, only to be remembered rather than positively influential on posterity. Luckily, I became a man. I cannot say the same for you.

H.M. None of this serves any purpose. If I pardon you, will you give me your word—

H.H. Don't even speak it. I cannot give you my word. If you exile me, I'll return. If you blind me, I'll find men to lead me and so lead them. In the name of God, kill me or jail me, because I see now there is no other choice for you or for myself. I cannot be other than what I am, nor you whatever it is you wish to be. I cannot be silent and you cannot tolerate my noise. I cannot be ineffectual and you would only use me to ends with which I cannot agree, in methods I could not bring myself to execute. Make me your Heir, your Caesar, listen to me in everything as you promised so many years ago in Cilicia, or cut off my head or let me rot somewhere. I'm weary of this.

H.M. You talk like a suicide.

H.H. The first Romans believed suicide, pursuant to one's disgrace or uselessness—as one follows the other—most virtuous.

H.M. They were heathen.

H.H. They were men, Manuel—like you and I. A man was useful or not; if he was useful, he lived, if not, he was irrelevant, dead or alive. Whether or not I agree with such a philosophy, the fact remains it is suitable to a conquering state. Christianity, from which you condemn them, is not. The moment a Christian lifts a sword, he is condemning himself. If he still believes himself a Christian as he wields it, he is an apostate. If he doubts and wields it still, he is a hypocrite.

H.M. How can you speak of morality?

H.H. Because I have nothing else, whereas you have absolution.

H.M. You would destroy everything. Even what is beautiful and harmless.

H.H. Show me the beauty which is not the prerogative of the fortunate and the envy of the oppressed. Such beauty belongs to the times in which it was horded. It must go. Men can make new beauty.

H.M. The loss is irreplaceable.

H.H. The keeping is bondage. If it must be replaced, one ought to strive to equal or surpass it. But it must go.

H.M. What is civilization but such heritage?

H.H. According to the Church in which you and I were born, our only aspiration is to be free of matter. Very well. We are born naked and die naked in our skins. We bring nothing with us and take nothing with us when we go. We do not possess what we cannot keep forever. We only possess what we create, truly new, from nothing, by our own genius.

H.M. What you do not seem to realize is that you have an idealist's sense of insurrection, not the politician's.

H.H. And what you do not seem to realize is that revolution is, first of all, not political, but therapeutic. Create the storm, then calm it—and then we have the particulars of rule.

H.M. Like that crypto-mystic outlaw Arnold of Brescia.

H.H. Manuel, the difference between outlawry and revolution is victory. Save the epithets for your courtiers. I am nothing like Arnold of Brescia. He is, as you say, a mystic. That, at any rate, is the impression I've received from witnesses. Very interested in tithes and damnation and democracy. I have nothing in common with him, save enormous sympathy.

H.M. If you are so certain of oppression of the poor and the rich and the peasant and the aristocrat in an autocracy, how is it your logic has not carried you, indeed, as far as democracy? Had you ever thought such ultimate reasoning might go against your own ambition and catch like a fishhook in your throat before you speak of it? Look at Athens: democracy, there, was a confusion of selfish motives. Such a form of government becomes a unity only in a crisis, and sometimes not even then. If all men are the state they may confuse their ambition with the good of the state, and there is only chaos.

H.H. At least that confusion of motives is more representative of the many wants of the millions under your foot than those few who supply the peasants to pull your war chariot or participate in the vulgar spectacle of your court.

H.M. How deluded you are. The peasant is as selfish and obtuse as you believe the aristocrat.

H.H. Then educate them. If the rich use their intelligence to hoodwink the poor, give the poor the same weapon to defend themselves.

H.M. A noble venture. Where would you find the money?

H.H. Where you find it and with it, erect palaces, pay for Persephone's whim, and cross from East Europe into the West.

H.M. Can you honestly tell me that is all you believe I have accomplished since my accession?

H.H. I believe you meant to do much good, Manuel. I know you have it in you to be compassionate and sympathetic. But only from incident to incident. You're not urged by example to investigate any more deeply. For you it is not *ex pede Herculum*—it is merely a foot. What you've done that I can approve, you've done well. I needn't tell you that. But Irene has done more, whatever her propitiation to a heaven which is not merely deaf, it simply isn't there.

H.M. And what have you done that you may pass judgment on my wife and myself?

H.H. Nothing.

H.M. Andronikus, the more I forgive you, the more you seem to test me. My authority suffers, which I must pass intact, as charged by God, to my successor, whoever he may be. Were you merely a rakehell, it would scarcely matter to me. But your mischief extends to politics, and time and again you have disobeyed me and even reversed me. The longer you exist as a free agent, the more I am undermined. It seems we are completely at odds. A while ago you made your intentions clear. You will not repent your ways but continue to attempt to undo me. Whether or not you would have it so, as you contest me, you contest the state as it exists. I fear this more than were your argument one entirely personal and jealous. Then I could expect a certain discretion, a line beyond which you would not go, but that you would reconcile yourself eventually to a fate which has placed me upon the throne to do quite as I see fit with or without your approval. If it were not a duel to the end, then, at least, I could blind you or execute or exile you with a clear conscience. Now I see I am irrelevant and it is not that you would be harsh with me personally—I would imagine quite the opposite—but that you will stop at nothing to do what you mean to do. Free, you are an example of my irresponsibility, in which case, I must disown you for you shall be my downfall and the state's as well or cause so much havoc in the meantime as to nullify all I am attempting to achieve. If I incarcerate you rather for what you might do than what you have done, at the risk of the justice I have always prized by my name, it is because I have no choice. To do less would be a greater evil against the state than I do to you.

H.H. Have you anything further to say?

H.M. Nothing. God have mercy on you. Good-by.

H.H. Good-by, Manuel.

The Emperor then departed.

Twenty-three years would pass before either man—so mutually and eccentrically beloved—would see or speak to one another again.

XV

A year after Andronikus' assumption to the throne, I had the transcript of his last interview with Manuel, at Pelagonia, drawn from the archives. I presented it to him. He read it with an absolutely blank expression, then handed the document back to me. He mused and, as was his habit, pulled gently at his short silver two-pronged beard, and said, "Uncanny. Listening to one's own voice out of lost time. And his, too, now that he's gone, as for that matter is the young man who was myself so outrageously self-assured in all he did, it never occurred to him he would encounter a venture over which he had no control: himself as prisoner.

"Believe me, I forgave Manuel almost the moment he left the pavilion. Really, he had no other choice. He had hesitated so long, out of generosity and because he feared what he would feel if he undid me. But it turned out the bruises of his injustice were easier than he believed to endure, weren't they?

"Probably I could have achieved my release, sworn my fidelity, and spared myself—at least before the interview took place. Afterward I was trundled off to Constantinople and forgotten. But, oh, the difference between accepting punishment and suffering it: traveling to imprisonment and realizing it is the end of everything—luxury, women, whim, choice, the end of arranging one's life as one likes it, of friends, of pastimes, of the open air. I can still see that ride through the countryside, and the pall which seemed to have extended itself over everything, between myself and the world as seen indeed 'through a glass darkly.' I asked myself: Could this be happening to me? Was I truly losing everything, become an object to be locked away? I had lost the simplest private rights of a human being. I would, in the most rudimentary sense, no longer be my own.

"That alien entrance to Buceleon—the entrance to the dungeons—which I had never before noted. The descent three fetid stone floors below ground level. The overwhelming smell of lye, excrement, vomit, the unwashed, the rotting carcasses of rats smashed dead in the corridor and left to the cockroaches. I remember I was ingenuous enough to say, 'There must be some mistake. Not this.' I had, with reason, consoled myself I would be placed in one of the apartments for highborn criminals in the Tower of Anemas or the Buceleon Lighthouse."

I asked Andronikus if he knew by whose orders he had been thus appointed. "I don't know. There are no records. They were obviously destroyed. If we knew when—after Theodora's father's death in '74, or John Sergius' in '76, earlier than that or shortly before or after Manuel's death or close on or shortly before my Regency for Alexius—we might be able to pinpoint the culprit. Obviously, it was out of the ordinary.

The governor of the prison section himself, who accompanied me, said, none too comfortably, to his credit, 'I'm sorry, Your Highness. Truly.' 'But here?' I repeated, disgusted with my panic and still enough of a prince to wish to appear imperturbable before 'inferiors.'

"The Buceleon Ravelin. Do you think any name could strike greater terror in a man's heart? For the first time in my life I knew frenzy, the true frenzy, creeping fear, which does not recommend itself to any alleviating action. I would have run, but the corridors were too well guarded and, for all I knew, one of John Sergius' agents might have been instructed to kill me at the least excuse. Odd, isn't it, how existence was preferable to death, even as ghastly as it promised to be? Over and over in my mind, the thought recurred, 'You are being put away, far away, deeply away, forgotten. Anything can be done to you, any cruelty can be inflicted upon you by these sentries and there is no appeal, for they are the agency between yourself and the world. Now you have not one god, but many, and equally as inscrutable, and all to be propitiated.

"Down every corridor we passed, you could hear hammering on the inside of massive old oaken doors, or the muffled beating against iron, and the moans, the pleas of those within, the very palpable sound of despair. I tried to conceive this hell as part of the world I had just left— a warm starry Easter Eve—but nothing could seem more unlikely side by side much less one within the other. And then with more sadness than I had ever known and a sense of self-accusation which seemed beyond any act of repentance, I realized all the years I had spent in the world above, in luxury and light and privilege, this perdition had existed and would continue to exist after me. Be sure the majority of its inhabitants were not counts or dukes or princes, usually exiled to their estates, but the recalcitrant slave, the tenant, the peasant, the beggar turned thief or murderer, here—by divine irony beneath the former home of the highest in the land—to learn the difference between inflicted deprivation and free sacrifice, between self-denial and comfort denied. Truly what could a man do to be so outrageously, indifferently buried alive? Was there such a crime equal to the punishment?

"I had the answer in myself. This was not punishment but the materialization of the fears of chastisers, punishment which has no limit because the fears are undefined. This is the secret and the darkness, the chaos, the depravity, the unnameable terrors which exist within the heart of vanity and glory, fanatic admiration, pomposity, deity, and the state—all that which can only exist against free will, compassion, and logic, the denial of mercy and enlightenment. (It has pleased me since to send to those horrible corridors several of my more fractious nobles. I am, I believe, doing them the favor of gross expiation and pray their sojourn will be as instructive as was mine. Of course, it is now put about I am only another senile Tiberius I. Strange, that when it was the untitled and the penurious who occupied those cells stacked one atop the other, no one raised a cry of tyrant against my grandfather, my uncle, or my cousin.)

"At the entrance to the ravelin, which occupies the space, half submerged in the Bosporus, between the harbor walls and inner seawalls, I was searched, stripped, searched more shamefully in full view of a dozen guards curious to see a Grand Duke come to such an unlikely fate. A ring which my father had given me was taken away and I never saw it again. They left this icon about my neck. Then I dressed myself, my name was entered into the rolls, and I was escorted to my cell. I was told, 'We have been ordered, Your Highness, to forgo certain regulations. You will be allowed candles at any hour of the day or night, two meals, not one, each day—prison rations, of course—a bath twice a month, reading material if you wish it, two changes of clothes between Sunday and Saturday, and underwear, as well as the services of a laundress on these articles once each week. Visitors are forbidden, of course, but you will have longer chains.'

"I looked at the governor as though he were lunatic. (And in that moment, I remembered him at a palace reception several years before, probably around the time of his appointment. I had remarked on him then to myself, only because this husky, sad-eyed fellow, standing quite alone and uneasy with a cordial in his hand, his tense expression—head down, eyes up—suggesting all too obviously the fear of doing *something* wrong, engaged my sympathy. I had meant to go up to him, then, and put him at his ease. I wonder what difference it would have made in 1154 had I done so. But someone called me away and initiated a cause whose consequence—or absence of it—would not close the circle for fifty-six months, and then, in a most unlikely setting.) 'Yes, Your Highness,' he said, 'longer chains. To walk about the cell. We've found prisoners who are fixed to their pallets tend to atrophy. They die sooner. We have our instructions.'

"(And, to my surprise, they were fulfilled. At length, you see, how little it takes to please a prisoner. I myself could not imagine why these men, who stood between complaint and resolution, between their own mischief—should they be so inclined—and its discovery, would extend themselves beyond their own miserable, minimum tasks, even on orders, for the requests of one unable to retaliate if they were not fulfilled.)

"In the next moment the governor, himself, lit two candles—large ones, and nearly smokeless. My legs were secured to fetters twelve feet long. The company bowed to me, if you can imagine, backed out, slammed the iron door and locked it. It was done. The first thing I did was to see if my chains would allow me to reach the threshold. They would not.

"There was nothing, any longer, between myself and death, but time: no chance, no surprise. I was, at last, beyond Fortune's wit, but then, to be beyond her, is to be beyond life. I could only exist. I remembered the family tales of the hatred of my great-grandmother, Anna Dalassena, for my maternal ancestor, the Caesar Justin, after her own jailing at his instigation. Now I understood its intensity. Yet I can say I knew rather a bitter calm, which did not exclude love of my cousin, else I would not have felt such betrayal. In chains a man has no choice but to be resigned, or he cannot even die of a broken heart.

"All I could hope for now was a circumstance unexpected as this jailing, which would free me. When a year passed and I was at odds with myself for having grown to the *habit* of imprisonment and even accepted the possibility of a lifelong sentence, I exerted myself from despondency to begin to read again—and for the first time, to write. Nothing political, I assure you—aesthetic, philosophical, and historical essays on my father's wonderful models and those of Tetzes. I understand they made a splendid bonfire after my first escape. Perhaps that awful resonance is what has since prevented me from ever again taking up a pen.

"In any event this diversion took me through another year and then there was only a frenzy to escape. Rest assured, the thought taunted me there had been many men who, breathing their last in these cells, had still been designing their freedom, which was about to arrive in quite another fashion. Incredible how the human mind refuses to accept the likelihood of incessant misfortune to the very end, that somewhere the toss of the dice will not balance one's suffering. I was foolish enough to believe this because I was still strong enough to believe nothing worse could happen to me. I had to believe the universe winks.

"One thing more: I had always feared—I still do, I don't know why—insects, small crawling things upon me, as though live, I were, nevertheless, carrion. One thinks of rats with their tiny teeth, the small, the incisive. My nightmares were legion. The rashes I developed tortured me by day, while by night the itching was transformed, I was certain, into the bites of lice or cockroaches. I had never before slept in the light, but I called for another candle. I have never been able to sleep since in the dark."

The consequences of the sequestration of the youngest lineal grandson of Alexius Augustus were unexpected, which is to say, terrific. The sentence was so ferocious and unaccountable upon a man the Emperor had famously loved, the foolish, effete, innocuous courtiers were simply dumbfounded. This display of crushing power and resolution by one they had previously believed as epicene as themselves left these poor toads as anxious and quiet as spinsters who have just been threatened with death by a burglar. The Emperor's sisters and nieces, led by Eudocia, or else in sympathy with Anastasia (whose kingly brother refused to offend Manuel by defending his brother-in-law), were exquisitely outraged. ("Baby must have lost his mind," wrote Helena Porphyriogeneta Anemas to Juliana Porphyriogeneta Cantacuzena, "to jail an Imperial prince for the murder of a Varangian lackey. I can't *imagine* how Andronikus is taking it, though I understand a few cracks have appeared in Buceleon's foundations.") The Grand Duke Basil wrote the Emperor he intended to leave Constantinople and the Empire and offer his services to the King of Hungary. When Manuel made no answer, but reassigned Guiscard to Anchialus, the latter, his will less apt than his integrity, obediently traveled to his new post. In a private audience Andronikus' mother implored the Emperor to return her son to freedom to no avail. (His brother Philip, calling in Michael from Iconium, took it upon himself to break the news to Isaac II, who succumbed at once to a despondency from which he was released only by death, three years later.)

Outside the palace walls, the army's morale sank in proof of their affection for the Megadux. Their archons, who had alternately loathed and respected Andronikus, remaining sensitive to their men, began to divorce themselves from Manuel, and from court life, the first sign of such a trend since the accession of Alexius. For them, the Comneni were now Constantinopolitan Grandees, fratricidally jealous, without honor, no longer possessing the right to call themselves military dukes. Among the city poor and the peasant of the countryside, certain the Grand Duke had been jailed because he was their known champion—his reputation having exceeded his acts—Manuel's popularity, and their tolerance of his lavish ways and his wars to the exclusion of internal reconstitution, suffered immeasurably. Rather, woe betide the parish priest who did not mention Andronikus explicitly in the *Domine, Salva Fac* for the Imperial family.

Ironically, Manuel's authority became greater not because he was resolved all the more by criticism, but that if it were not the Emperor, alone, who had acted so vindictively, and rather under the baleful influence of the Protovestarius, then John Sergius was to be dreaded all the more and obeyed as though he were the Basileus, his hold over the throne complete. The Emperor would not be brooked because his servant struck terror in the hearts of his subjects.

But most ironic of all was the gain in authority—moral authority—of the Grand Duke. Previous to his imprisonment, Manuel's indulgence, by its very definition, had threatened to belittle Andronikus' every act. What need not be punished cannot be serious. Obversely, what seems serious and is not punished arouses egregious resentment. Andronikus, after a decade, was in danger of becoming an antic clown or a despised, but inviolable pest. But now, because born at the summit of aristocracy (indeed, its rarest flower as his renowned luxury, which seemed to conflict with his personal philosophy, his physical beauty, which, even during his affair with the Grand Duchess Eudocia, had served up a dozen cuckolds via susceptible wives, and his wit on which more than one fellow had found himself impaled, became transfigured by their contrary fate), the thought of this man buried in the ravelin, which held for all Byzantines the unimaginable hideous terrors a child experiences awakening from sleep in the dead of night, certified Andronikus' legend, as surely as Manuel had hoped to prevent it.

What the Emperor failed to realize is that incarcerating a man in a dungeon which might as well be a coffin, condemning him to a living death instead of an instant one, is far more a constant reproach to the chastiser than a lesson to the chastised, especially when the nature of the crime for which the subject is punished is not explicit, or explicit enough. A corpse is buried, canonized, and dismissed, and only recalled incidentally and inspirationally. And while it is true men do not live for long periods in grief or outrage, the constant knowledge Andronikus was alive somewhere within stone, in chains, in Buceleon, was a nagging injustice, a warning against arrogance, a reproach in triumph.

His elevation was an infinity of small gestures: an anecdote which ended in reminiscent smiles rather than laughter; the sudden silence and following reverie at a banquet; the flowers—perfect bouquets and wreaths, or wild sprigs, hastily plucked—laid at the foot of the Icon of St. Paul, the patron saint of the day of his birth. At no time was this universal unease expressed more obviously than when Anastasia appeared at Easter services, for the first time, publicly, in 1157.

The one woman who would win the final commitment of love, if not marriage, from Andronikus, which neither Anastasia, Eudocia, nor any of his flirtations could expect, the Grand Duchess Theodora, described the occasion to me: "Before Divine Liturgy began there was a great swell of whispers throughout the floor and the galleries of Holy Wisdom. Of course, it was Anastasia. I've always admired other women who can draw attention to themselves with perfect grace. She won me at once. I could not take my eyes from her. She wore her gown in the latest style, but her hair was covered in the Georgian manner, a white silken kerchief entirely framing her face and knotted at the nape of the neck, its long, almost sheer tails reaching down the length of the back, the whole secured by her diadem as a Princess of Georgia, which was a violation of Church etiquette, for all she cared, I imagine.

"Holding her hand was their son, who must have been about six at the time, looking very much like the icon of his great-grandaunt, Mary of Alania, on the opposite wall rather than the century-old, stooped hag on my father's arm: blond hair, huge, black Oriental eyes, skin like milk, and the promise, even then, of his father's height. Behind them, a governess led Zoë who was—let me see, three, four—four at the time, and even then so much like her father, his strong nose and great forehead and pale eyes. One had the extraordinary sensation of looking at an actor's mask, that his voice would come laughing from that little rose mouth.

"Apparently it was the crown which got the better of the Patriarch. He whispered to a canon, who came up to her and no doubt suggested either she remove the fillet or, respectfully, that she leave the cathedral. It was obvious she demurred. She collected the governess and her daughter and started to leave. Suddenly from the congregation there rose this great hissing in the direction of the canon and the Patriarch. I was quite certain my uncle would be incensed. Quite the opposite, he seemed very distressed, called the errand boy, my father, to him, and bid him bring Anastasia and the children back, on the condition, I learned later, they remain in the second gallery, which had the unfortunate effect of drawing all eyes from the liturgy upward and to the right, where, it would have pleased Andronikus, Anastasia stood among the lowly, who were not allowed to mingle with the court on the floor and first tier of the cathedral.

"When liturgy was ended, I left my family, gathered my skirts, and hurriedly passed upstairs. I arrived before her, breathless, curtsied, said 'Christ is risen,' and kissed her on each cheek and then the lips. The poor around us were eager as I—though for different reasons—to give the Easter Kiss to the wife of Andronikus and they pressed round her and the children, and myself as well, in a great horde. Do you know, Count, it was my first experience among them? I think Andronikus confuses their helplessness with innocence, their vulnerability with the inability to be cruel themselves, and their crude minds with the simplicity of real wisdom. But between the fine robes, the cynicism, the hysterical intrigues of the courtiers to place themselves as close as possible to the Emperor on this holiest day of the Church calendar, and the luminous, elated look of real piety in the eyes of these poor, you may imagine which celebrants I preferred to indulge. I must be frank: The smells, especially the grease they used to slick their hair—animal fat, nothing less—stank appallingly. I have to confess there really was something quite perverse in my willingness to accept their kisses. It was so unlikely for me to be among them. They were like a new breed of animal of which one has heard but never seen close. I was fascinated by them, down to their vernacular Greek which, raised to speak court Attic, I could scarcely understand. I certainly hoped my uncle and my mother could see me."

I asked the then Queen Dowager why she included her mother. She leaned back in her chair and touched the tips of her fingers together, as though in an attitude of prayer, and brought them to her lips. Her smile had vanished and she was looking down and away from me. Her expression seemed at once meditative and belligerent. She sighed, she shrugged, she cocked one brow, drew away her fingers, and without looking at me, said, "It's not very pertinent." I did not pursue my inquiry. But a few weeks later I asked Andronikus if the Sebastocratrix Francesca had been a member of John Sergius' faction. He said, "After a fashion, everyone was. Formally, however? No. Why? Whatever put that idea into your head?" I explained to him the Queen's curious hesitation.

He said, "Francesca, as you know, was born into the Latin rite and, to compound her uneasiness, was also a foreigner. Brought to Constantinople and installed in what amounted, virtually, to the position of Vice-Reine of the Empire, she experienced the usual disquiet of an alien who fears she will be resented by those over whom she, a stranger, has been placed. So, of course, she attempted with a vengeance to prove herself more Greek than Greece, more Orthodox than the Patriarch. With her elaborately theatrical personality, this was fine from a distance, which often lends enchantment to high color. Close to, it was rather a trial. Of course, she never argued because she never listened to you and so her contradictions were incorrigible. After Baldwin's death, when the Sebastocratrix preferred her daughter as a widowed queen to my mistress, Theodora brutally dressed her down in front of me. Francesca fled in tears. Afterward I said, 'You must never, never do that again. She's as simple as a peasant, only she has the means to seem complicated, which you mistake for strength. What she believes of herself is none of your affair.' She said, 'It offends me.' 'Does it?' I said. 'And so long as it no more than offends you you must learn to be gracious and above all patient. You are acting like a common bully who cannot distinguish between opinion and interference.' She said, 'Why do you defend her? My mother is everything you despise.' I told her, 'God in heaven, Theodora, if you were less certain than you are intelligent, you would not seem so stupid and prejudiced.'

"You must understand, Francesca was one of those not precisely against anyone as for herself. She was an entirely selfish creature, which does not mean she was ruthless, only unthinking. She followed power as a sunflower grows toward the light. When Theodora's father was shown to be a cipher and John Sergius presumed his place, the Sebastocratrix's uncanny nose directed her to her daughter at Jerusalem. I hear she adored Baldwin. I can understand why. His artlessness was the perfect foil for her complete artificiality. Finally with only power—her widowed daughter's—to complement her, she would sooner Theodora the lonely mistress of her dower city, Acre, than mine, and a renegade, as she could only be. Her conclusions were sound, if not the motives which led her to them."

XVI

In October 1154 Venice abrogated its alliance with Constantinople and ordered its merchant fleet and all nationals to return from the Imperial capital to the Republic of St. Mark. A heart-rending exodus followed—by men, women (some of them Greek wives), and children who considered themselves more Greek than Italian and scarcely looked to the North Venetian Marshes as their home, save in the vague, now contemptuous, now defensive fashion of all émigrés. Many of the greatest merchant families, having resided at Byzantium since the early years of Alexius' reign, were forced to make the crucial decision— which is to say, fiscally sacrificial—to forsake Venetian citizenship and pledge allegiance as subjects of the East Roman Emperor (and more specifically, enter themselves on the tax rolls). Manuel, much moved, offended native merchants by granting these New Greeks the same tax privileges they had enjoyed as Imperial guests, a gesture—like the change of citizenship itself—more gracious than practical.

Two months later, while Roger of Sicily lay on his deathbed (the papal legate waiting without in hope of a last-minute reconversion swore he saw Satan, in the company of twenty-five horned attendants, enter the King's chamber), an alliance was signed between the Doge and the Crown Prince, William, as Regent, by which Venice was granted such extravagant trading privileges as made Constantinople seem niggard, and Sicily acquired, in turn, the defenses of the Venetian armada. Nothing could have served more effectively to reconcile the new Pope, Adrian, with Frederick, who in turn wrote a most conciliatory letter to his *Imperial* brother, at Constantinople, suggesting the re-establishment of the Alliance of the Two Empires, which—with an abrupt exchange of ambassadors and a speed magnificent in its cynicism—was done.

In March 1155 Manuel received a letter from Henry II of England,

Duke of Normandy—in itself a response to the Emperor's exchange of congratulations on Henry's mounting of the English throne—warning him, on the advice of his wife, Queen Eleanor, not to trust Frederick of Germany in any alliance. Manuel's reply—and the true initiation of that extraordinary twenty-six-year correspondence between two men who never met and did not even speak a common language (their letters were translated by secretaries into respective Greek and French) —ran in part:

> You must not imagine that I am in any but a watchful state as regards my nephew. In the years since we have met and Frederick has ascended the throne I have been aware of his unscrupulousness, his immoral cleverness. He deceives no one but himself if he believes he deceives anyone. Soon, I have no doubt, he will desert me and join Sicily, or, for all I know, Louis. He has need of the alliance for the moment, and so have I. It is a race to see which one of us will break it to his own advantage. It has, by the way, come to my attention, he is dealing with Reynald of Franche-Comté to marry that King's daughter, Beatrix. Is this certain? If so, will Burgundy fall under his aegis on the old man's death? Certainly such an outcome would affect all the port cities of the Riviera.

Manuel did not join the Sicilian expedition of 1155, but sent instead Nicephorus Paleologus who joined forces with Count Robert of Loritello, an immensely wealthy and ambitious former subject of King Roger. (He need not also be described as an opportunist of the first water.) The combined armies moved farther north, while Adrian, with Frederick's assistance, hunted down the last of Arnold of Brescia's communists and set afire, at the stake, their leader.

Byzantine possessions by the year's end were gained as far north as Ancona. Four fifths of the West Adriatic Coast, and nearly all of the East, now formed a Greek corridor through which Venice must pass on her way to the Mediterranean. It is at this point, Manuel made his most costly strategic error. In 1153 Andronikus had written him from Hungary:

> If you are intent in this conquest, and if you are successful, then for God's sake, make certain thousands of lives are not sacrificed purposelessly in the aftermath. The greater portion of the Western Fleet must be set to patrol the Adriatic lanes. Venice must be asphyxiated into accepting your hegemony in Italy. The only way you can do this is by cutting off her access to the Mediterranean.

Nicephorus Paleologus believed as Andronikus and urged the Emperor to "smother the Adriatic with ships so that I may pass from Ancona to Spoleto without wetting my feet." With most tortuous logic, rather, the Emperor decided Venice, surrounded now by Byzantine allies, would remain sufficiently intimidated not to fulfill her obligations to Sicily or stretch her own ambitions in war with two empires, the papal princedom and the Hungarian Kingdom.

The argument between the Basileus and his greatest general is exemplary in its prejudice. Nicephorus wrote the Emperor: To depend upon the concerted strength of allies rather than one's own risked the weak link of a friend's ambition—and blackmail. Too blinded by the victory consequent of the alliance to note the disaster implicit in its subtleties, Manuel responded: The seafaring legs of the Republic would stand poorly in a land battle and it was this disadvantage which would give her pause. Thus, "day after day," as one of Paleologus' ADCs later described it to me, "the general would stand on some promontory at Ancona and watch ship after Venetian ship sail ostentatiously unharmed along the west shore, south to Sicily, and north again, and he knew they were carrying more than grain and textiles. He would come away saying, 'Bad. Bad. We're going to lose everything, watch and see. Bad.' I asked the ADC if Paleologus was aware of his cousin's, the Grand Duke Andronikus', letter of 1153. 'He never mentioned it, but I think he should not have been surprised.'"

The deeper truth was that Manuel was not so much intentionally overextending himself as events were stretching him. With the loss of Cilicia, he was anxious about an alliance between Reynald of Antioch and Prince Thoros. Against that possibility, he sent a poorly spared preemptive armada to guard and warn along the South Asia Coast.

The crucial year was 1156, which saw newly enthroned kings at Palermo and Iconium—each as ambitious, vigorous, and militaristic as Manuel and Frederick. The latter was now in complete accord with the Pope, and both were alarmed by the success of Byzantium in Italy. Unctuously, Adrian questioned Frederick on the advisability of an alliance with Greek Schismatics. Ponderously, Frederick agreed as to the threat of unholy contamination, and shortly after his marriage to Princess Beatrix of Franche-Comté, 9 June 1156, he recalled his ambassador from Constantinople and declared the feckless Alliance of the Two Empires nullified yet again. (His device was superb: the only manner in which it might have been saved, he repined, was for Manuel to have ceded those Italian territories which, previous to Greek and Sicilian conquest, had belonged to the Holy Roman Empire. Manuel might have counter-argued Byzantium's still previous possession, but rather than dignify a burlesque with reason, he turned away entirely and told his generals they would do well in the future to consider one of their prime objectives the destruction or diminution of the House of Hohenstaufen, whose members afterward he referred to—in speech and correspondence—as the Pretender Saxon kings.)

In July of that same year there took place the battle which stands with Myriokephalum as the greatest military disaster of Manuel's regency, the only difference that the Battle of Brindisi had been presaged and could have been avoided. For two years, openly—and insolently only if one chooses to believe Byzantium had no alternative—Venice and Sicily had contrived the means of eradicating Constantinople's huge Italian achievement.* It was achieved in one ferocious week-long onslaught. Greek soldiers never set foot upon that land again.

William moved north, from Sicily, and Venice, south, by the sea. No fleet could match the armada and no army could survive with its lines of communications broken and supplies blockaded. The month of August was a mere mopping up by William's army: the destruction of enclaves, the taking of bravely defended, but inadequately garrisoned citadels and subjecting the final Byzantine retreat to relentless sortie. By 22 July our entire Italian venture had been nullified and the lucky remnant of the army rounding the Peloponnesus bound for home. The unluckier veterans (mostly infantry) were forced to trudge the entire breadth of North Greece without money or provisions, subject to local harassment by those farmers who did not appreciate their meadows trampled and their imminently harvestable crops rolling into the starving bellies of defeated soldiery. Naturally, these poor men were only a little less cursed than the Emperor, who would leave them to pillage,

---

* In March, at Constantinople for his daughter's wedding, Paleologus argued openly with the Emperor for more troops and ships. At the reception in Palace Paleologus, which my father attended as a friend of the commander and marshal of the Greek nobility of Iconium, Duke Nicephorus was heard to warn the Basileus, "If we lose Italy and you presume to charge me with the fault, disgrace me to distract the blame from yourself, I promise you, there are many colleagues who will not stand for it." The Emperor gave Paleologus his back and did not receive him before his return to Italy. N.A.

and it is a fact Brindisi marks the lowest point of the decline of Manuel's popularity, which began its descent with Andronikus' imprisonment.

Most tragic of all, however, was the fate of Bari, the first city of the province of Apulia, which Manuel had intended to make his capital in the West. On the first capitulator to the Byzantine war machine, William had gross revenge. That splendid metropolis of churches, art treasures, and bursting libraries, marble palaces and charming stucco villas, was reduced to submission, which is to say, ashes. The majority of the 200,000 population, that is, the poor and middle classes who had no part in the decision which turned the city over to Byzantium, were either slaughtered, bankrupted, or sold into slavery. Some one hundred or more of the most aristocratic families—many with holdings at Constantinople—bought their freedom with their fortunes and emigrated to Byzantium, fully expecting their remunerative due from the Emperor to whom they had sworn loyalty and for whom they had suffered. (Manuel, let it be said, championed their entry into the highest circles of Constantinopolitan society—than which there is none more closed—and, more significantly still, welcomed them into the government.) †

Cognizant of Paleologus' warning, the Emperor did not dare to cashier the Praetorium for whose heads the people were calling, appalled by the waste of lives and money and, no less, the final Barian brutality. But he did rigorously and obviously disassociate himself from his Greek administrators and generals, whom he kept powerlessly at their posts until death, infirmity, exhaustion, or personal affairs claimed them. And by their side, with John Sergius' assistance, he raised to power a personally selected body of civilian and military advisers almost entirely Latin and in the main composed of refugee aristocrats from his short-lived Italian conquest.

When the truth of this bicephalic government became known, many Byzantines, disgusted with native jobbers and in great guilt over the suffering and ruin "they" had brought upon Southern Italy, cheered such a Westernization of the Imperial government. In an excess of penance, they agreed with their Autocrat, heard to publicly comment

---

† In commemoration of the city, the Pope celebrated Requiems for thirty consecutive days. Even Frederick showed some sensibility. His first words on receiving the homage of the Burgundian nobles at Besançon the following year were: "Is it the whole truth about Bari? Is it really gone?" N.A.

he could not longer abide his lethargic and effete Greek aristocrats in comparison with these resolute Latins, who, to be sure, owing to none but the Emperor, served him with a single-mindedness and lack of criticism which became the single, most significant danger for the balance of Manuel's reign. (Thus, it may be seen the emptiness of the charge that Maria-Xenia Augusta introduced hordes from the West into our government. Pathetically the most visible, she was overwhelmed, rather by a wave of anti-Latinism born of a quarter century of Imperial-sponsored Latin domination. Manuel's second Empress was merely a symbol—a result, herself—of his policies, and symbols need not act, merely exist.)

Now with his defeat in Italy a most certain and irreversible fact of history, Manuel accurately predicted that move would be made against Byzantium on many fronts, as hungry cats would gather on a wounded deer. He correctly surmised William and Venice were, for the moment, satisfied by the enormity of their victory. Through the Foreign Ministry rather than his Imperial Italians (who were traitors to their fellow Westerners—presumably they ought to have died at Bari or lived to be slaves in Sicily) the Emperor instructed his agents at Palermo to turn the King round to the idea of an alliance. Feelers were also put out to Venice and gifts exchanged with the Pope. A letter to Henry of England requested that he soften Louis for a diplomatic kill and learn as much as possible about Frederick's ambitions. Geza was flatteringly entertained at Constantinople. In fact, the aftermath of Brindisi marks the beginning of Manuel's relentless diplomatic offensive which in less than twenty years accomplished with the pen what he could not gain by the sword: the domination of all Europe and the ruin of Frederick of Germany.

Just as the Emperor believed the worst had been endured and survived—it had, for the time being, in the West—disaster struck again, in the East. Thoros, and the parvenu Prince of Antioch, Reynald, striking the alliance Constantinople had dreaded, sailed against the Governacy of Cyprus, which had been intentionally undergarrisoned for the purpose of *not* antagonizing nearby Antioch. Too late Manuel lifted Michael Branas from his "exile" and dispatched him to remedy the defenses of the island. In the ensuing devastation, Michael and Prince John Vatatzes, the Emperor's nephew, were taken prisoner and all Cyprus laid waste: churches burned, palaces sacked, whole towns razed, women raped, Greek priests castrated or crucified—including the Patriarch—children slaughtered, and the fathers who defended them cut down without remorse. In the countryside the harvests were destroyed, flocks stolen and extortionately resold to their owners, and hostages taken in lieu of a staggering war indemnity.

It was a ravaging from which Cyprus never recovered. Imperial novels are vague in their statistics of the catastrophe, only because of its size. Something like two thirds of the population of the island—nearly 250,000 people—were murdered. The economy was ruined, the Church and aristocratic hierarchs, the leaders, desolated. Not the Turks at Manzikert nor Nureddin at Edessa had acted so vilely. By comparison, William's fist upon one city was an example of political discretion.

When the news reached Constantinople, crowds gathered at street corners to repeat the horrors or, in churches, to pray. The Emperor canceled all appointments for a week and went into retreat. With his wife and Imperial sisters setting the example, festivities were canceled until after Christmas and, under these dynastic patronesses, collections of food, money, and clothes taken up. But such charity was to no avail. It was learned the island was garrisoned by Antiochenes who would allow no commiseration in material form—or, presumably, spiritual, if they could have stopped the ascent of prayer—from passing through the lines of the victims.

Internationally, the repercussions were sympathetic to Cyprus and Constantinople, if not otherwise effectual. No less than William of Sicily, still only a few months fresh from the annihilation of Bari, singled out one lone and frightened millionaire Greek merchant at a palace reception and asked if there was anything he could do in behalf of the Cypriots. (The merchant hadn't heard of the disaster and was, thereupon, informed with full relish by the King.) At Paris, Louis, freed by death of his anti-Constantinopolitan saint, Bernard, wrote to Reynald's bewildered father declaring his son the incubus of Satan. Henry of England suggested to Manuel that after he capture Reynald—as he was certain the Emperor would—he initiate the English custom of binding the miscreant to a public post in the middle of the city and allowing any passing Constantinopolitans to carve him apart, piece by piece. (This brought the first smile to Manuel's lips in many weeks.) At Antioch the tender Constance dared to berate her invidious husband, and even threatened to divorce him. With the exhilarated barons on his side, however, Reynald beat his Princess with a leather belt and shut her in a tower to consider her imprudence. Only when his by now very obviously nominal liege, King Baldwin, threatened invasion if his cousin were not, at once, released, did Reynald return his wife to the palace. Thereafter, it is said, the Princess was as one in mourning. She never again wore her jewels, which were legend, nor the increase her husband spilled into her lap, snatched from the coffers of Cypriot aristocrats. She dressed as became a nun and denied her husband her bed. Oddly, this Prince who had raped and ordered rape throughout Cyprus, refrained from taking his wife without consent and turned miserably to mistresses, and then boys.

The man most revolted and eager to put amends to action was Baldwin of Jerusalem. To one so ingenuous and gallant the devastation of a Christian population was beyond comprehension, or penance. As Advocate of the Holy Sepulcher, moreover, he rightfully held himself the watchman of the morality of the Latin states, which, by Reynald's cruelty—indeed, blasphemy—had been seriously compromised. "He knows what he has done," Baldwin wrote to his mother, the Dowager Queen Melisande, "and now he is acting the perfect tyrant who, having committed the unthinkable, dares you to accuse him so that he may also eradicate the critics of his deed. I fear he would be obliged to destroy the whole disapproving world." With the wasp-bitten Antiochene Patriarch, now a refugee at Jerusalem, he discussed the possibility of petitioning the Pope for Reynald's excommunication. Aimery, no champion of Reynald, opened his empty palms to the King and said, "On what grounds, Your Majesty? How has he offended the Church?" Offended himself by this canonical, cold logic, Baldwin relinquished the idea of disassociating himself from Antioch and turned to the possibility of a community, instead, with Byzantium. Within a year, the path he would take was clear to him.

Still, the bottom of the abyss had not quite come up to meet the Emperor's feet.

On 3 March 1157 Andronikus' father, the Great Sebastocrator, Isaac II, died at Constantinople. He had been extremely ill with the quinsy since early February, and from the beginning, little hope had been held for his recovery. He was then, as he had been since Andronikus' incarceration, profoundly dispirited. There are those, indeed, for whom the lack of will to live in some way encourages their physical death. The Grand Duke Philip spoke of this to me: "Nothing could have saved my father, I should think, with the exception of Andronikus' presence by his bed, and, in that, I may be raising the miracles possible only to hypothesis. But he truly longed for my brother, and in the hope my cousin would reprieve Andronikus if only a few days, to attend Isaac's bedside, we moved him from Vera to Constantinople, despite the harsh winter, in a wagon set with braziers, surrounded by torchbearing Excubitors, who had volunteered their assistance, they said, expressly to honor their former commander's father. I dispatched a post to Iconium, to my brother Michael, and that messenger no doubt crossed—how closely, I wonder?—one from Rabia that my younger brother had died from injuries sustained in a fall in his bath. So we sang Requiems even before my father died. And still we hoped Manuel might yield on Andronikus. But he did not."

Probably, Manuel had no choice. Andronikus' fame had swelled rather than diminished. We must remember the Emperor's state of mind at this time. He had lost Italy and Cyprus and he had no doubt the Grand Duke, however distracted by his father's death, would not forsake the opportunity of misusing his brief freedom. But unavoidable as the decision was, it was small, and the family loathed him for it.

Philip: "I think only of the snow falling on Constantinople outside my father's rooms at Palace Comnenus. It was the worst storm since the last decade of the previous century. And then his delirium: of the snows the night we left Constantinople in 1129. I wonder if his blind eyes saw again in those memories. Or do the sightless forget what it was to see as legs atrophy from the lack of usual exercise. The end came unexpectedly. I was standing at the window, alone with my father, who I thought had been sleeping. He said, 'Who's there?' I came up to him and said, 'It's I, Philip, Papa.' And he said something curious. 'Be a good boy. Take away the candle, will you? The light hurts.' I was about to answer, but everything had stopped. The chest emptied and did not fill again; the mouth remained half open, the eyes seemed about to blink. He was gone.

"The Emperor offered a Requiem and burial at Pantokrator Cathedral, which, I suppose, was unprecedented. My mother and I refused for him, and my father was embalmed and sealed in lead and the following morning, preceded by the Patriarch and a company of Varangians and Excubitors, we set off with Isaac to return him to the Monastery of Christ at Vera, where he had wished to be ensepulchered. The snow was still falling and it was an arduous journey. I recall the torches by day and by night. But the storm ceased on the afternoon of our arrival and the cold crepuscular sunset and the tolling of the bell as we entered the gates was quite lovely.

"We had decided not to get word to Andronikus. It could not ease his suffering. It was not until many years later he told me a guard had informed him of Michael's death and that our father was dying. My brother said that truly brought home to him the full meaning of being caged. He was torn by the thought any moment he might get to Papa before the end, and never knowing in the same moment if it was already too late."

Once speaking of the midcentury, Manuel Augustus said to me, "I seemed to swing as subject myself between extremes of intense hatred and intense sympathy," meaning, presumably, no sooner had he roused the world or his family against him than some other event, taken up by heaven to undo him, earned him their reconciling compassion.

Two months after his uncle's death, the Emperor suffered the passing of his youngest daughter, Magdalena Porphyriogeneta. She was four years old.

Theodora: "I had become a great favorite with the children and my aunt Bertha. She was a very conscientious mother and she performed many duties which a sovereign's wife would ordinarily have left to governesses and ladies-in-waiting. Still, she seemed grateful for my regularity and quite delighted to share with me both Catherine's and Magdalena's affection. In the spring of 1157 I asked my aunt if I could take the children with me to the estate of my sister, Martha, who had married one of our distant cousins, the Grand Duke Andrew, a great-grandson of the first Sebastocrator. It was their first excursion away from their parents, if only to Chrysopolis, and they were ecstatic. Three days after we arrived, Magdalena came away from playing with her sister and my nephew Isaac and the other children invited from neighboring estates. She complained of a sore throat and dizziness and so we put her to bed and notified the Empress.

"In the morning there was an ugly masklike pall around her mouth and nose which my sister's physician described as the symptom of a serious, feverish, possibly terminal disease he had seen only once before. My aunt, who, I know, had always dreaded the least illness touching her children, arrived that afternoon with the court physician, who concurred in the diagnosis though he cautioned it was not *necessarily* fatal. But in the corridor the Empress grasped my hand and said with real terror, 'Oh, Theodora, I just know God will not spare me this cross.'

"And still the next day the child's entire body was covered with a fine purplish rash and the area, here—and here—on her throat was terribly swollen. The Empress and I waited by her bed. Sometimes she held both our hands but she was never in pain. My aunt waited as long as she could and then sent a messenger to the Emperor to come at once. By the next day, Magdalena's face was so puffed up as to be unrecognizable. During the night she had bled urine and she was almost literally burning to the touch. My uncle arrived that fourth afternoon and I remember he winced when she placed her small hot fist in his enormous jeweled hand.

"It was thought advisable to give her Extreme Unction, but when the wine was spooned into her mouth—her first Communion—she convulsed, became unconscious, and never opened her eyes again. The following night she passed from coma into death.

"It was the strangest group of mourners one could imagine. The Empress still sat with the little girl dead in her arms, rocking a little, back and forth, without tears. She had dared heaven to spare her and it had not. The priest was in his own world, chanting softly. And the Emperor stood by the window, opened out now so the desiccated smells could leave the room. I suppose he was less apt to be consoled than most men because he was keen to the illusion of power. The absolute ruler, body and soul, of so many millions and he could not prevent the death of his own child. I went up to him, prepared to be hideously platitudinous, thought better, took his hand and kissed it as I swept him a deep curtsy. He said to me, 'I know what you have done for your aunt and myself, my dear. I know how happy you made our daughter and I promise you you shall have your reward.' Can you imagine? He'd become so divorced from the normal run of humanity he was incapable of any longer comprehending an act which expected nothing in return. He no longer understood generosity, save his own, only petition. I was appalled, and I pitied him. My aunt, at least, remained recognizably human. A few days after the funeral, she said to me, 'The other night I was sitting in my villa and there was a sudden chill draft. It was about the time the children retired, and I knew my child was not in her rooms where she ought to be but lying elsewhere, cold in a stone crypt.' I thought, 'But where is she? She should be here, in her home, not somewhere far away in the night, when she had never been but asleep.'"

To all intents, their child's death was the end of their marriage. The Emperor kept more than ever to his niece, Persephone, who truly consoled him, while Bertha-Irene more than ever preoccupied herself with her charities and her remaining eldest daughter. The Imperial couple had recourse to one another only during state ceremonies or when the Augusta's works touched on state business, such as the establishment of a Moslem orphanage and almshouse, for which she had to gain the Emperor's consent over the Patriarch's vivid objection.

His child's death, however, marks the end of Fortune's assault on the Emperor. For nineteen years, thereafter, Midas-like, everything Manuel touched became unalloyed gold. The first achievements of this new era were gained at Palermo and Rome. First, the Pope was astonished to receive a second ambassadorial party within a year, this time with the purpose of opening negotiations, in absolute secrecy, pursuant to a reunion of the Greek and Latin Catholic churches. No less surprised was King William to receive a request for parley in the achievement of a nonaggression pact between the Sicilian Kingdom and the Byzantine Empire. The first mission was meant to affect the Pope and his Curia without offending the Emperor's own subjects. The second was meant to announce to all the end of Byzantine military ambitions in the West.

For once events were subtly considered before Manuel acted. Now, William did not gloat over the Emperor's defeat as his father might have done. He was several generations safely beyond his ancestor, the adventurer Robert, a true prince, cognizant of his honor rather than a soldier of fortune with no scruples owed but to his own ambitions. He might attack his antagonist viciously at that point when retreat for the enemy is its defeat, but defeat of an opposing army did not become carnage, nor a rout a massacre. He was amenable to Byzantine friendship because, with peace, he was beginning to realize the appalling price he had paid Venice for her fleet. The Republic of St. Mark virtually controlled the markets of Sicily, a hegemony as dangerous as conquest by force. (Ironically, it was not enough. Concessions in the Imperial capital, Venice had found, were worth literally the ransom of a kingdom. The loss in Asiatic and Russian routes was intolerable.)

Adrian IV, meanwhile, the former English Prelate, Nicholas Breakspear, who had given Henry II the overlordship of Ireland as something like a coronation gift, received a letter from his former King, praising Manuel to the skies as the most pious and gallant knight under heaven. If the Pope remained less than blandished, he needed, nevertheless, little prompting to suspect Frederick of Germany, whom he had met and despised on sight three years previous ("Everything about that man is soaked in brine"). The Holy Roman Emperor would respect neither the Holy Office nor its prerogatives and with his Bolognese legalists was preparing a brief to be presented at the Diet of Roncaglia (whose rumor all men knew before it was set to formal script), which would effectively emasculate the semi-autonomous finances of his Italian possessions. This was another way of announcing he intended to tax and toll such cities as Parma and Milan into slavery, grist for his German mill.

Rather than the Pope, the North Italians turned to Manuel for the promise of aid should it come to secession. This was given. In consequence, the Patrimony of St. Peter had now to recognize the possibility of Byzantine influence from the north rather than the south, if not military, no less real. Thus Adrian was prepared to take quite seriously— or appear to—the Emperor's suggestion of union. The negotiations did not really succeed, but then few had expected the Pope to consent to the still greater hegemony of a Basileus who believed himself, and not his Patriarch, the arch-hierarch of the Church. Nevertheless the parties remained in negotiation so long as the possibility of alliance served to encourage a rebellious Imperial Italy and, incidentally, gave Frederick pause at the thought of the challenges given to his own position by a brother *Roman* Catholic emperor.

The negotiations with William, on the other hand, were altogether less illusory and more successful, and on 5 January 1158, at Constantinople and Palermo, a Thirty Years Peace was signed between Sicily and Byzantium, the copies to which Augustus gave his signature and sign manual, previously sealed and signed by William, as were William's, similarly, by the Emperor.

XVII

By the autumn of 1157 Baldwin III had finally broken with Reynald of Antioch. This strange occasion of a king disowning a vassal rather than the vassal himself becoming a rebel actually shows the extent to which Reynald's brutality and arrogance were a success rather than a limitation. This was how the rupture occurred.

Baldwin and Reynald had combined their forces with a small crusading army under the aegis of Thierry of Alsace, Heir to one of the greatest fiefs in West Europe, the County of Flanders. In military consort, the armies overtook Shaizar and by implication the whole province of the Munquidite emirs. There was never any question but that Thierry would rule the new Latin state as suzerain. The armies had acclaimed him— handsome and brave, he had won their hearts—and the artless Baldwin, adoring as a dog in the presence of any man more daring than himself, was ready to accept Thierry's vassalage. But Reynald, on whose territory the Shaizarite province bordered, refused to allow the conquest to the great noble unless he swore vassalage to Antioch.

To a man the war party was stunned by this demand. Thierry, not notably haughty, nevertheless informed Reynald, a count of Flanders, the kin to kings and emperors, placed his hands between those of a lineal sovereign, not the whelp of a catchpenny knight no matter the dower by which he shined. From infantry to aristocracy, the whole feudal tradition was threatened by Reynald's unbelievable—though no longer surprising—insolence. Still the Prince would not relent and Thierry would not debase himself. Shaizar, under siege, at the end of its resources and ready to capitulate, was abandoned. Reynald returned, truly empty-handed, to Antioch, as Thierry to Europe and Baldwin to Jerusalem.*

As he took leave of Reynald, Baldwin had told his cousin's husband,

---

* Shaizar, nevertheless, remained under an ill-star. Two weeks later, battle-weary, it fell to Nureddin, who was convinced the Latins were not unholy, but simply lunatics. In December an earthquake leveled half the city, burying in the rubble three quarters of the population, including the entire ruling house and most of the aristocracy. When it was rebuilt, Nureddin installed as its Governor his foster brother and lover, Majd ed-Din, a most competent and clement figure, who, in the ensuing years, was revered—and perhaps overestimated in his virtues—by a people understandably dazed by those apocalyptic months of 1157. N.A.

"I warn you, Monseigneur, it is my intent to ruin you and, if it must be, I will join with the devil to do it." Whereas Manuel had lived long enough to realize a man's rash acts speak to himself as well as his victim, so that his own guilt will set his mind to wondering when or if, and how, the victim shall have his revenge, Baldwin, with all too childish excitement, had thus given Reynald unusual and undeservedly fair warning. Probably the Prince of Antioch laughed. If so, he forgot—himself a very estimable example—the single-mindedness and energy of youth.

Thus, shortly after signing the Thirty Years Peace with Sicily, Manuel was overjoyed to receive at Villa Rufiniana two notable ambassadors from Jersualem: no less than the King's Constable, Humphrey of Toron, and his Captain General, William of Barres. Their uncommon mission was to assure the Emperor Baldwin had disowned Reynald, to initiate a mutual assistance pact, and to join the Houses of Comnenus and Lotharingen by marriage of their King to an Imperial princess.

For two weeks, at Rufiniana and Blachernae, the Emperor lavishly entertained his visitors. Finally, in late February, on an unseasonably warm day, while the two ambassadors and the Emperor were walking in the fantasy gardens of Philopation Park, Manuel said, "Tomorrow we will sign a treaty. In a month, you will return to Jerusalem and take with you and present to His Majesty, who is very dear to my heart, his new Queen." Then, anticipating the pleasure of his visitors, and their curiosity, he said, "Come with me."

They walked ahead to a circular garden within a little wood, where, amid fountains and statuary, his daughter and her elder cousin were at games with their ladies-in-waiting.

"At first," Count Humphrey told me, in 1179 during his visit to Constantinople with Bishop William of Tyre, "I thought the Emperor would offer the child, at which my heart fell." He corrected himself. "That is to say, though a great honor, it seemed extraordinarily impractical in the light of my lord, the King's age, twenty-seven, and his already too extravagant reputation with women, which could only grow as he awaited Catherine Porphyriogeneta's coming of age. But then, Augustus called to a young woman whose back was turned to us, momentarily. 'Theodora,' he said, 'come here.' The Princess turned round with a ready, though questioning glance. It was like the stopper on a vial of perfume being opened in a small room: one smiles helplessly, and there is a sense of being lifted into sudden enchantment. That was my first sight of Her

Majesty and my heart leaped and I laughed as I treasured the surprise which awaited my King. She was tall, taller than one would have expected in a Greek woman, but voluptuous. Her carriage was incomparable—graceful, stately, but never stiff, always feminine. She seemed to move with a smoothness between a glide and flight—like a swan over water. Though her skin was unusually fair, her features were aquiline, Levantine, and her hair was black as a raven's wing. Her teeth were so white they were almost shimmering and her eyes as pale as a blue moon. She was not conventionally beautiful as we Latins would have it, or, I suspect, as Greeks. In fact, her features were almost Persian. Her brows seemed perpetually arched in an expression of distress, but the eyes were too merry and the lips too amused. It was the look of a young woman of hauteur and wit. In truth, her person combined, as I have rarely seen, the aloof and the provocative. When she arrived before us, she took her uncle's hand and began a gesture of curtsy, which he stopped with an ironic smile, as if to say they were equal now. Then with great relish he presented her to us, 'Gentlemen, your Queen.' We knelt, and in a curious, trancelike fashion, she offered us her hand, which we kissed."

Many years later Theodora stared at me with those blue-moon eyes rather less merry by virtue of what they had seen in her years with Andronikus, as I recounted Humphrey's lustrous memory of their first meeting. She smiled and said, "I suspect he was infatuated with me. As he once told me, between Mary and his own mother, he revered me. Of course, after my husband's death, all Palestine was quite certain we were lovers, which left him more crushed than outraged.

"Two months after that meeting—I was given, by the way, only a week's warning of my elevation (my uncle has a great weakness for surprises)—two months, not one, as Humphrey said, I was Queen in a city which was for me, as all men, a legend, and, by virtue of protocol, beyond any hope of familiars save my ladies and my husband. I was quite miserable, separated from my friends and my family, from the court and the city in which I was born and which, to me, represents everything civilized and gracious in the world. For all the veneer at Jerusalem, I was constantly reminded by subtle and oftentimes not-so-subtle occasions I was not at Constantinople. There was consideration only between equals, the courtiers and the barons. Their sense of etiquette was more elaborate than refined. Voices were loud—always—like children at games. At banquets, language was unimaginably crude and spittle and God knows what else were deposited beside one's chair, on the floor. The nobility would treat their women with a respect bordering on worship, but servants of either sex were mustered under a brutality which would shock any Greek. Even my husband was criminal. I should say he was indeed adored by the common people, but only those who did not have to deal with him. His legend is one of great generosity and gallantry. But who writes these legends? These people never conversed, they argued. They wept like babies when reversed and acted like homicides at their tournaments. Never a contest, always a war. The women had the contagion as well as the men, save for a few like my husband's cousin, Princess Constance, and even she had a sharp and sometimes unlikely demeanor which could be most alarming."

For all Theodora's demurrals, it was a famous marriage: the dashing young King and the most beautiful Princess of the Imperial court. In truth, advised of his bride's great beauty, Baldwin did not await her as King, at Jerusalem, but, impulsively took horse and met her disembarkation at Jaffa. At first sight he fell abruptly and irrevocably in love.

Theodora's first lady-in-waiting, the exquisite young Princess Veronica Melissena, great-granddaughter of Alexius Augustus' sister, Eudocia, and sole heiress to the immense fortune of the senior line of the family, remembered "how frightened Her Majesty was, even if she did not choose to show it. In fact, in proportion to the degree she is frightened, I would say, she pretends disdain. But then, what else might a young bride feel who had never seen her husband? As we left the pavilion, she kept her eyes down. His Majesty sat on a white stallion at the bottom of the gangplank. Theodora could not bring herself to look. She whispered, 'What's he like? You mustn't lie.' I was staring at the handsomest and kindliest-looking man on whom I had ever laid eyes. He was surrounded by priests and soldiers and standards and crosses. Everyone was silent, waiting for the long-anticipated Queen. Evidently, His Majesty had had enough, for to no man's surprise—from the looks of it—he dismounted and ascended the gangplank.

"As we left Constantinople, I remember Theodora had said to me, 'This is simply awful. They're going to surmise me like a side of beef.' Well, in the bright spring sunlight of that Sunday afternoon so many years ago, the King and the Grand Duchess frankly remarked on one another. His Majesty's expression passed from a willingness to be pleased (apparently he trusted rumors) to ecstasy. My lady's expression passed from apprehension to wonder. Count Humphrey, who was beside us, took Theodora's hand in presentation and moved up to the King. He said, 'Your Royal Majesty, I have the honor to present to you Her Imperial Highness Theodora, Grand Duchess of New Rome.' The King offered her his hand, but as she was about to curtsy His Majesty made a small warning sound and grasped her forearm, leaned to her and kissed both her cheeks. In Greek, in flawless Greek, he said, 'As once Ruth chose Israel and lived to be consoled by her decision, so, I pray, will you.' Now without a word, Theodora insisted on sweeping him one of her magnificent curtsies, for which she was so famous, and of which she was so vain at court."

If the Grand Duchess had been anxious about her welcome, her fears were put to rest as she rode beneath the Royal and Imperial devices and the escutcheons of the Houses of Comnenus and Lotharingen to Jerusalem. Elated with the reality of his betrothed, Baldwin was seen to speak to her repeatedly and intimately throughout the journey. At some point, surely, he told her the fanatical crowds were cheering the beauty with which she promised to grace the throne. Knowing Baldwin, he probably believed his own diplomacy. Knowing Theodora, born of a family whose women were as instinctively political as the men, we may be equally certain she knew the deeper cause of her future subjects' joy: the implication of an heir.

But that tumultuous welcome had a significance beyond its subjects. Garbed in the purple mantle sewn with tiny gold eagles at the edge, which her aunt Bertha had worn the day of her own investiture and given to her niece on the day she left Constantinople,† Theodora, riding beneath the bicephalic, tri-crowned, orbed, and sceptered eagles of the Byzantine Empire, represented the coming of age of the Latin states. Baldwin had gambled in two ways: that his house had ruled long enough to become in the minds of the people an entity separate from the crusading idea, from the concerted prejudices of the Principate, a state, autonomous, frankly prideful and self-interested; and that his people were as revolted as he by Antiochene conduct at Cyprus and Shaizar and considered the House of Guiscard, under the tutelage of Reynald

† "She seemed so weary and pathetic, indifferent, almost, since Magdalena's death. She helped to arrange the stoa, then embraced me and said, kindly, but unsmilingly, 'There. Now we are sisters.' It was the last time I ever saw that poor, sad woman." N.A.

of Châtillon, an imminent danger, against which Byzantium would offer succor, as present in the person of his betrothed. He had gambled twice and won twice. With the Constantinopolitan Autocrat now their King's uncle, there was nothing to fear. What had begun as an argument between gentlemen became a national policy.

Of course, it must be pointed out, the gain worked both ways. As Manuel could now count on Jerusalem not to interfere—in fact, perhaps even cheer him—he marched on Cilicia and Antioch late in the year, 1158. Behind him was the greatest land army the Empire had seen since the salad days of the Macedonian dynasty: 150,000 horse and foot. If these men, with an eye to booty—and assured of victory which leads to loot, by the size of their company—were subsequently disappointed by the events of the following months, their Emperor was not. Without captured treasure, the maintenance of such a force was an exorbitantly expensive proposition; yet when Manuel returned to Constantinople the following year, he could claim before God, not a drop of blood had been shed in a military venture which gave him hegemony over the Levant and revenged the rape of Cyprus.

Kilij Arslan II had hoped for an engagement with the Greeks until his scouts reported the size of the war train, which was passing with pointed ostentation close by his borders. Thoros had intended to make a stand at Mopsuestia. On the basis of intelligence reports, his generals advised capitulation, the end of independent Cilicia, with not one man an Alexander willing to face Darius' million at Gaugamela. When Manuel arrived before the ancient city, Thoros and his family and their suite attempted to flee by the back gates. He was easily recaptured. On his entry into the vast Imperial encampment, he dismounted, removed his boots, and walked to the praetorium, where Manuel made him wait on his knees the rest of the day and the entire night.

In the morning, as the Emperor left his tent, he told the insurrectionist, quite curtly, to come up off his knees and follow him to Divine Liturgy. Midway during the service, Thoros was signaled forward. He approached the enthroned figure, jewelless in a velvet robe of deep purple—so deep as to seem black—prostrated himself, swore his fealty, and begged forgiveness. He would accept any penance the Emperor wished him to make. Manuel raised the man, kissed him in a gesture of absolution, and summarily confiscated Thoros' title, his personal estate, and placed him under arrest.

Forewarned of the Emperor's intentions, Reynald of Antioch, his forces depleted since Shaizar (even at full strength they should hardly have been a match for the oncoming Roman colossus), made against his will probably the most statesmanlike decision of his life—at least the only one recorded. With Thoros gone and his brother princes estranged, he dared not submit the ancient capital to siege. Donning his crusader's cloak, which as Regent of a Latin state, he was privileged to wear, *in perpetuum,* and taking with him his greatest barons, Reynald rode north to Mopsuestia to submit himself to the Emperor's clemency. Ambassadors had been sent ahead to inquire on the conditions of pardon. They were these: The Prince must walk from the gates of the city to the Main Square, barefoot and bare-armed, with a length of rope about his neck. At the foot of the throne, he would prostrate himself and present the hilt of his sword to the Augustus, publicly ask for pardon, and otherwise say his piece. If Manuel chose to forgive him, he would raise the Prince and state the conditions under which, then and there, he was to swear vassalage and pay homage.

One can sympathize with the pride of this man, born not very well, succeeding beyond his wildest dreams, and unable to contain his arrogance before others who faulted him not because of birth, but that he, supposing they were given much from their own lucky cradles, underestimated them. The bully and the tyrant, it may be said, are closest to despair all their lives long. They know their own way with conquered antagonists and when they are themselves conquered or promised defeat, dread the victor's revenge from their own frame of reference, dread with a loss of will and dignity which is shameful. It takes little imagination to summon up the haunted mind of Reynald of Châtillon as he lay shivering between Antioch and Mopsuestia, in the finest bed of the Monastery of St. James Major that January night over a half century ago.

The following noon he arrived, anonymously, at Mopsuestia and was established at the villa of a millionaire merchant, beside himself with entertaining the Regent of Antioch, disgraced or not. (One can infer what surely must have been Reynald's first experience in the exercise of princely condescension—gratitude balanced by distance—before this volatile social climber.) His wife's spiritual adviser and friend, the Bishop of Lattakieh, was sent to the Emperor to confirm Reynald's submission and plead—that is William of Tyre's word—Manuel accept this humiliation and thereby forgive him and Antioch. The Grand Duke Robert Roger—Basil's brother, and himself half Guiscard—speaking for the Emperor, guaranteed nothing but tapped a finger against the Archbishop's chest and said, "Your Excellency, we *know* your Prince."

The Emperor waited a week before setting the date of homage. It was not until Reynald approached the Main Square the very day of capitulation he discovered why. To his horror, below the dais, on the same cold stones upon which his bare feet trod numb, stood Italian ambassadors to Constantinople, representatives from every Byzantine dependency or client—from the Carpathians to the Caucasus—as well as agents from Egypt, Abasgie, Iconium, Iberia, and Persia. The humbling was complete. From these men, who would be quick to write to their sovereigns or superiors, there was no escaping the publicity of Antioch's precipitous fall from authority.

Before these men, he threw himself at the feet of the Emperor and presented his sword hilt. Manuel did not move. He waited for Reynald to speak, and, at length, the Prince wailed his sorrow, not from cravenness, which all eyewitnesses attribute to him and his whole life denies, but, one suspects, from the depths of the despair of a proud man debased. William of Tyre, his politics more apt than his charity—even for the errant man, which is the very tale of Christianity—described the moment in the most contemptuous terms: "He cried for mercy and he cried so very long every man present was revolted. With good reason the Frenchmen present disdained him and blamed him for rendering Latin glory despicable before the whole of Asia."

Finally, one may ask why occurred this unexpected breakdown by men who, the previous years, had micturated on the altars of Orthodox Cypriot churches. Was it merely the numbers of the Emperor's army? Only in part. More's to the point: Cyprus served as a warning to the Levantine world. Thoros and Reynald were not to be tolerated or encouraged against Byzantium because they had passed beyond the farthest bounds of atrocity which men will accept so long as it remains at a distance—and this, in an age which knew massacres as a matter of course. Then again, Thoros and Reynald were Orthodox and Latin, collusive to the occasion, not in general interests. Their unity was in their guilt; their fears of punishment were their own. Not their guilt, but their fears, overwhelmed their daring and broke their resolve.

Two days after this exhibition of Byzantine might, the Emperor received a priority dispatch from his brother, the Sebastocrator. Andronikus had escaped.

XVIII

"All my life," said Andronikus, "I had slept on silks. In my majority, I made sure to procure the best chefs and tailors, had a groom for every horse—I think I owned five hundred at one time—and a servant for every room in every home I owned—as for instance, at Hieriea, which had several hundred apartments—even those unused. I had thought I could scarcely live without luxury. A few months at campaign or an afternoon hard at polo were enough to test my endurance to my satisfaction. I know this sounds hopelessly ingenuous (still, one man's platitude may be another man's insight, if only to his own increase), but I realized this: allow any man the condition into which he was born and there is always one worse. In my case, there was nothing better and anything less, intolerable—or so I thought. So I thought.

"In time I grew used to the open bath, a pail near my bed filled with my own detritus, the insects, the dampness—though never the rats—and the straw pallet. Rather it was the change within myself I did not expect. For five years, Nicetas, I never saw any human face but those of my guards. Though at first I refused to be friendly from rage, then disappointing princely pride, and then because I did not wish these men— through no fault of their own, my tormentors—to become real to me as I might have to kill them (as my first thoughts of escape vaguely proposed), inevitably, out of loneliness, out of the silence which weighed on me too terribly, out of curiosity for the world above, I talked to them and finally extended some affection. Against every ordinance, I am certain, they would sit for hours in my cell. Some were literate, some not. One fellow had hoped to attend the University of Constantinople and conveyed a most pathetic desire to learn. Once I recognized the bounds of their interests and the complexities of vernacular Greek (they found my Attic effete), once I ceased to expect an opinion on Cicero's *Tusculanae Disputationes*—which is another form of pride and introverted as illiteracy—I learned more myself than I thought possible or likely.

"I had heard of brutality at the bottom. I rather thought I had been given an example of brutality at the top—more articulate, better dressed. And while there is just as much pretension at the bottom, as at the top, there is also, for better or worse, no more, no less, an equal apportion of wisdom. One day one of my guards, who loved to chew the beeswax leavings of my candles, said to me, very meditatively, 'Your Highness, do you know what's the worst thing about being poor?' I asked him what and he said, 'When a man must humble himself like a clown in the presence of his family to gain a little money. And none of your talk, if Your Highness will permit me, about inner dignity. Obsequiousness is obsequiousness. His dignity is a man's last strength, and nothing is worse than when it dims in the eyes of his children. My father used to tell how once his father scrambled for a gold coin tossed him by St. John Augustus as a child. After that, for all the great Emperor's famed piety, he could never like him.' He may not have put it quite so elegantly as Juvenal, but it contains the same pith as the famous remark in *Satires,* III, 152, 'Poverty, bitter though it be, has no sharper pang than this; that it makes men ridiculous.' I remember, Nicetas, the guard then winked at me and said, 'A word of advice, Prince. Don't ever be too gracious to us poor folk. After all, you can afford to be and we have to accept your charity because we need it.'

"I began to be appalled. I was left to wonder how much human potential these millennia have wasted in this imbalanced scheme of things wherein, everywhere, in every epoch—including Greece—a few score families and their few hundred progeny are coddled, bodily and spiritually and intellectually, from the cradle to the grave. Whilst others. . . . What is more hideous for a man than to yearn for a completeness he can never have for no better reason than the aspect of falsely irrevocable circumstances says it must be so.

"In those years, if I experienced any suffering, it was not for myself but for the many who knew the same fate as I in this world which could so disintegrate a man's life. How strange we will not accept ourselves in the role of tragedian—for that would probably mean suicide in the most literal sense—and yet it may seem imminently likely and heartbreaking in others. Perhaps because the aspect of tragedy is always more hopeless than the experience, the difference between the helpless spectator and the actor who means only to survive.

"When I grew bored with reading or conversing, I would lie on my pallet, my feet weighted by the chains I no longer noticed, and preoccupy myself with plans of escape or thoughts of my children. These two little phantoms agonized me most unjustly. The thought they would grow to maturity knowing me only by hearsay—and God knows whose—was unbearable. Worse still was the thought they would become adults knowing nothing of what I might teach them, the thought that I had peopled the world with two more indifferent, self-indulgent aristocrats. A few years ago, Sandro, my eldest son, said, 'You know, Papa, there's a great dichotomy in your attitude between my friends and myself.' I said, 'There is, and what might that be?' 'Tolerance,' he said rather smartly. Of course, I had no answer for him. It's a prejudice I suppose I will keep against them to my grave.

"Well, 25 March 1158, the chains were taken from my feet and never replaced. Obviously this was done on orders. But whose? Do you know, it seemed incredible to me I was still reckoned by anyone in the world above? In fact, it was the first direct action from that world upon myself since my jailing. And then, the moment those chains were taken away, I had only one thought: escape.

"Since the first days of my incarceration I had been intrigued by a sound at the corner farthest from my pallet which I had not been able to reach previously. The plash, the hollow plash, of water, which I would have hardly expected in the half-submerged portion of the ravelin, through fifteen feet of stone. The water seemed to flow with a certain regularity, and as I marked it on a candle, sleeping several miserable nights without one to prove my theory, later and later each day, I was certain, then, it had something to do with the tide. But what?

"Then, it must have been in early summer, I dreamed that Persephone, of all people, and my brother Philip were carrying my father's corpse through empty streets of Constantinople. All was cold and all very gray. I was with them, mourning his death and wishing myself dead. When we reached the Square of Savior Pantepopte—you know it: where the students immemorially and enigmatically gather at one tavern one year, and the other in another, to drink—Persephone said, 'Do you want to see him before we bury him?' Her body and Philip's hid all the cadaver but one leg, chalk-white and stiff, and I said in something of a panic, 'No.' Then, quite suddenly, we were elsewhere, I don't know where, and they were attempting to stuff my father's body into a drainage pipe. And I knew. I knew. Even in my sleep, I knew. I awoke at once.

"I took the candle from its stand and went to that corner where the sound of the breaking water was manifestly strongest. Amazed at my own stupidity, I tapped the slate slabs, each about eighteen inches square, which, with my great loss of weight, would accept me as a cavern a mouse—well, an elephant. All the slabs gave a dense sound but one. That at the corner seemed hollow, to rest above space, and that space somehow led to the sea. You know, my very first thought was a vision of gulls whose cries were mocking the alarm of John Sergius.

"It took the next half year, the better part of every night, to file a groove on each side of the slab, which centuries of grime and damp—besides the perverse precision of the original stonecutters—had fitted so perfectly to its members and the corner wall. It was, need I say, the most ineluctably tedious work I have ever performed. All I had as tool was the sharp prong of the candlestick. It was necessary, of course, to work as quietly as possible and, insofar as I was resolved, with as much care to conceal what I was doing. I have to confess, as the possibility of freedom deepened, I became somewhat vindictive, for instance liberally mixing bits of slate dust into the warm beeswax my philosopher-guard so enjoyed chewing. He never noticed the difference. At the end of six months I had worked a slender space on all four sides, and with ease, using the same prong, I pried loose the slab. It had rested on a shelf following a right angle and at least three inches wide. I should never be able to slip through. That was unhappy enough after so much work. What's worse, beneath the shelf was a mysterious sloping surface, the drainage canal, no doubt, in perfect repair. I should have recalled, if I could hear the sound of the sea through two layers of stone, it could not have been very thick. Instead—luckily, perhaps—in fury, I smashed the iron end of the candlestick against both the shelf and the pipe, and they shattered with a terrible noise and the cold, moist January air, the wonderful smell of the sea, filled the putrid dungeon, probably for the first time since the age of my ancestor, Alexander—a propitious communion.

"It was dawn, it had to be, because low-angled sunlight filled the canal, about three feet high. I stepped down, and crouching, I saw, at the far end, for the first time in five years, a morning sky. Could anything have seemed more like rebirth? Sometimes I can still summon that moment, the taste of purity, of elation, of beginning again, perhaps wiser than before. I got to my knees—reached over and easily replaced the slab above me. Wisely, I decided to remain hidden and not attempt an immediate escape. The first day of my disappearance would see the most commotion, as indeed it began when the guards, searching cell to cell the origin of the crashing clay, discovered me vanished without a trace. Oh, the amazement, Nicetas, the stream of visitors. Once I thought I recognized John Sergius' voice. I was never bored."

Perched in an unused drainage pipe, a yard in diameter, a few feet above the Bosporus, and then half submerged in its winter waters, Andronikus gained only the merest hint of the sensation caused by his escape. Among those voices were the governor of the bastion's, the Constantinopolitan Prefect's, and then, indeed, John Sergius'. Almost unprecedentedly—in a time of peace—all the gates of the city were closed throughout the day, causing a sensation and raising more outrage against the government than the escaped Imperial Prince. Anchored vessels in all harbors were ransacked. Philip and his wife, the Grand Duchess Martha, and his sister-in-law, the Grand Duchess Rabia, were placed under house arrest at Palace Comnenus (a move which later required a personal apology to His Majesty, Shah Kilij, Rabia's brother). At Vlanga Palace a small war ensued while the entire staff attempted to prevent their mistress and her two children from being carried off by black-gloved Scholarians. The Protovestarius—more paranoid than vindictive in his certainty Anastasia had assisted her husband in his escape—detained the Grand Duchess, Alexander, and Zoë in the same cell in the Buceleon Ravelin from which husband and father had vanished.

When, the following week, Bertha-Irene learned of this monumental pettiness, she confronted her nephew and told him to release the Grand Duchess and her children, at once, to Vlanga (which had been searched and in some measure pillaged). John pointed out to the Empress the wife's probable complicity, and the fact the Basilissa was thereby making herself accessory. For once, however, he had played too hard on Bertha-Irene's known demureness. To John's surprise, before his own very creatures—he had by now an unofficial court—Irene rose from her chair to her full height, which was, unfortunately, greater than that of the Protovestarius, and on one of the few occasions in her life, raised her voice and said, "John, you know very well, any warrant of arrest for a member of the Imperial family is null without my signature. This you did not procure from me. You would not have had it in any event. If Stana is not returned to Vlanga by nightfall, you will answer to me before a meeting of the Sacred Consistory. Is that understood?"

It was done: the last great generosity the Empress extended to the man—or, here, his kin—who, more than any other, had eased the first of her unhappy days at Constantinople. The following morning Anastasia was returned to Vlanga with her two children and, as she would soon discover, a third in her belly.*

Andronikus: "The first evening, to my astonishment, I heard my wife's voice, unmistakably, and those of children in the cell above. I pushed on the slab and peered up from the floor. Stana had embraced the children and was cowering with them by the pallet, trying to cross herself against the evil eye, which is only slightly more amusing than the aspect my head rising Baptist-like from the depths must have presented. I hoisted myself into the cell and my wife drew back. I put my finger to my lips, then whispered, quite moved to see her, 'How are you, Stana?' Rather more logically, she asked who I was, our first words in the six since before Hungary.

"In that wretched cell, for the first time, I met my daughter, Zoë, who has been a joy to me, and reacquainted myself with my son Alexander. Zoë shrank from me as I stank abominably, and Alexander, who perhaps dimly remembered me, was fascinated by the loss of my beard and my cropped hair, which I explained was necessary to diminish the available nurseries for lice. When we put the children to bed, their heads on my spare prison garments, wrapped in Stana's sable-lined cloak, my wife and I talked till late in the night, and then I said, quite abruptly—alas, such circuitous charms as a seducer I had lost—'You know, I've wanted a woman for so long, I can taste it,' and thereupon we made love.

"I mention this macabre tryst because it was now vital to my escape. Each night I penetrated my wife I reasserted myself over her. Of course,

---

* Inseminated by Andronikus, though at first the Grand Duchess announced her pregnancy boldly as the work of her lover. It was not until her death Andronikus claimed the third of his five children and middle son, Julian, as his own. It may be, this toss between two fathers, between bastardy and legitimacy, more than any other reason explains the indulgence the Grand Duke extended to this distressing young man, who embodied all his father loathed in the privileged and, quite beside, sins ingenious enough, of his own devising. N.A.

she still loved me with the same jealousy as before, only now she had me probably as she had always preferred it: hidden by day and in the night by her side, quite captured. But—to the point—I suspected she would inform on me if I did not reaffirm our alliance. I had no idea, you see, how much she had become estranged from me and the influence her lover had upon her; still again, how much she resented me. In effect, I was obliged to let her possess me in order to escape.

"At the end of five days I swore my wife to secrecy, kissed her and kissed my children—and to please their mother made the Sign of the Cross over them like a proper Orthodox father (though I coldly refused when Anastasia asked me to give Alexander my stoicheion, the gold icon about my neck). I slipped through the opening in the floor and jumped into the waters.

"They were frigid and their shock nearly killed me. My strength was gone. The exercises in the cell throughout the years had scarcely prepared me for a swim across the winter Bosporus on a moonless night. Yet what one must do to survive, one must do. Perhaps I was sustained by no more than my anger against the indifferent invisible. I reached Chalcedon and collapsed on the beach, for an hour, for two, I can't say. When I was able, I crept through the streets, my head lowered, my knees ready to give way. My garment was thin and drenched and I was profoundly tempted to beg a bed at one of the monasteries. The risk, however, was unthinkable. During those five days beneath my cell, a proclamation of outlawry had been made against me throughout the Empire. Nearly every door of every public building in Chalcedon was so posted.

"I remember passing Hieriea Palace, brightly lit, flying its pennants and well patrolled by mounted Varangians. I was transfixed. I tried to recall the man I was who had been lord of that vast house. There was, quite simply, no connection. The cord had been snapped between myself and that Imperial Grand Duke who congratulated himself on his independence which usually took the form of petulantly antagonizing the Emperor and shocking the Patriarch, by holding dinner parties on Sunday. Strange, isn't it, how distant from me now Manuel seemed, going about his elegant, ordered life, full of alternatives and great gestures, how very distant, as though I were his poorest subject and he were, as they say, somewhere between earth and heaven in magnificent isolation. In a manner of speaking, of course, it was all quite true as I stood shivering in the street before my former home which was now closed to me, as to a beggar. I marveled how I had descended from its numerous magnificent apartments to a point whereat I would have given a year of my life to sleep, dry and warm, beside the furnaces in the cellar I had never seen.

"I was out of the city, as I had to be, long before daylight. I slept in the forest north of Nicomedia the better part of the day. I had decided to proceed southeast to my mother, who had been living at Christos Gennate since my father's death. Do you know, for the first time in my life, I dreamed of food? I cursed the tables we used to set at Hieriea, groaning with goose and venison and lamb, sweetmeat, tarts, fruits, and soups as thick as lava. I had heard the peasants, in time of famine, stripped the bark off trees and consumed it to stay their hunger. I considered that when I awoke in the late afternoon. I must have stared at one trunk till sunset deciding just how one goes about entering the tough skin into one's belly. At length, I decided against it, which says more for the peasant's starvation than my discriminating palate. You know the wood in that area teems with game, but I was too weary to chase it and too weak or too distracted by hunger to think of any other way of getting it. I ate some grass and vomited, and cursed Manuel. Do you know why? A few years before, he had told me when he was a boy and subjected to the cruelties of his older brothers, he had run away from the family villa at Oeneum and, in the night, eaten grass with no ill effect. Certainly, with my abstemiousness and my prison palate I should have been able to more easily digest such roughage. The answer, later, became obvious. All a matter of timing. My cousin ate fresh —one might almost say nourishing—spring grass. I had gorged on brute winter turf.

"When evening came an aurora appeared in the skies. I watched from beneath a leafless tree by the roadside. It seemed to me, in Manuel's behalf, heaven had opened out the night into great soaring vaults of radiance to search for me. Odd, as I learned later, Manuel stood on the balcony of the Magistrate's Palace at Mopsuestia and in the same moment was thinking quite the reverse: that the heavens were lighting my way through what otherwise should have been a moonless pitch.

"I was elated with my fortune when I came upon a farm and begged entrance. It was given me and I thought it extraordinarily charitable of that family as heaven knows what might have been knocking on their door in a night when the sky was afire. The reek of unwashed bodies and the animals gathered with the family for warmth and the hard-packed floor (the peasants tamp the earth with excrement, new as it comes to them, for it makes an excellent vinculum)—well, you can imagine it: a stink worse, if possible, than my prison cell. Nevertheless I had a blanket, a fire, some bread, and some soup.

"They questioned me, at which I tried to be evasive in my best vernacular Greek, which still fell artificially on my ears, as though I were mimicking and certain to be resented. The following morning, after those people had betrayed me, I asked if I had been recognized merely by my height. The farmer was frank, in an offhand way. He said, 'Only in part, Your Highness. Your height, yes. But so too, you didn't act like a vagabond. You weren't shy. You thanked us without excess. You had no stories, you wore your blanket like a mantle, and even though you were starving, you ate like no starving peasant eats. You broke your bread instead of biting it. And, look, when you lifted the bowl you did not grasp it like so'—he grabbed a bowl from the inside with his fingers—'but thus'—he placed his thumb, rather awkwardly, on the rim and fanned his fingers along the side and the bottom. 'No peasant, no vagrant, and not a lot of snotty merchants I've seen hold earthenware like a goblet. We just put two and two together.' I could not resist telling him he'd earned his reward.

"And then I was taken off in chains by soldiers, including one—the farmer's son—of the Malagina Garrison, nearby, whom the old man had warned while I slept. I remember as I left the hut I slipped on a frozen puddle and fell. The soldiers tried to help me out of the mud and the ice. I said, 'I don't need anyone's help.' But of course, I did. I was hobbled by my chains. The soldiers were all young, local, not very experienced, and, I could see, simply overwhelmed by their prisoner. One of them leaned over me, saying, 'Please, Your Imperial Highness. Please. Be good enough.' And they raised me to my feet, and— I shall never know why—I began to cry. No sobs, no sounds. Only tears. I must have made a sight—eyes rheumy, nose running—to the peasants who lined the road of my return to Constantinople. That was very harrowing—not the recapture, but to learn, to my surprise, I had not been forgotten. One peasant turned me in, but it seemed so many more of them—and not a few of their masters, some of whom I recognized—came to witness my journey, not to jeer, I think, but really to offer their encouragement.

"I chose to recognize no one, not that I was ungrateful, much less contemptuous, as once I might have been, by their concern, but because I could not bear the mirror of my future in their eyes.

"And do you know what altogether undid me at the very last moment? As we were crossing the Augusteum I saw a group of countryfolk, pilgrims, crossing the Great Square toward Holy Wisdom, *on their knees,* led by a priest as poor and probably as illiterate as his flock, holding high an icon they had brought with them to be blessed by the Patriarch, no doubt, whom I could well imagine dining at that moment on gold service at St. Michael's Palace. The thought of the unrelieved misery of these people, of their never having known one moment's—I could not name it—splendor, contentment, the extraordinary, *something,* of consolation, of succor, made my trials, by comparison, lucid, even justifiable. Theirs were the lives of Sisyphus, not because the Patriarch or my cousin, for that matter, were intentionally oppressive or without compassion, but because they suffered rulers who lacked the irony which perceives iniquity, who did not know, did not care, did not care they did not know, who believed a government—of the Church or the state—something separate, fixed, to be preserved at all costs rather than altered at any moment to avoid the smallest injustice, the least suffering.

"As the gates of Chalke closed on me, I looked back once at those dark, swaying figures, their prayers mute from the distance, and I thought myself well rid of such a world." *Explicit: Nicetas Acominatus.*

XIX

As the five-foot bronze horns are lifted to mouths of the Varangian trumpeters atop the Magistrate's Palace at Mopsuestia, they simultaneously catch the reflection of the sun in a brief, silent burst of incandescence, which anticipates the blasts to come. Below, on the steps of the palace Manuel Augustus waits for the oncoming center of the thousand-foot procession of the King and Queen of Jerusalem. At length, Baldwin and Theodora arrive: Only the more unsentimental observer would have noted this stunning young royal couple—he fair-

*haired and sunburned, she pale-skinned and dark-haired—is a com-
bination of opposites unreconciled. She is drôle, sensuous, self-possessed,
haughty, and cerebral. He is serious, ingenuous, jealous, tractable,
and merely intelligent. She is—with the double superiority of femininity
and a fine intellect—fondly contemptuous of her husband. He is, in turn,
intimidated by his wife's self-containment and within eight months
of marriage has begun again to visit with his former mistress who loves
him with the humility of illiteracy and social inferiority. The King
and the Queen are assisted in their dismounting and, sprightly, ascend
the steps to the Emperor. To Baldwin's surprise, his Consort takes his
hand. She is dressed in the Western style, her hair free beneath a small,
gold fleur-de-lis coronet, the lilies repeated in gold on the blue-black
velvet of her ermine-trimmed robes, nipped at the waist and the wrists.*

BALDWIN. Your Imperial Majesty. At last we meet.

*The two shake hands in the Western fashion with a mutual nod of
the head—esteem, rather than submission, though Baldwin, in fact, is
Manuel's vassal. The Emperor turns, eyes agleam, to his niece and
kisses both her hands and her cheeks.*

*They ascend the stairs, made way for, then followed, by their suites,
and enter a huge marble reception hall, designed—and monogrammed
—in the Heraclean age. Until now, from the looks of the scaffolds of the
Grand Chamberlain's workmen, neither walls nor pillars have been
washed.*

MANUEL. Your journey, I trust, was without incident.

BALDWIN. Felicitous, Sir.

MANUEL. We've had terrific thunderstorms, one after the other, the
last three days. I was worried for your safety on the road.

THEODORA. What's the news of Andronikus, uncle?

Manuel is startled and irritated.

MANUEL. How did you come by that?

THEODORA. It's all the talk. Genoese ships brought the rumor to Jaffa
from Italy.

MANUEL. I see. Well. In the meantime he's been recaptured.

THEODORA. Do you intend to blind him?

MANUEL. You're entirely too morbid. It hardly entered my mind. I'm
not at all pleased about the attention this incident has received. The
exaggeration seems to swell with the distance. Your father received a
letter from King Henry, whose questions, to hear tell it, suggest An-

dronikus has usurped the throne and I was in refuge at Cilicia gathering an army to march on Constantinople. Much the same comes from Yaroslav of Galicia. I rather sense some men's wishful thinking.

Incipit: Nicetas Acominatus: Baldwin of Jerusalem took advantage of the Emperor's proximity to meet with him, in the company of his Consort, for the first time. His arrival had a most salubrious effect on the air of vengeance and acrimony at Mopsuestia. In part, this was due to the distraction to which Manuel always readily consented to entertain a guest. Nothing could more genuinely lighten his mood than attention to the detail and the creation of wonders to amaze a visitor. Then, he could be benignly amused as an indulgent father by his children's excitement. But it is also given that the Emperor, helplessly charmed by Baldwin, as once he had been by his cousin, consented, on the young King's urging, to reconsider the cruelty of his stand against Thoros and Raymond.

Now, though he thus credits his sovereign's clement intercession in his history ("I could not but do otherwise; there is a point where legend not merely overtakes the truth but crushes it, and to insist upon fact above elaboration is to assume the role of pedant, explaining the magician's tricks, too conceited and too dull to realize his audience is not merely uninterested—they are resentful"), William of Tyre had quite another opinion in private. And well he ought to have known, since in that, his thirtieth year, he was attached as Chronicler and Confessor to the Court of Jerusalem (and soon by his brilliance to become adviser and premier diplomat, as well).

Once he said to me, "You know, Count, under the rule of a virtuous king, everything good is attributed to him, just as in the reign of a tyrant everything bad is surely the curse of the malefactor. After a fashion, perhaps it's true. The Sovereign sets the temper of the times. If he's a beast, the lesser beasts crawl from beneath the stones. If he's an angel, the virtuous take heart. But really, the generosity which my master is supposed to have introduced to the Emperor at Mopsuestia as regards Raymond and Thoros is quite false. Far more than His Majesty, Queen Theodora immediately grasped the implications of the Augustus' policy and it was she who convinced the King to warn Manuel that the effect of beating both princes to their knees without compensatory gestures might in the short term prove Byzantine might and make men fear, but in the long run would cost the Empire its last allies. The only friendship founded in fear is opportunism."

Thus, Thoros II was rescued from his dismal fate and instated as permanent Governor *in* Cilicia, which was more than he deserved. The lucky man knew it and was humiliated rather than grateful. In time, we shall see the result of his resentment. Reynald's punishment was politically more harsh and personally as lenient. He was bidden to sign a protocol which reasserted his vassalage, promised forces on demand, and—most prized and disputed point of all—gave to the Emperor the right to appoint a Patriarch of Antioch of the Greek rite rather than the Latin. The Prince gave his seal to this and, at once, returned to his capital to prepare for the Emperor's entry into Antioch on Easter Sunday, in April. Significantly the dissatisfaction was as great in the Imperial as the Antiochene praetoriums: the one because Manuel did not insist on a Greek administration; in the other because the Prince had ransomed his power at the price of Holy Church.

The entry into Antioch—the Emperor announcing he had come as friend, not liege or conqueror—was unexpectedly acclaimed. Some have suggested, and it is not so unlikely, the Antiochenes had come to loathe the policies of their Prince and found this a splendidly safe means of expressing their contempt for him.

While the Frankish aristocracy either took part in the procession or stopped their ears behind closed doors, the people were—really or artificially—beside themselves with glee. The Emperor rode his favorite horse, his limpid-eyed white Egyptian mare, Yasmin. He was preceded by the Nemitizi, eight abreast, then the Excubitors and Scholarians and the Archontopuli, and immediately by the legendary Varangians. Behind him walked the Prince of Antioch carrying the emerald and pearl Sword of Constantine, blade upward. Beside the Prince, but mounted, rode King Baldwin. The Emperor's safety was feared for in such sensational excitement. The crowds, everywhere, wished to touch him—his spurs, his hem, even his dainty (and probably frightened) steed. When he entered the Cathedral of St. Peter, he was met by an avenged Patriarch Aimery. Throughout the long Te Deum, all eyes were on Imperial Majesty rather than the iconostasis. As he left the church, on signal, Imperial banners—which would fly the whole of his Easter week stay—were raised over the city. It was the culminating, triumphant moment of Comnenus foreign policy vis-à-vis the Latins. It should have ended then and there.

Instead, from Antioch, the Emperor, at the head of a still greater army—Latins and Byzantines uneasily together—marched against Aleppo and Nureddin. In truth, Manuel had no heart for initiating full-scale war with the Prince, for, if he were any judge of a man's intentions, Byzantium's more imminent Moslem enemy was in Lesser Asia rather than the Persian Mesopotamia. Then again, he had progressed so far and so high without shedding a drop of his soldiers' blood, it must have seemed obnoxious in the extreme to chance carnage at the last moment. He gave in, nevertheless, to Baldwin's entreaties against Palestine's principal enemy. Ironically, what should have meant the end of Nureddin's hegemony—even that redoubtable warlord expected the worst—concluded at Manuel's instigation with a mildness and charity serving to dim some of the luster in which Baldwin had beheld his Queen's uncle. Manuel committed the Imperial army only in a reserve capacity and though Aleppo was lethally besieged, offered in behalf of all his vassals to end the campaign in return for the release of all Christian hostages now held by the Prince. Eager to be rid of the Byzantine colossus, which was just as eager to depart, Nureddin readily and unconditionally agreed.

In a letter to his Queen Regent, who had returned to Jerusalem, Baldwin wrote, in part:

Your uncle is a lily—a damned Greek lily. While we were fighting for our lives, he invited some fool archivist of Nureddin to his pavilion (everyone believed the fellow a spy)—for an interview, if you please, with the possibility in mind of the infidel assuming the post of Imperial librarian at Constantinople! I am not entirely unaware of what is said of me, but beside Augustus I think I am a model of responsibility. At least I listen to my advisers. He does not. He is unpredictable enough to drive one mad. He is not a great strategist, only lucky. He has reigned so long without criticism, his prestige is now so immense, he cannot be approached save in flattery. And he cannot—I repeat, cannot—be moved. Oh, all his great humility is a pose. I have found if you treat him precisely as he seems to beckon—familiarly—his manner would cover hell with hoarfrost. He has become in his own mind—and he is *not* so very old—what? Thirty-nine? Forty?—a great old man, with all that implies: pomposity, caprice, and mountainous self-esteem. His ideas are vague and without wit. I may not be the most inspired fellow alive, but I know the difference between one who is great because others consider him so in the light of the man's activities, and one who is great against the measure of his own book, which may or may not be valid; in this case, *not,* as his creatures subscribe to the manuscript without reading it. And now, what on earth has he done, but, fancying himself the Prince of Peace, released upon us seven thousand Christians, most of them nobles whose sons have succeeded to their name, complicating appallingly the political situation, whilst still we must battle Nureddin, who might have been undone at this one blow. This is intolerable and I am not moved by my freed brothers, not one bit.

But Manuel was, quite to tears by the sight of these thousands of Christians whom he preferred to believe had suffered for the faith of Jesus Christ, when, in truth, most of them had been taken in battle, offered as hostage, and been denied ransom by their own kin. In truth, the Emperor was bewildered by the hostility of the Latin barons and asked his Basilissa in a letter, "Should I have refused? Should they not be satisfied? To avoid war and regain their loved ones. Is this not good? Truly they are a fickle and mysterious people and beyond my comprehension. I am coming home."

On his arrival at Constantinople, the first order of business which the Emperor attended was the commission of a board of inquiry into Andronikus' attempted escape. He appointed Michael Branas and his nephew, Prince John Vatatzes, as co-chairmen. It was well he did, if his only reason was to honor and keep in his suite these men who had so hopelessly and courageously defended Cyprus and suffered for it in Reynald's dungeons. Politically, however, it removed the taint of initial bias against his cousin. Michael was, to put it mildly, sympathetic to Andronikus, while Prince John, a former playboy who had been made Governor of Cyprus—a sinecure, then—to prevent him from impregnating any more of his mother's, Eudocia Porphyriogeneta's, ladies-in-waiting, had a new sympathy for the conditions under which a man endured his imprisonment.

Their report was given to the Emperor in July, a month after his return to the capital. Rewritten by the family's acknowledged diplomat, the Grand Duke Philip, it remained, even in tempered form, an implicit condemnation of Manuel's treatment of his cousin, who, since his reincarceration in January, had been subjected by his jailers to cruelties and indignities unacceptable to a slave, let alone an emperor's grandson. ("Interestingly," the report states, with serene, but deadly criticism, "there are laws regarding the mistreatment of slaves, and these laws, initiated by the dynasty, are part of its shining record of justice. Why, then, one is prompted to ask, is there no Dynastic Charter?") For seven months, the Grand Duke had suffered random beatings, periodic starvation, weeks running, when he would be awakened throughout the night by dousings of cold water, days of enchainment when he was allowed to lie in his own offal and urine. These were only the more blatant tortures, and the recommendation was for immediate release to house arrest.

It may be said Manuel was amazed—and probably alarmed—by Andronikus' increasing fame—even at court he now had bold sympathizers —and uncomfortably aware the treatment he extended his cousin was unconscionably harsh, if not altogether unjustifiable. Not unknown to him, moreover, was a comment made by the mild Grand Duke Philip, when he had finished polishing and ameliorating the blunt soldier's language of the commission report. Handing it grim and whey-faced to Michael Branas, he said, "If after this His Majesty, my cousin, does not better my brother's conditions by leaps, I intend to undo him—by any means. I promise you. You may repeat that to whomever you wish. It is a threat." (He was banished to his estates for two years.)

Wanting to be kind, or to seem kind, yet unwilling to appear subject to public opinion—and with thoughts, no doubt, of that last chilling interview at Pelagonia (only the Emperor and his secretary knew how far beyond mere criticism of policy Andronikus had progressed)—Manuel ordered the apartment atop the Tower of Anemas, overlooking Blachernae, luxuriously reappointed. There he decreed Andronikus would spend his days, free to receive his wife and children, all meals from the kitchens at Vlanga, whatever clothes he wished, the services of his valet, a laundress, a barber-masseur, a physician, and to keep a dog if he liked. In short, imprisonment still, however lenient, not house arrest. Command was given the Grand Duke was to be translated in absolute secrecy between midnight and dawn on a date known only to the Emperor, the Varangian lieutenant, and the hand-picked squadron which would accomplish the task.

Not unexpectedly, Andronikus was scarcely in condition to mount a horse, let alone ride a half-dozen miles to his new prison. A closed wagon was brought up to meet the litter emerging from the dungeons of Buceleon under a summer's bright midnight moon. As the guard and wagon left Chalke Gate and crossed the Augusteum, they encountered several thousand torchbearing citizens intent on accompanying the Prince's person. (The guards were later interrogated but acclaimed their own silence, with no proof to the contrary.) My elder brother, among a host of seminarians and university students present, vividly recalls how Senator Leo Monasteriotes, a red-haired giant, stepped forward, glowering beneath his torch, and said, or rather bellowed—as I never knew Leo to merely speak—to the Varangians, "What's the matter, fellows? Why do you stop? Nothing to fear. Now we'll spread it about the Emperor, our August Majesty, has kept his word. But first, let's *see* His Imperial Highness." Warningly, the crowd took a united step forward. The lieutenant commander, sensibly, had the curtains drawn back. Andronikus' valet, allowed to attend his master for the first time in nearly seven years, helped to raise the emaciated—and possibly delirious—figure. Then and there, the commander should have taken the responsibility of altering the original plan, placing the Grand Duke on a yacht at Buceleon and sailing him the entire length of the Golden Horn to Justinian Bridge. Instead, the original schedule was followed, the crowd, as anyone might have expected, grew—years later all Andronikus could recall were startling shadows on the curtains of the wagon—and the Emperor, learning of the demonstration while it was still mid-city, ordered the people dispersed.

It has never been satisfactorily proven whether the Emperor personally selected the Nemitzian Regiment to be released into the city, or it was the carelessness—or zeal—of one of his ADCs. In any event, the most savage fighters in the Imperial army—those who are brought up only at the most lethal moment of battle—cannot be expected to have acted otherwise than they did. The Nemitizi, like the Varangian, are foreign born, but left as much in their semi-barbarous state as possible. This plainly peaceful display of favor for the Grand Duke, in the first, need not have been dispersed at all, but if it had to be, it was a more likely task for the Constantinopolitan constabulary, used to handling crowds without fatality, or, at worst, the city garrison, native born and unlikely to fratricide.

Ironically, at Virgin Pammakaristos, the church built to commemorate the marriage which founded the dynasty, the Nemitzi massed, allowed the wagon to pass through their ranks, then, without any warning, rode down the populace. Five hundred men and women were butchered and perhaps a hundred more trampled to death in the rush to safety.

By morning, while the whole city cursed the Imperium, Manuel, in one of his rare displays of petulance, complained to a courtier, "Everything that man touches or which touches him is contaminated." And then he swore no argument on earth could convince him to give his cousin his freedom.

On 2 March 1160, the same day Pope Alexander III excommunicated Frederick of Germany for the rape of Milan (which Manuel helped to rebuild), Bertha-Irene Augusta succumbed after three months' illness to malignant fever.

In decency the Emperor had broken off entirely his failing liaison with Persephone shortly after Christmas. With the court physician, he personally and expertly attended his wife. During that time, Imperial rule was assumed by the Sebastocrator and the Protovestarius, who, it is said, approached the Empress' deathbed and implored her to forgive him, for she had not spoken to him since the incarceration of the Grand Duchess Anastasia. The Emperor himself, passing between the sickroom and the Imperial chapel, in those months, took on his first gray hairs.

Late in February, Queen Theodora arrived from Jerusalem. She was appalled by the change in her uncle. "He had a pathetic, hunted look. His eyes previously were pronounced, though not unattractive. But now they seemed to be pushed by two thumbs from the inside. On my arrival, he asked me to see him in his apartments, privately. We sat in chairs, at angles to one another, he with his elbows on his knees, lowering his head now and then, running his fingers through his hair, miserable. I remember he said, 'How I've mistreated and humiliated that good woman. From the beginning. And now there's no time to make amends. She's dying, Theodora, with all my sins against her upon my conscience.' I said, 'Oh, uncle, more than anyone I know, she has had a short memory for these things. You must remember. She forgives you. She does so with no bitterness and nothing but gladness you are so devoted to her.' But he would not be consoled. After a fashion, I grew impatient with him. What's done is done. One would assume then, he had learned too well a lesson against indifferent cruelty the next time he was tempted to it. After a fashion, I felt a small revenge in my aunt's behalf, though that scarcely lifted a moment of the eighteen years she had suffered with us."

Of others, the Emperor asked, "What will happen to us without her?" and in the emotion of the moment, the courtiers wept and replied they did not know. With the Emperor crumbling before their eyes and no great figure in his place to console them for *that* loss, they believed, indeed, the Empress was the irreplaceable pillar being irrevocably felled. Closer, and more pathetically, to the truth, the Empress had ceased to be a relevant figure in anyone's life or thought, save, perhaps, her daughter's. Diplomatically, with Frederick's accession, her marriage ceased to have meaning as a bond between the two empires. As a public figure, she was profoundly respected, but not really loved by the people, who almost never saw her in public, and then, only ill at ease—scarcely the Consort for such a dazzling husband in his dazzling court. (But then, that same public never saw her during her lengthy, numerous private visits to hospitals and orphanages.) The Empress, above all, had not produced an heir to the throne—perhaps the most damning criticism and, too, the most irrlevant—and even the wonderful, if cold beauty of her youth had, with middle-age and disappointment, become the sharply drawn, hieratic wanness common among German women. Human beings, such as they are, however, grow weary of pitying their fellows. In time they grow irritated with the object's unchanging misfortune and cease to believe it unalterable. In the end, it may be said Irene Augusta was, in a small, but real way, resented, as though the quiet horror of her life was somehow of her own devising.

A month after her funeral (at which, unprecedentedly, the Emperor followed his wife's coffin on foot, his daughter to one side and on the other a heavily veiled Queen of Jerusalem, whom some mistook, in outrage, for the Grand Duchess Persephone) the Shah of Persia, Nureddin of Aleppo, and the Fatimite Caliph of Egypt jointly requested Manuel allow them to finance and decorate his Augusta's tomb in tribute to her work in behalf of the Moslem poor and orphans within the Empire. The Emperor, who the night of his wife's death requested immediate commencement of beatification proceedings, agreed to this singular honor (and was not too distracted in his grief to comment anxiously on the absence of Shah Kilij in this mourners' cartel). Thus, for the next ten months, Constantinopolitans were treated to the previously unthinkable sight of Moslem artisans at Cathedral of the Almighty, creating for their late Despoina, as one courtier put it—accurately—"not a crypt but a jewel box."

Queen Theodora remained with the Emperor and his child until summer. Manuel protested when his niece left him ("I think he feared he would go back to Persephone the moment I was gone"), but it is likely Theodora, whose sensibilities were enhanced by insight, preferred to remain only so long as was necessary to lift her uncle and cousin from grief, and then depart whilst still appreciated.

Princess Melissena: "She said it was time to leave when rumor reached her—kindly ones, mind you, and a tribute—she was considered the unofficial Empress. She had absolutely no desire to become a second Persephone, if only in some man's too lively imagination. Her Majesty was very aware of her dignity and her reputation. As Sovereign Queen, moreover, she could not be kept beyond her personal discretion."

While she remained, she was invaluable to her uncle. She presided over the dispersal of her aunt's personal estate and the execution of her personal papers, reorganized the Empress' charities and their staffs, the palace staff itself reassigned—or retired with handsome annuities—her aunt's ladies, maids, equerries, secretaries, and pages, approved the new tutors and curriculum for Catherine Porphyriogeneta and urged the Imperial Majordomo to create entertainments which might distract the Emperor, who may have had all these favors in mind when he introduced his niece to the Genoan ambassador as "a pearl beyond any price."

All of these duties, of course, were officially those of the Protovestarius, John Sergius. He was frankly enraged by the Queen's presumption or else merely jealous of the praise and place with which their uncle attended her. He took time from his unofficial duties as the "second busiest man in the Empire"—duties which would have prevented him from instrumenting his aunt's estate with a fraction of the Queen's discretion—to throw his cousin at every turn. Now, Theodora was one of those women who quite knows her own mind and brooks no affront to her common sense. She was called imperious, when, more accurately—and less emotionally—she was better described as assured. (As Queen, this faculty was only encouraged.) She despised her cousin, the Protovestarius, or so Andronikus insisted, not because he was wicked, but "puerile"

—volatile, jealous, small-minded, egotistical—in short, predictable—a bully capable of disproportionate retaliation for the least infraction he believed his dignity to have suffered. If Theodora, as Queen, was beyond his pale, it was all too conceivable he would strike at the nearest object —which might be human—or wait the day when he could avenge himself on the actual perpetrator. Without depth, he was incapable of change and so he was long on revenge.

Princess Melissena told me of a confrontation between John Sergius and Theodora, more chilling than amusing as the Queen did not seem to realize the very virtue of her position—as well as blindness to the possibility she might not always be inviolable—made her vulnerable. "I've forgotten how Her Majesty offended the Grand Duke, but he had, as usual, placed some obstacle, in turn, in her way. One day, she approached him, and with that reasonable voice and charming smile which her Latin servants had learned to fear as it concealed the degree of her anger, she asked her cousin why he had done such and such a thing and he made an evasive answer which was a small triumph of admission and impugnity. She considered the Protovestarius a moment, then said, 'Stay close to uncle, John. You're half his size and half dead anyway— and without his altitude, half buried even now by your enemies.' He started to speak, but Her Majesty moved on and he was left looking after her, looking murderous, surrounded by a chorus of titters."

Manuel remained grandly above this feud between his niece and nephew, favoring one no more than the other. On her embarkation to Jerusalem, he bid the Queen to a task surprising from one so freshly aggrieved. She was to compile a prospective of the marriageable princesses among the Latin aristocracy. Unlike his father who was—by three years—younger, when he became a widower, the Basileus had no intention of remaining unmarried the rest of his life, especially when universal politics promised any number of advantages to the Byzantine Empire via negotiations for a foreign empress.

At Antioch, Theodora found her husband's cousin Constance as close to a widow again, as ever she would come, but still ineligible for what the Queen amusedly called the Selection Panels, referring to the ancient days of Empire when the Basileus or Crown Prince chose his wife from among the assembled, suitably beautiful daughters of the aristocracy. For the third and last time in her life, Constance came near, but not near enough, to marriage with the Imperial house she so intensely admired.*

The Queen's report from Antioch to her uncle ran thus:

Constance, as you know, has two daughters—those girls presented to you at Antioch last year. To refresh your memory. Philippa, the younger of the two, fourteen, obviously is unready at the moment, and yet she has, even now, the beginnings of a splendid maturity. She is a serene, perceptive, wonderfully educated girl, demure, compassionate, devout. She is tall for her age, seems older too, and has red hair like Grandmama's, blue eyes, and skin of miraculous smoothness. I think Constance rightly fears for her because she is extremely beautiful and hopelessly trusting and would suffer terribly by an unkind husband. Maria, the older girl, is quite another story, believe me. She is both sentimental and opinionated, or perhaps too open to first impressions, too impetuous and then too stubborn. She says she intends to read no more books when her education is finished (with that attitude it was finished before it began), but she means to learn life afresh, if you please, by personal experience, which, insofar as I'm concerned, is a declaration of suicide. I mustn't convey that she is in any way hateful, because she most certainly is not. She's an impertinent little minx and at the same time she could charm the devil into heaven. What's worse, she knows it. I want to be impartial, so I shall tell you: this girl is the most beautiful creature I've ever beheld. This is the opinion of a jealous woman, as you've sometimes teased me, uncle. She has blue eyes, pale as a robin's egg, her mother's golden hair and flawless complexion and a figure too full for its own good at sixteen. But this is nothing. Save the skin, a horse may have the same qualities in kind, including two even rows of white teeth. Rather her perfection must be seen to be believed. I would hesitate to say the girl is stupid. I think she is only exceedingly willful and what she dismisses no longer exists for her, including discipline, con-

---

* Her husband, Reynald, was, as I have suggested, as good as dead, somewhere in Nureddin's dungeons, yet not perhaps as dead as he might have wished. He had thought it a fine escapade during maneuvers to cross the border from Antiochene Syria into Aleppan territory and rustle a herd of cattle. He was caught by soldiers from a nearby garrison, who did not realize the size of their capture until they brought him before Majd ed-Din of Shaizar who sent at once for the Prince of Aleppo, long past wondering at Latin idiocies, but delighted with his prize, whom he promptly jailed for the next sixteen years. Baldwin, needless to say, was not so gallant as to ransom this detestable vassal, nor did Constance possess a love equal to the price, but oblivious of the rights of her son, Bohemond, by Raymond of Poitiers, assumed herself the regency, while her husband, perhaps longing for the cool mistral of his youth in the heat of Transjordan, may, at last, have come to comprehend the ominous warning of the *Sic Transit*. N.A.

tradiction, and unpleasant advice. It is always a pity to see cleverness
uncultivated become the dangerous illusion, and self-delusion, of intelligence.

From Tripolis, she wrote of Raymond's sister:

Melisande is of perfectly marriageable age and a jewel: lovely features
of the same, trembling doelike dignity as my mother-in-law, who is also
her aunt and namesake. She is intelligent, quiet, a faultless hostess in
her brother's behalf. She has a charming wit which is at once surprising
and a perfect antidote to her usual and, if the truth be known, sometimes cloying sweetness. It redeems her and gives her mystery, for
then you realize you haven't quite plumbed her depths. Unlike the Antiochene princesses who seem to have inherited their mother's eye for
men—and an impractical one at that—Melisande, whatever her inner
feelings, is impeccably decorous. She is one who recognizes her responsibilities, that her life is not her own and affection is irrelevant
in the choice of husband because her person is of political consequence
as shall be her marriage. If my opinion is of any note, uncle, this is the
one for you to marry, if marry you must.

                                    XX

Now the Seljuk campaign of 1160 was one of those dreadful ventures
so beloved of military advisers in the anticipation and so readily disowned by them when the Homeric sweep of conquest does not occur,
but rather the battle bogs down in a series of bloody and seemingly
pointless engagements, war as attrition, from tree to tree. Here was one
of those evils which both sides desire and both sides get, begun haphazardly and executed relentlessly—this time, for a year—in unremitting
carnage which left thousands dead and tactical advantages much the
same as before, all that was changed, the faces of conscriptees. Neither
side wished to begin as aggressor but both sides were eager to consummate in aggression. A dreadful little venture indeed, which ended in a
treaty of peace, and, by a subtle shift (nothing moves without consequence), unforeseen, sowed the disaster for a future time.

The Seljuks attacked Laodicea in late July on the pretext that the
city was harboring enemies of His Majesty, the Shah. In point of fact,
a score of Moslem brigands of no great threat to the royal government

had crossed into the Empire and asked for sanctuary at the nearest town. Iconium did not present extradition papers to the Magistrate of Laodicea, but peremptorily demanded the return of the robbers, loudly proclaiming His Imperial Majesty succored the greatest robbers ever to plague Iconium.* The city was attacked, ostensibly to regain the brigands. The signal to march in its defense was given to a suspiciously ready Imperial army, at St. George's Palace, Nicea, within three weeks. The war, with and without the Emperor's participation, continued for nearly ten months, concluded only when the inevitable enemy of the Seleucid Dynasty, the Danishmend Emirate, attacked Iconium's virtually undefended east flank.

In July 1161 the Shah sued Constantinople for peace, which Manuel relievedly and graciously accepted, straight in the face of a warning Andronikus had given him long ago: "Allow Arslan to destroy the Danishmends and you will have a unified Turk state, without distraction, against you." Happy as always to set a precedent, Manuel invited the Shah to Constantinople, where, for eighty days, the Emperor dazzled Kilij with tournaments, chariot races, a naval festival, and banquets. Spectacular generosity was the watchword. Twice a day food was brought to the visiting royal suite in gold and silver vessels which were not taken back to Blachernae's pantries but left to the guest's personal disposal. At one extraordinarily memorable dinner, the Emperor's arm swept across the golden banquet hall to include all the plates, vessels, and decorations of every manner tooled in precious metals and gems, with which he thereupon gifted the Sultan, who was understandably overwhelmed, though when he returned to Iconium, he told my father, "Well, well, it seems the greater the damage I inflict on his Empire, the more magnificently I am gifted by the Emperor."

The leave-taking of these two men, who were never to meet again though they would affect one another in untold ways, is interesting for the very future its earnestness contradicted. "I eagerly anticipated our coming together, and I am not disappointed," Manuel is recorded as saying. "My blessings, Sultan, on your house and your family." At which

---

* One of my earliest memories is Shah Kilij's youngest son, Prince Suleiman, the favorite of his grandfather, Mas'ud the Blessed, and like him a pacifist, saying to my father with droll irritation, "In heaven's name, if the Emperor really wanted to give sanctuary to the greatest robbers to plague our Kingdom, he'd want to begin with my father's Grand Vizier, not those Troglodytes at Laodicea." N.A.

the Sultan responded, "May we, Your Majesty, who have been previously unknown to one another, having met, hereafter accept between us that truth which is dear and treasured most in all men's hearts though they be strangers to one another: peace. God's will that it be so." Manuel tapped the King's hand, resting on his pommel, and staring meaningfully, said, "God's will we cannot presume to know. My own, I do, as I would hope you do your own. Therefore I say, *we* will peace or war."†

Six months previous to the farewell breakfast at which those words were spoken, Imperial ambassadors and Count Raymond III of Tripolis had concluded a betrothal for the hand of his sister, Princess Melisande. Implicitly, this was a complete victory for King Baldwin and Queen Theodora who had urged the match for several reasons. In the first, Tripolis was a more tractable vassal than Antioch and even more closely related by blood to the House of Lotharingen. In the second, Antioch was too controversial, if not unpredictable, swearing simultaneous allegiance to Jerusalem and Constantinople, which was not unprecedented legally, but certainly provocative. No less the usurpation of Bohemond III's rights by his mother made an already unstable political situation only more tottering still. The union of Tripolis with Byzantium was at once more serene and useful—especially since Tripolis had become the major trading center of Palestine.

Baldwin and Theodora contributed lavishly toward Melisande's trousseau and Raymond quite literally put his whole domain in mortgage to build and equip twelve galleys, their shells gilded from stem to stern, to transport his sister, as befitted an empress, to Constantinople.

Needless to say the Protovestarius was disgruntled. Many years later a

---

† Even more interesting is a conversation recorded later that day at a meeting of the Sacred Consistory to ratify the alliance with Iconium. John Sergius told his uncle, "He will turn on you in the first moment it most benefits him." Manuel said, "Odd, I rather had the impression you liked the King." "I do, uncle." "Then trust *my* trust because I think him an honorable politician and detest the rest of him." "As you say, uncle." But Manuel insisted on making his point clear. "Would you prefer war to diplomacy?" "I would prefer, Sire, the revenues of Lesser Asia. We cannot afford to be without her." "We cannot afford too much war, nephew, to live with her, if we must be elsewhere in the world. The provident man counts well lost what is lost if he can keep what else he owns. Pray God, we do the best we can." "I will pray to God indeed, but He does not very often speak in miracles." To which Manuel responded in a manner which might have pleased Andronikus: "Miracles are for children and the hopeless. I would hope we are neither." N.A.

courtier explained his displeasure. "The Protovestarius would have urged Andronikus in a wig to the nuptial altar, so long as the Queen of Jerusalem was against a marriage between Antioch and Byzantium." There is every possibility—and, of course, no evidence—John's creatures under his direct orders affected the following intrigue.

The barons of Antioch were, in any event, unhappy about Constance's assumption of the power in her son's name. Byzantine agents, therefore, on the one side convinced her generals to contest the Princess, while those at her court urged Constance in turn to seek the support of the Imperial throne, which she did. She sent an ambassador to Manuel offering to surrender Antioch to complete Imperial suzerainty, and her daughter, Maria, as well. (Hence, even if she lost to her vassals, she was protected as mother-in-law of an emperor.) In all, this disgusting example of cellar diplomacy worked—to the increased prestige, of course, of John Sergius. With unlikely callousness and predictable impracticality, the Emperor chose the expensive reclamation of Antioch to the fiscally beneficial alliance with Tripolis and Maria to Melisande, who before the world was humiliated by the annulment of her betrothal. *Explicit: Nicetas Acominatus.*

Accompanied by two scampering pages, the beautiful young Princess crosses the huge vaulted main corridor of the Palace of the Caesars at Antioch. She is highly flushed, and her small, but full bosom heaves against the gold whipcord of her V-necked, green velvet gown. She stops short—one page colliding with the other—when a plump woman, lifting her skirts, running along the hall calls softly but urgently.

LADY. Your Highness, Your Highness, *Your Highness!*

She arrives by Maria's side, takes the girl's hand, bethinks herself, and with a triumphant smirk—as though she had got the best of some unseen antagonist—curtsies with unusual grace for one so large.

LADY. Oh—madame—I have just this moment arrived and heard the news. Can it be? Our little Princess? An empress?

At this, even though she despises the woman, Maria's excitement rises to all-forgiving condescension. She offers her other hand in raising the older woman.

MARIA. Yes, it is true, Alais. And how kind of you to think of me.

Abruptly the Princess turns her back and trips on, leaving Lady Alais with her smiling lips half begun to form her next word. Like silt spilling in a relentless, elegant swirl through clear water, the woman's mouth curls into an ugly smirk of disapproval, then downright loathing such as many jealous matrons, from generation to generation, allow young girls, whose youth seems freer than their own, therefore more scandalous, when it is neither. Rather age and marriage have closed about the older women, and from a cage, even a slave seems free.

At the doors to her mother's apartments, Maria delays the guard with a graceful little gesture of her upraised hand, which, in the same motion, directs her pages to one side. She adjusts her hair and dress unnecessarily, then nods. The doors are opened. Within, the Bishop of Lattakieh and Constance are laughing with the sort of derisive look which indicates the expense of another man's reputation, or his dignity. His Excellency is a tall man, neither fat nor thin, only large and soft with a lifetime's escape from labor or athletic diversion. His face is schizoid: the lantern jaw and ascetic slash of lip suggesting cruelty, the eyes dark and very large, suggesting compassion. By this contradiction, he stares men into his confidence, and, afterward, manipulates them to his purpose. Constance is dressed in black velvet and wears a white silk tassled shawl, as close to a nun's garb as she prefers. For all her trials she has aged enviably well. Her disinterest in concealing her years has left her younger, on first impression, for not reminding others via cosmetics of the decline. Demurely, Maria curtsies before the Bishop. His eyes glisten. He is old enough to confuse lust with tenderness.

BISHOP. Soon, my daughter, it will be for me to bow myself before you.

Maria is at a loss how to answer.

CONSTANCE. That shall never be, Your Excellency. My child is a faithful daughter of the Church before whose priests she is but a humble lamb.

Constance brushes back her daughter's hair from either side of the middle part, then places the back of her hand against the girl's forehead. In unutterable glee, Maria takes the hand and kisses its palm rapturously.

MARIA. Think! Oh, I am to be Empress!

The Bishop of Lattakieh frowns, not harshly, but quite touched.

BISHOP. Listen to me, madame. It is an honor and a glory beyond anyone's dreams to be raised to the Roman Imperial throne. But I must warn you. You are being given over to the most immoral, mendacious, unscrupulous society on earth. I beg you, Your Highness: restrain yourself. Give yourself to no one.

MARIA. Your Excellency, don't you want me to be happy?

BISHOP. Only more careful, my dear.

Incipit: Nicetas Acominatus: Queen Theodora, on learning of the nullification of the betrothal, traveled at once from Jerusalem to Mt. Pelerinage Castle, to console Melisande. To her husband, she wrote:

It is all very ghastly here. Raymond is simply transformed. That wide, flat, likable face, which I'm told so much resembles the face of your grandfather, Philip of France, is unrecognizable. I'd often thought it a literary convention that one's features could be "twisted with hate." It is not. There is no more of sweet irony in the eyes, and his kind mouth pouts. Raymond was never handsome to begin with, and I find him now even a little repellent. Melisande looks ravishing: pale, trembling, thinner than ever, miserable, exquisite. You know, of course, *he* means to use his golden galleys against Cyprus in retaliation for the superseding of their original use. If you cannot stop him, I really wish you would disassociate yourself from him and from this venture as loudly as possible. Both your cousins love one another dearly, but I'm afraid Raymond's revenge will alienate Melisande. This afternoon, even in my presence, they argued. She said to him, "You must not do this; do nothing, leave me be." He protested he could not. "Not like this." She said, "There is nothing you, or anyone else, can do for me. What you *intend* to do has *nothing* to do with consoling me. It shall only pronounce more clearly my humiliation, the extent of my shame swelled by the size of your anger." He was like a boy. "My shame, too." "No one is thinking of that, Raymond." She said this as harshly as I've ever known her to speak. Then she became soft again. "I only want to forgive." He said, "If that is what you want, it concerns your own heart which is beyond argument or reproach. We will honor you the more for it. As your brother, I would follow you. As Count of Tripolis I hold that man at Constantinople in perfidy." And then he stared bluntly at me, waiting for a defense of the Emperor. Melisande said, "What will it matter to Theodora's uncle if you do not forgive him? How could you repay him his scorn of me save by giving him the wit to know his own iniquity? Even if you could repay him in kind, what would that serve, but to give him the rights of a victim and you, in turn, the fear of a mean man's fate.

Oh, Raymond, if we could only see the beam in our own eye. I told you: I want only to forgive. It is not easy for me, but I want to forgive. I have no other alternative." But she does not really want to forgive. She is only beaten. Yet her despair takes her upon a course wiser—and with more dignity—than she knows.

So golden war galleys, re-outfitted with battering rams, catapults, and heliopolises, appeared in a shapeless blaze of light beneath the high sun of Cyprus. Witnesses tell us the gilding was not very seaworthy, but blistered from the wooden hull, and in large, glittering flakes left a fabulous, unlikely trail from Tripolis to Famagusta. *Explicit: Nicetas Acominatus.*

Beside Manuel, who wears the Imperial tiara and divitavisson, holding orb and scepter—herself wrapped in her coronation cloak, heavily trimmed with jewels and holding steadily two honey-colored candles— Maria rides horse across the crowded Augusteum. The first stages of the procession from Holy Wisdom glitter with gold: gold-decked capes of the Senators, the gold breastplates, helmets, and spearpoints of the Varangians, the gold casskins of the patriciate, the gold stoas of the ladies-in-waiting. Next follow the ministers of state wearing mauve and pink chalmys, then eunuchs in white silk and palace officials in sky-blue robes. The Emperor, the Empress, the Sebastocrator—the Sebastocratrix is absent at Jerusalem—all the Grand Dukes and Duchesses, pass between lines of pages—two thousand of them—in blue and green and yellow brocade, stationed so as to lead directly into the inner propylea of the Hippodrome and the silver doors of the Imperial kathisma. At the threshold the young Empress makes a genuflection before an elaborate cross held by the Patriarch, then kneels with the Emperor and— after both are blessed with holy water—kisses the Virgin Icon of Blachernae. Slowly she regains her erect posture, her hand resting lightly on the Grand Duke John Sergius' arm as she does so. She tosses back her head so that her emerald and pearl earrings and the diamond and pearl pendulars of her crown tinkle and glint. Now on Manuel's arm, she passes up the stairs of the kathisma, preceding the Imperial family. They cross the reception room—its walls pastel murals against gold, the floor covered with carpets of exuberant color, bowls of hyacinths and roses everywhere. The doors, of ivory and gold, leading directly to the Imperial box, are opened. The roar of assembled Constantinopolitans

*reaches the party with physical impact. Maria winces. With an encourag-
ing smile Manuel guides his new wife forward and down the flight of
stairs. Pandemonium is greater than ever, while the herald uselessly
bellows the official acclamation.*

HERALD. Glory of the Purple, Delight of the World. Hail: Chosen of
God. Welcome. Protected by God, Greetings; Basilissa, Empress, Des-
poina, Autocratrix, who has embraced Orthodoxy and will be called
Xenia Augusta.

*The standards of the Empire are brought forward in the arena below
by one hundred horsemen. They are waved sinuously, left to right, then
lowered to salute the new Empress.*

Incipit: Nicetas Acominatus: The chic, more vicious—that is, the
younger—matrons of Constantinopolitan society, with their millennia
pedigree (which, as Manuel angrily pointed out, "promises absolute
quality in dogs and absolutely *nothing* in a man—or a woman"), liked
to say the daughter of "the Guiscard parvenus" arrived at Blachernae
with a single change of underwear. This might have hyperbolic reference to the speed and controversy surrounding her abrupt betrothal.
Probably it was meant more personally and unkindly. But it was an
imputation which adhered to Her Majesty's reputation, as did any word
about her, for her or against her, in jest, malice, or flattery.

The Latin Aphrodite, as she was called by her worshipers, was one of
those extraordinarily glamorous women who, even as a maiden, could
not help but attract adulation bordering on fanaticism from those genuinely awed by her beauty or those wishing to partake in her celebrity by
championing her—with the suggestion of real or pretended intimacy—
and, on the other hand, drawing haphazardly against herself critics
whose very violence suggested something deeper than aesthetic, social,
or intellectual proportion. In the end her athletes increased their devotion—and her critics became more shrill—so that fair judgment became
impossible. It became a war to the death, both sides attempting to reach
and convert one another from rank apostasy. In the end there was no
longer a possibility of reaching a compromise—i.e., a measured verdict
upon the actual human being—since one was obliged to accept her as a
paragon or a Jezebel and pursuant, follow for or against her, with complementary political stands.

I do not pretend to intimacy with, or, for that matter, dislike of, the

Empress. Our relations were always cordial. As one, if I may say, whose vanity, since childhood, has prevented him from joining crowds of one persuasion or another (which Andronikus sometimes mischievously suggested—though for all I know, he may have been correct—is my only qualification as a historian) I would like to attempt some sort of balanced portrait.

For one thing, it is useless to compare Maria-Xenia to Theodora, though everyone—save Andronikus but including Theodora—found it diverting to do so. In fact, the two women could not have been more unalike. They both achieved legend, but even their paths to that questionable elevation could not have been at greater antipodes. Maria's beauty was fair and classical, usual only insofar as it conformed to the standards of the day and nearly stood absolute, apart from the personality. Theodora's beauty, on the other hand, was dark, asymmetrical, if it was beauty at all, in need of all her inner fires—and they were numerous—to ignite it, leading Andronikus to remark once, with much impropriety, "The Queen, asleep, is very ordinary looking, if not downright unbecoming, save for her hair." Maria's intellect was limited. Theodora's was sharp—and hard—as steel. Maria was responsive to any affection, quickly extending an almost smothering friendship which, if not returned in kind and degree, became irrevocable indifference. Theodora was, by miles, unapproachable. In her person were the inheritable arrogance of the Comneni and the wariness of a dynast burnt once too often by affection which, in the end, wanted only favor. Maria-Xenia was blind to any situation which was not placed directly in her line of sight. Theodora was a busybody before she began her alliance with Andronikus, and thereafter suffered her imagination to be extended by her lover. Maria-Xenia needed the constant attendance of maids, advisers, counselors, friends, taking a great delight in being cared for. Theodora could fend for herself, often preferred it so, and brooked no contest once she was decided. Maria insisted on her way as a child insists: she would charm, and when charm failed, she icily demanded; but she was without any malice whatsoever, vengeance or grudges. Theodora more than was necessary dictated when she might have seduced, and she never forgot her enemies. (Then again, hers was not merely charm, when she chose to display it, but some incandescent effusion of personality; and when she forgave—usually by a deathbed—she was an angel of solicitousness, leading Andronikus, once, to remark, "I'm afraid her harried enemies, or those simply brokenhearted, rush their own deaths to feel again the touch of her remorseless hand.") In sum, Maria's legend is passive and at last, pathetic. Theodora's was of her own making and thereby, at the end, celebrated both adventure and tragedy. "The difference," said her son, Prince Christopher, "is not that Maria-Xenia was a cow and my mother a lioness, but that Her Imperial Majesty was raised in the tradition of Latin Mariolatry, and Her Royal Majesty in the tradition of Antigone."

For twenty years, Maria-Xenia, helpless and beguiling, lived at the center of storms, miraculously unscathed, until, finally, inevitably, the power which raised the fury and deflected it from her person fell into her hands to manage as best she could, become like the nectar which attracted the wasps to Patriarch Aimery.

Yet, as any legend would have it, what ended in darkness began in light. If the Emperor's love for his new wife could be measured by his lavishness, then it was all-consuming, and, it may be said, the majority of the people were as infatuated with their new Basilissa as their Emperor. All men respected the memory of the new St. Irene (as she was already esteemed by the laity), but what was that stiff, painfully shy, duller-by-the-year woman—no matter her goodness—beside this raving beauty who fed on pleasure and applause as bees feed on flowers? It was high time the family, whose eye for mistresses was incomparable, break its long-standing tradition of crowning pious dullards and commemorate revivified Byzantium with a commensurately spectacular empress.

Maria-Xenia was that, with a vengeance. In the first great rush of her popularity, one noticed admiringly, rather than resentfully, her uncanny pleasure in personal adornment—jewelry by the tubful and daily commissions to the Imperial tailors. She was a wretched organizer but a splendid hostess as she had merely to *be*. She was the first Comnenus Empress in over eighty years to take not even a semblance of interest in charitable work, but again, in the beginning, this was put down to her unfamiliarity, which, in time, would assuredly vanish. (It was forgot Manuel's canonized mother virtually on arrival assisted in the establishment of Orphanotropolis.) New villas and palaces began to rise with alarming frequency far from Constantinople, involving the requisition of construction corps from throughout the provinces and the capital, gorgeous mansions, occupied perhaps a week or a month and then abandoned to other members of the Imperial family (who called the buildings "Xenia's Crumbs"). Even John Sergius, the instigator of this marriage, two years after the nuptials was heard to say to a courtier, "She's a vulture disguised as a bird of paradise," and himself began to be unexpectedly cool to her, warning his wife, the Grand Duchess Nina, to do likewise.

Palestine, meanwhile, was violently shaken by this alliance. One wonders the admiration Cypriots felt for Xenia when, in retaliation for his sister's humiliation (Melisande took the veil in February 1162), Raymond ransacked what remained of the east end of the island with that unlikely gold armada. In Antioch the elevation of its Princess to the oldest most august throne in Europe did not allay the troubled political situation but exacerbated it. When Maria left for Constantinople in late October 1162, the possibility of complete Greek hegemony seemed real and, what's more, unsated. Therefore Baldwin, who had regarded Manuel unkindly enough since Shaizar and with a completely cold eye since the jilting of Melisande, took horse, with a small escort, the more than three hundred miles to Antioch.

In the capital of Latin Syria, he met with Constance's barons for more than two days, following an ostentatiously brief interview with his cousin. When he emerged from the parley, he exerted his rights as liege lord and presented Constance with this ultimatum: she was to renounce her Regency in favor of another until Bohemond III could assume his responsibility. The eminence to take her place was none other than the Latin Patriarch Aimery of Limoges, who had obviously spent his exile to good effect. When Constance ironically protested her son was, indeed, in his majority, Baldwin probably smiled returning cynicism for cynicism, as the mother's argument confessed her own illegality. Bohemond was too much Constance's son, and in this perilous time, the King wished a more trustworthy—which is to say, anti-Greek—agent guiding the destinies of Antioch. If the Princess did not step down and retire with an annuity—and all honors, of course—to her estates, with her remaining children if she liked (a mistake, and a gross one, as she retributively turned them into Grecophiles one and all), Baldwin stressed that he could not otherwise be responsible for her person. With this implicit threat of harm—not by the King, personally, but rather his promise not to lift a finger if her barons decided assassination was the only solution—Constance abdicated, never again to regain her power.

She died three years later, a month after Melisande of Tripolis and a few months before her son's revenge.

The King remained at Antioch another month. On 29 January he started back for Jerusalem, as one of his courtiers described it, "in the best of spirits, like a boy again, even turning the escort into a hunting party when the mood took and the game passed by." One may surmise, however, the King's cheer was less a return to childhood than the elation of a man, who had arrived at full responsibility and found it not burdensome, but good. In the years since his accession, this Prince, who began by winning more plaudits for his smile than his ingenuity, had assumed the destiny of the principates—endeared and obeyed—and become a man of some independence, subtlety, and force. He was generous in praise of his Queen, whose intelligence—if not her rather off-handed affection—sustained and emboldened him. "She is my eyes and my ears, all I say and do, the premise of my goodness and my logic," he had said the year before. Yet as many men under the same conditions and even such a benign influence might have become puppets. It was Baldwin's achievement to translate his Queen's almost abrasively realistic insight into firm but gentle policy which kept the barons of the land in check without arousing pernicious resentment. His Queen, knowing her own genius and its influence upon her husband, was not wrong in the estimation of Baldwin as one incapable of true growth. That is unfortunately true. Rather she neglected to add in his behalf that with the proper guidance he remained an intercessor—between the idea and the act—of unsurpassed energy, integrity, and charm. Among warring parties, the agent of compromise may be more crucial than its architect.

When Baldwin died, then, of a heart attack, at Beirut, 7 February 1162, the loss was acute and irreplaceable. The Kingdom might survive, but that rare combination of pride and love and confidence in the King was gone, and with it, the rare and peculiar unity which sometimes occurs between all members of a state, from courtier to beggar, when no fellow and no caste seems imposed upon the other. All decent well-being symbolized in the measure of one man had vanished with his death.

Theodora: "I remember just before he left for Antioch, he came to my chambers and we talked in the usual way of a man and wife before separation: half-sentences, incomplete thoughts, indifferent things which needed only a few words or perhaps no more than a consenting glance.

"We're born to our homes, or married to them, which become part of us. Yes, we dream of the variety of adventure, which is the departure of the norm beyond our doors. But it is also the unknown. What is out of the ordinary tests us—the whole meaning of adventure—and every test carries with it the possibility of death. Therefore every good-by—no matter how indifferent the errand—is an intimation of death. The King was very sensitive to this, though, I suspect, he could scarcely articulate it. He merely called it his superstition. He never used the term 'farewell' or 'good-by' or even 'adieu.' Always, 'God willing, soon,' or 'Write to me at such-and-such a city.' Because those terms troubled him, I never used them, and, I suppose, myself became superstitious.

"At the doors to my suite that last day, he seemed loath to go. I remember, he had the flat of his hand—like this—along the edge of the door, and between conversation he would stare at it, and say, 'Well,' and clear his throat. Now, I am not a demonstrative person. I don't know why. I feel deeply, I know I do, but I really can't show it, unlike Andronikus. Not that I'm contemptuous of emotional gestures in others— from those I love, I welcome it—but they seem to me, especially if in distress, a protest against the inevitable. Usually, if the situation is too fraught for my taste, I insist on saying something sharp or, I will admit, tastelessly light, which invariably shocks the person opposite me and no doubt makes them think me cold, unfeeling. But at least it takes us from beneath the weight of the moment which is oppressive.

"Well, the King delayed, and the foreboding grew worse, so that finally I said, stupidly, with a half smile, 'What on earth *are* you waiting for? There's no lover in the cabinet now, and none shall pop back in when you return.' He stared at me with a look of sadness, even disaffection, smiled woefully, slapped the panel, and gently under his breath, said very quickly, 'Yes, well, good-by,' and left the door croaking like an alarm on its hinges.

"My heart turned to ice. I wanted to go to him, but I thought that should make matters worse. I saw him along the corridor, taking warm leave of my mother, who was blessing him with an icon. I ran to the little chapel which I had dedicated to my grandmother, but I felt it was too late. The curse had been applied. Of course, after a few days the incident was forgotten, and after a month, dismissed entirely.

"We exchanged letters, my first to him, of a rapturous Christmas at

Bethlehem, his first that he missed me more than he thought possible—which finally, for me, forgave my horrid quip that last day. It was the most intense correspondence, fittingly, on which we had engaged in the years of our marriage—some of it charming, some of political matters. I was even pleased to tell him that Lady Henrietta, his mistress, had given birth to a daughter, whom she was wont to call Margaret. To write those words in passing fashion took very much out of me, since I was certain, as were many others, though I never brought it to His Majesty's attention, Henrietta had been complicit with our sister-in-law, Almaric's wife, that detestable little strumpet, Agnes of Courtenay, in murdering my son, stillborn, supposedly, the previous year. But I was determined not to trouble the King, and I knew Margaret's birth would please him.

"In my last letter I remember writing, 'On your arrival, I shall have a surprise, a great one, for you.' My husband, you see, was an ardent student of poetry, and for the past year I had been in contact with Queen Eleanor of England, who had promised to send me a sufficient number of troubadours to hold a tournament in competition with our own, my husband as arbiter. The Aquitanians had arrived while His Majesty was gone, and I was having great fun playing the flirt to their flattery. On the morning of 9 February, I remember, I was sitting in the garden with my appointments secretary, when Count Humphrey came running down the stairs, stopped at the landing, leaned over the balustrade, and simply stared at me.

"I found my words fading and my body rising almost of its own will. He came down the last stairs and walked up to me in a curious way, hunched forward, his hands folded over one another. Then he kneeled and kissed my hand. I recall thinking, in Greek, how beautifully the folds of his robe trailed behind him on the grass, while he spoke, in French, but so garbled I scarcely caught his words. I heard snatches of phrases, something 'terrible duty,' something 'inform you,' something, something, and then the unmistakable *mort*. I looked at him stupidly, straight in the eye, and said, 'What did you say?' And he burst into tears, pulled on my hand like a dog, and said, 'Queen, the King is dead,' and in a trice my life was changed forever. Or rather it had changed long before, and I knew only now, having lived complacently in the wreckage of my own destiny for two days."

Like her great-great-grandmother Anna Dalassena, on her way to her dying son Manuel at Heraclea Pontica nearly a hundred years before, the Queen thought nothing of riding without stop the 150 miles to Beirut, accompanied by Count Humphrey and a score of soldiers.

Seventeen years later, he told me, "It was the eeriest homage ever paid a dead man. As Her Majesty's ride became known, we were followed by more and more horsemen—I don't know where they came from—by hundreds, thousands, perhaps, all led by this beautiful, resolute, absolutely silent creature, robes and hair flying, caked with dust. The sound of our passing, and the feel of it, was like an earthquake. Perhaps it was the Queen's way of purging herself of grief. In that, she is very French—or very Greek—or we are not so unalike.

"We arrived at Beirut at dawn, 11 February, and she went straight to the cathedral, to the King's bier, his body having already been eviscerated, embalmed, and sealed into lead. You know what that infernal climate does to a corpse. Well, Her Majesty ordered the lead seal broken. When I made the move to leave—I have little stomach for cadavers, save fresh on a battlefield—she said, 'No. Stay,' and took my hand. I knew she was reverting to her Greek customs and I did not want to see it. The coffin was opened. The stench was indescribable. What seemed most awful to me, I don't know why, was the white silk band which secured his chin and was tied at the top of his head. I tried to reconcile this putrescent object with the naked, golden, shimmering young King I had seen emerge from a swim in the river Jordan only a few months before. It was appalling. But the Queen, undaunted, kissed the dead man's lips—or what was left of them—and hands and whispered something at a high pitch over and over again. I made move closer, to hear, but one of the barons, quite awed, drew me back. I saw her pull something from her neck. I heard the snap of a chain. Why she did not lift the object over her head, I cannot say. I think she wanted to feel pain. She placed the object in his hands, kissed the King once again, left the dais, and walked blindly away, as stone, till some of us came up to guide her.

"The journey back to Jerusalem took seventeen days, a Requiem at every church. The crush of the common people was unbelievable. One day we considered ourselves fortunate to have made ten miles. Moslems descended from mountains and added their keening to this incredible display of grief. And no one, Count, who saw the Queen in that time, boldly unveiled, mounted by the side of the bier, shall ever forget her."

It was at this time, Nureddin's generals urged him to undertake a major effort against the Latin Principate. The Moslem Prince decisively refused. "It is not my policy," he said, "to take the ax after men blinded by tears. I leave that infamy to Christians." Something, moreover, in Baldwin's just and angelic reputation struck a cord in this normally insouciant Prince, who sent a letter of condolence to Theodora, which, adjured, in part, if "the Dearest and Most Worthy Queen of Jerusalem" were ever in need of aid, she had but to alert the nearest Mosul agent or ambassador, who would, in turn, communicate her wishes, at once, to the Prince. "I promise you, madame, this is not idle consolation, but an oath I have taken in the name of Allah to become your protector."‡

Not a few colleagues and courtiers at Jerusalem and Constantinople have suggested, by this promise, it was Nureddin's devious intention to win a "client" at Jerusalem or, possibly, an ear at Constantinople. I fear, then, these cynics underestimate Theodora's grief and, curiously, her disinterest in power, almost her fear of it, without the mooring of her tempestuous nature and companionship for the loneliness of a singular intellect, which only a faithful lover could provide. They also underestimate the nature of Baldwin's successor, whose subtleties his sister-in-law knew, the low susceptibility of the Imperium (if the Imperium was John Sergius) toward the Queen's advice, and, finally, the sincerity and sympathy of Moslems before all bereaved—no less one so lovely and courageous—and their respect for an honorable enemy.

There is no doubt Nureddin was a religious fanatic, but fanaticism—here, at least—works both ways. Just as in war the Prince would not hesitate to convert ten thousand Christians to Islam—or condemn them to death—just as he did not hesitate to roast Moslem heretics in spectacular autos-da-fé, then, whenever his propagation of Islam was not affected, or the purity of the faith directly threatened, he was free to practice its most pious and charitable aspects. Nothing proves the man's word more certain than the sanctuary he extended to Andronikus and Theodora five years later.

‡ I am told there was some controversy at the Mosul court averse which language to address the letter, a subtle but telling point. Arabic, it was felt, would suggest either arrogance or ignorance, i.e., a lack of civilizing social intercourse, besides seeming ungracious. Greek would place too much emphasis on the Queen's origins rather than her present station. Latin was the Lingua Franca and standard for official communiqués, but this called for something more intimate while at the same time recognizing Her Majesty's role as Dowager Queen. The above excerpt, then, is translated from the French, the language of the Jerusalem court. N.A.

Shortly after the obsequies at Jerusalem, to everyone's surprise—and grudging shame, for they had been prepared to resent her presumed bid for power after consoling her—Theodora retired to her dower city of Acre and that Cyclopean castle fortress, whose walls are the only rival of Constantinople's in the world. The Queen's seclusion and, thereby, her refusal to return to Byzantium, was less surprising than at first it would seem. According to canon and state law she was the anointed dowager wherever she lived, so long as she did not take another husband. But at the Imperial capital, the sense of failure—returned a childless widow of no diplomatic account—would have been acute, if not oppressive. She would have had to live in a court dominated by Maria-Xenia, of whom she disapproved, if not downright disliked (Melisande's heartbreak was, for her, an irrevocable grief), and endured the malicious condescension of John Sergius.

Here, in the Kingdom of Jerusalem, she was beloved, respected, and unique, and here she would stay. She wrote to her sister Maria, Princess Boris of Hungary:

> These people are something less than the last word in civilized finesse, but they are eager, brave, ingenious, gallant, and kind, and I have a real bond with them through Baldwin's life and death. There is not the variety of experience and intellect here, as at Constantinople—or even Stuhlweissenburg—yet, can you understand, here my life has more meaning than at Constantinople, which I miss all the same? I would not presume to interfere with my brother-in-law's regency, but perhaps in some small way, if only tacitly, I can see to it Baldwin's course is followed. How terrible it is to discover so late how deeply I loved him, as a friend and a husband. God, how it makes me sick to think of his beauty festering in a stone vault. I eat very little these days. Food makes me think too much of death. I walk a great deal along the sea by my palace. I'm afraid I tire my poor ladies overmuch.

So long as she remained in the Kingdom, devoted to her husband's memory, she retained the goodwill and the benefits—the awe, even—of that legend. She was the living reminder of a beauty of state now beyond recapture. Once she had declared herself beyond the interests of politics—which is only improvisation and mundane—there was absolutely no reservation in the adoration accorded her. At times it bordered on the blasphemous and then again the morbid. But even King Almaric, who, at first, as was likely to his nature, suspected his sister-in-law, at last consented to the possibility, her love of power could not be divorced from the love of his brother, and revered her—or, knowing the man, thought it politically prudent to do so.

It is indeed likely had not Andronikus, as he himself put it, "wrenched her from that necrophile melodrama being played out on the shores of Palestine," Theodora, by virtue of her enormous personal prestige, would have once again become political, if only to be opportuned for her imprimatur upon any later regime. Instead, by the year 1166, the empty immense fortress-castle of Acre stood beneath the incandescent silver sun as the final, mute reminder of the years of Baldwin and Theodora, perfect for having been so brief, more lustrous in its silence from the turmoil of the distance.

XXI

Baldwin was all a king ought to seem. Almaric was all Baldwin was not: obese, ambitious, cunning, autocratic, cynical, and illiterate—or nearly. Here is a very good example of what occurs when a king dies without issue and a younger member of the family, in no way prepared for the throne or ingratiated with his nobility (who were to become antagonized when he treated them as an irrelevance), accedes to the throne.

It is not too much to say a crisis took place at Jerusalem. For a month the barons were loath to swear fealty to Almaric, a hesitation the King never forgot. While Count Humphrey served as president of the Accession Council and virtual ruler of the Kingdom, both the Constable and Theodora, sometimes in unaccustomed tears, pleaded with the nobility to acclaim their new King.

Theodora: "A month after my husband's sepulture, I took aside Hugh of Ibelin and begged him to pledge his fealty to Almaric. 'For Baldwin,' I said, 'and to indulge me.' He said, 'Madame, how can you ask us, who love you and would die for you, to become the liegemen of such a woman as the Lady Agnes? Do you hold our affection so feckless and general, you believe we could give it in the same kind and degree to that base whore?' Perhaps in the emotion of the moment, the barons truly believed their excuse, and I, a stranger, was, of course, flattered. Yet I know, more deeply, they dreaded the future in the knowledge Almaric was less tractable than Baldwin. Of course, they did not realize by concerting against his accession, which was always quite likely, they were hardening my brother-in-law still more against themselves."

Finally, in late March, the strangest document an heir ever received was presented to the King for signature. In it, he was instructed, previous to his coronation, to divorce his wife, Agnes of Courtenay, the daughter of the ill-fated Joscelin II. The motives of the barons were deeper than even Theodora imagined, deeper than disapproval of Agnes' vicious behavior, her intrigues and sexual notoriety. Her brother was Joscelin III, Titular 4th Count of Edessa, who had never forgiven the barons' reluctance to save his patrimony.

Nothing loath to repudiate his wife in order to gain the throne, Almaric sent a bill of divorcement on grounds of consanguinity (their grandfathers were first cousins) to Alexander III, who, against his better judgment, annulled the marriage to avert a civil war (with which threat the King, already seeming too resourceful for comfort, had instructed his ambassador to alarm the Pope). In truth, Almaric was relieved to be rid of Agnes. The barons could not have taken him on a more malleable point, if it had been their attempt, by this, to stop him short of his honor, of which he had none to maintain. Agnes had been forced upon him by his mother, who, to her surprise, but consistent with the character of the emerging King, found herself even less consulted than in her eldest son's reign. Bluntly put, Agnes repelled her husband. (Nevertheless, the new King did not like to be told what to do and three years later found the means of inflicting this alarming woman on the ringleader of the recalcitrants, Hugh of Ibelin.) With a real flair for cruelty, Almaric removed from his wife her one pretense to commendability, the children she loved. Baldwin, the Heir Apparent, received what his father had not, a crown prince's tutelage. Princess Sybil went off to be raised by her grandaunt, Joveta, Abbess of the Convent of St. Lazarus in Bethany.

Seated on his throne, guaranteed of allegiance, Almaric sent a letter to Manuel suggesting they meet at some later date to discuss the most dazzling possibility of the day: the conquest of Egypt.

It is interesting to watch the progress of this idea, from incredulity to conviction, as expressed in Manuel's letters to Henry of England, from casual mention of the political situation at Cairo, where, as Almaric has said, "The Fatimites are rotting on the branch and filling the miles around with their enticing stench," to the Emperor's ultimate dreams of a new dynasty at Cairo, even a Christian one. While the Prince of Aleppo and the King of Jerusalem parried round one another in an effort to reach the Nile, like one man attempting to prevent the other from entering a room, Manuel, with an eye to a new Rex Aegypticae, convoked a synod of all patriarchs and metropolitans and commanded them remove the anathema from Allah. (The bishops knew the Emperor's intentions were not entirely matters of tolerance. They failed to realize they were not entirely self-aggrandizing either. While the Eminences hesitated to call His Majesty a heretic, they refused him his "request.")

One evening, shortly before his death, the Protovestarius, with uncharacteristic irony, told me: "At the beginning of 1163, His Majesty had thoughts of sending me to Egypt, if you please, as the successor to the Ptolemies. He foresaw, if he gained that land, removing the capital from Moslem Cairo to ancient, and Greek, Alexandria, where, of course, we still appoint the Patriarch. Sometimes he talked of treating Egypt as the prelude to assumption of the Imperial throne. That is, the Crown Prince, at birth, would become King of Egypt, its real ruler till his majority, in the creation of a new office: the Grand Regent." The Protovestarius shook his head and laughed softly, following with his unpleasantly affected boyish smile. "Later, before he joined Almaric, even that unlikely dyarchy had swelled—or diminished, as you will—to a Greek autocracy from Russia to Ethiopia."

Onto the scent of war in Egypt's entrails, the Emperor began rebuilding the armies he had disbanded after his smashing, bloodless triumphs of 1158–59. Our land magnates, however, were not so willing to offer their men or beat unwilling conscriptees from the peasants' huts. Manuel had become too public and too personal in his ambitions. They were no longer historically founded (Antioch) or defensive (the flint of a common border with Iconium), but vainglorious, if not megalomanic, which is to say without urgency save to their architect. Assistance was therefore negotiable. Meeting in Consistory at Ephesus—and including in their number civilian aristocrats and members of the Senate—the archons "respectfully" suggested the Emperor "exhibit some measure of concern" over the mounting confusion taking place in the Government Land Office. This was a euphemistic demand that Autocratic Majesty put a stop to the purchase of Imperial land grants by a prospering merchant class, on the one hand, or outright settlement of peasants—gratis, their tenancy paid for by the State Treasury—on the other.

> The result of this situation, Divinity, is perilous. Merchants who cannot tell a hoe from a scythe or a spear from a shortsword, buy up the countryside for the vanity of owning it, and thereafter leave it indifferently fallow. At the same time, peasant proprietors and their plots and free villages make the organization of state defense nearly impossible. Whether they are misled by troublemakers or simply challenge the Princes, Dukes, and Counts they formerly served in a conspicuous exhibition of independence, they seriously affect the integrity of provincial government. Your Majesty's intentions are, as always, noble, and, in theory, attractive: the greater number of your subjects who own the land, the more willing participation the previously dispossessed or indebted will show in the state. In fact, what has happened is quite the opposite. Each man is a little king with the consequent anarchy of too many kingdoms and too many disparate ambitions, no less the prevailing suspicion (among the lowest orders especially) any sacrifice is not in their own behalf but to their neighbors' advantage. The Empire, to use an analogy, instead of preserving the unity of the whole egg, is disintegrating into the thousand separate chips of a broken shell.*

Manuel took the declaration for what it was: an ultimatum. He proceeded to commit what Andronikus later called "one of the most crucial and invidious acts of his reign." On 8 February 1163, an Imperial chrysobull was promulgated in which "We, Manuel, Autocrat of the Romans, have found it good to prohibit to any citizens but those of senatorial or military rank (civilian aristocrats and archons) the right of transfer of any immovable property." In this dull legal phrase was the most spectacular example of imperially sponsored recidivism since Basil I's nullification of the Isaurian legal codes. The law was retroactive to the accession of the present Emperor, which is to say, to that period of splendid prosperity engendered by the economies of Alexius and, more especially, John Augustus, when so many men who had not hoped to own even so much as their graves—or therein, only, to find release from debt—suddenly aspired to be gentry, farmers, or free. Be-

---

* This analogy, by the way, announced the authorship of the document as none other than Theodore Prodromus, who, by now, was growing dizzy with distraction between adulation in the halls of the great—on recommendation of their wives—and adoration at the feet of the new Empress. Tetzes: "Appetite for his swill is born of bad taste made for him in heaven." N.A.

cause the Emperor did not concomitantly place a moratorium on the continued issuance of land grants, the gross enlargement of aristocratic domains continued.

A week after promulgation, Andronikus wrote a letter to Manuel. Here it is, in full:

My dear Manuel. In your latest chrysobull, I am moved to warn you, you have, with a stroke of the pen joined this great Empire—with its immeasurable capacity for good—to the dark forces of the world. We are now oppressors in fact as well as principle. The Latins have their serfs, the Moslems their slaves, and we, something more sinister still: an ostensibly free, in fact, legalized and perpetual downtrodden. They will be consumed for sure now by your aristocratic carnivores, who, one day, I promise you, will come back, hungrier than ever, in turn to rend you. You believe, by this, you have strengthened the Imperium. You have removed its foundation. You have a price, and when next you wish the armies or monies of our great dukes they will have new demands. You have set in motion again the very decentralization which Grandfather took the throne to prevent—and of which his rise was a symptom.

But this does not concern me. Imperial government as it is now constituted is a looting party. What you have at last removed from its recommendation is the remotest semblance of compassion. We who are the oldest nation in Europe, who could have benefited from our maturity to practice greatness of heart, to rise from the desuetude of superstition of bloods and gods by which a few men are pampered and most men trudge, now fall back, decadent. We regress. We are fit for barbarians again. And we have not even the excuse of senility, not so long as one man thinks as I do.

All men know the truth—even if they deny it—or there would not be guilt. They see all the colors of the human spirit, not the few to which their place in life, their birth, their training, make them apt. You see what I see, Manuel—I think too much of you to believe otherwise—but you convince yourself against all that is humane within you, all is as it must be. This is cruelty all the more insufferable, as you do not mean to be cruel, unless, that is, you have altered more than it is possible for me to imagine in the nine years since we have seen one another. I know, too, what you will say of this letter—or rather, how you will treat it, with derision, as the thoughts of a madman or a political ignoramus.

But that is no answer. I am reminded of a sermon Augustine of Hippo once gave on the creation of the world. A man interrupted him, saying: "This is all very well, sir. You have told us God created heaven and earth and that He is immortal without beginning or end. May we ask, then, what God was doing before He created heaven and earth?" At which the Great Doctor replied—or, probably, snapped—"He was creating hell for people who ask that sort of question." I can well imagine the fury and silence in the mind of that one questioner, whilst numberless faces—especially the women's—already contorted with the intolerance of prejudgment and a predisposal to believe what they are told—turned to him with a look of triumph. And I can imagine one other mind somewhat troubled as well—Augustine's. For you and I know, don't we, from his own writings (*verba volant, scripta manent*) how troubled he was by similar questions. Certainty is a public and general standard and rare in a closet.

I neither congratulate myself nor any longer question my right to deny the state as it is now maintained. To be universally contrary requires, it is true, a terrible faith in one's deductions. But to deny those conclusions is to deny oneself, which is hell in its purest form. If I have no other choice left to me but this, it is that I need not lie to myself.

I fear, Manuel, your ambitions and your success are rather like the setting sun which swells as it falls, while its light becomes attenuated. Grandfather became the first Roman Emperor to institute legislation in behalf of the treatment and sale of slaves, and with your father established Orphanotropolis. Your father reinstituted, for the first time in centuries, the sale of crown lands to the poor. Is it not to the point they considered these accomplishments among their proudest? My dear friend, have you so lost all sense of yourself that you can only be defined by the mere aggrandizement of your name? Yet it is not only yourself you are corrupting. By giving in to the worst impulses of the aristocracy, you are denying them the least and last excuse for existence in the eyes of a just man. Truly, I beg you to reconsider what you have done. There is no shame in contradicting oneself to a virtuous purpose. Andronikus.

Surprisingly, the letter was answered, but by John Sergius. There is no record whether or not this was done at the Emperor's request, indeed, whether or not Manuel ever saw the above quoted document:

My Dear Andronikus. The Emperor has read your letter and wishes me to tell you this: He has been clement in lightening the burden of your imprisonment because he does not intend to make you an object of veneration, as even a fool becomes a martyr when he is persecuted. There are those so empty of responsibility and reverence, of a decent humility for the ages which have preceded them, they fill their empty lives with the determination to destroy rather than reconcile. The Emperor wishes me to tell you your actions and your attitude toward himself and the state have made him heartsick. He is the most generous of men and the necessary sequestration of a Prince of the Blood and one whom he loves is forced upon him rather by your continued recalcitrance than any abusive desire to withhold from you your freedom. John Sergius.

Surveillance was increased on members of Andronikus' immediate family, since either the Emperor or John Sergius was certain an escape was in the air. Precisely describing himself, the Protovestarius said of his cousin, "I know that man's wits and this is the prelude to something. In many ways he is like a child whose excitement betrays the surprise before it is given."

For two years, with a wink from the Emperor, and on orders from her husband, Anastasia had opened the doors of Vlanga Palace to the poor and the petitioner, whose requests she carried to Andronikus. He would consent to given sums or tell his wife where to go, to whom, or how herself to remedy any problem in question. On orders from Blachernae this practice was stopped. A detachment of Excubitors was sent to Vlanga to turn away anyone who did not carry papers personally applied for from the Protovestarius, and provided only at his discretion. One may be certain no matron or her highborn spouse was about to submit to such an indignity or otherwise risk the suspicion of the Heir. (After all, if papers must be issued, one could only be but suspect, and something was *very* wrong.) The petitioning poor, of course, had not the remotest chance of gaining access to the philanthropic Grand Duchess.

On 5 March, Andronikus was forcibly drugged, placed in a sack, and carried in the dead of night across the city to the old Sacred Palace where he was incarcerated in the topmost cell of Buceleon Lighthouse. Portable manacles were secured to his feet, but not his wrists. His privileges of correspondence, various comforts, and visitation rights were curtailed or rescinded.

"Thirteen years later," he once recalled, "after our reconciliation, I asked Manuel what difference it made to him whether I was at Anemas or Buceleon. He said, 'Come here,' and I followed him onto the terrace. There, rearing above the opposite palace apartments, beyond Philopation's groves, was the accusing obelisk of my prison. I knew, then, my cousin's reasoning. He had only to step out for a breath of air and before him was the monolithic tower with its bluish conical roof. In all likelihood, never a day passed but that he was reminded of me. Nevertheless I said, 'That wasn't your only motive, was it? You've more wits about you than that. Besides, the manacles.' 'Manacles?' He was sincerely amazed. At that moment I could have begun his re-education in the obnoxious malevolence of the late Protovestarius—indeed if the process had not already begun with the assortment of his papers of which Manuel was executor. So, too, I probably could have determined to my own satisfaction the exact portion of my cousin's guilt in my persecution. But I demurred. I can only suppose revenge, like some foods, must be taken fresh.

"All reconciliations after long absence are the memorial of something deceased, and usually mourned, as common bereavement brings together former enemies. Love may survive, but it bears relation to its earlier form only as the grandchild to the grandfather. Love as we know it is based on an infinity of small things, day-by-day familiarities. It can survive the separation of a few months and even a few years. Beyond that, the alterations of the constant ripening of the soul to whatever purpose become too sharp, too obvious, too alien. Then, I should think, friendship or affection cannot be resumed, only refounded. I had not the heart for any more accusation and so I told him, only half seriously, I was for so long in chains, I seemed to have confused those periods when I was not.

"Marvelous, isn't it? Not until I was removed to Buceleon Lighthouse did escape become a distinct possibility. Anemas, you can see it, is virtually inviolable, with its wide, winding single stairway posted with sentries who are changed every two hours, twenty-four hours a day, to keep the men alert. As for its façade: well, a sheer drop of 180 feet is practical only if one has wings, or a rope. But can you imagine? The tower is everywhere visible. I used to have a repeated dream of escaping and being skewered with arrows, and falling, falling. Vivid.

"But Buceleon is quite another story. For one, the centuries-old trees hide its west wall, which faces Daphne and Buceleon Palace. Only its tip is visible from Magnaura. For another, its east wall is almost tangent to the seawall. Now, while there was no means of egress from my apartment directly onto the fortifications—only a tall slender window through which an unwilling cat might squeeze—there was at least the advantage of being hidden as I climbed the inner façade and lowered myself to the Bosporus.

"My plans were at once simplified and complicated by the end of visiting privileges for my family and the censoring of correspondence. We were now forced to work through one agent, my valet, who was thoroughly searched and suspect though he was still allowed to enter and leave the lighthouse at any hour. The means of communication we devised were the only amusing moments of the whole episode. In fact, it became something of a contest—and, at that, suffered whimsy and carelessness—between my wife and myself as to who could conceal a message or an implement with more cunning. Once I remember I was eating my dinner sent from Vlanga on our gold service and furious my wife had not answered my last communiqué which had been every third word of a letter in which I had claimed to have found God again. Well, as I cleared away the heavy gravy—besides wondering how after twenty years Stana or my chef could forget my loathing for rich food —I noticed the golden surface of the plate was badly scratched and peered closer, and saw it was incised with a message. After a time, I'm certain she imagined my smiles as I imagined hers.

"Then again, most momentously—at length you see what had become moment in my life—Leo brought a huge amphora of wine and I quite thought my wife had lost her mind. I drink little enough and that watered down. Leo set the container on the floor in its stand and said, 'It had best be consumed as soon as possible, Your Highness.' I looked at him as if to ask if he had become lunatic as his mistress. But he made a twirling gesture with his forefinger, then pointed to the amphora, then pantomimed climbing. That night we accomplished the two most important preparations for escape. I removed the immense length of rope from the amphora and with the wine remaining Leo had the entire time —another advantage over Anemas—to put the guards in a thorough drunk, including him whom the prisoners call the Peter Guard, the keeper of the keys.

"While that fellow lay in a stupor, Leo took two wax impressions: of the key to my cell and the key to the lighthouse door. I don't know how that fellow had the courage to do such a thing. The guards would have had no compunction in killing him on the spot. I can still feel the panic, a feeling of being brushed with moist feathers at the back of my neck, pacing back and forth in my cell, waiting on every moment for the sound of scuffling, pulled swords, screams, the end of everything.

"Of course, in the morning, there was a terrific hullabaloo. My guards were sacked, poor fellows. I really did feel sorry for them. I had *used* them and what future had they after discharge, if they were not themselves executed or become outlaw after my escape was accomplished. After that, wine was altogether banned and something like the Anemas schedule was initiated, though the guards were five hours at their posts, with a break for the afternoon sentries between five and six o'clock when the whole lot had dinner in the Mess on the ground floor. Thus, though I was assured of rope and key, I was forced to wait three months until late December '63 or January '64, when, at that hour, there was pitch-darkness. Perhaps the delay was to the good. There was the usual increased alertness after the drinking incident.

"On the night of 4 January 1164, between five and six o'clock, then, I effected my escape. Leo brought my dinner in the late afternoon, and, as he had made it his custom, sat beside the door in the corridor. When the guards had themselves gone down to supper, he unlocked my door. I left, nodded good-by, and began to go. He stopped me, and in the silence, reached for my hands. He knelt, he kissed them. He made the Sign of the Cross as I started down the stairs.

"With those manacles it took me, of course, an absurdly long time to navigate the flight, noiselessly, as it had to be. It was our plan Leo should wait until the guard returned, re-enter the cell, remove the remains of the dinner, and leave as quietly as though I were napping. I'd filled one of my robes, which I'd been careful to wear that day, and placed it on the bed, back to the entry, to produce that effect. The rest was simple. I left by the front door taking care to lock it with the key my valet had given me. The longer nothing seemed amiss, the longer the distance between myself and my pursuers.

"Outside, I rounded the tower, took the huge loop of rope from my shoulder, and collided with our first lack of foresight. How was I to secure the rope on the wall before climbing it? In all our invention I'm certain he could have smuggled to me a grappling hook, a prying bar, in the least. The trees, all cypresses, were out of the question. All I had left to do was walk the hundred yards to the nearest stairs leading up to the battlement. Once again the time element was exaggerated by the manacles and more so, by my panic.

I was unshod but for thin leather slippers. My feet were already cut by the rough ground and were growing numb in the cold. At the battlements I passed the hundred yards back to the lighthouse. I must have seemed ridiculous. I could only mince in my chains, like an ingenue in Menander.

"Well, I secured the rope round one of the crenellations, seated myself, turned, and started down. Another point forgotten. The rope had not been knotted and I dropped of my own weight for twenty feet, cutting my fingers and palms almost to the bone. After that, I had still to catch myself and hand over hand work my way to the bottom. I set foot on the outworks about a yard above the water and, in agony, abruptly dashed my hands into the cold Bosporus, looking about for the boatman. He was, exact soul, fifty feet away and looking in the opposite direction. I dared to whistle. He turned and rowed up to me. He was dressed in Vlanga livery, which meant he was a snob rather than efficient. I cursed my wife. He wanted to take my hand and kiss it, but I pulled away. At once, I felt too unutterably unkind. This man was risking his life for me. I explained, then, my palms were lacerated. I told him to rip off the insignia on his cloak, which manifested him a member of the Imperial staff as were all servants who attended the family in any one of our palaces. We started along the Bosporus toward the huge tower at the junction of the inner walls and the seawalls.

"Now, over two centuries ago, if you remember, old John Tzimisces assassinated Nicephorus Phocas—and crowned himself thereafter—by entering the palace in the night and from the sea. Ever since, a surveillance has been maintained at that corner and charged expressly with preventing boats from passing that point. Carelessness again. We were apprehended by a monoreme, taken aboard, and arrested.

"From the first, I knew by the *feel* of the arrest, my escape had not been discovered. These guards, moreover, had scarcely any idea who I was. It had been too many years since my last appearances at court with my family. As we were leaving the boat, I told Stana's servant—I never thought of Vlanga as my home—to follow my lead. He was positively mute with fear and could say nothing upon interrogation. Finally, I piped up with a heavy Russian accent—which so many Greeks seem to find amusing (all to the good as it helped in part to disarm these marines)—'If you fellows must know, I'm a slave, though I was born well enough among the Khazars. You can see it in my bearing. Look at me. Can't you tell? I'm also a poet. If this detestable master would let me, I could teach his illiterate brats the beginnings of an alphabet, but he prefers to keep them bookkeepers, like himself. Instead he uses me for heavy work, which I'm not used to.' Moment by moment, I was becoming frantic with the lengths to which I was allowed to speak. No master would allow such a diatribe from a servant let alone a slave. But the lieutenant seemed amused more than anything else. You could see what he thought of the boatman: one so timid as to be terrorized not only by the constabulary, and a good thing, too, but his own servants, as well, probably deserves what he gets. The officer looked at me sourly and said, 'That's quite enough.'

"He turned to my boatman. 'What are the manacles for?' The man finally found his tongue. 'Look at the size of him, sir. He escaped my house and I could only get him back at a whale of a price. He's a liar, besides. They're all former princes, aren't they? I don't mistreat him. Anything short of a silken sheet and I suppose he *would* think so.' The lieutenant announced it best to take us ashore to the guardroom. 'I'll kill myself first,' I said, and I may have meant it. 'No, you won't,' he responded, and he meant it, too.

"The voice and manner of my boatman, which at first irritated me for their mildness—quite unlike the aspect of an inconvenienced master —suddenly seemed a virtue. Reasonably he said, 'Now, fellows, can't we settle this here? I've a long night ahead of me getting back to Chrysopolis. I've a business to tend in the morning. What law have we broken? I don't understand.' The lieutenant explained the prescript of Tzimisces, who, naturally, was not about to suffer the same fatal vulnerability as his predecessor. My boatman was genuinely amazed. 'Mother of God,' he said, 'you must be teasing us in your boredom, sirs, with all due respect. For one thing, Manuel Augustus is five miles away from here. At Blachernae.' The lieutenant nodded: 'That may be true, but members of the Imperial family still live at Daphne, Buceleon, and Magnaura.' 'May I ask you,' my boatman said, 'do the two of us look like assassins? Look at my boat. Where are my weapons? Search me if you like. Be sure to search this lug, too.'

"One of the lieutenant's aides, God bless him, said, 'Really, sir, I think they're what they seem. The law isn't very well known. It's a preposterous waste of time.' His superior seemed indecisive. I recognized him as one of those men who might rise by luck or lack of offense, but always subject to a cleverer subordinate, who would surpass him. You see such specimens in old age: bitter, resentful, egotistical, and dull. I was certain I had his mark when he suddenly manifested boredom with the properly pretentious contempt of the military for civilians. 'Very well,' he said, 'I'll let you go. But let this be a memorable warning for you.'

"Something perverse made me insist, 'Take me back with you. You don't know what he'll do to me. He's not the lamb he seems.' The lieutenant turned away. I was out of his life. I said, 'You bastards are all alike.' He turned abruptly and struck my face with the back of his hand. I lowered my head. Not all my renunciation of caste nor all my fine thoughts and talk had accustomed me to the shame I experienced and the fury I could barely contain, when I was treated so by men who were not of my blood. I could not help but think to strike me was to strike my grandfather, my uncle, my father. Logically, I might make the distinction between their accomplishments, which were admirable fact, and their sacrosanctity—no less presumably, my own, as a dynast—which is so much nonsense canonized by religion and tradition. Emotionally, I still could not consent to it. I don't know why. I am Comnenus and that is all there is to it.

"The lieutenant took a regulation shortsword from a rack and tossed it to my boatman. 'Here,' he said. 'He's an unlikely one. You may need this. You're more of a fool than you seem to sit in so small a space unarmed, with an oaf like him. Make him row.' My hands, of course, were gone, but I wasn't about to resist. I only wanted to be away, without further explanations or delays.

"When we were round the front wall, I said, 'Here,' and shoved the oars so hard at the boatman they struck his chest and he lost his wind. Again I lowered my hands into the water. The walls glided by. 'Your Highness, if you can find it in you to forgive me.' 'Never mind,' I told him. 'Never mind. You did well and Her Imperial Highness will never forget you.' I could not resist adding, 'Nor will I, I promise you that.' But the whole way to the Vlanga Quay he bemoaned his blasphemy against me. God knows, these people. They will bathe you, wipe you, barber you, and yet in any other situations hesitate before you, not daring to touch you unwontedly, or speak to you familiarly, and their bodies are held a little hunched, as though they were ready to glance a blow from you you do not remotely intend. At length, as he rowed, this man who had saved my life began to simper and cry. I *was* tempted then to strike him, but I asked him quietly—for it was my station which had created such wreckage—*now* what was the matter. He said he could not bare to have let me row after all I had suffered. I said, 'I've suffered very little for my escape. Can't you understand that? Had you rather I returned to the dungeons?' No, that was not his wish, but nothing would have removed his sin, he said over and over again, until finally I threatened to pitch him into the drink if he did not restrain himself. 'Go give your complaints to a priest. He'll give you ready absolution. You've done nothing I can forgive you for.'"

Over forty years later, the Grand Duke Alexander continued for me that moment in time: "My mother, my grandmother, two of our most trusted servants, and myself were waiting on the little quay, with its sea gate, which leads off from Vlanga. My father approached us from the east, along the Golden Horn. He embraced my grandmother, first of all, at which I could see my mother was notably put out, but then dutifully, if brusquely, he kissed her and under his breath, as he kissed me by her side, commented unfavorably on the boatman. He straightened and said abruptly, 'Now, where's the smith?'

"The irons were struck from his feet and dropped into the water. When that was done, then and there, in front of everyone, in the unbearable cold, he stripped off his clothes, down to the skin, put on fresh underwear, Persian trousers, splendid boots, an overdress to the knees which he belted, and over that, a curmantle lined in fur. At one point, he said to my mother, 'Stana, help me.' It was then we saw his hands. They had been horribly injured by the ropes as he escaped. My mother exclaimed at this and he remonstrated her. He continued dressing and asked after my health, my tutelage, and my catechism. He kissed the top of my head, and I kissed both of his hands, awed by the tolerance of pain he must have felt from them. At a glance from my mother, which I could not then understand, he made over me the Sign of the Cross. Then he kissed me once again, on the forehead, and whispered, 'I will see you again. That is my promise.'

"He put one arm round my mother's shoulder and the other around my grandmother's and the three of them walked to the edge of the dock. They talked quietly for a minute or two and then both women bent their heads toward his chest. I watched from the back as he lowered his between them, then looked up, and up, at the stars, and once again lowered his head. At length he released himself and turned and waved to the servants. He seemed to bethink himself, then unexpectedly beckoned me forward and embraced me, pressing my face against his chest, his hand, now gloved, on the back of my head. (The smell of freshly laundered and scented clothes brings back that night to me in a flash.)

"Suddenly, my grandmother burst into tears. My father released me and went over to her. Very gently he said, 'Mother, there is no alternative. For God's sake, have courage. This is not the last. We will be together again. I promise.' He grasped her shoulder and embraced her. I cannot say with any certainty whether or not he joined tears to her own. My mother came over, kissed his hand, his cheeks, his lips. He said good-by to her and his voice was broken. Then he descended to the boat and was off. Of all my early life, that is the only way I remember him. He entered our lives unexpectedly as a rainstorm, demolished everything, overwhelmed us, revivified our love for him, and vanished again."

Andronikus: "At the end of every epiphany is a question. To what use it may be put? When the exhilaration of my escape was spent, I was haunted by the problem of my inutility, more pronounced for my freedom. Until I returned to Constantinople, it cannot be said I found an answer commensurate with the value of my liberty. . . .

"The reunion on the quay at Vlanga, and the departure again, I would rather pass over. It is very difficult for me, to this day, to speak of it. I never saw my mother and my wife again. Twelve years later when, in principle, I had the freedom of the streets of Constantinople, they were dead, no doubt taking to the grave with them a sense of betrayal founded in the stories which reached them. Of that night, between the frenzy to be away and the desire to linger with those who, above all, had remained loyal to me, a loyalty which I cannot really be said to have compensated, I was, as you can imagine, at odds ends. In any event, I was given clothes, money, food, and I crossed the Horn to Galata, where one of our agents was waiting with a horse, a sword, a bow and quiverful of arrows. I took all and put off at once for Russia."

The escape was not discovered until the following morning. As the renegade Grand Duke's whereabouts were, of course, unknown and in the likelihood he might be in the city, on his way to revenge himself, guards were doubled round all members of the Imperial family. (At this, one of the Emperor's sisters—we are not told who—protested indignantly to her brother, "Don't you treat *me* as though I had anything to fear," and ostentatiously went about with none but her ladies-in-waiting.) John Sergius would have once again arrested Andronikus' immediate family, but the Emperor forbade it. It is unlikely, anyway, the detachment could have penetrated the citizens' guard round Vlanga. Like her husband's great-grandmother, Anastasia, surmising the possibility, had sent agents about the city with news of imminent confinement. As expected several thousand Constantinopolitans, like all citizens of a capital city, bored with majesty and sated with gossip, arrived to protect the Grand Duchess and participate with impugnity in this insolence toward the throne. The guard, sent months before to detain the family, found themselves detained.

The best the government could do was follow precedent. Writs of outlawry were signed, proclaimed, and posted throughout the Empire. Any man giving aid and comfort to the Grand Duke would be considered complicit in his crimes, subject to arrest and to prosecution. The guards at Buceleon were, of course, cashiered, but the citizens' guard made it impossible to arrest and—if necessary—torture the Grand Duke's valet, Leo, for information his mistress could as surely have given. (Five days later the people had proved, truly, to have served a purpose when it was known the master had passed through distant Anchialus and the servant was halfway to sanctuary in Sicily.) The Grand Duke's recapture, quick or dead, promised a reward for which any man would have been willing to risk his life: 15,000 Imperial bezants, or, equivalently, 450 pounds of pure gold, which is to say, precisely the annuity the son of an emperor or a sebastocrator receives from the State Treasury.

Finally, to this event belongs much the most enigmatic remark Manuel ever made as regards his duel with Andronikus. On being awakened the morning of 5 January to the news of his cousin's escape, the Emperor—vulnerable to bluntness as any man rising from sleep—was heard to say, "Perhaps this was the only way."

XXII

Andronikus: "I arrived at Anchialus three days later, having taken care not to run my horse to death, since I couldn't afford another. I'd read stories of the great battle my grandfather had fought before those walls by the Black Sea. All my life I hadn't but imagined pandemonium and blood. Strange, then, to approach those bastions as I could not have conceived them until I saw them personally: only the noise of merchants, hawkers, runners making way for a closed sedan, children at play, beggars, soldiers from the local garrison, bleating sheep on their way to slaughter. It was quite uncanny. A shock. What had become of the men and the years since my grandfather had ordered those morning-to-night vigils in the unnerving silence, taunting the enemy forward against the forbidding Byzantine line stretched from the walls to the sea? What had become of the blood he saw soak the sea? I leaned in my saddle and watched for a time, and for a time was a little amused.

"But, you know, as a renegade, you mistrust everything, almost the air you breathe, and the worst moments are when you find yourself at a moment's repose. I caught myself up, and entered the city. Like any stranger, I followed the traffic for about a mile to what I supposed would be the main square. The press of people was unusually heavy and there was a great deal of chatter, eyes which danced with expectancy, a sort of furtive, cheery anticipation, which I recognized at once as the look of those about to witness an execution.

"Nothing more than morbid curiosity drew me on. I could have turned away. I didn't. There were several thousand people in the square facing a jerry-built stage. To one side was a sort of grandstand, on which sat Basil Guiscard, dressed like a peacock, his aides, his wife, her ladies, and what I took to be a few members of the local aristocracy, everyone chin deep in fur-lined silks, surrounded by guards and braziers to keep them warm as possible under the circumstances. The rest of the spectators simply stamped their feet and huddled in their homespun.

"At a signal, the Bishop moved forward with two acolytes and somewhere from the opposite distance arrived the condemned—not a single man, as I'd expected, but a woman and five children, bound and chained. I thought, then, a flogging was to take place. Yet again, what could this emaciated group have possibly done to merit even so much as public whipping. Then, from another direction still, the hooded axman and two assistants, carrying a basket and the scooped-out executioner's block, were moving forward. All very symmetrical: state, church, and the chastised moving from opposite ends to convene in the common ground of capital punishment.

"Even from the distance one could see the three boys and two girls, the eldest not much above fourteen, were utterly bewildered by the jeering and the curses and the fate which awaited them. The youngest—perhaps eight years old, a little girl—was to all intents pulled on by the rest.

"My heart hardened: I was certain theirs was some misdemeanor: their animals grazing on an aristocrat's land, poaching, or, at worst, burglary. I looked over at Basil from whom I had hoped aid, and I conceived for him and for his party a loathing beyond words. In that moment, there was a huge, hysterical roar as the victims mounted the platform.

"At closer inspection, I was even more appalled. The mother's eyes were bulging, her nose was running, and she was shaking perceptibly. Her hair was cropped, as were the children's, for the headsman's benefit. One of the boys became incontinent, staining the front of his clothing. There were, at that, great hoots. Nothing, Nicetas, can compare with the anonymous brutality of a mob, come at the state's consent to witness murder.

"The Metropolitan of Anchialus arrived on the platform and gave the condemned a last blessing, but they were in another world. To do the man credit, he seemed distressed, his manner was gentle and he did not shout the benediction for all to hear, but as nearly as one could tell spoke it with great intimacy to those whom it most and only concerned. Then the chains were dropped from the mother and she was led forward, the children crying and calling after her and held back by the guards.

"I thought to myself: *Do* something, anything, but do it now. I did nothing. Had I attempted to stop what was happening, I would have fallen under the crowd, quite surely, and been torn to bits—not as an obstructor of justice, mind you, but pleasure. Even had I been rescued from the crowd's corrupted fury, I would have so incurred my cousin's outrage as to insure my remanding to Constantinople. But no matter. The quality of a man's actions are in no way concerned with their effect, only their cause. I who had railed against injustice, especially the peasant's; I who knew suffering at first hand, was allowing this atrocity to take place. Never mind the hopelessness of whatever I should have done. At least it would have been the publication of my disapproval.

"The mother's head fell cleanly on the first stroke, and while the crowd cheered one less of their own undone before Basil's fashionable party—the women turning their heads away *after* separation (even Basil's wife, Princess Taronites, who I'd previously thought a good sort) —the condemned children became frenzied. Two appeared to go on the spot from apoplexy. The mother's headless body, twitching uncontrollably and spurting blood from the neck, was lifted by the axman's assistants and dropped from the side of the platform into a wagon, the horses ready to bolt at the scent of blood.

"I wanted to run away, but something rooted me: whether the taste for distant horror we all have—and which, then, I might not have admitted—or the truth of the voice within me, which said: 'All *you* need do is watch. Watch then, watch helplessness and feel your own, be appalled. Remember. The ax came down on the head of the fiendishly struggling fourteen-year-old boy, came down badly, severing only part of the neck and most of the shoulder. Three more strokes were necessary. Even as the head was held up to the crowd, then dropped after the body into the horse cart, the mouth continued to move.

"Then the chains were dropped from the eldest girl, who sobbed and in attempting, though still bound, to get to her knees, fell on her back. Her head shook violently and she was perhaps begging for her life, though it was impossible to hear above the crowd, as she was carried to the block. I looked over at Basil, heard the ax fall just once—at least it was quick—and saw my cousin's wife turn white and begin to shake. She leaned over, said something to my cousin, and rose to go, assisted by two ladies. There was a great hissing in her direction until Basil frowned and with one finger signaled his horse guards forward. Silence followed at once and there were only the pitiful sounds of the three remaining children.

"This, which they had not heard before, brought the crowd about. They became aware of their own mercilessness. The festival was spoiled. The wailing of the second boy was the sharpest possible remonstrance. No more hoots, no more cheers. The full majesty of death was upon everyone, and majesty, as everyone knows, little becomes a child. Four strokes of the ax were necessary and finally a sinew was sawed away before the fourth head fell. The two youngest were left, but the ghastliness of what they had seen had put them beyond mortality, beyond hope —terrible to apply those words to a child—and trancelike they went to their deaths, only it might have seemed as though they were the noblest of men, grown men, reconciled to their fates and aware nothing could save them, assuming the last dignity we may hold is to disappoint the merciless circus of public execution and to admonish the insensible. The final death was particularly cruel. The headsman was, by now, himself affected and landed his weapon in the child's spine so that the body went slack in paralysis before the head could be severed from the body. A low, compassionate moan rose from the people, who were the quietest crowd imaginable as they left the square.

"I weaved my horse through their numbers and rode up to my cousin as nearly as his escort would allow. I called his name, which made him start. As a Grand Duke in this godforsaken place of exile, only his wife had sufficient rank to so address him. He turned and looked round and his eyes glanced off me, then darted back. His expression fell. I dismounted and came up to him. '*You*,' he said. '*How?*' As meaningfully as possible I stared at him and said, 'I'm on my way to Galicia, Basil.'

"He took but a moment to decide and the clemency he did not show the six corpses he showed to me. He nodded with a commanding look of resolve and grasped my hand emotionally. The Proclamation of Outlawry, by the way, did not arrive at Anchialus till that evening, but it changed nothing.

"He signaled an aide to take care of my horse, said, 'Walk with me,' and we stepped ahead of his party who, I saw with a glance, were straining to see me and mostly at a loss as to who I was. 'Pull up your hood,' he said, and I did.

"He indicated the square, with a look of pain and disgust. 'Hideous business. The woman and her children owned a farm not far from here. My lot it should fall to my jurisdiction. As nearly as we can piece it together, they would sequester anything human, young or old, and not of the neighborhood who came to their door—vagrants, beggar children —and thereafter systematically torture them to death in rites involving some sort of devil worship.' 'Not the children,' I said. He must have seen the look on my face, for he nodded, as bewildered as I. 'Yes, the children, too, which is what most shocks me. Most have such a natural compassion—or at least a fear which recommends itself against cruelty and pain. Yet one wonders. What is it Solomon says? "Man is *born* wicked. . . ." It's been an ordeal for everyone. Had you been free at Constantinople, no doubt you would have heard it. The Metropolitan of Adrianopolis threatened to petition Uncle against our good Bishop because he decided to bless the condemned. He was marvelous. He said to me one day, "My brother Bishop at Adrianople chooses to presume I suffer the entry of the condemned into heaven by blessing them. I bless them to confess my own inadequacy in judging them. I merely commend them to God for Him to judge with His all-seeing heart. Rather it is the Adrianopolitan Bishop who would give or withhold his blessing as though he were council for the prosecution." '

"Yet Basil's explanation and the truth changed nothing for me. According to what I had seen, I had not acted on it. I had done nothing but allowed what appeared to me an atrocity to pass. I have been troubled ever since by that day, by my own selfishness—or my lack of integrity. And to be sure, the crimes of that family, in a purely objective way, quite haunt me. It is negation of humanity such as I have never otherwise encountered. Basil II's blinding of the Bulgars, the rape of Edessa or Cyprus or Jerusalem, seem to me perfectly understandable in their passion. But this was the calculated infliction of pain, with no apparent motive excepting the savoring of another's agony until the tortured bodies gave out their last eek of pain and failed forever. When Basil's stepchildren greeted us at the entrance of the Governor's Palace, beautiful children, attended and indulged, I was sick at the heart. Those infant criminals whose bodies were being drawn away seemed all the more vulnerable for their depravity than these progeny of aristocratic loins, raised to the glittering life which would be theirs as heirs of an Imperial stepfather.

"Basil, by the way, had quite deteriorated in those years. It was no longer an 'unofficial' exile. But then, he had nothing to recommend itself to him at Constantinople, certainly not the military brilliance of one such as Michael Branas. He could have returned at any time to the city, but he suspected the outcome: no doubt as one of Manuel's gold-brocaded sycophants. Not that Basil was above sycophancy. Rather at Anchialus he was Captain General of the Paristrian Province, the head of all social, military, and—as the Emperor's representative—religious life 300 miles north to south and 150 miles east to west.

"Unfortunately, since there were only three other major cities in this area of jurisdiction—Mesembria, Dorystolon and Peristhlaba—neither the social nor military life amounted to very much, but sooner that than anonymity among too many Grand Dukes at Blachernae. Of course, as his post was not usually occupied by an emperor's nephew, he was doubly idolized. If that consoled him, well and good; but I suspect he knew the littleness of it all. There were indications which let slip his bitterness. Worse, so much of his mother Magdalena's good nature was gone, and his father's Sicilian imperiousness and short temper had taken hold. In many ways he moved like a tyrant in small. He had collected a court and conscripted a guard, all quite smartly turned out—a little *too* smart, if you gather my meaning. He drank too much and he was a satyriac on an order which in comparison with my own early reputation would make me to seem a celibate. Yet what I found most reprehensible of all was the aspect of a scion of royal and Imperial blood involved in gross peculation, which participation he seemed delighted to relate to me mistaking my argument against privileges of aristocracy with my very real, if singular, admiration for the one virtue, if none other, in which a well-born man may make at least a partial excuse for his luck: absolute moral and social honesty. (I didn't quite understand the whole of his swindle, but it seemed to involve his pocketing of immense funds by bribing the Chairman of Revenue for the province who, in turn, was obliged to meet the predicated assessment of the district by forcing still more taxes from the already destitute peasantry. The sum sent to Constantinople was always on the mark. Basil was, therefore, always praised for his integrity—as what else can one expect of a dynast—and his name was cursed among the farmers, scarcely allowed to own a cow without having to sell it to pay for the right to possess it.)

"My first evening at Anchialus, he sent a priority dispatch by relay post half a thousand miles north to Prince Jaroslav at Galich, informing him of my arrival within the next two weeks. He bid me remain and rest a few days. You may understand, Nicetas, why the thought repelled me even had I wished it more or trusted Basil less. I felt as though I were bathing in a pool of slime and I was eager to be away. I told you once I ought to have liked Basil better, with all he has done for me, but I could not. I have intentionally used few people in my life—in the sense of asking favors of one for whom I hold, in whole or part, contempt. Basil was one of that number. I suppose it was this very secret loathing for him which kept me at Anchialus four days, very crucial days, while the writ spread like a thousand eyes and alerted the Empire to my escape.

"When I left, Basil presented me with changes of clothes, a packhorse, an extra riding horse, gold, provisions. It was a truly royal progress compared to that nightmarish escape six years before. On 27

January I crossed the Danube. It was my intention to follow the Prut to its northernmost point, cross the Transylvanian forest to the Dnieper, and continue west to Galicia.

"Not that I had become careless, but I believed myself, at last, free. I was elated. The sun shone each day and glanced off the snow and winked between evergreens, so old and so tall their branches began fifty feet from the forest floor. I suffered no want. I was warm. My horses were good mounts. If I was lonely, at least I had time to think, as a free man, not a prisoner—there's a difference—to collect my experiences of the previous ten years and bring myself to some reconciliation of the loss they represented—or the gain. . . .

"On the evening of 2 February I roomed at the Monastery of St. Cyril. I had wanted to sup alone, but I thought it better not to make myself conspicuous by my absence, and so I went to the refectory and sat at a table with several monks and a group of merchants who had arrived north from Adrianopolis and were, themselves, on their way to Galicia. Those fellows were full of talk of my escape and the staggering reward—which pleased me—the Emperor was offering for my recapture. I noticed that one of the merchants eyed me silently for a long while. When I stared him down, he remarked, somewhat abashed, on my resemblance to the renegade Grand Duke (indeed, I had regrown my beard, and my hair, deliced, was long again)—height, eyes, general expression.

"I pretended to be amused—after a fashion I was, proving myself not myself—and said, 'How would you know what His Imperial Highness looks like? Had you ever seen him?' To my surprise, he nodded. 'A few times, in one Imperial train or another. He was quite unmistakable.' Now, I had escaped the Bosporus guards because the unimportance of the incident to them had been inversely proportionate to its incidence to me, which is why I did not think it would succeed, why perhaps I had been so careful. Here, on the other hand, the proportions were turned and I was careless. I said, 'Well, I loathe to disappoint you, sir, but I'm not the Megadux. I'm not even Greek. I'm Georgian.' 'Incredible. Your Greek is flawless.' 'It ought to be, as my father would have had it. He paid enough to educate me at Constantinople.' One of his colleagues piped up, 'Indeed, sir, I've been to Tiflis many times. May I inquire your name?'

"Somewhat impatiently, I revealed the name of one of my wife's

maternal cousins. This was a mistake. The merchant was well informed.
'Then you're related to the royal house. In fact to the Grand Duke's
wife,' he said. I attempted to be both wry and critical, 'You seem to be a
veritable almanac of these things.' Another mistake. He became offended
and so did his colleagues, for they suspected a ruse, themselves dupes.
Greed, I'm also certain, swelled their righteousness. Boldly, he said, 'I'll
tell you, sir. Your knowledge of Georgia is undoubted but not so native
as your Greek tongue.' And then the other fellow shouted, 'It *is* the
Grand Duke!'

"There was a melee next. I know what I felt; the *killing* violence of
absolute despair. To have come so far and to be threatened once again
with recapture was simply too much. But that constituted another mistake because in my rage I was not merely defending myself. I was tearing
up the refectory in a fury such as I had never known myself to suffer.
Smashing, wounding, striking anyone—a sort of morbid exhilaration.
About a dozen monks joined the fracas. I believe two oaken chairs were
smashed against my back. I scarcely felt them. I was drooling. I was
monstrous in the most literal sense. Finally I was hit hard with something incredibly dense on the back of the head and I fell unconscious.

"When I awoke I was being tended, but I was also bound with enough
rope to decimate an army by hanging. The following afternoon a captain from the nearest Imperial garrison arrived with an escort to accompany me back to Constantinople. The soldiers were respectful, even
solicitous, but you may understand I was beyond caring. Perhaps that
saved me. I was so completely tractable they decided not to chain me
when we started out the following morning. (The merchants incidentally had their certificate from the captain and were on their way to
Constantinople—with the vegetable I'd made of one of them—to claim
their reward. When news of my escape preceded them, they started out
once again empty-handed for Galicia, where I myself had preceded
them. Jaroslav wanted to cut their throats. I demurred in their behalf.)

"I swear to you, the escape I made was one any fool could have contrived and only fools or the ingenuous would have suffered. The first
day we had not reached an inn by dark and were obliged to continue
by torchlight. I had been complaining of a stomachache all day and indeed I was suffering something like dysentery. Each time, on request,
the escort stopped obligingly while I passed a short way into the trees,
alone, my privacy deferred to as a Grand Duke. That first stop in the

dusk, I realized the very elegant alternative open to me. The epiphany was so quick and likely I nearly giggled aloud.

"I removed my mantle, broke a branch from a tree, set it into the snow and the cape around it, with the hood raised, spread the hem about to look as though I were crouching, saluted the unseen soldiers by the road, and set off in the opposite direction. The glee I felt, however, soon gave way to three days of travel which constitute among the most dreadful of my life, more so, even, than my escape of 1159. Then I had, at least, been surrounded by civilization. I knew my way, population centers were never very far, and even the farmer who betrayed me, it must be remembered, at first took me in. Now the solitude, which had pleased me so long as I was comfortable with Basil's provisions, was oppressive and nearly fatal.

"My objectives were simple and seemed to me, at first, almost insoluble. I had to rediscover the Prut, find food and the means of crossing the 250 miles of increasingly more severe winterscape to Galich. All that sustained me was the vision of my welcome should I arrive. I was, as Basil reminded me, now famed in Russia for being complicit—or at least sympathetic—to Jaroslav's late uncle, the King of Hungary, who was in turn allied, of course, to the Prince's father, Izyaslav; and loyalty runs like blood vengeance, from generation to generation, amongst Russian families. Indeed, it was believed my years in prison were suffered for no other reason than my Russophilism, which, of course, was nonexistent.

"In any event, at the end of those frozen, foodless insomniac three days I found the Prut again. I was in a condition, by then, as close to subhuman as I ever expect to be. I wept if I stumbled. I chased rabbits with a club. I vividly remember the unlucky one who came under my truncheon. We were both on the move and I got him in the back instead of the head. He lay there twitching, and I had not even a knife to put him out of misery, much less to skin him. So I brought the club down again and it was such a nauseating sight, I ran, and stopped close to the road and vomited water.

"As I sat beneath a tree exhausted, I espied a Russian knight—as big as myself, but healthier—on a horse, going north. Strange, I never thought to ask him for food or favor. In my desperation, I wanted all. I knew myself too weak to challenge him so I conceived a plan of rank cowardice to which no honorable man ought to admit, but then, where's

his honor if he does not admit its denial? I followed the fellow the remainder of the day, from the roadside, from tree to tree, like a wolf.

"The analogy is apt: My head was empty of any thought remotely
resembling that of a human being. What soul I might have possessed
to distinguish me from an animal was quite gone. Probably I would have
tracked the knight by scent had I the capacity. When evening came I
remained about fifty feet from his encampment. Eerie it is to study a
man you are about to kill. He was unknown to me and I to him, yet a
millionfold coincidences had brought us to this cold desolation and the
certain oblivion of one or the other. I still see him: huge, with a large
full face, pale hair, pale eyes. He moved with ponderous dignity, nothing wasted, crossed himself before his first mouthful, and ate his food
in very civilized morsels. Who knows but that once he may have been
offered commission as a Varangian—he was a likely one—and refused.
Had he accepted, he would have been at Constantinople now, and I
should have died, perhaps, in his stead, in this wilderness. He fed his
horse, crossed himself again, prayed before a little icon, kissed it, rolled
himself in his mantle and a blanket, also fur-lined, and closed his eyes
—forever—on winter stars. I waited perhaps an hour, came up to him,
and in the silence clubbed him to death. He never awoke and insofar
as I could tell, never experienced pain. He prayed, he slept, he dreamed,
he died.

"What desperate man does not believe his life is more valuable than
his victim's? That dead Russian knight is beyond my debt, my consolation, or my penance. I stripped his body, pulled it deeper into the
woods—leaving a trail of blood across the snow—donned his mantle,
ate some of his provisions, mounted his horse, nearly as big as a
Percheron and perhaps deceived by my size into thinking it his master,
and started off again, at once, into the night.

"Betimes I fell asleep in my saddle and shook myself awake. I did
not dare purchase a bed at a monastery until the following morning,
and once asleep slept through to the next. I ate the tack and pork in the
knight's bags. I wanted no communion with a world of men whose recognition of me was but to accuse, to claim, and to sell me.

"On 11 February I ascended the east spur of the Carpathians, which
bars the way to Galicia. From its heights, before me, below me, was
Russia. A light snow began to fall. Before I descended I looked back,
to the south, with the knowledge of Constantinople somewhere beyond

the horizon, and I was overcome with devastating reverie. I looked forward again. Could it truly be the same earth whereon both Constantinople and that vast, unpeopled expanse before me prevailed? Where was the civilization of man? What, then, was civilization? Rather all that I carried in my head? Was it repose, contemplation, frivolity, art, trade, government? And what did it mean in the face of this solitude?

"I descended the Carpathian range into Russia, and the wind which the escarpment had deflected assailed me at once, a cold wind such as I had never known, bitter, palpable, which scorched like flame. The second day, when the snow abated, I passed through a village, if you could call it that—some log huts, others of mud and stone, low as a kennel. One could scarcely believe humans lived within. Only a little church—and then, only in part—was made out of stone, a cream color, beautifully carved in places, which led me to conclude the work of a Greek journeyman. My eyes actually ached for the relief of color, but there was none.

"That same afternoon I found myself crossing an enormous, limitless plain of snow. The sense of line to infinity was uncanny. Above was an oppressively seamless sky of gray so deep and rich as to nearly be blue. And yet I sensed not expanse but suffocation, as though all the world had been sealed in this monochromatic casket and I would very soon become aware of a lack of air. I could hardly imagine the sun, the blue sky, great clouds, and the stars. I tried to estimate the time of day and I could not. But imperceptibly it became darker and a real panic, like nightmare, overcame me, until, in the distance—I was moving west —a failing crepuscular light appeared just above the edge of the world, much as a city in flames will illumine the cusp between land and sky.

"Then, quite like magic, the immobile sky began to shift. Racing clouds drew beneath the darker and darker gray dome, light little puffs, some the color of iron, some a ghostly white. Then that massive cupola began to give, to break, and patches of the deepest night blue I have ever seen appeared. Within minutes, the sky was clear, Jupiter gleaming regally, Orion's symmetry asserting itself above all other constellations, the Pleiades as wistful as ever. I was still haunted by the emptiness I had experienced at the Carpathian spur, but now, if not transcendence, I felt a child's wish to be taken up to the repose of those stars, beyond struggle, beyond fear, beyond inquiry.

"The next day it was brought home to me quite how far from Constantinople I was. I encountered a woman carrying a child, the both of them blue from the cold. I offered her one of the gold pieces—with Jaroslav's stamp—which I'd discovered in one of the knight's knapsacks. She took it, looked at it, and handed it back, and with what under other circumstances I might have called remarkable ingenuity, pointed in the direction I was going, supposing I was looking for the Prince of the land. I shook my head, handed the coin back, and said to her in Russian, 'No, no, Matushka, this is for you.' Once again she returned the coin and this time grasped the rolled blanket behind my saddle. 'This, my Lord,' she said, 'if you're giving.' Not gold in these parts. A man's treasures were his pelts, his food, and his herds, the thickness of his walls—and better stone than wood.

"Here it was: this absolute primal state on the same continent with Constantinople, which seemed, of course, unreal to me, now, a dream. I gave the woman the blanket. I had no choice. Warmth, not purchase, was the meaning of any charity she could appreciate, and I was obliged to abide by her terms or call myself a hypocrite.

"On 15 February, in the late day, I reached Galich, the capital of the Principate of Galicia. Round a huge belly of rock was the circle of walls which surrounded the city, more nearly a town by civilized standards, but enormous in comparison to what I had previously seen. All was wood, wood everywhere, used like stone, carved, lacquered, laminated, twisted to unexpected heights, coated with gold or in extraordinarily vibrant colors. Accented profusely and unexpectedly with immaculate traceries of snow, the aspect was one of charm rather than foreboding. Above the city, like a crown, was the great kremlin of Galich, one of the most astonishing sights I've seen in any country. Its bastions rose sheer from the rock, mighty walls of wood not stone, but a credit to any engineer. Within their encirclement was a profusion of roofs, fifty, a hundred, some sloping, some diamond-shaped, some domed, some bulbous, of red and green and gold, and to the last, each topped with a gilded cross.

"I was enchanted. Throughout the streets of the city, deep with snow, there were numbers of people such as one would have scarcely imagined from its size. As I passed down the main thoroughfare the door of one establishment was thrown open—it was a bathhouse, I learned later—

and following on a dense cloud of steam were six naked men on the run, who threw themselves into a mound of crushed ice, a common practice after sauna. No one but I gave their nudity a second glance. Beggars, merchants, minstrels, priests, whores, a dancing bear, hawkers, grocers, butchers. Men and women almost literally carried their professions on their backs. At one spot along the street, which had a graded surface composed of thousands of circular sections of logs, numerous corpses were laid out in coffins while a gong was struck continually to summon relatives of these otherwise unidentified cadavers—all men who had probably frozen to death in their drunken stupor, a nightly fatality during winter.

"I made my way slowly toward the kremlin, which, not much to my surprise, was surrounded by a moat, quite frozen over (in the summer, the stench of raw sewerage and detritus from the castle was quite beyond belief). I presented myself to sentinels, saying, of course, I was Andronikus, Grand Duke of Byzantium, and I wished an audience with His Highness Prince Jaroslav. It was all quite hopeless, I need not tell you. I was dressed in the garb of something like a Russian knight, and personally none too well kept, quite emaciated and ridden with lice, which are the true natives of Russia, and ineradicable. Though I argued with the first sentinel, then the second, and an oncoming half-dozen more, I knew they were lost to my persuasion.

"You must understand: In Russia, Constantinople is not merely Tsargorod, the City of the Caesars. It is something like heaven and—though their princes know better—among the people the Byzantine Emperor is second only to Christ. He is real and he is unreal. If you think the devotion of our own lower orders is impressive, you would find it as nothing compared to Russia's for the successor of Constantine—or his kin, for all that, as I was quick to discover. Surely, in sum, the cousin of the semidivine Basileus should have arrived in panoply, amidst thousands, clothed in gold and jewels, winged and incensed, an ambassador from heaven—not this ragged soldier of little fortune, filthy, beside his faithful, tired horse.

"In any event, I kept control of myself, bid the men inform the Grand Chamberlain—'if His Highness has one,' I couldn't resist adding—who I was and that I wished an interview with the Prince. I asked after the nearest monastery where I could stay the night.

"As I arrived at the establishment to which they sent me, a Vespers procession was leaving the church. You know the last light of day, some time after the sun has set, when the whole world seems lit by a curious blue-green-silver radiance. Well, imagine against this light a long line of similarly garbed priests carrying golden tapers with their amber flames, and icons, some bejeweled, glittering dully.

"Perhaps because it was the end of day, a time I find most melancholy anyway, I was quite moved, remembering the days of my earliest childhood and later as an adolescent returned to Constantinople my part in festal processions of indescribable beauty—and expense, which, of course, is why I have eliminated them since my accession. I remember looking up when the darkness was complete. The moon was haloed by a vast wisp of a circle which covered nearly the entire sky. All seemed auspicious, so long as I did not allow myself to think in terms of long futures.

"Later in the evening, one of the monks, wary and very shy, asked me in Greek if it was true I was the Grand Duke Andronikus, Kyr Andronikus, he called me, or Lord, which would have made my cousin, so jealous of his titles, blanch. I answered him in purest court Attic, an incredible feeling to speak one's natural tongue after such long silence in other languages or dialects. (And I must admit, however artificial it sounds to the people I rule—makes me suspect, perhaps—it is the tongue of my birth and most comfortable to me.) The monk answered me in a less pure tongue, but he knew the language of the Imperial aristocracy and this seemed to impress him.

"The following morning I returned to the kremlin. While the sentries had changed, the reception was the same. I returned once again to the monastery. The monk, who had questioned me the previous evening, diverted me by taking me through the monastery library. I pored through several chronicles, crudely illustrated, but lovely in their colors.

"Then at midday meal in the refectory, there was the sound of horses in the courtyard and, following, a commotion within the establishment itself. The doors burst open and, followed by a troop of courtiers, in walked Jaroslav. He could be no other. He looked like a frantic hawk, which, as I was to learn, was a deception of appearance serving well his authority. In truth this descendant of Rurik was lackadaisical, good-natured, nerveless, generous, loyal, cunning, benign, and literate. Yet his person seemed quite the opposite: a splendid long face with an imperious beak of a nose, high-arched blond brows joined as one—Octavian Augustus' great vanity—and, as I say, those quick darting movements and a glance which never wandered but passed constantly, instantly, and particularly from object to object, of a hawk, a very hawk, the blind pulled off suddenly. Only his mouth, small and perfect, and his long slender hands betrayed languorous aristocracy at the removal of centuries.

"He said, or rather, taunted out loud, 'Where is he who says he is Kyr Andronikus of Byzantium?' While the priests bowed and quivered like plucked lutes, I rose from the bench and said, 'He is here, my dear Prince. In good health.' He nodded, considered me from head to toe, and said, 'You expect me to believe you were born in the purple.' I said, 'I would remind Your Highness only an emperor's son or daughter is born in the purple, as was my father, His Imperial Highness, the Sebastocrator Isaac II. You would be more exact, Prince, to speak of me as *of* the purple, as an Imperial Grand Duke. That fact of birth cannot fall from me, whether or not I wear the rags of one of your obliging knights or you consent to it or you do not. My kin, the Governor of Anchialus, the Grand Duke Basil, wrote to you to expect me. None save you and he knew my precise intentions and you would have done well as an obliging host to inform your sentries to that effect. You are aware of the circumstances of my immigration. How did you expect me to arrive? Rather I was refused at the gates of your palace like a beggar.'

"Once again, he nodded. Then, abruptly, he said, 'Who reigns in Georgia?' 'My nephew, His Royal Majesty King George IV.' 'What are the names of the children of the first Sebastocrator Isaac?' I had to think for a moment, and then I said, 'George, Sophia, Adrian, James, and Alexius.' He nodded. 'Correct.' I said, 'Incorrect. My granduncle never had a son named George. That was John.' 'Very well. What is the relation of the present King of Hungary, Stephen IV, to Lord Manuel?' 'He is the youngest son of Bela II, who was cousin to Lord Manuel's mother, St. Irene.'

"He proceeded to the middle of the room, handing his horsewhip to an ADC. He faced me, looking up but not consenting to my height, his hands locked behind his back. 'What is the chief rule of cavalry when taking a charge?' I responded, 'Cavalry receiving a charge at rest will take a greater shock and greater losses than cavalry in motion. Therefore the only possible tactic is to be moving forward when advanced upon.' 'What are the conditions one must consider in mounted battle?' 'Infantry dispositions, the ground over which the horses shall advance, dips in the land and so forth, the advantage and disadvantage of hill-side posts, the exact danger from soft moss in the land around creeks.' 'The types of horses to be used?' 'Bigger horses can carry thicker armor and are better able to withstand the impact of a lance, but they are nei-ther as agile nor as sensitive as ponies, who also eat less. The larger the horse, the greater the necessity for the best grain, a great deal of it, which means limiting the use of such animals to a harvestable time of year or else diverting monies from soldiers' provision to pay the cost of transport of such cereals from one's supply base. On the one hand, the smaller steed stands formations well, but losing its rider in battle, be-comes hysterical and will seek the companionship and safety of other horses, attempting to rejoin formation, which is a danger to the mounted knight, thus jostled. On the other hand, the Percheron is more independ-ent, but becomes so used to the idiosyncracies of its rider, it is, for all in-tents, useless without him. Hence, I might add, your ancient custom of killing and burying the Percheron with its rider was not merely an act of ceremony but practical, too. To put a healthy animal to pasture is clement. It is also exorbitant. Am I boring you?'

"He smiled, came forward, and said, 'You couldn't. You are he. Only one trained at Constantinople, and a general, would know of such things. And a general would not look as you do unless he were a rene-gade Grand Duke, who, as we say, is swaddled in trumpets, cradled in helmets, and fed at the end of a lance.' He threw open his arms. 'Wel-come, brother.' We embraced. He smelled, curiously, of lemons. 'Felici-ties, Your Imperial Highness.' 'Felicities, Jaroslav, and God bless you.' 'God bless *you*,' he said, with real emotion. 'You are welcome to my house. But I beg you. My Greek is better than your Russian, so speak your native tongue, if I may be so bold, since our purpose is to be under-stood in all things.' 'It is, is it, Prince?' He smiled. 'Ah,' he said, 'that is the famed deep Greek. There is no second meaning in my hospitality. Is there, my lords,' and he turned slightly on these words, eyes hooded, with an almost feminine look of cunning. The courtiers muttered their expected assent. Jaroslav nodded, satisfied. He turned to me clear-eyed."

XXIII

In the two years which followed the assassination of the Caliph al-Zafir (1161), his son, in the minority, became the pawn in a series of revolutions which were, in realty, aristocratic massacres. Every man, of course, claimed he was fighting for the young King, every man intent on "liberating" him from the corrupt clutches of the current self-proclaimed Regent. Finally, in 1163, Prince Shawar, the Viceroy of Upper Egypt, marched on Cairo, slew al-Zafir's last favorites, and proclaimed himself Grand Vizier in the child's behalf. Like his predecessors, like all men in his position—including, nineteen years later, Andronikus—his concern for the state was as sincere as his ambition. But in the frenzy of the times, the integrity of his rule was undermined.

Shawar maintained his power for a year and was deposed, in turn, by Prince Dhirgham, Governor of the Alexandrian District. Unreconciled, Shawar fled to Nureddin, who sent his greatest general—which is to say, his most merciless—a Kurd, Shirkuh by name, to re-establish the former Grand Vizier. At this news, Dhirgham appealed to Almaric, who had scarcely dreamed of—and was not, thereby, prepared for—intervention on such a scale. While the Latin King assembled an army, Shirkuh deposed Dhirgham and Shawar was once again Regent. Then, with his country's independence most in mind, Prince Shawar turned volte-face and sent emissaries to Almaric who was still crossing Sinai, unaware his mission had been once nullified and was suddenly saved again. With astonishing honesty—perhaps he had no alternative—the Regent, through his ambassadors, spoke of his fears of Nureddin, primarily the founding of a puppet state by the Governor of Mosul. Shawar assured Almaric he had gone to Aleppo "as a friend seeking a friend to assist me in the rescue of my country from invidious hands. Instead, it appears His Excellency Nureddin received me as a traitor, willing to forfeit Egypt as his agent, to keep a position which, for me, is thereby tainted and meaningless."

Almaric, imaginably overjoyed as the pivot on which the Moslem world turned, proceeded to Cairo, aware that for the moment, Manuel's participation—and his ambitions—had been surpassed by a timely event. Daunted by the size of the army of Jerusalem—which conscription had cost the new King much in popularity—Shirkuh and his nephew, Saladin, retired. So did Almaric. Shortly before *he* could take control of Egypt in the guise of a mutual assistance pact—and risk Shawar's renewed alienation and another civil war—the King was obliged to take his army, at forced march, north, and defend the now masterless principalities of Tripolis and Antioch.

On 10 August 1164, at the Battle of Haranc Castle a combined army under Bohemond III of Antioch, Raymond III of Tripolis, Joscelin III, Pretender to Edessa, Prince Thoros of Armenia, and a man who was later to become one of my mentors, Count Constantine Colomon, Imperial Military Adviser to Thoros, was defeated by Nureddin in such a manner as brought chill to the blood of most Byzantines.

In a tactic-by-tactic repetition of Manzikert in 1072, the Greek and Latin cavalry had been lured into pursuit of the retreating Aleppan forces. As Count Colomon later told me, "While we moved after the enemy, Prince Thoros repeatedly muttered, like a man bemused, 'Something is wrong. Something is wrong,' and then, in horror, he actually shouted the name Manzikert. Others looked round as though he were mad and I told him so. I thought he was suffering sunstroke. Perhaps he'd learned his classic battles too well at the Scholarian Academy. Nothing could stop him. He sounded the retreat of his own forces and started back, and I hollered after him that he was the goddamnedest coward or else the most bold and venal traitor who ever lived."

But treachery and cowardice or prudence are only a point of view. Manzikert, as it might have been, was averted by a humiliation. At the precise moment Nureddin's forces about-faced and surrounded the Latin and Greek cavalry, those men, knights all, threw down their swords and "in misery and shame" watched the foot soldiers behind them massacred. Colomon, Bohemond, Raymond, and Joscelin, their aides, the cream of Latin aristocracy "and the curds of the Greek," as Colomon described himself and his men, were taken to Aleppo, paraded through the streets, and incarcerated in Nureddin's by now thoroughly Latinized dungeons, Joscelin where his father had died a Christian martyr disowned by Christians, Bohemond only the space of a few walls from his still live stepfather, the choleric Reynald, who, insofar as we can gather, never knew of his successor's presence.

In all the world, however, there was one power which gave Nureddin pause, and that power was Byzantium whose suzerainty over Antioch was grown more and more assured. So much so, that when the Kurd, Shirkuh, urged the Prince of Aleppo to attack and quite likely destroy the fourteen-hundred-year-old city, he was met with a reply of such political consideration as would have shocked and delighted the dead Zengi, who went to his grave despairing of his youngest son's impetuosity. "Sooner the Guiscards than the Comneni as neighbors," replied Nureddin, meaning that as a world of conquest had shifted, Antioch now occupied the same buffer position between the Byzantine and Aleppan Empires as Aleppo when a semi-autonomous governacy between Persia and East Rome. It had been useful to preserve that balance—though no man could have seen the end to which it would be put —and now it was useful to similarly establish Antioch.

Thus practicality born of fear gave Nureddin to graciously receive Manuel's emissary, the Grand Duke Philip, the only remaining scion of the junior Imperial branch of the family at Constantinople. Philip's instructions were—as politely as possible—to demand the release of the Emperor's brother-in-law, Bohemond III, Count Constantine, and all remanded knights. More pointedly, Philip was to express His Imperial Majesty's pleasure if the Second Ravager of Cyprus and Great Intriguer of the Jerusalem court, to wit, respectively, Raymond III of Tripolis and Joscelin of Edessa, were also repatriated. Nureddin surmised at once, and correctly, the latter Princes were of no account to the Emperor and refused to negotiate their release. (That was for Almaric to do, and he took his good time about it—eight years—since it better profited his treasury, his army, and his peace of mind to be Regent of Tripolis and undoubtedly rid of his former brother-in-law, Joscelin.)

On their release, in January 1165, Bohemond, Colomon, and the Grand Duke Philip—whom the Prince of Antioch praised as lavishly as he was to execrate his brother within two years—were bid to rest several weeks at one of Nureddin's most magnificent country seats— al-Fadila Palace—where, again, within two years, Andronikus and Theodora would find haven. (Al-Fadila means "ideal." Considering its silver walls encrusted with emeralds, turquoises, and diamonds, the name was, perhaps, no mere pretension. "I asked to see the Prince's apartments," Philip once told me. "The steward explained there were none. Only a small bedroom off the observatory roof. I asked to see that. An infantryman's tent is furnished more lavishly.") From al-Fadila, the party proceeded at once to Antioch where Bohemond ordered numerous Te Deums, in the main to display himself and reassure his people. Then, leaving the Principate under the unexpectedly responsible Regency of his eighteen-year-old sister, Philipa, the Prince proceeded to Constantinople, "to personally thank my liege and sister's husband for his efforts in my behalf."

In truth, it was something more than a courtesy call. Lacking chronology, authority, or experience, the twenty-one-year-old Prince was all but commanded to come to Constantinople and settle the fulfillment of the Emperor's suzerain rights—specifically the introduction of a Roman administration and a Greek Catholic Patriarch. At Blachernae Bohemond was alternately blandished and diplomatically brow-beaten, his Imperial sister now among the flatterers, now among the bullies, as the Emperor bid her. It was a revolting example of intimidation by all concerned, and one for which Bohemond never forgave Maria-Xenia. Seventeen years later, his revenge was abject.

On 30 June 1165 the Prince returned to Antioch with a new Patriarch, of the Greek rite, Athenasius II, who was solemnly enthroned in St. Peter's Cathedral, despite riots beyond the doors and the interdict of the Latin Patriarch, Aimery of Limoges, now in self-imposed exile at Qosair Castle.

Satisfied, and nothing loath to delay, Manuel returned to his Hungarian campaign, amidst rumors he was about to exercise the Orthodox spouse's right to a second divorce and a third remarriage. Nearly four years since the Imperial nuptials, and the Augusta had suffered that number of miscarriages. Midwives and physicians had variously described her as carrying too high, too low, her tubes too small, her diet too rich, too thin, but the Emperor, himself practiced in medicine, would hear of no quack remedies which would disfigure or in any way discomfort his young Empress, by whom he was infatuated, helplessly, more and more, day by day. He abided by Hippocrates' and Galenius' observations—sensible in the particular, majestic in the whole—and called most physicians "otherwise barbers, butchers, and monkeys with razors—in that order." In truth, if the Emperor seemed distracted his perplexity may have had more to do with the nature of his war with Hungary and her allies.

Despite betrayals, broken treaties, and attacks, now upon the Empire, now received upon the pate of his own kingdom, Geza II had died in alliance with Constantinople. His brothers (who became Stephen IV and Ladislas II) were rather willing to accept Frederick's hegemony if he sponsored their enthronement, which he did. The patently legitimate successor, Stephen III, Geza's son, was deposed by Ladislas, who died and was succeeded within a year by the equally pro-Hohenstaufen Stephen IV. It was at this point Geza's son—brother-in-law to the Grand Duchess Maria, Princess Boris, and Queen Theodora's sister—fled to Constantinople to seek aid in re-enthronement.

Now, it is too facile to argue Stephen III was exchanging German for Greek hegemony, and Manuel went to war on that point. Rather, at stake was the integrity of Hungary as a buffer between the East Roman and Holy Roman Empires. Of course, we cannot exclude the possibility of Byzantine influence. Yet in the choice between the open fact of Frederick's outright overlordship and the likelihood Manuel would minimally interfere preferring, in the tradition of the Comneni, a neutral zone between himself and his first wife's Imperial kin, Stephen, in wisdom, chose the more subtle patronage of New Rome.

It will be remembered during civil wars involving the Kievan succession in the late forties and early fifties, Manuel, abiding by the Rota system, had supported the legitimate George Dolgoruky rather than his contesting nephew, Izyaslav, whose sister Anne was Stephen III's stepmother. This led to the alliance between Izyaslav and Geza II. When that Prince died, he bequeathed his political hatred for Manuel to his son, Jaroslav. Virtually as a matter of course Andronikus' protector committed his armies—as early as spring, 1164—to Stephen IV against Stephen III and the Emperor. Now, a year later, Manuel, on the information of agents at the Galician court, expected to find his cousin in the Russian contingent. As Michael Branas told me, "His Majesty spent as much time searching for Andronikus as defending himself—often in notorious risk of his own life."

Andronikus was, of course, wiser than that. Having trained Jaroslav's cavalry in Greek techniques and—"My lord, you are costing me a fortune"—done away with the hardy, scruffy, but lamentably dumb step ponies (degenerate descendants of the Attilan horde), replacing them with imported Arabian steeds and Hungarian Percherons, the renegade Duke was content to remain at Galich, while his host pursued war. Thus the incidental hope of recapturing his cousin was thwarted. The Emperor, nevertheless, was not so disappointed as to be impervious to the new discipline, heretofore absent, in Russian armies, which, joined to their proverbial ferocity and stamina, constituted a newly ominous northern threat.

Worse still, it was reported to Manuel from sources he did not doubt, Jaroslav was so confident in his "Imperial Prize"—and charmed by him as well—he was proving himself that most unstoppable omnivore: the excited pupil, listening in everything to Andronikus' counsel. It was no difficult task to imagine the ultimate intent of that advice, and while the Emperor scarcely feared a Russian conquest, he was of no mind to waste money, men, or effort in defense against such mischief.

Albeit, Jaroslav's improved forces were not enough to keep Stephen II on the Apostolic throne. Four weeks after the siege of Stuhlweissenburg began, the population rioted, the soldiers mutinied, and the usurper-King, weakened and abed with measles caught from his grandson, was deposed, entering a merciful coma after signing the instrument of abdication.

By September 1165 Manuel had returned, indifferent with usual triumph, to Constantinople.

Michael Branas told me many years later: "When we returned from Hungary, the Emperor seemed unaccountably—well, if not despondent —dejected, unlikely quiet. Nothing seemed to raise him. At the annual banquet given for His Majesty by the Scholarians, Excubitors, Candidate, Archontopuli, and Varangians—and hosted by their generals— even then, he seemed pensive, his good humor effortful. And this, mind you, was a man whose self-control, whose ability to put on the best public face, no matter his feelings, left us all in the dust.

"During the masques, in the semidarkness, I told him I had noticed he seemed troubled these days and did I dare presume, not only as his concerned subject, but the husband of his niece, to inquire the nature of his grief. He had been listening profile, but now he turned, half his long, handsome face with those enormous, vulnerable eyes drawn into shadow. He stared in silence for a moment, then said, 'What are your appointments tomorrow?' 'At Your Majesty's service,' I said. He said, 'Can you break them? Good. We'll go to Rufiniana.'

"The next day, a gorgeous day—early autumn—we hunted the entire time till evening, scarcely at all conversing except in the discussion of our game. At dinner, at last, he began to speak of himself, of his moodiness. He was certain he had, lately, been a burden to everyone and through my agency begged our forgiveness. I said, 'Sire, I can only say it is we who have failed you somewhere.' He shook his head. 'No. Nothing of the sort.' He paused, he sighed. 'It occurs to me what good I do gets less of heaven's blessing than another man's work because, in the end, to do good is not my choice—it is my only justification before God. There is a *world* of good I ought to do and do not; therefore what good I do at all is little enough.'

"I leaned forward in my chair as he sat back. I asked him, 'Can I be of no help? None at all?' His elbows on the arms of the chair, his hands lifted, while he twisted his golden marriage band and looked away, he said, almost wearily, 'Yes, I ought to tell you. You are his friend. I have it in mind to pardon my cousin. I would like to bring him home.' I was astonished. Still looking away, but moving his elbows to the table, he spoke more to himself than his company, 'But God, it pains me to think him among those savages.'"

What is obvious to us at this distance is that the possibility the Emperor's affection for—if not dread of—his cousin had been sharpened by the expectation of seeing him face to face—and, yes, capturing him if that were so—after eleven years, at Stuhlweissenburg. Michael could not have helped but be surprised. Nothing had indicated such a turn of mind in the Emperor. It is almost certain his reconsideration was more emotional than political, though neither aspect is mutually exclusive.

Needless to say, Manuel was forced to confront the implacable opposition of John Sergius, and this led to the first breach between the Emperor and the Heir Presumptive, no mere difference in principle but a complete if temporary dissolution of their relationship. Frantic, the Protovestarius pushed too hard. Had the man some insight, he would have perceived at once this was scarcely an occasion to be fought with a public truncheon—via his sycophants—but one internal, to be fought insidiously, quietly, in the privacy of a chamber, inciting fear to overcome forgiveness.

The court was in an uproar, now falling on one side, now on the other, with consequent snubs from the Emperor or reprisals from John Sergius. Not unexpectedly, the Protovestarius, sensing he had overreached himself, refused to concede and withdraw, as well he might have done. He had only to realize the Emperor knew Andronikus would never return to Constantinople as mute courtier, that if exile were to be lifted, the reprieve could but be conditional, and therefore without threat to his person or position. But alarmed by the Emperor's independence he failed to see his uncle's forgiveness was ambivalent. Even after the Emperor lifted Andronikus' prohibition, the Protovestarius acted with appalling petulance; so much so, Manuel—in no mood to have his shining charity tempered by his own resurrected dread—no longer spoke to his nephew save on public occasions, refused to meet with him on government business save in the company of "council," and had his name as Heir Presumptive stricken from the *Domine Salva Fac.*

On 31 October and 1 November 1165, an Imperial Prescript was read in all the churches and all senates of the Empire pronouncing the pardon of the Grand Duke Andronikus and restoring to him "all liberty, safety, and dignities as befit his rank Imperial."

Michael Branas: "I was in Holy Wisdom the morning reprieve was announced. The Deacon, Eustathius, could not even finish the name. A roar went up between those golden walls unlike any I have ever heard in my life. I glanced over at the Protovestarius. He was looking down and away with an odd, drawn, almost sad expression. That afternoon when the Emperor appeared at the last games of the season in the Hippodrome, he was adored like a god."

On 7 November, Andronikus received his brother at Galich, carrying his pardon and orders to proceed at once to Cilicia, as Captain General against Thoros II, the only survivor, unscathed, of Haranc Castle, who had, yet again, rebelled.

XXIV

Andronikus: "I was astounded by Manuel's pardon. It was one of the few times in our lives when he took me completely by surprise. Of course, by that I realized his sincerity—however puzzling its source—since whenever he set great things afoot against me, their delicate steps usually set the earth trembling. Odd, I thought it as purposeless not to accept as to accept the pardon. I must admit, I was, by then, tired of Russia, which is still forming out of chaos, of the renegade's life and one's inability to dare the future by planning for it, of the rebel's punishments—and I was lonely. Yet this was scarcely the motivation to return to the Empire.

"You see, what I had to keep in mind—the very hardest thing to retain—was some sense of moral outrage, which comfort will always dull. This is, in any degree, difficult, if you are singular in your insight and, at the age of forty-three, have done nothing constructive to effect its conclusions. In any event, what purpose could be served by exile from the land I sought to change? If Constantinople was the light of the world, there—in upheaval and rebuilding—the elimination of oppression and the reconfiguration of society must first be tended. In exile, I was only an intruder, and the most barbarian land has not the sense of itself which is the integrity answerable to the world's expectations. There could not have been even the contemplation of a Platonic Republic, without Athenian Greece, its magnificence and its flaws."

The journey to Cilicia was indirect to say the least. The two brothers were instructed to pay a state visit to Jaroslav's second cousin, Andrew Bogliubsky, Grand Prince of Kiev, then sail south along the Dnieper, cross the Black Sea, and disembark at Sinope, where Philip would return to Constantinople, and Andronikus, having met with his army, would cross Lesser Asia—north to south—to Tarsus, a traversal of some seventeen hundred miles. Validity of forgiveness, in effect, was kept sincere by distance.

Philip: "As we were leaving the Galician kremlin, Jaroslav, who truly loved my brother, turned on the stairs to his apartments, came back to our horses, and patted Andronikus' hand. He said, 'I have a sense about these things, my friend. One day you will wear a crown. It is scarcely conceivable you were born for anything less.' To my surprise, Andronikus took Jaroslav's hand in both his own—a gesture almost unknown to him—and smiling with wit and sadness, said, 'An Imperial crown or a crown of thorns, my brother? One is the only alternative of the other.' 'Well,' Jaroslav said, 'I need not tell you which is the more glorious.' I had begun to say, 'Pity then he's not a Christian,' but Andronikus, sensing something the like, cut me off at the first word with a tiny furious gesture of his hand, leaned from his horse, and embraced the Prince."

Michael Branas: "The army arrived at Sinope 1 March. Andronikus was expected on the morning of the fifth. I cannot describe to you the anticipation of the soldiers, even the General Staff. No one had seen him in ten long years and in that time—I know why, perhaps, but not how—he had become a legend, which, one may say, is all things to all men. Well, promptly in the morning—having disembarked the previous night and gone into seclusion at the Governor's palace—he arrived on the field of Mars where we were encamped, about six miles from the city.

I had had lookouts posted and when he was in sight, they were ordered to sound their trumpets. In all the Empire, possibly in the whole world, he was the only man who could raise a frenzy comparable to that in the Emperor's presence. As he passed through the camp, his face was stiff, but his lips were trembling perceptibly. Now and then, rather blindly, he would pat one man's head, one man's shoulder—but looking straight ahead—until that head or shoulder dipped and another replaced it, or hands reached up, took his, and kissed them. I'd seen to it that the majority of the infantry were veterans who had served under him or served to be inspired by him in the years before his fall. If this were his homecoming, I meant it to show he was welcome. He embraced me at the entrance to the praetorium. No reunion in my life has moved me more."

In all this, personally incited, it is not surprising Andronikus took but a month to subdue Thoros. On 24 April 1166 he dispatched a letter to an immensely gratified Emperor informing him of the Prince's capture and the disestablishment of recidivist citadels. Three days later, posts crossing, surely, he received a message from his wife which informed him of his mother's death. Andronikus sent on a second letter to the Emperor in which he declared his intention of a forced ride to Constantinople to attend the Sebastocratrix Emerita's obsequies. He was bringing with him Thoros for Manuel to do with as he wished.

Andronikus: "I took with me only a small escort besides the Cilician Prince and Michael Branas. We changed horses at every military garrison. At Laodicea we were met by an Imperial agent, who handed me instructions to put Thoros in his charge and return at once to Tarsus. Several years ago Michael Branas told me he had never expected I should take so calmly what he called that 'unfeeling, unforgivable order.' He persisted in believing—he still does—it was given by Manuel in the consideration, dead, my mother was beyond need of my presence, and I would do better to be on hand in the late-won calm of Cilicia, than to kiss her corpse farewell before she was put away from me forever. Michael, unfortunately, has a soldier's mind in the very deepest sense: any insight proceeds from a direct reference of his career. (He once wrote, quite straight-faced, a treatise on the merits of military tactics as found in the Bible and the *Iliad*.)

"As for me, it was as though I had been sleepwalking since the pardon arrived at Galich. Manuel may have been unfeeling and unforgivable, but rather before than after the fact. Now he was only consistent. There would be no entry for me, ever, at Constantinople. In effect, I was still in exile. Now, I had in my hands a man who was the source of much strife in the Empire, captured by me in the Empire's behalf. To relinquish him would be to accept my cousin's deceit by ellipsis—I had never been *told* I could not return to the capital, nor I think had Philip. I was, in sum, being played as both a fool and a tool, a tool in the fullest sense of function without compensation. I resolved to wait.

"I instructed the agent to return to Constantinople for more detailed orders and further convey to his superior, whoever he might have been, I would surrender Thoros under no conditions to anyone less than a general of the army. A week later, there arrived at the Magistrate's palace, where I was headquartered, no less than John Sergius' brother, David, which I took as a direct affront. The orders were the same, with one significant addition. In my cousin's presence I was to take the Oath of Allegiance to Maria Catherine Porphyriogeneta and her betrothed, Prince Bela of Hungary, as Heiress Presumptive and Consort. I had heard rumors of this match—with visions of a Greco-Hungarian confederation from the Vistula to the Euphrates—but I had scarcely believed Manuel was serious. Perhaps he might disinherit Johnny, yet with a herd of Comneni males, no less myself, it seemed to me errancy in the extreme to sacrifice the dynasty to a cossack if only to satisfy the pride of his own loins.

"That was the curious thing about him, you know, the mixture of personal limpidness and megalomanic politics. This, I should say, more than any, stands as the reason for the inconsistency of his foreign policy. (Hence, my first necessity when I assumed the Regency was to design some comprehensibly uniform attitude toward alien countries. I inherited, after all, all the animosity Manuel engendered and none of the alliances, whose point was buried with him.) In any event, the oath itself did not trouble me. I suspected revolution would ensue among the General Staff—or what was left of it—before Hungarian intervention within the Empire would be allowed should Manuel die. Rather, I sensed I was being pushed, intentionally, to the limits of tolerable humiliation, as a pupil displaying the extent of obedience his chastisement had taught him. And so I dispatched my own messenger with a reply, in which I categorically refused to take the oath.

"I sent copies to Anastasia and various key members of the court, which is, of course, a flagrant violation of correspondence with the Emperor. To be sure, a crisis ensued. To prevent an Imperially inspired kidnapping, I placed my own guards round Thoros.

"In his reply, Manuel attempted to present a reasoned argument for the pledge to Maria Catherine, and, with an archness very unlike him, attempted also to play upon the animosity between John Sergius and myself. He could be a compelling liar—or else stupid in his sincerity. I maintained my stand, especially after I had word from Anastasia that she was receiving a daily, secret stream of visits from the family, as well as representatives of our most powerful houses, requesting her to convey to me their support in this matter. I remember vividly, in one of her communications, she said, 'The pity of it is, these poor men have been so entirely dominated by Manuel for so long, they seem unable, even in their disagreement, to act independently and so turn to you since one of their own cannot—or dare not—lead the way.' Nothing pleased me more than to be distinguished, instinctively, from those lamentable devils by the damned themselves.

"One day I asked my cousin David—who was living in the opposite wing of the palace—why he supported the oath in the face of the family —and his own disinheritance as much as mine. For what must have been the only time between us, that mask of defensive arrogance fell from his face, he stared at me straight on, shrugged, and said, 'Christ, what else is there to do?' I said, 'Do you really mean that? Contest him, man. What's wrong with you?' 'And if we failed?' he asked me, which is some indication of the indomitability he would bring to such a challenge. 'Yes,' I said, 'if we failed? What've we lost?' He shook his head. And I knew. He would lose all that ever really mattered to him: the accouterments of power rather than the power itself."

When word reached the Laodicean Magistrate's palace a full company of Scholarians was on its way to take Thoros by force, if necessary, Andronikus committed an act which tested the loyalty of even his most abiding admirers, who could not, at the time, follow the consonance of his logic. During the night of 28 May 1166, the Grand Duke and the Prince of Cilicia vanished.

In 1180 Michael Branas told me: "I guessed—correctly as it turned out—they would resurface in Cilicia. I was astonished and furious. I felt betrayed. Only much later did I realize, against my will, while Andronikus was by this acting with supreme *political* irresponsibility, he was first, and perhaps justly, remaining responsible to himself. If a man has not that right, he cannot live. It was the sort of action other men might think upon but never commit. If once you had told me I could make such a distinction I would have thought you mad. But His Imperial Highness does have a way of stretching one beyond the limits one thought possible for oneself, not by what he makes you do, but what he makes you *think* in reaction to what *he* does. Of course, in a more practical, even compassionate sense, I can't quite approve of that gesture. After all, he *did* set loose to more havoc that Armenian fiend with the final irony that not Augustus or Thoros suffered most from his 'clean ledger' —the refusal to offer the Emperor faithful service in return for mendacity —but the conscriptee and the city and suburban poor whom it behooved Andronikus to champion."

("Have you heard," my brother exclaimed to me the day I arrived at Constantinople to begin my matriculation, "the Grand Duke Andronikus has run off with Thoros the Bloody, and it's said they're going to raise an army and take the whole of East Asia." Michael was always willing— and is still—to fly on the wings of his own exaggeration, to carry every premise to its logical apostrophe. On the other hand, with pretensions to scholarship and the last detail—twelve-year-olds make the most exacting bureaucrats—I was appalled by this "brigandism" and confidently predicted the Megadux would rot in hell for his treachery. In truth, I was rather more impressed—if not enchanted—that afternoon to watch from the roof of Palace Cantostephanus, where my brother and I were lodged by our father's friend, Duke Felix, the funeral cortege of Maria of Alania, who had ascended the throne as the betrothed of Emperor Michael VII ninety-nine years before. Nothing seemed to me to confirm more surely the age, the heritage, the holiness of Constantinople than the long line of Grand Dukes and Grand Duchesses, heavily veiled, led by the Emperor and Empress, following the purple velvet and gold catafalque of this woman who had lived beyond her own legend and spanned from the moment of her birth, to her death, the last of the Macedonians, the Time of Troubles, the rise of the Comneni in an empire reduced, virtually, to the city itself and their present, foremost glory. Only since that day have I wondered what can it have been like— what loneliness beyond the imagination to endure—for one to live on and on, who was already old when old men now were born. We believe nothing is more precious than life, nothing more awful than annihilation.

Yet what can be said of existence in the face of Mary of Alania who was forced by some cruel indestructability to repeat nearly every one of her first, illustrious sixty years, one by one with fifty-one more; alone, to survive a life, when she found herself beyond the possibility of further experience, and all experience which she had endured, locked into history and judged by it to survive, alone, when all whom she had loved —and perhaps their children and even their children's children—were portraits, memory, and dust.)

"Not that he is himself inclement," said Manuel of Andronikus after the kidnapping and release of Thoros, "but that my cousin believes any clemency shown him is a weakness. No matter how just I attempt to be, even on the side of dangerous excess, my generosity is metamorphosed into weapons for him to use, in turn, against me. You cannot be fair with that man." (When many years later, I reported this verdict to Andronikus, he smiled and said, "His powers of deduction could suffer an enviable amnesia when he needed to justify himself; rather like a matron's prompt illness whenever her divorced husband arrives to visit with their children. He could not see both the whole and its parts. He would rather have forgotten his conditions pursuant to my return to the Empire and remembered only the graciousness of the *idea* of forgiveness.")

To provide the worm which would feed on the Grand Duke's renewed fecklessness, fate selected this moment for a lunatic attempt to assassinate John Sergius. He escaped unscathed and, seemingly, more than ever entrenched in Imperial power. The Emperor, appalled and chilled—with almost superstitious intensity—by the repetition of incidents which had brought about the death of his nephew's father, confused personal concern for the Protovestarius with political self-abnegation. John Sergius had warned him against Andronikus' incorrigibility, and he had chosen to disregard that voice. The Protovestarius was restored to power and Andronikus' fate was, in part, sealed for the next decade.

The first word from Cilicia was that Andronikus had freed Thoros at once upon arrival in Sis and—an act of apparent madness—resumed his post to contend, from the beginning again, against the Prince. In complete bewilderment, the Emperor, for the moment, took no measures against his cousin, though Michael Branas, still at Laodicea, requested transfer from the Grand Duke's forces or else threatened to altogether resign from the army. But a week after Andronikus' resumption of duty, he again vanished, and along with him, his valet, Leo, returned from Sicily, as well as three thousand pounds of gold—taxes of the major cities of Cilicia—carried away on twelve horses.

Andronikus: "I had procured that fortune from the treasury by virtue of my authority as Captain General, with the indifferent excuse of translating it to Constantinople. Obviously I could not take with me a guard in quite the opposite direction, east, and so, like poor Abul Kasim and his gold-loaded mules in my grandfather's reign, I went off, blithely unprotected in search of refuge. While it's perfectly apparent I wasn't strangled in my tracks like Abul, I might have been. I find my irresponsibility to myself, both physically and historically, grotesque. Had I been killed, it would have been a sordid end. Now that I am Emperor, it is among the most often sung of my adventures. Indeed, the anarchy of my acts thenceforward is, more often than not, celebrated to the exclusion of those twelve previous years, which seem to be of interest only to myself. Why these antics? It is too unctuous to call them the conscious retaliation of my disgust. I know only that while some men pretend to truth and justice and forgiveness, few are otherwise motivated save by self-aggrandizement. I acted the criminal by ordinary standards of honor and propriety, but I did so openly. Had I acted the honest man, I would have been considered a fool and a victim, to the gain of other men. I resolved, not so articulately as I now believe, to be bound by no law and no compunction but my own, forensically, as other men act in secret.

"From that moment, and for many years, I believed any further struggle purposeless—whether in my own behalf or others'. For the oppressed I'd done little enough and—from extreme to extreme—believed those gestures invalid, the excuse of ambition. Of course, in the swim of that sentimental and flatulent disgust and self-disgust, I did not stop to ask myself what had been the nature of this ambition. Power. Or why I had wanted this power. Scarcely for the pomp, which, I'm pleased to say, is even more absent in my court than my uncle's. Scarcely for the reassurance of my own worthiness. I know my worth—or at least the worth of my judgments, which is all a man is before the world—and, save this once, I never doubted them. I wanted power, particularly to the purpose of ordering the world as it ought to be, logically and compassionately, but always to the side of compassion even at the expense of logic. And now that I should never know the fulfillment of my ambitions against a scheme of things of which I did not approve, what did it matter what became of the world or myself?

"Well, if I am appalled by the idiocy to which I have sometimes descended, constantly believing myself to have reached a final maturity, only in retrospect to discover I was the more grossly immature for certainty, I forgive myself, that man of eighteen years ago. It is too deceptively simple—and therefore the more attractive—to believe the final answer is anarchy—of the mind, which is cynicism, or of action, which is loutishness. But then, no man knows what is happening to him except in retrospect. Consider that in this abysmal state, I also found Theodora, who was the greatest—and perhaps the only—gratuitous consolation in the course of my life."

I am certain my surprise at the emphatic—one might almost say artless—emotionalism of his last words was obvious. He squinted at me and looked away. "You have done me a great disservice, Nicetas, by coining that sobriquet in one of your monographs: the 'New Proteus.' I know you meant it as an ideal, but it is an inaccurate ideal, exceedingly unkind and perhaps pernicious. By that, I am removed from human experience, the integrity of my reactions is called into question. I am denied myself compassion. I seem only to condescend to other men. I seem not to act from a basis of reality, but in a sort of sublime whimsy, from role to role with an eye to the absurdity of the world, which I would readily admit, but not at the expense of the humanity—mine—which makes that judgment. I can guess why you have done this. You wish to make sense of me according to your own convictions of what a man should be. You wish to believe you understand me. To do this, you have removed me from the pale of other men. In effect, there is nothing I can do to prove to you that I am only a man, that I love, that I don't want to die, that I act only as I see it, as it is given to me to be."

I said, very quietly, "But you are not like other men, Lord, though I am not about to believe some of the stories your enemies have put about —as for instance, you entered Buceleon sane, and emerged a lunatic." He laughed shortly at this, genuinely amused. It was the warmth, I think, of that laughter, without connivance, a simple relish, which brought me up short, whereas his words a moment before had only scratched at my credulity. I remember, as though it were a moment ago, thinking perhaps I *had* done him a disservice. I remember once, shortly after our first meeting, he had good-naturedly described my imagination as "caught in a bureaucrat's body." He had said, "You are obsessed with detail and category, which is good up to a point in a historian. You will catch the incident the Olympian misses and for that, perhaps, tell us a great deal more than you yourself realize. But you mean to capture the whole, and that is impossible. You sense the chaos beneath and you would lie rather than confess it, by pretending to understand what you cannot, simply because there is too much to understand."

I am still haunted by that conversation. I see him the following year in those days of his death, which no man who was alive to witness shall ever forget. I see his grandeur in the midst of the horror and chaotic brutality, the hysteria and the unspeakable desecration of his person, and it seems to me now, as I was too blinded by his light to see it then, no man can carry whimsy, however philosophically founded, to the point of enduring what he endured to the shame of us all. Fear and grief and love were the only possible source of his dignity in that terrible September of 1185.

Too much a legend at the court of Manuel Augustus, perhaps he became unreal for me before he had the opportunity to be real. It is no difficult task to fix a personality without the constant contradiction of the actual, variable human presence. I preconceived him, and this prejudice, while he was alive, remained, so that I refuted all I saw in reference to what I had expected. Indeed the worst mischief may have been engendered the first day I met him and the day following his death when I consented, in grief, to the symmetry of legend, hardened his life, presumed a balance from one experience to the next; for this is what I wrote while the ghastly cadaver which had been he was still exposed and denied burial:

NOTE: September 1185. . . . Recall the first time he received me. I, having carried some papers—of what nature?—from Con., quaking, waiting for the Manifestation to enter the anteroom. Steps (a muffled call to someone—a short laugh—the voice higher than expected). The doors open. An equerry announces, "His Imperial Highness." In he strides—vigorous, curious, with that assured, almost offensively aloof air the whole family possesses. Beyond the family there are only petitioners. His face is both blank and alert. All that has occurred since intercedes between that moment and yesterday's monstrous event. He stands before me, at Oeneum, in 1178, not in second flower and miraculously vigorous (it is almost inconceivable he is but two years the Emperor's junior), only preserved superbly for swords, arrows, axes, whips, and stones. I see the vulnerable hand, the vulnerable bright teeth, the handsome mouth, the outline of the vulnerable thigh, the gray eye, the planes of smooth skin where the weapons will lacerate and enter the internum. . . .

Some men, they say, see visions of their own future in fire, a pastime I do not trust and to which I have never surrendered. The presumption is invalid because no man will voluntarily anticipate his own pain. If it were possible, moreover, to see the future, then we should be obliged by it to act against it or to fulfill it, which precludes the most precious premise of intelligence: free will, choice. Once Andronikus said to me, "Nothing is fated, but that does not mean magic—real magic, which is the evocation of awe and wonder—is removed from existence. Rather it must be appreciated in the coincidence of our lives, in the possibility of so much having not happened had this and this not preceded it. That is a source of terror almost too immense for the mind to tolerate. We dare not think factors upon which our lives come to depend are born of anything so frail as chance. Would I have met the Queen of Jerusalem had I not first seduced Philipa? Would Philipa have been as seduceable had not some young man I never met died suddenly before my arrival at Antioch?"

He was referring, of course, to the fact Maria-Xenia's sister was deep in grief that summer, 1166, in retreat, praying for the soul of a knight for whose death she felt in part responsible. It seemed the young man had quite a deft way of throwing dates into the air, catching them in his mouth, and swallowing them, all at once. According to a letter to her sister—which Her Majesty graciously allowed me to remove from the archives—Philipa was so charmed by the feat, she insisted the poor worthy repeat the trick that one last time. He choked to death, like Terpander, before her eyes. The Princess was inconsolable.

Hearing of her unhappiness, who, as a child, with her sister and mother, had received him so kindly during his "first idyll," as he called it, at Antioch, in 1152, Andronikus dipped into his bags of purloined gold and came up with an enchanting diversion. "Within two weeks, I had got silversmiths and seamstresses to equip and accessorize ten of the prettiest ten-year-old orphans from St. Peter's, whom I sent to her dressed in blue velvet, silver-whipped soutanes, carrying silver bows. I admit to a little conscience at using these poor children—in principle, if not fact—as clowns to divert a privileged woman, but at least as her servants they would be bathed, fed, and dressed."

Philipa was swept out of her misery like a lark. She sent for Andronikus, who was renting an enormous villa at Daphne. Within a week, an affair was commenced between the Princess and the Grand Duke. Her brother, Bohemond, abraided by his visit to Constantinople, was of a mind to spite the Imperium at his sister's expense. Criticized by his Greek Patriarch for allowing the devirginization of his unmarried sister, the Sovereign Prince snapped, "Philipa is lovelier than Maria, and more intelligent. All she lacks, which Maria has had too much of, is good luck. Insofar as I am concerned, Maria can go hang and Philipa can do as she likes."

"Infatuation, nothing more, more on the Princess' part than mine," said Andronikus. "Because it ended abruptly, men call it a calculation. I should think nothing else could prove it further from the truth. If, however, seduction is the cynical manipulation of another human being for purposes of one's own pleasure—with indifference to that other's happiness—then, yes, I am in some ways guilty in my alliance with Philipa. But if those principles stand, then, believe it or not, my boy, that was the single seduction of my life. She was young, and I was at an age when men confuse youth with sensuality only because the first signs of decay in one's own body are the first speculations of death, of which sexual pleasure must be the antithesis or it is nothing. I liked the Princess immensely and she loved me. Even if I could do nothing to assuage her unhappiness when I left her, she remained generous of heart and never afterward spoke ill of me. I adore and revere her memory for it."

Those are the words of the man whom Michael Branas called (many Constantinopolitan husbands agreeing with him), part in admiration, part in disapproval, and—who knows?—jealousy, "the most heartless and notorious philanderer since Leo III Augustus." (It is a tradition of the army the great Emperor and Iconoclast—morally impeccable according to historical report—was an indefatigable womanizer. It may be, as history is sometimes more exact in its stage whispers than its open theater.)

Significantly, not one of Andronikus' mistresses ever spoke out against him. Indeed, Philipa, with better reason than any, is a most notable example of this curious fidelity. Famed, I suspect, as much for the political implications of the alliance as the tender and melancholy languor she suffered after Andronikus left her, and, of course, her early death, the Princess wrote the following letter to her Imperial sister in 1168, a year after the Grand Duke fled to Persia with the Dowager Queen of Jerusalem:

> Dearest Maria. It has, however belatedly, come to my attention that the Emperor's cruel edict against Andronikus and the excommunication from Orthodoxy of both Andronikus and our dear cousin, Theodora, shall stand and that it suits your husband to do this in my behalf. If this is so then I am, forthwith, asking you to tell Manuel to lift both the edict and the religious interdict at once, for, in the one, he is at peril of my displeasure, and in the other, of his own immortal soul. I was not soiled by Andronikus, though it is not too much to say, I think, I am being soiled—insofar as gossip and reputation are to the point—in order that your husband's virtuous reputation may remain unimpaired. All men know his persecution of Andronikus is a matter of personal vindictiveness and questionable politics. But this is for Manuel to accord with his own conscience. In the meantime he is besplattering my character. I know you will ask how it could be I should prefer silence to vendetta. I can only say men will, in any event, draw their own conclusion: that I am so grief-struck and little in heart, I would prefer Andronikus more dead than alive, hunted down if he will not love me. But I am not so wretched in my unhappiness nor lacking in forgiveness I would feel it so and it is intolerable to be thought so. I shall love him always—at least for a very long time. He loved me only a little, only a little while. But lucky enough I was to have that. Before he left, he said to me, "You must be in no man's thrall after this. They will make you subject to their own designs by telling you you are dishonored and lucky to be kept from a convent by their own superb charity. This must not be. I want you to leave Antioch, as I do." That is when he consigned to me the monies he had brought with him, which, of course, I have returned to the Imperial Treasury. I have tried to be strong in this because I know he is alive, somewhere, and will hear of me, and I want his respect, if that is all I can have. Not that I shall seem indifferent, but that I cannot bear the thought he will think me a weak fool and regret whatever affection in which he held me. I do not need revenge—not by Manuel, not by Bohemond. Nor do I want suitors such as the new Governor of Cilicia, whom Manuel sent to me to win my heart. Your husband must think me an idiot if he believes I would relinquish immorality with a hero for the virtue of a husband. If a woman may be unhappy and

content, I am so, and I beg you to intercede with Manuel in behalf of a man of whom we were both so fond as children and who shall be with me, in my thoughts and my dreams, for all of my life. Philipa.

(A few months after the dispatch of this letter, she was married to the elderly, elegant former Constable of Jerusalem, Theodora's platonic adorer, Count Humphrey of Toron, who himself may have been reeling from the fate of the former Queen whom he had so devotedly worshiped. Their marriage, which lasted ten years and was childless, remained a curious mixture of affection and mutual consolation: faithful, serene, and, ultimately, enigmatic. The Princess died in 1178, after suffering horribly from cancer of the spine. When he heard his was the only name she repeated on her deathbed, Andronikus asked to pay for the purchase and decoration of a porphyry sarcophagus for her sepulchre. But Bohemond would hear none of it and Count Humphrey was indignant "at that man's boldness." And so the Grand Duke designed himself and had constructed a small chapel in the Princess' memory at Oeneum. The reader this day may still see it—a memorial of discreet beauty, in the Latin manner, save an iconostasis. Its walls are of pure Russian rhodonite, the rose effect carried into the decoration in quartz, chalcedony, pearls, opals, and red gold, used far more sparingly than is the custom of Greek architects [presumably Andronikus learned well from al-Fadila]. I have visited the little church several times these last years and it is strange to think, since it still serves the purpose to which it was assigned and conceived by the imagination of the late Emperor, it is something where nothing would have been, save for his existence; it is an act of his imagination, of the inner man, a portion of him which goes on forever.) *Explicit: Nicetas Acominatus.*

XXV

ANDRONIKUS. You're much smaller than I remembered.

THEODORA. I was only tall for a child.

ANDRONIKUS. And tell me: What is the purpose of having me called to you?

THEODORA. Uncle thought it perhaps best if I gave you fair warning.

ANDRONIKUS. Against what?

THEODORA. He means to have you excommunicated. Apparently he feels you must decide between Philipa and your hopes of heaven.

ANDRONIKUS. He need only say it and I would decide in favor of the lady and damnation. I had thought to break cleanly with the Princess. Now I see I should never have left her side.

THEODORA. Then there's no more point to what you do than to make mischief and be contrary like a child.

ANDRONIKUS. Madame, there are those who are born dead and pass from mother to undertaker with their eyes closed, accepting everything, denying nothing, never initiating, *like* the dead, merely acted upon. Then again there are those who are born to die, who find their own way through the world.

THEODORA. While the riddle of existence shines like bright blood from their eye—is that it?

ANDRONIKUS. Riddles must have their answers. I expect none, believe me.

THEODORA. I had always thought you too cynical to bake in a passion.

ANDRONIKUS. Only old men bake since they cannot be served. Theodora, I suggest you cease to treat a private interview as though it were being scored by your courtiers in a formal audience. This—or I will leave at once.

THEODORA. Oh, do as you like, for God's sake. I'm not made for this sort of errand. But you *have* tormented Philipa.

ANDRONIKUS. Come now. A man never intentionally torments a woman as much as she by nature torments a man.

THEODORA. You're right, you know. Let me tell you a story. Once, I recall, I was—oh—seven or eight, and I accompanied my father to a military review. I remember, afterward, one of his ADCs lifted me and I could feel the pressure of his forearm on my thighs, more pressure than necessary to keep hold of me. I can still feel the hairs of that arm on the back of my legs, even through the thin silk, and a very slight movement, barely a movement, as much as the poor fellow dared, up and down, little by little, up and down, and the folding of one hand around my leg. I had a sense of what he was going through and I said nothing. I delighted in it. My father was speaking to him and I'm certain he was hardly able to listen. His eyes were half asleep with pleasure and he was sweating like a pig. He kept swallowing noisily and his mouth was slack. It was an expression of pain or bewilderment or panic, for all I know. He did not look at me, at first, but when he did, I stared straight into his eyes. He held me then, even more tightly. But then I complained sweetly to be let down. Like the glowing little angel I pretended to be, I said how very glad I had been to see him again and embraced his sunburned neck and kissed his mouth while my father looked on appreciatively. I can still see that young face beneath the beautiful silver and ostrich-plumed helmet. He was faint. I let myself slide the whole length of his body. Once on my feet I embraced him a last time. A few days later, at Sebastocrator Palace, on God knows what pretext, he sought me with my playmates in the garden. I smiled at him, but I decided I barely had time for him. Still I knew he was watching me and every movement I made I exaggerated to show my limbs against my dress, to enchant him and tantalize him. But I never let him touch me again even though I loved him afterward for a whole year.

Incipit: Nicetas Acominatus:

We condemn you, Theodora Comnena Lotharingen and Andronikus Isaac Comnenus. We reprove, reprobate, and utterly reject you. . . . Likewise we forbid the faithful of Christ to associate, to praise, to give you counsel and sustenance or to defend you. . . . We condemn you, Theodora Comnena Lotharingen and Andronikus Isaac Comnenus as notorious and pertinacious sinners, incestuous and rebellious against the law of God, and therefore, We, Theodosius, Patriarch, Bishop of the See of St. Andrew, First among the Princes of God's most Holy and Orthodox Church, do excommunicate and anathematize you and condemn you to hellfire for all eternity. . . .

—From the Interdict of Excommunication of Theodora and Andronikus.

There is some controversy as to why Andronikus departed Antioch for Jerusalem. One version says Theodora commanded him to come to Acre. This is inference based upon records in the Imperial Archives in which the Emperor, as a last resort (and after Philipa's return of the Cilician revenues), requests his niece to convince Andronikus to voluntarily present himself to his cousin, Nicephorus Paleologus, now Governor of Crete. Presumably, Imperial clemency was the reward. But such occasion would not explain Prince Bohemond's outrage *before* the summons to the Dowager Queen's court. He could not, by any man's standard, complain his sister had been jilted, if the Grand Duke had been called from her side.

Guiscard's anger becomes more understandable, and Manuel's letter, too, if one considers the more mundane explanation. Andronikus grew bored with Philipa and left for Jerusalem of his own accord, shortly before King Almaric left for Constantinople on a state visit. Thereafter, the Imperial Secret Police, whose business it is—among many errands—to spy on visiting ambassadors or potentates, with no regard to rank or privacy, presented the Emperor with a short memorandum which informed him of Almaric's alarm "that womanizer, embezzler, and mischief-maker" was loose in the Court of the Holy Sepulcher. In effect, then, Manuel's letter to Queen Theodora, of which he made a great show to Almaric, becomes a matter of diplomacy between the two sovereigns, regardless of the subjects in question.

In private, the Emperor was exasperated. This was a new Andronikus. Absolute perversity reigned. Previously—and this quite possible, knowing Manuel—the Emperor held his cousin's gestures in grudging esteem. They were carried out with sweep, dash, gallantry, elegance, with an indifference to self and a willingness to accept legal consequence which could rise only from a dynast's ego, that arrogance and selfless duty of one whose family is the state. Now, his actions—criminal irresponsibility, criminal plunder, criminal philandering—were scarcely those of a well-brought-up farmer's son, let alone a gentleman. These were the doings of a common brigand, whose birth, unfortunately, gave him access to the highest circles, where his damage was magnified beyond a gangster's wildest dreams. A thousand miles away, moreover, in an autonomous kingdom, he was beyond chastisement whose nature the Emperor had not yet even allowed himself to guess. Free, he was an offense. Exiled, a danger. Manuel could only wait until his rebellious cousin's actions brought about a downfall of their own weight. It was not long in coming.

This is the woman, as I saw her, in 1178, who entered into the most famed love affair of the previous century. Once again, I present the note to myself as I wrote it after the first meeting. I was then twenty-four, and duly in awe:

I had got the repute of her beauty, and beautiful she most certainly is. Yet there remains in her features a harsh, almost mannish definition, which seems common to the women of the Imperial family. The nose is too strong, almost hawklike, the mouth too set. She has a curious, even charming, habit of speaking with her eyes cast down, and an almost frowning expression of earnestness. When she looks up—it seems to be an unwilling gesture—she smiles helplessly. The eyes blaze, the cheeks rise high and pronounced, like an infant's, the mouth opens very wide to reveal white, perfect—if slightly too large—teeth. Then she is radiant, sensuous, vulnerable. Whether or not it is recent of these unexpectedly adventuresome years with the Grand Duke, or a characteristic born to her, she seems at moments—while one speaks to her—to withdraw. Her expression becomes inward and impenetrable as one of Praxiteles' statues, yet she can repeat to you every word you have said. She possesses, for all her temper, her willfulness, her sharp wit, and lack of convention, the immemorial qualities of the true aristocrat: that inward melancholy of one with too much time to think, whose privilege has given her everything she could ever desire and nothing to look forward to. Her sense of honor is impeccable—as well it should be—for she knows the integrity of her name is, indeed, her passkey to her privilege. Her personal standards are exquisite, those which only assured wealth and position provide as there is no need to hoard sensations or momentary luxury. That is the frenzy of one who has only lately gained and may lose again. There is the usual revulsion before vulgarity which overwhelms emotions thus refined. There is the usual disillusion in the face of power brokers, whose cynicism and eagerness, the lady cannot realize, is the inevitable striving after that which she possesses by birthright. Flattery is, of course, abhorrent to her, since it is both unnatural worship, insincere, and an auction for her favors, an objectification. She is amused, when not disgusted, by the parvenu's exaggeration, for it is a caricature of her standards, the practitioner's self-abasement before models which are unnatural to him. There is about her a transparency, tolerating no guile, and she is quite without guile, herself. She has purity and repose. She is regal because she is self-contained without being indifferent. She possesses a countenance and dignity, unself-conscious as a child's—she is now forty-two years old—and against which her notorious reputation seems absurd. . . .

Andronikus: "I was forty-four years old when I met the Queen. I had not so much consciously forsworn love as believed myself to have surpassed it. I was quite taken with the glamour of negation, I rather think, after the ardency of my youth, which is the source of my reputation. Penetrating one woman after another, I discovered I thought, no difference between a princess' infatuation and a prostitute's competence.

Naturally if one concentrates on mere sexual satisfaction, all women are undifferentiated. We love, don't we, for what we believe is the singular in another human being. I looked for similarities to prove my point, and finding them, became cynical, forgetting it was my polygamy, not my mistress' humanity, which rendered a pattern to their behavior and, for me, nullified their integrity. I trust I was never cruel to any one of them, but I was never more than condescending.

"I may as well say, I was at first attracted and no more than that to my cousin and thereafter made the usual declarations to win one side of her bed. In truth—though I would never have admitted it—she irritated me. There was a distance about her—there still is—which was, and remains, frustrating. She was, and remains, too brutal in her treatment of those to whom she owes nothing and too sensitive, herself, to all criticism, especially that of her victims. She is not unkind, but she is arrogant. Once, this quite repelled me. But then, I was almost looking for flaws. The older one becomes, you see, the more self-centered one grows, so that love seems an intrusion, and if not doubted, then willfully denied. Sometimes that love is never contested. Mine was, I was punished for that love before I knew I truly felt it, and so I was committed to defend it, on principle, without any choice. Its consequences caught me before its nature became real to me."

Now, it had long been agreed between the Emperor and the King of Jerusalem, a final Armageddon would be engaged against Egypt. Manuel had proposed to rendezvous both an armada and an army with the Latin forces, in the spring of 1169. The *promise* of such a contributive force seemed, at first, enough commitment for Almaric. But as time passed, he became both wary and suspicious of Constantinople's lack of enthusiasm in joining this sacred crusade for a re-Christianized Egypt ("or Christianized, anyway, at the top," as Andronikus said. "The peasants could believe what they liked.") Hastily, then, but to the point, the King and his counselor, William, now Archdeacon of Tyre and Nazareth, were invited to Constantinople to conclude a certified military treaty and to seal it with a marriage. (This was the cause for Almaric's absence when Andronikus descended on his sister-in-law's court.) The King remained several months, while it pleased Manuel still in the ascent of his glory to show his fellow, fledgling Autocrat just how small a puddle he ruled in comparison to the Byzantine Empire. When the King returned to Jerusalem, he brought with him a new wife, John Sergius' eldest child, the Grand Duchess Maria Anna.

Andronikus' distant cousin, Count George Angelus, now a general of the army, wrote to him at Acre:

There is always another Comnena to occupy a throne. What is not so common is the armada Manuel intends to build and the monies which must be raised to pay for it. I tell you he means to impress Almaric by the sheer size of it all and thus remind His Majesty the delay in participation of this venture was not born of disinterest, but lack of proper attention due to otherwise pressing matters. What those might have been I cannot even venture to guess. It is the same as ever. Our august Emperor has an imagination more vivid than ripe. He scarcely embraces one project with his usual excitement than he is diverted by another. We had thought, of course, he had desired to dominate West Europe. Well, last October when Frederick stormed Rome, enthroned Paschal against public clamor, then sojourned too long until his army vanished in the outbreak of pestilence—*that* was when our worthy Sovereign should have struck. But last October he was busy with his lackeys discussing the guarantees he should give Almaric. He had grown bored with his visions of Italy. Egypt, if not any more easily captured, was something new.

There is a great deal of discontent here. Everything is begun, nothing resolved. Many generals are turning to John Sergius, but I do not think for very good reasons—at least any which would hold on a very honorable examination. H.I.H. is against these ventures, as you know, and it is supposed because he disprizes what my colleagues disprize, because he is personally incorruptible—who among your family, save yourself, needs more money or property?—(he is not loath, however, to purchase favorites with immense portions of public funds) because he loathes the same external enemies as any Roman, he would be a superb alternative. The truth is, if you will permit me, the Protovestarius, your cousin, is an ass—and a mean one—and he is superb *only* as an alternative, that is, an untested hope. . . .

Explicit: Nicetas Acominatus.

Andronikus, by the window, briefly scans the rest of the letter, held an unnatural distance from his eyes, then looks over at Theodora, sitting cross-legged beside him on a silver bedstead, her abundant hair awry, her body wrapped in a scarlet silk blanket lined with fox fur.

ANDRONIKUS. What do you think?

THEODORA. Almaric arrives home this week. How old is that letter?

ANDRONIKUS. What . . . forty days. He explains, he laid it aside.

Theodora shakes her head and sighs.

THEODORA. The Arabians have a legend of the Afreet—the monster incarnation of chaos—who once summoned cannot be put back in hell. It can't go on.

ANDRONIKUS. But it *will* go on.

THEODORA. It's immoral.

ANDRONIKUS. I'm certain Manuel thinks his activities the height of morality.

THEODORA. If that's morality, there's more contortion in it than a worm on a wheel. Why *don't* they turn to you? Why Johnny? None of them have forgot you. They write to you. They know you will appreciate what they have to say.

ANDRONIKUS. Precisely. They write to me. And by that they're certain they've done their day's work. But you see, between favors and threats he's emasculated the whole lot.

Theodora looks away toward the thin, bright slice of light of the window. After a moment, she squints thoughtfully.

THEODORA. Strange, isn't it? Since the influx of the Latins into the government he's *turned* from the West. I never thought of that before.

ANDRONIKUS. I suspect his precious émigrés are hoping one day to return in Roman-sponsored triumph to their estates. The less war about the premises, the better. But again, it's less a conscious policy on his part than the direct result of his inaccessibility to any except the most self-seeking or sycophantic advice. That's the pity of it. The others write to me. They hope for John's accession. They neither move nor are they moved.

He stares at her profile until, aware of the silence, she looks at him. Andronikus watches her with a fascinated, anticipatory half-smile. She lowers her head. Her hair falls forward concealing her profile. He goes to her, places both his hands upon her hair. She bursts into tears and he embraces her, hushing her and rocking her like a child.

THEODORA. It's nothing. It's the child. It's nothing.

ANDRONIKUS. It isn't the child. Marry me.

THEODORA. No.

ANDRONIKUS. You must marry me. I'll divorce Anastasia. I want *you* for my wife.

She draws away from him, shaking her head.

THEODORA. So long as I am Queen, and remain here, I'm myself. Here I am loved and those guards protect me—and if it should become necessary, they shall protect you.

ANDRONIKUS. Or protect you from me. I *want* to be bound to you.

THEODORA. We're bound by this child I'm carrying. It's enough.

ANDRONIKUS. Theodora, I've left a string of bastards from here to Russia. It's not enough. What's a title?

THEODORA. What's marriage? If you leave me afterward I'll have nothing at all.

ANDRONIKUS. Marry me.

THEODORA. If we had no choice in loving one another, we still possess the choice of loyalty which marriage would deny. It would not prevent you from leaving me.

ANDRONIKUS. It is my word.

THEODORA. And I trust it. I trust you would keep your word even if you came to loathe me, which I could not abide. I shall have you till you go. I promise you: it's enough. Until you go.

ANDRONIKUS. Look at me, Lady.

There is both command and entreaty in his voice. She turns to him. He takes her hands. He stares at them. To her amazement, he blushes and cannot look at her.

ANDRONIKUS. I'm certain only that I grow older day by day, that it is so very simple a thing to live an unhappy life and a lonely one—as day by day slips by without consolation, much less love. It is the uncertainty of everything else, which, without you, now seems to me to make my life unbearable, where before it was tolerable, perhaps because one day I had hoped to find you.

THEODORA. To find me?

ANDRONIKUS. To find what you personify for me, as it can only be you now that I have found you.

THEODORA. I'm weak, Andronikus. I'm insufficient.

He pulls round her more tightly the fox fur and scarlet silk blanket.

ANDRONIKUS. I ask nothing of you. I will not borrow or steal your strength. Your sufficiency for me is merely that you exist. That is my strength.

THEODORA. I mistrust all this.

ANDRONIKUS. I implore you. Believe me.

THEODORA. I mistrust the world. Not you.

ANDRONIKUS. Why? Tell me why and what it is you fear.

THEODORA. The intensity of the offense we give is the proportion of our happiness. If they should ever capture us, they will separate us. What good's my love for you or yours for me if you're not there, nor I to receive or return it? No bird flies on a single wing, Andronikus.

ANDRONIKUS. Must you fly?

THEODORA. No. But you must. And that's what frightens me. If I cannot guarantee you my life, I hesitate to let you guarantee me your love.

He smiles, nearly amused.

ANDRONIKUS. You have no choice. If you love me as I love you, all that you are, all that you experience, all roads you take to escape me lead you to me again, as everything leads me to you.

XXVI

Incipit: Nicetas Acominatus: Michael Branas left me with what I should call a most unlikely description of the Emperor and King Almaric together:

> For once, the Emperor's charm was to no point. Augustus was one of those, I think, who find it impossible to work with other men save on some confirmed emotional basis. Of course, the danger with such sovereigns is rather that they will take an act of state as a personal offense and vice versa. Well, His Majesty simply could not get through to Almaric and, I fear, wound up looking like something of a lackey himself. The King was gross, humorless. We've sergeants of the infantry much like him. Nothing amused him and he never smiled. He was completely unapproachable. The temptation to make a contest of the man's humor was irresistible and ought to have been resisted. This, the Emperor refused to do. It made me want to vomit. In self-defense I was rather defensive about Manuel and conceived an irrevocable loathing for Almaric.

With one condition ringing in his ears—that he was to make no further stand against Egypt, by himself or in co-operation with other allies in the period until 1169—Almaric returned to Jerusalem, the first week in April 1167. At once he called Andronikus to an interview. To everyone's surprise, the King—having heretofore only known him by reputation—conceived a great affection for the person of the Grand Duke.

It ought to have surprised no one. Andronikus' sheer physical size, his Imperial manner, and incisive mind could give pause to any bully, as the King was. But there is more to it, still. By virtue of his size, a distance between himself and the subject was almost always enforced and intimidating. If he chose to bridge that distance, then the delicacy of his charm and his wit, in contrast to his gigantism, left the object of his beguiling with feelings of awe, protection, and delight, precisely that of a votary before a benign god. Presuming, however, Almaric's hostility, he chose to meet the King's impassivity and dourness with his own, before which the King folded. "I decided at once I did not like Almaric," Andronikus said. "He repelled me on sight and without question, as certain animals will any man. Avaricious—not inscrutable, only empty —but too cunning for his own good. Crude. Everything blunt and unfinished. When I say he was not quite human and by no means inhuman, I mean precisely that: a man the Queen, his mother, would have done well to keep in her womb a little longer. When he congratulated me on Theodora's pregnancy, I thought him a clod. When he earnestly thanked me for bringing light to her life, too dark too long since his brother's death, I knew he was beyond any suggestion of good manners—or redemption."

It was Andronikus' belief, and Theodora's, too, Almaric had, on return, carefully gauged the Kingdom's general disapproval of the "spoilation" of their treasured Dowager Queen, and, thereafter, sought to encourage the affair to his advantage. His was, as we have said, an unpopular Regency, swallowed hard by both the barons and the people. Something of a misanthrope, he relished being despised so long as he was obeyed. In the same contrary vein, he could respect Andronikus and entertain suspicions of collusion with his sister-in-law.

Thus, when Almaric, the following July, crossed the incandescent Sinai Peninsula, he left the inexperienced Maria Anna as Queen Regent, knowing even so soon, this young woman, bland in her even temper but vicious, jealous and imprudent when angered, would strike against Theodora at the least sign of political mischief; and he took with him the Grand Duke as much to witness the legendary soldier in action as to prevent conspiracy.

Why did the King march against the Fatimids not five months after he had promised Manuel to wait two years before a concerted effort? Had Almaric his way, he would have desisted. But his barons, with visions of spoils as an incitement, feared Constantinople's share would be too large. As for the immensely wealthy and nearly sacrosanct Order of the Knights Hospitalers—whose influence in matters military Almaric could not any more forswear than the Emperor a Synod of Patriarchs —it was their opinion the proclamation of an alliance had been foolish, a blunder. Nureddin and his Commander in Chief, Shirkuh, now had fair warning and in twenty-four months could prepare for major war on Egypt's soil, war as the Prince of Aleppo preferred it, as jihad. The Grand Master of the Knights, therefore, informed the King the Order would go into battle at once rather than give the advantage to the Moslems and, if it needs be, would do so without him.

Unfortunately Almaric was not merely breaking his oath to the Byzantine Emperor, but to the Vizier of Egypt. Prince Shawar had relied on the King as protector, not plunderer, of Egypt, and plunder was the egregious intent of the Latin army. Rather lamely he explained to Shawar's ambassador, who met him in Sinai, "Men from beyond the sea have come among us, prevailed in our councils, and set out to take Egypt. In dread that they should succeed without our hand to control them, we have taken up their company. Trust us, I beg you, to assure their discretion." Now, surely, with the words "men from beyond the sea" the King meant the Knights Hospitalers, whose organization is, of course, pan-European. (He did not add, however, each chapter was autonomous.) When Manuel read the transcript of the meeting, sent to him by Almaric to prove his innocence, he read only one name in the phrase *"homines ex partibus transmarinis"*: Andronikus.

The invasion of Lower Egypt which followed was a disaster in its consequences. The occupation forces which Almaric had left earlier in Shawar's behalf had done little to enhance the Latin reputation. Indeed, these soldiers were so insolent, so brutal and presumptuous, they had effectively ended in the Moslem peasants' minds the alternative of Latins in preference to Shirkuh's Kurds. And so, in the first battle at Bilbeis, the army of Jerusalem was met by resistance from the most unexpected quarter: the common people. Angered, frenzied, the Latins took the city in the only possible manner, the classic manner, when bastions are defended not by soldiers but citizens. On capture, the population was slaughtered to the last man.

The alarm was sounded. Cairo, which the Grand Master had assured Almaric would burst like a dropped persimmon, defended itself under the leadership of Shawar, with predictable ferocity. To exacerbate from irony, the Vizier now pleaded with Nureddin—i.e., Shirkuh—as Moslem to Moslem, come to Egypt's rescue, reminding him, "while the Latins are intolerable interlopers with no claim but the thief's to this land of immemorial submission to the One, True God, and their resources are limited, if ferocious, Constantinople's claim has, at least, a legal tradition preceding the Prophet's lifetime. Their treasures and people, moreover, are vast beyond accounting. We should be overwhelmed."

When Egyptian collaborators, with great risk to their own lives, brought the news of Shirkuh's approach to the Latin encampments beneath the Pyramids at Giza, Almaric, after interminable deliberation with his General Staff, struck camp and announced his return to Jerusalem. After Bilbeis, and the long siege of Cairo, his forces were too depleted to fight on two fronts.

Andronikus, meanwhile, had presumed on the King and returned to Theodora at Acre. He had taken part in the first assault on Bilbeis, but once "Cry Havoc!" was called—the expostulatory order dreaded the world over as the signal for obliteration without quarter or mercy—he retired to his tent and refused to partake in the massacre and sack. Now, while Manuel fulminated against his cousin, the King took it into his head, the Grand Duke was Manuel's cleverly arranged agent at the court of Jerusalem. Unable to prove his suspicion, he sought, as cleverly, to separate the man from his commission and, "in regard for his services to the King," presented Andronikus with the fief of Beirut, 150 miles to the north. The city, however, was never occupied by its liege.

On 14 August 1167 an order was promulgated throughout the Empire—including all vassal states such as Jerusalem and Antioch—commanding the capture, and blinding on capture, of the Emperor's cousin. Though no punishment or remanding could be taken against Theodora, a Sovereign Queen, Manuel took the singular measure of joining his niece's name to her lover's in the excommunication interdict issued by the Patriarch. "He knew the depth of Theodora's piety," Andronikus once commented to me, with rare bitterness. "He knew. It was the meanest act of his life, which in so much else was contrary to such smallness." *Explicit: Nicetas Acominatus.*

Andronikus bursts into the bedroom chapel of the Queen, who kneels, sobbing before an icon of her grandmother, St. Irene of Hungary. He is flushed, enraged. She does not turn to him. It is obvious this is the extension of an ongoing argument. Andronikus pulls the icon from its stand, while Theodora makes a small desperate sound. He smashes it —once, twice, three times—jewels popping, the frame twisting on itself, the wood splintering.

ANDRONIKUS. What are you doing? What do you think you're doing? It's nothing. It's stones and oils and gold. It's idolatry. Who are you praying to? Your grandmother? I knew the woman. She held me on her knees. She smelled of violet and she hated children. That's what you're praying to, you idiot, that's what you're praying to!

She watches him from her knees, cowering, her eyes bursting. Suddenly a metamorphosis takes place. The fright becomes a frown; she gnashes her teeth, rises and rushes toward him, drawing three perfect lines of blood along his cheek. He grabs her and boxes the side of her head, once, with his fist.

Incipit: Nicetas Acominatus: The Writ of Outlawry against the dynasts and their excommunication caused nothing short of a sensation, everywhere, and in a stroke, gave the lovers the glamour of solitude. Whereas, previous, there had been the usual wags' comments on the Comnenus inclination toward incest ("Their arrogance carried to the logical absurdity, as they are no more apt to share their blood than a man can share a thirst"), now under the penalty of Church and state all humor was silenced. Yet, true to human contrariness in their very real danger, having set themselves against canon—in challenge to which all men aspire—they were cheered rather than condemned, covertly within the Empire, openly without.

Andronikus: "For one reason or another, I shall never know why, Almaric did not act on Manuel's command. Certainly he knew of the Emperor's fury against his preemptive attack on Egypt. Perhaps it was no more than daring the punishment he knew my cousin was not prepared to meet. In any event, Theodora dispatched an emissary to Nureddin who was at Damascus. She meant to test his promise given her on Baldwin's death. Three days later with a sweep and hospitality which made me suspicious, he gave us his answer: 'Damascus is yours.'

"We were instructed to proceed at once to the Jordan River where we would be met by a detachment of His Highness' Own Horseguards, who would conduct us to safety. With this message, Theodora was elated, triumphant, and belittled all my doubts. Yet her assurances were only all the more irritating to me. We could take with us virtually nothing we possessed—which is to say, in the main, what the Queen possessed. Theodora was allowed some clothes, all of her jewels, and one lady, Veronica Melissena, whose disapproval of me I found rather tiresome. But credit must be given. It was unsaid and understood the sacrifice she was making. Manuel would, in all likelihood, confiscate her fortune, which, some have said—and I little doubt it—is greater than our family's. As for me, I had nothing but my clothes and my valet, Leo, which simplified our baggage and complicated my feelings since I was now entirely dependent upon the Queen's resources. I'm afraid in those first weeks I was quite frightful to her."

The elopement was executed on 21 August 1167. From that day forward, throughout the years of wandering, the lovers ceased to be of political note and became legend, unseen and ever-present, the subject of rumor, gossip, song, and exaggeration.

Andronikus: "We approached Damascus in a thunderstorm. We were greeted, officially to my surprise, by Prince Ridwan, one of Nureddin's bastards, and like the sons of most megalomaniacs, quite the opposite of his father: full of quiet decency, which some might mistake for weakness, and a gentle but pointed wit, which, on the other hand, everyone is all too ready to accept as solid grounding in reality. In all, he exhibited the serenity of one raised lovingly and conscientiously, which might bewilder those who called his father Satan Incarnate. But many a tyrant —and Nureddin was nothing if not a tyrant—is usually, too, an excellent family man given to very ordinary pleasures. I suppose because the truly sanctimonious despot knows he can be a monster of depravity any time he likes—and such a course would confirm his political monstrousness —he desists somewhere and thereby excuses the rest.

"We were settled in Ridwan's villa, and while we waited further word from his father, the Prince conducted us on a tour of Damascus. Muhammad al-Idrisi, Roger of Sicily's geographer, says, I quote, 'Damascus is the most delightful of God's cities.' I must, then, commend God the Father's aesthetic sense. Damascus lies, as you know, at the convergence of five local rivers which transform it into a hothouse of flowers and trees. Even in the poorest quarters there's more dense greenery than in any one of the parks in this city. Fountains are everywhere and bathhouses, too, which, in the main, are gathering places for pederasts. The Great Mosque is stunning. Everything it had been reputed to me to be. Ridwan procured us entry, though Theodora had to view it from the women's gallery. Did you know—of course you do—it was built on the site of the Cathedral of St. John the Baptist, which Theodosius had built over the ruins of the Temple of Jupiter. I think there's a lesson in that, somewhere. . . . By the way, the moment I entered the building I was disturbed by a sense of déjà vu, and commented on this to Ridwan. He explained the ground plan and decoration scheme had been modeled on Holy Wisdom, at which, I don't know why, I was filled with awful nostalgia. I should say, however, the Great Mosque seems more simple and unified, perhaps because in the choice of marbles the Moslems did not vary, but selected a pure white stone. With our onyx and malachite and verd antique and heaven knows what else the impression is initially more startling, but at length tiring and, I think, chaotic.

"As a culture the Moslems are a good deal more alien than I would have guessed from those numbers who live at Constantinople. But here they have the wariness and circumspection of guests though they're full-fledged citizens. In many ways it is a civilization like Old Rome's, established, at least in civil life, almost entirely upon a foundation of slavery, and so it is at once physically magnificent and morally repellent.

"The aristocracy is exquisite, living in lavishness by which even Byzantium pales in comparison. Still, none of this would be possible without an intolerably narrow concentration of power in the hands of a very few. We Greeks are in some ways as guilty, but not to such a degree. And, as you well know, I am doing my best to assure that a middle class shall survive both myself *and* our aristocracy.

"What most interested me, however, those slaves are treated alternately with an indifference which chills the blood and a consideration, on the other hand, which exploits the absurdity between bonded man and free. For instance, during their month of Ramadan, which is much like Lent, all Moslems must fast from food and water during the daylight hours. Well, when the Prophet first decreed the custom, the period of renewal fell in winter and such abstention from dawn to sunset was penance but not persecution. But every thirty-three years, according to the lunar turns of the Moslem calendar, the days of fasting fall in midsummer. Then, while the rich sleep away the day, the peasants and slaves, without food or water, must continue at their tasks. Yet they do not complain, and no one appreciates the dichotomy and no one would think of a dispensation.

"Still again, a slave woman inseminated with her master's child and a free woman who carries her slave's child give birth, both, to free men. Imagine that state of affairs in Byzantium where a matron aborts the fetus of a slave she's fancied or forces him to wear contraceptives. But then, here, where slavery is a negligible factor, it takes a certain turn of woman to introduce a man she owns into her bed and the consequences are to be expected.

"'Prayer,' said one of their kings, 'carries us but halfway to God. Abstinence brings us to the gates of heaven. But it is charity alone which gives us entry.' *That* is civilization from any aspect.

"Of course, the society is male-dominated. Indeed, from the look of it in an open street you would think it a land entirely of males and parthenogenetic in nature. Save for a few extremely powerful princesses, who entertain the great of their day from all the arts and sciences, the women are in purdah and female homosexuality is rampant and lethal if discovered. This is not the case with the men. Pederasty is frowned upon by law, but it is ineradicably a part of the culture. I think I am not mistaken in saying this lends an effeteness to the males, even the greatest warriors, and it is not at all, or, at any rate, rarely, to the good. One would expect a greater clemency among their fighters, but not really. The same general who melts before his roses handily lops off heads with a nearly feline pleasure in his own savagery. Of course, since access to women is strict and singular and concubinage an institution, the husband soon grows bored—sated—and takes to aphrodisiacs and pornography and, with greater occasion, little boys. All of this lends a sickly sweet languor which seems to pervade the whole society.

"I must tell you, though, the women, when you can get at them, are marvelously alien in their customs. Surprise one in her bath and do you know what she covers first? This." And he placed his hands over his face, peeking between his fingers like a shy girl. When he revealed his face again, his smile was full of reverie. He shook his head, the smile lingering. His eyebrows lifted, once, in a quick, hopeless resignation to things and days beyond recapture.

"I am sitting with you now, discussing events which are a part of history, and they seem, in retrospect, important, symmetrical, calculated, the war of wits of many men who knew what they were about at every moment. How very unlikely. If I awoke with a headache, complained of the heat, cut my hand in the morning, and grew ever more aggravated by Nureddin's refusal to receive us personally, all these things obsessed me, if momentarily, far more than resolving methods of revenge against Manuel or ways of returning free to Constantinople. I'm certain Theodora and I discussed my children, and the child we were about to have, flowers, the weather, poetry—more often than not in Arabic to revivify our grasp of the language—than the danger and adventuresomeness of our position.

"And later, what did it mean to be pursued? To be deported by the next potentate, and the next, with due apology? Nothing more than the discomfort of breaking habits, of surviving, with as little tension as possible communicated to the children in tow, the dangers present until we found new succor, the humiliation of being beggars and beholden to too many.

"We received word in mid-September to proceed to Haran and await further instructions. The delay seemed to me ominous and only by indirection did I learn its cause. Nureddin's counselors, who previously had not given much credence to their Prince's fears of Constantinople, had succumbed to the contagion and were against harboring members of the Imperial family who had simultaneously offended the Roman Autocrat, the King of Jerusalem, and the Prince of Antioch. Of course, it must have been a difficult decision for Nureddin. I mean that in all seriousness, since it is unthinkable for a Moslem to break his word or renounce the sanctuary he has extended. No less, it can only have been repellent to him to succumb to Christian threats, on the one hand, or his ministers and generals, on the other.

"It was knowledge of this controversy which caused me to beg Theodora to return to Jerusalem. Once again my life was reduced to dangerous uncertainty and I could not bring myself to take her—pregnant especially—through heaven knows what peril. We argued violently, and against my better judgment I capitulated. A dowager with a bastard in her belly, for that matter, was scarcely the acceptable curator of a legend. Really, we had no choice. And so we left for Haran."

"It was a terrible ride," the Queen once recalled for me. "To no purpose, it seemed, the Grand Duke made it a gallop through those narrow, dizzy passes of the mountains of Lebanon. I rode by his side. I knew he was, in some way, attempting to draw from me, from the others, a protest of fear, by which he might lash out and so express his own. Every so often I put out my arm, not quite touching him, but a gesture to stay him. After a time I stopped, for I surmised this would increase his fury all the more without yet giving him an excuse to open anger."

At Haran, the Queen gave birth to twins, later styled Princess Irene and Prince Christopher and Serene Highnesses. To leave the parents no uncertainty as to the acceptability of their "incestuous progeny," the Patriarch of Constantinople, through John Sergius' auspices, sent on to Haran a letter of condemnation, declaring the children "unnatural bastards of consanguine adulterers and ineligible for baptism."

The Imperium would have done better to let well enough—or worse enough—alone. At first, the birth of the children had removed some of the Catullan luster from the lovers and turned attention to "Poor Anastasia," now irrevocably deserted—as well *her* children—by the husband she had served so faithfully. When, however, the interdict was proclaimed against defenseless infants, onlookers turned—perhaps gratefully—from the murky nuances of blame among the actors to the Church and the throne. Writs of Outlawry were one thing, capricious and persistent cruelty another. The Empress Maria-Xenia, whose pregnancy was proclaimed 1 February, met a stony silence at the Divine Service held to petition God for the birth of an heir.

On 27 February Andronikus received word of his wife's death. She had awakened on the morning of 15 February and, as usual, proceeded at once to her bath, only having complained to one of the servants of a severe headache. A few minutes after she entered the waters, she suffered massive apoplexy. Since it was her eccentric custom to bathe unattended, she drowned within minutes.

Andronikus: "In the letter Philip sent me, I was informed that though Anastasia's will had named my brother as guardian in the event of my absence—how provident of my wife—Manuel had removed Alexander, Zoë, and Julian to Blachernae and decided himself and Maria-Xenia their adopted parents. Prince Ridwan provided for me an agent to carry a letter to Philip in which I asked my brother to gain my children and send them to me at Haran by any means. It was a favor, at much danger to Philip, I really had no right to ask, but I knew I should be forever grateful if it were accomplished—or so I told him—and it was and I am.

"Theodora had the same fears as I. Though Manuel might demur and even John Sergius—I will give him that—any one of a number of their creatures, with the brutality of the small, might bring my sons and daughter to harm in a too zealous pursuit to please the Emperor and the Protovestarius. They would not be pleased, but by then it would be too late, and small consolation.

"To be honest—which is to say, unflattering—I did not think Philip would abide by my wish. I love my brother. He is an eminently decent man, with surprising strengths, as I've discovered. But he is—well—so very unassuming, those strengths must constantly be proved again and again to me. I suppose I have always underestimated him. For a very long time, I believed he disapproved of me and this did not encourage my opinion of *him*. Well, in parts, he did; in sum, he did not. His views are quite the opposite of mine. But he is not mean and he is open to novelty if it can be proved worthwhile. And his sense of justice is eminent. In every sense of the word, he is a gentleman. Recently, my sister-in-law, Martha, told me from the beginning there was no doubt in his mind as to my rights to the children and he was in fact furious—if you can imagine Philip furious—at Manuel's assumption of guardianship. It appears he asked to take them for a week to Christos Gennate, and, once there, sent them on with servants and a small escort the 650 miles more to Haran, straight through the Sultanate where my sister-in-law Rabia had procured them safe conduct from her brother, Kilij."

For this act of insolence, which Manuel pronounced "uncharacteristic," the Emperor banished Philip and his family, including his eldest son, Isaac, and *his* wife and son, to one of the Sklerus estates, inherited by the Grand Duchess Martha, near Athens.

Theodora: "We received the children at Haran. Alexander remembered his father but was shy. Zoë was willing to make the best of it but she was sad and distracted, only dimly remembered me, still less her father. Julian knew neither his father nor myself. He missed his mother beyond words, wept often, threw tantrums, had nightmares, and confided only in Alexander and Zoë, who, alone, could control him. Andronikus indulged him, then as now, to little good, I think."

On 2 April 1168 the refugees, their number swelled by children, governesses, and grooms, left for Aleppo. The city rises at the junction of the Great Southeast and Eastern Trade Routes and is nothing short of a wonder with its stone streets, nighttime illumination, hundreds of mosques, five colleges, dozen hospitals, and population of nearly a half million. They were established at al-Fadila Palace and given to understand the Prince—whom they never met: a diplomatic necessity, but an insult nevertheless and one to be borne quietly—was making arrangements with his nominal liege, the Mussulman Caliph of Baghdad, for their permanent asylum.

Andronikus: "After Haran, Theodora seemed resolved, whatever happened to us, to make the best of it. The only time afterward I ever again *saw* her tears was on receipt of the really awful news of her nephew, Crown Prince Baldwin."

In the spring of 1168 five physicians, called from Egypt, Italy, Spain, and Constantinople, confirmed for Almaric the incontrovertible truth, his ten-year-old son and Heir had leprosy. Since infancy the child had been subject to those dread, rust-colored maculations of the skin which, upon maturation of the disease, become nodules, then ulcers, then decadent rot. While the little boy's beautiful face, so reminiscent of his uncle's, and in turn that of Joscelin II, had not yet taken on the hideous, leonine appearance—due to the thickening of the skin round the eyes, nose, mouth, ears, and forehead—his complexion already possessed a warning dusty hue, and his voice was unnaturally hoarse, indicating the disease had even then worked its way into his throat.

Jerusalem's fate will soon diverge from Byzantium, and we shall not otherwise be able to tell the tale of the young Baldwin unless here and now. It is instructive. He stands as one of the eeriest and most estimable examples of moral fortitude for all time.

All men know the future which awaits a leper. On confirmation of the disease, he forfeits all rights, personal, civil, and inheritable, and must take up residence in a state leper colony, where he will be cared for for the rest of his days. Not so much that Almaric refused to acknowledge his son's disease, it is more accurate to say the leper would not consent to the law which condemned him to a living death.

William of Tyre, who was Baldwin's tutor, told me: "For the first time ever that I knew Almaric, I pitied him, though he did not want pity, only some means of rescuing his son from the Calvary which lay before him. It was exquisite cruelty to watch the Crown Prince while he was still young. Handsome, gregarious, charming, insightful beyond his years, never forgetting an injury—no saint in that respect—and still less a kindness. Unlike the previous Lotharingens, who seemed to pass from generation to generation only a tolerable seat upon a horse, Baldwin's was not only elegant but daring and, seemingly, beyond peril. He was restless, passionate, inquisitive. It is horrible to realize that at this moment he has neither hands, nor feet, nor face, no one sees him and he is carried about in a curtained litter. Yet, at this moment, he is more a king, just and adored, commanding to be obeyed, than ever his father was. Still, it must be said, it was his father's will, as strong as his own, which insisted that the child remain Heir. Whether this was wise, I cannot say —it seems to have been. Hardly any longer recognizable as human, he has made more of his life in his brief years than whole men living fourfold his time. But the Leper King cannot last much longer and the issue of inheritance is at stake, and with it, perhaps, my country. We may have forfeited our future to indulge a gallant present. Perhaps we had no choice."

On another occasion, the Bishop said, "Throughout his tutelage I had never known a child, so condemned, less given to self-pity. I remember once I finished a discussion with him with the words 'this land, which you shall one day rule.' And he responded with a hard glint in those still clear eyes, 'And well I will, Monsignor, for I am given nothing else in this life.'"

There has been the tendency in the years since his death—six months before Andronikus', March 1185—to portray the King as a saint of the military species, such as John Comnenus. To my way of thinking this belittles the man and the accomplishment. To the end, Baldwin IV was willful and temperamental, one for whom disobedience was intolerable and punishment, more often than not, summary. Like his father, he suspected plots at every turn and was harsh in undoing them. Yet here we recognize the impatience of a doomed man who has no time to play cat's paw with his servants; and, then again, in the vulnerability of a king without heir or kin in the male descent, we catch more possibility than paranoia.

In the beginning when the disease was showing only superficial effects, but he was easy to exhaustion, he rode into battle at the head of his troops. He knew soldiers are more zealous to sacrifice in the presence of their Regent who is the living state than in the van of his appointed commanders who tend to act like the kings they are not, and thus arouse not inspiration but resentment. Besides, he meant to make himself a living image to be remembered before disfigurement forced him to withdraw from the sight of the living. In the end, with stumps for limbs, a misshapen clump of a face, blind, and nearly insane, he still summoned strengths from the depths of his soul—whose nature, at this point, one only dares to imagine—to strategize battles and decree wise, and long-delayed, internal legislation in his people's behalf.

A few months before his death we are given the image of captains of battle responding to froglike growls from behind an enclosed palanquin, as the King, still so young, repels no less than Saladin from the walls of Jerusalem. A month before his death he summons his barons and commands them obey his choice of Heir—who is not theirs—Baldwin V, son of Raymond III, still Count of Tripolis and long recovered from his eight years in Aleppo's dungeons.

What is left of Baldwin IV dies, thereafter, at the age of twenty-seven, mortified nearly from birth to death. What is awesome in all of this is not so much the victory over flesh—though remarkable in itself—but the triumph of purposeful resolution over apathetic bitterness, the inconceivable struggle against final insanity, the will to use the power he was given, virtuously, over the state to which it applied, the sublime vitality which would use its generous genius in spite of the meagerly given body which was its vessel. Baldwin's real glory is something from within—that variety and surprise of human genius—which responded so magnificently and selflessly to the challenge he was given. When he told William of Tyre puissance was his only legacy, it may have been his only display of bitterness. He was also too modest.

In a world wherein each man's suffering, though relative to the next, is huge because it is exclusive, there are those few before whom our own miseries seem small indeed. While it is no consolation to those people we revere them for the gestures they have made beyond despair, it is also true, the model they have set for us, in the face of pain, selfishness, or indifference, is not wasted even as it does not practicably survive: rather it lives, as Baldwin's, as Andronikus', transfigured by the inspiration it extends.

Like Andronikus, I am ordinarily wary of inspiration, especially when it is worship of one who, given everything, triumphs or, beginning with nothing, gains great fame, without conscience or justice, through wealth or amassment of empire. That is merely cupidity, on the part of the admirer and the admired, and we are poorer for the reverence.

Gaining such ourselves, we have not increased the capacity of our own souls or those souls of other men who move in our name. Only suffering, because it is the destroyer of complacency, the initiator of struggle—as it is man's nature to struggle, which is movement, dynamism, the crucible which, by heat, by pain, produces synthesis, something greater than before—only suffering is the valid example, the valid prototype, the valid inspiration, suffering so indisputable it gives us pause. If we are blessed, it teaches us our luck, and in that lesson, compassion for the luckless; if we are too prudent, it teaches us there are those few who have overcome more than ever we must ourselves, and though our souls be petulant—and on the surface, rebel—they absorb the lesson helplessly, tempering the estimate of their own misfortune and overcoming it.

Once Andronikus said, "Always to go on, in the face of questions to which we would have answers and never shall, but to go on." In the light of such a success as Baldwin's—or such a failure as Andronikus'—is seen the cautionary reality: there is no summit, and no stillness in life. To believe oneself to have attained either is to precipitate the fall. To believe oneself fixed by the circumstances of one's life is to accept death, to cease to move, to ripen. Only as we believe ourselves small can we begin to be stupendous.

XXVII

When it became apparent to Manuel Augustus his Empress would, at last, reach full term, he decided, for historical reasons, to translate Maria-Xenia from Blachernae Palace to the old Sacred Palace, and the hallowed Porphyriogenetum, where every heir, previous to the Comneni, had been born since the foundation of the city.

To accomplish this, all streets leading to the Mesa were blocked to traffic and pedestrians for an entire morning. The Empress was assisted from her bed—where, she complained, she had "lain like a sow" for the majority of her pregnancy—to an enormous silk-and-eiderdown mattress which was carefully placed upon a still larger closed palanquin, and lifted by twenty-four carriers who, though trained for weeks in their route, were popeyed with tension. (They were followed, in turn, by several hundred colleagues, who would relieve them at staggered intervals every several hundred feet.) The entire length of the Mesa had been scoured in the previous weeks for holes, loose or cracked slabs, and proper gradient. All flaws had been rectified. Now, surrounded by Varangians, the Emperor, and her ladies, the Basilissa traveled the many miles to the old palace complex as had, it is quite likely, none of her predecessors.

On entry into the Augusteum, the litter was blessed by the Patriarch —a safe journey nearly accomplished—then carried through Chalke, across Daphne gardens, its roses in full, marvelous bloom, past fountains, ancient and new, through the ivory arches of the Pavilion of the Porphyriogeneti, past the jeweled mosaics, the marble pillars, into the most famous and least penetrated apartment in the world, the Porphyriogenetum, with its sloping ceiling and purple-stained walls constructed from portions of the monuments of Old Rome. There, three weeks later, 14 September 1168, Maria-Xenia Augusta, daughter of Constance Guiscard-Hautville and Raymond of Poitiers of the House of Aquitaine, bore to Manuel, son of John II of the House of Comnenus and Irene of the House of Árpád-Orseolo, a son, at last, baptized in indescribable splendor at Holy Wisdom Cathedral, by the Patriarch of Constantinople, as His Imperial Highness, Alexius Manuel Porphyriogenetus, Grand Duke and Sovereign Heir Apparent to the throne of Constantine the Great and Octavian Augustus.

I was an acolyte that day, near the great font, and though I am ashamed to confess it, more than thirty years later, I acknowledge my thoughts were of the most worldly and jealous nature. I envied that squalling blond infant in the arms of his godmother and cousin, John Sergius' wife, the Grand Duchess Nina. I envied him the cynosure of all attention, surrounded by this blinding pomp, his birth its initiation, his future resplendent as the bolts of sunshine driven through the cathedral's golden cupola above his head. After this public display—for that is what it was—he would vanish from our view to live God knows what indulged existence and emerge one day, a little boy in purple raiment, on a white pony, beside his father, whose pride was enormous, ingenuous, and oddly moving.

How I envied that child, indeed. And yet, could I have foreseen his pathetic end, I would have shrunk from that envy as from the very precipice of hell itself. What I did not then realize, I know now all too well. Ceremony is but the lavish visible gesture of invisible political power, as it was then potentially embodied in the Crown Prince. So long as he existed to give it meaning he was the locus classicus of all authority and contention of that authority to come. He was, of course, his people's future, and they would adore him as they could not adore his father because the child was amelioration beyond present miseries. But he was also the future of his father's courtiers, and their hopes were not passive and undefined. They were real, practical, and often as not, ruthless.

I wish now, in retrospect, I could be more sympathetic to the Porphyriogenetus, the vision of his magnificent baptism still before my eyes —the smell of frankincense is an unfailing reminder—the feel of the heavily jeweled cross still in my hand, the soaring beauty of the choristers still in my ears, the knowledge of his brief, hieratic life and abysmal end, virtually crying for one lone note, somewhere, of sympathy. But taken up, myself, by the mighty, I saw rather more of the humanity behind the façade than I expected to see or, perhaps, wanted to see. Not so much that what I saw was mean as all too human and fallible, an interruption of the order of panoply I had previously known and which suited my incipient historian's demand for seemlessness. (History after all is the lie of its time—the prejudices of those who record it, as well as those who live it.)

What I feel for that child now is an ambiguous mixture of pity and revulsion. I doubt that he was ever happy. He was not so much loved as prized; prized by his father as the continuation of the dynasty, prized by his mother as the confirmation of her position and fulfillment of her duty to the state, and, at the last, prized by a specific faction as the vessel of their power in the years to come. Though he could be charming (most often in his father's presence)—with that precocious self-esteem of an heir, taught duty while still in swaddling—he was, on the whole, a more disturbing mixture of insolence and vulnerability. That is, his insolence was the inevitable consequence of one never reprimanded by elders because it would be presumptuous to forgive him, and his vulnerability, the wound of a child who knows he is not loved. Yet here, even, at his most touching point, there was corruption. Unloved, he knew, nevertheless, he was invaluable, irreplaceable, unique, and so he developed an uncommon, bitter arrogance, which took no note of another man's dignity, as other men, keeping their distance, were the source at once of his solitude and his authority. In time, he knew himself to be despised. Yet he also knew none dared show their dislike. What could he feel for such men but contempt? He was the master, the tyrant of the implicitly insulting gesture. Unloved, beyond warning, knowing he ought to be warned, he passed from act to act of great personal recklessness to test the patience and the concern of others. (At the age of eleven he was an astounding horseman. All Comneni were born with a superb seat, but this child was death-defying, literally.)

While on the subject of Manuel's children, it is well to discuss the Crown Prince's far more personable, and no less interesting, half-sister, Catherine Porphyriogeneta, and his half-brother—Manuel's son by Persephone—Demetrius, whom, against all tradition of bastardy, the Emperor had raised to the Caesarship since protocol would not allow him a Grand Duchy. Indeed, it is almost heartbreaking to speculate on the course of our now vanished Empire—or for that matter, Andronikus' destiny—had either one of these elder children inherited the throne.

Demetrius was, and is, one of the most ingratiating, kindly men I know. When the Heir was born, he was twenty-one years old and resembled his father to a startling degree. While his young half-brother was fair and blue-eyed and diminutive like his mother, Demetrius was tall, slender, dark, with Manuel's delicately chiseled features and his father's wistful, penetrating eyes. Everyone loved Demetrius, including his stepfather, Michael Branas. In fact, that affection—Demetrius was helpless not to return it—was the cause of a small but real jealousy between the Emperor and his greatest general. All the Caesar's impulses were good, his patience inexhaustible. He could even provoke the semblance of an affection—or, in the least, the gestures of affection—from his cousin John Sergius, who believed any man attempting to approach him in good nature, for no more purpose than affection, was a fool to be tolerated. No one was beyond the Caesar's perfect manners. The lowest menial in the palace—and there was an excess to maintain Blachernae —would, in his quick-stepped passing, receive a nod of the head and a distinct "Good morning to you."

There were flaws. Some were innocuously distressing such as his disinterest in clothes, his inability, at best, to seem anything but poorly tailored and untidy. Another was the foundation of many an anecdote which in retrospect might seem hilarious, but in passing might be harrowing: the animosity all inanimate objects bore him—tables which danced in his way, braziers which crept up to him to be tipped over, chairs which wound like vines round his legs, plates which tipped like drunkards into his lap.

Yet I must stress this is not to make the Caesar seem an object of ridicule (as John Sergius, with his reliance on appearances, was apt to do —though for once without acrimony). He was serious, intelligent, if not deathlessly intellectual, and much like Andronikus at the same age, gave aid to anyone high or low, wherever and whenever it was necessary. But to these merely alarming and endearing foibles, we must add the far more serious imperfection which was a lack of initiative, whether to act against the worst events or believe the worst of his fellow humans.

His faith, I think, was too strong on the better side of man's nature —which, we must face it, is the exception which proves the rule—and the tendency to patiently allow occasions to set themselves aright—pardonable in the old who have seen too many cycles, positively frustrating in the presumably energetic young. Then as now, he lacks the imagination to conceive of the imagination which makes for ruthless ambition or evil in others. Then again, he had almost a child's view of the recompense of events. Nothing could continue in so wretched a state before *someone else* with a more blithe aptitude for authority than himself— or else God in heaven—would turn tragedy on its heel. It must, however, be said, he could discern good advice from bad—and always sought the best—and he was not loath to use power if he were absolutely obliged, as once it came about. And then, one only hoped it was not too late. For that is what is most condemnatory about the languorous nature: not that it refuses to rule but seldom realizes the judicious application of power involves the pre-emptive as well as the prompt.

In a recent letter from the Grand Duke Alexander, I noted he referred to Catherine Porphyriogeneta as "Poor Catherine," as a whole generation had called her mother "Poor Irene." Somehow, I am certain, the Caesarissa would have rejected the title, though not without a wince of momentary recognition. Before she ever descended to self-pity, the overwhelming common sense and her sense of estate invariably took hold. She possessed neither humor nor much optimism. She never suffered her canonized grandmother's conviction or her own mother's implication, this world was a vale of tears, to which one reconciled oneself with demure patience and resigned unhappiness. Nor had the Porphyriogeneta any illusions about power, save it was there to be used —sensibly, legally, and always to the good of the state—for she had inherited, indeed, her German mother's practicality—almost to a fault—and the formidable force of most of her Comnenae ancestresses.

She was not without charity, but she was not profligate about it. Every coin was followed to its destination, not because she feared herself a dupe or was parsimonious, but because she was one of those women who, with the best will in the world, believe none could fend for himself without their supervision.

She was the most Imperial of her father's children—not merely aloof and rude like her youngest brother, but regal, sharp, austere, knowing her prerogatives and using them, impervious to obsequiousness, and purposefully kind to those too intimidated by her position. She was most comfortable with her father and he, of his children, with her; and toward her bastard brother she was singularly tender. With other members of the family she was rather a ubiquitous and benign despot. Something in her nature brooked no contradiction. Lurking like a baleful eye within her manner was the suggestion of awful temper, which everyone suspected and none had ever seen, and, merely as legend, served her well. Even in her youth, she could draw up the most formidable matrons of the city, who dared not retaliate, and she otherwise terrified any other socialite not old enough to remember to the last detail the funeral obsequies of Irene of Hungary.

I am not entirely certain we can discount the rumor that a portion of Catherine's hatred for her stepmother was founded in jealousy of the Empress' beauty and easy charm, though, assuredly the intent of such gossip is more likely spite than accuracy. A plain, pale girl, she knew herself raised to desirability by her position alone, and that knowledge, I suspect, quite offended her ordinary womanly vanity. Not for Catherine Porphyriogeneta the question of many a naïve heiress: is she loved for herself, or the luster of her position? The Grand Duchess knew well there was no distinction. Power endows one with a glamour which is indivisible. Her misfortune was that she was born with an instinctive need for guileless affection. This, and her pride, assured her refusal to be used. To that end, there was at least one parallel life of happiness which might have been hers and followed her like an accusatory ghost to her grave. For one of her father's ADCs, Prince Eugene Catacalon was —unlikely as it may have seemed to many at the time—deeply in love with her, declared himself, and was rebuffed. Her own affection was obvious, but so was her suspicion—only exacerbated by his extraordinary

good looks in contrast to hers—he was rather intent on marrying the
family than herself. When, ten years later, she went to her marriage bed
a virgin, Catacalon resigned his post and took the tonsure.

With the birth of an heir, the Emperor seemed renewed, one might
almost say smug. Now there was nothing he would not and could not
do for a future which would be passed into the hands of the son of a son
of a son in an unbroken line from the founding of the dynasty. And to
the woman who by her fruitfulness had given him this prerogative, he
was grateful as few emperors have been to their basilissae. It did not
matter—despite the example of his first wife's personal maternity still
fresh in mind—that Maria-Xenia, no sooner recovered from her difficult
labor than she gave her son willingly, if not indifferently, to the host of
nurses and wet nurses and governors. Rather the Heir was born, he
thrived, his mother was the most beautiful woman in the world, and,
in middle age, when he scarcely expected to find it, the Emperor was
blessed with a completeness, an ecstasy sooner come by in youth, before
experience of the world teaches us that hope is something *against,* not
for.

Nothing could stay him. Even his contests and his challengers were
struck at with peculiar joy. In 1167, for instance, Frederick returned to
Italy and captured Rome, at which Pope Alexander III departed for
sanctuary in France. The North Italian cities, sooner than submit to
the German Emperor, resuscitated the Lombard League, to which Manuel contributed generously through Genoan agents with the double purpose of countering both Frederick and the Republic of St. Mark. (In the
time since the Sicilian campaign, Venice had reintroduced itself to
Constantinople's harbors and warehouses and was once again crushing
its competitors, fellow Italian merchants and Greek hosts alike.) Outraged by this intrusion into the internal politics of his Empire, Frederick
sent a letter stating, henceforward, he would regulate *his* conduct in
Byzantine domains according to the example set by the Greek Sovereign.
If it must come to war, so be it, though, Christ as his witness, he would
sooner come to amicable terms. Finally, as salutation the German Emperor bids his cousin realize his superiority, submit to it and to the
Latin rite, and recognize that he, Frederick, was ordained to rule Europe
—East and West—in its entirety, which included the Greek Kingdom
(*"ut non solum Romanum imperium nostro disponatur moderamine,*

verum etaim regnum grecie ad nutum nostrum regi et sub nostro gubernari debeat imperio").

Whereas, in his youth, Manuel would have taken offense and moved an army north, now, celebrating his twenty-fifth jubilee, was too long on the throne to doubt his own prestige. Nor was he blind to the edge he possessed in that it was Frederick who complained to *him,* puffing up his own claims. His reply to his first wife's nephew stands as a model of irreverence and bluntness in the usually pompous business of formal correspondence between chiefs of state. Its peroration is sufficient example:

> I find your accusations against me vis-à-vis the Lombard League quite typical, which is to say, puerile. You accuse me of interference, to which I readily confess. But take note of its nature. I have given the city-states merely the means to be independent of your depredations, your cruelties, and your indifference to their welfare, save as it accords with your personal ambition. I have no intention of undermining the premise of monarchy, anywhere, but I would show any mistreated slave in a neighbor's house the way to his freedom. As I am a Christian, it is all I may do. As for your orb and scepter, with which you claim all Europe, you will note its Constantinopolitan hallmark. You will further recall no less a predecessor than Carolus the Great, feigned to consider himself the true successor of Maximian Augustus in the West until the tolerance of Constantinople was extended. Even then, he preferred to recognize himself as the junior Augustus—gubernans romanorum—and subordinate to New Rome. Legally we have a precedent and your legitimacy depends upon our recognition. If you chose to keep the regalia at any time, hence, when we have requested its return, your chrism would be invalid, and you would only be a thief. Pray my regards to your fertile Empress. May Alexius II and Heinrich IV find more in common as brother Emperors than you and I as kin. The worst espionage between the comity of states is their ignorance of one another.

No sooner, with such jollity and imprudence, had he put the German Emperor in his place, than, true to his earlier word, Manuel made war on Egypt. I have often thought the siege of Damietta most perfectly appropriate as the prelude to and symbol of the final decade of the reign of Manuel Augustus. A promise was given and a promise delivered despite the contingencies which had arisen between inception and execution.

Now shortly after Almaric had returned to Jerusalem, the Kurd, Shirkuh, and his nephew, Saladin, marched through the gates of Cairo, where they were officially received as "Deliverers" by the Regent, Shawar, and the child King, al-Adid. Believing Shawar had set Moslem against Moslem only to the profit of Christians, Shirkuh commanded the Regent summarily executed. Two months later, the great general was himself dead of a heart seizure, while seated at his desk. His thirty-five-year-old nephew, Yūsuf, or Joseph, called Saladin (Ṣalāḥ-al-Dīn, Defender of the Faith), was now, in all but canonical recognition, ruler of Egypt, in behalf of Nureddin, who, though but a prince, was overlord of two Caliphates in a sweep from the Nile to the Persian Gulf.

Pressed by his courtiers to assume the title Sultan, the Prince of Aleppo unequivocally refused. "There is," he said, "too much to do and too little time in which to do it. I leave the divertissements of pomp to those with the leisure and the inclination." It has been said the Prince was, in fact, disappointed he had not been requested to assume by *favat*—the highest religious authoritarial consent decree in Islam—the title Emperor, Shahanshah, successor of the Sassanid's last Basileus, Yazdegerd III. But this is to misunderstand the nature of the man.

Egypt was the key to the doors which opened on an Imperial title, but Egypt had come beneath his sway in a manner wholly offensive to him as a devout Moslem. No such member of that creed consents to war any more than a pious Christian. (Jihad is not a contradiction in terms, but a dispensation.) Corrupt Moslems—as there are corrupt Christians—make of it a hypocrisy, rather, by transfiguring self-aggrandizing slaughter into penalty against infidels. ("If God would punish men as they deserve," said the Prophet, who, like Jesus, has suffered his sense of humor to be lacquered over by the sanctimony of his followers, "there would not be left so much as a beast upon the earth.") Nureddin was, like Leo III Augustus, that rare and unimpeachable—and perhaps alarming—sort of man, the warrior-mystic. We may, objectively, question the dichotomy, but not the man. His ambition was so closely bound with his piety the one cannot be extricated from the other. In the beginning, he had been appalled at the prospect of Moslem Egypt re-Christianized. In the end, his anger was more manifest—an avenging priest rather than a potentate—toward the collaborating aristocracy of the land. They were to him pariah, contaminate, and he had no desire to be their liege. So he refused the crown which would have set him above these people, while through Saladin, as his Governor, he maintained his hegemony. His religion was satisfied, and his ambition. (Perhaps, like the awesomely cunning Octavian Augustus, he preferred the power to the principle, knowing, as with gold, it is the glitter and not the power which attracts the more superficially ambitious.)

There is every evidence the Prince did not trust for a moment the subservience of his Governor. Though Saladin quite sincerely revered the Prince as "the noblest of men," he believed Nureddin, betimes impractically devout at the expense of state and safety (witness the edict which commanded soldiers remove their swords from their belts, which were conveniently at the ready, and replace them in scabbards since the Prophet had used a scabbard). It was an open secret the Prince had not recovered fully from an attack of consumption earlier in the decade and at any moment his regained, but frail, health might give way. In that event the power would fall to a regent in the name of Nureddin's infant Heir, Malik.

Now, the Prince was powerless to prevent the eventuality of the civil war he foresaw in the aftermath of his death, save by proclaiming Saladin Regent—in which case he feared for his son's young life—or having him assassinated, which neither conscience nor politics would permit. Like Manuel's, his last years were a torture in the face of chaos which he knew was nearly inevitable and he was helpless to prevent since alive, his prestige precluded it, and only with his elimination could it arrive.

Nothing assured Nureddin the likelihood of his suspicions fulfilled than the cold and merciless fashion in which Saladin—soon to be called the greatest gallant in Christendom or Islam—asserted authority throughout his governacy. When the Caliph al-Adid's Royal Guard, a fifty-thousand-man army, was incited by the still surviving Fatimid faction to revolt, the Defender of the Faith retaliated by surrounding their vast barracks outside Cairo and burning alive their families—more than seventy thousand women and children. Attempting to save their kin, the guards were driven into the flames by Kurd regiments. The following month His Majesty's Own Armenian Guard was locked into its barracks and all members therein—some twenty thousand—incinerated, or else impaled alive if they were unfortunate enough to escape cremation. When the Royalist faction, still miraculously unpunished, began secret negotiations with the Jerusalem court as well as Constantinople—hence Manuel's miscalculated confidence—Saladin had the "Kinglet of Egypt," as he called the last of the Fatimids, quietly poisoned, thus removing the banner beneath which he was contested.*

This, then, was the Egypt toward which the colossal Byzantine armada sailed in 1169, the greatest native fleet founded since the Macedonians. At Damietta, the Imperial navy and army rendezvoused with a halfhearted King of Jerusalem, discouraged by recent local defeats, still bewildered by the tragic news of his son's affliction, suspect by his own barons and loathed by his own subjects. The siege which was commenced against the important commercial city lasted eight interminable months. Half the King's forces were destroyed by plague as were a third of the Imperial army. Supply lines were overextended and subject to blockade. The combined Latin-Greek Praetorium, when not split by prejudice and suspicion, could not anyway agree on a uniform strategy. The common soldiers were bored to tears and roasting in the Egyptian summer. The nobility on either side held tournaments which became gladiatorial combats. An expedition of Latin and Greek regiments was sent into Lower Egypt and never heard from again. Spoils were nowhere to be found for the city had not surrendered, salaries were delayed and, when issued, lost in gambling as there were no other means of spending them. Food was infested, leather harnesses were turning into mold, quartermasters nowhere to be found.

At the end of the summer, the siege was lifted, capitulation acknowledged. Almaric returned to Jerusalem and the Imperial fleet began its thousand-mile journey home, morale near the point of mutiny or suicide. On the island of Rhodes a storm sent three quarters of the armada to the bottom of the Mediterranean. Of the sixty thousand men accountable from those ships, it is estimated no more than ten thousand returned to Constantinople. Those who had not perished in the moist inferno of the Egyptian Delta died in the cold green world beneath the

---

* No official proclamation was made of the death. Instead, without any ado worshipers throughout Egypt were stunned one day by the absence of the Fatimid Khotba (the equivalent of our *Domine, Salva Fac*) during religious service. It was replaced by the Alid Khotba in behalf of the figurehead Caliph of Baghdad, al-Mustadi, the nominal liege of Nureddin. As for the Prince, he watched these events but, weakened by illness, by work from dawn to dusk, too many hours of prayer and fasting, and foreboding, which trips us upon what we most dread, chose to do nothing. In fact, Saladin's dominance of Egypt was the guarantee of his son's life. N.A.

sea, trapped in holds, crushed by horses or cracking timbers, or beaten back into the water from overcrowded ships by their fellow soldiers.

The perfect symbol: enormity of gesture, irrelevance of intent. Or, perhaps more accurately: the intent was the gesture. Manuel Augustus was by no means a superficial man, but the court he had created served him nothing but superficialities and concealed the rot which was dissolving the Empire from the edges inward. Living too long in a world run perfectly to his own accord, he could scarcely comprehend the world without which did not. Unwittingly, he assured that at his death, with the removal of a strong hand, there would no longer be a functioning Imperium, but a bureaucracy, locked like a decapitated body in violent spasms which had movement but no meaning.

XXVIII

"One day," Theodora recalled, "while we were still at Baghdad, Alexander came to my apartments and lolled about waiting to speak to me. In the few short years he had been with us, he had grown nearly as huge in breadth and height as his father, though the resemblance was somewhat vitiated by the stoop of his head and his shoulders, which made him seem as one about to glance a blow. This gesture and his gentle manners and soft voice had a way of irritating me, which, I suppose, was unreasonable. It was not a want of masculinity, nor was it humility. He possessed no force, no fire, no point. It is rather like clouds: They are interesting by chance and eventually dull.

"I paid no attention to him, which he did not seem to mind. He listened as I dictated some thankfully lost essay on what I thought was a startlingly original connection between the mysticism of al-Ghazzali and St. Augustine. When, at length, I turned to him, he waved a letter roll, ribbon and seal sliced. 'Constantinople,' he said, 'and I think Papa will want to read it.' I dismissed the secretary. And then I said, 'You know your father wants no news from Constantinople.' He said, 'Oh, now, that's not quite true. He expects me to tell Leo all the news Uncle Philip sends us and then as Leo says, "he presses and sniffs, like a man taking up a date and throwing it aside, and eating it when no one's looking."' 'Do you find that amusing?' 'Not at all, ma'am. I find it apt. I miss Constantinople, too. Perhaps more than he does.' I said, 'Do you?' I asked him to please sit straight in the chair, which he did, blushing. I fear my sharpness and his malleability found themselves irresistibly attracted. I said, 'Well, you're free to return whenever you like.'

"He leaned forward, laying the letter aside, absently, on a table. 'What would he say?' 'Why should you care,' I asked. He said, 'There's no longer any reason for my being here. I'm not exiled. Why should I be forced to share his? Otherwise, perhaps, I shall never again see Byzantium.' 'Well, for God's sake, tell him this.' He looked up at me dolefully. 'I couldn't. It would crush him.' 'You have a very exalted opinion of yourself, don't you?' He made no remark, but rose and went to the arched quartz window. You simply could not reach him. Rather he responded, imperturbably, 'No opinion counts for him but his own. But he loves me. And he seems to think that obliges me.'

"I remembered myself then—I was even fascinated this boy should be thinking just so. 'Doesn't it oblige you?' I asked him. He smiled, almost ironically. 'He makes it seem so, doesn't he? He can't see through himself to me, or to you, for that matter.' 'Careful,' I said. 'My life's my own. I do as I please.' 'Do what?' he asked quite reasonably. 'You allow yourself to be included in the complications of his existence. What sort of life is that?' 'More than you know. Whatever portion of his existence he wishes me to share, if only to help him to endure it, I am flattered more than I can say.' " *Explicit: Nicetas Acominatus.*

ALEXANDER. What good do I do by your side?

ANDRONIKUS. What good will you do by Manuel's? So long as you remain with me here, there is a point you make which is valid enough for a lifetime—and well taken—against the corruption and desuetude of the Grand Court. At Constantinople, as a dynast, you have no other choice but to be a courtier, a parasite.

ALEXANDER. What point can it be to merely waste away in an alien empire far from home? I want to return to Constantinople.

ANDRONIKUS. Then go, my boy, and be damned to you.

ALEXANDER. Why must you curse me?

ANDRONIKUS. Why do you need my blessing? What difference would it make? If you wish to be my son, you must suffer my disapproval. If you say I have no claim to you, then that is the price you must pay.

ALEXANDER. Why must you reduce every man's argument to terms which affect yourself solely?

ANDRONIKUS. In what other fashion should I be concerned?

ALEXANDER. I *know* you. If I return to Constantinople, it is certain you will think I have entered the enemy's camp and betrayed you.

ANDRONIKUS. And I know *you,* so that is *not* what I will think. But other men will. That is what I cannot abide and you are consenting to it.

ALEXANDER. I'll stay.

ANDRONIKUS. You're a damned milksop, then. No man has the right to cut the edge of loyalty on another man's freedom. If it is your gift, I take it happily, but I will not hold you to it.

Incipit: Nicetas Acominatus: Not too long after the conversation with the Grand Duke Alexander, as described by the Queen, there took place the famous estrangement between Andronikus and his eldest son. The younger man in an act of singular independence quitted his father's exile and returned to Constantinople. Of this event, both Andronikus and Alexander remained reticent.

Alexander, in his own behalf rather than against his father, explained, "You know my father well. It should come as no surprise to you that he treated us, his children, as not quite pets and not quite slaves and not quite free. He was, I think, too perceptive and too honest not to realize he had no right to order our existence according to his own. Ordinarily, though, he seemed never to recognize the integrity of our acts or our persons. Somehow he felt they were his, or else reckoned to him—that all we did, we did in his name."

Andronikus was almost as regretful and unenlightening. "I've never ceased to love my eldest son, but I've never trusted him since the exile. He does not dissimulate, I must point out, and he is not without some resolve, but he is not to be depended upon. It is one thing for a man to say one thing—and mean it—in the emotion of the moment, then turn and do quite the opposite. But suppose he is taken on his word, at once, and sets in motion a series of events from which he cannot extricate himself or does so at the risk of certain chaos? That is the nature of weakness, not indecision, but introversion. The weak man makes decisions aplenty, but without any sense of responsibility, of the consequences beyond himself, like a child who plays with a toy only for so long, grows bored, and leaves it aside for someone to trip themselves upon."

Manuel happily welcomed his cousin's son and gave him Vlanga Palace. Beyond that, recognizing the young man's reticence—not enmity, but the hesitation to slander, or even appear to slander his father—the Emperor, with exquisite tact, refrained from associating him too much with the family or palace life.

After Damietta, Saladin became intent on securing a system of alliances, however ephemeral, with the Latin states, to maintain his authority in Egypt and—pursuant to Nureddin's death—utilize the country as a base of operations for nothing less than the capture of Moslem Syria if it would not be given him in the form of a Regency, which each day seemed more doubtful. Saladin was not about to discount the rumor which reached him that Nureddin had expressed himself perfectly willing to see Damietta, even Alexandria, fall to the Greco-Latin armies, and with those cities, the Viceroy's prestige. The antagonism between mentor and protégé was something short of open war, but only by a little.

Not so much anti-Christian in his foreign policy as fanatically pan-Islamic, Nureddin—to the purpose of crushing his Saladin—hesitated to initiate a mutual assistance pact with Constantinople against the Egypto-Latin consortium. He nevertheless believed it prudent to come to some sort of understanding, if only implicit, with the Imperium. To this end he heeded, at last, the dispatches from John Sergius which, for more than two years, had reminded him of the Basileus' displeasure "that an errant and rebellious excommunicant is unconscionably succored by the Great Prince." Thus, without any previous warning, Andronikus, his family, and suite received notice, shortly after Alexander's departure, to prepare, within two days, for removal from Baghdad to the Ortoquid Emirate and the city of Mardin, three hundred miles northwest and one hundred miles directly east of Edessa.

There is every reason to believe they were notoriously unwelcome in their new refuge. The Emir was given the choice of offending the Military Governor of Trebizond or else suffering the pulverizing retaliation of his Zengid neighbor to the south. He chose to welcome the Grand Duke and his family, however coldly, and provide them with a residence, which became his revenge for such an imposition.

According to Andronikus, the fortress in which he was established was built at the turn of the tenth century, during the first Turk invasions. "I leave it to your imagination," he once said, "to consider the circumstances in which those people built, and with what lack of subtlety. One room led into another. There were no passages. The large central hall might have been warm enough, save the disrepair of the place made it a funnel for numerous drafts whose origins, like creation, were innumerably suggested and ultimately untraceable.

"It was a classic citadel: the walls extended to the well of the courtyard, which was merely tamped earth. The apartments themselves, if you could call them that, were part of the walls. The roof was the palisade from which the fort had been defended. Of course, the infants needed constant supervision, not merely from entry to the roof—walking had given their curiosity wheels—but from the rats and vermin which infested the place. The observatory—I can't imagine what one was doing there—had to be closed off entirely. Luckily I was the only one to see what was inside. It had become a haven for bats, thousands of them, and the floor was ankle deep in their detritus in which lived some sort of insect, by the millions, so that this sickening morass seemed alive. It gave me nightmares for months.

"Indeed, a full refurbishing, even a cleansing, was impossible. We had no staff but our own servants and only a small allowance—no, not small, but insufficient—sent to us by our dear friend, Ridwan.* We hired a few citizens from the city of Mardin, and a few men as guards, all of whom we had to fire punctually, for drunkenness or thievery. Only one wing of the fortress was cleared—all we could humanly do or afford—and that was our home for the following two years. After that—especially after al-Fadila—I never again so long as our exile lasted took for granted luxury and the luxury of attendance. For the first time in my life I hunted not for the sport of it but to put extra meat on the table."

By the 1170s—it becomes clear in hindsight—Manuel Augustus was like Aeolus, creating a swell of resentment, act by act, which would

---

* Andronikus neglects to mention, perhaps understandably, the expenses of their stay at Baghdad had been supplemented by the Queen's jewels, which were now gone. Like all refugees, they had underestimated the term and expense of their exile and spent too lavishly. The Grand Duke also fails to report the substantial sums sent periodically by his son—of which more—and each time returned without comment. N.A.

break upon the Empire when he was no longer present to cross the skies and with an alternate wind keep the waters back.

Late in the first year of the new decade, he dispatched one of the Sebastocrator Isaac I's great-granddaughters, the Grand Duchess Anna-Eudocia Comnena, as ambassadress to the Vatican and, concomitantly, marriage to its wealthiest and most powerful supporter, Count Odo Frangipane. This was nothing less than another intentional affront to Frederick, who had done everything but kidnap Count Odo in order to marry him to one of the collateral Hohenstaufen heiresses. "I warn you," Frederick wrote to Alexander III, who was scarcely about to listen to the sponsor of his supplanter, Paschal, "this is but the pointed end of the Greek wedge, and you will pay dearly for it. I will not know you then, when you ask to be rescued." (It might be mentioned in passing Anna-Eudocia found the freedom of Latin women a revelation, no less they found her learning, her sophisticated pleasures, frequent baths, imperious ways, and sharp tongue formidable and refreshing. Today, she is the Grand Dame of the Pisan aristocracy as the wife of Count Guelfo di Paganello, with whom she maintained a notorious alliance during the life of her first husband. Her enemies—i.e., the disinherited Frangipanes—insist to this day she indulged too readily Count Odo's tendency to dipsomania and her bed, which weakened his already frail constitution. The doyen, on the other hand, insists she could not turn her husband from craving what he could afford or what he owned.)

In the same month, God, guilt, and nature conspired to set back in the east the comity of the Latin and Greek rites which the unlikely Princess Comnena was to win in Italy. In point: While Patriarch Athanasius was celebrating Divine Liturgy at St. Peter's, an earthquake struck of such malicious energy that in a few minutes, half Antioch and all of its suburbs were reduced to debris. The loss of life was immense. Villas and palaces—some back to and preceding the Great Constantine— were destroyed. The elegant bulbous domes of St. Peter's crashed to the floor of the cathedral, killing most of the congregation. Athanasius was rescued, more dead than alive, and thereafter subjected to a most excruciating spectacle of cruelty and superstition such as few men have been forced to endure.

The humiliation he was served at Constantinople several years previous had not been forgotten by Prince Bohemond. Though indifferent to the Greek or Latin rite save as a political dignity, he took up his people's cry of "the Lord's Revenge," and in a gesture of ostentatious theatricality, shaved his head, dressed in a hair shirt and sackcloth, and, barefoot, to the fore of thousands of Antiochenes, walked to Qosair Castle to ask forgiveness of the Latin Patriarch Aimery for the installation, in his place, of a Greek. Overwhelmed by his own humility, Bohemond prostrated himself, confessed his certainty Aimery's interdict had found righteousness in God's eyes and for that heaven had punished Antioch. ("If it took that long for retribution," declared the Emperor, "we can only suppose the celestial bureaucracy is as slow as our own.") Bohemond begged the French prelate's return to the patriarchal throne or all his lambs would be lost.

Aimery's condition was the expulsion of Athanasius. Now suddenly drawn up—and probably reminded of his earlier antipathy to Aimery—Bohemond somewhat uneasily protested the Greek Patriarch was dying of "every injury imaginable to a man crushed between tons of brick and timber." To Aimery, who had, apparently, forgotten his own painful turn with Reynald's wasps, the victims of heavenly wrath were beyond compassion. Thus Bohemond ordered the mortally injured Greek priest to be carried from the city on a litter and—either intentionally or carelessly—forgetting to provide a guard, learned too late, Athanasius' helpless body had been pelted with offal and belabored with all too available broken stone. The deposed Patriarch died that same night and his body was shipped to Constantinople in a cowhide sack.

On receipt of the cadaver, which was properly embalmed, dressed, and enthroned at Holy Wisdom for formal obsequies, Manuel commanded the Prince's immediate personal attendance to explain himself. "Any conniver," he wrote, "would have acted as you acted till Qosair. After that your inhumanity would have given lesson to the devil." But Bohemond, like so many, having committed the unthinkable, found it conscionable, and even gained against the Emperor, would hear nothing of journeys or explanations or any further subservience to his brother-in-law. ("So," Andronikus wrote to Michael Branas, "that detestable little sneak has learned the secret of the tyrant. If unpopular, find an enemy everyone can hate in unity with you.")

With unexpected subtlety and foresight, Almaric realized Bohemond's actions were certain to alienate Constantinople from Latin Palestine. The danger was long-term, but real. Should Saladin ever overtake Aleppo's vast holdings, nothing would prevent him from turning on the Latin allies he now surrounded, and crushing them. Should that happen, the goodwill of Byzantium would be crucial to any rescue. His Majesty, therefore, sent an ambassador equal to the occasion, one of Manuel's favorites, William of Tyre, to arrange a second state visit, accomplished in September 1171. As usual, the Emperor entertained the King with renowned splendor, and seemed touched by Almaric's new eagerness to express his faith in Constantinople, as a factor and guarantor of the destiny of the Holy Land. Yet even Almaric, not much given to looking beyond his own nose in matters which did not directly or indirectly relate to him, commented to William on Manuel's distracted manner throughout the month-long visit. The reason became apparent the moment the King returned to Jerusalem.

The Grand Prince of Serbia, Stephen Nemanya, who had inherited a state in semi-vassalage to Constantinople, had been urged by ambassadors from proximate Venice (openly disturbed by the Emperor's leaning toward Genoa and Pisa) to declare his independence from the Empire. Warned by Hungary but blandished by Venetian money and assurances of a naval blockade of the Adriatic (where, Stephen forgot, the theater of war was not only strategically unlikely but practicably impossible due to the loss of the Damietta armada), the Grand Prince declared himself secessionary.

With the last great army levied before Myriokephalum, Manuel marched north and in a brief, brilliant campaign centered around Scutari—and strategized by Michael Branas and Michael Gabras—forced Nemanya to capitulation before Christmas. He exacted neither indemnities nor corvee, but merely ordered the Grand Prince and his men march behind him at Constantinople as had Reynald of Châtillon in 1158 at Antioch. He believed he was being clement. He could not have been more wrong.

"I told His Majesty," said Michael Branas, "a nearly illiterate race in semi-barbarism has no sense of self or state, no pride, but in its prince. The unity is terrific and indivisible. He would do better to increase taxes, burn farms, and steal sons than humiliate Stephen. In the one, resentment was diffused and helpless; in the other it was categorically centered and far more mischievous. But he was too moved by his leniency to be dissuaded and he called my criticism 'eccentric.'"

When the Serbian abscess burst, it was in the reign of Andronikus, wherein too much poison without and within served up the final tragedy.

For the moment, however, it seemed the Emperor's usual triumph against reasonable prediction. The Senate—in the name of the people and the army—urged him to enter Constantinople in state, as a warlord. It was an honor Manuel had cherished and never dared allow himself, perhaps in awe of his father's greater right to it and that man's only reluctant consent.

Now with the confirmation of its power over Serbia, Constantinople controlled the entire East Corridor of the Adriatic. Should, at any time, formal alliance be made with Sicily, it would dominate the Gates, too, and Venice's access to the Mediterranean. Whether the Emperor had foreseen in his absolute suzerainty over Serbia the first feint of a stranglehold is moot. The point is, the Republic of St. Mark—which for that very reason had supported Nemanya's policies—at once recognized the danger and rather like the victim whose heavy breathing gives his hiding place away to the killer by its own alarmed activities drew the Emperor's attention to his superiority. A final confrontation became inevitable.

Let us look at the Empire in the year 1171, through the eyes of Eudocia Comnena Frangipane's husband, Count Odo, an ardent Grecophile. In the letter he wrote to Pope Alexander III, the criticisms may not be entirely accurate—they may even be superficial—but in many ways they are comprehensive and have the acuteness of one who has loved from afar and now must reconcile the legend with the reality:

> You have, Your Holiness, advised Louis of France to ally himself with the East Roman Empire, perhaps even to the point of marriage into the Imperial house. On the face of it, I would say this seems an ideal thrust against Frederick. It is only as one plumbs beneath the surface one perceives such an alliance, were it real, and not merely an oath of mutual accord, might entail the danger of pernicious contagion.
>
> You know my feelings, Your Holiness, toward the beauty, the glory, and the achievements of this ancient Regency. Yet I would be remiss if I did not warn you, I am appalled by what has become of Byzantium since the late reign of John II. This is and this is not the land described by my father when he visited here in your predecessors' service. Manuel Augustus will, in two years, celebrate his Thirtieth Jubilee. He no longer rules, it may be said, if rule is in the interest of the people, whose care is commanded by God. There is literally an army of clerks—generally

underpaid and living on bribes—to carry on the day-to-day business of administration, like an infernal perpetual-motion machine. There is no longer initiated legislation of the least interest to any class but the chambers of the highest aristocracy. All rolls on as it has since the first burst of promulgations in the first years of the Emperor's reign. His day, which I have been privileged to follow, begins at dawn and usually ends after midnight—for he often returns to his offices after a banquet or entertainment—but I cannot believe it is in the continual exercise of his imagination in behalf of a stronger internal state—only one more glorious, which is not the same thing. He seems to rule without knowing why or to what end his deeds must be accomplished. And so he promotes his prestige beyond the borders of the Empire rather than, by deed, within.

I must point out, however, he is neither a tyrant nor a military hysteric nor aloof from the people he cheats of his attention. He adores every Byzantine to the last native slave. Though he derides them as enervated with too much civilization, he calls them fondly his "children," and beyond this land, he believes the world not only awaits but deserves the benefits of the Mission Civilisatrice they have represented for a thousand years. He is, in short, anomalously the most melting of universal conquerors, a megalomaniac of great gentleness and charm. Believe me that. You would fall under his spell in a minute.

But behind him, as far as the eye can see, are the legion ghosts of flaws and failure. The provincial aristocracy is nearly in ruin. The Grandees are rich, but without influence. Ministers, whether Latin or Greek, vie against other, as one or as a group, and almost never concert themselves to their tasks. They do not attempt to be efficient. They mean only to please the Emperor, whose power—by virtue of the army, the Secret Police, and quite simply, his longevity—is indisputable. They are not men but lackeys, with all the dishonesty, obsequiousness, and the arrogance of lackeys. He has shown to his entire government, by the example of treatment of his critics, that, with the best will in the world, he does not want independence of mind and personal initiative. He wants, apparently, the obedience of slaves, and that, precisely as possible, is what he does not get—only ambitious men who pretend to be slaves.

Whatever goes wrong, whether in the administration or the military, whatever fails from inutility or breaks down from senile irrelevance to the times, is never rectified, nor ever a source of complaint, for that would be to the detriment of the reputation of whatever minister or general or clerk is called to question. Not that the Emperor would hesitate a moment to set things aright or, without a second thought, merely command the man to do it himself. Simply, he does not *know*. In their pretense at slavery, his people have come to think like slaves, who fear because the master has the whip, he will use it.

In this way, also, the Emperor never hears of criticism against him, nor of the cracks which are becoming chasms and which will swallow the Empire in ultimate failure and darkness. His Majesty sees only the gold and none of the squalor. In fact, what he rules has degenerated to gilded squalor and nothing more. It is all very well for him to present the Basilissa Maria-Xenia with a Madonna and Child of solid gold, her blue mantle of sapphires, the babe's swaddling of pearls, but there are hunger riots in several provinces because the crops have been poor and the Imperium has initiated no relief. (Presumably, the Minister of the Interior has decided the report of poor crops to the Augustus would reflect unflatteringly on God, who, one surmises, is also in the Emperor's pay and eager to keep His sinecure.)

It is, meanwhile, among these wretched, ordinary citizens that the greatest toll in taxes, land, and—quite literally—lifeblood is taken. They are without hope and, really, someone ought to fear their potential mischief, for there is no damage done like the damage of men who have nothing further to lose. But at least the peasant is in the open air, near game to satisfy, partially, some of his hunger, amidst natural beauty which might temper some of his misery. His predicament is virtually as nothing compared to that of the city dweller. The filth, the lack of any alternative whatsoever, the dismal slums side by side with the huge palaces of the great are as tinder and flint. A little motion one way or the other, and there is bound to be conflagration.

This city which, under Alexius and John II, was as safe by night as day to walk abroad is rapidly becoming another Rome or Paris. Crime is nearly unmanageable and citizens fear to travel in the evening save in a group or with their own guard, if they can afford it (the guard, as you might have guessed, often is composed of the very extortionate rowdies who would otherwise prey upon their employers). Bread riots have become a matter of fact. The task of charity seems so immense as to give it pause—what difference will it make?—and so those who would give are discouraged, and those in need go from bad to worse. Infanticide is becoming prevalent since orphanages are full. Beggars are everywhere. Streets it is certain the Emperor or some high minister will never see are an adventure in summer and impassable in winter.

In all this, of course, the aristocrats do not suffer; their palaces have become, in fact, fortresses. But the middle class is grossly affected. This group, of course, covers every sort of fellow from the moderately successful merchant, to the clerk in the Imperial administration, to the cobbler in his corner. These people have not the resources to protect themselves and they hold the dearer what they have. They must endure, moreover, not only the hooligans from below but favored aliens from without. This is especially to the point, now, as the Emperor attempts to battle the fiscal hegemony of the Republic of St. Mark, with newer and more lavish privileges granted Genoa and Pisa. (To be sure, the Latin Quarter is the most carefully tended and guarded portion of the city, as the best rooms of a once splendid palace ought always to be set aside for guests.)

Wherever this will lead—the corruption and inefficiency just beneath the top and the boiling, gratuitous violence at the bottom—I cannot say. This journey to the Empire I have all my life dreamed about and admired has been, to say the least, a revelation.†

Thus we were seen by one man, and perhaps many more. Beyond the seemlessness of life at Blachernae, where voices never rose above a whisper and servants walked shod in kid on tiptoe and the world seemed to accord with the Autocrat's ambitions, the very Empire on which his conquests were founded was giving way.

Occasionally, however, the rumbling beneath his feet was so obvious, while Manuel remained impervious, as to produce the effect of farce, if one did not know of the broken bones after the pratfall. The Emperor, for example, took it upon himself to write letters to his friend, Henry of England, consoling him for the nullification of the Constitutions of Clarendon which denied the King authority over the Church, a state of affairs Manuel could scarcely imagine (but then neither could he imagine assassinating his Patriarch, as had Henry his Primate, merely to prove a point). His own bishops, meanwhile, were preparing a less lethal form of resistance in reaction to Imperial ecclesiastical ambitions with Rome. Having previously summoned a synod to discuss the causes of disparity between the Latin and Greek rite, with the intent of forcing concessions from the priesthood whose pontiff he was, the Emperor was met by hostility which bordered on open revolt. Listen to this exchange between the Emperor and the Patriarch Theodosius:

---

† Unknown to Count Odo this letter was confiscated by the Secret Police and placed in the Imperial Archives. N.A.

HIS HOLINESS. With all due respect, I would suggest Your Imperial Majesty would do well to get out a little in the world. Your Majesty's information via his Latin servants has no basis whatsoever in the reality of public opinion.

HIS IMPERIAL MAJESTY. May it please Your Holiness, I rule this Empire so that it is meet with the opinions of the best of my counselors, not the least of my subjects.

H.H. Then I would as respectfully suggest Your Imperial Majesty look to the nature of his counselors and then to his least subjects, for it is upon their backs that the whole weight of the Empire rests. And to be blunt about it, there are more of the least whom he must satisfy than the great to whom he must pay court.

H.I.M. It is precisely by such condescension, Bishop, mediocrity triumphs.

H.H. I find it singular, Your Majesty, Christ Our Lord believed quite the opposite.

H.I.M. That is a specious comparison. Christ spoke of the simplicity of the spirit, which is quite another matter.

H.H. Is it indeed, Your Majesty? From the spirit of each man all his actions proceed.

H.I.M. Since it is Your Holiness who presumes to defend the downtrodden how is it, may I ask, you are among those who have importuned me day by day, month after month, to the total reinstitution of monastic privileges? There is a contradiction here.

H.H. Only without reflection, Your Majesty. I have said it before and shall say it again. Unless monasteries have monies and endowments, not a noble's son—or an emperor's—would join the Church Spiritual. Without such men we will have none of the leaders necessary to organize and propagate the faith. A church directly dependent upon governmental emolument, as you would now have it, would helplessly intrude itself upon the workings of the state, and there, no doubt, sully itself with intrigue and greed born of self-interest.

To unrest in the Church—in part justified by wariness of the Emperor's motives—one must add as well the degeneration of the courts, glutted by the injustice each man suffers—or believes he suffers—when a society begins to crack. Ancillary to this failure—indeed, both born of and exacerbating it—was the notorious moral decadence of overworked, underpaid judges who could no longer resist corruption which is the end of justice at the source, that is, its agents.

"Beyond belief, isn't it?" Andronikus Augustus said, thirteen years later. "It was so obvious who was culpable. But, as the Autocracy is constituted, loyalty toward it is to accept it in whatever form it thrives, obnoxious or virtuous. There is no criticism without the implication of revolution. If the Emperor is God's Vicar, he can only be right. If he is wrong, he is wrong in all things, for God has withdrawn his infallible aegis. To praise him is redundant and to warn him is blasphemous. What was it Alcuin said to Carolus Magnus? *Vox populi, vox Dei.* Within their context those are wise words—or else an invitation to anarchy. You see, to a man, even the people who were not blinded by my cousin's display hesitated to blame him because the conclusion of the argument was too fearful. To blame him was to take it upon themselves to replace him. But such was the state of the aristocracy—so weakened by intimidation and corrupted by favors—there was no one to lead, and, even had there been, none dared follow. Finally, it came down to this— don't you think? In many minds, though none dared speak it, the people began to realize Manuel no longer knew what he was doing and was liable, therefore, to do anything. It is at such a point personal dread converges in mass apathy."

"Well it is, the citizens of Venice ought to fight for Constantinople," ran the old joke. "They own it, don't they?" The point was more serious than laughable by a half.

Naturally as a society begins to fail, the most evident desperation— if not the primary one—is financial chaos. If taxes are raised, if food is scarce and twice as expensive, if arrows snap before leaving the bow and ships are improperly equipped, if a man is maimed or jailed because he cannot afford to bribe a judge, if His Grace hoards while his peasants starve, all descends to a question of money, and whether one is destitute by birth or falling to destitution from great wealth, the inevitable answer, founded in the symmetry that as one man lacks another gains, is a search for the thief. By 1171 the evidence suggested only one culprit, and that one, more symbol than reality, was Venice.

While the Emperor envied—and dreaded—the unconquerable Fleet of St. Mark, his people rather envied and abominated its citizens in every city in the Empire. They were millionaires—aliens got rich on native gold—their bejeweled wives and arrogant young heirs ensconced lavishly behind high walls, estranged from the society in which they reaped and lived, entertaining among themselves and appearing for display each Sunday as they made their way to the local Roman Catholic church for Mass. In truth, Manuel was amazed by the favorable reception his legislation in behalf of Genoa and Pisa was—at least initially—accorded. As estranged from his subjects as they from the Venetians he could not realize all Byzantines were transferring their fearsome disapproval of his rule to more bearable hatred of Latins, and very specifically citizens of the Venetian Republic.

It is curious, then, the events of 12 March 1171, as initiated by the Emperor and accepted by most Byzantines, were, quite literally, two entirely different stories. At noon, on that day, a moment prearranged with unexceptionable secrecy, local authorities everywhere throughout the Empire, from the Adriatic to the Georgian Caucasus, arrested all Venetian nationals and subjected their property to confiscation to the crown. Save for isolated incidents, no harm was committed against any man's person. This absence of violence is not accountable to Venetian passivity, but more than likely, the shock of the event and the lack of complicit mobs, itself due to the lack of publicity and the clandestine manner in which reserve troops were quietly introduced into each city's garrison months beforehand.

There were injustices, of course. Many Venetians who had declared themselves subjects during the Italian campaigns of the mid-fifties but continued to live in the familiar comfort of the Latin Quarter were pell-mell arrested with the nationals. A few were able to convince their captors of Roman citizenship; most suffered the same fate as their former fellow countrymen, and, embittered, did not hesitate, on return to Venice—and once overcome the initial hostility and sometimes pitiful hardship—to enter again the councils of state as the most ferocious and unappeasable enemies of the Byzantine Empire. (Among them was Enrico Dandolo, who proved to be so lethally enraged, Greek official action was taken against him in the form of blinding by reflected sunlight in a concave mirror. He was, at the time, sixty-three years old. It is not too much to say, sheer venom forced the blood in his veins for the next thirty-three years, until, at the age of ninety-six, as initiator of the sack and dismemberment of the East Roman Imperium, he arguably knew a revenge more complete and apocalyptic than any man in history. Yet Dandolo was but an incident and unnoticed. He had experienced—and by that, represented—what I should call the contingency of human exist-

ence: that one extraordinary or scarcely recognized moment which forever deflects a man's life and the lives of those dependent upon him, who
do not even recognize that dependence.)

A small portion of the nationals at Constantinople, the very richest,
with friends at court (primarily Latin), escaped along with the entire
population of the colony at Halmyros in Thessaly, in a fleet of twenty
ships. So skittish and frightened were they that as a trio of Venetian trading vessels passed them at twilight, the refugees, without warning, attacked with fireballs and stone missiles. For the rest, there is a vivid
description of their arrest and deportation in a letter from the Grand
Duke Alexander to his exiled uncle Philip. His vantage was especial
since Vlanga Palace borders on the Latin Quarter:

> We heard commotion—very distant—terrible cries, as one sometimes
> catches out of the night on the way to a fire. I drew on a cloak, left the
> palace, and crossed the courtyard to the gates. I asked the guard on the
> rampart if he could see anything, and he said, "I certainly can, Your
> Highness. Soldiers. Hundreds of them." Then he smiled. "And Latins.
> Lots of them." I told him to open the gates. He told me he didn't think
> that was wise and I told him to go to the devil and open the gates. I hope
> never again in my life to see such a sight as I beheld. While I stood in
> the cold, huddled in my fur curmantle, men, women, and children, of
> every age—many wearing no more than the robes they had donned that
> morning—were being marched away by *étape,* chained like criminals,
> regardless of sex or station, between mounted members of the Con-
> stantinopolitan Garrison. The Latin Quarter had been surrounded, its
> villas, palaces, and tenements ransacked, its inhabitants summarily ar-
> rested, whose only wrong was the nationality marked on their papers.
> They were not allowed to bring anything with them—not food, nor
> clothes, nor money. It was a sight of such misery, Uncle, as to defy
> description. Some women walked sobbing against their husband's backs.
> Children, speaking the only language they knew, Greek, called fran-
> tically for their parents from whom they had become separated. One
> lovely girl—a noblewoman from the looks of her—stared at me as she
> passed, and said, "Oh, please, sir. Tell me what will happen to us?" I
> thanked God above she did not know who I was. What greater self-
> disgust or helplessness can one feel than to stand witness to such injus-
> tice? I am ashamed of our house and the fatherland. It is a desecration
> of all that the family and Rome itself has ever stood for. It is the end
> of honor, insofar as I am concerned.

Alexander's attitude, it may be said, was characteristic of the aristocracy and the intellectuals in all major cities, who were appalled by the brutality and unaccountable ignominy of the act. It was simply without precedent and an assault on the international comity and the integrity of social intercourse between sovereign countries. Michael Branas' aged father, Marshal of the Constantinopolitan nobility, spoke for nearly every member of his class when he said, "His Majesty has detained a great many people, some very rich, all innocent. All have suffered the confiscation of their possessions. He has now imprisoned them in a great crush under inhuman conditions and is holding them for ransom. If any man can distinguish between this Imperial edict and the activity of a common thief, I defy him to come to me and explain it." Shortly thereafter, he resigned his official dignity, and for once, gained the support of his daughter-in-law, Persephone Porphyriogeneta, who for the first time openly criticized the uncle who had been her lover. (Perhaps she was a little too round in her condemnation; some believed she was quite put out by the Emperor's extravagant attention to his son by Maria, over and above their own, poor Demetrius, who bore that double onus of bastardy and incest.)

But the aristocracy and the learned were, of course, a minority. The poor Greek, and the Greek merchant, for differing reasons, welcomed this act with great thanksgiving, the poor because it was believed the taunting burden of a pampered, alien group had been lifted from their backs, the merchant because he believed the Venetians had been privileged to cheat against him. Though conditions remained substantially the same—which is to say, in decline—the Emperor's popularity soared.

As for Manuel, his yield was, at once, immense. Despite that early emigration of several millionaires, their ships, much of their gold, and their agencies were left behind, along with most of their colleagues who were to suffer so ultimately. Within two months, the Office of the Finance Minister was able to transfer to the Imperial Treasury, now perennially empty between indictions, gold and notes in excess of the cost of one year's annual expenses for the maintenance of Empire. And there was the promise of more to come, as Venice, prompted to honor, however unwillingly (i.e., to take advantage of a policy at which the righteous world without was aghast), ransomed its people from the Byzantine beast.

What can Manuel have been thinking of? All records of the event were, apparently, destroyed on receipt. Certainly the tradition of the Comneni and Venice was too long, riven with need and hostility on both sides, too complex for the Emperor to be ignorant of the consequences of his act. After ninety years of uneasy alliance, he was like a man tossing himself from a cliff to flee from a lion. The rescue exceeded the risk of confrontation.

It is among the most culpable acts of his long Regency. As alliance with the Republic had been a heritage of father to son, so now, from father to son, and cousin to cousin, was a tradition of inescapable acrimony. Manuel had been, as always, fortunate enough to break a habit, gratuitously, with his people's encouragement. Andronikus, in need of turning a new custom on its heel, to save himself and the Empire, would, in the chaos which provoked that necessity, find himself against his subject's prejudices and, for that, their victim. *Explicit: Nicetas Acominatus.*

XXIX

In the blue light of the moon, Andronikus and Theodora sit atop the walls of Mardin Fortress. The old stones which form the vertiginous drop of the bastion are transfigured silver. From the courtyard, shared by horses, dogs, chickens, and three cows, an occasional animal complaint arises, magnified by the deep well of the building. The Queen and her lover are laughing softly, and every so often, with the dying amusement at some previous comment.

THEODORA. I wonder. Would it have made a difference, if you hadn't the children, myself, all the poor souls we're bound now to keep about us or what would become of them if we were to let them go?

ANDRONIKUS. Probably I should only have been more reckless, and stupid. At least I have this—and I am not lonely—and that is saying a great deal. I regret nothing as nothing will alter for my regret. What's done is done.

THEODORA. Perhaps. Aristotle said the past was beyond even God's power to change.

ANDRONIKUS. Agathon said it.

THEODORA. Aristotle *said* Agathon said it.

ANDRONIKUS. Then he did him a disservice to repeat it.

The Grand Duke is silent awhile.

ANDRONIKUS. I've asked myself to what purpose I would struggle. No man cares, and if at the end I do not accomplish what I set out to do, it is of little matter. There will be others, and, in the end, there's only the grave and it makes no difference, whatsoever. Why struggle against the animation of a chaos which is greater than yourself?

THEODORA. There's no answer to such a question.

ANDRONIKUS. Why struggle? Why not?

THEODORA. That's worse than a bad answer or a false belief. It's apathetic.

ANDRONIKUS. No, it's an answer of sorts. Other men resign themselves by choice. I choose not to. It's as simple as that, because believe me, I might just as soon cut the chain and willingly, even gladly, relinquish myself to the night and submerge.

He smiles at her, at once mischievous and wistful.

ANDRONIKUS. You see before you a very tired old man, quite ruined.

THEODORA. I prefer your ruin, Sir, to the apotheosis of other men. Remember that.

ANDRONIKUS. Consider: The sun is visible on the other side of the world, but to all our intents it might just as well not exist at this moment. I am a Greek, a Byzantine, which is more than Greek, the very reconciliation of Greece and Rome—of art, law, and science, of morality and politics—and yet here I sit beneath a Persian moon. I know there are men alive who would be happier to be alive if I were Emperor, if I could promulgate my beliefs in reality—that is, hard law.

THEODORA. Andronikus, can't you see, men as they are, if oppressed, would not oppress less if freed, but attempt, in turn, to oppress their oppressors?

ANDRONIKUS. I know. And what's worse, such men would still be oppressed, bound by their former agony. And yet, if they could be taught forgiveness of their former tormentors—they would be free in principle as well as fact. Without understanding forgiveness is only indifference.

THEODORA. That is the power of illumination. God's gift or godlike.

ANDRONIKUS. Don't be ridiculous. It is no more beyond any man's grasp than mine. It is truth. I think it. I feel it, and if I speak it to other men, they will understand. It is with such misplaced humility as yours most men refuse to consent to their own conclusions which are probably the more painful for being subtle.

THEODORA. Each man's truth according to his own experience is anarchy.

ANDRONIKUS. Is it? If we were all so dissimilar, how is it we are commonly moved by the intent of the artist? If we were all so dissimilar, how could love or compassion exist? I want more than most men presume for themselves: to act upon what I believe. If men shall *see* more clearly because I lived, then I die justified.

THEODORA. Why should you need others to justify your existence?

ANDRONIKUS. Don't be so defensive in my behalf. Let me explain. It occurs to me poets and philosophers and theologians write of *meaning*. The poet describes those who pursue it; the philosophers are those who seek it and theologians believe they have found it. Yet all remains moot, I do not think we shall ever know why we are born, live, and must die, with the definitiveness which would make birth, which we do not choose, life, in which we are at the mercy of coincidence, or death, which is an annihilation—and has nothing to do with us—acceptable. Something tells me, not meaning, but justification, alone, is accessible, possibly because "justice" is relative to time, place, and circumstance. I may convince myself life has meaning, but it is all quite introverted. There is no agreement, no consent from beyond my own soul and senses. Justification, on the other hand, is not only more tenable, but most certainly, extrinsic. The city of Catania, for instance, was just recently buried under an eruption of Mt. Etna and fifteen thousand people were ensepulchered in the lava. Had I, on a moment's notice, found my way the two thousand miles to Sicily and assisted but one survivor with money and comfort from his desolation, my life would be justified, past, present, and future, for I should have acted positively against all riddles —existence, coincidence, meaning—which are torture enough against any man without the added and indifferent brutality of nature. In any event, justification, insofar as I can see it, possesses as many definitions as there are acts we may, in any way, call good.

THEODORA. I could accept your deserting me for another woman, but not a religious epiphany. You sound as though you're about to take orders.

Andronikus laughs shortly.

ANDRONIKUS. That's highly unlikely, though, you may be sure as I am famed for, and not myself accustomed to, doing things by halves, if I were so inclined, you would be the first to go. I would settle for nothing less than the Patriarchate.

THEODORA. And more than likely you would make Christians of Christians at last. To see that day, I would leave you voluntarily.

ANDRONIKUS. I want—or I wanted—to be great, but in the precise sense of greatness, not genius. Julius Caesar was a genius, but he was not a great man. The cynicism of his ambition forfeited the dignity of other men, and that nullified the possibility of comparison with them which would make him great. For myself, the only true greatness is to enhance the earthly life of man or give it to him to accept what is possible and no more. Nothing is irrevocable and not everything is soluble.

THEODORA. What a wonderful contemplative you would have made.

ANDRONIKUS. I doubt it. I've always thought of contemplation as a diversion one must earn, the supreme pleasure of absolute rest after final accomplishment. I have neither.

He pulls her to him, taking her head gently to his shoulder.

ANDRONIKUS. I remember when I was a boy, my brother Michael told me if I got upon my father's horse, Helios—a giant, seventeen hands— and gave him free rein, he would leave the earth and fly. The horse was so divinely huge, as I say, nothing seemed impossible to it. And it would have been a lovely thing to do: to soar in the warm afternoon, high past the trees in autumn, high into the firmament, to race between valleys of clouds, to ascend fleetly to heaven, the angels—and God.

He pauses. His eyes glisten with reverie.

ANDRONIKUS. So I climbed upon Helios' back and started off—and suffered rather the nightmare of the runaway until my father saved me. It is only now that I am so very much older, I know the rushing away is, perhaps, all there can ever be, the wind indignant, the muscle raving, the noise of the earthbound in frustrated speed. I remember the misery I felt, the panic, like the brush of the sodden, cold feathers of the raven of death at the back of my neck. I was without hope and no knowledge of my destination, or any assurance I would be alive on arrival—until, that is, I heard my father's voice arriving on another steed beside me. Now when I experience such fears, there is no rider at my back except Time, reaching over to flail my horse's flanks. Death, but no light. And even were there a voice, it would not be enough. I have become too aware of my own solitude to be consoled by another man. But the tangibility of that moment when Michael told me I might fly—the vision of soaring above the trees and beneath the blue sky and perceiving the banked clouds from an alien aspect—has remained with me to this day, so detailed and so perfect as to seem almost to have happened. It is the memory of that vision, the suffusion in bliss, of tenderest spiritual sweetness, and the promise of final stillness in color and light, toward which I would aim to return in contemplation and never shall. So much for my grounding in reality. Perhaps I'm no more and no less a dreamer than Manuel.

THEODORA. My uncle's no dreamer. He hasn't the strength for it. But he could have been great. That's why his corruption is so pathetic. You *would* have served him, selflessly, I know it, as your father served my grandfather. It would have been superb.

ANDRONIKUS. That's good. You ought to feel that way. It would suffer me to see you bitter.

THEODORA. I was. For a while, longer than you knew. But I was afraid what you would think of me. I suppose I knew, even then, I was wrong.

ANDRONIKUS. You've learned that much. I learned it much sooner. To excoriate Manuel served no purpose, as it serves no purpose to become anyone's conscious enemy with no more point to your existence than revenge. Any factor which shackles one's perceptions, inhibits change, is a worse oppression than that any man can extend over another.

A processional of vast, white racing clouds, their edges glowing beneath the light of the moon they conceal, their underbellies luminous with the refracted light of earth, cross the clear, profound night sky. They pass beneath Orion, concealing all the constellation but Betelgeuse and Bellatrix, a red and a blue eye, which seem—fixed and impassive— to stare down upon the lovers.

Incipit: Nicetas Acominatus: Once Andronikus said to me, "Ambition is no more than fury, a man's revenge against his birth, or fate, or both. To be sure, fury leads to exhaustion, the sort of which you are unaware until you yield to events—and forced rest. By 1172, indeed, I was not so much disgusted as exhausted with life, somehow indifferent. It was not the same as my years in prison. Then, however desultory my day-to-day existence, my very survival was somehow participation in the event of my challenge to Manuel. But in 1172, in the seventeenth year of estrangement from my cousin, my former hopes were spoken of in terms of regret, as unfulfilled prospects congealed beneath the gradually incrementing surface of time, lost with my youth and my middle age. At fifty, it seemed as though I had been successfully deflected from my ambitions. I was now given only so much time to return to the course, more distant than ever. I believed then, in fact, the progress of the state was now too far ahead for me to recover."

In 1172 Queen Theodora wrote to her sister, Maria, Princess Boris of Hungary, now sister-in-law to the new King, Bela III:

It is too harrowing to watch him, day after day, exerting himself to the breaking point in little pursuits, simply to forget, to sleep, to allow the monstrous wound to heal. Everything is too intense. Every encounter with him is exhausting. Yesterday he fell into an abandoned wolf pit exploring the castle. His leg was badly sprained. He couldn't walk, couldn't climb, and he called for help for hours (he was in the uninhabited wing). When we found him, he made light of it. Looking back at the pit as we helped him away, he said, "Life imitates art." I asked him what he meant, and he only laughed. Well, his words are his words; but the thought of him lying there, in the darkness, in pain, unheard, simply breaks my heart. His life has been so full of misfortune. It is too much to think how the small frustrations of those hours must have seemed to him—the very end of tolerability. There are times when I think I will go mad watching him, listening to him, because he is a great man who is wasted, and he *knows* he is both great and wasted, and the misery of it all eats at him like a cancer. There is nothing I can say that he will not refute, and so I am silent and wish I were dead for my helplessness, and his. But he must talk or he will go mad himself. He says I am his consolation, and he says it often, and it is enough I am with him. Probably, if he knew how much I loathed those moments when he speaks of his thwarted life, so failed, how much I wished myself elsewhere, never having met him, he would be stunned, more than ever forlorn and so I must never tell him. I am confirmed in one thing—perhaps in all this desolation all that I am left—that he must never be alone again. If I could take upon me all the years he ran, alone, I would do so. It is a small price to pay to be loved—and I think I am loved—by so exalted a man. Papa says I have given up everything meaningful in my life—my name, my church, my treasure, and my prestige. What foolish things he speaks. I will longer be honored, I know, as Andronikus' mistress than ever I was as Baldwin's Queen or Isaac's daughter.

His son, the Grand Duke Julian, however, tells, if not a different story, then one complementary in the light of the whole Andronikus. "I fear," he said, "my father was so roundly persecuted for so long over matters in which he believed himself in the right, he came to believe himself incapable of wrong, and now justifies nearly any action he takes, quite out of hand. All autocrats are anarchists and my father is both. I think in his heart, he welcomes the excuse to forbid or, at any rate, discount all criticism. It is interesting, you know, his rebellion against Manuel Augustus—I mean the early years—is taken as a sign of his integrity. Manuel adored him and my father is subtle beyond description—or anyway, used to be. He could have accomplished anything he wished under his predecessor."

At these words, I reminded the Grand Duke that the late Emperor, for all his melting charm, was extremely self-willed and opinionated. "That may be true," he said. "But so is my father and, as you have called him, an actor of extraordinary persuasion. To be sure, I cannot possibly know what he was like previous to imprisonment and exile. From the descriptions, from contemporary accounts, I gather he was a different man entirely. All I know is that at some point in his emigrations he altered completely from what he must have been. Only his acting was consummate in concealing the metamorphosis. I think all love and compassion and the check of his own good sense died then. It can be explained away by his humiliations and deprivations. It cannot be condoned. Previous to 1155, 1165 even, my father would have made a great emperor. Afterward"—he shook his head lugubriously— which is to say affectedly—sighing.

I asked Julian if perhaps it was not events which were overwhelming his father, but, quite the opposite, Andronikus' refusal to forgo reforms at the very moment when he should have been giving all his attention to rectifying the damage of two previous reigns. The Grand Duke shook his head again, and then, with a condescending smile which seemed to pity my defense—as perhaps he would condescend to smile on any defense of his father—said, "But there, Count, don't you see? You are calling it stubbornness, noble miscalculation. I call it for what it is: a self-centered vendetta against the aristocracy who, he believes, did nothing to save him or the fatherland from Manuel's shriving. You and I know"—I winced at the complicity: the ploy of the opinionated—"he didn't give a damn for his precious oppressed by the time he assumed the Regency for Alexius. He wanted then, as he wants now, merely to destroy the archonate and the Constantinopolitan Grandees and all members of our family, who, he chooses to believe, tormented him or allowed Manuel to torment him. Perhaps as you say, events are overwhelming him. If so, he must realize he made a better critic than he does now an Emperor. He hasn't the least idea how to rule, just as it happens in a child when a teacher delegates real authority to him, and his mind, of a sudden, goes blank. My father is clumsy, too old to learn, and, anyway, only interested in preserving the throne for Sandro or me. Failing this, and he senses now he is failing, he will bring down all our house with him. Watch and see."

(Added: Michael Acominatus: In the original manuscript, beside the above words from the Grand Duke Julian, was a notation to delete the entire passage. My brother wrote: "He has more accurately described himself. His conceit is so unbounded that nothing and no one emerges from his perceptions without resembling him, not greater for it, but belittled, like a string of not too attractive bastards left behind by a philanderer." The conversation with the Grand Duke took place in October 1184, of which, my brother told me, "I knew perfectly well what he was going to say and I dreaded every word from beginning to end. There is nothing so quick to exercise one's self-discipline, one's patience as giving full attention to a highly placed bore who confuses politeness with consent. Julian is not evil, only bleak, petty, and stupid. If it is not stupidity, then call it the predictability of the dull. He is like too many men who use their minds not as a lamp, but a hearth." I have gone against my brother's judgment and allowed the passage to stand. Though in most respects I agree that the portrait of the father by the son is quite invalid, it remains to say something of the son, and, thereby, indirectly, the father. As for myself, I must, in all honesty, state I found in Andronikus—who, I am willing to admit, may have been the most stupendous prince produced by the House of Comnenus—an alarming, brooding, ominously infernal side which he may have been at pains to conceal from my gentle brother. His rages were notorious, and, more often than not, unexpected. He could be rude, suspicious, calculating, relentless, just as intolerant of criticism as Manuel, and occasionally unfeeling in manner which was completely alien to his cousin. He was, in some measure—just as his son suggested—self-centered, even selfish, demanding unexceptionable loyalty and the constant commiseration of a petu-

lant child. It was quite plain he believed no born prince had ever suffered as did he in order to reach the throne. Supreme power, therefore, was his to do with as he wished, and woe betide the man who attempted to stay him. For all his amazing ability to charm and move, without condescension, the lowest peasant, he was every inch royalty in that he expected the loyalty of servants to the Imperium, without question, whatever its policies. But in this, also, was the danger any regent has yet to be too apt to escape: sycophancy. There is the world of difference between true adherence to a throne, wherein one seeks to serve the state, regardless of the Emperor—men such as Manuel's confidential secretary, Michael Hagiotheodorites, who became Andronikus' Plenipotentiary Undersecretary, Michael Branas, his Commander of the Armies, and my brother, his Secretary for Foreign Affairs, men who were intrigued by if not resolved upon his ideas—and those who simply feigned interest and devotion to their own advantage. I am speaking of course of the sinuous, invidious Stephen Hagiochristophorites, who more than any other man blacked the name and reign of the Emperor by whom he profited.)

Four years passed.

Bela III of Hungary reminded the Emperor the betrothal to Catherine Porphyriogeneta was still valid and he intended to see it through to marriage. Manuel nullified the betrothal and the Apostolic King, deflected from visions of a Greco-Hungarian Imperium, never forgave Constantinople and, in the reign of Andronikus, put his grudge to work.

Riots in the Bulgarian Province, unexpected and savage, served notice of an autonomous movement under the Asen brothers, the mediatized Princes Peter and John.

Four years passed.

Almaric died—on the same day as the Sebastocrator Isaac III—leaving as the last Lotharingen Advocate of the Holy Sepulcher his valiant, passionate, decomposing son.

Nureddin died, and Saladin, true to his mentor's fears, became supreme in the Orient.

Isaac Aaron, Manuel's official interpreter, commissioned to initiate a reconciliation with Venice, accepted a bribe as double agent, returned to Constantinople where he was confronted by the Secret Police with evidence of his perfidy, was blinded, and waited to spread his poison under Andronikus Augustus.

Four years passed.

Frederick Hohenstaufen, his Italian policy a complete failure, chose to imitate Manuel's diplomatic wiliness by inaugurating ambassadorial relations with Kilij II of Iconium. Rather than invoke and substantiate the treaty between the Sultan and Constantinople, Manuel, in a dudgeon, sent ambassadors to the Danishmend Emir, Saltouch, and following the advice of the latter's agents, broke alliance with Iconium, preparing the way for Myriokephalum.

Four years passed.

John Sergius died.

Andronikus and Theodora and their children moved from Mardin to a magnificent villa, the gift of the Emir of Khelat, who, by this gesture, infuriated his neighbor—precisely the point—Saltouch, now allied with Manuel. When the lovers had outlived their usefulness—after seven months—they were wakened in the night and escorted north across the border with but their clothes and a purse of gold hurriedly snatched by Veronica Melissena. With their suite, they made the hundred-mile trek on foot to Tiflis, where they were received by Andronikus' nephew, George IV, scarcely pleased to antagonize Constantinople or succor the woman who had humiliated his aunt. Yet to refuse anyone who had come to him for sanctuary would imply politically that he was less Byzantium's client than its henchman, which no proud Bagratid could tolerate. The fugitives remained a half year, whereupon they were offered formal asylum, to the astonishment of nearly everyone, by Saltouch of the Danishmends. The Emir had reconsidered his alliance with Constantinople and found his dignity wanting as a diplomatic incident in the nearly quarter-century duel between two Christian Emperors. He was, moreover, openly intrigued by the legend of the Comneni lovers, the tale of their extraordinary personal attraction, their hardships endured in the face of Church and state, and he was desirous of meeting them. He proved their last sponsor, their most lavish, and quite without condition. He established them with a staff and guard in a gigantic, handsome citadel near Colonnea. From that castle, now reverently visited by sightseers, a small war issued between Andronikus at the head of Danishmend soldiery and troops of the Governor of Trebizond, the Grand Duke's cousin, Nicephorus Paleologus. Without the slightest hesitation, Andronikus sold all members of the Imperial army whom he captured into Oriental slavery.

XXX

On 29 May 1176, at Legnano, the Holy Roman Emperor was se-
verely wounded and his entire army defeated in a battle which won complete victory for the Lombard League, their ally, the Pope, and their
generous supporter, via the agency of Pisa and Genoa, Manuel Augustus.
That summer, then, proved to be the heyday of Byzantine power, such as
it had not been known—or feared—since the reign of Basil II. With the
exception of the Seljuk gouge in Lesser Asia and the provision that
Manuel's authority in Italy was rather one of personal prestige than
territory, the sway of Constantinople in fact exceeded the last of the
great Macedonian Emperors. From Sardinia to the Caspian Sea, the
light which shone was the last, refulgent burst of the Greek sun.

Who does not know the story of Alexander the Great? How he conquered Persia, but Persia was not enough, and so from Hecatompylos,
marched easterly still to the Indus. Persia had never stood as the
living symbol of impossible ambition. It had merely been an immemorial and great enemy which must be undone. When its walls were
down and the way clear beyond it, the true chimera of the young King's
demon could be witnessed: India, perhaps the edge of the earth. But
at Pattala, on the Indus, in July 325 B.C., the army refused to march
any farther. Alexander waited three days to be certain of their reluctance, erected twelve altars on the shores of the Hyphasis River in
thanks to Olympus for his victories, and started home. I have yet to
read the poet or historian who suggests, as it seems to me so likely,
this astonishing young man, perhaps the greatest military genius of all
time, believed himself, in the recesses of that onyx, inscrutable heart,
a failure. Persia had been the shield. So long as Persia existed, there
was Persia to undo. Impossibly, Persia fell. Beyond that, there could
only be the siren of universal conquest or suicide for the littleness of
things. Alexander died and Greece, in the end, died with him. His
brilliant and finally hesitant army was not the source but the agent
of the unforeseen, the element of chaos introduced into all lives.

So, too, the West, though he could not know it, had been Manuel's
shield against ultimate ambition. A massive final assault against the
Seljuks, entrenched for a century in Lesser Asia, had never been pos-

sible so long as there were considerations of Germany, Italy, and the Latin states. But during the summer of 1176, the Emperor, "a second Justinian" (who, so many forgot, had presided not at the apotheosis but consummation of the old Roman Imperium), could look left and right and, finding no equal, collect an army with the intent of marching on the premier chimera against whose advent the Comneni had taken the throne: Turk Lesser Asia.

Two days before the Emperor crossed the Bosporus, I received an unexpected embassy from the Sultan, which I was at pains to bring before Manuel without the least delay. They were commissioned to reassert the alliance between Constantinople and Iconium, in any manner whatsoever pleasing to the Emperor, including abject vassalage of the Moslem King of the land in which I was born. I shall never forget the thought which struck me as I listened to Prince Mikail and his aides: "These are frightened men. They haven't the forces to contend both Saltouch and the Augustus. His Majesty needn't make war."

But Manuel would hear nothing of peace. He complained of border skirmishes too long endured by Constantinople, much less Arslan's presumption in going over to the German enemy camp. I remember the ambassadors seemed particularly alarmed at this. Distressed by their distress, the Emperor smiled kindly and plighted his goodwill toward all Moslems and demurred any religious or personal animosity. The gentlemen before him were to understand such impertinence as the Sultan exhibited, who had long ago, it might be reminded, sworn vassalage to the Imperium, was no longer to be tolerated.

Prince Mikail said, "Your Majesty, is there nothing we can do to avert so ghastly an alternative?" I remember he ran his bejeweled hand along the thick edge of his brocade robe, meanwhile concentrating his fierce, beautiful eyes on the Emperor. Manuel looked down and away, obviously uneasy. His eyes, recessed and encircled by age, were more haunting than ever, though somewhat unlikely beneath his still miraculously scarcely grayed hair. His refusal to meet the Prince's gaze told all. He was quite sensitive to the difference between the obsequiousness of a coward or a petitioner and the helpless imploration of the righteous. No man of essential goodwill wishes to be reminded, in small, of the absolute power he holds to move with or resist war, which is his ultimate power over life and death. He said, "Sir, can you give me your word that were Iconium prepared for war you would still be

here?" The Prince stood silent. The Emperor continued, "If there were
any other solution, I would take it with a ready and gratified heart.
Iconium must recognize the final extent of Constantinople and the
limits of its own daring." Mikail took a step forward, "But, Lord, I
beg you. This is not reason. It is belligerence. *Delenda est Carthago.*"
Manuel shook his head and rose from his chair. They bowed, and so
did I. When we looked up, he was gone.

Michael Branas said to me, several years later, "After Myriokephalum,
I wrote to Andronikus, saying, 'No one wanted this war, and now we
learn that it could have been avoided. I ask you, how dare even an
autocrat rule against reason?' His first words by return post were:
'Now you have it, my friend.'"

The army reconnoitered at Miletus to which the Emperor sailed at
the last possible moment, wishing to attend the Empress who was ill
at Blachernae. His General Staff had believed the campaign involved,
solely, a forced march on Iconium and a long siege, thereafter, with
the possibility of taking the city before winter. During the leisure of
his sail southward, Manuel changed his mind and decided to take
Philomelion, which had lately fallen into Seljuk hands, thus opening
for the Imperial army a new base of supplies at Dorylaeum and Nicea,
and a speedier line of communication with Constantinople.

"It was absurd," said Michael Branas. "By this we were forced to
waste men and supplies—and time—moving in a great loop, north to
Sublaion, Sozopolis, Myriokephalum, then east to Philomelion, and,
thereafter, if we took the city, south again to Iconium. The whole Praetorium objected. Our lines of communication were open to the sea.
What did it matter if there were a little delay in dispatches and supplies? The object was not worth the expense. But the Emperor was
one of those who reasoned this was just the sort of detail, which, in all
its subtlety, everyone might overlook, and would prove to be the key
to victory if the siege lasted longer than expected. He confused fussy
caprice with ingenuity. The more we objected, the more he became
convinced, the one standing against the many, his clear eye against
our blind glance. Finally, impatient, he suffered it as a test of his authority, a command from the Autocrat rather than a suggestion by the
Imperator."

India did not defeat Alexander, but the bemusement and suffering
of his own army, who could no longer understand his purpose. So

ambition did not defeat Manuel, but rather the desperation of his enemy. "Hideous," continued Michael Branas. "In retrospect, hideous, tragic, inevitable. Like Oedipus, who senses the ghastliness of the final truth long before it is revealed, and, for all warnings—each as much the knell of his own oncoming doom—goes on, impetuously, to the end. I have sometimes thought the Theban King stands as allegory for the root truth we would find at the bottom of our souls dare we look. At Sublaion, a last embassy appeared from Iconium to gain a peace and was, last of all, refused. The rest, you know."

To use one of Andronikus' favorite expostulations: A child would understand. Strange, how much one would choose, if choice were possible, to fit complexity to an occasion of such moment as Myriokephalum, to posit that it was a battle of military wit commensurate with its consequences. But it was not. It was merely a crude mistake exacting a crude penalty. Eight hundred years of military tradition were undone, never, never to recover. In two hours, a century of effort was nullified.

Now, approach to the fortress of Myriokephalum is guarded by a long deep gorge which renders the citadel, at the far end, impregnable. By definition it is a snare. Larger, for instance, than the world's most famous clefted passage—that leading to Petra in Jordan—Myriokephalum is wide enough and lengthy to accommodate the very greatest armies. "Simply put," Michael Branas said, "the bigger the trap, the bigger the game." The tips of its steeply slanting walls—which permit descent of only the most sure-footed men and horses, but scarcely any possible means of ascent, in turn—form perfect bastions from which to attack.

Thus, 17 September 1176, Manuel was in the company of his 180,-000-man military colossus as it proceeded ahead to the citadel. There had been no adequate previous surveillance by scouts. Shortly before noon, the entire army for a period of about an hour would be ranged along the floor of the defile. Ten thousand Seljuks ranged themselves before the fortress. Twenty-five thousand, evenly divided, took the summits, right and left, on either hillside. When the sun reached its zenith, the signal via a system of mirrors was given. Arrows, spears, missiles, fireballs, fired logs, and boulders rained down on the huge, vulnerable Imperial forces.

"From the corner of my eye," Michael Branas told me, "I saw something in the sky, quite brilliant. I looked up. You cannot imagine what it is like to raise one's eyes toward that blue which one always turns as a haven of peace, and behold brutal, tumultuous, helplessly falling instruments of death. Since that day, whenever I hear sudden, loud noises, I look not behind, but up, and the sky no longer seems to me celestial.

"It was a disaster so great it cannot adequately be mourned: pits were filled to the top with corpses; in ravines were heaps of slain. One galloped over dead bodies in a frenzy for a cover or escape. I remember Michael Gabras, on my left, said, 'Oh, my God, we're like pigs in a pen.' The Varangians surrounded us, and we lifted our shields above our heads in something like a turtle formation, and started back. There was never any question of defense. I had said, 'We must stand, we must do something. This isn't war. It's murder.' And George Angelus said, 'This isn't murder. It's massacre and there's nothing to be done.'

"All the while, the Emperor, at our center, said nothing. He was being crucified and he knew it. His entire reign, everything he had achieved or hoped to achieve, was being swept away in this inescapable insanity of gore and noise. Wounded horses, struggling to rise, were dragged out of our way. Soldiers were calling after their comrades, some merely dazed, others walking corpses, dripping torrents of blood as they stumbled. Dust, carnage, wails, war cries, and a continuous, infernal never-ending rain of missiles from above. That is what I remember.

"Hallowed standards were tossed aside: here the Nemitzi, there the Archontopuli, the Excubitors, the Scholarians, the Candidate, the Maniaces—the legions of St. George and St. Demetrius and St. Michael. Men were crawling under mountains of corpses to save themselves. But worse was to come. The Turks descended the hillside. I rather can say it now that it *was* a thrilling, awesome sight to see that cavalry take the incline, the steepest I'd ever encountered.

"The army, already in chaos, was now cut in half and completely savaged. Our own Varangians were beginning to fall. We speeded our retreat, followed by thousands of confused cavalry and infantry, most of whom collapsed by the wayside to be hacked to death or captured, at battle's end, and sold into slavery. They would have followed anything which had the semblance of destination, of human plan. Hands reached out to us pitifully, some beseeching a final blessing from God's anointed, some for assistance, some for rescue—whoever gave it—and some to wave a curse as the blood ceased to pump from finger to pulse to shoulder to breast and stopped irrevocably at the useless heart.

"We had been traveling at the center of the army, along with the Emperor's hundred wagons of accompanying luxury, which, needless to say, we left behind. We must have moved a mile in retreat to save Augustus from the major theater of battle. That mile took us an hour and a half—a minimal approximation. The party included the Basileus, his generals, and about two hundred members of the Varangian Guard, the rest of whom were still in the gorge, probably dead, along with all the Emperor's personal field staff. To our amazement, when we set down our shields, our horses and their underbellies, our persons from head to toe, were coated with blood—not from combat: there had been none—but the traversal of that butchery.

"The Emperor, I remember, as soon as we were escaped, spurred his horse, as in the same moment I caught the reins and stared at him, only stared, but stared with a hatred which was at once insolent and unconscionable. God knows what he must have been suffering. He looked at me, his eyes narrowing a bit, said hoarsely, accusing and self-accusing our cowardice and self-serving, his blindness and his vainglory all these years, these many years: 'What would you *have* me say, Michael?'

"At that moment, a lad—a peasant by the looks of him—in the Nemitzi colors, wandered out of the gorge. Blood was streaming down his face and he was holding his head with both hands. His expression—but I shall never forget it—had the stunned and fearful look of a child. It was so obvious he knew he was going to die and he was afraid to die. Suddenly he spun, turning his face up to the sun. His arms flopped to his side, and as he fell to the sand, the whole top of his head came away like a cap, covering a perfectly little bowl of brains and blood, while the two great gushes of the carotid spewed out onto the ground. The Emperor watched fascinated, his face tragic. He continued to stare long after the youth was obviously dead. Then he looked off to one side, turning his profile to me, so elegant a figure—even besplattered—in purple and silver, with his white-plumed, encircleted helmet, distracted, unapproachable, for he, as the ultimate power, bore responsibility to God for what had become of us. I thought of a line from Ovid when Rhea implores Apollo after Phaëthon's catastrophe: 'Is *this* your will and is *this* my reward?'"

BOOK THREE

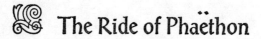 The Ride of Phaëthon

I

The Emperor and his escort were granted safe passage to Miletus or Constantinople, as they wished, by Kilij II, who was present for the battle. He asked no more of the Basileus than that the walls of Sublaion and Dorylaeum be razed. He could afford to be generous. Scarcely believing the triumph which had begun as no more than a preemptive strike, the Sultan knew Lesser Asia was his for the taking. Constantinople as a military power had been destroyed in an afternoon. For the moment, Iconium's King had not the men to occupy the land, but a levy would not be difficult. As the full import of the occasion affected the world, as Manuel's prestige failed, that of Arslan would rise to unparalleled heights.

Broken, speechless, beyond prayer or tears, Manuel consented to the Sultan's demands and on the way to his yacht, anchored off Miletus, razed the walls of Sublaion. Apparently the Sultan misunderstood the Emperor's intention to likewise order the disarmament of Dorylaeum on his return to Constantinople. Believing Augustus to have failed on his word, Arslan sent a force of more than twenty thousand infantry and cavalry, with war machines—designed in his father's reign by Byzantine engineers—and the walls tumbled while the entire North Meander Valley was put to the sack.

At Constantinople, we heard rumors of a great disaster somewhere near Lake of the Forty Martyrs. "Where is Myriokephalum?" someone asked me, knowing I was born to the area. Now, of course, not a man is unaware of its location and children tossing rocks from roofs onto their playmates, in alleys, pretend to be the valiant Arslan. After the full scope of the disaster was learned—and a day before the Emperor's arrival at Constantinople—a former classmate of mine from the university, Daniel, Duke Sklerus, who had become all too friendly with me since my entry into government, ran into my office, shouting, "You *said* he shouldn't go! You said it! Now look."

I met the Emperor, along with a delegation, at Buceleon Harbor. Wherever he got the iron control, I don't know. I expected a man crushed, hooded, ushered down a gangplank, and sped off into seclusion. Instead, he greeted us familiarly, personally—if not jovially—and invited us to a light meal with him, while we awaited the dromonds from Blachernae which would transport us to the new Sacred Palace. After dinner, the Emperor excused himself, took up several of his numerous Cantacuzenus nephews, and passing along the room, tapped my shoulder and Michael Branas' with an indication to follow him. Surrounded by Varangians, we crossed the still lovely gardens beneath autumn trees to Thecla Church where Divine Liturgy was celebrated. I shall never forget, as the dead were commemorated, the Emperor suddenly buried his face in his hands. I was so moved, I burst into tears and had to be led from the chapel by a disapproving usher.

William of Tyre, who visited us three years later, was stunned by the change in the Emperor. Later he was to write, *almost* accurately: "From that day the Emperor is said to have borne, ever deeply impressed, upon his heart, the memory of that fatal disaster. Never, thereafter, did he exhibit the gaiety of spirit which had been so characteristic of him, or show himself joyful before his people no matter how much they entreated him." But there are calamities so enormous, so consequential, their weight and effect can never, at once, be comprehended. Rather the Emperor's first quick response of grief was mixed with that which the merely bereaved—who have suffered the worst—can never know: dread. In September, returned from chaos to the serenity and magnificence of Blachernae, he could, almost by nature, remain gracious. In February his imperturbability while writing to his wife's cousin —and corresponding intimate—Henry of England, was an effort of will.

. . . Now I must assure you, my brother, things are not so dolorous here, as portrayed in rumor. I fear the gossip is more wish than fact. Besides, let me tell you, in the tradition of the British race who have so long and nobly served Roman emperors, many of your subjects were with us at Myriokephalum, either as picked soldiery or members of my personal guard, and they comported themselves with authority and courage to the end. Proof of their excellence is that I am here, at Blachernae, writing to you.

(I recall thinking, from the look of his face as he dictated those words to a secretary, while absently petting one of the hounds Henry had sent from England to amuse him, the implicit conclusion of the sentence ought to have been ". . . when I should be dead, in the gorge, with eight-score thousand others. . . .")

In time, rather than at once, despair began to tell as surely as a disease suddenly strikes a robust man and progressively disables him. Though there was some success under his brother-in-law, Stephen Cantacuzenus, in sending back the invading Seljuks from the western half of Lesser Asia, the Emperor had no illusions. Without the massive forces which had previously been at his command, it could be no more than a holding action.

Within a year of Myriokephalum, his hair turned almost wholly gray and his temper, so imperiously suppressed all these years, became pronounced, though, as always, he was quick to apologize. He slept poorly, he ate meagerly, and his health began to fail. He was not a hypochondriac, but perhaps in a certain simplicity from which he was never free, he mistook despair for a curable illness. The headaches, the poor stomach, the listlessness and disinterest in things were all too obviously the toll of a dementia from which there was no escape.

He was incapable of accepting the fact the accomplishment of a life-time had been ruined by chance. "Had he done so," Andronikus said later, not without sympathy, "he might have accepted the measure of coincidence and, with the same vigor and self-confidence as before, rescued and even regained something of what had been. To believe in chance, however fearful, is to accept it at length at its best and worst. But Manuel took his anointment too seriously. He believed God had withdrawn his chrism, his validity, and against that there was no challenge."

The Grand Duke was most certainly correct. The Emperor's despair was that of a man who believes, not that he has been the butt of his own self-confidence, but that such conceit became the agency of a vengeful God, not that his personality, and chance, made such a fall, at some point, at any point, inevitable, but that his pride conspired with heaven to the moment of Myriokephalum. He could not be roused from such a conviction, perhaps no man could. He wished only to re-treat from a life which had been harsher for its splendid promises. Yet it was also the will of God that he should live and suffer and endure his subjects' curses.

Still, I think it not too much for Andronikus to have said, "At the end, Manuel did not really care what happened beyond Alexius' succession. The future was God's business—the God who had given him a throne when he had not expected it and the God who had punished him so awfully—and my cousin was too tired to care. He was a good man, which I am not, if I take the good man to be he who looks for good in others, whereas I am mostly mistrustful. But his good was scarcely artless; it was self-aware, and, at the end, perhaps a means of self-excuse for any act and self-pity for any punishment. His final passivity and disinterest, in a way, exhibited his profound irresponsibility and the lack of any passion or vision beyond himself. He had failed in his dreams and cared only to hold what little he had. Is it not strange in those last years, on his occasional visits to me at Oeneum, he seemed, if not fascinated, at least unusually interested in my ideas of reform? I sensed then, this was the end to which the confusion of the state and himself had led. Further effort was inconceivable as it was against God's decree of punishment. He wished only death, now, with—if I may so call it—a serene desperation."

Perhaps most poignant and torturous in those last few years of his life was estrangement from his one source of consolation, the Empress. It was not a willed separation. But what does volition or involition matter, at least on a personal scale? The separation occurred, it was absurd and it was unnecessary. It tortured the Emperor and no less his Consort, bewildered by the remoteness of the man she adored, if not loved, for the indulgence and the honors with which he had described her life. Its origin was directly the result of spiritual fanaticism and subjugation to priests—understandable in these circumstances—to which the Emperor gave himself.

Unwilling to live with his misery and unable to die, Manuel sought surcease where it had been immemorially found: in prayer. He made pilgrimage, in February 1177, to the wonderworking shrine of Sts. Cosmas and Damian, where he conversed, at length, with its abbot, Monsignor Isaac, the holiest living man in Orthodoxy. It has been said since—with extraordinary meanness of spirit, or cynicism—the Patriarch directed the good priest in the advice he should give the Emperor, and that prescription was founded in Theodosius' notorious anti-

Latinism, which antipathy included the Empress. I believe this is to be at once discounted. I would accept nearly any rumor of intrigue among Constantinopolitan religious, less readily provincial diocesan fathers, and not at all, one such as Isaac, whose piety and integrity were impeccable precisely because, in his spiritual authority, he had nothing to gain by becoming the Patriarch's instrument. He was, moreover, an ascetic who constantly decried the Church's ownership of vast properties, the insinuation into government affairs by men of God (and vice versa), and—unfortunately, but significantly—toleration of any religion outside Orthodoxy.

Rather, it may be said, by receiving Isaac's counsel, the Emperor put himself in the way of churchmen, beginning with the Constantinopolitan Patriarch, who would, thereafter, use him. As for Isaac's advice—it was famed and simple—all evil directly resulted from the proto-sin of Adam and Eve. Woman's domination of man through carnality was the beginning of wickedness. It may be, then, as Manuel remembered infatuation for his wife had inspired him to his conceited deeds, including military ventures, to win her praise, that the Emperor consented to this torturous simplicity.

I suspect Manuel was one of those who believed the more arduous and unlikely the cure, the more certain its success must be. He secluded himself for a week at St. John of Studion Abbey, and emerged, declaring himself, at the age of fifty-seven, a celibate. It was pathetic. The Empress, as has been said, was a most certain, intimate consolation to a man still vital. With the loss of that intimacy, the Emperor was rather more melancholic than regenerated, and with a likely swing from antipode to antipode, gave himself more and more to spiritual advisers, sent to his side, in legion, by an obliging Theodosius, who, himself, did not hesitate to reassert the old patriarchal prerogative of dining nightly with the Sovereign.

By this, of course, Theodosius' influence increased day by day, and it is certain, to this scrupulous but reactionary authoritarian—a former provincial noble—we owe the ugliest and the meanest aspects of the end of Manuel's reign: the re-establishment of the Index Expurgatorio, of censorship, of increased Secret Police surveillance, hearsay trials, and obligatory state-stamped papers for travel (an excellent way for the government to know where any citizen is at any given time).

It must be said, however, if the record is offensive, the man was not. Theodosius was brilliant, if brilliance may be to the purpose of willfully rejecting what did not support his bedrock, archconservative convictions. He was witty, austere, of enormous charm when he chose to convey it, though—to some—it seemed less the gregariousness of Christ's servant than the condescension of Christ himself. Theodosius possessed, as few men do, immovable faith in his own high-mindedness. He never retreated from a step taken, no matter the cost. He never blinked. More often than not such an attitude leads to power as most weak souls beside him will convince themselves such self-confidence is born of truth, and bow to it. Occasionally, unnecessarily, it leads to tragedy because there is no possibility of compromise. I know there were times when I thought I could have befriended the Patriarch, but five minutes in his presence, when he was far from smiling, speaking rather in those clipped, precise syllables of the gentry imitating court Attic, his mouth moving beneath an absolutely immobile face, and I knew there was no possibility of trading pleasures and knowledge with an irrefutable oracle.

So the Empress was forgotten. From the day of his birth, the only child of her marriage had been given over to his own vast staff, who, themselves, had little affection for a charge on whom their appointments depended (sick, he was looked upon not as one to be cured and coddled, but as a deliberate and ungrateful assault on all their years of attention). There was no likelihood on Maria-Xenia's part of succumbing suddenly to a maternity she had not felt at the beginning, and could not feel now. Manuel could not face her and chose to live instead at Buceleon or the Irene Villa in Philopation Park. Deserted by the court which took its cue from the Emperor, she was left with a few faithful friends, among them the late John Sergius' younger brother, the Grand Duke David, who, rather from resentment than affection (for as the Protovestarius' power had slipped after the birth of the Crown Prince, so had his own), became the Empress' champion and probably her lover, as early as June 1177.

There is some evidence Manuel, however distressed, consented to the affair between his wife and nephew. His own denial, his wife's infidelity and the permutations of incest—collateral, at least, and not consanguine—were, he no doubt believed, continued and just penance of a world gone mad against him at God's behest. Himself, too in love with the Augusta, he could scarcely be expected to perceive, as a woman of little inner resource, the Empress' very reason for being depended upon heartfelt adoration. Simple women often resort thus to a personal cult of sentiment and affection. Well aware her beauty had always been the source of quick and unconditional affection for which others seemed to strive—often hopelessly—she would seek elsewhere and soon what her husband denied, not merely to end her loneliness, but to satisfy herself the key to its eternal banishment—that beauty—was still intact and supreme.

The court itself was of two minds: For once, with all its superficiality, cynicism, and ambition, it was truly moved by the purposeless estrangement of two people, obviously devoted to one another, by the same forces which had worked upon the Emperor, also, to transform the world's most dazzling court into a monastery. On the other hand, these same people forbore with dread—should Manuel die—the rise of the Grand Duke David, a man of far less integrity and political sense, whatever the faults—and they were many—of his dead elder brother. His ascendancy was practically assured when the Empress was proclaimed Regent Absolute till her son's majority, according to the terms of Manuel's will, sent to the Patriarch and the Senate, 4 June 1177.

II

On 1 July 1177 the most sensational news since Myriokephalum, and far more delectable, reached Blachernae and—somehow—the streets before night. The Governor of Trebizond, Nicephorus Paleologus, was sending under guard to Constantinople, Queen Theodora, her two children by Andronikus, Princess Irene and Prince Christopher, and her two "stepchildren," the Grand Duchess Zoë and the Grand Duke Julian. Rumor was—and perfectly true—Paleologus had lured Andronikus to a battle two days' distance from his castle, having previously sent the major portion of his army to storm the citadel and by any means, at any cost, take hostage the Grand Duke's mistress and his children.

In a brief note, which Nicephorus Paleologus kept for many years, Andronikus wrote to his cousin:

You people have ground me down to the nub. You have taken from me my station, my usefulness in life, expulsed me from my native land, and now robbed me of the Queen and my children, who were my last bastions against despair and the loss of dignity. To remain here, alone, would be to become no more than a clown and a thief. Be good enough, cousin, to dispatch a force to this place and I will present myself for arrest and remanding to Constantinople and whatever punishment awaits me.

On arrival at the Imperial capital, the Queen and Andronikus' children were established, under house arrest and in strictest seclusion, at Villa Rufiniana. One day shortly thereafter, the Emperor asked me to accompany him on his interview with his niece, whose political status—was she to be recognized as Grand Duchess and subject to Imperial law, or Sovereign Majesty and immune?—remained in doubt. As a member of the Foreign Ministry, I was to be entrusted with "sounding out" the Lady before her meeting with her uncle.

She met me with her children—and to my surprise, the Grand Duke Alexander—in the small private refectory at Villa Rufiniana, where passion was declared a century before between Mary of Alania and the then general, Alexius, Duke Comnenus.

His great-granddaughter, at forty-two, tended to plumpness. She was, indeed, a tall woman, seeming short, more than likely, only to her lover. While she affected the deep décolletage of Western dress and rejected elaborate Byzantine hairdos as did the Empress, there was no mistaking her middle age. I was even a little disappointed. Her face was beginning to tell, and her bosom, though still firm, was matronly ample. She seemed to me not at all the beguiling mistress. But there was serenity in her person like a glow. There was not a trace of smugness about her. Her wit and intelligence were obvious in the eyes, which seemed to convey the belief no situation, however benign, is without its debts, nor abysm without its humors. Yet—and I cannot say precisely how it came to me; it may only have been her history as I knew it from the dossier I had read the previous evening—there was also an aura about her of vulnerable and tragic weariness. She had been loved by two of the most fascinating, handsome, and admired men of the century—and others, perhaps, unreckoned. But the love of one and the dreams born of that union had been abruptly ended, and of the other had led to interdict, exile, and want. Profoundly intelligent, she had lived a life, by the standards of the mind, most unlikely. Aloof, jealous, beautiful in no ordinary way, one who made her decisions and lived with them without regret, she had known adoration and adventure such as most women spend their lives in the wish rather than act, but at the cost of repose for which her femininity and any true intellect might yearn. One sensed, as a result, her soul had been tempered almost beyond tolerability. One sensed any further misfortune or disruption in her life would be consequentially disastrous.

Alexander sat to her right, and her affection for him, considering his generous nature, was only to be expected. But it was Julian over whom she hovered. He was not the sort of personality to whom she ought to have been attracted, but he, not Alexander, had suffered his maturation enduring exile with her. Andronikus' middle son was perfectly beautiful, a Bagratid rather than a Comnenus. He possessed Alexander's coloring—the blond hair, the green eyes, and pink skin—but the features were almost feline—small, drawn, aquiline, exquisite. He was alarmingly vain, with self-conscious mannerisms as though he were reciting poetry to an adoring audience.

His sister, the Grand Duchess Zoë, was a frail young woman, unusual in Comnenae. Her plain but regular features were, if not redeemed, then distracted attractively, by that frailty. One was quite drawn to her delicacy, which itself was rescued from the nondescript—of bones too brittle and organs too near the skin precluding overt sensuality—by a strong, almost peasantlike mouth which opened into a dazzling smile—unexpected and all the more bewitching—merry gray eyes, and the curiously pleasing hoarseness of her voice. Her father's favorite child, her words to me concerning her relationship with the Queen most nearly convey her character. "You know," she said, "I'm not very brave or adventurous, but I am prepared to be—or to pretend to be—because my life is worth nothing if I must live it without my father's approval. I suppose by that, I've survived experiences and opened myself to people from whom I might otherwise have preferred to remain aloof. He taught me my only limits are those I place upon myself. For his sake I was prepared to accept the Queen. Accepting her, I loved her for fear Alexander and Julian would not, because I could not bear to see her humiliated by my brothers' disaffection. In time, I realized what she meant to Papa. As I grew older, I could not help but love her for herself and what she suffered to love my father."

My interview with the family—which, unlike most dynasts, surprised me for its homeliness—was uneasy and inconclusive. I am a poor diplomat for such situations. In retrospect, I often believe myself to have acted more awkwardly than in fact. I doubt in any way I truly offended the Queen that day. Rather, I count her implicit dislike of me thereafter, conveyed by the regal distance she put between us—and when that failed, downright petulant resistance, but never arrogance (probably because Andronikus would not have stood for it)—due to my association with this most unhappy episode, and her presumption, at once, I was one of the Emperor's courtiers instead of a member of his government.

I conducted the family to the Emperor on the following day. He received them informally in Rufiniana's gardens, which saturated all the senses with its thousands of roses. I suppose what touched me so deeply was the alteration of the Queen's expression on sight of her uncle. Until that moment, her glance would have frozen fire. But as we approached the Emperor, who was seated on a marble bench, his hands folded in his lap, looking away with his—by now—usual goatsong mask of unhappiness, Her Majesty actually seemed to bend a little from the waist and *peer* at him, amazed. It was not hard to understand why.

She had not seen him since Cilicia in the early sixties, in the company of her husband, when all were in flower. The change, in totality, was profound. He was not dressed in Imperial purple, but priestlike black, which only accentuated the pallor of his skin. He wore no jewels, not even his Imperial sigil. The perceptible bulge beneath the chalmys was for anyone to guess, a hair shirt as much as the unhealthy bloat from lack of exercise on which his otherwise lean body thrived. His almost completely gray hair was no longer shoulder length and thick, but barbered short and combed straight back from the forehead, revealing a receding hairline. There was a curiously hunted, hunched, vulpine attitude in his posture—not alertness but a coming closer toward some vision he perceived from within which replaced what was before him. (Indeed, in any conversation during the previous ten months, though he missed not a word, he seemed to retreat—I can only call it that—the moment he was finished speaking, and thereafter to fade, gently as the color goes out of the world when the sun passes behind a cloud.) His charm, his goodwill, his hesitancy to offend, were a part of him, natural as speech, but it was all that was left of Le Chevalier Manuel, the momentum of a lifetime. The fire was quenched, and the soul in darkness.

With this apparition, and because he made gesture to embrace her as he rose, the Queen greeted her uncle perhaps more warmly than she had expected—certainly so. The words which she had no doubt intended to toss at him, like knives, were served up with a sort of grudging, bantering tone.

The Emperor had said, "I assure you, if Andronikus does not come for you in a reasonable amount of time, I will let you return to him." In response, the Queen said, "You know I could never return. Does it please you to put me through a test of his loyalty?" "Nothing of the sort," said His Majesty, and he meant it. "It never entered my mind." "If Andronikus does not surrender in my behalf, then I've lost, for under no circumstances would I follow him if he betrays me. If he surrenders, then I've lost him, too, for you have used me against him."

The Emperor was about to reply, but she looked at me meaningfully, and with His Majesty's nod, I withdrew.

Shortly after the reconciliation between the Emperor and himself, Andronikus said, "Curiously enough, in taking me back, Manuel showed himself strong, for he had not treated me very well, and to deal justice, which is freedom, to one's victims is an act of faith and courage, too. I commend him for it."

He arrived in chains at Constantinople on the night of 25 July 1177, and was conducted to the Tower of Anemas, where he was visited almost at once, by his eldest son, the daughter-in-law he had never met, Euphrosyne Paleologa Comnena, and his first grandchild, who today rules as Alexius I, Grand Comnenus of Trebizond. When, by letter, he asked that the Queen be allowed to visit him, the request was denied. Shortly he would have his freedom, but first he was obliged to make his peace with the Emperor before the entire court, which was being held for the first time since Myriokephalum, with this lugubrious errand in mind. I curse myself I was ill that day with the worst hangover I have ever suffered, penalty for the previous night which had begun as a symposium on poetry (old Tetzes and I could scarcely look one another in the eye for months thereafter), and so I missed the reunion between the Imperial cousins which was both real and formal.

Michael Branas: "He was taken manacled before the Emperor. I don't know whose idea that was but it was tasteless in the extreme, unkind to His Majesty's reputation and humiliating to the Grand Duke. It would scarcely be expected that Andronikus would assault Manuel. But, really, what an unforgettable moment when the doors at the far end of this very audience hall opened." Branas' words now echoed throughout its dim, golden enormity, lit in the night by a few auxiliary torches and alternate rows and candles of the chandeliers.

"I was standing behind the Emperor," Branas continued. "He was actually shaking, and he started when those doors over there began to move back. Well, you know the protocol of an Imperial audience. Absolute silence. As far as my experience goes, this was the only time that rule was broken. There were murmurs, gasps, half-stifled 'ohs.' Don't forget, many of these people had not seen the Grand Duke for twenty years or more, when he was scarcely turned thirty. And now, here he was, a spectacularly handsome man verging on old age. He was what? —fifty-five. But his active life had weathered him superbly. Look at me. I'm the same age now as he was then, and I *look* my age.

"He approached the first porphyry circle—never moved an eye— bowed and moved to the second circle, bowed again, moved to the third, bowed, and passed up to the foot of the dais. His bearing was simple and majestic. He was neither artificial in his submission nor obsequious. His pride was personal rather than political and without insolence. At the dais, he looked up once at Manuel, then at the Empress. There was a small, shocked, almost amused trace of surprise at what had become, I suppose, of the infant Princess Maria he knew at Antioch a quarter century before. He fell to his knees, and despite the chains, prostrated himself, falling against the marble with a sound—the impact of body and metal—which I can only compare in that silence to a clap of thunder. It was so fast, so startling. Right here. Here is where he was.

"With his face to the floor, he said, 'August Sovereign, from the bottom of my heart, I beg your forgiveness for any wrongs I have done you, and they have been many. I implore you to spare from punishment, if punish you must, my Lady and my children who are in your custody. They are guilty, if it is guilt, of no more than giving solace to a wretched man such as you see before you.'

"I watched the Emperor. In a movement so small, so imperceptible, I'm certain very few saw it, his head was moving from side to side in woe or dismay. I could not, as I say, see his face. Then he spoke, against all protocol, the Emperor himself. He said, 'Rise, cousin. We've both our sins to live with and only God alone can forgive them, for alone, He knows the motive.'

"The Grand Chamberlain descended the steps and assisted the Grand Duke to his feet. Augustus said, 'Come. Come closer to me.' There was a moment's hesitation on Andronikus' part. You know that gesture, the wry smile at the corner of his mouth—tiny as the shake of the Emperor's head—and it told everything. Implicitly, now, it was for Andronikus to forgive Manuel by taking that first step. I think it must have been very difficult. There is no doubt in my mind that he loved the Emperor, but His Majesty had made him suffer so very deeply, and Andronikus wasn't the sort who made such a clean breast of things. Even when he seemed to forgive, it always impressed me, rather, as exasperated indulgence to a tiresome child. But for him, loyalty and love were indivisible and irrevocable. They might be repaired, but their unity would never again be seemless.

"Still, he gave Manuel, if not his trust again, then something like a tolerance beyond that which he extended to anyone else. It's true, you know. We've often repeated the usual truth of Manuel's clemency, but there existed on the part of Andronikus quite as much the nature to yield, in turn, to his cousin, in here"—he tapped his chest—"even if it were not explicit in his actions. In many ways, it was the graciousness of a respected enemy. Well, you know the rest. He remained a month at Rufiniana with Theodora and the children. Manuel visited him constantly and even roused himself from his penance long enough to initiate the hunts in his cousin's honor. Still, the Emperor had the wit—or the wisdom—to realize they could never exist side by side."

He shook his head and smiled at his own words. "What am I saying? That's rather as legend would have it. The truth, as you and I know it, is that the Manuelian Regency was in ruins and there was not a man among us—well, every other man—who did not expect Andronikus, even then, to succeed to the throne. The Emperor had the wit, all right, the wit to perceive his own unpopularity, that it was real, not fickle, not a momentary dissatisfaction, that the splendor of his reign had been bought too dearly, its flaws totally exposed in the process. Only his longevity—that, after thirty-four years on the throne, one could scarcely imagine someone else in his place—forestalled chaos or revolution.

"Many, many years ago, the Emperor said to me, 'You know, Michael, I've begun at last to feel like an emperor.' This was, oh, about 1151. You can imagine how startled I was by this confession. What on earth had he felt like the previous eight years? I asked him what he meant, and he said, 'Well, I was never destined for the throne. All my young life I was obliged to consider my elder brothers—and my sisters—before

me. The Imperial throne was, itself, something to which *I* looked up to
as exalted, unobtainable. Since my accession, I've felt like nothing so
much as a charlatan, a monitor, at best an actor. Now I've become a
little used to it. I've ceased to *play* at being Emperor.'

"Indeed he had. By 1177 the Imperium was no more distinguishable
from himself than the color of his eyes or his hair. I cannot escape the
feeling he positively consented to Andronikus' capabilities, that he knew
they were the only fit weapon against such times as would come following his death and, in secret jealousy or, perhaps, a kind of possessive-
ness—to whose meanest, most selfish aspects he blinded himself—went
ahead with primogenital succession and excluded his cousin from the
Regency Council. One wonders, if Andronikus had been named from
the beginning, rather than at last, whether the whole mad murderous
catastrophe from 1180 to 1185 would have occurred, and the boy and
his mother might still be alive today. One wonders. I see it myself as the
last of the many fatal gestures His Majesty made.

"To be sure, nothing could have confirmed him more in his course
than the effect of Andronikus' few appearances in the city, especially
that fantastic moment when he appeared by the Emperor's side in the
Hippodrome. He was legend become reality, and that legend was his
role as contestor to the Emperor. Now manifest and so incredibly youthful, he could not help to give hope. That was something his august cousin
could not tolerate. All their lives, it seemed, Andronikus was the only
man who could draw from Manuel this otherwise concealed streak of
pettiness. Why is it, do you think? In any event, the contrast between
the Emperor's failing Regency and the light which Andronikus offered
—well, the contrast was too bold. So he gave him the governacy of
Oeneum and established him lavishly there—and, of course, there were
now two courts in the Empire. Significantly, for all the Emperor had
become priest-ridden, he broached neither the subject of excommunication nor the dissolution of the affair between his niece and his cousin.
There may have been more purpose than tact in Manuel's silence. So
long as Andronikus was excommunicate and illicit, his participation in
a regency was unlikely.

"Well, there he was, at Oeneum, remote—revered like Jupiter and
his lightning, resting in that calm and splendid retreat from his past
adventures. And let me tell you—a truth you surely know, for you acted

no differently than I and a thousand others—we all of us made 'the pilgrimage' for the purposes of salting away our own futures."

Branas frowned, looking about the vast, domed, aureate enclosure. There was a look of pain as he shook his head. "Gone. What does it matter now? Suffering every one of them to the last. You wouldn't remember, but around midcentury, there was a popular phrase, 'lucky as the Comneni.' They possessed all a man could reasonably—or even unreasonably—desire in a lifetime: great flair, great good looks, great intellect, the very image of princes with the throne itself to magnify their virtue and the intolerable, infuriating brilliance to accomplish what they promised: to revive an empire lying in the gutter when they became a dynasty. They had their saints, their wantons, their gallants, their artists, their military captains, their fools, their wise men, their master builders, languorous princes, and monsters of ambition. They were the living definition of hubris. Offer them wings and they would still prefer to take the abyss in a leap of their own feet, even with the certain knowledge it was too wide by any human standard of endeavor."

Andronikus: "The Queen had quite convinced herself she had betrayed me. 'They used me against you,' she said, and I tried to explain that was for me to mourn, not her. 'By loving you,' I said, 'I enabled others to use you. There is a penalty in everything. I reckon any risk I must take according to its compensation.' But she would not let me console her. Quite frankly, I grew weary of fruitless attempts to do so.

"As for the Emperor. I had come to genuinely pity rather than reject him for his faults. He never sensed the continuity of events, their metamorphosis, which is constant, from effect to cause. Perhaps one is fortunate to possess such a mote. You may suffer without hope, but you live without dread.

"When Manuel allowed me to return, he did so, I think, with a disregard rather than a conscious absolution for the past. All would be well again and we would return to the good companionship of our youth. He was beyond ambition, which is a personal sense of the future. Quite naturally, I must be also. I think he was contemptuous of neither my trials nor my ideas, but only indifferent in a profoundly egotistical or introverted fashion. I may as well tell you, by the way, I was genuinely horrified by the change in him. If I had resented him till the moment of our reunion, I had nothing but sympathy for him afterward. He was like a great wounded animal and no one cares to see anything proud in size fail. Unfortunately because he was omnipotent, his inattention was causing an empire to expire, but that did not in any way lessen his personal tragedy. For all I know by that, it was increased.

"But how in heaven's name do you lecture or remonstrate a man who is at once good-natured and presumptuous, who wonders why the entire world is against him for wanting to rule it? Still his was not petulance but real pain. Amazing: He had the subtlety to perceive absurdity and self-contradiction in all but himself. He could distinguish between real compliment and rank flattery, yet he had not the strength to be indifferent to either. In the beginning he had a child's fixation with appearances—and in the end, appearances served too easily to console or to grieve him.

"He listened to me, expressed interest in what I had to say, but he did not act on his interest and he was only grateful for my affection. No force on earth will convince the weak and stubborn to take the advice of the strong and yielding.

"At one point I said to him, 'You know, by lavishing privilege on the nobility, you've ruined them.' He smiled and said, 'Oh? And since when are you their defending attorney?' I said, 'Oh, but I'm not and never shall be. Yet I mourn the use they might have made of themselves, to preserve themselves, which now is lost. By dispensation of taxes and, in most cases, of military service or trial before a common Judge of the Vellum instead of the Sacred Consistory—where they're certain to be favored by colleagues who would not set a precedent punishment in case of their own peculation—you've removed them from all responsibility within the state.'

"He seemed genuinely interested. He said, 'What could be done to save them? Give them a greater voice in government? You know where that would lead, back to the time of troubles before Grandfather's accession.' 'It's too late for that. Their privileges, quite simply, must be revoked and the entire patriciate abolished. Let there be the Emperor, the Senate, in something like an electoral form, the people, the army, the Church divorced from the state. Nothing more. No more nobility. The very concept is obsolescent. Times have left them behind. We're too old and too ordered and too sophisticated. The Latins need an aristocracy because they're not entirely arrived out of barbarism. They need their helots, too, because save the mercantile cities, the people are scarcely beyond bartering in kind. Our currency has been acceptable from Scandinavia to Ceylon for centuries.'

"He said, 'Do you also suggest I altogether emancipate our slaves?' I told him that would be implicit if the crown purchased or confiscated the domains of the Grandees. If the tenants were allowed to till the land for their own profit, slavery would become even more irrelevant than it is now. Byzantine economy, unlike Rome's, had almost never been dependent upon human thralldom, but the initiative of the free employee. Constantine assured us that when he chose his capital at the crossroads of world trade. He said, 'Fascinating. Even possible. But this is not for me to accomplish. Perhaps the boy'—Alexius—'in his time.' 'Manuel,' I said, 'you're fifty-eight years old. You might die any day or live half your life more. You have an obligation to act now, if not to the Empire, then to your very son. If you died within the year, you know what would occur during the Regency which followed. Those same aristocrats you have indulged would set upon the child and Maria. They'd eat alive the Imperium for more prerogatives. They know something's wrong—I even pity them—like a man in the agony of undiagnosed pain, unaware it's a terminal illness he's contracted. They're raging and they'll continue to rage, and they don't know why.'"

From the moment Andronikus crossed the border into the Empire, he was "sensed" the way an apt farmer senses in the stillness of a summer's day, despite a clear blue cloudless sky, an oncoming storm, or all men uncannily "know" in the last calm moment when they are hardly aware of the tremor stinging their feet, an earthquake shall be upon them. In consequence, without so much as a move on his part—indeed, he seemed to watch with an amused complacency which suggested it was only his due—factions began to form both for and against the Grand Duke, hardly knowing to what purpose they were about, rather by natural force than logic, as clouds gather round a mountain summit.

The lines were easily demarcated. Since the Latins were primarily in power in the administration, and the Constantinopolitan aristocracy identified with the court, those folk marked their action against the Emperor's cousin and quite literally stocked the government with their own supporters who, nothing loath to accept a post and pay without commensurate responsibility, quickly turned that massive, eminent bureaucracy into a nest of sinecures. The acknowledged head of this faction—with contempt for every one of its members—was the Patriarch

Theodosius, whose argument against Andronikus was as much religious as political. As an aristocrat, he did not care to see the confiscation of his family domains. As a priest, he feared the Church fortunes under an atheist regent or—worse—an atheist emperor. If the devout Alexius I could loot Church gold, heaven alone, or the devil conspiring, knew what his grandson would do. His Holiness, then, found himself in the singularly uncomfortable, or at least, compromising bed of the Latin Catholics whom he abhorred.

I suspect he could only watch in dismay as the Greek Catholic—the "Patriotic"—party, at whose head he ought to have stood, formed against himself and his clique and in behalf of Andronikus. These included most of the Imperial family, otherwise disempowered by the Sovereign, who chose as their object of loathing Maria-Xenia rather forgetting she was the consequence, not the cause, of Latinization; the Grandees of the provinces, who failed to understand Andronikus' argument was not merely against the Metropolitan aristocrats, but perhaps especially, the exurban; the oppressed poor, who still passed on the tales of the Grand Duke's philanthropic youth—stories which had quite got out of hand— the wealthy Greek mercantile class, who abominated their Latin compeers and the court as a nest of iniquity; and, finally, the native bureaucracy, outraged by the Latin intrusion and the attempted corruption engineered by the aristocracy. (This most crucial strata were especially resentful, as the bureaucracy was essentially the prerequisite of the middle class. While a noble like myself was not resented, he was expected to serve an apprenticeship as humbly as the baker's son or the priest's, much less the millionaire's youngest, denied by primogeniture his father's business interests.) The trade guilds, it need hardly be added, were overwhelmingly in the patriot's camp and against the dangers of foreign importations.

Andronikus did nothing to incite or to disband the factions in his behalf. He was in the enviable position of being influential without exerting himself to influence. He need not lift his votaries to action, no matter how frustrated they became, so long as the Emperor were alive. It was no plan on his part, but mere circumstance. He could afford to act in accord with his thirty-five-year-old oath to the Emperor. To take the throne, to supplant Manuel, would lose a large part—the least reckless, the most conservative—of his incremental following. So long as his circumstantial loyalty was never put to question, the Empress Regent's faults would serve to make her far more culpable. (Warned by several members of the family—primarily her sisters-in-law—to make some approach toward her childhood hero, she was on the other hand dissuaded or actively prevented from doing so by the Grand Duke David.)

One would have expected, then, those years at Oeneum something like an interlude, and a pleasurable one, with the anticipation of great things to come. Yet, if I may add a personal note, I sensed quite the opposite during my infrequent visits. Certainly it had less to do with politics than the plain fact of the humanity of the occupants of the Imperial villa. As I could nearly gather it, there was some latent animosity between the Grand Duke and the Queen—sparks, if not fire, gestures, corrections across a table, a sharp word, the snap of a glance when the other was looking the other way. As her lover's authority grew, and his future became again full of shining possibility, she became more than ever jealous of her position, now as the woman for whom he had sacrificed all, now as the Queen who had sacrificed all for him. Only many years later, when both loved and beloved were dead, did the logic of her irritation and her jealousy become clear.

As explained to me by the Grand Duke Alexander, Theodora was now willing to become the wife of Andronikus, for which a dispensation from consanguinity would be required from the Patriarch. Whereas once, it was rumored, shortly after Anastasia's death Andronikus had been willing to join the Latin Church to marry the former Queen of Jerusalem, he no longer found it acceptable to petition the acknowledged chief of the faction ranged against him for removal of the excommunication interdict and permission to marry his first cousin's daughter. In that, at least, he was manifestly sacrificing a personal pleasure—if pleasure it any longer seemed—to a political end. But it was to be several years more before the alliance had reached such a desperate state, the Queen would be forced to the elegant, ingenious, and decadent solution which, with unexpectedly hard humor, she would call the Peace of Maupacta. In that wit her pain was barely concealed and the laughter was coarse because its origin was a refined soul, irrevocably injured and driven by pride to accommodate the abhorrent.

At least on my early arrivals, there were other small crises. Theodora, distracted by her affair with Andronikus, had given her children over to too harsh governors. The Grand Duke was eager to be rid of them, but the Queen would hear none of it, not because she approved of their harshness, but by demanding resignation, would thereby confess a fault before her lover.

The Prince and Princess Comnenus, nearing the ages of ten, quite exhibited their father's obstinacy and their mother's verve. Neither parent ought to have worried that the children would be broken by any nurse or pedant. His Highness Prince Christopher was as bumptious and precocious as his second cousin, the Crown Prince. His habit of calling older people his "inferiors" and by their first name, with a low note of majesty in his voice, was amusing if it were not allowed to become a habit, and, with mature rationalization, a conviction. Princess Irene was as beautiful as her mother was reputed to have been as a child, with bold eyes and pretty lips. She was then suffering the adolescent's usual and first confrontation with the concepts of eternity and death, and at each dusk she retired to the garden—where her father, as a youth, walked by himself while his contemporaries partied—there to burst into abject, inarticulate, despairing tears such as no adult ever knows—and lucky for him.

It may be said children, late in a man's life, preclude the onset of senility. Yet I noticed at fifty-six, robust as he was, enchanted by and very attentive to their upbringing, the Grand Duke now and then seemed a little distracted, even bewildered, by the notorious energy of these scions, more like him than his heirs by Anastasia, the only bastards he ever acknowledged and loved as truly as his legitimate brood. But for me, when I might come up to him standing on a balcony, watching the Prince and Princess by the sea, a secret smile upon his face, his eyes lost, I would have given my right hand and my left to know—sooner than his most intricate political motive—the nature of his thoughts. It is in the anecdote rather than the finished action we will find the man. There is more of Alexander of Macedon in his dialogue with Anaxarchus than in all his triumphs from Memphis to India.

III

It has come time, now, to draw to its natural close, in death, the reign of Manuel Comnenus.

At the end, the swell of consequences directly attributable to Myriokephalum occurred as the Emperor feared they would and only the most complicated series of alliances and promises stemmed the tide —or appeared to—at least so long as he lived and it was a point of simple gallantry to honor a man—a broken old man—who had sat upon the oldest, most august throne in Europe for the better part of four decades. Indeed, his performance in those last years exhibited a finesse and purpose, impossible to any but an old master in the craft of Kingship.

By August 1177, when the entire continent knew the full scope of the disaster in a previously unknown gorge in Lesser Asia, there arose in the mass mind the first considerations of a Europe without Constantinople, or a Constantinople so weakened as to be irrelevant. Nothing could have moved men sooner to action. At once enemies within the body Latium sought concert at the Congress of Venice, convened in the late summer. Ten thousand nobles attended, but only two were significant: Pope Alexander III, and his ancient archenemy, Frederick Hohenstaufen, who knelt to kiss the papal boot.

We cannot accept this new alliance as anything but cynical. The Petrine Prince still despised and feared the man who, more than once, had put Rome to sack and established his own Bishop at the Vatican. Frederick, as long as he lived, would never forgive the Fisherman's successor for support of the Lombard League—in concert with Manuel Augustus—against him. But with their mutual peace, and a treaty of accord arranged by Alexander between the league and their choleric sovereign, the way was clear for a concerted effort against the Greek Empire. For Frederick, it was a matter of precedence, not loot, a refusal to recognize any but his own Imperial imprimatur. For Alexander, it was a utilitarian means of expulsing Byzantium—no more to be trusted than Frederick—from Italy. For the Lombard League—no less their host city of Venice—it was the enticing possibility of an economic stranglehold on the untold wealth of their former sponsor.

Reports of the Congress regularly arrived at Constantinople, and by October 1177 Manuel was resolved to commence what he only halfamusedly called his "War of Marriages." His first duty was to insure the East—or what was left of it. After appointing Theodora's nephew, Isaac, Governor of Cilicia, Manuel bid him pay a courtesy call on Bohemond III of Antioch, recently widowed, and inquire into the possibility of remarriage with an Imperial grand duchess. Quite to the Emperor's surprise—since he was realistic enough to suppose Bohemond had little to gain by further alliance with his brother-in-law's crumbling Asian portion of the Empire—the Prince accepted, and the late John Sergius' youngest daughter, the Grand Duchess Stephanie—a pretty thing, with sad, enormous blue eyes, unlikely red hair, and poor teeth of which she was exceedingly shy—was dispatched to Antioch and a short unhappy marriage, whose fate we will presently describe. It is quite likely Bohemond found her dower, the city of Tarsus, by far more enticing than the lady. Certainly for the previous ten years—and throughout one marriage—he had been happy enough with his concubine, the notorious Sybil who, unknown to the Prince (but known to the Imperial Secret Police), was a double agent for Saladin, now King, at Damascus. (To the Defender of the Faith, by the way, the Emperor paid in full for the ransom of Bohemond's notorious stepfather, Reynald of Châtillon, and settled the former Ravager of Cyprus in a magnificent villa in Thrace, thus holding an effective hostage against any lack of the Prince's outward continence.)

So, too, the last of the Sebastocrator Isaac III's daughters was wed. Theodora's youngest sister, Eudocia, was sent to marry Alfonso of Aragon. Here, unfortunately, it was less a matter of the young Grand Duchess left waiting at the altar than her entry into a deserted church long after the last echoes of ceremony had been absorbed by the stone. Insufficient information—to put it mildly—had reached Constantinople, via the Aragonese ambassador, as to the marriageability of the King, who took a wife during Eudocia's arduous journey to Spain. Somewhat to make amends, the embarrassed monarch commanded his greatest vassal, William VIII of Montpellier, to marry the would-be bride. Like Bohemond, William was quite happy with his mistress and only sullenly obeyed the King. Eudocia's fate was as miserable as, if not more than, her cousin Stephanie's.

The next marriage was the most controversial, internationally.

Now, Frederick's most ardent supporter in his wars against Lombardy and the papal states had been William V, Marquis of Montferrat, generally recognized as the most dominant noble, virtually a king, in Northwest Italy and the Southern Alps. To Frederick's purpose he had borne the brunt of the league's wars against the Holy Roman Empire. (While the German Emperor could always retire north, William was surrounded by the enemies he made.) He had been against participation in the Congress of Venice. As he feared, so it happened: he believed Frederick to have betrayed him in the truce called between the great Italian cities and their Emperor. The Peace of Venice did not include his name—and not by his choice—nor was he asked to be a signatory. "He used me like a dog," the Marquis told the Emperor's kin, the Countess di Paganello. "I kept his sheep in line and when that was no longer necessary, he took them off and left me to my own poor devices." In some respects he was not exaggerating.

This extraordinary oversight—or lack of foresight—which gave the German Emperor to disregard the wishes, let alone the safety, of his most powerful supporter was well taken by the Countess who, at once, wrote to her former sovereign suggesting it "the perfect opportunity to exhibit your Imperial concern whereas Frederick does not." For an alliance of such profound importance, Manuel could offer nothing less than the highest terms in the person of his own daughter, Catherine Porphyriogeneta. Whichever of William's sons was chosen to marry her would, moreover, become Caesar and sit at Thessalonika. In return the Marquis was to strike the chord of rebellion in Italy, against Frederick, which he did, effectively nullifying the German Emperor's gains since Venice.

William sent his youngest son to Constantinople. Renier was a youth of seventeen years, cupid-locked, sapphire-eyed, and a spectacular athlete. At once he won the heart and head of Catherine, who felt herself suddenly, miraculously rewarded for twenty-six years of spinsterhood, now as barter between Hungary and Byzantium, now between Byzantium and Sicily. Unfortunately Renier's apparent ingenuousness in all things did not extend to seduction by the Caesarissa, with whom he preferred to remain no more than a friend. Rather he surrendered himself as catamite to the Empress' lover, the Grand Duke David and, to parity the factions, the Grand Duke Julian. (Once, during an interview between David, Catherine, and Renier, when the Porphyriogeneta corrected her young husband once too often, David is reputed to have silenced her—and won her enmity forever—with the words: "Ma'am, it seems you can bully your husband beyond any threshold but the bedroom. I suggest you remember that when next you mean to condescend to him.") Indeed, the new Caesar was not by any means artless, but closed and stubborn. His manner mistaken for a lack of guile was merely the lethargy of demeanor, common to the Riviera temperament. His indomitability—on the occasion of its use—was bewildering to those prepared to control him.

The same embassy which brought Renier to Constantinople had within the same month negotiated at Paris the most important marriage, the final one, of Manuel's design.

In 1178 Philip of Alsace, Count of Flanders, stopped at Constantinople on his return from the Holy Land. As the relationship between Flanders and Byzantium was a tradition back to Alexius' friendship with Count Robert, the Emperor invited the great aristocrat to Rufiniana, where, during a walk in the gardens, myself present, the Augustus asked the vassal of France if Louis Capet had any marriageable daughters. "Indeed, Divinity," he said, "but one small and very young." The Emperor said, "Well, you have met His Imperial Highness, Alexius Porphyriogenetus. He, too, is young. I shall tell you, Count: I have it in mind to put in your company a few of my ambassadors and you must attest with them to Louis that if he sends this little Princess to me, I would have her married to the Heir, as soon as she arrived, and permit her to wear a diadem. What would your King say, do you think?" Flanders hesitated not a moment. "Your Majesty, he would be beside himself. And it is to Louis' liking against Frederick, for as you are friends with my most eminent Lord, Henry, and would be kin with Louis, it will place all westernmost Europe from the Tweed to the Ebro quite in a position against the German Emperor."

As Flanders had foretold, Louis was indeed overjoyed at the prospect of an Imperial title for his youngest and most treasured child, born of his beloved second Queen, Alix. As the emissaries brought fabulous gifts from the Emperor, so Capet looted his kingdom to bequest Manuel in turn and equip the betrothal party. The Princess who was the object of this silver flurry, Agnes, then eight years old, felt quite equal to the occasion. As she told me two years later, "Monsieur, at the age of five I burnt all my toys as unbecoming a grown-up maiden." When I repeated the anecdote to Andronikus, finishing with the words "Adorable, isn't it?" he simply stared at me as though I had lost my mind.

The royal child bid good-by to the King and Queen of France, whom she would never see again, 2 March 1179. She set sail from Genoa surrounded by a fleet of twenty-two ships, excluding her own, all flying the Imperial eagles, the dragons of the House of Comnenus, and the Cross of St. Andrew. (The galleys were loaned to the Imperium by its most fervent Genoese agent, Count Baldovino Guercio.)

It was fitting the last months of the last full year the Emperor would live were celebrated with a return to the pomp he had loved so well and which, one could tell, still dazzled his eye after nearly forty years as its cynosure. While little Agnes made the long journey to Constantinople, stopping frequently along the South European coastline to be honored and feted as the next Basilissa, the marriage of her betrothed's half-sister, Maria-Catherine Porphyriogeneta, was accomplished in Cathedral of the Almighty. The nuptial feast—the Imperial Majordomo's recompense for the past, parched three years—was held in Philopation Park. Enchanting enough in late summer, this wood within a city was transfigured with cloth of gold and silver, white roses, priceless antiquities transported from Athens, Thessalonika, and Imperial palaces throughout the Empire, and ten thousand milky doves in ten thousand golden cages. (Unfortunately when the cages were opened at the climax of the festivities and the birds released skyward, nothing less than an ocean of excrement was deposited upon the guests. William Bishop of Tyre, sitting beside me, who, till then had been stupefied with awe, at last burst out laughing.)

Still, as the women say, corners were cut, though it would scarcely have been apparent to those outside the Imperial circle. The Emperor, for instance, decreed the city celebration of his daughter's wedding would be postponed until after the betrothal of the Crown Prince and Princess Agnes. As one event virtually tripped over the other, this was accepted as more than sensible. But not a few years before the Emperor would scarcely have hesitated to expend sums on two—or three or four—public celebrations within a season. In 1179 the Imperial Treasury was nearly empty, due especially to the loss of so many provinces in Asia. There was no alternative but to economize and only a very few knew how this embittered His Majesty.*

* The only other unfortunate consequence of the day was the widening of the breach between the Empress and her stepdaughter. Initially, they had attempted to reach some accord. Maria-Xenia had, herself, embroidered Catherine's wedding mantle and Catherine, greatly moved, had sent the Empress an extremely precious, ancient icon, which had been her mother's. There was a promise of mutual decency in the air until the Grand Duke David, who despised Catherine both personally and politically—she was not a member of the pro-Latin party—ordered one of the Grand Duchess' ladies-in-waiting, his creature, in fact, to convince Her Highness the lack of public celebration was due solely to Xenia Augusta's influence on the Emperor. Quite simply she did not want her son outshone (not that she cared about her son, only her prestige as Empress Mother). Catherine was of a

Princess Agnes arrived at Constantinople in late September, and once again the round of ceremony and feasts took place, including magnificent spectacles at the Hippodrome, where the Emperor and Empress sat with the Caesar, Caesarissa, Crown Prince, and Crown Princess Designate. The betrothal itself was solemnized in the Trullan Chamber of the old Sacred Palace, where the massed court had their first close look at the little French royalty who, twenty-five years later, would preside at the last Divine Liturgy on these grounds before the fall of the city and the Empire. They saw an unusually tall, slender child with dark hair and eyes so brilliant as to seem filled with tears. Her expression was not the child's imitation of hauteur but, unnatural in one so young, quite the real thing.

Thus in the space of two years Manuel allied the House of Comnenus to Italy, Spain, France, and Palestine. To leave no doubt as to what he expected of these alliances, he was pleased to receive William of Tyre, returning from the Third Lateran Council at Rome, and commissioned him as something of a special envoy to the courts of Antioch and his own, Jerusalem. There he would stand proxy for the Emperor, while the Crusading Sovereigns took an oath of filial loyalty to the Heir. "In effect," Andronikus said to me when he heard of it, "he is giving Antioch and Jerusalem, as well as Iconium—for he is not too proud to extract a similar oath from Kilij—the right to interfere with the Imperium should a hand be raised against Alexius. Well and good, if the child were not a child, but a man and an upright one. But, you know, if His Majesty should die, others will rule in the boy's name and they will be inviolable, no matter how wretched their purpose or performance. And if the Empire lies in ruin, these foreign potentates can claim its wreckage. But if a citizen shall attempt to stop the fall, he will be roundly subject still to this legal device by which Arslan or Bohemond or Baldwin could march on Constantinople as 'Liberators.' You know why he is doing this, don't you? To stop me. He would sacrifice the Empire under his son's aegis to prevent my ruling it. Another contretemps of the blind." He sighed. "We can only hope it is his last." It was.

---

mind to believe the story, treated her father's wife thereafter and throughout the ceremony with a correct coldness, which was returned in kind, and so on, one to the other, until neither woman remembered the formal source of her loathing—or cared. N.A.

Four years later, enthroned himself, he spoke of his final meeting with the Emperor: "I saw him for the last time, briefly, in March 1180. He was returning from the rescue of Claudiopolis in Bithynia. He had dispatched a messenger to Oeneum I was to meet him, wherever possible, on the road to Nicea. I had heard rumors he had collapsed several times in private audience, spewing blood. They were true, the rumors, weren't they?"

I nodded.

"Yes. I thought it was so. The request was completely unexpected. It must have been a last-minute decision. I took horse at once, to be sure." He was silent.

I said, "May I ask what was said between Your Majesties?"

He was looking down and away, his features in a little frown. He shook his head absently. "Nothing, Nicetas. I rode fifty miles in half a day, killing a horse in the meanwhile, for a few words. But nothing. Nothing by which history might be measured. Only a few words. Our last, after more than forty years during which, I think"—he paused, raising his eyes to clouds of the end of a summer's afternoon—"I think, perhaps apart we were more united than together, as two men chained, attempting to draw away from one another become only that much more aware of their bonds. What was it between us? I shall never know. Perhaps a vision, though I always blamed Manuel for his visions and congratulated myself my reality. What vision? Who can say? Beyond the Indus they believe in reincarnation. Perhaps we were the broken halves of the same person, for, at bottom, he was utterly without the practical and I, without the fantastical. Neither totality—because each is an untempered extreme—can, perhaps, act, save in the extreme, and extremes are not tolerable in a world which seeks a balance between earth and air and fire and ice. Creation is lasting, but it is not everlasting. It is lavish, but to survive, it cannot be profligate." *Explicit: Nicetas Acominatus.*

The war train of 5,000 men—800 cavalry, 4,200 foot—waits along the road, the dust still settling, as the rider and his small escort arrive from the north, galloping beneath the Imperial and Pontic Gubernatorial escutcheons. Manuel, fatally thin, ravaged by tuberculosis, watches his cousin's approach with an eager eye. Andronikus stops within thirty feet of the Emperor, and an unexpected volley of cheers—

startling in all the open air—greets him. So swiftly as to pass unnoticed, a look of alarm crosses Manuel's face. Andronikus is oblivious of the army's goodwill, even angered by their display. Ambition is small, if not irrelevant, before finality and he has no wish to remind the Emperor of a future he will never see, to taunt him with a possibility he dreads. He approaches Manuel, like any subject, on foot. For one embarrassingly revealing moment, it is obvious he cannot believe his eyes at the terminal change which has overtaken his cousin. His expression becomes one of distress. All at once he lowers his eyes, his head, his body to one knee, and kisses Manuel's dusty scarlet boot, embroidered in gold with the bicephalic eagles.

ANDRONIKIUS. August Lord.

MANUEL. Thank you for coming. I want to walk.

To Andronikus' surprise a short flight of steps—covered in purple velvet, embroidered exquisitely with flowers, besooted from travel—is brought forward. The Grand Duke offers the Emperor his hand. When the Emperor grips it, Andronikus' arm shakes under the unexpected weight. His had been a gesture of courtesy; obviously the Emperor cannot take the stairs without it. Duke Michael Branas and Count George Angelus watch as Andronikus places his near arm around the Emperor's shoulder, and with his right hand, supports the Emperor at his elbow. They walk off slowly.

COUNT GEORGE. Pity. They've never reckoned how much they mean to one another except in their farewells.

ANDRONIKUS. You must know I have nothing whatever to do with that nonsense offered in my name at Constantinople.

MANUEL. There's a story shortly before his death, Grandfather complained to old Bryennius factions were forming as though he were already dead. He feared if they completed their strategies too soon and became impatient, they would perhaps rush nature a little.

ANDRONIKUS. You mustn't let it disturb you.

MANUEL. I suppose it does. I'm quite helpless as any man. I don't want to die, to be beyond action, to be helpless. Somehow, though, I sense if I were to take too overt precautions against those I mistrust, I would be their laughingstock. "What the hell's he about?" they would ask. "Can he be unaware he's a corpse and beyond obedience?"

ANDRONIKUS. Do what you must, what will give you peace of mind. Forget what other men will think.

MANUEL. Are you happy now?

ANDRONIKUS. What a question. I've never been happy.

MANUEL. Oh, now, never? Never at all?

ANDRONIKUS. Not if happiness is total freedom from dread. I've never believed anything inevitable, so I've never been at peace, never happy. I can't anticipate.

The Grand Duke relents, he smiles with utmost charm.

ANDRONIKUS. But there are times when I would confess to enthusiasm, and once in a while, to contentment.

MANUEL. Good enough.

The Emperor sighs and the sigh is a whistle lifted from his clotted, sodden lungs.

MANUEL. I've failed, Andronikus. It was all a waste. God has abandoned me. I know it.

ANDRONIKUS. You know nothing of the sort.

MANUEL. We have a very simple way of knowing it. There is no warning. Only disaster. In that, the Autocrat becomes aware he has lost the will of heaven.

ANDRONIKUS. If every Emperor who preceded you failed because heaven abandoned him, then, with little exception, we've been roundly cursed from the beginning and we have no right to be here. Manuel, what's done is done. All the unhappiness which has followed was never intended. You pursued everything with a just heart. In you, there is nothing mean. In the end, it may be all that matters, and it is the truth and it will survive.

MANUEL. Who knows but perhaps you were right so many years ago at Paphlagonia. Perhaps I ceased to serve the people. It was a divine vanity which has brought me to this. With the best will in the world, we may sin, and if we do, then we are culpable, more so, as it is the sin of indifference.

ANDRONIKUS. Is there nothing I can say?

MANUEL. I believe in a vengeful God who watches over his kings and punishes them, above all, their betrayals, for the sake of personal aggrandizement, of the great captaincies in which He leaves them.

ANDRONIKUS. Is a God less just than his kings, who punishes the kingdom as well as the king? There is a perversity in events which is the many dreams of many men.

Suddenly Manuel turns his eyes from the horizon to his cousin.

MANUEL. My dear friend, I implore you: When I am gone, do not add to the chaos which is already upon us. Promise me in the name of anything you hold holy. On your father's memory.

ANDRONIKUS. Is this why you called me to you?

MANUEL. Andronikus, I have nothing left but the hope my son may one day outgrow the Regency and serve this Empire better than ever I did. It will be the one consolation for having existed—if only to father a hero.

ANDRONIKUS. Will you never care more for those served than the servant?

The Grand Duke bethinks himself and modifies his tone, which had become somewhat too harsh.

ANDRONIKUS. I love you and I grieve for you whatever pain, spiritual or physical, you must endure. But I must tell you, no sympathy on earth will force me to accept a silence in my father's name.

MANUEL. Do you realize what you are saying?

ANDRONIKUS. Do *you?* You've named a Regency Council? Very well, why was I not included? Or Philip, at least. After you, we're the senior Princes of our House.

MANUEL. I have given you other responsibilities.

ANDRONIKUS. Oh, come now. Lies? Like a little girl?

Manuel breaks free and coughs. He coughs again, the spasm more violent, and again, and once again. Andronikus moves up to him, but the Emperor, in disgust, in self-disgust and pique, pushes his cousin aside and brings up bloody phlegm, which he expectorates on the sand. Both men are silent, as the Emperor, sweating with the exertion, his eyes rheumy, attempts to collect himself, standing perfectly still, swallowing often and noisily and quite out of breath. When he speaks again his voice is hoarse and he pauses occasionally between words, sniffling and driving still more phlegm into his stomach.

MANUEL. How many times might I have had you done away with?

ANDRONIKUS. Many. And many times you nearly succeeded. No. You would not sign the document to the effect of my execution or the commission of rowdies or your Secret Police against me. Nothing overt.

But you would have let me rot in a dungeon for the rest of my life, or die elsewhere in exile.

MANUEL. And does my constant forgiveness prove nothing to you?

ANDRONIKUS. Only ambivalence.

Andronikus speaks those words curtly. He is looking away from Manuel.

MANUEL. But, there, are you blind that you cannot see love won?

ANDRONIKUS. Not love. *I* won. I cursed your ambivalence and made the best of it. I saved *myself*. You merely consented to the rescue. That was weak of you. Were I in your place I would have made murder by all means, by any means.

MANUEL. Has everything, then, between us been false?

The weariness, the tragedy, in the Emperor's voice forces Andronikus to turn to his cousin. As he speaks, his eyes narrow in a squint of earnestness.

ANDRONIKUS. That would depend upon what you wish to call up as proof of my mendacity. For myself, I swear to you as there's a blue sky above us I was prepared to serve you as my sovereign in the least capacity so long as you listened to me.

MANUEL. And what would have given your decisions a value above mine?

ANDRONIKUS. Disinterest.

MANUEL. And when was your desire to rule ever so selfless?

ANDRONIKUS. So long as I might have been content to serve you. But that cannot be proved, I agree, because you never gave me the opportunity. But your stubbornness and your vanity and your suspicions taught me a pure lesson. Now I would have it that posterity not condemn us abject slaves willing to join the Imperial suttee with your corpse.

MANUEL. How cruel you are.

ANDRONIKUS. Perhaps. If truth is cruelty, then I am that brutal. Yet however hateful it may seem to you I would pay the love between you and me the tribute of pain.

MANUEL. And now, as you would have the power, it is for the people, not yourself? Would you have me believe such nonsense? How can you love me if you would hold me in such contempt?

ANDRONIKUS. Am I any less fallible than you? In death, as I believe it, I go to far less than you expect for yourself. I've only the here and now and probably whether or not I'm remembered shall make little difference to my corpse, to my obliterated spirit. But sooner at least the future reckons me, knows that I lived, I died, I contested. You fear dying. I don't. I only fear anonymity.

MANUEL. And for that you would make civil war? Where is the difference between you and me—or myself as you believe me to be?

ANDRONIKUS. You have no idea what I would do, nor any right to presume. You used the state, yourself, to pursue the imitation of another man's glory. Rather than *idées reçus,* you would have done better to take stock of the world as it was and rule as necessity would have had it.

MANUEL. Once again, I ask you: Accept the Regency as I have established it. Accept my son as your sovereign lord.

ANDRONIKUS. So long as it seems to me provident to the state, I will. I promise.

MANUEL. That is not the honor of an Imperial prince.

ANDRONIKUS. It is more honor, Manuel, than you can ever know, and that, I think, is the pity of it all.

MANUEL. God hardens a heart to all admonition before he releases it to the devil.

ANDRONIKUS. In God's name, spare me that—and yourself.

MANUEL. Will nothing move you? I'm humbling myself. I'm begging your pity as a promise.

Andronikus faces Manuel with the dead-eye stare of an absolutely mature spirit.

ANDRONIKUS. You're humbling yourself. You're glorying in the role of ostentatious humility. That—or greed has got the better of your dignity. Shodless and throneless, you could never be humbled so long as you are what you are or what you were. You're asking me to consent, in the last, to what I've condemned in you since you mounted the throne. So long as I live I will not put you or your heirs or myself or my reputation before the good of the state. The state is the people, not you. The state does not exist except as the people. It is their servant, not their overlord, not an entity apart from or symbolized by the Emperor.

MANUEL. That is republicanism and anti-Christ.

ANDRONIKUS. That is the way of people like you. Poison an idea by dismissing it in invidious category. Call it what you will. I've given you my probationary promise. You have the choice of placing me on the Regency Council or leaving me as critic to judge those you leave behind.

MANUEL. I have another choice.

ANDRONIKUS. Yes. You do.

Impassively, Andronikus releases his scabbard from his belt and offers it, pommel forward, to the Emperor.

ANDRONIKUS. Go ahead. Take it. Arrest me.

Manuel looks from the sword to Andronikus' eyes, from one to the other, repeatedly. Broken of all illusion, the last portion of hope with which to console himself, his expression, set in the rigidity of apathy beyond despair, he speaks, scarcely audible.

MANUEL. Good-by.

Andronikus moves to assist him.

MANUEL. Go away.

The Emperor walks back, his breath harsh, his feet barely lifting from the sana, nearly an old man's shuffle. Andronikus is alone, watching his cousin, still offering his sword to the empty air beneath the sun.

IV

Incipit: Nicetas Acominatus: Andronikus: "I wasn't there for those dreadful last months, which robbed him of the dignity, at least, of resignation to his own tragedy. I think of him now with utmost compassion. I think of him with awe because he has made that irrevocable crossing from the living into oblivion. What an unhappy state that we cannot give such unimpeachable respect previous to death. But then, if we did not spend our lives denying to ourselves and to others we are fellow victims, I suppose we would expire in the stagnation of mutual deference—too considerate to be ambitious, too thoughtful to correct an error, too kind to argue.

"Between March and September, there is only one ray of light, one moment of lucidity, a passage in a last letter, which Manuel sent to me, along with the regular dispatches for the Pontic governacy. 'You once said to me,' he wrote, 'so many years ago words I have never forgotten: "The only man in the Empire who has true freedom of choice is the Emperor himself." Let me assure you, in some ways, to live without choice is to be happier. To choose is to be responsible, to suffer frustration for the knowledge one might have fallen on one side of the question as easily as the other.'" Andronikus looked at me, shaking his head. "Blind to the end, but brilliantly."

Epicurus has said: "That which is the most awful of evils, death, is nothing to us, since when we exist, there is no death, and when there is death, we do not exist." He was not wrong, but he did not follow his thought deeply enough. We are beyond awareness *in* death. By its very definition, we are all *too* aware of life. The only animal given a sense of the future, the penalty has been foreknowledge of our demise, which is literally unthinkable beyond the moment of its overtaking. To one in flower, death is an abstract. To a man in the throes of terminal disease, the failing of the body each day is notable, traceable, cruel. Death is prevalent, inescapable. Day by day, from moment to moment, one is preoccupied with one's own decay and not all the will in the world will stay that failure. If exhaustion does not accomplish an easeful sinking as into sleep, then the pain makes one to most awfully wish for death as the antidote.

As many men fear the turn of the world from day into night and are helpless to prevent it, so the decadence of this body becomes something alien, apart from the human essence, which is helpless to have back the vigor which carries the spirit. What is this body, one asks oneself, which dies against one's will, against the desire—and the capability—of pure thought to live forever? Thus the carnal becomes an enemy, which is alienness by definition, something apart. All the care, all the ablutions, the periods of activity and rest, the sensuality with which we indulged it at the expense—there were times—of logic and virtue, has been for nothing. The body is a brutal, selfish tyrant, which promises nothing, gives little, and, at the end, like the stupid, destructive, vulgar omnivore it is, surveys the desolation it has made, and, itself, curls up and dies without so much as the leave of its animating soul. As the earth pulls all along with it into the cold, blue night, as the most intolerable despot will destroy the world along with himself, so the dying body kills the living soul, too much ultimately crude matter and insensate to know the value of what it annihilates.

The man who is dying and who is too subtle to any longer bring himself to a confession of faith—if he cannot otherwise momentarily forget his fate in his tasks—is left to the vagaries of introversion or superstition. In the one, he somehow reaches, if not accord with inevitable death, at least the inner consent it cannot be averted. That is a great leap for him, though he continues to resent pity or consolation, any outward concern for his condition which once again confirms the objective reality of his obliteration—you will go on and he will be gone—plunging him once again into despair. Death is something within, between the soul and its fractious body. Acceptance must remain within maintained by delicate balance if its victim is to remain vivacious rather than merely wait and lose what life is left.

The fantast in Manuel smiled when his astrologers promised him fourteen years more of rule, of lovemaking and triumphant war. But he sat bolt upright and listened earnestly when they foretold in his reign the conjunction of the seven major planets in seven months: an omination of catastrophe. In fact, the conjunction did not take place until a year—to the day—following Andronikus' death, when, during an eclipse, twelve degrees of sky were sufficient to encompass all the wandering stars: the sun, Mercury, Venus, the moon, Mars, Jupiter, and Saturn. To an only mildly skeptical mind, wanting to believe but too exquisite to believe, this was impressive, and in an entirely "reasonable" way, wondrous. If such an awesome event could predictably occur, then who knows what is possible in this unpredictable existence? Throughout spring, he dared to hope some small measure of his necromancer's predictions—perhaps his survival, if only that—might be vindicated. He could no longer believe in the Resurrection, but in his own tortured mind, he seemed convinced of some sort of perdurance of the spirit. When the Patriarch reproached him, he merely said, "Who has come back from heaven to prove the resurrected soul." To which Theodosius, more apt than logical, said, "Who would *want* to?"

Indeed, of all people, it was the Empress who reconciled the Emperor to his priests—Her Majesty, and, perhaps his own weary spirit, discouraged by the all too obvious degeneration of the body, clear-eyed and already taking leave of the earth. The Augustus yielded to the Empress' pleas, accepted Theodosius' visits, and closed his doors to the canonically interdicted astrologers (who, nevertheless, made a spectacular financial killing, as the new rage among the courtiers, bored with the deathwatch).

In late August, Manuel left Constantinople for the last time, passing from his beloved jewel, Blachernae, to the fresh air and isolation of Damalis Palace at Chrysopolis. It was my privilege to be with him in those last days and to attend him with the Empress the last time he walked upon the Greek earth.

Because he believed, as I, he was the Viceroy of Heaven, touching this man was nearest on my fingertips to material proof of God and the celestial realms. He grasped my hand with his left, the Empress' with his right. He was nearly as tall as his cousin, who was, of course, a giant, yet in those last days, it was, most literally, painful to behold his wasted frame, ravaged, quite undone. The walk round the private garden of Damalis Palace—which is not really a palace, but an enormous mansion built by Alexius I in his last years to commemorate his famous victory— served to exhaust him. Too weary and nauseated and scarcely able to breathe, to return on foot to his specially prepared sickroom on the ground floor, he asked for a litter to carry him in, for the last time, from the open air. Dispatches went out to all members of the Imperial family, save Andronikus and Queen Theodora, to attend him.

The following three weeks he was subjected to the martyrdom of the privileged and ill. So long as he was too important to die without accusing physicians of ineptitude—as the heirs of a man too wealthy and dying unattended would be accused of murder—all participants were forced to play their roles before him at the expense of final serenity. The physicians bled him and constantly ripped the blankets away to administer enemas. The Empress told him he would not die and by her tears removed his last will to live. The Patriarch blessed him, morning, noon, and night, and told him he would go straight to heaven, each time more perfunctory and less convincing. The Crown Prince was brought forward to hear words of advice he could scarcely comprehend. Churches and cathedrals remained opened day and night at Constantinople and all the major cities of the remaining Empire as prayers were offered up for the Autocrat's recovery—liturgies which, at any moment, might become Requiems. Magistrates and governors the length and breadth of the land reassured their charges of the Emperor's health and had their soldiers, priests, and administrators at the ready for the taking of the oath to the new Basileus. Beyond the Empire, messengers passed between kingdoms as regents, allied to Constantinople, maintained their loyalty and began to formulate their strategies on a continent soon to be bereft of its most dominant figure for thirty-seven years.

On 13 September he called me to him and gave me a dispatch to take to the Patriarch. There was a weak smile upon his face, which I thought curious. As he spoke, I leaned closer to hear the whistle which had replaced his superb voice with its uniquely caressing consonants. He whispered, "Do you know what this is, my boy?" I said, "I can hardly imagine, Divinity." "It is a chrysobull," he said, "raising your brother to the Archbishopric of Athens." Speechless, shaken, I burst into tears and kissed his hand. Almost at once, the Empress circled around the enormous, eagle-winged golden bedstead and grasped my shoulder as an indication to rise, then assisted me to the Grand Chamberlain with the words "Come, now, Count. The Emperor is tired." I remember looking back. Propped on pillows—he found it difficult to breathe lying on his back—he followed me with his eyes. He nodded and formed the word *Good-by.* When next I approached him, he was ermine-and-purple-shod clay, surrounded by a thousand candles, sung to heaven by choristers hastily arrived from Cathedral of the Almighty.

The Grand Duke Philip: "On the morning of September 24, he was sinking. That, as you remember, was when the order was given for all traffic to be rerouted as far as possible from Damalis Palace so as not to disturb him. Naturally, the Chrysopolitans guessed the worst, and before noon rumor reached Constantinople the Emperor was dead. Johnny Kamaterus, the Prefect, had to call out the garrison and send heralds with bulletins, which, of course, should have been done long before.

"We were admitted into the chamber, and I was astonished to find the Emperor, without blankets, stretched out upon a made bed in a monk's robe. Later Xenia told me he sensed the end and expressed the wish to die as a priest of the Church, which right he had, as on accession he was Pontifex Maximus. He was dressed in a hair shirt which he had not worn since the inception of his illness. Having been tonsured at his coronation, it was necessary only to confirm his ecclesiastical name. He died, then, not as Manuel Augustus, but Brother Matthew.

"Toward noon, he wept a little and when Xenia, who was a jewel, asked him the nature of his tears, he said, plainly audible—surprisingly—'The boy. What will become of him?' He whispered something else to the Empress, and, insofar as I remember, those were his last words. He fell asleep, and from sleep passed the short divide into death about three hours later, according to Divine Purpose, as they say, at the age of sixty. He deserved that final clemency of an easeful end."

I remember I was sitting on the grassy, rose-patched bank of the little lake behind the palace. Everywhere were great heaps of fallen, golden leaves. The air had turned chill during the afternoon. On the surface of the waters, swans floated with an elegance as curvaceous as the mist—forming and ascending—through which they passed. On the opposite bank a peacock lifted its gigantic concave plumage and shook it so vigorously, the eyes seemed to detach themselves in a fantastic, shimmering illusion of deep blue and sea-blue jewels. Then the great fan was still, and the cock began to turn slowly, on exhibition, its extraordinary gold tail feathers also extended. But no peahen arrived for mating. Instead, three of the English hounds sent by King Henry II pulled free of the leashes held by a too small groom from the Imperial kennels and made a dash for the gorgeous fowl, who closed his tail like a shot, and ran. The dogs did not stop at the water but dived in precipitously and started for the swans, one of whom, with a hideous noise, shattering all belief in the tranquillity of its appearance, lifted itself above the surface, exhibiting ungainly feet, and made to attack the insolent dog, then scurried not quite airborne, in the opposite direction, its huge white wings flapping with uncanny languor—it couldn't possibly fly—and rose against the background of the sunburst trees and cypresses, and up, up, into the unbelievable azure of the afternoon sky.

Someone had been calling my name. I looked toward the path. It was Bishop Eustathius of Thessalonika. As I came toward the Metropolitan, he stared straight at me and said, "He's gone. Her Majesty asks that you be present at prayers for the dead this evening." Without another word, he grasped my shoulders and began to cry.

The dogs had returned to shore, the swan to the surface of the lake, the peacock still strutted, but His Imperial Majesty was dead. All went on seemlessly. Not even his death could stop it. Which, then, was irrelevant? Men's lives or the earth itself? Neither. There were the lives of men and the life of the world, the two indivisible, the parts extinguished but the whole remaining. Leaves die, and dogs, and the birds that flew—and men, too. But the tree lived on, and the beasts of the earth and the air left their heirs, as did man, who, individually and irrevocably, altered the course of existence upon the planet for having lived at all.

The cortege across the Bosporus took place three days later, on another balmy day of a summer which refused to yield to autumn, though the solstice was passed and the trees were long revealing their branches. What particularly troubled me about the enormous funeral party was, to use that word again, the irrelevance of its object, the dead

Emperor. At prayer eyes shifted to one's neighbor. Little groups constantly collected for whispered conversation, unseemly family arguments—usually over the prospect of new distinctions, new monies, some article of inheritance—which would make the devil blush for shame, all the greed, the unwarranted ambition—and perhaps clandestine fury against the man who so dominated every member of the Imperial house —restrained by Manuel's life, were released with his death. And at the center of this monstrous assault upon the Imperium was not His Imperial Majesty, Emperor Alexius II, aged twelve years, nor the Regency Council, with its Patriarchal President, but the ineffectual, intellectually limited, surpassingly beautiful, unfortunately ingenuous Dowager Empress and Regent Absolute, Maria-Xenia Augusta.

V

Only a few days ago, I received as visitor—for the last time, I fear— my good friend, the Caesar Demetrius, illegitimate son of Manuel Augustus and Elizabeth Persephone Branas. He asked after the progress of my history, and when I told him I had recently described the events of his father's death, he said, "Remember, if you must praise him: he was a good man. Whatever the faults of his rule—and perhaps they were inevitable—he was a good man. Since the Empire he left behind is no more, perhaps the memory of his goodness is what most matters. It is by far the more worthwhile judgment. Nations die, customs fail—and then, all we may remember is the virtue or lack of it in which a man lived."

In the days following the Emperor's death, my own thoughts were never far from such a consideration. In truth, as the Empire was still viable, still with us, my appraisal was even more generous than his son would recommend, more than thirty years later. It seemed to me a man both good *and* great had been taken from us and we were quite lost. He needed not, then, as now, to be divorced from his magnified actions as a ruler. I do not think it too much to say I was one among legion who were despondent. The loss of Manuel Augustus struck us all, very hard, on a personal level. For a while we were overwhelmed.

Everywhere, by absence, were his phantoms: his patience, his decency, his graciousness, his lordly extravagance, his sure way, and the unparalleled authority of nearly four decades as head of state. There have been emperors whose death was celebrated in the streets—Andronikus was one—but Manuel's was genuinely mourned. It was not simply the men and women who threw themselves in the way of his cortege, prostrate and weeping, but the feeling of true desolation, of one gone who was loved and irreplaceable. I myself passed from day to day not with the sense of awed unreality which followed the sack, not as one who has stood nearby a sudden stroke of thunder and lightning simultaneously, not with the numbness and shock which followed the death of Andronikus, but with a sort of weary gloom, uninsistent but abiding, a tolerable but certainly discomforting pain, which limited pleasure and emphasized the sadness of things.

Something glorious had been taken from our lives—one who, by his very existence, enhanced ours. Gone was that not quite definable human splendor on which we thrive, personally or vicariously—as it is enough to know there are the superb among us, who raise before our eyes the vision of what it means to live in the ultimate chambers of civilization: *raffiné,* graceful, unhurried, cultivated, exquisite, contrary as one likes, and enigmatic with the perfection of self-containment. Perhaps that above all was the greatest loss, for the denial of spiritual glamour is the absence of irreplaceable beauty, which is first of all unique. Then, all that is left is yearning, which is the inability to possess at last or resume former possession, and grief, that what was possessed, for a fact, was not treasured as it ought to have been, or, just so, could not be kept forever.

A month after Manuel's death, the Empress called me to her apartments, a signal privilege, more so, as she received me with only one of her ladies in attendance. It is quite possible she was more beautiful in her grief than in her days as the high-spirited, indulged young Consort whom the Emperor adored spoiling, as she adored him for spoiling her. I give her that praise in the understanding it had nothing whatever to do with increased physical beauty, but that her mourning, for once, lifted her out of herself and one might judge her attractiveness on one's own, without the insistent, if never irritating, prodding of the lady's very genuine narcissism (a curious vanity, which was almost objective in its self-appraisal and naïve in expectation of your similar aesthetic excitement).

"Count," she said, "I have heard you pray daily at the Emperor's tomb." (He had been buried beneath the great stone slab which had barred Christ's sepulcher and, more than thirty years before, he had trudged on his back to Pantokrator Cathedral.) I could give no reason; none was expected, I presume. She smiled sadly, but not warmly. "More than that, I have heard you go about with a long face, that you are quite distracted, sleep and eat little, so that you shall become ill. If you do, you will no longer be able to serve us. That is a loss we cannot face. His Majesty, my son, is but a child, and I am only a poor woman. We require your attendance far more than Manuel Augustus. It speaks wonderfully of your personal devotion to my husband, who loved you truly and saw in you the promise of great things. But it would serve his memory little to fail in just those talents which attracted him to you, and of which the state is in such great need."

Prepared for a harrowing emotional encounter, I found myself rather more sobered and fascinated. Somehow I had the sense of rehearsal, a prepared speech, or words tripped upon—like bright stones at a beach— from one interview to the next and rearranged, from one to the other, as seemed fitting and precluded boredom. I had the sense of correct gestures and the heart gone out of them, of repetition before too many ministers. Whether this was the Grand Duke David's idea or Maria-Xenia's, it was failing in the face of her disinterest, or, perhaps, exhaustion. Previously she had never taken any part in government. Now, like it or no, until her son's majority, she *was* the government, forced to schedules and signatures, even if the full weight of rule had, at once, and almost totally, been assumed by her not too competent lover.

Perhaps the grief for Manuel was something quite beside what I saw —real, but secluded from the world. Perhaps what I saw—and all the world—was rather the dismay of a woman quite crushed by responsibilities she had no desire to assume (for it must be kept in mind in all which follows, Maria-Xenia held to her power as a shield, not a weapon). That sense of distraction, of detachment between errand and conviction—unsettling, if not offensive—may have been grief for the end of happier pastimes or the lack of seclusion to recover from her loss.

She may have meant every word she said. Rather it was her misfortune to be incapable of subordinating her feelings to duty, of realizing herself and the state one and the same. In the end, the consequence was the same: she alienated more than she encouraged.

When Her Majesty completed her well-meant admonition to me— gentle reproof and a flattering plea—there was a momentary silence, not awkward—or only a little—but touching, for her face seemed to lose its composure, to go slack with exhaustion and reverie. In a nervous gesture, as though becoming at once aware of where she was and what about, she drew the tips of the fingers of her right hand across her forehead and looked up, smiling momentarily, wanly. She extended her hand to her lady, who placed upon the upturned palm an absurdly small, exquisitely carved ivory casket, which, straight arm shooting forward, the Empress then offered to me, as a shy child offers a gift, or is thus instructed to offer it.

"Open it," she said. "Please do."

I lifted the lid. Within, no larger than a robin's egg, was a scale model, in solid gold by its weight, of the Parthenon, now of course, the Cathedral of the Holy Virgin, my brother's "parish" church. "Oh, madame," I said, "it is too lovely."

She responded with some real emotion, "He had planned as early as last January to make your brother Bishop, and he commissioned for you this memento."

"Lady, I could treasure nothing I own—save my personal memories of the Emperor—more than this."

To my surprise, and nearly in conversational tone, she said, "Isn't it a sad business, the giving and receiving of gifts of one"—she hesitated —"quite gone?"

"Truly, madame, it is, perhaps because in most cases we know they carried the tokens with them and it may be a little of their spirit is instilled in the object."

She said, "Yes, it must be so," but I do not think, for one moment, she had any sense of the words I had just spoken—or else she was too preoccupied or too rushed to risk an actual dialogue. Royalty seldom wishes to converse even when it seems to. At most, and then rhetorically, they ask questions. I was abashed; it was a mistake a courtier would not have made. She said, "The Emperor left many personal effects, as you may imagine, but he was especially insistent his sword, his shield and dagger, which were his father's, as well as the icon he wore about his neck, and several other articles, be placed in the hands of His Imperial Highness, the Grand Duke Andronikus. I would like you to take them to him as soon as possible."

The following week, I journeyed to Oeneum, where the Queen received me, and before I was risen from my knees, said, "He'll never be rid of him. He's more pervasive now than ever. In life, at least, the Emperor's person was confined to Constantinople. But now his ghost is everywhere." She shook her head and sighed. She remained standing, indicating she did not wish to extend the interview by offering me a seat.

"It was terrible when we received the news. I told him. Then he paced back and forth, rubbing his hands like a lunatic. His expression was desolate and so *fierce*. I knew better than to console him. He left the palace on horseback and did not return until the following night. I have no idea where he went or what he did, but I dared not send a search party after him. Once home again, he went straight to bed. I thought he was sleeping, but he lay there with his eyes wide open the entire night. Yet it wasn't grief. Somehow, I knew, it wasn't grief."

She surveyed the table where the Emperor's artifacts lay—mementos, all that was left of a man's life. She lifted the Emperor's icon and handed it to me. Not without a little bitterness, I thought, almost imperceptible —like the taste of urine in the most succulently prepared calves' liver —she said, "Why don't you bring it to him. He's in the lower garden. He would accept it from you."

It was an unnaturally warm day following a cold, rainy night, and the lower garden was still shrouded in mist, which reached the first branches of the tallest trees. The aspect was enchanting. As I descended the stairs the dampness on the pavement of the lower terrace suddenly caught the sun and momentarily blinded me so that I was forced to stop and wait until my eyes became acclimated to the brilliance. A sentry asked if I was all right, and I said I was. I descended the last flight into the garden, and the mist—from above, white and pure and seemingly still—appeared to be moving in golden volutes, refracting the sun's rays, sometimes iridescent, mostly citron, spinning beneath a dimly perceived sky, round trees, phantom and gleaming, almost pulsating in an imitation of breathing. Man's pomp is oppressive because it is heartless, designed, and pretentious, created to dazzle the eye. But nature— whether as an alabaster thundercloud, east of the sunset, or a field of madonna lilies grown in a lava bed—is nothing if not elating because she is the coincidence of perfection, an excess without the *intent* to arouse jealousy, or fear or awe, or admiration.

I stood rooted at the foot of the stairs, as I beheld, with a start, a huge figure coming at me in the mist, at first indistinct and dull amber-colored, then gradually resolving itself. It was Andronikus, lit peachlike, pink-gold, unnaturally luminous, without shadow, in the all-pervading light of the irriguous air.

"Nicetas," he said with surprise. I had never seen his face so completely devoid of wit, of subtlety, of that sensational control which allowed the world to see what he would have it see and no more. He looked indeed, as Michael Branas was to suggest many years later, like a brooding Jupiter. His was not the sadness which behooved the onlooker to consolation: this was a melancholy beyond the possibility of simple pieties, or even deep ones.

"Your Highness," I said, and, indifferently, as though those words were a call to the world of customs and position—so much irrelevant vanity—he extended his hand for me to kiss.

He said, "What is it? Why have you come?" unexpectedly gentle, truly curious.

"I've brought these personal effects the Emperor wished you to have."

He said, "How very good of you."

"The Queen thought you might like to accept this particularly from me. I have no idea why."

He extended his hand again and I placed the beautifully incised icon on its long, fine filigree chain in his palm. He considered it a moment. The mist was swiftly dispersing, his body losing that eerie glow as the sunlight reached us straight. Now he squinted, hand to eyes, looking up at the sun for an instant, then at me. A little beguiling smile played about his lips, while he considered again the icon, now gleaming so lustrously—reflecting itself brilliantly on his throat. Without looking up again he said—and it seemed to me he was thinking aloud—"I could not help trying to win him to me, because I loved him, and he could not help insisting on his autocratic will, because he loved me, and it meant so much to each of us to win one another to the rightness of our individual ways. Now—what difference does it make?" He sighed, closed his fingers over the icon, and drew the back of his fist across his forehead. As he began to ascend the stairs, he said again, "What difference does it make?" And more softly still, yet again, no longer even a question, "What difference does it make."

Theodora was standing at the head of the stairs. He did not acknowledge her and I could only bow in passing.

By January the general policy of the Grand Duke David became explicit. It was to be more Latins still against the native bureaucracy against certain elements of the Church and the nobility, all the middle classes—i.e., the untitled rich and the wage earner and the peasant farmer—and the poor. The answer to the obvious question—why such senseless, impolitic moves at such a critical internal moment—is most disheartening because it is so simple and so unworthy of a dynast. The Grand Duke's point was nothing less than the looting of the Empire for purposes of his own remuneration. To this end, he was obliged to keep all power in his hands by means of highly placed creatures owed to him body and soul. This great-grandson of Alexius I sold posts like an auctioneer, dismissed "buyers" at the least sign of independence— some of them actually awoke to a sense of responsibility—arrested them if they protested, confiscated all their wealth if they were not thus intimidated into silence, and, on four known occasions, had them murdered in their cells. Naturally, with absolute corruption at the top, all license prevailed as men attempted to hoard what they owned, steal what they wished, or, at its most legal, resort to the thieves' legality, extortion.

Before the new year emigration from the city was proceeding at an extraordinary pace—rich and poor, noble and renegade slave alike. As the native population vanished, the Latin nationals and Constantinopolitan aristocrats bought up property at cost or summarily moved into more and more posts within the administration and the army, causing, round-robin, the disaffection of still more archons and provincial nobles. Theodosius' party was triumphant, but in a manner which appalled the Patriarch, too late realizing the nature of the Trojan horse to whose entry he had given his consent rather than like that other Greek priest, Lacoön, his warning.

Everywhere the Imperial administration was crumbling. From Athens, my brother wrote to me:

The whole of Hellas is being raped by these men, the caliber of whose appointments are not to be believed. It is no exaggeration to say there is only myself between their appetite and the people. And I have no doubt, were I not Bishop, I should have been suspended from the walls for archery practice.

Like their manifest leader, whose name I would not speak, these new jobbers—excrementitious wretches all—sleep by day, party by night, and sign whatever is put before them in the dark before dawn. To prove

I was not using hyperbole when, at a recent party I commented on the new Governor's illiteracy, a friend of mine placed on His Excellency's desk a document ordering the drainage of the Aegean Sea and the peppering of Mt. Parnassus. The document was duly signed and dispatched without a second glance to Constantinople. If you hear of it, see that it passes through the proper channels. It is bound, by example, to be salutary.

I need not add, I trust, the farce corruption in government would suggest were it not, at once, so tragic in its consequences. Services are at a virtual standstill. Jurisprudence is impartial to all—to be bought by rich and poor alike. The great collecting machines, meanwhile, are well engaged in their work. The newest order of the day is a prohibitive rise in inheritance taxes. Our official worthies, you may be certain, do not allow the bereaved to depart probate without a sharp examination of the fortunes left them. If the major portion of property is not seized at once, torture reveals all sources of wealth at last. In this manner, the death of the master of any household—rich and poor—becomes the signal for its dissolution.

The Grand Duchess Helena Porphyriogeneta Anemas, speaking of the Grand Duke David, said, "My nephew is as monstrous a rascal as his brother without the commensurate political integrity." A man as humorless as John Sergius would scarcely have perceived the irony of a fond memory. Yet it was true. In comparison with the younger brother, men saw the difference between the invidious fellow who seeks power —for what he believes—however mistakenly—is the good end of his own rule, and the offensive prodigy who seeks it and confirms one's worst fears.

We had all remarked upon David's balefulness in previous years without really looking more closely. Now his visibility exaggerated his flaws. He was not illiterate, but he possessed a mind so *literal* and crude that whether he could read and write made little difference. All the cunning, suspicion, disproportionate response, and complex but ultimately uninsightful strategy of the uneducated were his. He possessed a fancy for gorgeous clothes, more fitting for state occasions than everyday wear (even his hunting boots were sewn with pearls and there is a legend his claque practically fell from their saddles as they attempted to retrieve the jewels which burst from his shoes during the chase). He surrounded himself with half again as many attendants as his uncle at the height of his glory and he demanded all men—including members of his own family—kneel preceding and during his passage. When one of his aunts —as usual, the sharp-tongued Juliana Porphyriogeneta Cantacuzenus— laughed, half amazed and uneasy, and said, "He must be joking," and refused even to speak to him, the Grand Duke, in spite of a family peti- tion—and the physical threats of her eleven sons—had the august lady banished to the Chersonese. Thereafter, without further ado, he was accorded the reverence of an emperor. In short, this man, past the age of forty, was pretentious, conceited, insolent, vulgar, vicious, and im- moral.

Yet the indignation which, little by little, roared toward the throne from within and beyond the walls of Blachernae fell finally not upon the true culprit, but those in whose name he ruled.

Alexius II indulged his passion for the hunt and summarily dis- missed the tutors who should have prepared him for his majority. There was no one to reinstate them: he hardly knew his mother, taking her maternal prerogatives as plain presumption; he detested David as thor- oughly as his cousin cared little what became of him, so long as he was present for signature and seal. Maria-Xenia dutifully assumed public representation for the Imperium and frequently, gratefully retired to the Irene Villa in the company of the Grand Duke whose attraction was beyond anyone's comprehension (it was known he beat her unmerci- fully upon argument—shades of her mother and Reynald). The corrup- tion, the inefficiency, the degradation of the Empire was laid at the feet of the child Emperor and the Empress Mother. It does not matter who disservices a throne—or in what manner. Who claims the crown assumes accountability.

A landslide began. On 12 January 1181 Bela III, who had placed Dalmatia under Byzantine suzerainty in exchange for marriage with the Caesarissa Catherine, reclaimed his fief. Within the same week, Queen Theodora's nephew, the Grand Duke Isaac, was captured during a Cilician insurrection and tossed into a dungeon, removed only now and again for inhuman torture which, it is said, snapped his mind. His ransom was offered in terms of formal secession from the Empire. When his father, a collateral Comneni, attempted to parley with the ambas- sadors in behalf of his son, David promulgated a chrysobull which dis- missed and banished his kin to the family's estates in Thrace. Rather than east, however, the Grand Duke George and Grand Duchess Militsa passed west, to Oeneum, where Andronikus was boldly amassing a mercenary army against any attempt by David to persecute him or enter any Latin or paid creature into the Pontic governancy.

The landslide continued. The previous year's abundant grain crop, having waited too long for sufficient ships and wagons from Constantinople, was pronounced, on arrival, spoiled by cold and blight and infestation and dumped, ton after ton, into the Bosporus before the eyes of thousands of destitute to whom no explanation of cereal disease would serve to condone this atrocity. Hunger riots followed, as they had occurred in other major cities waiting for the produce. Hooligans wandered the capital and initiated a pogrom in the Jewish quarter on 25 January, in which three hundred members of a congregation were burned to death in their synagogue (the rabbi's charred corpse was found to cover their Sacred Scroll, which was undamaged). Burglaries among the rich increased. The old and poor, if not victim to the lack of social services and absence of philanthropy, suffered as the most common victims of the roving bands.

On 1 February I asked an interview with the Empress and received, in turn, a note from the Grand Duke David, asking me the nature of the subject I wished to bring to the Autocratrix's attention. In the following seven days the same procedure was repeated by the Patriarch, the Caesar Demetrius, the Caesarissa Catherine, the Prefect of the City, the Grand Duke Alexander and his sister, the Grand Duchess Zoë. It was nothing less than an attempt to reach the Empress and protest to her the state of affairs to which her late husband's nephew was reducing the Empire. The alternative would be hers, but she ought, at least, to have the choice of disassociating herself from the Grand Duke.

When our camarilla met again at Vlanga, the Caesarissa Catherine perhaps accurately if uncharitably said, "She made her choice the first day David beat her and she did not have his fists lopped off. Now she is in mortal fear of him. We'll never again have access to her and I think we ought to act accordingly."

Others find conspiracy against an entrenched power a heavy, exhilarating experience. I noted this curious elation in the Caesar Renier and the Grand Duke Julian, especially, when they chose to desert their former sponsor. For myself, I was, if not actively frightened, tense to the point of physical nausea from the moment I accepted the Caesarissa's invitation until the annunciation of Andronikus as Regent, over a year later. The likely truth that we were on the side of justice and Imperial integrity gave me no courage at all, for there are none so brutal in their retaliation as those who suspect their own wickedness and must confront its would-be chastisers.

Once, in that hard, forward way of hers, Manuel's daughter actually smiled on me and said, "Nicetas, you're an awfully small man, cursed with a conscience which forces you to act larger than you are. You'll be very unhappy but you'll do very well."

At any moment I expected to be arrested, judged, and executed. Men whose politics I had placed second after their appeal to me as human beings I suddenly rejected as sycophants or I suspected of spying. I was uneasy along corridors and, for the first time in my life, no longer walked the city I loved so deeply, but took horse with an aide and carried a dagger beneath my cloak.

We were a privileged society of conspirators. Unfortunately, we were also quite inept. For one, we allowed too many people into our schemes, and we were too apt to receive any man who bore a grudge against the administration. For another, we had been too scrupulous in effecting some conciliation with the Augusta, who was now called by the people the Foreigner, a ready indication of the alienation of the Empire from the Imperium, and probably precluding all hope of maintaining her in the Regency. The order of our request for an interview had set the Grand Duke David's nose to scent and, unknown to all of us, we were under the surveillance of the Secret Police. Finally, and most to the point, a priest, whose allegiance to the throne was real if misguided, revealed our plot to one of the Grand Duke's minions.

21 February had been set as the date to assassinate the Empress' lover during the annual court pilgrimage to the shrine of St. Theodore at Bathys Rhyax, a few miles from the city.

I arrived at the ministry offices the appointed day and lived in a state of anxiety such as I had never known. Every sound startled me and I could scarcely concentrate on the conversation at hand. Several colleagues later remarked at our mass trial on my extremely odd behavior. Often I would lose myself in reverie remarking to myself the inescapable guilt I felt in the knowledge the man whom I had watched leave Blachernae that morning might, at any moment, be dead or rescued. And then, I would remonstrate with myself: What was I about? I was complicit in murder, in taking another human life. Even now, perhaps,

I could save a man from annihilation. Why was I unmoved? A man alive that morning would be dead as much by my hand, which held the pen, as the assassin's which wielded the knife. At a pitch, I would tell myself I must not allow such an event, not because I feared punishment, but because I must not be the intentional agent of another man's death, as, most certainly, I was by remaining silent and still. And then again, the purpose of this awful act took hold. I would remind myself of David's corruption, his vindictiveness, that he had murdered more citizens by his ineptitude and greed than I had hairs upon my head. And so it went: He was a human being; nothing would be served by killing him. There ought to have been some other way. But there was none. So long as he lived, with the Empress in his thrall, he had the loyalty and the might of those sworn to his mistress by oath—such as the Varangians— and those moved to him by expediency—such as Agnes-Anna Augusta's French Guard. I would hold. I would make myself numb. I would forget. I would allow time to pass. I would restrain myself until it was done, at the expense of mercy and my own fears of death extended to another man.

The first word—and the final one—the attempt had failed reached me, if I may say, in the classic manner. A man whom I had never seen before, an elegantly accoutered fellow, accompanied by two Varangians, entered my office, and while I was in conversation with several aides, interrupted us, with a brief but real apology, and said, "Count Acominatus?"

I knew at once. "I am he."

He said, "Will you come with me?"

I asked for what purpose.

He was Greek, and perhaps it pained him, "Sir, you are under arrest by order of the Empress Regent."

"On what charges?"

His manner remained free from belligerence. "You are under arrest, sir, for high treason in the attempted assassination of His Imperial Highness, the Megadux David."

Theodore Maurozomes, my chief secretary, started toward me with a gesture to protect me. He was an unusually sensitive-minded giant, who suffered the usual ribaldry against large, exceptionally gentle men, with a blush and much hurt, I think. He was older than my twenty-seven years by five. "No, no," I said, "don't come near me, Theodore," meaning, of course, the usual disgraced man's warning: don't touch me, don't be seen with me, don't attempt to protect me. I am pariah and you will implicate yourself.

The others, I was moved to see, were of no more mind to leave my side. My accusator, considerate as ever, refused to take offense. There was no violence here, only this passive resistance and momentary display of loyalty to me. He and I became complicit, then, to save my well-meaning subordinates.

"Count, I ask you to come with me."

I smiled—almost astonished at myself for the feeling of lightness I experienced, not at all what I had contemplated had I ever considered being arrested—and I said, "I *could* claim the immunity of the Senate, couldn't I?"

He smiled in turn. "I'm afraid not, Excellency. The law does not read so on express charges from the throne in matters of high treason and specifically, Imperial assassination."

I tapped the rolled document I held quickly against my thigh, turned and replaced it on the table. "Very well," I said.

Theodore offered to come with me.

I smiled again—the last time I was to smile for many months—and said, "You most certainly will *not*."

To my surprise, my aides all embraced me, quite a tribute to an aristocrat, who is resented on principle when he enters the bureaucracy, no less one such as myself who had risen so high, so quickly, through the most exalted sponsorship. Yet for every trust given me by the Sebastocrator or by Manuel, I had exerted myself twice as much as any man against just such antipathy and criticism. I *was* myself, moreover, who wished to excel in whatever I did. Nothing would have appalled me more than to be considered a pampered creature of the Manuelian Epoch. That was not illustriousness and the praise of history, but my own condemnation. Now, at the last moment, at least among my own, I learned I had succeeded.

The Grandees who had participated in the plot—to my surprise, I was included among them, probably because of my brother's great eminence—were conducted to house arrest in the throne room of Daphne Palace. Among a dozen, these included Helena Porphyriogeneta's son, Duke Andrew Lapardas, the Caesar Demetrius, the Grand Dukes Alexander and Julian, and the Prefect of Constantinople, Duke John

Kamaterus. Others were unceremoniously incarcerated in the Buceleon Ravelin. Only the Grand Duchess Zoë, suddenly bedded by menstruation, the Caesar Renier, and the Caesarissa Catherine, whose prestige was so immense as to make her arrest impossible this side of revolution, were, for the moment, allowed their freedom.

The lot of us at Daphne spent an uncomfortable night on makeshift beds, but warmed by the sense of failed comradeship in a good cause. Even the Grand Duke Julian won everybody's affection with his saturnine humor, as well by the surprising respect he accorded his elder brother, a privacy within the Andronikan branch, which few had ever witnessed. In the morning, unbathed, unshaven, and unbreakfasted, we were manacled and led out to wagons—hay wagons, a purposeful insult —and taken from the old Sacred Palace to the gigantic Basilica of the Ministry of Justice.

If David had intended to show his undoubted authority—to commit the unthinkable and inspire fear as he did in the extraordinarily petty exile of his aunt—he miscalculated. From the moment the wagons left Chalke and egressed into the Augusteum, we were surrounded by well-wishing Constantinopolitans, prevented from reaching us only because we were surrounded by the Imperial Horse. We were brought to summary trial before the Minister of Justice, Theodore Pantechnes.

The Caesar Demetrius, and Andronikus' sons, as well as Andrew Lapardas, refused to recognize the credence of the court. With Imperial blood in their veins, they maintained they could be tried only before the Sacred Consistory. Neither Kamaterus, nor the others, nor I, could claim such dispensation. For a fact, I was threatened with torture as the least of the aristocrats accused. At that point, the Grand Duke Julian, in one of the truest moments of imperiousness I have ever beheld, said, "Pantechnes, remember my words. Those things which you do today—to the least of us—place your life, not ours, in the balance." The judge, seated beneath the Christ-mosaiced apse, stared coldly at Julian. He was a true legal pedant, incapable of the genius which transforms the law from the inhuman generality to the humane particular. Man's justice was not his wings but a cage. He said, "Your Imperial Highnesses do not recognize the court, therefore the court's business is not of your concern." The Grand Duke smiled, so like his father, at that moment. He was charming, melting, condescending, "But of course it is. We are beyond your jurisdiction, though you are scarcely beyond our criticism, or its consequences."

He did not overtly insult Pantechnes, though insult was implicit. It was something beyond insolence, beyond the callousness of one who believes his inferiors scarcely worth the merit of his spit or his boot. Rather I think his contempt was nothing whatever articulate in Julian's own mind, but inborn, something Olympic, something like an irony experienced in inviolability. He was speaking from the disdain for death or threats or denial, from the fullness one knows as a dynast. Others, not always successfully, must ascend to the plateau of history. One such as Julian, merely for being born a Comneni, is cradled in cynosure. If our purpose is to be remembered, he knew he might have died before the age of reason and his name would survive the ages, if only on a genealogical table. Thus, all acts become superfluous after emission from the mother's womb. In that surety, what man would not act with a sense of distance, of the once removed, with regal imperturbability? (In rejecting the mystique of the blood, Andronikus forgot its consequences were all too real in a world which, allowed to unmake its gods, who made themselves vulnerable, could make new ones.)

Well, needless to say, I was not tortured, though for a few moments I knew that sense of nightmare unreality when we are suddenly presented with the possibility of unjust pain committed against one with no recourse. And, I may say, much as I was awed by Julian's gesture—at least as it was executed—I was a little angry that in taunting the court, he was begging a dare.

In any event, we proved too estimable a group to be punished in parts and without further consideration were returned to Daphne, a dozen men, who all their lives had taken luxury and dominion for granted, forced to endure one another in the space of a lady-in-waiting's abandoned apartment. We called it our Lenten Sacrifice, and perhaps suffered the worst of it only in the lack of air and exercise. Indeed, the puzzling inclusion of the Grand Duchess Zoë in our number, two days later—and with God knows what motive (after all, we were gentlemen)—may have been our saving motive. The Lady's presence insured our civility to one another and sharpened our gallantry (cheered to exhibit it, we gave up one precious room in its entirety to her accommodation). During this incarceration, it hardly need be added, was founded the relationship between the Grand Duchess and her second cousin, Demetrius.

Two days later still, Maria-Xenia signed the warrant for the arrest of her stepdaughter and her husband. A sympathetic courtier warned the Caesarissa, who fled with her Georgian mercenaries and Renier's Montferrat Regiment, to Holy Wisdom Cathedral, where sanctuary was at once granted by the Patriarch, who, indeed, had much amends to make.

Almost at once, David sent an emissary to promise amnesty for herself and the Caesar. "She was quite splendid," Theodosius told me later in the year. "She said, 'Tell my cousin an emperor's daughter takes nothing by halves. I *demand* amnesty for all my fellows and release from their detention at Daphne and the ravelin. That—or nothing.'" The Patriarch's expression glowed with appreciation. "Well," he continued, "the emissary returned about an hour later and suggested, quite out of line, in matters of treason, there is *no* sanctuary from justice. At that point, I interrupted him and said, 'You listen to me, young man, if Lucifer and his Rosy Light entered this church, he would be inviolable from all earthly law.' But the insolent little heathen was not to be put off so easily. He said, 'The Emperor is Supreme Head of the Church and may do as he likes.' I stared him down, pointed to the door and said, 'When you cross that threshold, you leave the Emperor's deputation, and enter heaven, which is God's.' At that he left.

"It was then the Caesarissa turned to me and said, 'You are with us, then?' I told her I was only concerned with the violation of the Church. She said, 'Come, come, Monseigneur. Yes or no? Do you join us? If David comes after us, as he threatens, we must take greater measures against him. You are already complicit. Consent.' I perceived a possible overthrow of her brother. You *know* that woman has never accepted his assumption. I said, with a coquettishness which, I fear, makes me blush, 'I am on the side of legitimacy.' She knew my meaning and drew herself up. 'So am I,' she insisted, 'and I detest its misappropriation.'"

Both Holy Wisdom and the Patriarchal Palace—St. Michael's—were reinforced in the next week, while the Grand Duke remained inexplicably inactive. Perhaps he believed Theodosius still faithful to the pro-Latin party. The Patriarch and the Caesarissa, then, took advantage of His Eminence's freedom to make a decision, whose consequences no man can say. They determined to distribute gold among the beggars, the toughs, and the poor of the city, in return for their aid. Whether the mob, which had been growing in noise and effect since the last years of Manuel Augustus, would have, anyway, made their presence felt, here was a formal recognition of their power, which, once given, could not be taken back. With this, the beast which had lain quiescent since the accession of Alexius I, in 1081, was risen again and suddenly the government was accountable to its roar.

On 1 March, the Varangian Regiment of the Guard appeared at the gates of St. Michael's demanding the surrender of the Caesar and Caesarissa. Refused out of hand, their captain gave the order and volleys of fired arrows were sent over the walls. In an act of stunning bravery, the Patriarch gruffly pushed aside those who attempted to stop him and appeared on the parapet in his full vestments and blazing miter. The arrows stopped at once.

For the next month, a stalemate ensued. On Holy Friday, 10 April, Theodosius refused to appear beneath the great canopy, erected in the Augusteum, there to exchange the Kiss of Peace with the young Emperor. Disappointed at the cancellation of the ceremony—David had proceeded on the supposition the Patriarch would scarcely refuse—the assembled crowd broke out in riot which seriously threatened the safety of the thirteen-year-old Emperor, his eleven-year-old betrothed, and the Empress Mother. By noon, unrest had spread throughout the city, probably incited by a rumor—its origins have never been discovered—the Grand Duke Andronikus was marching on Constantinople.

Now in complete panic, David called in not the Constantinopolitan Garrison, but the Nemitzian Regiment, who guaranteed brutality. The slaughter was hideous, on demand, and the Grand Duke's miscalculation assumed mountainous proportions by uniting the city against him. Palaces of the nobility known to be still faithful to the court were sacked —as well as those of creatures raised by the current regime, including (I cannot help smiling) Theodore Pantechnes' magnificent new establishment.

In the days that followed, huge crowds assembled before rabble-rousers in the great forums and squares, in the Augusteum and the Hippodrome. Now they were led by priests beneath icons, crosses, and portraits of Alexius II. When the Constantinopolitan Garrison was called in to disperse the demonstrators, many of the soldiers, native to the city, joined with those they were meant to disband. As a last, painful alternative—even David was, by now, sensitive to the charge of Latinophilism—the Empress' lover commissioned Agnes' Frankish regiments, whose loyalty was unquestioned. They were remarkably effective, achieving minimum fatalities. But the sight of Westerners threatening Greek mobs in a Greek city stamped the final damnation of the government, at least as it was constituted under the Grand Duke.

From 15 April to the evening of 8 May, short, sharp negotiating sessions were followed by longer and longer periods of stagnation, followed again by skirmishes between the Imperial troops and the Caesarissa's. The morning of 9 May proved to be the end of the "Holy War," as it was thereafter called. Twenty thousand of the Imperial soldiery—more men amassed than anyone had seen since Myriokephalum—fifteen thousand foot, five thousand horse—entered the Augusteum and drove the Montferrats and the Georgians back to the walls, quite literally, of the great cathedral.

The next recourse was slaughter on the very stones of Holy Wisdom, and storming it, or else, a truce. Catherine had put her hopes in the people, whose anger, zealous as it was, could not be matched against the discipline of the crown's regiments. And so, though she had endured three months' siege and was prepared to survive three years more to gain amnesty, the Patriarch crossed the city between lines of Varangians, midnight, 10 May, and met with Maria-Xenia, David, Count George Angelus, and his son, Count Isaac (who later told me in his wan, good-natured way, he "would much rather have been drinking with Julian and Andrew than ameliorating their reputations before the Empress"). The parley resulted in something like a semi-triumph for our party. The Caesarissa, her Caesar, and those incarcerated at Daphne were given total amnesty, but only on the condition that they remained confined to Constantinople on penalty of forfeiture of all personal properties in the capital. Those followers in the ravelin would be transferred to more comfortable quarters, but remained under arrest pending review.

No sooner were we free than David, in the Emperor's name, convened a synod for purposes of impeachment of the Patriarch on grounds of desecrating Holy Wisdom in its use as a fortress, and fomenting rebellion against the state. My brother, and our great friend, Bishop Eustathius of Thessalonika, undertook to act as the Patriarch's counsel. Their substantive defense: the Grand Duke, not Theodosius, was culpable, since His Highness had violated the privileges of sanctuary of Holy Wisdom Cathedral and St. Michael's Palace. Theodosius himself, with marvelous composure, and not a little wit in his eyes—especially face to face with some of his accusatory subordinate priests—spoke last and pronounced the synod "not a tool of justice, merely a tool, with the gestures, not the intent of justice." The Patriarch was cleared of all charges, but the Grand Duke had him removed to Terebinthos Isle in the Sea of Marmora, while a Priest-Regent was appointed to serve the Church. In the eyes of the people, nothing at all had been served but further Latinization of the government and the making of a new Greek martyr. (Predictably, it was rumored, the Procurator, David's confessor, was a follower of the Latin rite. He most certainly was not.)

On 10 June the former conspirators were obliged to present themselves to Pantechnes to demonstrate their fidelity to the terms of probation. Of their number, four were absent: the Caesar Demetrius, the Grand Duchess Zoë, Michael Branas, and myself. We had fled to Andronikus, now headquartered at Sinope. *Explicit: Nicetas Acominatus.*

VI

At the sound of the opening door, Theodora turns her head with the same speed and rapt frown of an owl. Andronikus enters her apartment. He is ostentatiously impassive. A tension is notable in the tremor of his cheeks. He refuses to look at the Queen.

ANDRONIKUS. I was told it was urgent.

THEODORA. Where are your clothes, your books, your papers? Where are they?

He looks away, his expression set, something between sadness and stubbornness.

ANDRONIKUS. Lower your voice or I shall leave.

THEODORA. You're disavowing me before everyone. You're saying to everyone you cannot even abide my company.

ANDRONIKUS. That is understating the case.

Now he gains her glance and holds it and does not seem in the least moved by the possibility of her tears. She notes his imperturbability and at once assumes a quieter manner, swallowing hard to control herself.

THEODORA. You've humiliated me more than I have the power to forgive you. But I still have my pride before the others, so long as I seem to be your companion. I'm asking you to lie. I deserve that much.

He bethinks himself, moves up to her. She is limp with amazement. He grasps her shoulders and kisses her forehead.

ANDRONIKUS. Yes, yes, you do. Forgive me. I will have my things returned before evening. That I promise.

She lowers her head, shaking it from side to side, her expression one of utmost pain. She breaks free, turns her back, and moves away.

ANDRONIKUS. I continue to love you and, it seems, I cannot make you understand that.

THEODORA. I thought I understood you. I don't. But I know myself, in some degree. I cannot survive without self-esteem. Do as you like.

ANDRONIKUS. This is what you wish?

THEODORA. Had I what I wish I should be dead.

He lifts her hand—still she will not face him—kisses it, and lets go. It drops back, like a puppet's, to her side. When she is alone, her eyes flutter, as one about to faint. Her mouth goes slack. She brings her hand to her stomach, bends a little forward, and, as her face visibly screws into a mask of despair, she emits a low wail, catches her breath in brief gasps, like a child at the end of tears, scarcely able to force a sound without suffocating herself, and wails again, louder, more guttural, and catches her breath and still again wails. The sounds, deepening in pitch and growing in volume, follows Andronikus down the corridor. He stops, turns. He is indecisive. One of Theodora's ladies comes running. He stops her, shakes his head, then relents and lets her go to her mistress. The ululations—suggesting dying animals and howling winds through empty rooms—continue.

Incipit: Nicetas Acominatus: The change in him was startling. In eight months he seemed to have become an old man. I asked myself if this were he, indeed, in whom we now put our hopes. He was alert enough and near to coming to a decision to march on Constantinople. Yet, when he was not given to strategy or, with me, reminiscences, he was distracted and listless. One of his courtiers insisted—swearing me to secrecy—this was nothing less than the effect of drugs the Queen had been administering to the Grand Duke to maintain his virility. In fact, I know with some certainty, aphrodisiacs were not the province of Theodora but introduced by the concubine, Maupacta. It was obvious, moreover, that the relationship between Her Majesty and His Highness had taken a new turn, by far a calmer one—if more cordial than warm—to replace the tinder-like animosity which had existed between them during my previous visits. I think, in truth, Andronikus' behavior, previous to the Great March, is more subtle and less romantic in origin.

One day, during a walk, he said, "I could have it now, couldn't I? The power. The form no longer matters to me. The Regency is the crown without consecration and consecration is for lackeys. It's within reach, it's possible." There was in his voice a measure of sad astonishment, an almost naïve disappointment. What could it have been but the sense of arrival at Supreme Power he had never believed he would attain, and so, in his soul, attributed to its grasp, satisfaction of all ambitions, of yearnings too deep for articulation, of that tranquillity, that finality toward which all men aspire and few achieve? This profoundest realist I had ever known, like all men—and whatever his demurrals—possessed a perverse, fantastical duality in his nature which alternately inspired and subverted him, seduced him forward—and forward a little more, promising, dissimulating, promising more still and drawing him on—until the final trip over the abyss into death. He would achieve what he had once believed to be the ultimate, the unobtainable—and it was not the inner transfiguration he had thought it would be.

During the summer, David attempted to more deeply entrench the Imperium by assuaging the crowds with spectacle in the marriage of Alexius II to Agnes-Anna and winning the clergy by extending tax privileges to the monasteries in Macedonia and Thrace and resettling the Patriarch—though still under arrest—a few miles from the city at Pantepopte Monastery. The effect was precisely what a diversion accomplishes: momentary distraction. The real point of interest was Sinope, where Andronikus continued to mass an army around a hard core of Paphlagonian mercenaries, who had scarcely crossed the divide between barbarism and civilization.

Somewhat come to his senses—however inadvised his policies in the long run—David was now acting in a manner to consolidate his power, at least in keeping with a sensible despot's designs. But it was too late. He was no longer acting for himself, but against the emergence of the youngest son of the Sebastocrator Isaac II. As an audience who knows a play by heart impatiently anticipates the entrance of the great actor or actress in the role which incites the rest of the piece, so now all men, with an eye to the east, almost to the point of inactivity, refused to commit themselves lest they be compromised or divert their attention from the master force soon to arrive in the heart of events and move all there-after. (Maupacta once told me actors usually display two tendencies in the scene which leads to the entrance of the premier tragedian or come-dian: either they rise to the occasion themselves and become scintillating or, overwhelmed by their own mediocrity, quite fold.)

When in September a rumor reached us from an undisputed source David was contemplating marriage to Maria-Xenia, quite prepared to proclaim himself Autocrat in a Co-Imperium with her son, and, to that effect, restored Theodosius to the patriarchal throne (the seven-mile trip across the city which conveyed the Bishop from the land gates to St. Michael's Palace was so tumultuous it took an entire day), Andronikus gave the order to march from Sinope 26 September 1181. Now letters and emissaries were smuggled out of the capital at an ever-increasing rate, as power perceptively siphoned off from Constantinople to the Andronikan Praetorium.

The march of little more than three hundred miles took six months. This incredible drawing out of an apparently straightforward journey was part of the Grand Duke's strategy. The slow progress would give the impression of a massive, cumbersome force, which it was at the end, rather than the beginning, when it numbered no more than 25,000. But a slow progress was also a necessity, as decreed by those generals—much the best—now in Andronikus' camp. The army, they insisted, must hew close to the shore, always within sight of the accompanying fleet—only a few warships among a host of cargo vessels and yachts—for protection as well as supplies, especially if Sinope were cut off as a base, an eventuality which never occurred since men such as Branas who foresaw the possibility were not at Constantinople to suggest it. Finally, the Grand Duke was publishing propaganda as he traversed Lesser Asia, in proclamation and in person before every senate which would receive him or city stadium opened to him, often vanishing for days in one direction or another to present his case to noble or peasant alike—leaving the army, of course, at a standstill. The decision these towns and cities or aristocratic domains would make for or against him was an enormous one, and he had no intention of coercion. As he wrote to me after a week's interminable wait at Dorylaeum:

> The Dorylaeans, especially, have every right to be hesitant, having suf-fered the loss of their fortifications after Myriokephalum. They are for

all practical purposes defenseless. I understand that and I am willing to be patient. Those who arrive at our encampment voluntarily are anyway disaffected. They are, of course, welcome, but they are already confessed rebels before they come to me. It's the fearful I want. It's the reactionaries I want, the modest men, the timid, too, and those who yield to the wind and support the Imperium whatever its character. They will be irresolute every step of the way, and to keep them we must measure our pace to theirs. Finally, I am a deliverer, not a rebel. I am a deliverer, especially, if David continues to discredit himself. We must give him the time, as he is sure to accommodate us, to spoil what little prestige, foreign and domestic, remains to the throne. Look at the state of things even now. At Montpellier, William has divorced Theodora's sister and placed her in a convent (I will do my best to rescue her as soon as I have the authority). At Antioch Bohemond has deposed Stephanie and returned to his whore, Sybil, apparently willing to provoke a civil war between himself and that wretch, Aimery, who much to his consternation, no doubt (he hasn't the wit to be amused), finds himself on the side of a Greek.

What most heartened me, however, during those six months, was the return of the superb and vivacious, magisterially self-sufficient—and seemingly ageless—Prince I had first met at Oeneum. All the assurance, the subtlety, the sophistication, and intellect of the man, his natural command among fellow aristocrats and his ability to consort with peasants without the least condescension—no less to express to them his real concern, which, of course, was not devoid of his ambition, but fired it—all seemed to surge in him again. No detail was beyond his attention, nothing was beneath his interest or beyond his amusement. His only real worry was for his sons, Alexander and Julian, who by their presence at Constantinople became hostages against him. He anticipated at any moment having to choose between a surrender—which would be the last of his life—and the lives of the two Grand Dukes.

I remember standing with Theodora on the balcony of the Magistrate's palace at Heraclea, watching Andronikus in the courtyard work at swordsmanship with his youngest son, Christopher. ("You're groaning. That means you're not breathing properly. You're doing something wrong and you'll tire easily. Try again. And again. And again. And again. That's it, there, that's it. . . .") The Queen considered her child with a meditative look and said, "Someday a girl will blush when he enters a room and envy the years she never knew him as a child and grow jealous when someone touches him and feel helpless when he is sad and become frenzied if he is alone. . . ."

It did not take much imagination to realize her point of reference and I attempted to change the subject. Our relationship was a wary one and it seemed likely she would later manifest resentment for opening out to me. But she would not be put off. "Does His Highness speak of me lately?" she said.

I responded that he did, as always, in the most gracious terms.

She smiled. "Is that sycophancy or sympathy, Count, because neither one is acceptable to me."

"Neither, madame, at that. Only the truth."

Her expression was one of indulgent contempt or unassuageable misery—they are similar—as she turned away from me.

By January 1182 the massive encampment was but one hundred miles from Constantinople and the marching followers swelled to 50,000 including private troops brought by complicit Military Grandees. It was at the boundary of the Province of Bithynia—in fact, near its milestone —the one pitched battle was fought against Imperial forces under the halfhearted leadership of the Angeli, father and sons, George, Isaac, and Alexius. Unfortunately they were strategizing against the greatest generals of Manuel's reign. The forces were primarily Latin and fought well, but were completely demoralized when the Greek detachments surrendered themselves to us. The end of the battle was a rout and three quarters of the Imperial army—or what remained of it in its international polyglot form—bathed in their own blood.

With this, the remaining cities of Greek Lesser Asia—save Nicea, Nicomedia, and Philadelphia—declared for Andronikus, along with their trans-Aegean counterparts, save Thessalonikan-dominated Thrace. In the next two months the Grand Duke received emissaries both public and private from as far away as Butrinto, the last great metropolis before Greek land slips into the sea and re-emerges as Corfu. Most of these men were of the nobility or, better still, millionaire mercantilists. They assured Andronikus of their support whatever he proposed to do to rescue the throne from the "dark forces" which were submerging it.

At Constantinople, meanwhile, David drew up an indictment against the Angeli, accusing them of misappropriation of defense funds—an absurdity in the light of their immense wealth—and, more seriously, of heading a pro-Andronikan faction within the city. The truth was rather ahead of itself. On learning of their imminent arrest, the family barricaded Palace Angelus and attempted to drum up support, at which they were less than successful. Shaking his head, on receipt of the news, and laughing, Andronikus said, "Only our Angeli could take a city on the verge of revolution and put it to sleep." But he received Count George and his sons, with all honors, if with a touch of mischief in his eye, when they came to him shortly thereafter. One wonders what he would have thought had he known, while embracing the two brothers, he was greeting the instruments of his own downfall—and his successors.

With the Angeli defected, the Latin mercenaries cut to pieces, there was nothing any longer to hold him back. Andronikus marched past Nicomedia and Nicea, reaching the shores of the Bosporus, and Chalcedon, 2 April. Pointedly, he insisted on making camp upon the heights *above* the city so that our fires in the night would be visible at Constantinople. Learning well from his grandfather's example before the walls of Thessalonika, he pitched more tents and lit more flames than he had men—though their number was ample—so that from the capital, the row upon row of fires against the stars seemed unending, Persian in its limitlessness. (It was rumored about the city, to the Grand Duke's satisfaction, his forces numbered 300,000.)

Catherine Porphyriogeneta: "It was almost sad to watch David those last few weeks. I wasn't certain whether he was emerging from or entering a trance. Perhaps emerging, realizing the depths to which he had reduced us: a state of civil war, division within the family, the humiliation of the crown before the whole world." She sighed, her eyes distant, her manner without its usual vitality. "Perhaps I've become a fatalist, a pessimist, but even though we've survived this time, I suspect our days are numbered. Something between the Comneni and the people has been rent and I don't think it can be mended." She shook her head again, as if to mark the parenthetical nature of the thought, and perhaps its lack of accord with vibrant reality since Andronikus had overtaken the Regency.

"Poor David," she said. "When an intelligent man fails or suffers, he may draw something from his tragedy, most likely and savingly, a sense of compassion or resignation. But when a stupid, prideful man such as my cousin is fallen, he has nothing but his tears and despair—no resources, no lesson, no consolation. David seemed astonished by his fate."

Reduced to the palace guard and a fragment of the Constantinopolitan Garrison, David possessed but one remaining triumph in the Imperial navy, which he took care to man half with Genoans—to assure some portion of loyalty to himself—and half with Greeks and thus allay the mob, whose anti-Latinism had become incendiary in the last month (mostly initiated by mobsters and priests in high anticipation of reward from Andronikus). It is at this point the Grand Duke made his final, wrong decision, and the gates swung back for his cousin. He had hoped to install a Latin commander of the Bosporite Squadron. Instead, yielding—when it no longer mattered—to the anti-Western element of the city, he granted the commission to Juliana Porphyriogeneta's son, Justin Cantacuzenus, who was, in fact, Grand Admiral and, despite his mother's exile, protesting his loyalty to the crown and demanding his prerogatives.

I will never forget the day when the armada, a proud one, sailed into guard formation along the Bosporus. We knew it would block transportation of the army, but the languid majesty of those ships moving into appointed place before the seawalls, their choreography performed beneath a concave, granite sky promising April rains, the golden domes and crosses of the World City gleaming evenly, lustrously in the white, indirect light stilled all talk of strategy and politics. A warm spring breeze lifted, and, indeed, a gentle rain began to fall, but none of us sought cover, standing in the hills above Chalcedon. Thirty years later, I can still recall Andronikus, wrapped in his mantle, his silver hair sopping above his virtually unlined face, swollen and pink with sunburn, his absolutely gray eyes—Paleologus eyes, scarcely a trace of blue—as huge and still as an icon's.

A week after the blockade began, and despite its success—perhaps because of it—all support for the regime vanished. Courtiers, fearful of stepping out into the city, under guard, left it altogether for Chalcedon. Merchants, infuriated by the delay of—and thievery taking place upon —trading ships, which had to be thoroughly searched on departure and disembarkation, added their own agents to the mob. Ordinary citizens waited in long lines at the marketplace for provisions, which, when they arrived at the stalls, were usually quite spoiled. Priests, legally nothing short of treasonous, called for prayers to bring down the Imperial family or at least those Latinophiles among them.

Resigned, David sent the Canon of Holy Wisdom Cathedral, George Xiphilinos, as emissary to Chalcedon.

In return for an end to "this odious rebellion," amnesty would be granted to all Andronikus' followers, without regard to station or crime, and the Grand Duke himself would be raised to the Sebastocracy with full plenipotentiary powers.

"The Sebastocracy, but not the Regency," Andronikus half-asked, half-commented, leaning across the table like a wolf, the gray of his eye in the dull light of the pavilion nearly blending with the white.

"No, Your Highness. No mention of that."

With a loud sigh, the Grand Duke seated himself, then sat back. "He grants. He does not relinquish."

Michael Branas said, "In other words, Father, His Imperial Highness, for all his powers could, conceivably, find himself acting against sanctified authority and liable to accusation of treason and dismissal from the government."

Xiphilinos, one of those men of unimaginative integrity who would serve the devil himself so long as his superiority was attained through proper legal channels, was not about to play the optimist before this shrewd counsel. "I would say it is possible."

Andronikus, drawing his forefinger from lip to chin, looked at me sidewise.

I turned to Xiphilinos. "The terms," I said, "are entirely unacceptable as they stand. You may so inform the Dowager Empress and His Imperial Highness."

Andronikus straightened in his chair. "You may also tell my cousin this. They are the last words I have to say in the matter. The Grand Duke must present himself to me and the members of my Praetorium and render a full account of his actions these past twenty months. Furthermore, I find the Regency as it is now constituted quite inimical to any settlement between us. So long as Her Majesty is Absolute, she may, at any moment, turn to the enemies of the state, both within and without the Empire, as she has previously seemed to do. She is not a very wise woman, but she has a very large heart, if not a good one, and it is open to every wind. She would serve too many people as a rallying point. The

Imperium must be freed of the uses to which her authority might be put, as it has been, most miserably, till now. Her Majesty must then renounce her title and enter a convent for the rest of her life, which—so long as she takes this course—will be a long one, and, otherwise, happy."

There was a stir among those present. We should have been warned by the Grand Duke's manner, but it was too late when he said, "Yes, gentlemen?"

Clearing his throat, obviously still surprised, Michael Branas said, "Your Highness, we had never discussed the deposition of the Empress." Andronikus lifted only his eyes, not his head. His forearms rested along the arms of his chair. "No, we had never discussed it, Michael, but I should think that would have been implicit. If Xenia does not become the tool of the aristocracy, she will become the marching banner of the mob."

Michael said, "The same mob which reviles her now and calls her Foreigner? That's very unlikely."

"It's all *too* likely, Michael. Several weeks ago Nicetas asked me why I delayed in taking Constantinople. David, he said, could only do more damage. I told him I was a deliverer, not a rebel, only so long as David made a botch of things and his fall became a matter of public opinion. I intend to assume the Regency as one enters an empty room. The people must clamor for me in their loneliness. A rebel is beholden to too many factions, whereupon, if he can keep any integrity, he must deny them all and become a tyrant, which I refuse to do, as I refuse to assume responsibility between two fires—final judgment from above or from below."

I said, "Are you *not* responsible to those who acclaim you, Your Highness?"

He was firm. "Yes, indeed. But there is a fine and crucial distinction between providing rule I know to be worthwhile and ruling as a semi-autonomous instrument, answerable to a rioting beast through the agency of their Empress, the roles quite reversed. We all realize the Empire is in a crisis such as it has seldom known and it would be purposeless, if not tragic, to leave the final prerogative to a woman who is culpable if not by design, then indifference. I am sorry for her precisely because she will never comprehend what she has done and why, for that, she must be—as it will seem to her—punished. I am sorry because she no more desires the life of a devout sister than I do that of a monk, and she will probably suffer the cloister terribly. But there is no alternative. It would be bootless for me to attempt to remedy the damage which has been done and allow the Augusta, herself or as tool, to exercise the right of veto. What I must do—the least I would have to do—would be controversial. I shall please few men once the enthusiasm which has raised me is past. And then this woman might easily serve as the symbol of complaint—perhaps among some of you sitting here." He drew a small semicircle with his finger to include us all. "And then where should I be? Where indeed would any man be? Does one among you truly wish to rescue the power of a woman whose sense of duty is so limited, she has served to confuse the Empire with a love token and handed it over to that prenicious debauchee, my cousin?"

Despite Michael's signal to keep silent, I said, "Is Her Majesty criminal because she is, shall we say, not very apt or subtle?"

He seemed to be very understanding, without vindictiveness. "Nicetas, I believe we are all born with the instrument of our destruction in our hands, like a caul. It is only more visible among dynasts. If the poor man is born with the curse of being better than his station allows, the dynast is cursed by the rank which magnifies the consequences of his ineptitude." He looked up at Xiphilinos. "Now go back, Reverend Father, to Blachernae, and tell its occupants it is no longer a question of my acceptance of their terms but their acceptance of mine."

Unexpectedly, he rose and accompanied the Canon to the entrance of the pavilion, whispering to him a last, few words. When he turned back to us he seemed altered beyond recognition.

His sheer physical size had never been so pertinent or pronounced. Merely standing before the entrance, he concealed it and by that seemed to seal it, to entrap us in something malevolent. Indeed it was so. Though we came to him in his role as challenger, his authority potential rather than real, there was now not a shadow of a doubt the autocratic power was his. And though, precisely as possible, we had supported him, suffered for him, worked in his behalf to achieve this moment, because we believed he would use command responsibly, he assumed in that omnipotence, caprice: the alternative with impunity of being grateful for or indifferent to our support, following our advice or rejecting it. Henceforward he was beyond the usual obligations of favor, benignity, apologies, compassion, or explanations. He might display any one or all of these virtues, but it was a matter now of his choice. If we had served to place him in command—and if it were to have any meaning—we were obliged now to retreat from him and submit. Now he was separate, aloof, and, in this, the halo of dominion was perceptible. For the first time since I had met the Grand Duke—perhaps it was the same for the others—I shrank from him physically and intellectually and in a visceral way I cannot even name. I remembered then the tale my grandfather told me of his first sight, as a child, of the colossal, rayed statue of Apollo-Constantine shortly before its destruction at the beginning of the reign of Alexius I. When I asked him his impression, he said, "Fearful, awful. A man who would raise such a statue to himself, or take it in his name, cannot have been much more human than the stuff of which it was composed. For months afterward, I had dreams it leaned down to consume me like Saturn his children. It suggested to me not majesty, which most certainly *is* human—and on occasion, moving—but chaos, because it was meant to intimidate by terror."

Without raising his voice, or exhibiting the least display of emotion—which served only to separate him from us all the more—he said, "It goes without saying, I presume, that ought never to happen again. In every one of you, I value your wisdom and those qualities which give to it temperance and compassion. But argument is for the closet, not a forum before our enemies. As I decide publicly, you follow. If you wish to change my mind even after I have committed myself, you may try—and you might succeed—but privately. I am not to be underminded. Xiphilinos will return to David and inform him there is controversy within our camp, which there most certainly is not. If he is foolish enough, my cousin will attempt still more measures against us on the presumption of our devisiveness. It does not matter now. The way is clear and he can only delay us. He cannot change things. But such counsel is intolerable in the manner in which it was given today. I will not change my mind as to the Augusta's fate. If it comes to that, someone must assume the role of chastiser. Gentlemen, you and I both know, whether we speak of Maria-Xenia or myself, the closer one comes to the throne, the sharper the division between the inner nature and the outward action. If you will not give me this—the lady's abdication—then I can go no further, and since I cannot, in any safety, return to private life, I will leave the Empire to your own devices. You may take that in any way you care to. Good day."

VII

On 23 April the Grand Duke David was seized in his bath by Latin sailors who had infiltrated his personal guard. These men were in the pay of the Archadmiral Justin Cantacuzenus, who had sent a secret message of capitulation to Andronikus the previous day. The son of the Grand Duke Sergius was bound and gagged (with a small green apple) and tossed into a chest where he remained the entire day. In the night, he was transported to St. Michael's Palace. Warned, Maria-Xenia, in distress, in tears, swept up her son and his twelve-year-old wife, and in secret departed for Villa Rufiniana. In fact, if not principle, the Empire was without an emperor. The flood tide had passed to Chalcedon.

Andronikus ordered the Grand Duke to the encampment. On Theodosius' orders, he was driven from the gates of the Patriarchal Palace, naked, seated backward on a donkey, his hair cropped and his head decorated with the entrails of a freshly slaughtered bull. At Buceleon Harbor, he was placed in the hold of a yacht and taken across the Bosporus to Chalcedon. When Andronikus saw his cousin's condition, he was genuinely shocked. "Whose work is this?" he asked the captain, and when told, said, "You return and tell the Patriarch he has the authority to bless—on that we all agree—but not to punish." As he turned away, he said to me in passing, "One presumed priests were about the dignity of man."

David, his nose running, his head covered with garbage, his body marked with blows, in tears of fear and exhaustion (his guards had not allowed him to sleep for two days until, ironically, the intervention of the Patriarch), appeared momentarily hopeful of a private interview with Andronikus or the opportunity to defend himself he had been promised. Nothing of the sort. He was condemned out of hand by a council of nobles, Andronikus sitting silently at its head. (And so condemning himself. By denying his cousin the dynastic right to trial before the Sacred Consistory and consenting to the recommendations of his advisers in plenary session, he gave precedent to the legal machinations of his own downfall only a little more than four years later.) Remanded to Pantepopte Monastery—a very pure revenge for the Patriarch—the

Grand Duke was blinded and tonsured. We shall hear no more of him. A year later he committed suicide.

For three days more Andronikus waited at Chalcedon, leaving the hills and moving into Hieriea Palace. There he received the last delegations from the city, including the chief rabble-rousers and popular priests, who assured him Constantinopolitans would lay themselves down upon the Mesa and make a human carpet for his entry. "On one condition," said their spokesman, a monk whose dark, ingenuous eyes, bulbous nose, great gray beard, obese frame, and deep, almost glutinous, voice suggested a good-natured phlegmatism, quite belied by his errand.

I will never forget Andronikus at the sound of that word, "condition." He had been lowering his eyes, now and then, from the delegation to the refectory table, catching phrases—you could see it—of the documents before him. At that notorious "condition," which rings in my mind like the first knell of a funeral, his glance shot from the table to the mobsters and priests. "On what condition? Be frank," he said. "But I warn you: I can match a highwayman's extortion with a highwayman's violence."

The priest shifted on his feet. "Your Imperial Highness, nothing we would ask of you would be less than in the state's good behalf."

"Indeed. What is it you have to say?"

The priest became bold. "Of the Latin Colony and the Latins, the people desire some revenge."

"A pogrom, you mean."

"We should not call it that."

"Of course not."

Andronikus rose from his chair. He glanced at me, momentarily, indeterminately. The priest said, "Great Prince, as a Christian, I would sooner take the path of forgiveness. But you cannot imagine the depths to which the people's hatred of the Westerners has descended. All men worship the memory of your august cousin, Lord Manuel, but they remain to decry his Latinization of the state. While aliens have waxed fat and drained us of all our resources, mocked our customs, presumed on our generosity, desecrated all we hold dear, we have been patient, tolerating these things as the throne would have them, because we revere the House of Comnenus. Now within the dynasty we find a prince who is truly meant to be a reformer, who is a patriot, and, I tell you, we look to you to rid us of these accursed people. We do not need them. We have never needed them."

Andronikus clasped his hands behind his back. His voice was low and he seemed to be speaking—gently, reasonably—as to a child he wishes to teach, not remonstrate. "Reform is change, not havoc, Father."

The priest nodded. "Perhaps. But we've learned well from the Latins, haven't we? The strong arm triumphs. Only the bully endures. I quote Plato: 'The more a child observes violence, the more likely he is to use it.' And now, till now, despite all, we have been pacific."

"And I will quote you back St. Jerome, and let you put the two together. 'Virginity can be lost by a thought.' If it has reached this state, then our people long ago ceased to be pacific. What you do not seem to realize, Father, is that we do, indeed, need the Latins. Surely not as the Empress Regent would have it, by inclination, or as the Grand Duke David preferred it—by expediency—but need them we do. Our fortune is in trade, and, in some degree, our sea power depends upon them. The people, moreover, of whom you speak—the residents of the Latin Quarter—are practically as Greek as ourselves. The Latins you would properly be done with—in the court and the administration—the real culprits—shall, believe me, face my justice."

"Your Highness, this may be, but the people cannot or will not distinguish between one Latin and another. They are alike as pines. They are *one* in the common mind and we want no more of them."

The previous year Andronikus had commented to me as how he marveled at the loyalty given a sovereign. Unable to see beyond the mystique of heavenly appointed kingship which he rejected, he could not imagine—save in the most literal terms of vested interest—why men would sacrifice their lives for the smile of their king or dedicate their lives, selflessly, to his service. When, the following year, he reached the throne, he carried that doubt with him and suspected every man's motive rather than accept their loyalty and adoration to him as the symbol and reposit—whatever he believed himself—of all earthly power and intercessor with the unseen. Now that blind eye to magic, to which men, whose intelligence he respected, readily submitted, compelled him to a decision of tragic dimensions: he allowed the mob free rein against the Latins.

Whatever his doubts, he had accepted the loyalty of the aristocrats, who were the first barrier to the Regency. In truth they were the only barrier and he had surpassed it without drawing a drop of blood. It has remained my conviction he could have drawn on the credit of his legend among the people—a legend more influential than the sacerdotal nature of the Imperium—and entered Constantinople with the same spotlessness of his march across Lesser Asia. He believed otherwise. This champion of the oppressed reasoned thus: "The aristocrats will remain faithful to their oaths because they are gentlemen and they respect their word in God's name. They take him seriously, and well they should as the evidence of his blessing is so tangible. But among the poor, among the majority of Constantinopolitan citizenry, there is no such obligation to honor or to be grateful to a heaven which curses every prayer they offer up and blesses the rich man's sin. They have been brutalized by their lives and they must be accorded the same wariness given any brainless, dangerous beast capable of frenzy."

To my way of thinking, that meeting at Hieriea was his last opportunity to give a resounding no to the wishes of the mob and thus nip in the bud its dangerous reassertion. You will never convince me an appearance in the streets—street by street if necessary (and he was not, as Manuel might have been, beyond such an action)—mounted on his huge stallion, the force of his eloquence raised to the occasion, could not have dissuaded these people of their anti-Latinism. Had he told them what he knew—that the most notorious millionaires and aristocratic émigrés such as Count Sclavo and Alexander of Conversano had taken ship to Sicily with John Sergius' son, the Grand Duke Peter, the moment his uncle, David, had been captured—had he explained the harmlessness, indeed the benefits of the Genoan and Pisan merchants at Byzantium, as he explained these points to the Hieriea delegation, he could have won Constantinople, I think, as he had won the aristocracy.

Instead, so near to his goals, fearing, at the last moment, the loss of power he had so long desired, he became convinced the dignity and decency, the capability of reason, the infinite educability he had posited in all men, was a fiction, or at least temporarily suspended at so torturous a moment in time. He convinced himself he could enter Constantinople only over the bodies of the Latin nationals. Whether vanity, calculation, or both, he could not bring himself to enter the city as an invader. He forgot, then, the accession of the grandfather he so much admired. Two weeks later and too late, Alexius occurred to him.

"My great-grandmother, Anna Dalassena, made my grandfather and all his generals eat only bread and water and attend Divine Liturgy for forty days after their entry, for the violence they had done the city and the people. Point was, it was initiated and atoned for by those in power who remained in power. I had not even war to make to gain the city, but rather to avert it. And if I could not do so, then, as my grandfather, I should have met its violence with my own, kept it the perquisite of the crown. Now it is loose, like an unleashed demon among the people, entering one body and then another and I don't know where it will end or whom it will invade next. It was a mistake on my part, a ghastly mistake."

Like the parallel lines which join at infinity, there is a point, apparently, where those of the highest and lowest motivations meet. The priests incited the crowds in the churches and church squares, and the rabble-rousers directed them thither to the Latin Quarter. What followed was the most indelible blot in our history, and like all pogroms effected for many reasons.

Among the poor and oppressed, who are not always the rabble but usually a tool, it was the explosion of the despair of their lives, the momentary revenge in violence for the misery in which they lived and which they were promised until death. In the smashing of things, beautiful things, of human lives, we take a short, sharp, orgasmic pleasure as we deny apostrophically all that has been denied us. In breaking beauty we destroy the symmetry which has mocked the disorder of our own lives. Among the priests it was nothing less than the physical eruption of the spiritual humiliation they had endured since the schism of 1054. Among the mobsters, the rabble-rousers, theirs was personal satisfaction in the sense of power, the power to move vast crowds, the depraved glee in the affliction of pain, and, quite simply, the loot gained in consented lawlessness.

And so, on a sweltering day in May, scores of thousands of Greeks poured into the unwarned and defenseless Latin Quarter. The first victims were those in the streets, no doubt bewildered by the oncoming crowds. They were torn apart, dismembered so violently and swiftly, as one eyewitness—exaggerating only a little—told me, "their hearts, tossed in the gutter, were still beating." Had any one of these doomed pedestrians in some last instant of life asked themselves, "Why me?" they might have taken solace—as any dying man in the knowledge the end of the world would follow his own demise—that sixty thousand more compatriots, as indiscriminately slaughtered, would follow them. For three days this hideous, inexcusable destruction went on. In the end, it was not suspended by a higher authority—there was none, save possibly the Patriarch, who had not the troops—but simply died of its own satiated engorging.

Every house was entered, its inhabitants murdered, its treasures yielded up, and no one spared, one can be sure, for volunteering their treasure in place of their lives. There is a maniacal violence beyond the corruption of bribery. Pregnant women were beheaded, the fetuses torn from their womb and besplattered atop Roman Catholic altars. Pope Alexander's permanent emissary was taken in his mansion, trussed, dragged down the stairwell, and decapitated in the street, his head tied to the tail of a terrified dog. The sanctuary of Latin churches was not respected. They were burned to the ground, their shrieking parishioners within. At the Hospital of the Knights of St. John—the largest in Constantinople (and perhaps the finest)—the sick were murdered in their beds. The old, the lame, women of all ages and description were not spared. The Latin cemetery was desecrated, the dead exhumed and abused.

It has been a point of the new Latin Imperium at Constantinople to keep accessible in the archives the reports of the commissioners whom Andronikus dispatched to record the damage through their own eyes and the reports of witnesses. (Naturally, when the massacre was ended, not a man would confess to his participation. The beasts had vanished into thin air, as, after a fact, it may have been true. Demons, expended, do leave the body.) One assumes the present government wishes to justify its own atrocities, twenty-two years later. Without attempting to exculpate my fellow citizens I must remind the reader those blood-curdling descriptions were compiled by a Greek government, accusing itself, and preparatory to making some sort of compensation. No such log of mortality and damage was initiated by the Latins, who sacked in its entirety the largest city in the world and slaughtered perhaps ten times their number killed in 1182.

I visited the Quarter with Theodore Maurozomes, Duke Michael Branas, and his young son, Alexius, two days after the riots had ended. There is nothing more shocking, more violent than the evidence of violence which has occurred. Imagination can manifest a greater horror than actual witness. Imagination replaces the glass in its casements and smashes it back into the street. Imagination crushes that bloody iron truncheon in someone's skull and tosses it aside again. (Why? Had the killer suddenly realized his crime?) Imagination exerts itself wondering at the caresses that lopped-off hand may have given. Imagination places the bloody doll by the child, murders the child, tosses the doll in the air, and returns it to earth to bathe in the blood of its mistress. Imagination resurrects the cadavers of horses and observes again their snorting, hysterical, akimbo deaths. Imagination draws up again the walls and brings them down again on a thousand heads, such vulnerable heads, battered by brick and marble. Imagination withdraws the stench of corpses, softens the charred skin, grows hair on the bodies burned in a church, then burns the church again—and once again, the stench of incinerating epidermis, the sickening inflammation of hair. Imagination replaces doors torn from their hinges, slams them again with a battering ram—some of them human—and again the gaping entrances through which a rush of brutes—or worse, maddened women and children—pass, from which emit the cries of the slaughtered, mothers and maids, fathers and their young sons, infants tossed from windows, grandparents dismembered, servants cut down. Imagination within incurs a pain against such monstrousness, a pain so great and inescapable as to render compassion meaningless. And when one suspects compassion is for nothing, then the only alternative is despair for oneself and one's fellow men.

We rode through those ruined, those devastated, streets, speechless, ashamed. The knowledge that at the same moment those Latins who had got to harbors and not suffered the last ill-luck to die on fired ships, but escaped, were now, eye for eye, committing the same atrocities—sacking, killing, raping—in coastal towns, in monastery and convent alike, along the Marmora and the Aegean—could not allay this awful indictment of our own sin and the unhappiness born of it. Victim—oppressor —victim again—oppressor again—all lost, nothing learned, only more inhumanity and still more.

Along one street, I remember, a young woman's corpse lay by the door of a building. Someone had been moved enough to remove a lovely white silk shawl, discreetly bordered in gold, and, with it, cover the poor maid's face and the upper portion of her body, fastening the delicate fabric in her clasped hands. (Who had done it? Her rapist? That is one story. A Greek woman suddenly shocked from her harridan's dance? That is another. A member of her family, a friend—a Greek friend who recognized her? A Latin stranger? That is still another. Perhaps the shawl was not even her own. And that is still another story.) Now, as the wind rose—harbinger of the rains which broke the heat spell—the scarf started, as if to life, undulated, lifted, undulated, lifted again, settled, undulated, lifted and fluttered, now without rest, like the girl's own ghost, almost parallel above her body. Her child's lovely, amazed face, with its ice-blue staring eyes was revealed, accusatory in its lack of accusation. (*"Was it to this I was born but a short while ago? I was young. What world was worth my death?"*)

I dismounted. Michael warned me, "Nicetas, the plague." I went up to the corpse and the sickly sweet smell was perceptible. I knelt and stretched forth my arms, which, for a moment, were lost in the billowing silk. I caught it and secured it beneath the back of her head. (That terrible limpness when we are used to the miraculous plasticity and self-assertion of another's musculature.) I left her there. There was nothing more I could do or need do. The undertakers' wagons had been in and out of the city all the previous two days—indeed those carts were its major traffic—carrying victims past their killers and beyond the walls to the mass graves at Hebdomen. I returned to my horse. (*"Wait, don't leave me. I had a name, a story to tell, a whole life. I had a name. Don't leave me among the anonymous. Please don't leave me. I had a name."*)

Though I had not approved of bringing along with us the young Duke Branas, his youth and extraordinary golden beauty seemed to have arrived like a benediction, physical perfection as hope amidst this heart-rending devastation. Many poor wretches came up to his horse—not his father's, nor mine, nor Theodore's. Some merely stood before him, stunned, others kissed his hand and wept. At a nod from his father Alexius smiled kindly—his eyes benign as those of his great-grandfather, John Augustus—embarrassed, scarcely aware what he was about. But that, perhaps, was as it should be. All angels must be imperturbable, the promise of something above earthly miseries.

At one house, we came upon a sizable crowd surrounding a young Latin, in tears, battered from one man to the next, while he pleaded he was only a troubadour, as was perfectly evident in his smashed guitar, an instrument lately come from Spain and enchanting in its sound and versatility. Of course, he was neither heeded nor absolved. I remember in heavily accented Greek, the cry, "Someone. Please. Help me. Have pity."

With Rachel's child, wrapped in her white silk shawl, still fresh in my mind, I lost any sense of the lethal stupidity of what I was doing (I can still feel the tumultuous pumping of blood to either side of my eyes). I was all too aware I might be set upon myself, but at the sight of that poor young fellow's desperation, it seemed to me to make little difference, for it was worth little to survive in a world of such heartbreak and malice.

I spurred my horse through the crowd—with the petty hope her hooves would cut someone—and heard Michael warn me again, then his own horse follow. "That's enough!" I shouted. "That will be quite enough."

There were catcalls and threats and questions thrown at us like stones as to our identity and presumption. Then Michael announced himself and that was quite enough indeed—our most illustrious general and the widower of the Grand Duchess Persephone.

The troubadour ran to my horse and clutched my leg. Tears, mucus, and blood covered his face and his thick black hair was matted by sweat and rainwater to his head. "Please," he said, "please, my lord, save me."

I asked him if he was badly hurt. He said he wasn't. I told him to mount up behind me. As my mare swung this way and that attempting to balance the increased weight, I began to shout, "Fine citizens of this great city you are," when Michael, who knew men as I knew Plato, said, "Senator, that's enough."

We arrived at Hieriea in the evening where servants and "courtiers" were in fear for their lives. The reason was obvious the moment one entered the cathedral-like entry. From behind the gold, silver, and ivory doors of the refectory, which Andronikus had made his office, was the sound of argument between himself and Queen Theodora. No one could escape their words.

Theodora: "You did nothing, nothing. You could have sent in the army."

Andronikus: "The army would have been slaughtered by the people."

Theodora: "But not before disassociating your name and purpose from those animals who presume to call themselves Greeks. *That* is what you have left rule. Not a city but a wolf-pit."

Andronikus: "Think what you will, but as my conscience you are a lit-

tle askew. Not that I failed to send in the guards, but that I did not altogether prevent the riot."

Theodora: "What—*possessed*—you?" Her voice was ours and the
question burned within our hearts and minds, too dangerous to be answered to anyone's satisfaction at a moment when we presumed to support its speaker for the Regency. "You're a poor ruler who loves men's
lives so little, or if you do, love men as men love fire—at a distance, un-
scorched."

Michael Branas had the presence at that moment to dismiss everyone
from the great hall.

I did not meet with the Grand Duke until later in the night, and as
I sat across from him during our interview while I reported to him what
I had seen in the city, it seemed to me, with his pale hair and high
cheekbones and deep blue velvet robe, he was indeed like some stark
angel of death. When we were finished, I accompanied him from the
refectory to the great stairwell. He said, "I should like to meet the fellow you saved. I should like to talk to him." He sighed deeply. "I wish
there were someone to whom I could apologize." He smiled ruefully.
"But then if there were, I'd too easily accept what I've done and forget
its lesson."

The Queen was coming down the stairs to meet us. The Grand Duke
gave her the look of coldest hatred I had ever seen, and started up the
stairs passing her without recognition.

Holding the marble banister, she stared at me, and in a hoarse voice
said, "I asked him to go into the city, secretly. I wanted him to see what
was accomplished in his name." Andronikus was still ascending. "He
wouldn't. He is keeping himself from the evidence which would lead
him to doubt his decisions. If he does not doubt, he will never feel guilt
—and that is the beginning of despotism."

The Grand Duke had reached the first landing, at which the stairwell diverged. "Madame," he called. She continued to hold my glance,
in tears. As gently as possible, almost in echo of Andronikus' command,
I said, "Madame." She turned, drew her skirts to one side, and wearily
trudged the steps to her lover.

Four days after the massacre, Theodosius crossed to Chalcedon to
make his submission. Michael Gabras called it "a meeting of the titans,"
as well it may have been—and not only because both men were of such
enormous size. It was the confrontation of two diametrically opposed

powers of unquestioned authority and personal self-confidence. On the one side, the Patriarch, representing aristocratic privilege, traditional values, and the Church, a good man, compassionate in his fashion, and of real integrity, but with an arrogant blood of position born and position attained. On the other, the grandson of Alexius I, born of the purple—and for that capable of dispensing with what he had always possessed—representing as best the most perceptive men could sense it, something new as the newborn child or, perhaps, as old as Christian philanthrophy and Greek democracy though it was to be presented in the guise of Persian autocracy, a profane superman, an atheist and logician, sublime in his contradictions, who aspired to the throne—or its power—by right as a dynast, yet rejected the concept of aristocracy, who believed in the civil rights of all men and the inferiority of most to himself.

On exchanging the Kiss of Peace, the Patriarch said, "I have only known of your ways by rumor, and now I see clearly and am certain—it is all too true."

Andronikus, appreciating the double entendre, smiled and replied, "Behold the deep Armenian."

I have reconstructed the salience of their interview from my own memories and the minutes which were on deposit in the Imperial Archives, constituting the first Imperial State Papers in Andronikus' name.

The Patriarch began by saying, "A great wrong has been done against the Latins these last days, Your Highness."

Andronikus had expected this. "Unfortunately true, Your Holiness. And could I but find the priests who helped to instigate it, I would certainly present them to your ecclesiastical court, as I am certain you would wish to subject them to your own rigorous justice." He smiled charmingly. It was the sort of banter both men detested—quite as thoroughly as they detested, or, in the least, were wary of, one another—but it was their only means of communication. Had they been frank, the breach would have opened between them at once. For the good of the state, this could not be allowed to happen.

Andronikus said, "Obviously your priests have a humor for havoc as the devil amidst dissent."

To which Theodosius, nothing daunted, replied, "Oh, I beg Your Highness, the devil abhors true dissent which seeks to rectify evil and reassure integrity. Those who criticize desire the ideal rather than possess it. Perfect loyalty is perfect docility, or don't you agree?"

"Considering my past life, I could hardly disagree. Without Your Holiness' own exquisite antipathy, I should hardly have been reckoned as a legitimate critic."

The Patriarch chose to overlook his participation in the Grand Duke's religious interdiction. Instead he said, "There is very little doubt you are an exceptional man, Your Highness. Prove worthy of what distinguishes you best. But I would remind you: The people expect a Messiah."

"They shall have a reformer."

The Patriarch was insistent. "Allow me to finish, if you will, Your Highness. The people want a deliverer from the evil and the chaos they have endured. A reformer is precisely what they do not want. They want rest."

Andronikus pointedly changed the subject. "On behalf of the people, Your Eminence, I wish to thank you for your efforts these last months in protection and tutelage of His Imperial Majesty."

To this Theodosius would not, or could not, reply. His lips worked, but he did not speak, and for a moment the reality of blazing hatred occurred between the two men. Andronikus turned away. The Patriarch said, "And now I shall pray for him as among the dead."

The Grand Duke's eyes met Theodosius' with the intense stare we occasionally grant those discussing something of unusual interest. In one such as Andronikus, the logic behind the glance was something else entirely: the almost too-well-mannered response of one born to the courtesy of royalty—given alike, high and low—who is nonplussed by effrontery. The silence which seems to shrivel and the glance which indeed seems unseeing is, in fact, the paralysis of embarrassment.

Even the Grand Duke Alexander was astonished enough to be roused from his good nature to say coldly, "My Lord Patriarch, you exceed yourself."

The Patriarch bowed. "I crave pardon if I have offended Your Highness"—but to whom was he speaking? His next words, without doubt, were addressed to Andronikus: "If I have, as Your Highness says, been an effective caretaker of the Imperium"—he seemed to dismiss the double-edged flattery as beneath his notice: it was there in his indifferent tone of voice—"that is all very well. I now deliver it unto you to do with as you best see fit, and for the rest, I wash my hands of it."

Before entering the city, Andronikus traveled to Rufiniana where the Dowager Empress and the as yet uncrowned young Emperor and Empress were residing. I was present among the Grand Duke's retinue and I am obliged to say my feelings were, to say the least, ambivalent. He accorded every respect to that infuriating august boy, Alexius (whom he described as "a really bad dog, biting whatever gets in his way"). Filled by her ladies with tales of a deliciously chilling caste (seemingly realized in this giant before her) Agnes-Anna nevertheless slammed the armrest of her chair and said, "This is my throne and you shall not have it!" Andronikus, amused—or pretending to be amused—said, "So it is, ma'am, and so it shall remain." But when he turned to the ravishing Dowager Empress—who shrank back perceptibly—he said, "You are still here, madame. Why are you here?"

She smiled nervously, like a child, and like a child, never took her eyes from him. He said, "My conditions were that you should take the veil. Is that not what you intend to do?"

She could not speak. She was terrified. It is not difficult to surmise the nature of her fear. All her life she had depended upon her great beauty, whether by assault or withdrawal, in the pursuit of anything she wished. The inviolability of her charms were a shield against punishment. She had seemed to possess all men by allowing them to believe they possessed her. Yet here she was confronted by a prince whose eye for women was infamous and yet before her he was insensible. She may as well have been plain as an egg or another man. He was unmoved. In the most literal sense, she was weaponless, for she had never the aptitude or the inclination to truly control men by knowing them. She was the true flirt—introverted, improvident—who had squandered her beauty rather than used it, very much its victim rather than its mistress. Very tentatively, with a pathetic hesitation, she said, "It has been many years, Andronikus."

He said, "Madame, I asked you why you are here, or what, then, are your plans?"

Barely audible she said, "To best benefit—"

"Please speak up," he interrupted.

"To best benefit the state in whatever I do," she said. It was too much of an exertion. She seemed about to break.

He said, "I wish by your example, Maria, you had followed that wisdom from the beginning."

At the mention of her Latin name—as he had always known her—they both winced and something flew between them, almost imperceptible, almost clement—like the brief abeyance, in a momentary zephyr, of cold winds in the late winter. Rather than succumb, Andronikus turned to the Grand Chamberlain, the eunuch Nicephorus, a slender giant, and said, "You will prepare Their Majesties' train to return with me to Constantinople. The Dowager Empress will remain at Rufiniana until further notice. That is all." He turned on his heel and left.

I was about to follow him when Maria-Xenia called me back. She offered me her hand, an unusual honor, or explicit of her desperation and need to flatter. "Count," she said, "what will become of me?"

"Your Majesty, I cannot tell you with any certainty. Perhaps if you are sincere in your wishes for the state, you would indeed do well to take the veil."

She broke then and closed her eyes. From beneath the lids perfect little tears burst at either corner. She pressed the tips of her slender fingers against her lips. I was no comfort to her. She wanted the impossible. She wanted indulgence, forgiveness, as she had always been forgiven. Her voice an animal squeak as she wept, she made a vague gesture of dismissal and said, "Yes, yes, you may go."

In the courtyard of Rufiniana, as I mounted up, obviously affected, one of the Grand Duke's aides moved to my side. "His Imperial Highness wishes to speak with you."

I went up to the Grand Duke and stood beside his horse as he towered above me. His head nearly blocked the sun and his face was in umbra. I had to shield my eyes and even then I could not discern his expression. I heard only the impersonality of his voice. "What did she say to you?" It was a command, not a question.

I knew him well enough not to prevaricate. "What any woman would in her position, Your Highness. She asked what will become of her. I told her—in everyone's interest, including her own—she ought best to take the veil."

"Good," he said, "very good."

He moved off and I returned to my horse. I knew—but he was beyond confirming it for me—that his resentment of Maria-Xenia was not entirely political and disinterested. Though founded in her acts as a political being, his reaction had become one of intense personal antipathy. She had, after all, inherited an empire which, if not entirely sanguine at her husband's death, was, in some degree, still viable. A strong, responsible hand at the source of power would have been the beneficiary, moreover, of the late Emperor's enormous international prestige. But the Empress dallied and rather than resort to competent men, gave over the Commonwealth, as victim, to her incompetent lover. Had Andronikus assumed the Regency twenty-one months before, his task would have been difficult enough. Now, through Xenia's agency it was virtually insuperable. All his hopes of reconstructing Byzantine society were delayed—and possibly precluded—by the greater imperative of first restoring the integrity of the state. Most ironically, in that restoration, he required the assistance and support of the class he wished to dissolve even sooner than disenfranchising the mob. His disappointment was bitter. He was sixty years old, at an age when each day of his life was gratuitous rather than taken for granted. In appearance, in vigor, in presence of mind, he might deny the apparent progress of his mortality, but it was relentless. He knew it. And he had little time to waste. His lack of mercy shown the Empress is unfortunate, but it is also understandable. She represented the final, mean turn against him in a life filled with the antagonism of the invisible.

That day at Rufiniana was the last time I saw the Augusta: her slender manicured fingers against her lips, shifted a little sidewise in her chair, her eyes brimming with tears, a frown upon her face—defenseless, bereft.

He entered Constantinople the following day, one, I trust, such as few men know in their lifetimes. That day, the little Emperor at his side, to all intents ignored, the Grand Duke came as close to godhead as a mortal might dare.

As the bronze trumpets and pummeled drums announced the Emperor's entry through the Golden Gate—the signal for Andronikus' formal return to the city of his birth—the roar of a million throats—inhuman in its totality—went up along the Via Triumphalis. Every Regiment of the Guard, the Constantinopolitan Garrison, and all available mercenaries had been called up to keep order, but they were scarcely expected to be sufficient. Mobsters, filled with officious self-importance, were also employed, a good deal more brutal—and perhaps effective—against the overexcited populace. The Grand Duke was greeted as the Patriarch had foretold: as a Messiah.

There was, or so men believed, not a moment of his life, from lovemaking to politics, which they did not know. He was the people's in ways Manuel—regal, venerable, aloof—could never be. Of the late Emperor's private life there had been only gossip. Of Andronikus', men sang songs. He was, indeed, Proteus, Man as Actor, before the Theater of the World. Had he not laughed delightedly when, but a week ago, a troop of students from the university sailed to Chalcedon at their own expense and, as name-day gift, serenaded him with a lengthy musical discourse which vividly detailed his philandering? Who would have dared—or desired (that's the point)—to confront Manuel's insuperable dignity with such mischief? Not that Andronikus was common. Rather he was stupendous, humanity magnified, all actions transfigured not by his station, but his very person.

He looked neither left nor right. If he did not disdain the cheers he did not recognize them either. His eyes were open on infinity, and his whole imperturbable presence—gigantic, majestic—seemed to say: "Yes, this is as it should be. You are mine and I am yours and we cannot exist without one another. I am your magic and you are my fulfillment. I am your hope and you are the credence of my ambition. I come to you as lover to the beloved. Without you I am lost; without me you are empty. Therefore as beloved to lover, you must accept me without question as you accept yourself, for I am what you would wish to be, the conjuration of your inmost soul. If you reject me, you reject your profoundest self. You *must* love me because I am yourself, the best that is within yourself. Raise me and you raise yourself."

At Cathedral of the Almighty, he dismounted. I noticed his eyes had a curious distant look and his mouth was set as he mounted the steps. The stop was unexpected, but he had decided on the visit to Manuel's tomb at the last moment. He followed his cousin's son, who looked patently bored, through the doors. When the boy turned and said something to him, I read clearly on the Regent's lips the words *Behave yourself.* The child stared up at his second cousin in amazement (that same look which, with others, promptly led into a snarl). He blinked. The Grand Duke took his hand and they descended into the crypt, where there was cool and dark and some diminution of the tumult. To our amazement, Andronikus sank to his knees before the porphyry sarcophagus. He remained in that position a good five minutes, his fingers intertwined at his chest, his head a little to one side, but unbent. It was not a tribute of prayer, but reverie. When he arose and turned, his eyes were moist. When he left the cathedral for the sunlight and the cheers, his face screwed up in a look of real pain as though he had been assaulted.

VIII

The young Emperor and Empress were installed with their suites at Blachernae. The Grand Chamberlain was ordered, in whatever circumstances possible, to prepare coronation ceremonies for Pentecostal Sunday, 16 May.

Andronikus, meanwhile, lived between the Irene Villa at Philopation and St. Michael's Palace. He could have had any apartments at any number of Imperial mansions, but it no longer mattered to him where he slept (though St. Michael's was frankly chosen with the object of keeping the Patriarch under his eye). As to Philopation, the Grand Duke threw open its miraculous beauty to the people—"Let them see what their labor and taxes have wrought"—and, sad to say, it quickly became a shambles. Golden Imperial eagles were ripped from posts—and the posts taken away, too, as they were also gold. Superb marble walks were defaced and ancient statuary damaged. The fountains of precious metal and stone, the waterfalls with their quartz and semiprecious boulders, were demolished by souvenir hunters and canny jewelers eager to reshape their mementos rather to their own profit. Flower beds were trampled, rare blooms plucked up, pavilions used as urinals, faience-lined ponds polluted with garbage and detritus, their fish caught and eaten or left to die in the open air, tame deer, peacocks, swans, the gentle animals of the Imperial menagerie, slaughtered and roasted or left to rot.*

---

* I must mention an episode which particularly distressed Andronikus. Ten days after the gates of Philopation were opened, a crowd, as usual, gathered before the Irene Villa hoping for an appearance of the Regent. It was late afternoon and the Varangians began to light the torches and braziers surrounding the lovely little palace. According to reports, one hysteric or another suddenly proclaimed the Regent would not appear because he was ill as a result of the spells worked up by an old beggar, now present, who had slept in the park since it was given to the public. At once, a young woman agreed that, yes, she had seen the crone in the night sticking pins into a wax image of the Grand Duke. The poor old fellow was set upon and before enough Varangians had been collected to save him, set afire. He burned quickly and when the lot of us arrived on the balcony to learn the origin of the commotion, I saw what I have long since hoped to forget: within a gigantic egg of flame, the reaching, agonized, still-standing, charred corpse of the old man before it fell over dead. Andronikus commanded the park closed the following day.

If May began tumultuously it ended in magnificent order. As commanded, the Imperial domestic staff accomplished its magic and in the short space of two weeks, to the last detail, prepared a coronation ceremony which, if now and then, hilariously displayed the effect of under-rehearsal—and something less than the intimidating perfection of splendor of Manuel's day—nevertheless recalled the genius of Greeks for ceremony. After the crowning, like Christopher carrying Christ across the Cydnus, Andronikus hefted the understandably stunned Alexius II, by Grace of God, Emperor, Augustus, Basileus, and Autocrat of the Romans, onto his right shoulder and transported him thus into the Augusteum.†

Nine days after the coronation, the son of the Grand Duchess Elizabeth, who had married Henry Jasomirgott, Leopold, Duke of Austria, on his way to the Holy Land, arrived in Constantinople, expressly to visit his Greek Imperial relatives. As the grandson of the Grand Duke Sergius, hence nephew to John Sergius and David, he was somewhat abashed his Comnenus blood flowed from a disgraced branch of the family. But Andronikus at once put him at his ease, reminding the young man of his affection for Elizabeth and suggesting "your uncles swallowed most of the brine at birth, leaving your aunts the sweeter for it," which is hardly how one would describe Andronikus' first great mistress, Eudocia, or the "family Aphrodite," Constantia. No longer the social lion of his youth, the Grand Duke scarcely had the inclination for entertainments, but he extended himself as host and spent lavishly in Leopold's honor. He took this visit quite seriously, considering it a first step in rebuilding the European reputation of the Byzantine Empire.

The Duke left Constantinople, crossing into Lesser Asia, in the company of Andrew Lapardas and a mixed army of mercenaries and conscriptees, which parted from him at Nicea and turned southward toward Philadelphia where Manuel's nephew, Prince John Vatatzes, son of Eudocia Porphyriogeneta—who had declared for Catherine during the rebellion of February—had declared against Andronikus on assumption of the Regency.

Unfortunately for Vatatzes, he became ill during Lapardas' siege.

---

† Later that same week, when His Majesty, alternately intimidated and charmed by the Grand Duke, suggested meeting his contemporary, Prince Christopher, Andronikus refused out of hand, commenting to Michael Branas he would sooner set his son in a nest of vipers than the Emperor's suite. N.A.

Strategizing from a hilltop, which always carries the danger of flatten-
ing the aspect of the terrain, he left his sometimes incomprehensible directions to be executed by his sons. Death got to him before defeat and
the Philadelphians, either sensing their isolation or unwilling to defend
the Vatatzes' family prejudices in the euphoric wave of sentiment
sweeping the Empire in Andronikus' behalf, capitulated to the dead
Prince's cousin. The sons were forced to flee to Iconium, where Arslan
—of no mind to offend the new Regent, whose nature he knew well—
rather than provide sanctuary, merely gave the brothers money and an
escort to the coast, suggesting they proceed to a "safer" haven at Sicily.
A storm forced their ship into harbor at Crete, where they were taken
ashore by orders of the Governor and thereupon extradited to Constantinople. Andronikus ordered the brothers blinded without further
review of their motives, after which they would be allowed their usual
position and possessions and complete freedom of movement.

The Imperial family was horrified by this brusque justice. When the
very conqueror of the condemned men, Lapardas himself, remonstrated
with the Regent at a meeting of the Sacred Consistory, Andronikus asked
him in that curiously subdued manner which had been his since the assumption, "What would you have me do, Andrew? They are my kin as
well as yours. Name their punishment. But remember this: Under
David's Regency they scarcely murmured their disapproval. Ask yourself why. Perhaps because their father was John Sergius' creature? That
may be. Or they would divide the dynasty and claim it, through kinship,
for themselves? Or simply that they feared the consequences of their
ineptitude and complicity and acted preemptively against the measures
I would take against them, which I hasten to remind you, would have
been not much more than removal from office. Finally, one is obliged
to point out they were contesting the throne in contesting me."

Lapardas' temper, which concealed his wisdom as a flame may conceal the treasure it burns, got the better of him. "They were contesting
you, Andronikus, and you know it, as Regent. Don't hide behind the
Emperor's skirts."

Still patient, the Grand Duke continued, "Let me put it this way. All
of you would do well to listen. Any man who strikes against me in these
first months, above all, and quite convinced of his own sincerity—"

"As all rebels are," Lapardas retorted.

Andronikus did not acknowledge him: "—is basing his disapproval on my reputation—and its attendant exaggerations—rather than fact. What I was forced to do and to be is no measure by which to predict my conduct as Regent. Any man who presumes to do so—whoever he is, whether Theodosius the Boriodite or John Vatatzes—is either bigoted or ambitious, or too stupid to be accountable. Believe me, I have suffered enough pain, myself, as all of you well know, to be a great deal more sensitive to it than any of you dare imagine. Yes, it is a terrible thing to blind a man, to strike the light from his eyes forever. But sooner that than kill him. Death is the end of everything. Blindness is not. It may, for all that, remove a man from the vanity of worldliness which, of course, is not really our concern, though we have the example of my grandfather's cousin, Constantius Porphyriogenetus Diogenes. Yes, granted, a life whole is preferable to one by halves, which is a life without choice, but sooner the choice within a constricted freedom than none and no life at all. I am prepared to take responsibility for my justice, but I remind you, I would be remiss if I did not demand it. You cannot reason with frenzied men in dire times. You teach by example. If I did not insist upon penalty for the Vatatzes, others would follow their insolent path. I am, gentlemen, more certain of my sincerity and my logic than you may be of your own, and of the course I must follow. I intend to stay the dissolution which threatens us, and I will not tolerate, not for a moment, not in the least, the degree of any man's panic—in whatever guise—as ambition, corruption, or for that matter treason with the best will in the world. The task before you and me is quite enough without our acting the policemen as well. I did not assume the Regency to loot the Empire or satisfy my vanity, as other men will speak of me while attempting to remove me and gain precisely for themselves the outward satisfaction of their greed or self-esteem. Believe me, I will ruthlessly distinguish between personal affection and political consequence in the suppression of any defiance against my will."

The silence in which his soliloquy had been begun was merely respectful. That which greeted its last words positively cracked, as men crossing carpets on a winter day will give off sparks. Some of those nobles present were indeed cowed or convinced by his words. If they remained troubled, nevertheless, one could sympathize with them, without in any manner desiring the resolve of their dilemma.

Among certain members of the Consistory, "each of as many minds,"

Michael Branas once said, "as the double-headed eagle," even so early, you could see the complicit glance, as if to say: Now what shall we do? They would not await Andronikus' rejuvenation of the Empire, presuming it could be accomplished. They would cloak their avarice in a mentality which emphasized the hopelessness of it all, and invite chaos, but better that than the end of aristocratic priority. In retrospect, it seems nothing less than the very same introverted thoughtlessness with which a neurotic man designs his own suicide with the intent of wounding those who have wounded him.

One day Andronikus came by my office in the Foreign Ministry. In his company were the ever-present Varangians and his fifteen-year-old son, Prince Christopher. "We're going on an expedition about the city," said the Grand Duke. "Would you like to come? I think you might find it instructive."

I could hardly refuse, and I told him so.

His smile vanished and he seemed genuinely amazed as he said, "Why couldn't you?"

Rather than state the obvious and destroy his excellent humor—which had been rare these busy days—I said simply that he was the final judge of how I might best dedicate my time. This pleased him. He nodded.

So we traveled to the Petrion Quarter, immemorially the poorest in the city, whose inhabitants, on notice of the Regent's arrival, came running from every direction. Surrounded by the Imperial guard, Andronikus and his brother Philip, who had also joined us, recognized the cheers of the people with genuine pleasure. (There was, by the way, especial interest in Prince Christopher as the love-child of the Grand Duke and the former Queen of Jerusalem, whose legend remained intact, perhaps because she had, as yet, made no public appearance at Constantinople.)

At the doorway to one tenement, Andronikus stopped and said, "Let's go in there." The Varangians made a path for us, and we followed the Grand Duke up a solid cement staircase, badly chipped, drawing our skirts out of the way of rats—I counted a dozen—and an infinite number of cockroaches and heaven knows what other insects.

In one of those rooms we found an old man, lying on a pallet, holding prayer beads. He was a Moslem. Andronikus got to his knees and bent lower still, questioning in whispers the crone, who must have been flabbergasted by the apparition of these lordly figures, robed, perfumed, bejeweled, and their magnificent gold-cuirassiered, scarlet-caped guard.

Aloud, the old man said, "It's no good. There's no work for old people. You're old, you don't work. Life is very bad."

At that, Andronikus rose from his knees and looked round the room, dropping his intent glance, once, on the old man. He espied a stove with a boiling kettle atop. "Is this what you eat?"

The old man nodded.

The Grand Duke lifted a ladle, scooped out some soup, blew on it, and sipped it. Almost at once he spit it out. He offered the ladle to Philip, who refused, then Christopher, who sipped and could barely swallow, then to me. It seemed to be a broth of weed and bad meat. The meat was not there, but the grease was, along with vegetables which I could recognize neither by sight nor taste.

Andronikus returned to the old man. "Why should you want to work? You've lived a long life. Wouldn't you prefer to rest?"

"Little things," said the old man. "I can do little things, Your Highness. Here I am in the charity of my son-in-law. I'm used to things my way, but I must be grateful—and I am—and so I'm my daughter's prisoner because I must keep silent. I'm not my own man. I have no dignity."

Andronikus asked if his daughter's husband complained. "No, Your Highness, but what does that matter?"

Andronikus said, "We will see what we can do." The Grand Duke extended his hand to receive several gold pieces from a Varangian whose head was bent beneath the low ceiling. These he folded into the old man's palm. "Take this. I promise you something will be done. You will give your name to that fellow over there."

Emotionally the old man grabbed Andronikus' hand and kissed it. "As the Prophet said in the name of Almighty God, 'As to the righteous, they shall have fruit. Thus is rewarded the doers of good.'"

On our return to the Irene Villa, we were greeted at the doors by Maupacta, Andronikus' "official" mistress, introduced to him by the Queen who had seen the young woman, the greatest actress of her day, in several private performances at the palaces of friends throughout the city, and selected her as successor, perhaps, by that, maintaining some participation in the subsequent affair and certainly a portion of influence as Maupacta's sponsor. One look at the young woman, however, and a little consideration of her person, and one wondered at the success of the Queen's schemes.

As the Grand Duke Philip's son, Isaac, once said, accurately, I may add, "To hear Maupacta's voice, to behold her energy and watch her breasts heave beneath a diaphanous blouse in the last declamation of Antigone is to experience the fine line between tragedy and comedy—or pornography."

She was tall and red-haired, with jade-green eyes and amazingly fine-drawn features. At first glance, she seemed a sensuous creature indeed. A more considered evaluation gave one to understand her sensuality was in her glance and manner, rather affected than real. Born the daughter of a butcher, she nevertheless possessed that inborn, high-boned, physical refinement of an aristocrat. Her carriage was superb and her diction flawless court Attic, the result of her training as a classical actress. The superficial sense of breeding was but heightened by her composure and her self-containment. It is said, Theodora, on first meeting, was astonished by Maupacta. With the naïveté of an Imperial Grand Duchess and Queen, whose life and station had precluded the company of notorious women, Her Majesty had been prepared for a strumpet.

She was something like Maria-Xenia in the obverse, her strengths the product of her background and for that beyond the reach of the Augusta. She had begun life as one of those urchins of startling beauty, sponsored early and often by obliging aristocrats and millionaires, who resolves, rather by intent than accident, to use that beauty very conscientiously to her own ends, to rise above a level of life she abhors but never denies, which is for nouveau riche. She was called an adventuress. Indifferent to epithets, she considered herself rather a success. She was not brazen, but amoral. She was not cynical, but unpretentious in the most literal sense. She was not hard because she was not sentimental. She was a woman who knew she was attractive, and drew nourishment from the admiration she evoked, in turn desiring to be more scintillating still. She had no opinions, beyond that, about herself and her body, therefore it could not be said she sold herself even in a spiritual fashion. She chose her "mentors" from among petitioners—and there were many —as they pleased her.

Ironically, her limited intelligence made possible the fabulous, even interesting, creature she was. Able to recite with perfection of nuance whole sections of the *Orestia*—whether as Elektra *or* Clytemnestra—she could no more discuss the literary subtleties of her words and the profounder issues of the trilogy than I, with any competence, can play a lute. In fact she was the perfect instrument, full of lovely sounds but incapable of intellectual initiative. But she also possessed the pride and silence of a confident woman and the clear eye to realize her limitations, and so the discrepancy was rarely exhibited. Not an internal creature, moreover, she could be what she chose to be without tortured introspection, which is the hesitation of the discreet.

She pleased Andronikus, as one would be pleased by an especially ingenious and entertaining pet. She may even have fascinated him because he knew she was his entirely by her own choice and yet she did not love him, indeed, she might, like a cat, be indifferent to him the moment he let her go. As for the Grand Duke, I sensed he looked upon this last of his trysts with some sadness and even a little irritation, if not tattered vanity. I sensed he was not pleased having to resort to a professional mistress—to the purpose, as it were—when once, this greatest rake of the twelfth century might have had any woman's heart for the meanest suggestion of his ardency—"and believe it or not," he said to me a year before his death, "it's her heart and not the body, which dulls, I would sooner have. I have always been enraptured—even made jealous—not by the sight of young lovers, but those old and long allied. For, you see, I have always suspected love is not so much the provenance of youth or the recapture of lost time, as that which, itself, makes time irrelevant."

Still the matter of the Dowager Empress was unresolved. On 29 July 1182 Andronikus ordered a public hearing—virtually unprecedented— to consider the deposition of Maria-Xenia, and her removal to a convent. He insured it would be well attended by holding the session in the cavernous New Basilica, himself present. In those first days, his every appearance was irresistible to crowds.

Leo Monasteriotes, President of the Senate, and the justices, Prince Demetrius Tornicas and Constantine Patrenos, presided. In fact, the Regent had convoked the hearing as something of a formality, to explain his position publicly and test its consequences among the people. He was unprepared, then, when Monasteriotes interrupted the proceeding and somewhat haltingly addressed the throne with—at long length— this question: "It comes to this, Your Imperial Highness. Is Her Imperial

Majesty renouncing her rights of her own free will? Is her remanding to a nunnery the express wish of the Emperor, her son?"

It was not difficult to imagine Andronikus' feelings. Neither Count Monasteriotes, nor Prince Tornicas, nor the patrician, Patrenos, were any great supporters of the Dowager Empress. They were, however, expressly against an Andronikan Regency. This was nothing less than an open challenge.

The Grand Duke turned on the Senate President with the most savage look of power and blatant contempt I had ever seen contort his features. I felt myself actually step away from his chair. The silence in that colossal marble hall was terrible, the bated breath of those awaiting the outburst of one who possessed the power of life and death over every man before him. If he was not a god, he had the power of a god. "I will not be impugned, Count," he said at last, with terrific self-control.

Monasteriotes, nearly as big physically as the Grand Duke and therefore not so easily intimidated, answered boldly, "Impugned? Your Imperial Highness, we only wish to know whether or not you are carrying out the wishes of the Empress and of the Autocrat."

Andronikus stared at Monasteriotes as though he were insane. In truth, had the question been asked seriously and not as a ploy—that is: Was the Regent obedient to the Imperial minor—it would have been a clear putation of the Count's lunacy. *"You* are the men," the Grand Duke said suddenly, but still with preternatural calm, "who dare to question me whilst sitting silently and pusillanimously throughout the twenty-one months when my cousin, the Grand Duke David, acted as Regent. Where was your legal probity then? Your record bears investigation, especially during that period, and your conduct here today is nothing less than insolence, if not short of treason. Until further notice, I suggest you return in the company of my guards to your respective homes and remain there, under their eye, until further notice."

But then as John of Norwich, Commander of Andronikus' guard, and several of his company started toward the tribunal, something untoward happened—and ominous. A few mobsters present among the crowd shouted, "No, no, we'll take care of them for you!" and rushing the apse were followed by at least a thousand other folk. The three justices attempted to escape, were caught and manhandled terribly before enough Varangians arrived from outside the Basilica to accomplish their rescue.

The trio was treated for wounds, none too severe, and placed under house arrest in Monasteriotes' splendid palace near Studion Abbey.

For the first time Andronikus was witness to the prerogative of the mob. That they acted in his behalf mattered not half so much as that they acted at all. When the Varangians had started toward us to protect the Grand Duke's person, he had gestured impatiently, "No, no, for God's sake, the justices!" He had never any illusions about the mob, save one, and that one the most lethal because it was the most comfortable: that he could control it. The New Basilican episode proved otherwise, and his active disenchantment, if not fear, may be counted from that day.

We left by a side entrance. I was near Andronikus as he was about to mount his stallion, when, in a gesture of purest submission, a fellow came up beside him, bowed low, and clasping his hands, offered his palms and locked fingers from which the Regent might step up to his horse. When the Grand Duke, holding his saddle pommel, did not move, the man looked up. I gasped—audibly—and so did Andronikus. The stranger, possessed, almost to the measure, the Grand Duke's broad forehead, even hairline, his cheekbones, his mouth, his chin, his deep gray eyes, all surrounding a leather artifact in place of his absent nose. His undoubted previous good looks only emphasized the ghastliness of the obtrusive object. When he smiled, the sensation of malice was indescribable, the death's head grin of teeth too much exposed without the accent of real nostrils instead of those grotesque leather moldings, the eyes closed a little by the squint of revenge against the existence which had so betrayed him.

"Terrible in there," he said, daring to break Imperial protocol and speak before spoken to. "You ought to impale a few of them above Chalke. That ought to settle them, Your Highness," which was precisely what Andronikus would not do. Even had he been less confused and uneasy by what he had just seen, a random decimation of the mob and a public exhibition of violence could only incite violence in turn and end in final alienation. Our noseless interloper's suggestion was the brute and stupid response of a man totally ignorant of politics—or perhaps human feeling—like a wolf on the scent of blood, with the difference animals may kill for hunger—as this man seemed to hunger—but without pleasure.

The Grand Duke looked through the fellow and mounted his horse. We were off.

"What on earth was *that*," Andronikus asked his Varangian Commander. Speaking in English, as the Regent had asked him to do whenever possible (he was eager to communicate, in his own hand, with Henry of England, and, with his uncanny ear for languages, was leaning far toward proficiency in barely three months), John of Norwich said, "He's a vagrant round the court, Your Highness, always to one side of a ceremony, forever thrown out of the barracks or the palace galleries where he oughtn't to be. A liar, a thief, some say a pimp. He's illiterate but a good storyteller, and a better archer. All of us know of him."

"What about the nose?"

"Well, he's poor-born, a tax collector's son, of no account. According to his own testimony, he fell in love with a very beautiful countess, who evidently reciprocated, although some say he merely opportuned her and she was offended by him. In either event, the lady's brothers contrived to have him disfigured. As you can see, they succeeded. He says, if you'll forgive me, 'Sooner my nose than my balls,' but it's all rather lurid and he's a scoundrel." (I marveled at how John had so easily assumed the superior airs of an aristocrat when, himself, so capriciously touched by fate, born a farmer's son in a land nearly two thousand miles away, taken up by an Imperial agent, deposited at Constantinople, educated, pampered, and finally given a commission in the most elite regiment of guards in the world.)

Andronikus—all too apt to believe that one, poor-born, was a victim rather than a pest—momentarily turned in his saddle, frowning sympathetically at the noseless man who watched us off, never turning away his eyes.

"What's his name?" the Grand Duke asked.

"Well, as a joke, Your Highness, we call him Antichristophorites, 'anti-Christ-bearer.' "

"I asked his name."

"Stephen," said John of Norwich, "Stephen Hagiochristophorites."

IX

On 1 August 1182 Maria-Xenia Augusta was deposed and remanded to the Convent of St. Diomede. I was present when Alexius Augustus put his signature to the promulgation of his mother's fall. The boy displayed no more emotion—if indeed he was aware of the seriousness of what he was doing—than he might proclaiming best wishes to his people on Easter Eve.

Among the mob, the deposition of the Foreigner was greeted as nothing less than a "personal" triumph. Unaware of Andronikus' true motives —and very reasonable ones—the rabble supposed its own strength achieved the longed-for diminishment of the Latin Princess who, during her husband's lifetime, had been the object of such flattery and luxury as would embarrass Cleopatra.

Now the victory may have been illusory, but the consequence of appearances was not. The numbers of the mob grew and became, in effect, professional. Men—and sometimes women—whose means of support were invisible, attended the Hippodrome in season or out of it and gathered—loitered—in the vast squares of the city. They were present for all public ceremonial, swelled then by the usual sightseers, and, to be sure, during any event of a political nature, when their cohorts, the parish priests, charged ordinary citizens to demonstrate with these wretches, for or against some policy, and always in "Christ's behalf."

Some theorists used to submit both Old Rome and New Rome suffered their mobs in part because of the dole. The state, they said, financed the vagrant, thus its internal policies were of primary importance to a people who depended upon governmental philanthropy, and who, by their freedom from gainful employment, had the opportunity to register their pleasure or displeasure, indeed, were behooved to do so in their own interest. I myself would say, these theorists have not looked very closely into the Imperial rolls, where the registration for bread or emolument is overwhelmingly among the perennially unemployable—the old, the lame, unmarried mothers, wards of the state, and so forth.

Rather, it would seem, mobs are usual to all great cities. I am not speaking, now, of those who, very infrequently, are prodded to some sort of civic demonstration by issues of undoubted seriousness. In centers of immense population, the world-in-small, one must expect, along with great neglect and suffering and unemployment—perhaps as a result of these—great vagrancy, with the consequent—unfortunately predictable—concentration of crime and anarchy. Given this, and the usual contempt—often good-natured, but lethal in times of crisis—with which all citizens serve the throne in any capital, and there is bound to arise a mob when occasion gives it spark, as there is bound to be, helplessly, inequity even in the most supremely administered state—so that each man's personal sense of injustice blends in the indistinguishable boil of mass anger.

The sheer weight of the accumulated reigns of Alexius I and John II and the brilliant, if misguided Regency of Manuel had served to distract, if not nullify, the idea of the mob. Only with the emptiness and corruption which followed the Emperor's death, the sense of no great power to insult or by which to be intimidated, did riot become a prevalent factor in the life of the city. Perhaps this, more than any of the obvious problems of foreign affairs, internal administration, and societal iniquities, may have constituted the most effective instrument—because the least predictable or controllable—in bringing about the fall of the House of Comnenus. Certainly the deposition of the Dowager Empress, by which Andronikus believed he realistically increased his power—and misinterpreted by the mob as indication of its own strength—was the first of the final crucial underminings of the dynasty.

While stories still circulated the city of Maria-Xenia's hysteria on entering Diomede—relished or horrified descriptions (depending on the speaker) of how she was carried up the steps, unable to walk, sobbing—I received, one day, the Caesarissa Catherine's Chamberlain who bid me visit—at my convenience, but soon—his mistress whom he described as "very much alarmed and ill." The man seemed mildly overwrought in that deferential way of old courtiers—too discreet to be frenzied, always inclining the upper half of their bodies with each reply, staring intently, a pleadful look in their eyes, but their voices serene as a calm sea, and as measured.

I asked him if the matter was urgent. If necessary, I could visit now with Her Imperial Highness.

The Chamberlain thought that would be most considerate of me.

I had not seen Catherine, or Renier, for several months. On assuming the Regency Andronikus had thought it prudent to sequester the Caesars, whose influence was great enough to be an alternative for malcontents, and whose ambition, he supposed—insofar as the Caesarissa, at least—was undoubted enough to make use of any agency which would allow Manuel's firstborn the power she had never previously been resigned to relinquishing. What the Grand Duke did not consider was Catherine's own disillusion with politics following her grasp for power in the Revolution of 1181, a failure she assigned in great part to the ineffectiveness of the mob she could incite but not control. Withal, Their Imperial Highnesses enjoyed a seclusion such as few men experience, given the freedom of Porphyriogenetus, all its staff, and its exquisite gardens. They had seemed to accept their fate with surprising patience.

I may say, then, I was scarcely prepared for the condition in which I found them. Thirty that very year, the Caesarissa appeared nearly twice her age. Her hair was falling out and what remained was stark white. She was skin and bone and the lesions on her arms seemed to be infected. Her teeth ached constantly and she had been running a fever for weeks. She could not walk save supported by servants. As for the Apollonian beauty of her husband, but twenty-three years old: it was quite gone. The few tufts of hair on his head were the color of bleached wheat. His face was bloated and his body emaciated excepting an unnaturally swollen stomach. He was bedridden and could scarcely summon the energy for conversation.

My horror was instantaneous and unconcealed. Indeed, polite pretense to the contrary would have been its own form of obscenity. Blatantly, I said, "My God, Your Highness, what has happened? Have you seen any physicians?"

Her tragic eyes boring into me, she said, "*All* of them, Count, the very best, those *he* sends us and my own. Don't you see what's wrong? He's poisoning us."

I asked if she was employing a taster, and if he was suffering so.

"No, he's unaffected," she said. "I don't know how it's done. Perhaps it's in our baths. Perhaps in our hair. Or we're drugged from sleep to a deeper sleep and it's introduced through our veins. Can't you see? We're dying." She grabbed my hand. "Nicetas, go to him. Plead for us. Help us. We'll do anything. We'll go away. Look at what's become of my Caesar. I don't want to die. Go to my cousin." I said I would, at once, and I did.

From Buceleon I made the short traversal to Philopation and the Irene Villa, hoping to speak alone to Andronikus. He was in the private gardens behind the palace, where a scene of extraordinary domestic confusion made privacy out of the question. He was sitting in a marble chair studying, I knew, two reports prepared by Michael Hagiotheodorites, the Chancellor of the Interior Ministry, Theodore Chumnos, and myself. (One document concerned the Prostagma which prohibited the transfer of land, and the second, positions, pro and con, on the abrogation of the Law of Wreck and Astray.) On the ground before him were three of his grandchildren by Alexander, their play ostensibly supervised by nurses, actually by their aunt, the fifteen-year-old Princess Irene. To one side Theodora was talking softly and earnestly with Alexander's wife, the Grand Duchess Euphrosyne. Nearer the Regent, at her embroidery, was the lady of the hour, as they say, Maupacta. Also present were two liveried servants, two secretaries, Theodora's ladies, Euphrosyne's First Lady and Groom. As I watched from the balcony, Alexander came out of the lower garden and kissed his father high on the cheek as he bid him good-by. When he arrived at the stairwell, smiling at me in recognition, I came down to meet him, told him the nature of my errand, and asked if I might be so bold as to request that he fetch his father to me. Rarely one to stand on protocol, he did.

The Regent knew by my look something was wrong and while presenting his hand, said, "What is it, Nicetas?"

I asked him if he knew what had become of the Caesars.

"I've received reports. Hysterical."

"No, they are *not*, Your Highness." I stared at him and something in my look convinced him.

"Go on," he said with a nod.

I described what I had seen and what Catherine had said. He leaned on the balustrade built for the woman who could give her husband but this daughter of whom we now spoke.

When I was finished, he said, "I have appointments until this evening, but I will definitely go to her." He paused. I was surprised by his next words. "Do you believe my innocence?" I hesitated not a moment, "Yes, Your Highness. The circumstances are extraordinarily unpropitious, but they are not extenuating."

He shook his head and folded his arms against his chest. A soft breeze ruffled his lustrous gray hair. He laughed shortly, humorlessly. "Who else will believe it?" He cocked his brows, momentarily, in resignation. "Well, there's nothing to be done. A public declaration would only exaggerate the matter. What is it Aristotle said? 'There are some tasks in which it is impossible for a man to be virtuous.' He should have said, 'seem virtuous' and added, 'chief above all, that of the ruler.'"

Two days later, I received by messenger the following note from the Caesarissa:

My dear Count. You know he came to me, at your behest, for which thanks. No dissimulation could so convincingly imitate the alarm and the concern he manifested when he saw the Caesar and myself as we unhappily appear. If it is one of his lieutenants who has done this terrible thing to my husband and me, then the Grand Duke is also a victim, for, I fear, he will be blamed and he is blameless. Logic is relentless, even when it is artificial. I offered to deposit a letter with the Patriarch containing my personal exoneration. He would not hear of it. I had met the Grand Duke a few times, and then briefly, previous to our lengthy talk the other evening. I can only hope his way will not be made more difficult for my misfortune. Catherine P.

I vividly recall reading that letter again by a window of a blazing autumn afternoon, shortly after the Caesarissa's death, and thinking my heart would burst with sadness. She died 12 October, eighteen days after her husband's passing.* Andronikus ordered Imperial obsequies for both Caesars and attended them with his entire family. The slander against him was atrocious and open and whispers followed him at Catherine's funeral from the entrance and along the entire length of Holy Apostles Cathedral. At one point there was a shout of "Hypocrite!" then abject silence. If the Regent heard the epithet—and he did—he gave it no recognition.

Prepared for the contumely which would follow these august deaths, he dismissed it beforehand, and proceeded apace in the most urgent tasks pursuant to the Empire's recovery.

---

* On the morning of 24 September, Renier had felt well enough, almost revived, and actually made it to his bath unassisted. His emaciated body was soaped down by attendants, he plunged into the water, and there lost consciousness. He was carried back to his room, followed by a tremendous commotion, and, as his wife arrived, expired almost at once coughing up black blood. To this day, the deaths of the Caesars remain a mystery, or else a coincidence of infinite proportion. From the onset of the illness, as the Caesarissa pointed out, a taster had been employed with no effect. In an inquiry which I unwillingly chairmanned under Isaac II Augustus, two court physicians testified, yes, Their Imperial Highnesses exhibited the symptoms of slow, debilitating poisoning, which, at the same time, were also the symptoms of a form of terminal cancer. In that event, the patient might pass from perfect health to a wizened, living corpse, and finally one dead, within three months to six. Yet men will believe what the times, or prudence, their own gain—or prejudices—would have them believe. What seems to have occurred out of all improbable numbers is that a young woman and her young husband, both suspect in the eyes of their kin, the Regent, contracted the same terminal disease within weeks of each other, and so died. Very few of Andronikus' friends, even, quite accepted this explanation. The theory of assassination was more comfortable, perhaps because it could then be denied we are all similar potential victims in the repetition of such gross, gratuitous misery. N.A.

First, there was the preamble: the purging of the bureaucracy, rebuilding the army, streamlining as well as appointing new provincial administrations, and, above all, immediately abrogating the most glaring laws of privilege of the two previous regimes.

To this end, throughout the late spring and summer and most of autumn, 1182, he personally reviewed the dossiers of every member of the Imperial administration at Constantinople. The number was staggering—more than twenty thousand—from High Chancellors to the lowest clerks. He had these documents read to him at meals, read them personally in any spare moment, and took huge sheaves, along with Maupacta, to bed with him. (Once his reader was halfway into a report before he realized he was condemning his own brother's peculations. Amused, Andronikus forgave and retained the lucky fellow.) Indeed, the secretary who followed him with that singularly identifiable, bulging portfolio became the object of only *half*-mocking assassination conspiracies.

In any event, the Regent had promised to purify the bureaucracy and that was precisely what he was doing—but according to his own precepts. This meant, as most Constantinopolitans had not foreseen, the retention of any Latin who had proved himself faithful to the Imperium and wise in his service, and—to the shock of various jealous colleagues who had hoped to advance by class sooner than competence— the retention also of aristocrats whose competence was undoubted. Let no man believe otherwise: it is because of this Augean-like task, the Empire was able to survive, as an administration, if not a government, the chaotic twenty years of the Angeli Dynasty which followed Andronikus' death.

The same care, contrary expectations, and begrudgment resulted from his work upon the army. Generals were sacked who spent rather more time at banquets than barracks. A chrysobull was issued describing the sons of the nobility—from the patriciate upward—liable to military service. Conscriptees from the peasant class would be limited to one son per four in a family. Latins were welcome, but only by quota, and their pay would be equal to—no longer exceed—that of native Byzantines. Michael Gabras argued it would be wiser to raise their pay but limit—say at a captaincy—the stations to which a mercenary could rise. Andronikus maintained he would imitate his grandfather and regain a native army, more responsible to the state and less to a single man who happened to hold the power. He did, however, create a new post, the Heteriarchy, or Command of the Foreign Corps, at whose head he placed a brilliant, bloodless young patrician, formerly a lieutenant of the Scholarians, Constantine Tripsychos.

As to the provincial administrations: they were the quickest to repair. A constant traffic which lasted nearly to the final months of Andronikus' reign, commenced between those governors, magistrates, and bureaucrats recalled to Constantinople—and sometimes to indictments—and those dispatched. "It's simply amazing," Andronikus said one day. "The extraordinary number of competent men, wasted all these years, while fools and thieves did their damage. That's all it takes, Nicetas: corruption, emptiness—personal, civil, moral—at the top for no more than a year, two years, and the rot becomes endemic. The state is such a fragile instrument of civilization, and the only instrument. It needs constant tending."

I asked him what had become of the anarchist he was reputed to be.

He said, "The anarchist I'm reputed to be and the one I am, in fact and principle, are two quite different men. Without civilization in the truest sense of all men civilized we will never enjoy the anarchy, which is perfection, all men deserve."

But the happiness of those first months of the Regency—the exultancy in positive action—was drawing to a close, never to be recovered. By November—so early—the consequences of the Grand Duke's rule began to draw reaction, and it was in the form of halfhearted cooperation or animosity. Everyone had expected miracles. Instead, the Regent's measures found each man still anticipating, no man content, and not a few grumbling betrayal, from the peasants who had hoped to be forever free from conscription, to the aristocrats denied the favors they had expected—whatever the public face of Andronikus' incorruptibility—for placing the Regent in power, to the provincial administrators, who, if incompetent, were cashiered, no matter the support they had tended during the Great March, to the Constantinopolitan mob which scarcely knew what it wanted and now scarcely knew why it felt denied.

On 2 November 1182, having mustered sufficient forces, Andronikus dispatched Michael Branas and Andrew Lapardas, as joint commanders, north, to counter Bela of Hungary, who, since his initial depredations, had occupied Belgrade and Brantichevo, marched along the Moravia, attacked Niš—carrying off the relics of St. John of Rila—entered the Bulgarian Province, and captured Sofia. There, with superb political subtlety, he received the Asen brothers and assured them his support of an autonomous Bulgarian kingdom. Continuing this policy—not unlike Byzantium's—of client states who owed their ostensible independence to him, his Apostolic Majesty allied himself with the redoubtable Serbian Prince, Stephen Nemanya, who declared the principalities of Rascia and Zeta independent of the Empire. Writing to Branas in the field, Andronikus suggested "a strategy of sorties until I can give you more men, as I fully intend, since it seems the Balkans will be our theater of war for the next several years. It will be worse—much worse, I fear—before it gets better."

The day he wrote those words—15 November—evidence confirming the high treason of Maria-Xenia Augusta and a host of aristocrats—many married to the Imperial family—was brought to his desk. Called the Second Great Conspiracy by historians, it is also the most lurid.

Enchanted by the former Empress, the Abbess of St. Diomede had agreed to act as go-between for the Dowager and my immediate subordinate, Prince Basil Dukas, also Count George Angelus, his sons, and the Grand Admiral Justin Cantacuzenus ("The perfect sailor," his mother, Juliana Porphyriogeneta had once described him, "trims his sails to every wind"). These notable personages were, in turn, in league with Bela III, welcoming him to the Empire and the prospect of marriage with a reinstated Xenia. The number of adherents to this lunatic scheme was enormous, and its leader, at the opposite end of the golden thread between Constantinople and Stuhlweissenburg, was Queen Theodora's sister, Maria, sister-in-law of the King.

Quietly, Andronikus spread a dragnet about the city, and, on the appointed night, surrounded the palaces of the Angeli, the Cantacuzeni, the Dukas, the Paleologi, the Exazeni, the Kamateri, the Skleri, and the Catacalons. The guilty parties were arrested and arraigned before the Senate, whose members were called out of their beds—those, at least, who were not themselves complicit—then remanded to Magnaura Palace, where they remained surrounded by guards day and night. The following day the Regent signed the order to blind Cantacuzenus and four of his eleven sons—those involved in the plot—since as collateral members of the Imperial family, they had broken both blood and civil oaths to the House. Also blinded was Prince Basil, who, by the delicacy of his position, was privy to secret documents and easy access to Bela III. Amazingly—perhaps the only touch of macabre humor—the usually slow-witted Angeli, forewarned, had escaped on a shipful of empty amphora vases bound for Syria, where Count George died on arrival of a heart attack and the sons, claiming him poisoned on the Regent's orders (he did not even know their whereabouts), declared themselves against the throne.

It is usually maintained a reign of terror began that night which did not run its course until Andronikus' death a little less than three years later. Whatever the later controversy of his regime, the arrests and meted punishments of November 1182 were not the intimidation of an ideologue, but the Autocracy's behooved response for treason, if treason has ever existed as a viable accusation. These people were collusive with a deposed empress, who had been removed against precisely the occasion of such complotting. The conspirators, moreover, had communicated with a foreign conqueror who was destroying Byzantine cities and calling them liberated, allying himself—with aid—to secessionist princes and implicitly consenting to the deposition of Manuel's legitimate Heir and the proposed assassination of the Regent.

The only argument lies in the means of justice which Andronikus initiated. Were the blanket arrests and blindings of members of the Imperial family collateral called for? It is a matter of personal opinion.

For a man at the age of sixty—no less an intelligent and philosophically sensitive man who happens to believe death is an end, not a beginning—the possibility he had missed oblivion by inches may have compelled him, helplessly, to strike too heavily. His alarm was understandable and not merely personal. He believed—without a taint of messianism—his person, at this moment in time, was the embodiment of the one given possibility of change as he believed change was necessary to the survival of the Empire. Should he die, both impetus and idea would die with him.

But terror breeds its own. If it was Andronikus' intention to warn others as well as punish the guilty, he may have succeeded too well. Those on the periphery of the conspiracy redoubled their ardency to the throne, sharpening their loyalty on the reported disloyalty of friends and relatives. What had begun as awe of the Regent swiftly metamorphosed into fear. What had seemed to him fitting punishment against the most abject cabal since the dynastic quarrel against St. John in the twenties, appeared to others persecution of a class or, even more unworthy, a jealous, ambitious, ruthless man's attempt to remove all familial competition from the possibility of rule. The reader may be sure these negative explanations gained currency among a discontented populace and have since found their way into several of my colleagues' histories.

Four days after the arrests at Magnaura, Andronikus visited the conspirators and addressed them, in part, thus: "It is said there would be chaos if each man acted as he wished, without regard for the other. Even if the law could not prevent such an eventuality, then, I suspect, human compassion would. But there is another sort of chaos, worse than the popular view of anarchism, and that is the ignorance men will willfully practice of another man's motives. As long as this persists the only possible outcome, in small and at large, is social convulsion. There are already people about who call your arrests an attack upon the nobility and, by these words, attack my right to punish you as criminals, so that you appear heroes and martyrs and I, the morbid tyrant. To prove the contrary in more ways than one, therefore, I am going to free some of your number in the hopeless hope you will speak otherwise. Gentlemen, the state cannot endure turmoil within if it is to succeed without against aggressors who will not hesitate, I assure you, to take advantage of our present weaknesses, our agony. If it is given to me, I am here to save us, but this I cannot do if I am, on all sides, beleaguered by kith and kin, whose duty to the state is perhaps more noble when given, for it is choice against inaction, which is a citizen's perfect right, and one—by blood, by heritage, by oath—I do not have. Many of you have known me my whole life long and I have never made any secret of my desire for power, of my will to rule. I would have been happier to assume a stronger state, but I am doing my best in circumstances which would tax the wit of Theseus. For your own sake—and for mine —do not allow your preconceptions or your ambitions to lead you to a frenzy of misjudgment as to my designs. I am no longer young. I have little time and I cannot tolerate distraction. I have little time and none at all to spare for inquiry into the sincerity of *your* motives. Men fighting a hospital fire will not pause to calm the lunatics in the asylum ward, but strike them and carry them out."

As Andronikus was leaving Magnaura, having freed at least a score of the conspirators, he passed Hagiochristophorites, lounging the main portal, who loudly announced his now famous remark, "How can it be such wicked men are advanced, while I, the wickedest by far, am not allowed to display my talents in His Highness' service?" The Varangians without a word from either Andronikus or their Commander set upon him with their heavy lances, bloodying his mouth, raising a welt on his forehead and lacerations upon his body. It was not until the Grand Duke was mounted that he realized what was about and ordered the beating stopped. He had Hagiochristophorites brought up to him.

I considered the two men: the Grand Duke, immaculate and magnificent in black velvet, whipped with fox fur, looking down from his frisky, gigantic stallion on this fellow with his own Paleologus eyes and mutilated, bloodied face. One's sympathy for Stephen was in that moment helpless: a wreck of a man, thwarted, impoverished, now surrounded by panoply, its painful victim. Andronikus shifted the reins in his gloved hands but did not look at the churl. He said, "I don't like impertinence," but he spoke mildly and there was even a trace of humor in his next words. "As you can see, neither does the Imperial Guard." Now he was stern. "I especially dislike impertinence when it stems from self-assurance rather than stupidity. Hagiochristophorites—that's your name, isn't it?"

"Yes, Most August Highness."

"And you believe yourself a wicked fellow?"

Stephen's bloody mouth laughed halfheartedly, uneasily. One pitied him a little more still. "Only a joke, Your Imperial Highness, I swear to you. If I have offended you, I am beyond saving."

"Royalty sets the measure of humor and of punishment. You've had your share of both. Let it be a warning." The Grand Duke pulled a fresh, fabulously embroidered handkerchief from his sleeve, tossed it at Stephen, who caught it handily, and said, "Wipe your mouth. It's bleeding."

As we were riding off, he said to his ADC, "Use him. Put him on Tripsychos' staff, here, in the city. One less rabble-rouser against the government—one less loiterer, too."

Was it whim? Sympathy? Or a blind scent controlled by fate? By this, by chance, was recruited the only man I've ever known I would call irrevocably evil. All pity I ever felt for him was that which one experiences before a creation of nature condemned to its own ugliness, a malaligned soul, living in unending darkness, incapable of light. After a time, Andronikus never doubted the make of the man Hagiochristophorites was and, I think, was himself in awe. Once he chided me when I remarked I felt very sorry for the fellow. "Nicetas," he said, "you would pity the devil and for that succumb to him."

I think, perhaps, it is quite the opposite. Compassion for the worst spiritual miscalculations perhaps allows us a shield against them. Andronikus' wary contempt, on the other hand, objectified the man. Objectifying Stephen, he was able to use him. To use Stephen meant but committing oneself to his perfidy, giving it license over others, even if one's own motives were not perfidious themselves in origin or intent.

Hagiochristophorites was an opportunist of the first water. Opportunists, by definition, have no large strategy themselves, but merely bend each occasion to its maximum personal profit. As such men rise, they are, virtually by instinct, loathed and plotted against. In self-defense they increase their ambitions and their unscrupulousness. They will, in a word, do anything to survive, since survival is much their only point. They become the janitors of a regime, willing to work in the filth to which any man in power must sometimes descend, and does, whenever he can procure the suitable agent. Employing such human refuse, the potentate will then defend him against his enemies. In turn, those who loathe the opportunist will come to loathe his sponsor. (Often the prime beast of any tyranny is not the tyrant, but his servants.)

I am not unaware, many men who lived through the Andronikan years called them a tyranny. I myself refuse to use this epithet. One of the first promulgations of the Regency was the establishment of Right of Address to the Throne—in effect, the right to argue an Imperial decision or suggest an alternative without previous behest or permission from the Regent or, as the case may be, the Emperor. Andronikus defined this prerogative as "the only antidote against the corruption of silence in the face of that with which you disagree." The first test of this address surrounded the condemnation to death of the Empress Maria-Xenia.

Perhaps it is some limited eye on my part. I would hope it is no lack of sensibility, but I find myself consumed by the same disinterested pity toward the Dowager as I knew for Hagiochristophorites. Yes, the end of any human being, short of its own appointment, is terrible. Somehow the death of a basically good-natured, if misguided, but above all beautiful woman is that much more unfortunate. We are a world, as I fear we shall always be, at once more indulgent toward, because we are no less in need of, beauty. Its elimination is always pathetic. For each man, no matter how distant from the source, the death of comeliness strikes an immediately personal grief. Yet hard as it may be to reconcile oneself to such a point, beauty is irrelevant, or dismissable, if it serves to cloak damaging self-interest which destroys others in the venture of its goals.

Maria-Xenia was, as Andronikus said, something like a victim, the victim of the power to which she was born or her beauty made her candidate. Her life was unhappy only at the end. Let us remember, there were countless lives subjected to a more miserable experience, without compensation or hope, to indulge her or preserve her in all the years preceding those last months. She was not a vindictive woman by any means, nor without sympathy in some degree. But she was without the density of thought and curiosity by which one overleaps himself. Perhaps she did indeed suffer a small tragedy—as do I for not pitying her more—and that is the tragedy of limitation. She was, at once, a vulnerable being and an incorrigible symbolic reposit of all power. If a way could have been found to erase from men's minds the acknowledgment of her Dowager Imperium, it would have been taken. But that was impossible. Despite her rights renounced, she was Autocratrix and the subject of veneration, real—for men who believed her deposition unjust—or presumed—those using it as a banner to contend the supplanting government.

Of all men, the Regent's son, the Grand Duke Alexander, was one of the few who spoke his piece openly against the execution of the Empress. This was on the occasion when his father asked him to stand as witness to her death, since no execution of a member of the Imperial family was legal without the presence of another member. "The execution of an emperor or empress cannot be legal," the Grand Duke told his father. "It is regicide. There is no law save heaven's above the Imperium and heaven has no provision for capital punishment."

"We are not speaking of a crowned head regnant, but one deposed."

"In all your wish to alleviate suffering and make change, sir, is there nothing of love or compassion?"

Andronikus, in the Emperor's chair at this meeting of the Sacred

Consistory, seemed to pucker and grow dark. "I'll settle for perfect justice at this point."

"Perfect justice, without compassion, is only relentless law."

The task of Imperial witness was delegated to the Grand Duke George, a distant cousin and great-grandson of the Sebastocrator Isaac I, a diminutive little man—unlike his giant impetuous ancestor—gentle and literary, content in his collection of icons and rare manuscripts. After the testation, he took to his bed for a month.

The execution was ordered to take place at Selymbria, the decapitated body then weighted in canvas and buried, with consecrations, at sea, to prevent subsequent martyriology. The Abbess of Diomede, whom Andronikus thereafter ordered into retreat at a convent at Trebizond, accompanied Maria-Xenia to the Imperial villa, where, in some sort of mordant recognition of the Empress' position, it was decided she would not be beheaded by a common executioner, but a general of the armies —appropriately, the Commander of the Foreign Corps, Constantine Tripsychos.

Many years later, the Abbess, a woman of greater sensitivity than her earlier conduct would have led me to expect, told me: "I shall never forget that ride from Diomede. A light snow was falling, the wispiest of snows, and it formed something like a dusting upon the road. When the wind blew upon it, it would move in great, veinous striations, rather like the last foam of the tide as it retreats. I remember watching the horses' hooves incise into the diaphanous stuff and I could not help but compare those hooves and that snow with Her Majesty's delicate life and the sword which would cut it. All the trip, she was pale but composed. I noticed, however, a small frenzied look in her eye. Probably she was thinking what anyone—you or I—would think at such a terrible moment: either she would be rescued or this was but a dream. How could she be going to her own death as if in a procession? A ride, a meal, a night's sleep, and she would be annihilated in the morning. How could there be such order? Why were the trees still? How could these people round her be so calm, as though nothing extraordinary would happen, when quite the most extraordinary thing would happen: she would not be alive one turn of the earth from that moment.

"In the evening, while she was served her last meal by the fire—she ate little—she explained to me how she had always feared snow, associating it with the cold and misty north, which she associated with death.

She was pale as a Dane and yet her blood was thick and her nature Levantine. She knew she would not be buried in sanctified ground, but dropped into the sea. Strangely, this did not disturb her or frighten her. Men have called her empty and foolish, but she had the wit to say, 'My death is my own and no man can follow me. I would that I be put away from all eyes and too many prayers and too much grief. I am weary of acclamations. I would go up to my God, quietly, in my innocence.'

"She slept little and prayed most of the night. Early in the morning her abundant golden hair was cut above the neck and burned, to prevent the propagation of relics, I suppose. She was not bound, but pads and a blindfold were applied to her eyes to keep them from opening after decapitation, which took place, as ordered, at the sixth hour."

"If justice does not work from the accused to the enhancement of the accuser, it is not justice, but vengeance and twice the crime it seeks to rectify," said the Grand Duke Alexander many years later. "Xenia's death laid a curse upon my father, and, subsequently, the family, from which all else proceeded. I am certain he had his doubts about her execution. Perhaps *because* the Foreigner's death pleased the mob, the decision was all the more difficult. But just because he overcame his doubts, he was hardened to the unthinkable—the next execution or blinding—and the next and the next. The Empress' death was omnipotent in its consequences. It set most of the family against my father whatever the motivations of their concern: sincere outrage or plain fear. It further alienated the Patriarch and offended the West, well pleased with a Latin empress, and intimidated still more the nobility which mistrusted his ultimate designs against it. If the anointed Basilissa was vulnerable, so was any man. Nothing daunted to depose and decapitate, he hardened his heart to other cruelties, lesser cruelties. When, for instance, the Caesar Demetrius came to him for my sister Zoë's hand, he gave instead Irene's. My father, the social iconoclast, was still enough of a dynastic legitimist to forbid the marriage of a grand duchess to a bastard. He wished, nevertheless, to unite the junior and senior branch of the family, as politic in the controversy following the Basilissa's execution, and so made offensive use of both my sisters and Demetrius by determining that he marry Irene, an Imperial bastard like himself."

After the Dowager Empress' death, if I may be permitted, something sagged. There was a quiet, a cheerlessness about things. Men were at once anxious and resigned. Anything could happen now, if the unthinkable had taken place. The enthusiasm for the new and untested was over and in its place was the unease and forlornness such as one experiences moving into a new home from an old one. One's heart is still fixed to the previous hearth to which he may no longer return, while obliged—because there is no choice—into this still alien establishment.

Indeed, we were no longer what we had been. With the first legal indictment and execution of a crowned head in all our history, we had passed into a previously uninhabited historical condition. With that, we could seek assurance we were not entirely lost only in the familiarity of the man who had brought us to this end—or this beginning—Andronikus. We were obliged to believe he knew, if we did not, where we were bound. The only alternative was to contest him and seek the past again. Those who did were to learn, as all men must, the past is irrecoverable because each preceding moment of our lives is more ignorant and, therefore, innocent, than the next. What is past can never be rejected. It must be incorporated. Any return to former conventions is, so to speak, invalid, a game, a pretense. Any return involves a confrontation with the same subtle lopsidedness of a familiar place in a dream. Once having seen the past from a distance—even a short one—in whole perspective, as one espies the city from without in which one has lived secure within its walls, and you cannot again, ever, feel *enclosed*. You have observed your previous vulnerability. The progress of time is the process of skepticism, gentle or crushing.

Yet, in a fell swoop, while Andronikus further alienated the powers of the Empire, he won more closely to his side the peasantry. Three days after Maria-Xenia's death, he presented for signature to Alexius II the abrogation of the Prostagma, which had prohibited, the reader will remember, the sale of land in Manuel's time to any but the civil or military aristocracy. Once again a peasant proprietor who had the means, or could post collateral, was allowed to buy the land he cultivated—for rent—from his liege. To be sure, the Asian nobility retaliated by promising to stand aside should those of a mind to be independent seek aid in the event of a Turk incursion. (The Europeans made the same threat in the event of a Balkan or Sicilian invasion.) This was a defiance which might have been meaningless when the Empire girded Europe and Asia from the Adriatic to the Euphrates. Now, it was quite another story. Yet Andronikus neither threatened nor warned.

Rather, in March 1183, when Prince Nicholas Catacalon, whose estate was nearby the Comnenus ancestral domain, Christos Gennate, forbid his soldiers to come to the aid of a dozen free peasant families attacked by a daring Iconiate guerrilla force, the Regent commanded the archon present himself for arraignment at Constantinople. The Prince refused and a force was sent against him. On second thought, he chose not to risk confiscation, lest his family suffer, and surrendered to the Imperial Guard. The Grand Duke Philip, a personal friend, urged his brother to be clement, "After all, he did at last surrender." Andronikus was unmoved. "After defying both my edict and any general measure of decency by allowing the massacre of sixty people beneath the walls of his own home. If I should let him go unpunished, ought I then to give every man a first absolution and a second chance?" The fortune of the Prince was placed in trust for his family, and the culprit sent to the Tower of Anemas where he remained until the fall of the dynasty a little over two years later.

Not all directives, however, were against the aristocracy. In February 1183 Andronikus intervened among the Constantinopolitan guilds at the behest of young apprentices who requested—and received—an audience with the Regent. It seemed during their heyday, Latin journeymen, willing to work for far less than the native rate of pay, had seriously affected the income of the guild craftsmen, with the result doors were closed to new trainees. What had begun as a preventative measure was now a confirmed policy—even with the disappearance of the Latins. Hence, disgusted, ambitious, talented young men were leaving the city for more prosperous climates or roaming it with an eye to the mob. No new blood, meanwhile, was entering the great guilds, which provided poorly for the future. Andronikus ordered the guilds to cease their exclusivity on pain of disestablishment, to allow entry of any newcomer who was properly qualified. He appointed Imperial commissioners to make certain no one was turned away on a pretext of unfittedness. (Pricked by this state of affairs, he inquired into the merchant guilds, where he found the same situations, relatively speaking: huge consortiums which cleared profits befitting their size against the lonely, private entrepreneur. The cartels were broken up, guild entry eased, and their charters rewritten. When resistance continued, the final threat of close investigation of any tax arrears was implied. The "self-improvement" thereafter was instantaneous.)

The following month, however, Andronikus gave with one hand as he had taken—or flattened—with the other, by abrogating the Law of Wreck and Astray. This chrysobull was greeted by merchants as nothing less than an epiphany. So long as a broker and his investors could not reclaim their goods on a shored or wrecked vessel which became the property of the scavenger, only the very wealthy could afford the risk —which might pay so handsomely—of such speculating ventures. With what amounted to an Imperial guarantee of original possession, the way was open to middle-class financing and the Greek dream revived of supplanting all foreign competition in sea trade, using Constantinople's immemorial position as world terminal.

When, at a banquet, I asked one of the city's richest merchants if small sums and too many investors were not a nuisance in terms of bookkeeping and client relationships ("after all, the clerk has less to give and more to lose and may pester you, whereas a sole sponsor will not"), he said—unaware Andronikus was standing within earshot, listening intently—"Senator, I'd rather match the sum of one bezant each from 300,000 Constantinopolitans than 50,000 security from any one man any day. In the first instance, I could afford twelve ships. In the second, but two." Behind his back Andronikus smiled and catching my eye, winked.

Unfortunately this burgeoning of a great native fleet was almost at once countered by one of the most baneful, long-term consequences of the Latin massacre. Pisa and Genoa, rather than requesting indemnities for that awful event in which their citizens were the chiefest sufferers, gave consent and encouragement to the formation of piratical fleets. As early as spring, 1183, these corsairs entered the Aegean and began a campaign of savage depredation. Within two years, many of the major isles were desolate and the minor ones transformed into brigands' havens. Indeed, when Andronikus made his first approaches to Venice as a makeweight against Byzantium's former West Italian allies, the Genoans and the Pisans had the insufferable effrontery to thereupon demand reparations for 1182. Our ambassadors at both cities were ordered to inform these governments Constantinople's injuries suffered by their marauders more than equaled those described in the massacre. Since these people could not officially deny the raids without appearing liars as well as thieves, they withdrew their claims. It was the last official dealing the Comneni had with Latins they had brought to Constantinople.

The Grand Duchess Euphrosyne Paleologa Comnena joined her husband in condemning her father-in-law's insistence on a marriage between Demetrius and the sixteen-year-old Princess Irene. "Perverse," she called it, "capricious and perverse." In truth, Andronikus' reasons for uniting the Johannine and Isaac factions in this manner were subtle and even too anxious, involving an assessment of the character of his two daughters. He recognized, above all, too much of himself in his favorite —and contrarily denied—daughter, Zoë. Though quieter and plainer than her spectacularly beautiful half-sister, the Grand Duchess, with age, exhibited definite signs of independence and a too certain ambition, which she might—however demurely, but persistently—pass on to the malleable Demetrius, a peril which Irene, as willful, but willing to be obedient in all things to her father, would never consider.*

In any event, either daughter's marriage to the Caesar required a dispensation since the children were prohibited within degree. This, Theodosius refused to give. His popularity—ironically, among those same people who cheered Andronikus—was such that he could dare and remain inviolable. In Alexius' name, then, Andronikus convoked a synod, which swiftly revolved into a war between the pro-Andronikan and pro-Theodosian forces of the Church. The sides were easily remarked. The patriarchs, abbots, metropolitans, and suffragens—usually aristocrats—recognized Theodosius' argument of consanguinity. The lesser hierarchy were willing to consent to any decree—short of state atheism—put forward by the Champion of the People. The Theodosian forces argued that canon law forbade marriage within the fourth degree consanguine (Irene and Demetrius were within the second and first, as their respective parents). The Andronikan forces argued that civil law

* Rather it was in Andronikus' mind to marry off the Grand Duchess superbly instead of symbolically, to the son of Princess Veronica Melissena's only male cousin. Prince Romanus was a violent-tempered—and occasionally charming—wastrel, constantly in debt from gambling, who might have made a splendid general had the necessity for a career not been precluded when Theodora's former lady-in-waiting and companion in exile returned to Constantinople, too old to trust any man's reason for marrying her, and adopted her second cousin in order to name him heir to the enormous fortune of the senior branch of the family. Apparently Andronikus would sooner see his eldest daughter bullied—and survive—than his youngest, as bold and free-wheeling, corrupted. N.A.

did not recognize the parentage of bastards, hence no impediment existed.

Now, those who rule would have it that fewer share the power and many suffer it. In most instances this is true. At a synod, however, something very like a democracy exists, wherein the ruled, by sheer numbers, enforce their will. With a few judicious bribes—or flattering invitations to dine with the Regent (whose boredom one dares not imagine)—Andronikus won several bishops to his side and together with the lower hierarchy, achieved consent for the marriage. Theodosius claimed the Regent, with this act, had "rent the Church up and down the middle like the temple veil," and refused to place his imprimatur on the dispensation.

Andronikus, in an interview with the Patriarch, threatened to depose him.

"You do that, Your Highness," said Theodosius, and he meant it. "Do whatever you like. I am weary of it all and cannot, for the life of me, endure the thought of remaining on the patriarchal throne until my death. It is a burden I never sought and never wanted. I am an eldest son, as you know, and need not have joined the Church but for the love of Christ. I sought the renunciation of power and instead it fell upon my shoulders like a cross. This is not the purpose for which I gave myself to tonsure. I desired not the cares and pettiness of the world, but release from them. I know the delight you take in power. I take none. I believe in God as helplessly as you do not. For you the summit of life is authority. For me it is resurrection before the Lord. You believe authority a treasure and—yes, yes—a tool. I believe it a vanity and the worst agent of mean distraction the devil ever invented to lead one away from God. In a position of command, you believe you are raised above the mundane. I tell you, a crown is only the mundane magnified."

The look in Andronikus' eyes was something to behold: delight at being rid of Theodosius—or the prospect of such—as well as objective aesthetician's appreciation for a well-articulated, profound position, he could understand but never himself assume—and perhaps even surprise at the seemingly real unworldliness of a man he had suspected of being quite the opposite. "Very well, Eminence." He could not resist, with some acidness, the following words: "I am only troubled you did not come to me sooner so that I could have relieved you of this intolerable burden. As it is, I cannot depose you, for that would be to dishonor you.

May I suggest a solution? You will shine for it, I assure you, and I will be blamed, as having secretly enforced it, but no matter. Presumably if you retire to the monastery you have built on Terebinthos Isle—something like an implied resignation—I might then appoint a Procurator, whom, in time, I would raise—or, rather, the Emperor would raise—to the patriarchal throne."

The Priest-Prince stood aghast at what he had just done. Not for one moment do I doubt the sincerity of his declaration . . . or his ambivalence. He had only forgot he was speaking to an antagonist with the power to act upon his words and end his inner battle—perhaps the only way: from without—between love of power and love of God. "That will do," he said. It was not difficult to imagine his thoughts.

In exiling himself—whether it appeared voluntary or involuntary (and amazingly he did his best to exonerate the Regent)—he was forsaking both common parishioner and aristocrat alike against a man he almost superstitiously mistrusted. Were he deposed, he could have served as a martyr, an alternative should the regime become untenable. A resignation—itself unprecedented—might have, in the long run, added a touch of impeccable saintliness to his reputation. In the short of it, however, renunciation seemed like desertion, and he had no wish to disillusion or dishearten his followers. But beyond these considerations—which may have served to show him how far he had passed from things spiritual—was the personal high pride before a man he loathed and whose contempt, for that, he could not have borne if he were to retract so much as a word.

It was, then, done. Somehow, I think the withdrawal of the Patriarch a symptom of the times. If men did not fight and fail, they folded, resigning themselves to that mystic, inarticulate languor which runs in the blood of every fatalistic Byzantine, even Andronikus. William of Tyre once said to me, "On the available evidence—none at all, really—I am attempting to decide whether you Greeks actually have second sight of disaster and forthwith relinquish yourselves to it, or bring disaster upon yourselves by deciding it is inevitable and suffering the apathetic paralysis of the doomed, thereafter."

Theodosius left the world a week later and remained in pious seclusion till his death in 1193. In late June, his suffragen, Basil Kamaterus, brother of the City Prefect and patently in Andronikus' camp, was named Procurator, and a year later, Patriarch.

On 25 April the Caesar Demetrius was married to the Princess Irene Comnena in splendor reminiscent of her father's marriage to Princess Anastasia of Georgia, thirty-nine years before. Unfortunately for all it implied, the resemblance ended there. In 1144, though still stupefied by the untimely death of St. John, the Empire was not only territorially larger but internally stronger than at any time since Basil II, the Great. The Imperial Treasury groaned with gold, and the reputation and prestige of the dynasty was awesome. Then Andronikus was the leader of the most fashionable society in the city, in whose van even the Emperor followed. Then his nuptials to the sister of the King of Georgia had allowed his young cousin to initiate the magnificent panoply which would become the signature of the new reign. Now, instead of the Patriarch of Constantinople officiating with a brace of bishops, there was, in lieu of St. Andrew's successor, the Patriarch of the Bulgars. Now, instead of a huge, unified family delighted to put aside mourning and partake in ceremony, all too many kin were divided, many present only so as not to anger the omnipotent Regent.

Ironically, with his marriage, Andronikus only alienated further the family he intended to bring together, and poisoned the relationships between his own immediate heirs. Alexander refused to attend. Julian had argued violently with Irene before the ceremony. The sisters were estranged. Demetrius was bewildered and resentful. (But he was soon to be surprised by the pleasure he took in Irene, whom it would often amuse to make him blush by some boldness, whereupon she would laugh merrily and kiss him, in public or private.) Most damagingly, perhaps, the Grand Duke not only raised enmity between the bride and her mother—all of Theodora's person revolted against her child in place of Zoë, whose affection for Demetrius was proved—but on this point broke with his mistress of nearly seventeen years.

According to Alexander, Andronikus had commanded Theodora appear at Holy Wisdom or that same wedding day leave the Irene Villa. An argument followed which lasted throughout most of a night, from room to room of the great mansion, now seemingly ended in forgiveness and a moment later begun again. In the morning, with the Regent's eldest son at her side and Prince Christopher by the hand, the Queen visited with Basil Kamaterus, adjured Andronikus, and confessed and received Communion for the first time since her liaison began at Acre in the mid-sixties. She never returned to either the Irene Villa or St.

Michael's, but took up residence at Vlanga with Alexander. Of course, she was not present at the wedding. Or rather she was, as they say, in all but her person. No man alive to see Theodora a quarter century before could help but be haunted by her daughter's resemblance. When, during the banquet, the Latin musician whom I had saved the previous year strummed an especially elegiac tune, I caught Andronikus most mournfully watching his daughter, who was, at once, strained and radiant.

Later, when evening had arrived beyond the windows of Blachernae's magnificent banquet hall, Andronikus kissed the young Emperor's hand, threw a simple white wool cloak over his robe of opus plumarium sewn with rubies and emeralds, took two guards with him and myself, and together, rather daringly, we walked the streets of the northwest portion of the city. "Plato was so very right," he said. "Music is a dangerous weapon. It is insidious. I feel quite my age tonight."

I thought of seeing him that morning in his bath. I recalled how this man, who had always been so inordinately proud of the beauty of his body, turned a little away—self-consciously—from Julian and myself. He was remarkably firm for sixty-one, but the age—or its deterioration—mostly held back by constant exercise strenuous enough to kill an adolescent, was evident nevertheless. The gray hairs of his chest and arms and pubic region, unlike the almost effeminately lustrous silver curls upon his head, suggested the patriarch he did not want to be, so too the webbing at the join of the arms and chest, the slight flabbiness of the teats, of the biceps when relaxed, the stretch scars upon the skin, the blue veins behind the knees. He could still bend a bezant between his fingers without a blush of effort, but one's delight was in the enormous strength still left to the old giant rather than the acceptance of such strength as a matter of course.

"The other day, in Philopation, I was sitting on a bench, in the sun. Maupacta was there. She asked me what I was thinking. Do you know, Nicetas, I was thinking of nothing at all?"

He watched intently as a middle-aged father and his young son passed us by, the child staring up at the old Hercules by my side. Both were dressed in homespun and the father was at least a day unshaven. The Regent sighed as we walked on.

He said, "I'll confess, when I took the power—at least in the first days—I was overwhelmed. Where does one begin, I asked myself, to rebuild a state?"

Where *did* one begin, I asked him.

"Well, one doesn't precisely begin. Oh, you can commission the reports of those matters which have particularly aroused your interest. But, really, the problems of state are seamless from one ruler to another, and it only depends upon the competence of the successor whether or not they will be solved. Of course, finding good men to serve you is perhaps the chiefest contribution toward change and solution one can, indeed, abruptly make."

"Good men," I said, "have a way of acting independently, don't you think, Your Highness?"

"Not really. I can't summon a single example wherein a great civil servant's independence, as you call it, was not in accord with the man who raised him—if that man, to be sure, was serious in his search for virtue. Even if ruler and servant diverge in method, the ends are the same. It is the flunky, in fact, who will act independently, whether actively by corruption or passively through inactivity. These men have nothing in common with their mentor, as I have nothing in common with my reputation. By the way, I noticed Hagiochristophorites the other day. He had a new nose. Silver, from the looks of it."

"Yes, indeed, Your Highness. I'm told he occasionally removes it in company and while everyone looks on bemused, polishes it."

Andronikus laughed uproariously, which pleased me.

I said, "His hygiene is as unedifying as your glee, sir."

"What's that?" he said. "You're too hard on the poor devil. Give him his little measure."

"I've always thought delight, like water, runs out as it is measured, Your Highness. God knows the origin of water. I would guess the source of Hagiochristophorites' silver pleasure a matter of extortion. I don't like the man. He loiters where he oughtn't to be. He's too eager to do any man a favor."

The Grand Duke stopped me with a touch on my forearm: "Leave him to Tripsychos and don't worry about him. He's the Commander's concern." He paused. "Now this is yours. I have it in mind to initiate negotiations with Venice. What do you think?"

"Rich and prodigious Venice."

"Do you disapprove?"

"I see its necessity. The people won't. You mean to bring them back, don't you?"

"Yes."

"Then the people will ask if a man should starve his family to feed his friends."

"Yes, again, if that friend helps to defend the family. Hunger for a time is infinitely preferable to death once and for all."

"Then," I said, "Your Highness will be obliged to explain that to our citizens as they watch the Venetians once again luxuriate while their own stomachs growl. The people want equity and have no mind for safety or antidiplomacy vis-à-vis Genoa and Pisa. The mob will take that up with us, I fear."

"My grandfather used to say a mob serves its purpose by pointing out injustices. It cannot solve them. In the noise and the sensations of riot, I suspect it is all too easy to feel a sense of action, to refrain from accusing oneself for not being constructive or clever enough to solve a problem at hand. Well, if one truly means to take command, one must expect to offend the some and the many: the intelligent who have ideas of their own, and the ignorant sufferer who has not the resource to be patient."

I had good reason to remember those words in the years ahead. As Michael Branas once said to me long after, when the azure mist of Andronikus' legend began to envelop us all, "I sometimes think because he did not believe in the supernatural, he was forcing himself to accomplish the superhuman. If one has no standards by which to take the measure of one's limitations—and that is the practical nature of humility—then you surely risk the danger of attempting to accomplish too much at the expense of the little which can be done. We are, after all, only human, and we *are* limited in what we can do. The frustration in the failure of great things distracts us from—and sometimes prejudices us against—those possible compromises by which we survive. I think it rather instructive—don't you?—that in the *Iliad* the mortals are, by far, more admirable than the gods."

That summer of 1183 was a fury of activity. He commissioned the repair—badly needed—of the aqueducts in all major cities of the Empire, a colossal enterprise for which, even at its abysm, his name was secretly blessed. He raised the salary of public officials in "that crucial middle shelf between great power and none, wherein incorruptibility and debt confront one another." His hope was to preserve these people from peculation, and it was mostly fulfilled.

He carried on a tremendous, unprecedented dialogue with his newly appointed governors and magistrates, sometimes dispatching as many as three letters in a day to the same addressee. Answers were, at all times, expected, and these epistles became something of a joke, then a trial. No detail was beneath his attention. (When Nicephorus Prosuchos, the new Prefect of Athens, arrived for a short visit at Constantinople, he came to my office and complained, "For God's sake, Count, can't you speak to him about those damn letters? He wants immediate answers and immediate results. We haven't the time for one if we're expected to accomplish the other.") He urged governors to travel about their provinces and woe betide the man who wrote once too often from the same residence.

Then, in July—the same day he issued a Writ of Outlawry against Alexius Angelus at the court of Saladin—he promulgated the great chrysobull on taxation, which bluntly shifted the major burden of taxes and assessments from the cities—primarily mercantile and middle or lower class—to the countryside and the vast domains of the monasteries and the nobility. It may be said, truly, if his proposed social revolution began at any moment—and, with any cause, set the aristocracy irrevocably against him—it was in this document, drawn up throughout winter and spring. Henceforward it was the singular ambition of the nobility to separate from the throne "this man," as an aged, outraged Leo Cantostephanus wrote to me:

> this godless blasphemer and regicide with his lunatic—if not syphilitic—visions of a Byzantine Republic. Only the Jew Emperor Michael I Rhangabe spoke similarly and the comparison is fitting. I have known the Regent since he was a boy and I shall never understand how so blithe, so witty, so effervescent, and, frankly, so indifferent a young wastrel could turn so dour, mean, brutal, and quite suddenly a reformer against his own class. Like all things in his life, I suspect dilletantism. And tell me, how does he propose—once we are gone—rule shall be effected? By an elected council? By a proconsul? By dictatorship? Does he intend to abolish the Sacred Throne of the Caesars along with the nobility? Does he intend to keep it? If he does, he will have a hybrid, at once unnatural, ugly, and weak—like all hybrids, as much a mongreli-

zation as one of his precious poor, and as offensive to God Almighty. I traveled to Iconium and held you at the font many years ago, Nicetas, as your godfather. I have known you all *your* young life as I have known him his and I will never understand how you could so thoroughly and unconscionably betray all you are and all your own in behalf of that conceited and senile murderer. It is more difficult to imagine he is the grandson of Lord Alexius—who was *my* godfather—than your father *not* to be looking down from heaven with disapproval. Somehow I feel myself responsible.

Two aspects of the chrysobull on taxation were most controversial beyond even the scandal of the document as a whole. One was the establishment of a judicial seat for each tax district, wherein the fairness of any assessment and the probity of any tax collector could be called into question. Governors and magistrates deemed the office an encroachment on their power and complained there was no guarantee against collusion with the tax collector; the poor feared they would—as in any court they entered—lose to bribery (and were consequently astonished when, in case after case, they did not). The second disputed point was the institution of the death penalty for corruption in any form by assessors or collectors.

He said, "I don't think many jobbers quite realize how important, at this point, is the maintenance of the government's reputation among its citizens for integrity, or the revenues necessary to a depleted treasury. Things are not as they were. I fear we are going to have a few men hanging at crossroads before the seriousness of my threat—or rather the ultimate intentions behind it—is realized. There is nothing to be done about it, however. I mean that punishment more as a dare than a practicing reality, but I know it will have no effect without a few examples. Surely there could be nothing more pathetic than one of these tax gatherers dead for a few coins. Most of them are low-born and manifestly *not* corrupt. They are merely doing as their predecessors have always done, cheating a little at the public till. But that's just the point. Habit can dull the edge of any vice. Because it is immemorial does not mean it is ineradicable. It is certainly the most notorious sin against any state, or any state which does not waste its treasure on panoply and privilege. One revenue agent and a few coins is nothing. But multiply the sum by thousands. This is thievery at its worst. Such money is given in good faith for services which the government must provide. I see no other way of ending this scourge. Maiming a man is the signal for his revenge not his regeneration. I would hope at this point to be taken at my word. They have the choice between ceasing to cheat and ceasing to breathe. I can only be comforted, henceforth, in the knowledge we will probably hang the worst of the lot or the greatest fools, in which case they have no business working for my government."†

Pursuant to the government's probity in the expense of revenues, Andronikus began slashing away at the court, its courtiers and its trappings, all of which had been inherited from Manuel's era, accepted and continued since his death despite the exorbitant cost at a time of widespread financial crisis. Later, after his death, it was said the disestablishment was the Regent's carefully strategized second step in assuming for himself the crown. Nothing could have been further from the truth. For those alive in the reign of John II, austerity was scarcely new or without its recommendations. At least until the Regent instituted reforms, not a few of the city's aristocratic aesthetes considered the court "antiquated and vulgar." The proof of Andronikus' duplicity supposedly rests in the remark he made shortly after the decimation of courtiers and the breaking up and melting down of a great deal of expensive paraphernalia—the proceeds handed over to the Imperial Treasury. When his cousin, John Cantacuzenus, remonstrated with him, "How can you destroy regalia—objects beautiful in themselves—sacred with the reigns of a hundred autocrats, turning them into coins which will be spent tomorrow?" Andronikus replied, "They will survive longer as money than as raiment. Besides, without his trappings, one would think you fear the people will not be able to read majesty across Alexius' pettiness."

At fifteen, His Imperial Majesty, Alexius II, indulged his obsession for hunting as much as the change of seasons and herds and harvests would allow. On all those occasions he took with him his fourteen-year-

† A codicil, by the way, was added to the chrysobull reducing the salt and grain taxes for the native population. Theodore Chumnos protested, "How shall we replace the revenue? This is luxury the Empire cannot afford." Andronikus rather too glibly replied, "So is the nobility. We'll get it from them." Unfortunately the reduction had not the desired effect of lowering the prices of these commodities. The speculators merely withheld the produce, creating a terrific demand, then raised their retail prices and reaped a tremendous profit. N.A.

old Empress, the slender, beauteous little Agnes-Anna, across whose inherent stateliness one could have read imperiousness had she been dressed in rags. (Often she complained to Andronikus of the young man's "spiteful" desire for her presence: "He commands me accompany him because it bores and annoys me, and if I do not want to go he threatens to put me away the moment he attains majority." At this, the Regent sympathetically replied, "He is your husband, madame, and you must be submissive to him in all things. Only rest assured, you shall never be obliged to take the veil.")

The Emperor's education had begun well enough in youth, if too early. Surely that was the result of his overeager father, too old to recall a child's hatred of matriculation by category, enforced hours, and the rigorous training of a naturally curious mind to unquestionable concepts. The late Emperor's precipitant application of tutors had, in fact, soured the august boy so that when, intentionally or unintentionally, his education abruptly degenerated during his mother's Regency, his resistance to books and crudity of mind became irrevocable. Andronikus sent the greatest jurors, poets, historians, rhetoricians, and musicians to the Imperial suite with no effect. This, too, may have been a mistake. Autocratic will can bend the greatest no less than the least to obedience. It is only natural to secure the most eminent teachers and practitioners to educate a child who will one day assume Supreme Power which is already his in principle, if not fact. Unfortunately, some exquisite contingencies arise. An emperor in his minority must be accorded the same respect in public and indulgence in private as in the years of his majority. If there is no figure of sufficient authority—at least out of the public eye—to keep the child at disciplines against which anyone his age would rebel had he the power (and Andronikus was understandably too busy to do this), the result is monstrous: tempestuousness, petulance, lassitude, secretiveness, cunning, even physical violence, which no man so honored in his field as to be selected an Imperial tutor—and thereafter insulted and exasperated in his dignity—is bound to endure.

Andronikus, reading reports of his cousin's matriculation, receiving tutors—bruised within and just as often without—unaware of his own mistake in the choice of too celebrated men and his failure to discipline the youth, could but be disgusted and begin to entertain a profound contempt—and a dangerous one—for the Emperor. Alexius, in turn, with lack of discretion and the ready susceptibility of the powerful, vain, and mentally undisciplined, began to listen to those who would use him for their own ends, true sycophants, who do not repeat the ideas of their masters, but train their masters to repeat their own.

Quite the opposite of what Angelian apologists suggest, Alexius, at the age of fifteen—three years before his majority—was *not* daring to assume the power in defense of Empire against the evil Regent. I knew that boy and he was for all his egotism—perhaps because of it—a tool. Like the Grand Duke Julian, he was also something of a melodramatist. It pleased him to receive the adoration—and wage none of the battles— of a champion. It pleased him, as did the hisses of conspiracy, its meetings in empty churches, its notes passed within the folds of a robe from palm to palm, and aristocrats four times his years kneeling before him to mystically venerate him and pledge their lives. Of course, the more seriously committed nobles were wisely mistrustful of the youth's loud excitement and had nothing whatever to do with him, save the strategy to promote his legitimacy at the end. Rather it was his more cynical manipulators who could not see beyond their own derision to the fatal position in which they placed themselves and Manuel's son.

From the beginning, through the Secret Police, Andronikus was aware of a plot, which itself was of no account—he combed it through with spies—but sufficient to bring him up shortly with the prospect he had perhaps too early dismissed: the Basileus' majority. At that point, Alexius was entirely within his rights—i.e., with the power to enforce them— in dismissing the Regent, who, if he wished to keep the power, could but then resort to usurpation. His only alternative was preemptive: a Co-Imperium.

"What do you think?" he asked me, among others—at least one other, I'm certain—after informing me of his intentions in counteracting the Emperor. "An honest answer now," he warned good-naturedly—or such as it seemed to be.

I smiled, "Your Highness, if I said no to what you intend to do, you would think me honest to be sure. If I said yes, you would think me a liar or a flatterer."

"Then," he said, "what is your opinion of its validity?"

I said it was positive. "Then tell me your reasoning and I will guess at deceit, obsequiousness, or conviction. Go on."

I looked directly at him and spoke. "It is quite simple, Your Highness. This Empire is in no condition to tolerate another Michael VII. You are a prince of the Imperial blood, closer in time, which is to hope the integrity, of Alexius I and John II. Primogeniture is a tradition. It is not an absolute."

He was amused by this. "Indeed? I thought you believed as the others."

"Your Highness," I said, "long ago, when I first read Thucydides and decided ultimately I should become a historian—all else to that purpose —I realized almost simultaneously, if I should make my prejudices too well known I should lose my freedom to argue and the right to change my mind. Let us say, I believe God acts through the Imperium in ways scarcely comprehensible to us. We have often posited our emperors fail or endure by heaven's decree, whatever appearances to the contrary which test that faith. We have the choice of abiding by tradition and perhaps suffering for it or striking out against precedent and rescuing the Empire. Let me put it this way. It is a point of Imperial etiquette that if I am walking with you, or with His Highness, your brother, or any one of your kin, and I encounter a friend, I am not allowed to recognize him or speak to him unless you do so first. But suppose that fellow were to come to some great danger—even his death—if I did not warn him. What ought I to do?"

"Warn him, I would hope."

"Precisely, Your Highness. I might offend you. I might be punished for it, but sooner that than offend myself to the bottom of my heart by allowing tradition to prevent me from saving one who need not otherwise have been destroyed. You must do what *you* will, Your Highness; you would otherwise deny the meaning of all you have done previously. I am no flatterer and no sycophant and I've nothing to gain for I've risen high, higher than men twice my age, and now hold power I should scarcely have expected myself to wield. I would, however, relinquish it the moment I suspected the crown's disinterest and my consequent irrelevance."

It took a month to make him Emperor, and then the accession was out of any man's hands, the consequence of events. For the first time, significantly, Stephen Hagiochristophorites was used, and importantly, because of his contacts with the chief mobsters of the city. Andronikus would have been satisfied to rely on those rather more sedate and influential elements for him—in the Senate, the army, the Church, and amongst the middle class—and through them force Alexius to proclaim him Co-Adjutor. There were, however, too many uncertainties in this alternative. He would, by precedent, leave himself open to the accusation of usurper since, by law, all initiation of legislation was his by empowering of the Emperor. Then again, if the crown came down from the top rather than arrive upon his head as a result of a ground swell, there was always the dangerous legality of the young Basileus' seniority. In truth, whether "given" or forced upon him, it would be a matter of prearrangement, of appearances, above all, but those appearances by which we live and act and the law so moves to judge us.

First, word was put about that the Regent, till his accession in excellent health, was beginning to tire after seventeen months of uninterrupted eighteen-hour days (perfectly true), and that he was discouraged by the controversy of his position, which forced upon him the burdens of an empire but left him vulnerable to criticism, plots, and indignities such as the throne would never be made to suffer (partially true). Then, Andronikus called a meeting of the entire Imperial family and, to the outrage of some and the relief of others who dreaded the majority of Alexius, frankly told them he wanted the Co-Augustate, believed he deserved it, and, while he would ask none to commit themselves, would appreciate what he called, almost humorously, a "consenting neutrality among those of you who doubt the providence of such a move, but not my qualifications." (It is said, on these words he looked at Theodora, who attempted to remain impassive but, at last, looked away. After the meeting, he was seen to speak to her.)

Finally, in late August, he went before the Senate and openly declared himself dissatisfied with being "an emperor in all that is expected of me, and otherwise treated as the Lord Steward of the backstairs. Either I am made co-equal in honors as well as expectations or, gentlemen, in the very near future, you may expect my resignation." At the end of the speech, several dozen Senators rose from their chairs, gave the Imperial salute, and shouted, "Long live Andronikus Augustus!" More than a thousand remained immobile and silent. Finally chagrined, my colleagues beseated themselves, blushing and coughing with the sightless eyes of men who have made fools of themselves.

I was sitting behind the podium with the Grand Dukes Philip, Alexander, Julian, and Prince Christopher, as well as Michael Branas who had returned from the battlefront—specifically for this speech—to make "a show for the army." I ached for Andronikus because he was a great man who had a right to be vain and the sensitivity to be easily humiliated, as surely he was now—*not* by the silence of the majority, but the absurdity of those sixty or seventy men whose consensus of the Senate was so ill-informed they had allowed the Regent to be thus embarrassed and even impeded. It did not take a seer to realize this scene would be repeated from mouth to mouth throughout the city and the Grand Duke's prestige would suffer for it.

For several days, Andronikus went about his work in the worst mood I had ever before beheld. Normally his self-containment was awesome and his anger, even real, measured. Now he was surly, given to drifting away empty-eyed in mid-conversation. He looked haggard and probably he had not slept. One by one his children tried to distract him, and failed, as did Maupacta. On the third night this most abstemious of princes got notoriously drunk and sought out Theodora at Vlanga. There he slept for two days, as he was to say, "closing my eyes a caterpillar and awaking a butterfly."

What had happened was this. At Nicea and Brusa in the governacy of Bithynia, the secretly returned Angeli, in collusion with several members of the recently chastened "Imperial" Cantacuzeni had declared rebellion "against the Regent, solely," which was legally impossible; one rebelled against the Emperor or not at all. Over and above Hagiochristophorites' preparations, mobs began to gather in Andronikus' behalf. Then, while Michael Branas was returning to the Balkans, his Co-Commander precipitously left the Praetorium and rode horseback, night and day, to Adrianople where he consulted with his family and the aged Bryennii brothers, sons of the great Caesar, who had been alienated from the Comneni since Manuel's accession and failure to release their mother Anna from her incarceration. With several of the Adrianopolitan nobility, Lapardas departed for Bithynia to join the Angeli and Cantacuzeni declaring himself against Andronikus' assumption of the power on the rather novel grounds of the Regent's well-known atheism. He wrote:

> You cannot claim the Sacred Authority, the Pledge of Allegiance, or the obedience all subjects owe to the Emperor so long as you are, self-confessedly, estranged from God Almighty. You cannot be a secular autocrat. We are bound by sacred Christian principles. You are bound by nothing at all. We should be giving ourselves not to the immoral, but the amoral. No man in his right mind would do this.

Lapardas' integrity was undoubted, for he was the first against David and the last to yield in the Rebellion of May 1181. But he was also a land magnate of enormous wealth, an eminent aristocrat, and had long been uneasy about Andronikus' policies vis-à-vis the nobility. "Why must you *destroy* your own people? Who will lead? Do you realize, truly, what you are about?" he had asked Andronikus only a year earlier.

The Grand Duke had answered patiently, "Andrew, I have no intention of destroying anything. I mean only to act with the complete logic and justice of which a man is capable. I cannot help it if the obsolescence of things is thereby perceived. What is ripe falls of its own weight, and to deny that fact is to fall with it."

And so it was the false rumor—raised and masterfully instrumented, I must admit, by Hagiochristophorites—Lapardas was taking half the West army with him to Bithynia, which brought to Vlanga a deputation of the Senate followed by 100,000 rabble, who well knew what Their Excellencies were about.

From noon to late afternoon to twilight, when God knows the number of the multitude of torches which were struck and raised, the crowd, filling the palace courtyard and spilling in either direction the whole length of the street—and swelling still—chanted Andronikus' name. Within Vlanga's walls (swarming with Varangians, whose politically sophisticated commanders knew when a shift of power was taking place), Andronikus consulted with every member of the government and the family which could be safely escorted through the tumult without.‡

Finally in the last moments of dusk, a blood-red, lurid moon rising in the east, the Regent came out onto the small balcony above the great central doors. The greeting which went up from the crowd was actually distorted as it entered the ear, an insufficient instrument to receive the sound. From within, near the doors, I watched his profile, flamboy-

---

‡ He also dispatched a commission to one of the Comneni's most faithful adherents, Count Eugenius Cephalus, great-great-grandson of Alexius I's valet, to secure Lapardas' imprisonment by any means. The Count, an aesthete and poet, as well as a magistrate, his sensibilities having long suffered the arrogance of the more ancient aristocrats who held the Cephali parvenus, seized the Duke, still on his way to Brusa, at the port of Atramyttion, blinded him the same afternoon, and sent him to Constantinople in chains. Lapardas never even convened with the Bithynian conspirators whose lot he suffered by joining them at a distance. N.A.

antly lit and flickering above the light of a thousand torches. He was absolutely expressionless. He did not speak, nor try to speak. Below him, horses of the Imperial escort were brought forward, the signal to leave the balcony.

Within the great room—to everyone's surprise—he sought out Theodora and embraced her, his face still registering no emotion. He gestured to his sons, his sons-in-law, several other Imperial relatives, a number of his chief counselors, including myself, and together we left the second floor and the palace itself—amidst stupendous acclamation— for Blachernae, where, in the great gold, domed Throne Room, Alexius had been prepared since midafternoon—however sullenly—to acknowledge the Regent as Co-Augustus.

Near tears of frustration, the youth bid his father's cousin retire to put on the purple boots, the divitavisson, and the diadem and sit upon the Empress' throne which he commanded be brought out and placed beside his beneath the enormous jeweled crown, suspended from the ceiling by golden chains. What should have taken no more than a quarter hour took two.

Three crowns were released from the Imperial Treasury: the Alexian, the simplest, of gold with a large single ruby; the Justinian, of ivory now reinforced with silver, of rubies and amethysts; and the Macedonian crown, a great bowl of emeralds, sapphires, and pearls—the "Sea Crown," as it was called, for its aquamarine colors. (Alexius II, in state, was wearing the Johannine-Manuel Crown, the most elaborate of all—of rubies, emeralds, sapphires, pearls, and diamonds.) Each was too small for the Regent's head. Finally someone remembered the Constantine Crown, high above the altar of Holy Wisdom, a massive seven-pound hoop of pearls and rubies in solid gold. A troop of Varangians was dispatched to procure it. As for the scarlet campagia, they had to be made on the spot by the Emperor's bootmaker—and there was not enough time to apply, as prescribed, the pearl eagles. Only the fabulous divitavisson, with its avalanche of jewels affixed to quadruple-weight black-purple velvet, needed no alterations.

But then occurred the unexpected. As several Grand Dukes were about to dress him with robe, crown, and boots, Andronikus held up his hand and said, "No. Wait," and disappeared into a small anteroom. Several minutes later, rather stunned and perplexed by his leisure, the

Grand Duke Alexander and I went to the door and slipped into the gold-walled closet. He was sitting in the half-light of a small brazier, his eyes in shadow but for a single eerie glint. *Explicit Nicetas Acominatus: Res Gestae de Comnenorum.*

XI

Incipit: Michael Acominatus: That is the point in the manuscript from which my brother could go no further. Wasted and exhausted by cancer of the spine, which may or may not have been founded in the wound he suffered escaping Constantinople, he forsook his pen, went to bed, and waited in pain for death. Perhaps it was just as well. The tale of those last two years, which, shortly, I will continue, is not one of fulfillment. There is no apotheosis save the manner in which His Imperial Majesty, my Lord Basileus Andronikus, met his death.

After a fashion, Nicetas' inability to complete the history was the chance analogy to his association with Andronikus. From the fall of the Emperor, in 1185, throughout the nineteen years of the Angelus Dynasty, my brother longed to explain his commitment to the last great Comnenus. But, besides the tactlessness of speaking the forbidden names, of recalling those tumultuous years in a time when men hoarded gold and emptied their memories, not dreading the future, but beyond dread—having lived with the worst fears too long until the edges of fear were worn—languorous and stupefied as the lotus-eaters, there was simply a lack of interest in my brother's ratiocination. If men were beyond dread, then, by definition, they were beyond guilt or innocence—their own or their judgment of others'. Whether the amorality was the result of relinquishing the great burden of Empire or the stunting of all emotion following the public atrocities committed upon the last Comnenus Emperor—in the end, the manner of his death having proved as consequential as his life—they could hardly be expected to care for or credit the personal culpability of one man, who, to all appearances, was free of malice and, in fact, still cared what became of crown and Empire. It was a call to self-preservation, if not duty, their cynicism would no longer allow.

Against cynicism, anxious idealism has no resonance. Most of these men condescended to my brother's impeccability, while Nicetas, who, like Andronikus, lived by logic, would not accept his own guiltlessness unless he could evidence its justice. Men do indeed carry the seeds of their own destruction, as he had said. Born to, if not of, the provincial aristocracy—Orthodox, conservative, circumspect—he lacked the assurance, the spectacular sophistication of the great Grandees—and *their* greatest members, the Comneni—whereby he could publicly, indifferently act without explanation or apology and then draw on his own cold blood against criticism. No one cared to hear his apologia while he lived, and this enforced silence only exacerbated his sense of a great guilt having been committed, himself complicit, but forgiven, which is not reconciliation. At the end, it occurs to me, he may have been as alone as Andronikus.

Nicetas was by no means a saint, but he possessed the innocence of the saint in denying his innocence. That he could not round out his history of Andronikus and the Comneni was, by itself, less unhappy than the fact, in failing to do so, he lost his last opportunity to investigate and justify his own motives, at least in those final two years of the dynasty. For it must be perfectly clear by now, as he told the story of Byzantium and of Andronikus, he was discovering himself, deeper and more deeply. No man can confront the better part of a century of events, of actions oftentimes alien to himself, without summoning his own soul to challenge them and be challenged by them. The true historian—and I believe my brother was among them—is not one who presents his history without interpretation—that is a mere clerk—but history through his sensibility, who is altered himself by the events he records. The man who commenced this work is not the same at the end of the manuscript as at the beginning. He has less hope, but he is closer to reality. He is less elegant, more intricate—so were Tacitus and Thucydides, his two favorite historians—but for that closer to poetry which is nearer epiphanies than the melodrama of Xenophon, the dense veneer of Cicero, or the indifferent precision of Sallust.

Andronikus' goal may have been power, yet he had the wherewithal to realize this power was the key to something still more personal and desirable: ultimate freedom of choice against the alternatives destiny presented to him. In Nicetas' chimera—knowledge complete, of others and of himself—the considered possibility, whether or not he acknowledged it, was the desire for reality beneath reality, ultimate motives. In both men, the final objective was the same: personal providence in a world of intrusion—for nothing moves in the universe save something else is displaced. And in each man, the failure to recognize the impossibility of his goal ended in the only fall which has true meaning, that which is self-inflicted.

The point of flame rides down to the earth, and incandescent obliteration.

In the following few, remaining pages, we do not mean to give short shrift to the fall of Andronikus. One may be certain my beloved, long-winded brother would have said amen to that. The two years nearly to the day in which he reigned as Autocrat comprise the summation of all that had gone before. In truth, what necessity and symmetry oblige me to do is the very obverse of the tragedy of *Oedipus the King*, which takes place before the play begins. What is written by Sophocles is a gigantic denouement, necessary because there is no redemption without the victim's consciousness of his fall. The play is the thought following the action. This history is action following on the thought.

We shall never know for certain what drove Andronikus from the anteroom of the Gold Audience Hall at Blachernae, or, on his return, prompted what my brother later recalled to me as "the strangest scene I ever expect to witness," to wit: The Regent, now Emperor, burst into tears and refused the Power. He had actually to be forced into his robes and boots and virtually shoved into a chair while the crown of Constantine the Great was lowered onto his head. Some called it his political sense—a false humility, which, unlike Caesar's, worked. Some called it his theatrical sense, others a practical joke, still others a devious plot to be certain who were his adherents at the last moment.

His first official act as Emperor, according to custom, was to choose his burial site. He selected Church of the Forty Martyrs in the poorest section of the city and, to that end, commissioned an architect to refurbish the establishment—to the pleasure of its parishioners—and a sculptor to erect his image near the North Gate. He was to be represented not in Imperial robes but as a worker, oppressed with labor, holding a scythe over his shoulders. The statue became a legend. There was talk of it throughout the Empire, and at a party at Athens which I attended, opinions were divided between derision, anxiety, perplexity, and—among the new bureaucrats and officials—a somewhat tentative pride.

In October he virtually separated the Church from the state by issuance of a chrysobull which declared religious dissension of any sort—whether between sects or within sects—that is, theological or prejudicial, on paper or with sticks—now punishable by law, whether the subject in question was Greek or Latin Catholic, Paulician heretic, Jew or Moslem. In one stroke, by implication, he declared Orthodoxy of no more special interest to the government than Euripides. In one stroke, he offended the entire Synod, whom, in his Coronation Oath—kissing the relic of the True Cross—he had sworn to uphold. In one stroke, he lost the pulpits of the poor priests, his most ardent followers and scarcely more literate or reasonable—or less bigoted—than the rabble they incited in his favor. In truth, with few exceptions, the whole of official Orthodoxy was now alienated: the monasterial landlords, whom he acted against on principle, the bishops disempowered from the throne, and the lower hierarchies barred from their mean-minded wrath.

Also in that same month, with the rebellion in Bithynia spread from Nicea and Brusa to a third major city, Lopadion, Augustus instituted a new Oath of Allegiance to the throne to be taken by all members of the aristocracy at Constantinople and duly administered by all Marshals of the Nobility in the provinces. The final sentence of the pledge was the most controversial: if one member of any immediate family committed treason, all would suffer jailing. Confiscation of property to the crown would be total and irrevocable. Men dared not refuse the oath for fear of making themselves suspect. At the same time, taking it, they considered themselves under no obligation to an atheistic anti-Christ. Donatism, apparently, had returned to trouble these Christians.

Nicetas:

The aristocracy is outraged by the pledge. Can you imagine such an attitude under Manuel or John? Rightly, of course, they suspect His Majesty to be other than their tool. At the same time they do not realize this renewal of allegiance is a guarantee against persecution. Or is it, they do not trust themselves? Yes, I understand the sincerity of their greed, which is unself-conscious. So many of them are decent people, merely confusing unjust tradition with sacrosanct right. But the path Augustus follows is to the good of all men, not a few, whose blindness may turn out to be the death of us all. Great or nefarious by their standards, Andronikus is our Emperor and to contest him is to contest the validity of the state. If they break him, then we, in turn, shall break apart. By that, what has any man profited?*

In November he paid a state visit to Thrace, the last province to consent to his Regency. He spent several days at the hunt "clearing his head," as he told Nicetas, "thinking nothing, absolutely nothing,"† then made a pilgrimage to his father's tomb at the Monastery of Vera, his first opportunity to do so since the great Sebastocrator's death twenty-seven years before. At Thessalonika, he stayed at Demetrius Palace and consulted with Michael Branas on the possibility of withdrawing the Army of the West to Asia to fight the Bithynian rebels.

> Michael advised His Majesty to leave him be at least a few more months. The stalemate against Bela and Stephen is working to our advantage. The native population has been heartened by the resurgent Imperium and come to join us, whereas Bela's army and Nemanya's are being slowly decimated. In their respective states, the war, as it goes on, becomes less popular, prospective conscriptees vanishing into the woods, volunteers few and far between.

Andronikus consented to Branas' strategy, believing, in the long run, the rebels less a danger than Hungary triumphant. But danger they were. Mid-journey his return to Constantinople, the Emperor was informed of a secret consent between the Bithynian rebels who had advanced on Nicomedia (which repulsed them) and the advisers of Alexius II, with or without the youth's consent, as much as it mattered. Many of the Co-Emperor's suite had been appointed by Andronikus, when Regent, and their collusion shocked him all the more. He ordered the entire staff of courtiers imprisoned and three men in particular blinded. Once arrived at Blachernae, he immediately convened the Sacred Consistory and demanded the deposition of Manuel's son. As Nicetas described it several years later in a monograph:

---

* This and the following quotations are excerpted from my brother's letters to me, or from his own notebooks. M.A.

† The hides and antlers of the animals he hunted were returned to Constantinople as trophies. Much later Maupacta persuaded the Emperor to affix the horns to the porticoes of the Bovi Forum, rather to twit husbands for their wives' infidelity. The ladies of the city had, then, the dubious pleasure of laughing with a woman who, they may not have realized, was also laughing at them. N.A.

How obnoxious legal fiction can sometimes be. Of course, he could not accuse his Co-Adjutor of high treason. The Emperor *is* the state and treason is impossible to him. Not a man present was unaware of this predicament. Blatantly, Alexius' counselors had sided with the rebels against the throne, which may be occupied by two men, but remains, nevertheless, indivisible. Still, several members of the Consistory questioned the legality of one Co-Emperor deposing the other. The true justice of the question was whether or not Alexius had given his name—or his name was given over—to rebellion, as a means of deposing Andronikus.

In the following days—having duly noted the names of Consistory members who refused him the Chrysobull of Deposition—Andronikus alternately raged, threatened, and bribed members of the Senate or, in more than one instance, sent Hagiochristophorites for parley, the menace implicit in the fact he was the most unlikely of intermediaries. On 25 November the doors of the Senate Building were closed to the public, an extraordinary measure taken no more than two or three times in a century. Within, a secret Imperial ukase was submitted, proclaiming the fifteen-year-old Basileus a bastard, his right to the throne nullified. It was imputed his father was incapable of producing a male heir and his mother, after six years of miscarriage, had turned to the Grand Duke David. The confused precedence of events was ridiculous and intentional, though many pointed out similar characteristics between the Grand Duke and his cousin—more likely the contagion of temperament. To make certain his intentions were completely understood, Andronikus added charges of sorcery and satanic worship, which are sufficient to be punishable by death. The Senate, nevertheless, refused to ratify the charges.

"Of course, I expected it," he told me. "But the defiance is moot. That execrable little beast has to be put out of the way. Deposed he would be visible more than ever, as a bruised hand swells. Even now they're putting it about as part of my campaign against the nobility. Well, it is, insofar as the nobility rebels. He's a mote in the eye of the Empire and I won't put up with him any longer." He said this to me in a corridor, for anyone to hear, holding in his arms his grandson, Maurice, Alexander's boy, the one born club-footed.

On 26 November, Constantine Tripsychos, Theodore Dadibrenos, and Stephen Hagiochristophorites—in a select company of Varangians

—visited Villa Rufiniana, bolted the doors of the young Empress' apartments, then entered the Emperor's suite and strangled him with a bowstring. Tripsychos described it to my brother:

"Hagiochristophorites, who is insatiable, started for His Majesty's valet. The Emperor at once put the fellow behind him. For me, that one protective gesture gave a conscience to my errand—and a bad one. Then His Majesty grabbed up his perennial riding whip from a table and struck Stephen several times, laying bloody welts and knocking off his silver nose. Finally Hagiochristophorites got hold of the whip and jerking it forward threw His Majesty off balance. Dadibrenos had meanwhile slit the throat of the valet. Then we fell upon the Emperor. Before Hagiochristophorites slipped the string around his neck His Majesty called for help from God and his mother, neither one of whom I think he knew very well. It was awful. This noseless man holding tight the cord staring into the bursting eyes of the young Emperor, bleeding at the mouth, the nostrils, and the ears. Well, it's done, and I ask God to forgive me if I've done wrong, though I think not."

The body was buried in the same sea which received the woman who had given it birth. The head and heart were placed in a reliquary and given for interment to the monks of Kalabatos Monastery. The death was posted the next day throughout the city and announced from the pulpits throughout the Empire. The cause: pneumonia, contracted during the Emperor's last hunting expedition. Among the people, he was scarcely mourned for he was scarcely known. Among the aristocracy, however, not only was the true nature of his death widely reported, it was also held to be,

as Uncle Leo calls it, the final corruption of the Comneni. He said he knew nothing about that "common monster," Hagiochristophorites, but he was certain the devil would arrange two eternities in hell for Tripsychos—one for the decapitation of the Dowager Empress, the second for the assassination of the Emperor. Once again he asks me how I can continue to besully myself as a member of such a regime. I think much of the mourning over Alexius II is specious, which is to say, political. He was, in every sense, a danger to the state, promising in majority a merry and pretentious lunacy we simply could not tolerate in our present condition. As the reposit of Autocratic Power—even renounced—he could not be put aside. Andronikus did what had to be against Man-

uel's son as Manuel did what he need not have done against Andronikus.
I grieve for Alexius Comnenus, not Alexius II.

None of the nobility, offended or forlorn of their august tool, dared
openly challenge the Co-Emperor's death. Within the next week, however, they were given precisely a lurid point on which to hang their
dissension. In a private ceremony in the Imperial Chapel at Blachernae,
the sixty-one-year-old Autocrat married the fourteen-year-old French
Empress, whose marriage to Alexius II had, of course, remained un-
consummated. The reasons for this nuptial were numerous and entirely political: it reasserted the alliance with Louis of France as a
makeweight against Italy and the Holy Roman Empire. It associated
the Emperor, formally, with the Johannine branch of the family. Above
all, however, it removed—without deposing—the young Empress as an
instrument of the anti-Andronikan factions.

Now, to be sure, the marriage, however necessary, was unpalatable.
Among the people it was received with surprised but reasonable equanimity. No one presumed the Augustus' legendarily virile eye extended
to maidens scarcely commencing their puberty. They were correct. Yet
the slander was put about His Majesty not only lay upon the virgin
Basilissa, but thereafter corrupted her morally. Even now it endures,
a squeamish point among those who would utilize the memory of Andronikus as an inspirational weapon against the Latin Empire. Tales,
at the time, were replete with descriptions of the girl dancing naked
before the Emperor, offering herself to guards, swallowing aphrodisiacs, and drinking to stupefaction under the invidiously delighted eye
of the degenerate sexagenarian. Since, as any empress, Agnes-Anna
lived in seclusion and was seldom seen, quite any imputation could be
true.

"Does anyone who truly reveres me believe I am or ever have been
so appallingly debased?" the Empress asked my brother many years
later. "Would I have acted thus in my husband's behalf during those
terrible September days less than two years later?"

The entire issue should have been beneath the remark of any intelligent man, save the nobility lifted the incident to a notoriety comparable
to that of Tiberius' homosexual pedophilia at Capri. It was a dangerous
and terrible publicity and the estranged priesthood fell to it, hungrily,
fulminating from their pulpits against the Autocrat. At this the people

in turn passed from indifference to delicious shock, then fear. The atheistic, philandering Imperial Grand Duke had been a taunt against the authority all men despise. But now he was animus epistasea and he had passed from adultery to depravity.

All his life the subject of gossip and awe, his self-confidence has permitted him to be amused when not indifferent to the exaggerations of his legend. But those were stories of a stupendous scapegrace. Depravity is alien to him. He is astonished and uncertain. He has never before had to deal with accusations of degeneracy and he does not know how to now. He is, I think, frightened by its meaning. Those priests who are banished for contumaciousness only make matters worse. They become heroes and martyrs and certify by their punishment the truth of the indictment.

The day after Christmas, when he appeared at the funeral of his trusted Undersecretary, Michael Hagiotheodorites (who was succeeded by Theodore Maurozomes), there was open demonstration against the Basileus as a child molester, usurper, and regicide. He departed the church between an impenetrable wedge of Varangians, while some worthy shouted after him, "You're too tall to use those boys as shields."

Something has snapped, woefully. He has never had the support of the aristocracy. But the people: *they* have been his bastion and now those mighty walls of common trust—that Great Secret between himself and the powerless—is beginning to crack. It is not impudence against Majesty which wounds him. Honors and prerogatives mean nothing to him. He is certain, anyway, it has nothing to do with the Autocracy, with politics. He is certain the people are going against him personally.

In February 1184 he ordered Michael Branas from West to East, reconnoitering with him at Atramyttion with the intention of crushing the Bithynian rebels. After two days of conferences, Andronikus and Michael diverged. The Emperor marched on Nicea and laid siege. Branas marched on Lopadion, which was quickly taken. He left it to his second in command in a state of martial law, then rejoined the Emperor. The Niceans, assisted by the private armies of their leading rebels and mercenary Turks, had proved unexpectedly bold. Day and night between sorties, they shouted through megaphones the same epithets Andronikus had recently suffered at Constantinople. Privately, the Emperor was enraged. Strategically, he remained temperate, for to alienate Nicea with a great pitched battle and much blood would be the ruin of one of the Empire's great—and most ancient—cities.

> Michael told me one morning before a day's battle, His Majesty was taking his usual constitutional on a new mount. About two miles from the encampment, a woman shouted from the road, "Well, Divinity, how do you like that horse of mine?" Augustus instantly dismounted and asked her what she meant. The accuser, a soldier's widow, pointed out that the fine steed bore her late husband's brand. When he died, the Quartermaster Corps did not return the beast, as per law, to his family. Andronikus restored the stolen property and standing amused rather than irritated among his escort said, "Well, gentlemen, it seems I cannot even take a simple morning gallop with a clear conscience."

Andronikus resorted to a stratagem. He ordered the mother of the Angeli rebels, Countess Mary, brought from Constantinople. The exquisite, dignified old lady was thereupon tied to a small battering ram of the sort used to clear defensive housings atop a wall. The weapon was set at the highest level of a small heliopolis which towered fifty feet above the ground. The implication was clear. If surrender were not imminent, the Countess would be pulverized against her own son's fortifications. Before this unlikely end, however, the lady was freed via the arrows of expert marksmen and thereafter rescued by ropes.

Fate intervened. On 13 March 1184 Theodore Cantacuzenus, chief instigator of the rebellion and the very heart of the tri-city strategy, caught sight of the Emperor, insolently unguarded, inspecting the front-line defenses. Impetuously, he left the walls and rode out to meet Andronikus. As Branas described it to my brother:

> "He shrieked the Emperor's name. It was not a warning, not a shout of defiance, but some ungodly disgorging of his insides. His Majesty scarcely had time to turn. All in a moment he registered surprise, unsheathed his huge sword, somehow drew his horse and himself aside, and—I swear to God, I've never seen its like before—struck so powerfully, the head of Cantacuzenus' steed burst cleanly in two. Cantacuzenus fell away with textbook battle technique. The Emperor took his own horse in a leap over some engines, and the infantry present finished off the Duke, who had been my friend, once."

With Cantacuzenus' death the rebellion ended. Isaac Angelus sent emissaries to offer unconditional surrender. The populace was spared;

the native nobles were exiled. But several of the Grandees in question were executed or blinded and the Turk mercenaries impaled upon spikes in a ring around the city walls. This gratuitous brutality was not meant to admonish the Niceans, but discourage Seljuks from ever again crossing into the Empire as soldiers of fortune. Only one of the great rebels survived. In a note to himself, dated 1195, the year Isaac II was dethroned and blinded by his brother, Alexius III, my brother writes:

> One asks oneself why Andronikus spared Isaac, after the Nicene Rebel-
> lion of 1183–84. "Harmless," he commented to me not much later by
> way of describing the man who would succeed him. "Isaac hasn't the
> wit to be but another man's instrument. He's not vicious, only too weak
> to resist what's against his better interests—or his better nature, for that
> matter." I reminded the Emperor he had taken part in the worst recorded
> rebellion against the dynasty. "I would sooner punish a child for follow-
> ing in the wake of his brothers in whatever they do. Besides the foulest
> culprits were at Iconium—that's Alexius—and at Brusa—that's Peter." It
> was among the most momentous decisions he ever made—a misreading
> of character, a matter of caprice.

Brusa was given the choice of surrender of its leading rebels and complete amnesty. To that effect, it refused. The glorious green city with its world-famous hot springs was thereupon besieged and bombarded and two weeks after the arrival of the Imperial army, was entered in force. The camarilla of nobles, forty-two of the forty-three, were hanged on the spot, while Count Peter Angelus was blinded, set upon an ass, and forced into the wastes to be rescued by Turk nomads four days later. At Lopadion, the Bishop, leader of the community, was deposed and blinded, fifteen nobles hanged and another fifty imprisoned.

> Branas said to me, "During our return to Constantinople, he kept repeat-
> ing the word 'waste, waste,' over and over again. It was only later I
> realized he may have been speaking of time as well as men."

Once again in the capital, he lifted the restriction on immigration to the city and voided the Manuelian chrysobull which obliged every citizen to carry official papers when traveling. He initiated the expansion of Orphanotropolis and—attempting to undercut unemployment— Municipal Work Programs. The rebuilding of the Hospital of the Knights of St. John, however (mostly financed from his and Queen Theodora's private purses), once again subjected him to controversy since the Constantinopolitan rabble believed—or so one would think—having destroyed the establishment in the Massacre of '82, they also owned the right to reject its refounding. When the hospital was reopened in January 1185, it was subjected to vandalism only further prevented by the appointment of a round-the-clock guard.

Also in this spring of 1184, he began pensioning the great writers and artisans of the state and those retired jurists whose honesty had left them with great names and no means in their dotage.

Beyond the monolithic walls, under his vigorous, imperious hand travel increased literally by leaps, as merchantmen and sightseers and kin who had not dared visit one another in distant cities for fear of highway robbers, journeyed between reassuring garrison posts. For the first time in forty years, due to fairer, more brusque and systematic taxation—and no less a rigorous administrative budget—the Treasury was beginning to take in more than it gave out. Several provinces, deserted during the Manuelian epoch or its immediate aftermath, were repeopled—more significantly: voluntarily. Agriculture flourished: superb crops bolstered by sure markets and assured stable price. "It seems indeed," my brother said to me with a smile, "as if the multitude of people who had been reduced nearly to the grave have risen to new life, as if the trumpet of the Blessed Archangel Gabriel had sounded in their ears."

Even the mob could now and then be pleased:

During a pause in the games yesterday, which Andronikus attended— and opened—for the first time as Emperor, a troop of clowns began to perform a burlesque as guests who badgered and bullied and made exorbitant demands of an innkeeper while the latter kept on making asides to the crowd, i.e., it was all in a day's work, any indignity for a little profit. But the guests proposed to leave without paying him and when he protested, the innkeeper was told: "Why worry, fool? This is only pretense. Besides, last week, His Majesty's Counselor, Dadibrenos, did the same thing and got away with it." At these words, His Majesty, quite bored, started in his seat. He beckoned a blushing Dadibrenos and asked him if the accusation was true. He denied it. Andronikus called to him the Hippodrome's Master of Ceremonies who explained the owner of a hostel in Chrysopolis had come to him with such a complaint and this ingenious plot to gain the Emperor's attention since, among Dadibrenos' duties was that of co-ordinating His Majesty's daily Right of Address interviews and it was highly unlikely he would grant an audience to his own accuser. By now, the entire Hippodrome, aware of some business in the Kathisma, had fallen silent. (But Maupacta talked on to me, quite oblivious: "When I bow, I bow low, very low, looking at the ground, and hold that position, prolonging the applause. If the audience cannot get your eyes, they will not stop cheering out of courtesy. Of course, you *do* sense the breaking point and that's the time to straighten bolt upright with a smile, for which they reward you with even greater applause. . . ." And so on.) Andronikus said, "I will ask you only once again, Theodore. Is the accusation true or is it not?" No threat, nor any preference for a yes or a no. Dadibrenos one last time denied it. Andronikus beckoned Maurozomes, who later told me what he said, "Tell the herald to announce at once Dadibrenos has been relieved of office, his property is to be confiscated, and that he will be exiled, as of this afternoon, to the Chersonese. Tell him to say, 'His Majesty believes if his own officials do not conform to scrupulousness and purity in their conduct, he can hardly expect the loyalty of the people. Let this be an example of his troth in his citizens and a renewal of inspiration for theirs in him.'" Translated into the vernacular, it was done. Before he had Dadibrenos taken away, he said to the condemned man, "I would not have tolerated your dishonesty to a humble man in any event, but I should not have been so harsh had you admitted it to me. You did not. Rather you lied, which leads me to believe you are not only a petty thief among the people but a deceitful servitor of the office with which I have entrusted you."

The following day when he appeared again for the games, he was greeted by a cataclysm of cheers, perhaps the most exuberant from the expensive reserved seats where sat the middle class and well-to-do, who had learned that morning of the publication of a chrysobull which reduced inheritance taxes to the level of the reign of John II. My brother did not find this antipathetic to the integrity of the people's champion.

It is superbly practical and just. The greatest beneficiaries of this law will be precisely that class which His Majesty wishes to perpetuate in place of an overweening aristocracy: the merchants and the successful craftsmen and clerks of modest income. It is this group which has suffered most insidiously the exorbitant death duties. No sooner does one generation rise by mettle and ingenuity than its heirs, in the next, are struck down. As usual, Chumnos complains, "Where shall we get the money?" As usual, the Basileus says, "Assess the domains of the nobility at a higher rate—and that includes Crown Lands."

The summer of 1184 marks the division between Andronikus' attention to internal reform and the turnabout to foreign affairs. It is strange, indeed, this most sophisticated, open-minded, and—if against his will—best traveled Emperor of the Comnenus Dynasty had little or no interest in international relations save as they affected the Empire. In part, it is probably a reaction to Manuel and, in part, a necessity. There was simply too much to do within the borders of Byzantium—let alone maintain them—without seeking the Justinianian hegemony—much less the Macedonian—which had been Manuel's chimera and his fall. As not one offensive battle took place from his accession to the Regency in 1182 to his death in September 1185, he is the least belligerent and most deliberate of a family, in the main, bellicose and impetuous.

Now, with good reason—and despite the Congress of Venice—Frederick of Germany mistrusted the independent Lombard League's capitulation and in the intervening years since 1177 had sought a counterweight in Sicily. To this end, he married his son, the Crown Prince Heinrich, to Constance, King William II's only—legitimate—offspring. The implications of the marriage were tremendous—nothing less, after the death of the King and the Emperor, than the amalgamation of Sicily and the Holy Roman Empire as one lethally mighty enemy against Byzantium. When news of the betrothal reached Constantinople, the Emperor, Nicetas, the Caesar Demetrius, several more Imperial kin—including Queen Theodora—closeted themselves at Rufiniana for five days. The result of this marathon session was a diplomatic offensive east and west. As a beginning, plans were rushed ahead for an immediate entente with the Republic of St. Mark, now quite eager to join forces against the Germano-Sicilian Leviathan perceptible on the horizon.

To the immediate satisfaction of the Republic, a down payment was made on the indemnities covering the 1171 confiscation and the 1182 massacre. When this became known, the feelings of the Constantinopolitan mob who had given the West witness to such brutality as would ruin any man's faith in his brothers could best be summed up in one word and that one, betrayal. The Emperor who had risen to the throne on a flood tide of anti-Latinism was now cousining with the very people our citizens believed had made them to suffer so throughout Manuel's reign.

They cannot see their way to blaming Manuel for turning to the West nor forgiving Andronikus for turning back to the Latins in defense of the very Empire which gives them identity. One wonders where it will end. He knows the mob is going against him and because he abhors the oppression which has made its members ignorant and frantic and hopeless, he blames the agents of the nobility—agents who do not exist, or if they do, in far fewer numbers than he believes. He sees plots, everywhere, now. Some of them are real, most of them are his own tortured manufacture. Last week at the closing of the games, the railing of the Kathisma fell into the stadium. He was ready to run. The fear of assassination could be read in the sweat which pasted the curls to his brow as he sat inhumanly still.

Over the objections of the Patriarch, His Majesty rebuilt the Latin Church and opened negotiations with the new Pope, Lucius III, granting renewed privileges for Latin Catholics throughout the Empire in the somewhat wistful hope His Holiness would use the threat of interdict—should it become necessary—against both Frederick and William.

He forgets all politicians are atheists. The best he can do is rely on the Pope to keep in line his own vassals and the North Italians. France and England, for all their influence, are safe—the one by marriage, the other by tradition, both by distance.

In truth, he gained nothing from these Western alliances, which in no way, as Nicetas suggested, could prevent the coming onslaught. At home, however, his loss of authority among the rabble grew apace.

For many months now the Queen has been pleading with the Emperor in behalf of her sister, the Grand Duchess Martha, whose son, Isaac, still wastes in a dungeon in Cilicia. The ambassadors whom Augustus has sent to Saladin have been instructed to visit with the Grand Master of the Knights Templar to gain His Excellency's word in the negotiation of a ransom.

Thus noted are two of the occasions bound to the failure of Andronikus—foreign policy in the East. The most powerful political force in the Levant was now, undoubtedly, that of the King of Damascus who had inherited from his mentor, Nureddin, a traditional and not entirely unfounded respect for Byzantium. (In our undeviant fall since the last of the Comneni, dropping apace for nearly twenty years, men forget how real the possibility of resurgency seemed under Andronikus—at least as seen from without. From within, it was all too evident the Emperor was destroying the military and civilian aristocracy too quickly, and only the time he did not have could raise a vast, wealthy middle class and a national army in its place. But surely it was the positive nature of *appearances* which prompted William of Sicily, with John Sergius' son, the Grand Duke Peter, in tow, as Pretender to the Throne, to initiate his daring campaign against the Empire.)

If politicians do not believe in a just God, states do not believe in international philanthropy. As early as February 1184, Saladin's ambassadors to the Imperial court had given the Basileus to understand the King's ultimate intention was dominion over the Holy Land and Persia. This could not be accomplished if he had Arslan at his back. It was therefore proposed as soon as humanly feasible—1186 or '87—hostilities would be opened against Iconium, a prelude to the restoration of the Johannine borders of 1142, terminating at Antioch. Saladin could expect a free hand in his conquest of the Palestinian coast and promised, as soon as it was feasible for him, to attack Iconium from the East. For the Emperor's diversion on the one hand and neutrality—vis-à-vis the principates—on the other, the King would not only recognize Byzantine suzerainty over the Holy Land—himself vassal of Constantinople—but, excepting taxation, guarantee the autonomy of the cities of Antioch, Tripolis, and Jerusalem.

> It is a complicated, fabulous plan—and *not,* as some think, the betrayal of Latin Christians. The Western Houses would remain in power as vassals of Saladin, who in turn would recognize the Emperor as liege, much as Henry of England, as the Duke of Normandy—which is his richest inheritance—is Louis' vassal, though this does not give France the right of interference in either Normandy or Britain. Our policy will, moreover, curb the ambitions of the Latins, who ought then to be somewhat more responsive to the policies of Constantinople and Damascus. What is envisioned, perhaps by the early nineties, is a Greco-Moslem colossus encircling the entire east portion of the Mediterranean. If it can be accomplished, it will ensure our safety against its makeweight—a unified Germany and Sicily—in the West.

The alliance was signed at Constantinople and Damascus in November, and the Emperor and King exchanged gifts and letters, finding in one another the delight of unexpected spiritual similarity, though, for myself—and contrary to my brother's view—I cannot think of two men more dissimilar. To be sure, both were capable of the large and witty gesture (who can forget during the Jerusalem siege of 1183 when, with wry gallantry, the King ordered his men not to fire on the castle, wherein John Sergius' granddaughter, Princess Isabella, was celebrating her marriage to Humphrey of Châtillon?), both sensed the absurd, both were capable of absolutely amazing ruthlessness and compassion. Yet while Andronikus, the atheist, all his life retained a peculiar, undefinable innocence—a purity of honor which may have been his downfall (for he continued to be surprised by betrayal and at the end, was violent in his revenge)—Saladin, the Defender of the Faith, treated men with the droll, exaggerated accord of one who suspects his fellows from pate to foot (and thus retained the serenity of the cynic, surprised by nothing and measured in his revenge).

But this last great dream of New Roman hegemony to which, I suspect, we shall ever aspire was not to be. No union between two men of ostensible—or, at least, diplomatically comfortable—similarity, no resurgent Byzantium in Asia, rescuing itself once again from Western menace, no lasting reform within the borders of Empire, nor any Comnenus, any longer, upon its throne. The "element of chaos" which leads one to believe the universe does not burn down but flies apart, now enters the realm of foreseeable event.

Martha's son, Isaac, through the mediation of the Templars, was released into the custody of Prince Constantine Dukas and Count Valentinian Dukas (the Prince was of the Imperial house collateral, the Count, of the junior line). With these agents, Andronikus had dispatched a guard and an enormous sum, in gold, for deposit with the Grand Master, who had advanced the ransom from the Templars' bursting treasury. Both the Prince and the Count maintained it was the Grand Duke Isaac who had conceived the plan to abscond with the funds to Cyprus, where, with forged papers, he relieved the present Governor, himself assumed the power, and, within two weeks, declared the island seceded from the Empire and himself King of the Cypriots.

The explanation is literally beyond belief. What of their guard? Could His Highness not be contained? How did he lay hands on the gold which should have been delivered to the Grand Master's emissary *be-*

fore meeting the Grand Duke to escort him home? No, it is much more likely Their Graces are in collusion. Either they believed it possible to deceive the Emperor and become Isaac's agents at Constantinople or they were paid handsomely to look the other way. Of course, there is still another explanation. Rather than dupes of Queen Theodora's nephew, he may be theirs. What is the rational motive for the Grand Duke to have acted so against the man who freed him—an initiative never taken by either Xenia or David. We shall never know what his custodians told him of the past fours years since his imprisonment, but it may be imagined. They could have urged him to the course he followed, while his parents and the aunt who interceded for him awaited his homecoming. Dissension anywhere is to the benefit of the anti-Andronikan factions, whose members are everywhere, even in the Emperor's service. In any event, this cannot have happened at a less propitious time. We have not yet the navy to recover this island and this, at once, throws into question the Emperor's alliance with Saladin. It also ends the use of the Cypriot merchant marine against the Genoan and Pisan corsairs who still plague the Aegean despite our proposed reconciliation with their sponsors.

There is a durable legend Andronikus at once arrested the immediate families of the Dukas' emissaries and—to meanly prove their faith—sent the respective husbands and fathers to bring back Isaac to Constantinople or suffer their women and children the penalties of disobedience to the Loyalty Oath. In fact, the Emperor gave the nobles the benefit of the doubt, pursuant to their remanding the Grand Duke by peaceful means to the capital. Their instructions were to offer Isaac unconditional amnesty should he renounce his rebellion and return. The Dukas families were not even placed under house arrest, though they were ordered to remain in the city.

Whether or not the emissaries made any attempt to convince Isaac to surrender, they returned empty-handed. That Isaac seriously considered their plea, if plea was made, is unlikely. By now, he was fully informed of the state of things at Constantinople, and, whether in guilt or fear, his rebellion became irrevocable.

The city passed under virtual martial law, as the Emperor grew more and more wary of the mob and its nocturnal maraudings. He was resolved to crush it forever. He also dissuaded himself from tolerating any longer a nobility even in its most docile form, disgusted and angered by their protesting activities since his accession to the power nearly three years before. Arrests took place daily of any man whose politics were subject to question, and many more who were innocent but unwilling to surrender to the extortion ring presided over by Hagiochristophorites. Andronikus, who once could have walked among the lowest of his subjects, unarmed, no longer appeared in public save with a fully armed bodyguard and those two famed ferocious, brazen-voiced mastiffs at his side.

The Dukases have returned in failure. The Emperor has not punished their families or confiscated their fortunes, as the breaking of the oath warns. The women and children have been banished to their country estates, their town houses closed, and Constantine and Valentinian placed in the Tower of Anemas. The atmosphere, here, is suffocating: a round-robin of plots, reprisals, and plots again, and more arrests.

Last night the Emperor called me to Rufiniana. He could not sleep. As he is in almost complete seclusion the worst possible stories are circulating the city: Imperial orgies, constant feasts, his inaccessibility to ministers, and the domination of Stephen Hagiochristophorites. It is only a pity the first and second rumors are not true since they might distract him. He is now obsessed by work, by mean details his lowest clerks could attend to. I enclose a list of his appointments for a single day. It speaks for itself.

As for Hagiochristophorites: he does not by any means dominate the Emperor, but rather pervades all that is done in the name of the throne. Augustus, unfortunately, cannot see he is giving his imprimatur to the most hated man in Constantinople, but then he knows little of the worst that Stephen does. I shrink from him. Michael Branas wants to waylay and kill the churl and asked me to join the plot. I swore to maintain secrecy but I cannot repeat the immorality I practiced—or nearly—against the Grand Duke David. Both men are wretches, but I cannot, for the life of me, commit any more crime in the state's behalf. To attempt to do so once was to suffer guilt, which is a warning; to overcome that guilt would be to begin a moral callus and initiate one's own corruption.

In any event, when I arrived at the Imperial villa His Majesty apologized for the lateness of the hour and the journey and asked me to walk with him in the garden, lit by bright blue moonlight. He is physically altering day by day. There are dark circles under his eyes and his hair is thinning in front. There are frown lines, and, betimes, he leans heavily against a doorway, a balustrade, a chair, as though, for a moment, all strength has gone out of him. "Behold," he said quietly, with a bitter smile, "behold the orgiast. I count myself lucky if, at the end of a day, I can make it to a bed and luckier still if I can sleep." I said surely he was exaggerating. "Only a little. I need no valet yet to keep me from tripping over my steps."

He dropped onto a white marble bench almost on the verge of gleaming in the ghostly light. I seated myself as he gestured. "Once, even when life seemed to be at its worst, I needed so little sleep. Now I would like to sleep forever. No sooner do I accomplish one task than another appears and some occasion cancels the validity of the first, and so on, and on and on." I told him he had attempted too much too quickly. "Is that it, do you think? Or is it simply the poor luck to be born and arrive upon the throne at a moment when so many forces of their own weight—and the weaknesses which have brought me to power—have struck us. History has, if not a logic, a rigor of cause and effect. In some degree, we're locked into it."

I am worried for him. He rules with his purposes still in mind, but he is also exhausted and disillusioned and fears if he lets down for a moment the burden of rule, it will be his end.

Well, we sat in the cold garden and talked, then moved to his apartments where the attendants lit a fire and the guards stood mute. At dawn we moved out again to watch the sunrise, which might have seemed refreshing and hopeful had we just risen from sleep. Instead, in the cold, one felt deathly drained, light-headed with a peculiar, morbid acuteness of perception but the lack of will to articulate it, "sharp thoughts and a slack tongue." I had managed to distract him, I thought, as we spoke of literature, of astronomy, and the assassinated Emperor Maurice, who fascinates him more than ever these days, the good Maurice, forced to rule against insuperable odds to preserve the aftermath of the age of the Great Justinian.

As I was preparing to leave for Constantinople, he did me the honor of coming out with me to my horse and escort. He said, "Don't go to the Ministry. Sleep the day. That is my command. You've served me this past evening."

I stared at him for a moment and said, I don't know why, like a child, "Oh, Your Majesty, don't be sad."

He sighed, he patted my shoulder, then looked away, absently holding the reins of my horse as though he were a groom. He frowned, he shook his head, he lowered it. "It can't go on," he said, "not like this. It will end in chaos if it continues. Something *must* break soon. . . ."

XII

Martyrologion, we Greeks call it. Literally the Book of Martyrs. In the end, its list includes Andronikus and all the Comneni—and so, too, the people they ruled. Perhaps the only difference between "the profane superman," as my brother called him, his kin and his people, is the suggestion, at the end, the Emperor may have been reconciled to his death, or the events which brought him to it.

The last months are repellent and heartbreaking. In early March the Caesar Demetrius, whom Andronikus had grown to love deeply and to whom he had delegated more and more authority as his reign progressed, goaded by two creatures in his train, the Sebastianos brothers and his secretary, Count Nicholas Mamalos, conspired to depose his father-in-law, blind him, and incarcerate him at Chele Fortress on the Black Sea. Tripsychos presented the indisputably incriminating material to the Emperor who beat his Commander of the Foreign Corps with his fists and, in a colossal rage, ordered the Caesar to share the fate he had intended for his Sovereign. When Theodora, then Irene and Alexander, attempted to intervene, they were ignored. The Princess joined her husband in his arrest and the Grand Duke Alexander, now completely estranged from his father, left Constantinople for Christos Gennate.

> Probably they would have done better to let his temper subside. They were confronting him not merely in the frenzy of anger but the heartbreak of betrayal by one of whom he was so enormously fond. Julian has been sent away by his father to the "purer air" of Thessalonika—away from the intrigue—and, as it appears now, he will probably be named Crown Prince in the very near future. Romanus, Zoë's husband, has been appointed Governor of Dyrrhachium in the hope he will rise to his responsibilities, as he is entirely capable when not self-indulgently lassitudinous. Only Theodora and Christopher remain. The Queen says she hasn't the least influence upon the Emperor, but he has indicated he desires her company and she has not the will to refuse him. The Sebastianos brothers have been hanged, by the way, and Mamalos burned alive in the Hippodrome.

It was Mamalos' particularly cruel execution which caused an outcry to reach the Senate, among whose members the late Count had formerly stood. Count George Disypatos was openly cheered when he accused Andronikus "of crimes in number and ferocity sufficient to dethrone Satan himself." The Usurper of Hell ordered Disypatos placed under house arrest.

Still the revolution by the crown continued apace. Disturbed by the vast amounts of useful funds bound to churches, the Emperor ordered several monasteries—the very richest—disestablished and their treasure surrendered to Imperial agents.

Kamaterus sought an interview with the Emperor. He argued jewels and gold glorify God. Andronikus riposted, "God, as you perceive Him, then, is a courtesan. As I would have Him, He must, at least usefully promise a better life to the oppressed who have nothing but their belief in Him as consolation for the misery they endure on earth. Those glorifications, as you call them, only bewitch, when they do not mock, the poor." Kamaterus became very bold, "What do you know of the poor, Sire? Of the illiterate mind? You've dispensed with the pomp in which they delight, for it brings color to their drab lives. Now you will shorn their God of His magnificence, which their dull brains cannot otherwise imagine. You believe we priests to be condescending. I tell you you haven't the faintest notion, Your Majesty, of the souls of those oppressed of whom you speak so confidently. They're beasts, beasts who speak and can carry weapons, and the moment you treat them as men, you court disaster. First teach them before you dare to treat them as equals." The Emperor was livid but controlled. "I've dared to *begin,* which, I suspect, is what most alarms you, Bishop."

Easter Sunday, 1185, the Patriarch laid an interdict on the Emperor, forbidding him entry into any consecrated building. When, nothing daunted, Andronikus arrived for liturgy, presenting himself at the narthex, the Imperial entrance of Holy Wisdom, waiting to be greeted by his bishops, Kamaterus remained on the ambo and declared to the entire congregation, he and all his clergy would leave the cathedral if Andronikus entered.

His Majesty turned from the door, his eyes dead, his mouth half-open, slack with shock. He told the rest of us to enter the church, since we were not under the ban. Some did—out of piety or fear of disobeying him. Others—Michael Branas and myself included—did not. The first half of the journey back to the palace, not a man spoke. When, finally, the Emperor broke the silence, he said, "Very well, I had planned to ini-

tiate mass education of the peasants through the church. No doubt it
would have meant some profit to Kamaterus' creatures. Now we'll do it
by secular means." The rest of the way, he gradually perked as we began
a discussion of ancient Greek academies and their methods. This emphasis on education is sudden, until now scarcely considered as part of
his internal reform. I know his interest has everything to do with his
last conversation with the Patriarch. It is plain Kamaterus' accusation
of his ignorance of the peasants' commensurate ignorance has struck
its mark. He seemed recovered and about himself when we arrived at
the Irene Villa.

Two days later news arrived from agents at the court of William II:

The King is preparing an offensive and means imminently to set sail
for Dyrrhachium. According to reports, he has been assured by the
Grand Duke Peter, whom he intends to set upon the Imperial throne,
abject rebellion will topple Augustus as Sicily approaches Constantinople,
that, furthermore, the Grandees of the West will readily collaborate
against His Majesty. The King's forces include 5,000 cavalry, 75,000
foot, and four hundred ships. Many of the foot are poorly trained conscriptees and some of the fleet, piratical vessels. Among the cavalry
are some picked French brutes who act like men in war and resemble
their horses in peace. Such rusticity is dangerous, not contemptible.

A meeting of the Praetorium was called at once, including Michael
Branas, his brother, John, Alexius Gidos, Duke Manuel Paleologus,
Andronikus' distant cousin, Theodore Chumnos—who had taken over
the post of army quartermaster along with his duties as Finance Minister—Theodore Maurozomes, the Grand Chamberlain Nicephorus,
Constantine Tripsychos, and Manuel Kamytzes. From that council, all
else follows.

Whether it was the usual jockeying for rank and Andronikus' fear of
offending any one man at such a crucial moment or his own confusion
and the belief two master strategists are twice as effective as one, he
divided the command of the Western Defense, so that perfectly competent men in a singular capacity, sincere—and probably correct—in the
confidence of their own genius, fought among themselves for the honor
of planning the master attack. Worst still, in three instances—in the
crucial cities of Dyrrhachium, Thessalonika, and Philipolis—he par-
celed authority between the military and civilian branches without detailed instructions as to who was to obey whom. Here the reasons were

more personal. His son-in-law Romanus was Governor of Dyrrhachium and unwilling to surrender his pride—he had long ago surrendered his competence—by surrendering command to John Branas. His cousin's son, George Bryennius, the grandson of the great Caesar, was Prefect of Thessalonika. Already suspect because of his uncle's collusion with the Bithynian rebels, terrified of his awesome Imperial kin, he refused to place his fate in another man's hands, to follow the perfectly excellent advice of Maurozomes and his military attachés. There is indeed, as William of Tyre suggested to my brother, a certain strain of fear—frantic for some sense of saving activity—which causes its victim to be indifferent to any assistance and rely on his own injured judgment, in the end meeting the fate he had all along dreaded. As for the Grand Duke Julian, it is doubtful anyone but his understandably distracted father could have set him to do other than he wished.

The end of spring and beginning of the Long Summer, as it later came to be called, accomplished more ruin, both public and personal. Ascension Day, 30 May 1185, the by-now golden-nosed Hagiochristophorites, who had assumed Maurozomes' duty as Undersecretary, arranged a public trial, which the Emperor would attend, of the "Cypriot Conspirators," Valentinian and Constantine Dukas. Queen Theodora, in her last intercession, attempted to stay Andronikus from appearing. She had never met Hagiochristophorites—or rather, he had never been presented to her—but knowing his reputation, and acute, as always, she realized the Emperor, who had never been publicly seen with Stephen, must continue this disassociation.

She said to me, "I told the Emperor, divorced from his people these last months, he could not begin to comprehend how mightily that man was hated. He said to me, 'He carries out my policies.' I told His Majesty I could never believe that. Hagiochristophorites was deceiving him like so many of his creatures. He was arresting men against whom the Emperor had signed no writ because they did not see their way to bribing that monster. He said to me, 'That is a lie.' I asked him if he believed there would ever come a day when I should be capable of speaking less than the truth to him. He yielded at once and said, yes, yes, what I had to say was true but only insofar as I had been listening to gossip. I told him the lower orders would never tolerate *His* Majesty consorting with dregs the likes of Hagiochristophorites. By that he would be vulnerable. 'And whom,' I asked, 'will you find to direct our defense in place of the archonate? Will merchants throw bags of gold and clerks stab at the Sicilians with their pens and use ledgers as shields?' He took this as a sign of my complicity with the nobility. I told him it was a sign of my distaste for any gratuitous act of cruelty, and in his behalf, above all. By his attendance next week he will give offense to offense. I said, 'The nobles you persecute are as deeply Byzantine as the meanest peasant. It is not the farmer who lives and dies never a mile from his land, but the aristocrat who has preserved our culture who has the spiritual means to love it, who contributed to its greatness and galloped into battle to protect it and died as definitely as any conscriptee. If there are injustices, they are part of the historical fabric, not a conscious evil.' I said, 'Men are born to what they must be, just as you. But you would destroy the loom rather than reweave the cloth. Teach rather than punish. In all your pursuit of your own free will, what free will have you accorded others to change their minds?' He said, 'There is no time. The persecution of the nobility was never gratuitous. Those men—who, I agree, are very much under the weight of the traditions to which they were born, *and* the prejudices, *and* the self-aggrandizing presumption—have committed acts against me which have left me no alternative but their eradication. Since I assumed the Regency three years ago, who among them has given *me,* by word or deed, an example by which I might reconsider *my* prejudices, which, I might remind you, I was not born to. Who among them has given me the least indication all my work will not fall with me if they are not now crushed?' I said, 'What has become of you? They are human beings.' And what do you think he replied? He said he was no longer responsible to his own conscience, only the state's relentless defense. It was then he commanded my presence. 'Or,' he said, 'do *you* now fear to be associated with me?' "

The trial took place in the Outer Philopation, a municipal park, separated only by a high wall from the formal groves of Blachernae. It was well attended by the mob, who, to his surprise, cheered the Emperor. Nicetas, present and standing by Theodora, often said afterward, this favorable reception was misinterpreted by His Majesty and Hagiochristophorites. They may have believed the people were against the Dukases —and wanted blood. When the Prince and the Count made statements in their own behalf, however, the crowd turned murmuringly sympathetic. Nicetas always insisted the Emperor himself, at length, seemed to realize his own mistake and was possibly inclined to mercy. His Majesty persistently looked over at Theodora, who was obviously distraught, her hands torturing a silken handkerchief. When judgment was about to be passed, Hagiochristophorites suddenly jumped to the dais. One of the straps holding his golden nose in place snapped. He tore the object from his face, lifted a good-sized stone from the ground, and shouted, "Why wait, citizens? We know what the Emperor thinks of these traitors!" He hurled the missile, which struck Valentinian in the chest. That was the signal. Some of the mob, probably Hagiochristophorites' agents, hurled their own stones and the rest followed suit, tossing anything at hand.

> Theodora buried her face in her hands, then looked up, got out of her chair—with which she was honored as Dowager Queen—took one step forward, and collapsed. The Emperor ordered the near-dead men drawn from the mob. Rather than publicly contradict Hagiochristophorites or risk the vengeance of wounded men, he commanded their impalement—Valentinian across from the Jews' Cemetery near Blachernae, Constantine, above the gates of Magnaura Palace. They were unconscious as they were taken away and it is my hope they never regained their senses. It seems to me His Majesty has merely covered the guilt he perceived in Stephen—in *his* name—with his own.

That night, at Vlanga Palace, the Queen Dowager was found dead in her private chapel. Family legend has it a small phial with a little poison remaining was found in her rigorous fist, and brought to Andronikus. The evidence of suicide was then destroyed as the Emperor insisted on obsequies and sanctified burial. No stake through the heart, no fire, no tricturation.

> He has ordered she be buried at Forty Martyrs. Tonight, he sits alone with her body in the great cathedral. He wants no company. He does not speak. She goes to her grave, I suspect, with more of the secrets of his troubled soul than he, in his grief, any longer recalls or will have the occasion—or the desire—to recall, henceforth. Once he said to me, "I was already beginning to be old when I met her. My old age is in hostage to her. Should she die before me I really don't think I have sufficient heart to much outlive the Queen." And once Her Majesty commented, "I had really never been so foolish as to believe in allying myself with the Emperor so many years ago, I was promised a very calm fate. It was not serenity I was to find with him, but adventure, sometimes perilous, with no promise I should survive and be with him at its end."

Three days after the sepulture of the Queen, my brother wrote:

He eats little. Work disinterests him. He sleeps little, but wanders the grounds of the Irene Villa. Yesterday morning he was found dozing on a bench beneath a statue of the gentle god, Nereus, grandfather of Achilles. Reluctantly, he has sent his beloved Christopher to Christos Gennate for his own safety.

On 13 June 1185 William set sail for Dyrrhachium, which was taken on the eleventh day of attack, leaving the ancient Via Egnata open as far as Thessalonika, where he planned to reconnoiter with the remainder of his fleet. Throughout the summer, in lieu of the Emperor, my brother dispatched one ambassador after another to Venice, pleading with the Republic to send an armada after that of the King of Sicily. Our emissaries were treated shabbily and, at length, pointedly refused. Obviously, St. Mark's citizens had no intention of offending the easy conqueror of Byzantium or alienating his markets. On 6 August, with only mild resistance in North Greece, due, as foreseen, to the collaboration of the Western archonate, William arrived at the walls of Thessalonika. Nine days later he greeted his fleet. On 24 August, despite the brave defense of Theodore Maurozomes and his military council—in truth, against their will—Bryennius surrendered the city to the King of Sicily. Neither the traditional mercies to those who submit nor the pleas of the Grand Duke Peter—who did not want to rule over an empire in ruins—were heeded. The city was put to the sack, the tomb of its patron, St. Demetrius, raided, churches defiled and burned, priests crucified, men, women, and children murdered individually in the streets, in their houses, or crowded into the municipal stadium and massacred indiscriminately with arrows and axes. In all some 200,000 citizens lost their lives and after three days, as Eustathius—who was taken prisoner —later wrote to me, "a third of the city was in rubble, a third in flames, and the rest a charnel house."

So long, nevertheless, as Constantinople remained untouched, the Empire, almost literally, kept its head. It was the eventual agreement of the Imperial Praetorium to follow the strategy of Alexius I, lure the Sicilians into the Balkans and perform a holding action. In fact, this is what was successfully accomplished though not soon enough to save Andronikus and only in time to confirm the usurpation of Isaac Angelus. Who rules claims his predecessor's strategies and his servants' victories though he does not turn a hair to their design.

How did the revolution take place ending a dynasty which had ruled more than a century, resurrected Byzantium from the grave, confronted and triumphed over an unprecedented invasion from the West, given the state a Silver Age of arts and architecture and letters, dominated Europe for forty years, provided the historical roll with three of its greatest Emperors, four saints, and a wonder of a man, Andronikus, unlike any the civilization had ever known, who, in turn, was murdered with a brutality unparalleled in our annals?

The revolution began—as they all do—by accident.

When news of Thessalonika reached Constantinople, 1 September, the city was plunged into simultaneous mourning and hysteria. Riots occurred daily and were put down brutally, seriously hampering the fortification of the walls the Emperor had commissioned. On the fourth day of the month, still grieving for the Queen, lonely for his family—either alienated or dispatched—given no peace by the citizens, he passed across the Bosporus to his favorite palace, Hieriea, where, two days later to his great pleasure, the Grand Duke Alexander arrived to be with his father. For another week the government went about its work while the people clamored for some reassurance they were not deserted by the Emperor. Neither words nor deeds would, of course, have been sufficient. A people in despair and frenzy want magic, not logic or deliberate action.

On the afternoon of 11 September, at Hieriea, during the midday meal served elegantly and efficiently, as usual, by liveried pages, a medium was introduced to amuse the Emperor. He called forth the spirit world and when Andronikus asked, almost too eagerly—though with the first trace of a smile any man had, in months, observed—"Who shall be my successor?" the fellow, his eyes rolled back, his mouth opened, his tongue "still"—Nicetas emphasized that point—produced from somewhere a voice which repeated the letter iota several times. This was well, though nothing remarkable. All men knew then of the prophetic Comnenian anagram, AIMA, and not a few were aware—though it had never been made official—of the Grand Duke Julian's position as Heir Presumptive. But then the spiritualist pronounced a second letter, sigma. Obviously: Isaac. His Majesty took this to mean Theodora's nephew, the Cypriot rebel. My brother described Augustus "leaning forward, the smile gone, fascinated," as he asked the question no one else dared, "When?" The medium's response was instantaneous, "Before the Feast of the Exaltation of the Cross," or 14 September.

At once, the Emperor was himself again, really smiling, entertained rather than provoked. The Cypriots had three days to arrive, which was patently impossible. But then John Apotryas, the Minister of Justice, suggested the IS might stand for Isaac Angelus. The Emperor, with the Comneni's born contempt for the Angeli, scoffed, and dismissed the subject out of hand. To everyone's annoyance, however, Stephen Hagiochristophorites, an ardent follower of astrology and mediums, kept urging the Count's arrest. At length, the Emperor told Stephen to be silent, thought again, and said, almost indifferently, "Very well, arrest Angelus, if you like, remand him to the Tower of Anemas until the morning of the fifteenth when he is to be set free. Tell him that or he'll quite collapse before your eyes. And no harm is to come to him physically." Hagiochristophorites bowed low and started off. The Emperor called to him by his Christian name. "Stephen," he said. The agent of Nemesis turned. "You are no longer welcome at my table," declared the Emperor.

Hagiochristophorites entered the city toward sunset, accompanied by two guards. He was admitted to Palace Angelus in the southwestern corner of the city, where he instructed the Count as to his arrest, Isaac swore later to my brother, without informing him as to its temporary nature. It is doubtful such knowledge would have made a difference. The most ineffectual of his brothers, famed for their ineptitude, a man who bathed morning and evening and tried not to wear the same clothes twice, good-natured but effete in that hypersensitive way of some men too easy to panic, the Count delayed, wept in his wife's lap, then kissed his children, and rather than wait, went to the stable where a horse was being readied. Between lap and saddle, he became Emperor.

With the daring of the despaired, Isaac armed himself with a sword, galloped into the courtyard, ran down Hagiochristophorites, and split in two the head of that misbegotten wretch. Thereafter, he kept on riding, probably appalled at what he had done and half mad with fear of the consequences. He waved his dank sword shrieking he had killed the Emperor's creature. As he passed down the Mesa, he gathered a huge crowd which followed him through the forums to the Augusteum and the sanctuary of Holy Wisdom Cathedral. At midnight, he was joined by his uncle and cousin, who, by virtue of the Loyalty Oath, were guilty as one member of a family was guilty. The three nobles implored the crowd to protect them and, swelling by the hour, it did. By morning, more than a hundred thousand people were gathered outside the church, no mob led by rabble-rousers, but a true uprising. Shortly before noon the first cries were raised calling for the overthrow of the Comneni.

We received word of Hagiochristophorites' death at dawn, and by midmorning, the first rumors of revolution.

The Emperor ordered the Constantinopolitan Garrison into the city. (They arrived—and joined the rebels.) Then he commanded the Imperial Stables, at Pera, ship parade horses with full trappings to Buceleon Palace. He intended, in his ignorance of just how much events had escaped him, to quell the uprising by showing himself in procession. As he retired, his galley was readied for the crossing of the Bosporus on the following morning.

I had left early in the afternoon, offering myself as intermediary between the Emperor and his distant cousin for whom, if the truth be known, I had always a somewhat offhanded affection. In any event, we still believed negotiation possible. I only realized the extent of the rebellion when I arrived at the Augusteum. There, and in the Hippodrome, the people were armed and calling for the enthronement of Isaac Angelus.

I was admitted to the cathedral where I found the proposed Emperor quivering with fear. "Isaac," I said, "what the *hell* do you think you're doing?"

Since I am not at all known for profanity, this made him shake all the more. "What will happen?" he said. "What in God's name will be the end of this insanity?"

John Angelus Dukas, his uncle, and the son-in-law of Helena Porphyriogeneta's daughter, the Grand Duchess Veronica, was decidedly more to the point. The Priest, as he is nicknamed by the Imperial family, said to me, "He must take the crown. It's a popular rebellion. The only alternative is massacre."

I said, "I see. You're doing this for the good of the people."

He shook an arthritic forefinger at me, "Don't you be insolent with me, young man." He bethought himself. "Besides, it's not like you. I know what you think of my nephew. Well, someday I'll tell you what I think of you, at least in relation to your marmorealization of that rank tyrant across the waters. But now, let me ask you this. Can you honestly say we *have* any alternative? Knowing him, what do you think his reaction to this will be? Will he grow more lenient, more yielding? Do you think he will merely punish my nephew, my son, or myself. He will bathe the city in blood."

"No, he won't. Hagiochristophorites is dead."

He stared at me with Olympic contempt, and began to say, "Do you really think . . ." But said no more and signaled two collaborating guards from the Constantinopolitan Garrison. They joined me on either side. "Take this man," he said, "to the Imperial Vestry and hold him there. Under no circumstances is he to leave."

"Let me go back to him."

"No, Nicetas, and I promise you, one day you'll thank me."

The Patriarch was bodily rescued from his residence and carried to the great cathedral, where, at sword point, he was forced to crown Isaac Angelus as Isaac II, Augustus, Basileus, Emperor, Autocrat of the Romans. Meanwhile, in one of those ominous coincidences which bespeak an ironic invisible, Andronikus' parade horse, a superb bay, gilded and decorated for the Emperor, escaped its groom at Buceleon Harbor and began running wild throughout the city. It was captured and brought for mounting to the new Emperor.

Andronikus reached Blachernae on the afternoon of the twelfth. The numbers of his guard were so small, all hope was abandoned of defense. None of his generals, his family, or his counselors were present. They were either at war against William, preparing for it at Hieriea, at Christos Gennate, Chele, or dead. As a last resort, he sent a herald into the Augusteum offering his abdication in favor of his son, whom he styled Alexander II Augustus. The mob treated the herald to a good-natured drubbing and chanted, "Down with Alexander, too!" though the eldest son had been a great favorite throughout the Empire. It was too late. The name of Comneni was now besplattered, and it is doubtful Alexander—kind, gracious, compassionate—would have had the decisiveness necessary to calm the city and lead the Empire from the Sicilian threat to victory.

In the golden, late summer afternoon, the mobsters, having infiltrated the people, led the huge crowd through Chalke Gate, tearing limb from limb any member of the Imperial Guard who attempted to stay them. Daphne, Buceleon, and Magnaura were all or in part plundered, as well as the galleries, the churches, the museums, the oratories, and the barracks of the guards. A deputation of nobles who arrived at Blachernae to arrest the deposed Emperor found that he had vanished.

Having thrown off his rich robes (the gold icon he believed his stoicheion was found among them), Andronikus had returned to Hieriea, dressed in the disguise of a Persian merchant. At the Chalcedonian Palace, he bid good-by to his staff and his son, whom he believed he was sending beyond harm to Christos Gennate. Taking with him Agnes-Anna Augusta and Maupacta, he boarded a yacht bound for Chele, where a ship had been ordered to take the Imperial party to the Cheronese. Once arrived at the citadel, he attempted to see his daughter, but she refused to meet with him. The delay proved fatal. A storm—one of those sudden, ferocious squalls so common on the Black Sea during summer—drove back the émigrés but a mile from port. They returned to Chele, where an escort, sent after his predecessor by Isaac II, was waiting. Despite the pleas of his ladies, Andronikus was separated from his Empress and his concubine, beaten, bound, and gagged, returned to Constantinople in secret, and imprisoned in the Tower of Anemas.

Among my brother's many notes of those days—"Indeed, it is all I may do and I have all the time in which to do it"—is this memorandum he rightly considered most precious, depositing copies with me, with a colleague at Adrianopolis, and still another—via a papal legate—with a corresponding friend in the Vatican Archives, at Rome:

Isaac II lived among the plunderers at the old Sacred Palace until yesterday. Now, at the behest of the nobles whom he has freed from their house arrest and all prisons, he has removed himself to Blachernae and ordered the great complex at the opposite end of the city "cleared of the rabble." (When someone in his train worried of the possibility of spilling the people's blood, the new Emperor commented impatiently that the "people can go hang.")

I requested an interview with Isaac yesterday afternoon, and it was denied. This morning, however his uncle, John Dukas—the Priest—came to see me. Strange man. That lean farmer's face—though a prince, he really *is* a man of the land—conceals what may be our only hope in the chaos I foresee. (Perhaps it is *my* only hope and what I take as astringent and disinterested subtlety, powerful integrity, and a solid, if uninspired intellect, may be but the stubbornness and craftiness of a terse, hard-hearted fellow bent on his own self-preservation and no more.) He said, "You made a request of His Majesty. May I ask its nature?"

I said I presumed I was not under house arrest.

"That is correct. You have your freedom. In fact, it is likely, at the proper time, His Majesty will have need of your undoubted services."

"If that is true," I said, "I have one favor to ask before I give them."

He was on his guard, but more interested than suspicious. "And what might that be?"

"I would like to see His Majesty."

"You have already been told that is impossible. At the moment he is exceedingly and understandably preoccupied."

I relented: "The deposed Emperor, John."

He smiled. He had got across his point. "What man does not?"

"He is alone. He has no one. I mean only to console him, if it is so given to me."

He looked at me curiously. "Are you really so ingenuous?"

I asked him if he was really without that much generosity.

He said, "Wasn't he?"

"Is that the Christianity we were taught, Your Grace?"

"Was he the Christian he was raised to be, Nicetas?"

"Is any sinner, as we so believe men sinners? Even a man condemned by the Church has the consolation of a priest at the last moment before execution."

"Shall you go to him as a priest at the last moment?"

"Mock me, if you like. Christ, either, had no consolation on the cross."

"Blasphemy."

"Irony, John. Let me go to him."

He departed without an answer, but toward evening, four Varangians arrived at my house to accompany me to Anemas. I knew one of them: he had been among those attending Andronikus. The tower was aswarm with more Varangians still, as well as Excubitors. A great, fractious crowd had gathered knowing perfectly well who was within and calling up for his death. My guards formed a wedge and took me through the evil-smelling humanity to the door of the tower, whereupon I was escorted by new guards to the uppermost cell wherein the former Emperor had spent so many years of his middle age.

He was alert at the sound of the doors opening and utterly consternated at the sight of me. Other than the bruises from the beating at Chele, he seemed well enough, in truth less drawn and drained than in the past months since the Queen's death. He was even prepared to be amused. His voice unexpectedly cracked and hoarse, he said, with that unforgettable, anticipatory smile, "Don't tell me they've sent you as intermediary."

"No, Your Majesty."

"I thought not. To be sure, there's nothing more to mediate. I doubt that they need an instrument of abdication. I hadn't thought that necessary for usurpers."

I told him I had merely come to see him. At this his smile broke, he rose from his chair, turned from me, and passed to the barred window. At once an indescribable howl rose up from below. He turned away with an indeterminate gesture of his arm, as though he were tossing something disgustedly aside. He sat on the bed. "Well, thanks, I suppose. But why?"

"May I sit, Your Majesty?"

"Whenever you like, Nicetas. I'm no longer Emperor. I'm not even a Grand Duke."

"Had you preferred to be alone, Your Majesty?"

"What difference would that have made? No, I'm being ungenerous. But how will this affect you politically?"

I said I was quite beyond caring.

He said, "But you ought not to be. My God, man, don't be a fool. You're what—thirty? thirty-one?—you've a whole life to live. Fate is quite impossible that way. Tyche can ruin a man in a minute, in an instant."

"What does it matter, Your Majesty? Whatever I foresee ahead is life without light."

"A few months, a few years, and you will think quite differently, I assure you. We have an insatiable, if not irritating capacity to renew ourselves." He was silent, and then fell to musing. "One of the soldiers who beat me at Chele. He was quite young—and not very well educated, I suspect—but I thought from the looks of him he might have been otherwise kind to me, save he was taught to hate me, and the unsubtlety in his fury made him the most brutal of all. I think that was what I could least abide. The gratuitousness of his hatred, not for what I had done, but because I was who I was. He was not beating me, but a rumor. Suddenly it was revealed to me what a hideous thing it is to live, if merely by living, by existing, one incites a man to loathing. There is no contest and no repeal and only by dying does one bring such contumely to an end, perhaps not even then. Once I was a source of ecstasy for many—or exasperation—excitement always, but never, I thought, hatred. Never hatred."

I told him there were still those who loved him well. I wondered if he was listening.

He made a little motion with his head and his eyes in my direction, as though merely acknowledging my words, but not their meaning. He shook his head, his expression a mild drown of wonder. "That I should be returned to this cell, of all places. It is really too pure in its theater. But I'm a better man now, I suspect, than I was during my first incarceration." After a silence he turned to look at me. I inclined my head to one side in question. He smiled. "A preference. I didn't like myself very much at the time. I was middle-aged and I find such men older than those who are presumed to be approaching senility, like a ditch, any day. They have not yet reconciled themselves, I think, to the eventuality of oncoming death or the distance from the vigor of youth. They are no longer young enough to hope or old enough to be weary. They are bitter with the loss of one and, in the other, fear the end of everything, but they are not near enough or far enough from youth or superannuation to be part of one or the other and so reconciled. Middle age is to be contemptuous of the elderly, jealous of the young, to be at a moment in time too early to relinquish everything and still too late to be ambitious. It is, I suppose, a disconcerting fire through which we must all pass."

I smiled. "But then, Your Majesty always preferred extremes."

He nodded, the merest trace of amusement on his lips. He was silent again, then laughed shortly. "So absurd. A rebellion out of thin air. Great things accomplished by accident. As I was leaving Hieriea, you know, poor Chumnos came up to me and said in that diminutive, furious way of his—exactly like an angry squirrel, I thought—'It was foreign affairs, Your Majesty, damnable foreign affairs. You had no time to get back to the necessary internal reforms.' Poor fellow, indeed. He cannot understand the indivisibility of events. One thing, only one. Oh, God"—it was almost a cry—"would that it were so. One thing, but one. Surely we would have no *need* for gods if it were 'one thing.'" He looked at me. "You know, a guard, here, a Varangian offered me a knife last night with which to kill myself rather than face"—he paused delicately, for my benefit, I am certain—"whatever it is they have in store for me. I refused him. I don't know why. Perhaps I'm a coward, at the last. But I cannot see to plunging *myself* into oblivion. I will take a few minutes more, like a beggar, even with the promise of greater pain at the end, by which I might sooner wish myself dead, but at least alive, wishing it so."

I asked him if he was afraid.

"Only of not being, Nicetas. In annihilation there will be no feeling, no thought. I can anticipate it, here with you. But for the moment of death? Nothing." His voice sounded fascinated and terrified, while something divine—or accepting—deeper within him—it was visible in the eyes—waited for the horror to pass. "What difference? We live only to reckon the day of our death. We love only because life ends. We believe only to be consumed by doubt. We have so many questions and not one answer and that is death in small. And when we die, we die without reassurance into an enigma. What difference can fear make indeed?" Once again, longer than before, he was silent. Then he said, "You know the practice I had of spending Christmas and Easter at Orphanotropolis instead of the court. I would have preferred the distraction of the palace festivals, I assure you. Otherwise, to stand witness to those poor old folk, or the young who must become disillusioned if they shall ever reckon them-selves against this world and reconcile themselves to eternal oblivion; to witness the lame and the lunatic, denied even the measure of a walk or one lucid thought in this the only life they have to live—" he sighed. "It's not to be borne."

I told him he had done much.

He shook his head, coughed up some phlegm into the handkerchief I immediately offered him, blew his nose, and shook his head again. "Too little, Nicetas, in a betrayal of all I had ever stood for. I laughed, a mo-ment ago, at the young man I was. He knew the ends. I believed I had found the means. I persecuted, even my own, because I believed I had so little time and a greater good was being accomplished. I had not found any means whatsoever—only an excuse to be inhuman, which is the temptation of all men. The excuse was my old age. I did no good what-soever. I used unconscionable means to accomplish what I knew to be good and nullified it, thereby. The agency of immorality not only encourages challenge—and ought to—which is positive, but negates any defense against itself when it ceases to be 'useful.' Nothing can be worth a man's life."

I said, "Suppose that man is Caligula?"

"Suppose he is Andronikus? We must be rigorous. I ceased to teach. I reproved and punished, and men resent both—as well they should. Neither reproof nor punishment are means, but ends. They are without aspiration and they do not counsel."

I rose from my chair, went to him, knelt, and kissed both his hands. "Sire," I said, "I love you, and however little it can mean to you, I will be with you in spirit in the days ahead. I wish only that I could pierce the pain you may feel and remind you you are not alone, that one suf-fers with you."

He smiled wryly, but with a trace of unexpected sweetness. "My boy, you are an angel and I love you, too, with all my heart, but my heart lasts only so long as my consciousness remains. I will forget your con-solation, and I will forget you, and, yes, I will be alone. I am sorry for that, but it is something you must live with as well as I, for as long as we both shall live. Not all the love in the world can penetrate the solitude of a man's death."

We were interrupted then by a guard. The Emperor frowned in that terrible fixity when a man is attempting to conceal his emotions. Perhaps, after all, it was cruel of me to go to him. Better he had been left wretched, but without the added salt of sympathy, which only exacerbated his disappointments and his anger. But no. It seemed obvious to me from his words he was neither disappointed nor angry, and for all the awful rise of exquisite sensibilities, he was grateful. Or perhaps it had been his last, gracious condescension as an Imperial dynast who must conceal his true feelings to the purpose of entertaining the subject who acknowledges him.

"Well, Your Majesty, good-by."

He did not rise. He was looking away. "Good-by, Nicetas."

I was still for a moment, awkward. I did not know what to do next. I said, "Yes," bowed, and left him.

Outside, it was night.

On 16 September he was shorn of his clothes, dressed in a loincloth, and brought to the great gold throne room of Blachernae, in chains. The passages and galleries were thronged with both nobility and the mob, who, hardly daunted by the guards, belabored the fallen Emperor with their fists, pulled at his hair, and tossed missiles of all sorts, including garbage brought up from the Imperial kitchens. In the presence of the newly enthroned Emperor, the condemned man's crimes were announced by the herald. Then, without a word spoken by court or Autocrat, he was scourged on his back, chest, and legs two hundred times. Thus lacerated, he was subject to the assaults of the nobility present. The women were especially avid. Most of his hair was pulled out and all of his teeth were broken. Still conscious, he was assisted once again to Anemas, through a crowd which threatened to kill both the captive and his guards.

That evening Isaac II received a delegation of mobsters who insisted, under the circumstances of the new Augustus' elevation, they could not be responsible for the activities of the people of Constantinople if "one Andronikus Comnenus" were not given over to them. At least that is as history would have it. There is too much evidence among private sources that the new Emperor and his counselors were indecisive as to the means of execution—which was forgone—and unwilling to openly

Against the Fall of Night

assume responsibility since too many Comneni—whether earlier refugees from Andronikus himself or émigrés of the previous days—were still alive and might rally to Agnes-Anna in counter-revolution, or worse, Alexander, to whom the Emperor had formally abdicated.

Three decisive steps were thereon taken. Alexander was apprehended at Christos Gennate and in the presence of his wife, children, and half-brother, his eyes were precipitously and clumsily torn from their sockets. Angeli agents at Philipolis incited Julian's staff to the same action, but the blade bore too deeply, penetrated the brain of the Grand Duke, and killed him. Finally, it was given out Isaac II had no alternative in saving the peace of the city but to allow its citizens the revenge against their deposed monarch for which they clamored.

The evening of 18 September, Andronikus was transferred to the Buceleon Ravelin, where one eye was gouged out, a hand cut off—and cauterized—and the wounds on his body doused with salt. For three days he was left without food, water, or any medical care whatsoever.

On the day of the Autumn Solstice, he was bound, naked, behind a camel affected with diarrhea and on his lacerated back dragged until noon through the streets of the city. Some beat him on the head with sticks. Others pushed dung into his nostrils and, adding to the camel's incontinency, squeezed sponges soaked in excrement over his face. Some thrust at his ribs with hot spits, some stoned him. One fine lady fetched a huge pot of boiling water from her kitchen which she emptied into his face. Finally the procession doubled back to the overflowing Hippodrome where Andronikus was slung upside down between two columns. Throughout the afternoon expert marksmen shot at his legs and remaining whole arm—but never his vitals—piercing his body with some seventy or eighty arrows. Some brave boys were allowed to escape the stands and carve obscenities upon his chest. Twice he lost consciousness, twice he was revived. He would not die, however, so great was his will to live or so colossal the last strength remaining to that giant's body. Toward sunset the multitude became uneasy. One woman screamed he was Michael the Archangel come to earth to test us and we had misunderstood him. Someone else shouted from the sphendone, the curved end of the Hippodrome, that he was Satan and there would be no killing him but this would go on for all eternity. Amazement, awe, hysteria, flew from head to head as the sun turned the enormous stadium into a bowl of scarlet light, and the silver crescent of the moon rose in the east.

Three or four soldiers, suddenly frantic, unsheathed their swords and began to hack at the thighs of the ghastly body. Suddenly the arm which had no hand began to move. In horror, the soldiers stepped away. In his anguish the deposed Emperor, thirsting, was attempting to drink his own blood. Now madness broke out in the stands. But that was not the end. From that arrow-stuck, castrated, lacerated, and hacked body bellowed the hoarse plea which resounded throughout the stone vaults: "God have mercy on me! Why will you break a broken reed?" One of the Latin soldiers present shoved his sword into Andronikus' mouth and pushed it upward into his entrails. The Emperor's body wriggled convulsively. There was sudden silence throughout the stadium. The sword dropped out of the mouth of the corpse. From the lips—or what had been the lips—emitted a gurgling, whispering wail as the huge lungs emptied, a wail which grew in intensity and volume into a piercing, appalling, blood-curdling shriek which went on and on, rending the air like a whirlwind. One man jumped the stands, picked up a sword, and struck halfway through the Emperor's neck. For one monstrous moment the cry went on. But it was only an echo.

The body hung in the Hippodrome for five days. The new Emperor refused to allow it burial, anywhere, much less sepulture beside Queen Theodora. On the morning of 26 September, the decomposing cadaver was cut down and tossed beneath the vaulting of the seats.

My brother convinced some monks from the Monastery of Ephorus near the Hippodrome to retrieve the body and, if they would not give it Christian burial, at least wash it, mend it, remove the arrows, and arrange for some sort of entombment. It was done. Without sarcophagus or embalming, wrapped in a peasant's leather cloak, Andronikus was carried to one of the subterranean vaults beneath the Baths of Zeuxippos, where for twenty-five years he lay in darkness, decomposing till but his bones remained.

Now that vault is ablaze with light and all that is left to materially prove that once Andronikus existed lies in a coffin of glass and gold, contributed by the Paleologi and Lascard Pretenders to the Restoration of a Greek Imperium. The small stone room has, in truth, become a secret chapel as in the catacombs of ancient Rome, with Andronikus its presiding saint.

Finally, it is well to close, not with my words, but my brother's. I have chosen this letter, in its parts, written to me from Trebizond, a year before the sack.

More than ever, Andronikus' death seems to me one of those events which turn the world, or, at least, which turned our world, from what it might have been. Yes, we can speak of the inextricability of events and that every man's death affects existence grossly. But some, I would surmise, do so more *visibly*, if not effectively, than others. His was a death larger than the man, or even martyrdom for an idea. Because so much power was embodied in his person as Autocrat, we were what he would have us be. As he died, so what we should have been and might have been died with him.

We believe that only the holiest and most wicked men have made us alter our view of the human condition; the holiest because they show the higher and highest possibilities to which we may ascend; the wicked, the depths of depravity of which we are capable. Perhaps evil comes more naturally to man—his tendency to brutality and greed—but that is no reason to surrender to it. Rather, because we recognize it—because we are able to recognize it as hideous and unworthy of rational beings —we are all the more moved to guard against it if we cannot eradicate it in ourselves.

I come by these thoughts because recently I confessed to the Grand Duke Alexander that since his father's death I have been *afraid* of the citizens of Constantinople. He said, "My father would never have permitted you to hate the Byzantines for what they did to him."

I thought this was Alexander's usual sentimental kindness. I said, "Wouldn't he? He was too frank to be so forgiving. Besides, what man, save Christ, forgives those who deny him life and deny it so horribly."

"And I tell you, Count, he would rather have you blame and be wary of the manipulators of those people, not the instruments themselves."

(Suddenly I remembered Andronikus' words to me in a letter dated January 1184: "Kings believe it is their nobles who keep them in power. It is a fiction, a coincidence really, of proximity. If kings lived in hovels— as have I—they would think differently, I assure you. There are fewer nobles than middle class, fewer of the middle class than the poor, fewer of the poor than the dirt poor, and it is these three groups who finance the Empire. When they suffer enough discontent to boil away the fat of apathy, the end is at hand. Arithmetic, my dear Nicetas, mere arithmetic. Nobles may merely do a king *personal* harm.")

"Let us have no illusions," Alexander continued. "My father wanted absolute power and the more certainly the aristocracy was destroyed the more his authority became indisputable, but for that, as he would have had it, the misery of the lower classes became less, their freedom increased. No. He would not have you hate them, and he would probably think a conscious pardon condescending. His destruction was precisely the consequences of what he was attempting to eliminate: bondage, exploitation, ignorance, parasitism, mendacity in whatever form." The Grand Duke paused. "His end was the sum of his failures."

"Of his greatness," I said. "It is never the arrival, but the way which makes any man great."

You see, Michael, between the extremes of mankind—the wicked and the holy—stands one more figure who synthesizes both, who enlarges in a way the examples and provocations of the celestial or the infernal do not, and that man is the pathfinder. He suffers the most dangerous existence of all, for not only does he move in previously unknown and unpeopled lands, he must live with the risk of being misunderstood when he returns to common ground and speaks of what he has seen. Neither an utmost devil nor an utmost angel, unchallenged, fixed in their sanctity or damnation, can aspire to godhead. The pathfinder—he is sometimes called the hero—can, and he sometimes does. But society has spent its millennia preventing men from becoming gods—omnipotent, magic, desired, daring, protagonist, antagonist, liberator—as men can only accept their freedom from gods, not from other men. We will tolerate one or some of those qualities, but not their convergence, for such a man is no longer a man, as we would have him, subject to usual human precepts. He is unstoppable, inviolable, and—beyond our standards—primarily disruptive. Rule is the rule of everyday life, not exploration, not revolution, not empyrean feats. With such men, there is no peace, no living with oneself. The lot of us progress by starts, but we much prefer the rest between. The angel we may only praise, and the devil condemn, but the pathfinder is most unendurable of all, for we must confront him, and the road upon which he leads us moves in only one direction. What he has disclosed to us cannot be forgotten and there is no going back. We may survive him, we may stumble for the lack of his presence, but the journey upon which he has taken us *is* ever forward, and only God knows its end.

ISAAC I, Sebastocrator   NICEPHORUS – M –   ALEXIUS I, C[...]
                          MARIA OF ALANIA   (1056-1[...]
                                              (REIGN: 1[...]

Generation I

CONSTANTINE ANGELUS – M – THEODORA   MARIA   SIMON
                2 Generations   M. NICEPHORUS
                                        CATACALON
     ISAAC II   ALEXIUS III
(REIGN: 1185-1195) (REIGN: 1195-1203)

Generation II

ISAAC III, Sebastocrator – M – FRANCESCA   HELENA – M –   JULIANNA –
                               OF HUNGARY   MANUEL ANEMUS   STEPHEN CANTAC[...]
EUDOCIA – M
THEODORE VATATZES   2 daughters   11 sons
    2 sons
                                                                     BERTH[...]
    MILITSA   ANNA   MARIA – M   OF SULZBAC[...]
                          BORIS OF
    ISAAC OF   HUNGARY
    CYPRUS   ALEXIUS – M –
              EUDOCIA – M   NATALIE MELISSENA   CATH[...]
              WILLIAM OF
              MONTPELLIER   ZOË   MANUEL = PERSEPHONE – [...]
BALDWIN III OF JERUSALEM – M – THEODORA   MICHAEL BRAN[...]
          ANDRONIKUS =   AGNES–ANNA CAPET – M – ALEXIU[S...]
                                      (Morganatic Union)

Generation III

                          JOHN – M –   CONSTANTIA
                          DUCHESS NINA
AGNES DE
COURTENAY – M – HUGH OF IBELIN
                                                     PETER
                                   STEPHANIE – M – BOHEMUND III OF ANTI[...]
    HUGH OF IBELIN – M – MARIA-ANNA – M – AMAURY I OF JERUSALEM